EVERYMAN, I will go with thee,

and be thy guide,

In thy most need to go by thy side

SNORRI STURLUSON

Born in Iceland, 1178. Law-Speaker of
the General Assembly, 1215–18, 1222–31.
In Norway 1218–20, 1237–9. Accused of
treason by the Norwegian king and murdered by a political enemy in 1241.

SNORRI STURLUSON

Heimskringla

PART TWO

Sagas of the Norse Kings

TRANSLATED BY
SAMUEL LAING

REVISED WITH
INTRODUCTION AND NOTES BY
PETER FOOTE, M.A.
*Professor of Old Scandinavian in
the University of London*

DENT: LONDON
EVERYMAN'S LIBRARY
DUTTON: NEW YORK

© Introduction and editing, J. M. Dent & Sons Ltd, 1961
All rights reserved
Printed in Great Britain by
Biddles Ltd, Guildford, Surrey
and bound at the
Aldine Press · Letchworth · Herts
for
J. M. DENT & SONS LTD
Aldine House · Albemarle Street · London
This edition was first published in
Everyman's Library in 1930
Revised 1951
Further revised 1961
Last reprinted 1975

Published in the U.S.A. by arrangement
with J. M. Dent & Sons Ltd

No. 847 Hardback ISBN 0 460 00847 1

CONTENTS

INTRODUCTION

OF THE numerous Icelanders who wrote or compiled works of history in the Middle Ages Snorri Sturluson is justly the most famous. He came of a gifted family, newly risen to a position of influence in the west of Iceland, but he was brought up at Oddi, the great cultural centre in the south. He went there at the age of three and did not finally leave until he was twenty-three (1181–1201). His education there and his subsequent career as lawyer, landowner, politician and poet ensured in him both a deep knowledge of the past and a close acquaintance with men and affairs.[1] His history of the kings of Norway was written between c. 1223 and 1235. It was the culmination of a century of historical composition in Iceland, most active in the generation preceding Snorri's own, and it is impossible to understand his methods or assess his qualities unless his work is viewed against this background.

1. SNORRI'S AUTHORITIES

(i) *Intelligent people and ancient poems.* In his Preface Snorri enumerates the sources which he regards as authoritative. His first reference is to what he has learnt from 'intelligent people,' and there can be little doubt but that he has his education at Oddi chiefly in mind. Snorri's foster-father there was Jon Loftsson, grandson of Sæmund Sigfusson (1056–1133), the first northerner known to have studied in France and the author of a lost Latin work on the kings of Norway. The tradition of historical learning begun by Sæmund was reinforced by an aristocratic family interest since the men of Oddi traced their descent from the Scylding dynasty of Denmark; Jon Loftsson's mother was an illegitimate daughter of King Magnus Bareleg of Norway (cf. p. 407); and they were on friendly terms with the family of the earls of Orkney, with whom they could claim kinship in that they too were of the blood of Earl Rögnvald of Möre (cf. p. 71). The dynastic genealogies and 'history-poems' mentioned by Snorri were the family pride and inheritance of his foster-home. He refers particularly to the poems *Ynglingatal*

---

[1] A full account of Snorri's life and other writings will be given in the Introduction to the forthcoming reprint of the *Olaf Sagas* (Everyman's Library 717).

and *Háleygjatal* and indicates their antiquity, the one composed by a poet alive in the time of Harald the Fairhaired and thus some three hundred years older than Snorri, the other composed for Earl Hakon the Great (died 995), some two centuries before Snorri's time. Their age gives them status as authorities, but Snorri is aware that he has no means of checking their information, and he can do no more to justify his acceptance of their authority than cite the precedent of 'old and wise men' who held them to be true. He was doubtless thinking of earlier scholars like Ari Thorgilsson (cf. pp. x–xi below) and the men who taught him at Oddi, but he may also have had in mind the great men for whom the poems themselves were first composed.

(ii) *Scaldic verse*. The next authoritative sources are the poems composed by poets at the courts of the kings of Norway, from the reign of Harald the Fairhaired onwards. For Snorri such verse was contemporary, often first-hand evidence, his substitute for the writs and charters, diaries and correspondence at the disposal of a modern historian. Snorri admits the dangers peculiar to sources that are eulogies on great men composed in the hope of reward, but he explains in terse and striking terms his acceptance of them as authorities: it would be 'mockery, not praise' if a poet gave a false account of the battles and expeditions of the very men in whose presence he recited his verse. The further danger of textual corruption in this orally preserved poetry seems to occur to him as a kind of afterthought, since it stands at the end of the Preface. This was a problem to which no definitive and general solution could be given, but Snorri's answer is a reasonable one: he says in effect that he accepts such verse as substantially authentic as long as it observes the rules of composition and makes reasonable sense.

Some acquaintance with the technique of the verse will clarify the nature of these problems. The typical verse-form of scaldic poetry is called *dróttkvætt*. The unit is a stanza of eight six-syllable three-stress lines, with a regular syntactic break at the end of the fourth line; stress normally depends on a combination of accent and syllabic length. Each pair of lines is linked by alliteration, two syllables in the *a*-line alliterating with the first syllable, always stressed, of the *b*-line. Within the *a*-line the third stressed syllable should make a half-rhyme (*-eyt-*: *út-* in the first line of the verse below), and in the *b*-line it should make a full rhyme (*eið-*: *-eið-* in the second line of the verse below). The following stanza by Einar Skalaglam will be

found translated at the bottom of p. 118. The alliterating
sounds and the rhymes, sometimes coinciding in the same
syllable, are italicized; vowels and initial *j*- (pronounced like
English *y*-) may alliterate with one another.

> Ok *o*ddn*eyt*ir *út*i
> *ei*ðvandr flota br*ei*ðan
> gl*að*r í Gǫndlar v*eð*rum,
> gramr sv*að*i bil, h*að*i,
> ok *r*auð*mána r*eyn*ir
> *r*ógsegl Heðins b*óg*a
> *upp* hóf *j*ǫfra k*app*i
> *etj*u lund at s*etj*a.

Some minor licences were permitted, but in general the above
pattern was rigorously followed by the professional scalds.
Corruption of any kind would readily disturb the metre, so that,
as far as this goes, Snorri's acceptance of correct composition as
a criterion of authenticity appears a reasonable one. It is
another question whether such verse is ever likely to have been
preserved and transmitted orally *except* in a metrically correct
form, and Snorri may also have been thinking of verse subject
to scribal corruption in manuscript sources. There is, in fact,
good reason to believe that the poets in whose hands lay the
preservation of earlier scaldic verse were capable of combining
half-stanzas originally separate, recomposing partly forgotten
verse, and even supplying new verse where the tradition failed.

Other rules of composition applied to word-order and the
use of *kennings*, and it is from these features of scaldic verse that
difficulties of interpretation largely spring. Great freedom of
word-order is allowed by the inflected language, poetic taste
and the exigencies of the metre, and it is not infrequently
possible to construe part of a stanza in more than one way. A
rearrangement of the first half of the above stanza, for example,
in straightforward order immediately translatable into English,
would read: Ok oddneytir eiðvandr [ok] glaðr hafði flota
breiðan úti í Gǫndlar veðrum; gramr svafði bil.

The other feature of the verse is the one that lends scaldic
poetry its peculiar splendour, the use of that type of meta-
phorical expression known as the *kenning*. A literal translation
of the above stanza gives: 'And the glad and honourable *point-
user* had a great fleet out in the *winds of Göndul*; the prince
suppressed all hesitation; and the *tester of the red-moon of the
shoulder of Hedin* raised his *strife-sail* to keep down the princes'
inclination for war.' The 'point-user' is the man who uses the

weapon's point, the warrior, here Earl Hakon. Göndul is the name of a valkyrie, one of the choosers of the slain of Germanic mythology, and the 'winds' of the valkyrie are battles. The 'tester of the red-moon of the shoulder of Hedin' is another *kenning* for warrior: Hedin was a warlike king of legend, his shoulder's red moon is the round red shield that hung from it, and the tester of the shield is the fighter, again Earl Hakon. He raised his 'strife-sail,' his shield, i.e. he made war, to dull the appetite for war of the princes, Harald Greycloak and his brothers.

It is clear that a later historian needed knowledge and skill if he was to make confident use of such verse as source-material. That Snorri was extraordinarily well qualified to offer a reasonable interpretation of scaldic verse is shown both by the *Heimskringla*, where he quotes verse by over seventy scalds, and by the *Prose Edda*, his handbook of poetics. In this work he brilliantly retells the mythological and legendary stories from which the *kennings* were created, and also treats analytically the kennings, poetic diction and metres of the scalds, with constant reference to the practice of named poets. Nor should it be forgotten that Snorri was himself a poet in the scaldic tradition and a man of the soundest literary taste.

For the most part Snorri uses scaldic verse in his narrative in the same way as he uses Einar Skalaglam's verse cited above. He draws a straightforward conclusion and gives in brief prose the import of the verse: 'Hakon had several battles with Gunnhild's sons,' citing this stanza and others to substantiate his statement. As far as we can tell, Snorri was the first to use these stanzas from Einar Skalaglam's poem to fill in the picture of the early dealings between Earl Hakon and the sons of Gunnhild, and he thus supplements or corrects his other sources on the basis of the verse. Snorri may himself err at times, attributing a stanza to the wrong poet or the wrong occasion, or even mistaking the import of a verse, but he always displays a most active intelligence and wakeful critical sense in his handling of scaldic sources. He was not the first to use scaldic verse as primary source-material, but he had a more extensive knowledge and a more clear-headed grasp of principles than any of his predecessors.

(iii) *Ari Thorgilsson*. The third authority to whom Snorri refers in the Preface is Ari Thorgilsson (1067–1148), the first Icelander to write historical books in his native language. We know little of his career, but he was educated at Haukadal, an important centre of learning in the south of Iceland, and he was closely associated with the outstanding Gizur Isleifsson, bishop in Skálholt, 1081–1118, and with Sæmund Sigfusson. The only work by Ari now extant in the form he wrote it is the second edition of his *Book of the Icelanders* (*Íslendingabók*).[1] From his prologue it appears that this second version has been augmented in the matter it contains, but that it represents an abridgment of the whole original work in that the 'lives of kings' have been omitted. It was, however, the first edition, containing these 'lives' of the kings of Norway, that Snorri knew and esteemed so highly.

It is not to be thought that Ari's 'lives of kings' were full biographical records. Amongst Ari's prime interests was the establishment of a firm chronology on the basis of historical facts for which he had reliable witness. It is likely that his history of the reigns of the kings was presented synchronically, important facts being related to contemporary events else-where within the Norse sphere of interest—Snorri refers to Denmark and England as well as Norway and Iceland. Later Icelandic historians, like many medieval historians elsewhere, did not have Ari's regard for any form of absolute dating, or were too acutely aware of the difficulties to attempt to estab-lish one. Snorri is no exception in this respect, and he follows the native chronological convention which depends on dating by reference to some significant and memorable event, often a battle, or to the regnal year or age of a king.

Snorri explains why he looks upon Ari as an authority, emphasizing first his age and the age of his sourcemen: through them Snorri could reach back to the end of the tenth century. The sourcemen are also prized on account of their good memories and intelligence. As can be seen from his extant book, Ari is extremely conscientious in citing the source from which his information is derived, and Snorri fully appreciated his method. Such citation of sources and eye-witnesses is not un-common in medieval works of history and hagiography—it was recommended in the textbooks—but Ari and Snorri distinguish themselves by their honest and serious application of the principle.

In Snorri's circumstances he could go no further in producing reliable sources for the history he was writing and in establish-ing their authority. He sees the problems clearly and solves

[1] Edited and translated by Halldór Hermannsson, *The Book of the Icelanders* (*Islandica*, XX; 1930).

them as far as he is able with sound sense and keen judgment. The scaldic poems and the work of Ari were to be the touchstones by which any information he derived from other sources was to be tested.

(iv) *Eric Oddsson.* The authorities mentioned in the Preface carried Snorri down to about 1120. For the following period there was one other source, apart from scaldic verse, which he could regard as authoritative in the same way as Ari, and this source he describes in the body of his work, again stressing the reasons for his acceptance of its authority: the intelligence of the author and the first-hand information of his sourcemen. The source is a book called *Hryggjarstykki* by Eric Oddsson (see p. 354), which appears to have recounted the history of the kings of Norway in the period 1130–61. The original work is lost, but it is known through *Morkinskinna* (see p. xvii) and *Heimskringla.* Eric's book filled to a large extent the gap between the end of Ari's work and Snorri's own limit of 1177, and it brought Snorri to within the reach of living memory— however unreliable that might be at times. For the middle period of the twelfth century Eric appears to have been Snorri's chief guide and source.

Eric's work has doubtless undergone alteration in the texts in which it is preserved, and Snorri particularly could be relied on to improve the phrasing and arrangement where necessary. It seems likely, however, that in chapters 2–12 of the Saga of the Sons of Harald (pp. 341–55), for example, we have a text substantially as Eric wrote it. He appears to have been able to present a vivid and reasonably well-ordered narrative, although the work undoubtedly suffered from that lack of proportion that was almost inevitable in a contemporary history. The personal engagement of Eric and his immediate sourcemen produces a less restrained, more subjective style. It is Eric's use of the first person on pp. 352, 363, 369 and 387. The author's enthusiasm and admiration shine clearly through in an outburst like 'Happy are they who have such praise!' (p. 352), and are no less evident in the description of Sigurd Slembedegn's bearing under his gruesome tortures (p. 355). One of the most affecting passages in the whole *Heimskringla* is to be found in the simple words that Eric reports directly from life: 'Ivar the bishop said that never was there anything that touched him so nearly as Ivar Dynte's going to the shore under the axe, having first kissed them with the wish that they might meet in joy hereafter' (p. 353). Eric was the first Icelander to write history in the form of saga, detailed descriptive narrative containing much of the powerful and artless immediacy of real life, though, as it seems, with but sparse report of the spoken word. He must be counted a figure of great importance in the early development of Icelandic historical literature.

2. OTHER NAMED SOURCES

Snorri refers to three sagas by name in the *Heimskringla*. Two of the references are of a bibliographical kind, where the reader is, as it were, told to look for a fuller account in *Skjöldunga Saga* in the one instance (p. 30), in a saga of King Canute in the other (p. 143). The third reference is in *Saint Olaf's Saga* (*The Olaf Sagas*, p. 230), where Snorri speaks of 'the Saga of the Earls,' i.e. of the Earls of Orkney, and plainly infers that this is one of his sources.

Of these sagas, the one dealing with Canute is lost and nothing more is known of its contents. The *Skjöldunga Saga* is known in a vernacular fragment and a sixteenth-century Latin epitome,[1] while the *Saga of the Men of Orkney* (*Orkneyinga Saga*) can be largely reconstructed from a number of later manuscripts.[2] All these works must have been written about 1200, and *Skjöldunga Saga* and *Orkneyinga Saga* have both been plausibly connected with the family of Oddi (cf. p. i above). The former was a work that traced the history of the Danish dynasty from its mythical origins down to the death of Gorm the Old (*c.* 936). Its sources were oral legendary tales, mythological and heroic poetry and genealogical lore. Without shunning the fantastic and marvellous that these sources contained, it still apparently succeeded in presenting a serious, orderly and exciting 'history' of Denmark's famous dynasty. Snorri used the work in his *Prose Edda*, in the *Ynglinga Saga*, and probably in the *Saga of Halfdan the Black* (it has been conjectured that the 'long saga' about Sigurd Hjort, mentioned on p. 46, was part of *Skjöldunga Saga*). The *Orkneyinga Saga* also begins its history in the remote past but it brings its narrative down to about 1170. It gives a detailed account of events in the islands in the period *c.* 1070–1170 and appears to depend chiefly on traditions from Orkney itself. The author makes noteworthy use of scaldic verse in support of his narrative. Snorri derived much material from this source in his

[1] See Jakob Benediktsson, 'Icelandic Traditions of the Scyldings,' *Saga-Book of the Viking Society*, XV, 1–2 (1957–9), 48–66.
[2] Translated by A. B. Taylor, *The Orkneyinga Saga* (1938).

accounts of the relations between the Orkney earls and the Norwegian kings, especially in *Saint Olaf's Saga*, but also, for example, in the *Saga of Harald the Fairhaired*, cf. pp. 66–7, 70–71, 72–4.

3. STAPLE SOURCES

The sources considered above could only provide Snorri with material for comparatively small sections of his history, and for most of the rest he made use of other written works which he does not name. These were anonymous histories that did not themselves claim to be based on first-hand evidence, and their contents were doubtless regarded as 'common knowledge,' even though 'research' had gone to their making. Some of these sources are extant in more or less the form Snorri knew them and others are found incorporated and revised in later compilations; others again are not extant but their existence has been certainly or plausibly demonstrated by modern scholars.

Eric Oddsson's *Hryggjarstykki* must have been completed soon after 1161 and parts of it were perhaps in circulation before then. Historical works produced in Iceland and Norway in the following half-century fall into four main groups.

(i) *Contemporary history*. An account of the reign of Magnus Erlingsson may have been written soon after his death (1184), but this is not certain. The greatest of all the contemporary histories is the *Saga of Sverrir*,[1] which describes Sverrir's struggle for power, beginning in 1178, and his reign after the death of Magnus down to his own death in 1202. The author of the earlier part of the saga, and possibly of the whole, was Karl Jonsson, abbot of the Benedictine house of Thingeyrar in the north of Iceland. He lived in Norway for three or four years from 1185 and began his work under Sverrir's personal direction. The *Saga of Sverrir* is one of the most vivid prose texts to be composed in medieval Iceland, written in a style that is forceful and colourful and particularly skilful in catching the superb irony of Sverrir's own rhetoric. Snorri ends his history with the battle of Re in 1177, when the faction of the Birchlegs, soon to be led by Sverrir, had recently raised its head. It was an appropriate moment and there was precedent for it in earlier works, but the existence of *Sverris Saga* must have made the limit inevitable.

The period from Sverrir's death to the accession of his grandson

---

[1] Translated by J. Sephton, *Sverrissaga. The Saga of King Sverri of Norway* (1899).

Hakon Hakonsson in 1217 was covered by a work known as *Böglunga Sögur*, and much later the histories of Hakon's long reign (he died in 1263) and of that of his son Magnus (1263–80) were written by Sturla Thordarson, Snorri's nephew and principal successor as historian and poet.

(ii) *Ecclesiastical biography.* The Norwegian Church was naturally intent on the glorification of the great martyr-king, Olaf Haraldsson, who fell in the battle of Stiklestad in 1030, and of almost equal interest to the Icelanders was the memory of Olaf Tryggvason, who in the five years of his reign, 995–1000, had converted five countries, including Norway and Iceland, to Christianity.

A purely hagiographic work was the *Passio et miracula beati Olavi* by Eystein Erlendsson, Archbishop of Nidaros (he appears in the *Saga of Magnus Erlingsson*, see pp. 404, 407–9). This was written about 1170 and at about the same time the earliest history of St Olaf in the vernacular was written, the so-called *Oldest Saga*, of which we have fragments only. The author of this text expresses caution in retailing stories for which there was no authentic witness, but in spite of this he includes much material that is of little relevance or of a completely legendary character. His style is breathless and his narrative badly ordered. Towards 1200 the *Oldest Saga* was revised in a version known as the *Middle Saga*. This text itself is not extant, but it was used in two later works, the so-called *Legendary Saga*, now known in a Norwegian manuscript from *c*. 1250, and the *Saint Olaf's Saga* of Styrmir Karason (*c*. 1170–1245), made about 1220. Styrmir was a distinguished cleric and a close friend and associate of Snorri. It was on the basis of Styrmir's work, now very imperfectly known to us at first hand, that Snorri wrote his own life of St Olaf, originally a separate saga (and still extant in this form), which he adapted later in the *Heimskringla*.

Olaf Tryggvason never received the honours of a cult, but his biography was first fully treated by churchmen who were primarily interested in him as the great missionary-king of Norway. About 1190 Odd Snorrason, a monk of Abbot Karl's Benedictine monastery of Thingeyrar, composed a Latin life of Olaf Tryggvason, which is now known in versions of an Icelandic translation made soon after the Latin text was completed. About 1200 another Latin life was composed by Odd's fellow monk, Gunnlaug Leifsson, whose work also appears to have been translated, in whole or in part, soon afterwards. Our knowledge of this life is again imperfect, based on excerpts and adaptations found in other much later texts.

This hagiographic treatment of the lives of the two Olafs appears to have had a liberalizing influence on the composition of history in Iceland. These works contain much valuable historical material, but their authors were not bound by the scholarly scruples and aims of Ari, nor by the common contemporary knowledge that would prevent free invention or gross distortion on the part of a writer like Eric Oddsson. Their chief concern was to illustrate the saintly character of their hero, and their pious motive fully justified the acceptance of any tradition, probable or improbable, as long as it was appropriate to that character; it justified too the invention of episodes or the arbitrary connection of facts to produce a lively and affecting narrative, at once entertaining and edifying. In technique it was especially important that they made much use of direct speech, for which they had good models in the contemporary histories as well as in such a well-known classical writer as Sallust and in the saints' lives they heard and read day by day.

(iii) *Norwegian synoptic histories*. Two such surveys of Norwegian history were written in Latin between about 1170 and 1185. The first is called *Historia de antiquitate regum Norwagiensium*, written by a certain monk named Theodoricus in Latin (probably Thorir in Norwegian). He gives a brief survey of the reigns of the Norwegian kings from the time of Harald the Fairhaired down to 1130. He writes clearly but about one-third of his text is taken up by various learned excurses. He professes to have used Icelandic sourcemen and doubtless did, although deference to the authority of the Icelanders, who had preserved the ancient poetry, appears to have been something of a commonplace amongst Scandinavian historians at the end of the twelfth century. Theodoricus's book was used by Odd Snorrason in his life of Olaf Tryggvason.

The second work from the same period is not extant but is known through two later works that are based on it. The one is the *Historia Norvegiae*, believed to date from *c.* 1220, which begins its history with Yngve (cf. p. 14) but differs from Snorri and agrees with Ari in making him Frey's grandfather and not the same person as Frey; this is followed by a genealogical list of the Yngling dynasty similar to the one that Snorri must have used in conjunction with his poetic and other sources in *Ynglinga Saga*. The extant text breaks off in the reign of St Olaf. This work does not seem to have been known in Iceland, but the other work derived from the same source was certainly influential there. This is the *Ágrip af Nóregs Konunga Sögum* (*Compendium of the Histories of the Kings of Norway*), written about 1190, which seems to have covered the period from Halfdan the Black down to 1177. The author knew Theodoricus's book and he also drew on Icelandic sources, probably written, and Norwegian sources, probably oral, particularly from the Trondheim district. Material from the *Compendium* is incorporated in several Icelandic texts from about 1200 onwards, including the translation of Odd's life of Olaf Tryggvason and the *Middle Saga of Saint Olaf*.

(iv) *Kings' Sagas and stories of Icelanders*. Scholars have assumed on plausible grounds that by about 1200 separate sagas dealing with the reigns of the Norwegian kings, other than the two Olafs and the sons of Harald Gille, existed in Iceland. There is a particularly good case to be made for believing in the existence of early independent works on Halfdan the Black and Harald the Fairhaired, on Hakon the Good, Magnus the Good and Harald the Stern. The difficulty lies in the fact that such works as did exist have largely lost their identity through adaptation in later works, and it is only certain sagas on the periphery of Norwegian history, as it were, that have managed to lead a more or less independent existence: the *Skjöldunga Saga* and *Orkneyinga Saga*, mentioned above, and the *Saga of the Faroese* (written *c.* 1220) [1] and the *Saga of the Jomsvikings* (earliest version not later than *c.* 1200).

The earliest known collection of kings' sagas, as distinct from the Norwegian synoptics, is called *Morkinskinna*, properly the name of the codex in which it is preserved. The manuscript is dated to the end of the thirteenth century, but the text must have originated *c.* 1210. It begins with the reign of Magnus the Good (*c.* 1035) and doubtless extended to 1177, but the text is now defective and ends with events from *c.* 1157. These limits would lead one to suppose that the two Olaf sagas already existed and perhaps the *Sverris Saga* also. The writer made much use of Eric Oddsson's *Hryggjarstykki* and he cites much scaldic verse. How much of his work otherwise depends on the adaptation of earlier sagas is an unresolved problem, although it seems likely that separate works on the reigns of Magnus the Good and Harald the Stern were available to him. Further difficulty lies in the fact that *Morkinskinna* in its extant form has

[1] Translated by F. York Powell, *The Tale of Thrond of Gata commonly called Færeyinga saga* (1896).

undoubtedly been expanded by the introduction of numerous anecdotes and episodes, and it is not always possible to distinguish what is original from what is secondary. The narrative in *Morkinskinna* is in general lively and entertaining, throughout somewhat more verbose and less formal than Snorri's work. For the period it covered, *Morkinskinna* was Snorri's chief staple source, corrected and supplemented as always by reference to his authorities. Thanks to the peculiar nature of the text translated by Laing, some episodes from *Morkinskinna* are found in the present volume (cf. pp. xxx–xxxi).

A collection which covered the history of a longer period is found in the codex called *Fagrskinna*. The original work was compiled by an Icelander working in Norway about 1220. Like the *Compendium*, which the author used, it begins with the reign of Halfdan the Black and reaches the usual limit of 1177. The author had a good knowledge of scaldic verse, but he does not seem to have been a gifted writer—he is most fluent in his description of battles—and compiles much of his history from earlier sources, including *Morkinskinna*, with little alteration or attempt to harmonize them. Some of the dryness of the narrative may be due to the fact that *Fagrskinna* represents a kind of official history. Although the work is so nearly contemporary with the beginning of Snorri's own composition, it must be counted one of his sources.

It was not only the history of the kings of Norway that was recorded in these early works. Towards 1200 a history of the earls of Lade was written. This great family, from Hålogeland and Trondheim, had played a decisive part in Norway's history, and from *c.* 970 to 995 and again from 1000 to 1015 members of that family were the sole rulers of the country, although they never assumed the kingly title and for much of the time owed nominal or real allegiance to Denmark. This saga is not extant but it was an important source for *Fagrskinna* and for Snorri. It probably extended from the mythical origins of the family, here doubtless based on Eyvind Skaldaspiller's *Háleygjatal*, down to the reign of Earl Eric Hakonsson, who left Norway in 1015, or to that of his son, Hakon, who died in 1029. A kind of continuation of this *Saga of the Earls of Lade* is found in the *Saga of Earl Hakon Ivarsson*, written soon after 1200 and now known in a fragmentary manuscript and through a sixteenth-century Latin epitome. Earl Hakon's dealings with Harald the Stern are told at some length in *Morkinskinna*, but Snorri preferred to follow the independent saga for his parallel account in chapters 39–53, 59–74, of the *Saga of Harald the Stern* (pp. 190–99, 203–18; cf. p. xxvi).

By the end of the twelfth century a number of short stories about Icelanders, especially poets, had been written, mostly describing episodes that arose out of the hero's dealings with one of the kings of Norway. They are often humorously told, even those which most give the impression of being written to illustrate a moral precept. In some of them the narrative is astonishingly smooth and well proportioned. Episodes of a similar kind appear in the *Oldest Saga of Saint Olaf* and in *Morkinskinna*. By the time Snorri began his *Heimskringla* a number of sagas with Icelandic heroes, again mostly poets, had been composed. Two of the earliest of these were the *Saga of the Foster-brothers* [1] and the *Saga of Hallfred*, both dealing with the lives of notable poets in the service of St Olaf and Olaf Tryggvason respectively. Snorri made use of the latter, but whether he drew directly on the former is uncertain. With one important exception it may be said that the other sagas written in Snorri's lifetime could have taught him little in the way of literary technique, although he doubtless valued the verse they contained. The exception is the *Saga of Egil Skalla-Grimsson* [2]— which many scholars now believe to be the work of Snorri himself. A large part of this saga is taken up by an account of the collisions between Egil's father and uncle and Harald the Fairhaired, which lead to the family's settlement in Iceland, and between Egil himself and Eric Bloody-axe, both in Norway and England. The picture of early tenth-century Norwegian history in the saga is essentially the same as that in the *Heimskringla*. The saga is a work of high artistry and contains the verse of the greatest of all scalds, but it is also important because it shows a traditional attitude of the Icelanders towards the history that formed the background to their own emigration—an attitude for which we must have some respect. From merely reading the saga's serious and compelling attempt at historical interpretation Snorri would have learnt much— not only about history, but about poetry, character-drawing and narrative prose as well. And from writing the saga Snorri would have learnt much more.

Snorri must have known nearly all the works mentioned in

---

[1] Translated by L. M. Hollander in *The Sagas of Kormak and the Sworn Brothers* (American-Scandinavian Foundation, 1949), 73–176.
[2] Translated by W. C. Green, *The Story of Egil Skallagrimsson* (1893); and by Gwyn Jones, *Egil's Saga* (American-Scandinavian Foundation, 1960).

this survey. To these written authorities and sources must be added the oral traditions that were either generally current in Iceland and Norway or were to be gleaned from particular informants. An obvious example of the latter is in Snorri's account of the Vends' attack on Konghelle and of the coronation of Magnus Erlingsson in 1164, where his foster-father Jon Loftsson was clearly his original immediate source (see pp. 328, 407). Snorri was in Norway 1218–20 and from there he visited Gautland in the summer of 1219; in both places he must have heard and seen much. His topographical knowledge is not always accurate, but sometimes, as, for example, in the description of the grave of Harald the Fairhaired on p. 82, he writes with the precision of an antiquary and is doubtless describing what he himself has seen. It will be noticed that he is not unaware of what may be called 'archaeological' evidence.

4. SNORRI AND HIS SOURCES: AN ILLUSTRATION

Since space does not permit consideration of the whole of Snorri's history in relation to his sources, a more detailed analysis of a single saga may serve as an illustration. For his sole account of the sole reign of Magnus the Good (pp. 127–59) Snorri had *Morkinskinna* and *Fagrskinna* (henceforth abbreviated *Msk, Fsk*) as his staple prose sources and he probably referred to the *Ágrip*; scaldic verse provided him with material and a means of controlling his other sources; and he drew on his own separate *Saga of Saint Olaf* and on information he had acquired in Norway.

In chapters 1–5, describing Magnus's return to Norway and the flight of Svein Alfivason, Snorri has added material to his staple sources. Most important and novel is his account in chapter 1 of Queen Astrid's efforts on behalf of her stepson in Sweden, for which Sighvat's poem about her is the chief source. In chapter 6 Snorri departs from *Msk-Fsk* and his own separate *Saga of Saint Olaf*, which all say that the Danes and Norwegians inflicted much damage on each other before peace was made on behalf of the two young kings, Magnus and Hardacanute. Snorri's reconsideration is probably due to the absence of scaldic evidence for this active hostility, and he may have thought it an unlikely development when King Canute and King Svein both died so soon after Magnus's return to Norway (ch. 5). Snorri's account here is much briefer than *Msk*, but nothing of value has been lost in the abridgment.

Chapters 7–13 have no parallel in *Msk-Fsk*, but much of it

is found in a somewhat briefer form in Snorri's separate *Saga of Saint Olaf*. For chapers 7–9 Sighvat's poetry is the chief source, but Snorri's text may here be directly based on Styrmir's *Saint Olaf's Saga*. The description of St Olaf's shrine in chapter 10 doubtless depends on Snorri's own visit to Nidaros, where he spent the winter of 1219. These chapters dealing with St Olaf's wife, mistress, poet and the establishment of his cult lead naturally to the following account of the fate of his chief adversaries in the battle of Stiklestad and, in doing so, return the narrative to the next great moment in Magnus's reign, the near-revolt of his subjects. Each of the chapters 11–13 begins firmly with the name of the adversary in question: Tore Hund leaves the country; Harek is struck down, with the king's connivance, by Asmund Grankelsson; but Kalv Arneson, in pointed contrast, 'had at first . . . the greatest share of the government of the country under King Magnus,' although it is at once made clear that Kalv's security was not to last. In chapter 12 Snorri says, 'many are the tales about the strife between Asmund and Harek's sons,' a phrase which most probably points to unwritten traditions from north Norway. It is also possible that the episode of Torgeir of Suul (ch. 13) depends on a local Norwegian story. This is the final incitement to remind Magnus of his father's death and to prepare for the striking account of his visit to Stiklestad in Kalv's company (ch. 14). In *Msk* the visit to Stiklestad is preceded only by two brief episodes that illustrate the strained relations between Einar Tambarskelve and Kalv. Snorri's new material and its arrangement steadily builds up a pressure which relentlessly forces the protagonists—and the reader—back to Stiklestad. The account of the visit to Stiklestad in *Msk* is vivid and impressive, but Snorri's text is characteristically briefer and more disciplined. Snorri's only addition here is Kalv's echoing reply to the king's words, a typical pattern in Snorri's dialogue. In *Msk* it reads: 'The king said, "Then your axe would reach my father." And at the same moment the king turned away and his face was blood-red.' Compare Snorri: 'The king turned red as blood in the face, and said: "Then thy axe could well have reached him." Kalv replied: "My axe did not come near him."'

The following episode (chs. 15–16) grows out of Magnus's harshness towards his father's enemies and others; the resulting discontent prompts Sighvat's 'Free-speaking Verses.' Snorri departs from his staple sources and to some extent from his separate *Saga of Saint Olaf*, where most of this was already written, in speaking of a more general mood of revolt in Norway, whereas the earlier works confine it to the Trondheim district. Snorri lets Sighvat's verses speak for themselves, citing only those that have a direct bearing on the complaints against the king and omitting others now known only in *Msk*. Snorri is the only writer to tell of Magnus's connections with the law-code called 'Grey Goose' (cf. p. 141, note 1): this forms a fitting conclusion to the 'Free-speaking Verses,' a kind of symbol of the king's amendment and reconciliation with his people which Sighvat's poem had brought about.

In chapters 17–19, on Magnus's succession to the throne of Denmark, Snorri's account is chiefly distinguished by minor rearrangements, which produce a more reasonable and orderly sequence of events, and by the introduction of new verse-sources. Two stanzas in chapter 19 (pp. 142–3) are new, for example, and Snorri learns from them the size of Magnus's fleet and the presence of the great Bison under the king's command. In chapter 20 Snorri stops to consider the reasons for the Danes' acceptance of Magnus as king. His reasons are plausible, although it has been suggested that he overlooked the most important, *viz.* that the Danes needed unity and a strong leader to ward off the aggression of the Vends. Snorri's statement that the fame and sanctity of King Olaf, Magnus's father, played a part in securing his succession to the Danish crown, reminds us of one of his major themes (cf. p. xxvii).

In the account in chapters 22–3 Snorri's most notable alteration is in the description of the ceremony by which Svein Ulvsson is made an earl. The episode is told in *Msk* thus:

> And one day when they were drinking, the king gave him his own cloak, made of the most precious cloth, and with it a cup full of mead and told him to drink a toast in return. 'And with this,' said the king, 'I am going to give you the title of earl and such share in the government of Denmark as I shall decide when I come there.' Svein took the cloak and did not put it on, but gave it at once to one of his men and turned very red in the face; and he himself put on an Icelandic grey-cloak. And when Einar Tambarskelve saw that, he said, 'Too great an earl, too great an earl, my foster-son!'

This brief, dramatic and foreboding scene can scarcely have failed to impress Snorri, but he evidently did not find it comely or dignified enough for such a great matter of state. He puts a kingly speech into Magnus's mouth, including that sort of historical reference and parallel which he constantly brings in, and describes a fitting feudal ceremony with the gift of sword and shield (p. 144).

In the following chapters, 24–8, describing Magnus's expedition against Jomsborg, the defection of Earl Svein and the battle of Lyrskog Heath, Snorri has abridged and to some extent rearranged the comparable narrative in *Msk-Fsk*. A typical excellence of Snorri's style may be noted in his description of events before the great battle against the Vends (p. 147): the economical way in which he introduces a sense of precise reality by careful reference to place or time. Whereas in his sources at this point there is either no indication of time or indication only of the crudest kind, we find in Snorri the following orderly sequence: the king was anxious as they lay under arms and slept little all night; towards dawn he fell asleep and dreamt his dream about his father; when he awoke he told his dream and the day was then dawning; and then they all heard the sound of bells in the air. His introduction of the dream is also typical in that he makes less of it as a supernatural visitation than does either *Msk* or *Fsk*.

Snorri describes the battle of Re (ch. 29) after the battle of Lyrskog Heath and thinks it was fought against Earl Svein, whereas in *Msk* the order of the two battles is reversed and Magnus's enemies are described as certain vikings. *Msk* is doubtless nearer the truth, since the place of battle (cf. p. 149, note 2) makes it extremely unlikely that Svein was engaged. In Snorri's account it becomes the first of three major battles fought between Magnus and the Svein, the other two being described in chapters 30–5. Snorri follows *Fsk* in relating the battle of Aarhus before the battle of Helgenes, while *Msk* again has the reverse order. Snorri found support for *Fsk*'s sequence in the stanza by Odd Kikinescald (p. 157), where the battle of Lyrskog Heath is said to have taken place before Michaelmas and the battle of Aarhus before Christmas in the same year: there was little time for a third battle at Helgenes between them. Snorri supplies Magnus's speech at the beginning of chapter 30, but thereafter almost all his narrative is based on the verse he cites. In *Msk* the account of these two battles takes 42 lines of prose with 7 stanzas and 4 half-stanzas; *Fsk* has 26 lines of prose, 3 stanzas and 2 half-stanzas; Snorri has 148 lines of prose and cites 25 stanzas and 3 half-stanzas. It is a striking example of Snorri's superior knowledge of the scaldic sources and superior skill in profiting from them.

Snorri ends the saga with the exchange of letters between King Magnus and King Edward (the Confessor) of England. In this he follows the order of *Msk*, while in *Fsk* Magnus prefers his claim to the English throne immediately after his succession to the Danish kingdom (corresponding to the end of chapter 21 in Snorri's saga). The order in *Fsk* is undeniably more plausible, but *Msk*'s arrangement gave the history of Magnus's sole reign an appropriate and noble end: king of Norway and Denmark, law-giver and warrior, the destroyer of the Vends, supported at home and abroad by the sanctity of his father, Magnus is now seen receiving King Edward's reply with all modesty and prudence. This is the last picture we have of him before we next meet him face to face with his uncle, the hard-headed and guileful Harald Sigurdsson (p. 174 ff.), where the contrast between the two is fully marked by Snorri. Snorri's treatment of the letters exchanged between Magnus and Edward is worthy of attention. In *Msk-Fsk* only Edward's letter is reported in the first person; Snorri gains much by putting Magnus's letter into the same form. Edward's letter in Snorri's version is less than half as long as that found in *Msk*, and whereas in the latter text Edward writes like a long-suffering saint, his letter in Snorri's saga reads like the considered utterance of a high-minded man of principle.

5. HISTORIAN AND ARTIST

Ut brevis, ut aperta, ut probabilis sit—is the Ciceronian prescript for *narratio*, handed down in the medieval school-books of rhetoric. No better description of the chief qualities of Snorri's narrative could be found. The discussion of the *Saga of Magnus* will have demonstrated his outstanding ability to organize his sources in a convincing logical order. His imposition of such a pattern, as in the description leading up to the visit to Stiklestad, can produce the effect of art. His orderliness leads him, in common with the authors of the best of the Family Sagas, to describe things as they happened; he does not often comment on the motives of men—these must be revealed in the action—and he does not presume to know beforehand whither the events will lead. This objective presentation often leaves much to the intelligent inference of the reader. An extreme example is found in the story of Harald Greycloak and his brother Gudrod and their attacks on Tryggvi Olafsson and Gudrod Björnsson, p. 121 below, where only at the end does one suspect that the quarrel between the two brothers was fabricated in order to allay the suspicions of their victims.

It is evident that Snorri not only records history but also reflects on it. He considers why or how such a thing came about and, in the manner of other early historians and the creators of epic, he seeks motive and manner above all in the characters of great men. He is as much of a rationalist as the period in which he lived permitted him to be, and where possible he discards the marvellous and supernatural in favour of natural causes, not least those that have their roots in human personality. Snorri's greatest achievement is in the portrayal of a 'developing' character, where an internal personal drama is framed and moulded by external historical events. St Olaf is the great example, but there are noteworthy personal crises, intimately bound up with important historical events, in the kingly careers of both Hakon the Good and Magnus the Good. And for 'mixed' characters, which medieval writers elsewhere found so difficult to portray, it is only necessary to think of Earl Hakon the Great and King Harald the Stern. Perhaps the most brilliant of all Snorri's brief chapters that weigh up the facts of a man's character and career are precisely those where he comes to grips with these two rulers (see *The Olaf Sagas*, p. 51, and p. 240 below).

Snorri is not unaware of other forces that go to mould the history of a nation: the influence of good and bad seasons, the natural conservatism of the bonder, the part played by wealth in the consolidation of authority, whether gold from Byzantium or booty in furs from a Bjarmaland-expedition. He also emphasizes with great firmness the element of oppression that lay in kingship and the element of liberty that lay in opposition to the monarchy. At its most extreme, the clash between king and subjects led to death or exile of one or the other. When the monarchy was successful in the early period, Snorri sees the results in the settlement of colonies abroad or the enlistment of foreign aid for a new struggle. In Norway itself he appears to see a delicate compromise between king and great men, always alive with the danger of conflict at any new assertive step on either side. In all this Snorri distinguishes a clear and not unreasonable pattern, but some over-simplification inevitably results. One root of the misunderstanding lies in Snorri's belief that in Harald the Fairhaired's time Norway was a highly organized kingdom, something which must be far from the truth. That King Harald in unifying the country under his rule attempted to impose a centralized order cannot be doubted, but only the beginnings of any effective organization can be traced to his reign and much more was done in the reign of his son, Hakon the Good. Snorri's neat and precise description of the feudal order under King Harald (p. 54) is certainly anachronistic. It is also certain that Norwegian colonization abroad had begun long before King Harald's reign—economic factors, 'land-hunger' at home and the attraction of profitable piracy, were among its chief causes. The major exodus to Iceland took place in Harald's time, and whilst the political factor was certainly important in the emigration of individual families, it cannot account for the whole movement. In his long study of the interaction of monarchy and people, however, Snorri can balance the two sides as an objective historian and contrast them as an artist. And if he sees in the great men and bonder the defenders of freedom and self-interest, the reverse of freedom's coin, he also sees in the kings the innovators and idealists.

Snorri's work is given a unity and interest not to be found in any of the other early sources by his ability to take a wider view of Norwegian history. In their speeches his characters often refer to precedents from earlier times or other countries. He is in particular aware of two great themes which transcend the bounds of any single saga. These themes naturally only appear in their amplitude if the *Olaf Sagas* are read in their proper place (see p. 126). The one such theme is that of the relations between the Ynglings and the succeeding dynasty of Harald the Fairhaired and the dynasty of the great earls of Lade. We see how Harald the Fairhaired allies himself with Earl Hakon Grjotgardsson and how that alliance is renewed between Hakon the Good and Sigurd Hakonsson, while in the reigns of Queen Gunnhild's husband, Eric Bloody-axe, and her sons there is conflict between the two houses. This leads to the sole rule of Earl Hakon until Olaf Tryggvason wins the throne, but Olaf himself soon falls in battle against Earl Eric Hakonsson. The rule of the sons of Earl Hakon ends on the succession of St Olaf, but the shifting pattern of alliance and conflict continues in Einar Tambarskelve, Earl Orm Eilifsson, Earl Hakon Ivarsson and Erling Skakke. The origin of these younger branches is quietly but regularly emphasized by Snorri. His awareness of this theme, running throughout his history, explains his preference for the *Saga of Hakon Ivarsson* to *Morkinskinna* as a source. In the latter there is no connection traced between Hakon and the family of the earls of Lade, and the motives and chronology of Hakon's feud with Harald the Stern are different from those of the saga, where much is made of the connections with the Lade-dynasty. *Morkinskinna* is probably right and the saga and Snorri wrong, but it is not surprising that Snorri should find in the saga's account a satisfying completion of his pattern.

The other great theme is the conversion to Christianity of Norway and the Norwegian colonies, chiefly seen through the personalities of the kings who struggled to bring it about. The period of struggle, success and setback culminates in King Olaf Haraldsson, who, in his sanctity after his death, is clearly seen by Snorri to play a part in the practical politics and international prestige of his successors. St Olaf is already prefigured in the dream described on p. 48, and the miracles recorded by Snorri in the reigns of the later kings, as well as the constant influence ascribed to him, particularly in the reigns of Magnus the Good and Harald the Stern, testify to Snorri's recognition of the peculiar strength lent to the Norwegian Church and monarchy by their national saint. In the period of struggle, in the time of Hakon the Good and Olaf Tryggvason, the theme of the Conversion is decisively linked with the theme of interplay between the descendants of Harald the Fairhaired and the dynasty of the earls of Lade.

It is probably not the larger themes that live in the memory after a reading of the *Heimskringla* but the single episode, even the single phrase. Such scenes exist in plenty, presented with Snorri's typical economy and precision of description, often containing a dramatic dialogue that builds up its own tension as it progresses, sometimes cut short by a single remark that suddenly reveals a deep insight into the character of the man involved. A list of such episodes would be pointless, but a brief look at two such against the background of his sources is illuminating. Both episodes are of small significance as history, but however much modern historical criticism may reduce the importance of the *Heimskringla*, such passages as these will ensure that it is always read as literature.

Harald the Stern fought Hakon Ivarsson and an army of Gautlanders, defeated them and captured Hakon's banner, a famous one that had been given him by Ragnhild, his wife, daughter of Magnus the Good. The separate saga of Hakon is unfortunately defective in this part, but we may see what is made of the following episode in *Morkinskinna*:

And as they rode on a path through the forest, a man ran out from the trees on one side of them, taking them completely by surprise. With one hand he seized the banner from the man who carried it, while he thrust him through with the spear in his other hand, and then ran off again into the forest on the other side of the path; they could not catch him and the man who was stabbed died. Then King Harald said, 'That must have been Hakon and there weren't many men capable of such a deed, and indeed I think he has gained no less a victory in this exploit than I gained in the battle. But then, I don't know my niece Ragnhild's temperament, if it had been easy for Hakon to climb into bed beside her if he had lost the banner, but now they will make it up.'

Snorri describes the action in much the same way (p. 216), but introduces it by saying that as they rode Harald's men were discussing whether Hakon had been killed in the battle. And in place of Harald's speech above, Snorri has only the incisive: 'When the king was told of this, he said, "The earl is alive. Give me my armour."' No amount of superlative adjectives could produce the impression we receive of Hakon's stature as a man of action and courage from this characteristically laconic prudence of the most experienced warrior of all the early Norwegian kings.

In *Fagrskinna* the description of the battle of Frædeberg, where Egil Ullserk plays such a valiant part, ends with an account of the honourable burial King Hakon gave the slain, laying them in the captured ships and heaping mounds over them. Snorri has a similar account on pp. 103–4. *Fagrskinna* reads here like a guide-book, and the passage ends: 'Where Egil fell there also stands a high bautastein.' [1] By the smallest alteration Snorri turns this into a sentence which has all the monumental simplicity, significance and dignity of those bare needles of rock themselves: 'High standing-stones mark Egil Ullserk's grave.' [2]

6. SNORRI'S TEXT AND THE PRESENT TRANSLATION

Kringla is the name of the codex that contained a text of the *Heimskringla* nearest to Snorri's own. It was written *c.* 1260 in Iceland; in the sixteenth century it came to light in Norway and thence it went to Copenhagen, where it was destroyed in the great fire of 1728. A single leaf had somehow got to Sweden and is now preserved in Stockholm; for the rest, its text is known through paper copies from the end of the seventeenth century: the best of these appear to have been accurately done. The most important texts related to *Kringla* are in manuscript *AM 39 fol.*, written *c.* 1300, and the so-called *Codex Frisianus* (*AM 45 fol.*, written soon after 1300), both in the Arnamagnæan Institute of the University of Copenhagen. The former is

---

[1] *Þar stendr ok bautaðarsteinn hárr sem Egill fell.*
[2] *Hávir bautasteinar standa hjá haugi Egils ullserks.*

fragmentary but seems to have contained a pure text, apart from one interpolation and the omission of a number of miracles. The latter is in a different case, for it does not include the saga of St Olaf and from the end of the saga of Olaf the Quiet down to the end of the saga of the Sons of Harald it has a conflate text based on a version of *Morkinskinna* with material from *Heimskringla* included.

Three other manuscripts, all written in Norway, contain interpolated texts and belong to a different line of descent from that represented by *Kringla*. *Jöfraskinna* was the name of another codex burnt in Copenhagen in 1728 and now known through paper copies. The original from which this codex was copied did not contain the saga of St Olaf, and this text was supplied from a copy of Snorri's separate *Saga of Saint Olaf*; four leaves of this part of *Jöfraskinna*'s text are now preserved in Stockholm (perg. fol. nr. 9 in the Royal Library). This manuscript must have been written *c*. 1325. The second codex in this group, *Eirspennill* (*AM 47 fol.*), was written about the same time. It contains only the last part of the *Heimskringla* (beginning chapter 252 in *Saint Olaf's Saga*, see *The Olaf Sagas*, p. 384), followed by *Sverris Saga*, *Böglunga Sögur* and the *Saga of Hakon Hakonsson*. The third codex is called *Gullinskinna*, also from the fourteenth century. It too was destroyed in 1728 and is known only from copies. Its contents appear to have been similar to those of *Eirspennill*. These three texts have in common a number of interpolated chapters, derived from a *Morkinskinna* text, and they omit many of the miracles of St Olaf. Other independent omissions and interpolations are found in each of them, and the last word has not been said on their mutual relationship and on the position of the *Codex Frisianus*, which contains much similar material.

Kringla has been properly made the basis of all recent editions of Snorri's work. Its readings can sometimes be improved in cases where it is faced by agreement between *AM 39 fol.*, *Codex Frisianus*, and the interpolated Norwegian manuscripts mentioned above.

The first edition of *Heimskringla* was published by Johan Peringskiöld (Stockholm, 1697). It was based on a less good, though still textually valuable transcript of *Kringla*. Additional material was introduced, retranslated into Icelandic, from a translation into Danish made by the Norwegian parson, Peder Claussøn (1545–1614), published in Copenhagen in 1633. Peder Claussøn had used a text related to *Jöfraskinna*, as well as other

sources. Still more material in Peringskiöld's edition came from
the codex *Hulda* (*AM 66 fol.*), a conflate text based on a version
of *Morkinskinna*; from Stockholm perg. 4:o nr. 2, the best text
of Snorri's separate *Saga of Saint Olaf*; and some use must also
have been made of a now lost vellum.

The second edition was prepared under the superintendence
of Gerhard Schøning and Skúli Thorlacius and appeared in
Copenhagen 1777–83. The basis of the text down to the end of
Saint Olaf's Saga was the chief *Kringla* copy in Copenhagen, but
for the rest of the work *Eirspennill* was made the basis of the
text. Other sources from which material was obtained were principally Peringskiöld's edition, *Jöfraskinna* and *Codex Frisianus*.

Samuel Laing's translation of this Copenhagen text was published in London in 1844. In his Preface Laing modestly dis-
claims any 'considerable knowledge or great familiarity with
the Icelandic,' and says he has often, when in doubt, referred to
the translations accompanying the Stockholm and Copenhagen
editions, as well as to the Norwegian translation by Jacob Aall
(Christiania, 1838); Aall's translation of the verse and his notes
have especially been laid under contribution. Under these circumstances, it is perhaps all the more remarkable that Laing's
translation is in general as lively and as accurate as it is. But,
although the basis of his translation was thus insecure in some
respects, Laing had a quality which is not necessarily given to
a better scholar with better apparatus: he could write English
that is plain, spirited, natural and confident, and in vigour and
clarity he thus comes near to doing justice to Snorri's style.

It is, however, important to know what Snorri did and did
not write in the translation of this work attributed to him.
Some of the interpolations in the text below are printed in
square brackets and others are indicated in Appendix iii
(see p. 433).[1] The following list covers the major interpolations
and shows the source from which they are ultimately derived.

Eirspennill is the source for the following passages (similar
texts are in *Jöfraskinna* and *Codex Frisianus*); the ultimate
source is a version of *Morkinskinna*. The text of some of these
passages has been influenced by Peringskiöld's edition, where
the corresponding passages are either derived from *Hulda* or,
more usually, from a conflation of *Hulda* and Peder Claussøn.
246–9, 256–61, 267–8, 269^{35}–270^{26}, 285–6, 289–90, 290–2,
293–6, 301, 303–7, 308–9, 316–18, 334–5, 336–7.

---

[1] Line numbers are only given where the interpolated text is not
bracketed in the translation.

Codex Frisianus has supplied the following passages, also ultimately derived from a version of *Morkinskinna*: 254[23–34], 282, 284[36]–285[21], 296–7, 310[5–11], 318, 338[5–11], 343[3–6], [12–15], 345[17–24], 345–6, 346[32–40], 347[35]–348[5], 348. Also from *Codex Frisianus* are: 140[43–51] (no earlier text of the whole verse is known); 148[32–7] (this quotation from the 'Bremen Book' is also in *AM 39 fol.*); 323[1–10] (the earliest text in which this verse is found is the *Orkneyinga Saga*); 323[13–30] (verses for which *Codex Frisianus* is the earliest source). *Codex Frisianus* has further contributed material to the conflate text of the 'man-pairing' scene between King Sigurd and King Eystein, pp. 298–301.

Peringskiöld's edition is the source for the following passages: (a) Derived from Snorri's separate *Saga of Saint Olaf* (cf. p. xv): 132[30–8], 146[26–31], 157[42]–158[17], 161[30–6]. (b) Derived from Peder Claussøn and no earlier source known: 235–7, 238–9, 281[28–35]. (c) Only in Peringskiöld's edition, presumably derived from a lost manuscript: 160[26–9].

The present edition has been reprinted from plates and revision of the text has consequently been limited. The verses stand unaltered: for the most part, the essential fact recorded in them comes through in Laing's artificial couplets. I hope that most grosser errors have been corrected, either in the text or in the additional notes. About half the footnotes have been re-written in whole or in part. It has not been possible to remove all the inconsistencies in the forms of proper names, many of which are not due to Laing but to his later editors. Not the least valuable part of this reprint is, however, the new index made by Mr P. Found, in which by cross-reference and by quotation of the original form every effort has been made to present the reader with a clear and reliable guide.

I should like finally to express my gratitude to Professor G. Turville-Petre, who has done me the kindness of reading a draft of this Introduction. On this occasion, as on others, I have benefited immeasurably from his scholarship and sound judgment. He is not, however, to be made responsible for any of the opinions expressed in this Introduction.

· PETER FOOTE.

SELECT BIBLIOGRAPHY

Full bibliographies will be found in two works by Halldór Hermannsson: *Bibliography of the Sagas of the Kings of Norway and
related Sagas and Tales* (*Islandica*, III; 1910) and *The Sagas of the
Kings and the Mythical-Heroic Sagas: Two Bibliographical Supplements* (*Islandica*, XXVI; 1937).

The standard critical edition of the *Heimskringla* is by Finnur
Jónsson (*Samfund til Udgivelse af Gammel Nordisk Litteratur*,
XXIII; 1893–1900). The best general edition, also of value for
textual criticism, is by Bjarni Aðalbjarnarson (*Íslenzk Fornrit*,
XXVI–XXVIII; 1941–51).

The following short list is restricted to works in English dealing
with the historical and literary background:

A. W. BRØGGER: *Ancient Emigrants*, 1929.

A. W. BRØGGER and H. SHETELIG: *The Viking Ships*, 1951.

J. BRØNDSTED: *The Vikings*, 1960.

T. K. DERRY: *A Short History of Norway*, 1957.

K. GJERSET: *History of the Norwegian People* (2 vols.), 1915;
History of Iceland, 1925.

L. M. HOLLANDER: *The Skalds*, 1945.

T. D. KENDRICK: *A History of the Vikings*, 1930.

K. LARSEN: *A History of Norway*, 1948.

L. M. LARSON: *The Earliest Norwegian Laws*, 1935.

A. MAWER: *The Vikings*, 1913.

A. OLRIK: *Viking Civilization*, 1930.

M. OLSEN: *Farms and Fanes of Ancient Norway*, 1928.

H. SHETELIG, ed.: *Viking Antiquities in Great Britain and Ireland*,
1–6, 1940–54.

H. SHETELIG, H. FALK, E. V. GORDON: *Scandinavian Archaeology*,
1937.

G. TURVILLE-PETRE: *The Heroic Age of Scandinavia*, 1951;
Origins of Icelandic Literature, 1953.

G. VIGFUSSON and F. YORK POWELL: *Corpus Poeticum Boreale*,
2 vols., 1883.

A. WALSH: *Scandinavian Relations with Ireland during the Viking
Period*, 1922.

B .GUÐNASON: *Um Skjöldungasögu*, 1963, with a full summary in
English. This book argues that the *Skjöldunga Saga* was bare and
scholarly rather than luxurious and marvellous. Cf. p. xiii above.

TRANSLATOR'S PREFACE

It is of importance to English history to have, in the English language, the means of judging of the social and intellectual state—of the institutions and literature—of a people who during three hundred years bore an important, and for a great portion of that time a predominant part, not merely in the wars, but in the legislation of England; who occupied a very large proportion of the country, and were settled in its best lands in such numbers as to be governed by their own, not by Anglo-Saxon laws; and who undoubtedly must be the forefathers of as large a proportion of the present English nation as the Anglo-Saxons themselves, and of a much larger proportion than the Normans. These Northmen have not merely been the forefathers of the people, but of the institutions and character of the nation, to an extent not sufficiently considered by our historians. Civilised or not in comparison with the Anglo-Saxons, the Northmen must have left the influences of their character, institutions, barbarism or culture, among their own posterity. They occupied one third of all England for many generations, under their own laws; and for half a century nearly, immediately previous to the Norman conquerors, they held the supreme government of the country. It is doing good service in the fields of literature to place the English reader in a position to judge for himself of the influence which the social arrangements and spirit of these Northmen may have had on the national character, and free institutions which have grown up among us from elements planted by them, or by the Anglo-Saxons. This translation of Snorri Sturluson's Sagas of the Norse Kings will place the English reader in this position. He will see what sort of people these Northmen were who conquered and colonised the kingdoms of Northumberland, East Anglia, and other districts, equal to one-third of all England at that time, and who lived under their own laws in that portion of England; and he will see what their institutions and social spirit were at home, whether these bear any analogy to what sprung up in England afterwards, and whether to them or to the Anglo-Saxon race we are most indebted for our national character and free constitution of government. The translator of Snorri Sturluson's Sagas hopes, too, that his labour will be of good service in the fields of literature, by bringing before the English public a work of great literary merit—one which the poet, or the reader for amusement, may place in his library, as well as the antiquary and reader of English history.

.   .   .   .

The translator believes also that it opens up a new and rich field of character and incident, in which the reader who seeks amusement only will find much to interest him. The adventures, manners, mode of living, characters, and conversations of these sea-kings, are highly dramatic, in Snorri's work at least; and are told with a racy simplicity and truthfulness of language which the translator cannot flatter himself with having attained or preserved. All he can say for his work is, that any translation is better than none; and others may be stimulated by it to enter into the same course of study, who may do more justice to a branch of literature scarcely known among us.

S. LAING.

EDINBURGH, 1844.

SNORRI'S PREFACE

In this book I have had old stories written down, as I have heard them told by intelligent people, concerning chiefs who have held dominion in the northern countries, and who spoke the Danish tongue[1]; and also concerning some of their family branches, according to what has been told me. Some of this is found in ancient family registers, in which the pedigrees of kings and other personages of high birth are reckoned up, and part is written down after old songs and ballads which our forefathers had for their amusement. Now, although we cannot just say what truth there may be in these, yet we have the certainty that old and wise men held them to be true.

Thjodolf hinn Frode[2] of Kvine[3] was the scald of King Harald the Fair-haired, and he composed a poem for King Ragnvald the Mountain-high, which is called "Ynglingatal." This Ragnvald was a son of Olaf Geirstade-Alv, the brother of King Halfdan the Black. In this poem thirty of his forefathers are reckoned up, and the death and burial-place of each are given. He begins with Fjolne, a son of Yngvefrey, whom the Swedes, long after his time, worshipped and sacrificed to, and from him (Yngve) the race and family of the Ynglings take their name.

Eyvind Skaldaspiller also reckoned up the ancestors of Earl Hakon[4] the Great in a poem called "Haleygjatal," composed about Hakon; and therein he mentions Sæming, a son of

[1] The Danish tongue is the name given in ancient times to the language spoken in all the three Scandinavian lands.

[2] Surnames were not in use among the Northmen, and are still rare in Iceland. Olaf the son of Harald was called Olaf Haraldsson; Olaf's son Magnus, Magnus Olafsson; and his son Hakon, Hakon Magnusson: thus dropping altogether any common name with the family predecessors. This custom necessarily made the tracing of family connection difficult, and dependent upon the memory of scalds or others. The appellations Fair-haired, Black, and other nicknames help in distinguishing individuals of the same name from one another. *hinn Frode* = the Wise, the Much-knowing (the antiquarians have translated it as Polyhistor, Multiscius), is applied to a number of men; it usually implies a critical historian, one reliably informed about the past.

[3] Kvine is the fjord and district about Kvinesdal in the south of Norway.

[4] In Norwegian the name is now written Håkon (or Haakon) and pronounced as if spelt Hawkon.

3

Yngvefrey, and he likewise tells of the death and funeral place of each. The lives and times of the Yngling race were written from Thjodolf's narrative enlarged afterwards by the accounts of intelligent people.

As to funeral rites, the earliest age is called the Age of Burning; because all the dead were consumed by fire, and over their ashes were raised standing stones.[1] But after Frey was buried under a mound at Upsal,[2] many chiefs raised mounds, as commonly as stones, to the memory of their relatives.

The Age of Mounds began properly in Denmark after Dan Mikillati (the Magnificent) had raised for himself a burial-mound, and ordered that he should be buried in it on his death, with his royal ornaments and armour, his horse and saddle-furniture, and other valuable goods; and many of his descendants followed his example. But the burning of the dead continued, long after that time, to be the custom of the Swedes and Northmen.[3]

Iceland was settled in the time that Harald Fairhair was the King of Norway. There were scalds in Harald's court whose poems the people know by heart even at the present day, together with all the songs about the kings who have ruled in Norway since his time; and we rest the foundations of our story principally upon the songs which were sung in the presence of the chiefs themselves or of their sons, and take all to be true that is found in such poems about their feats and battles: for although it be the fashion with scalds to praise most those in whose presence they are standing, yet no one would dare to relate to a chief what he, and all those who heard it, knew to be a false and imaginary, not a true account of his deeds; because that would be mockery, not praise.

The priest Are hinn Frode [4] (the Wise), a son of Thorgils the son of Gellir, was the first man in this country [Iceland] who wrote down in the Norrön language [5] narratives of events both

---

[1] Bauta-steinar. These are in Scotland called "standing stones" by the common people, and we have no other word in our language for those monuments.

[2] i.e. Old Uppsala (Gamla Uppsala) in Sweden, some two miles north of the present univsersity town of Uppsala.

[3] These stones, particularly common in Sweden, seem to have been raised over graves or as independent memorials from c. A.D. 300 to c. A.D. 1100.

[4] Are Frode was born in Iceland in 1067, and lived to 1148. Between 1122 and 1133 he wrote his Íslendingabók (Book of the Icelanders), to which Snorri here refers. Cf. the Introduction, pp. x–xi.

[5] i.e. norrœnt mál, the Northern or Norse speech, used of the language of Norway and the settlements made from Norway, principally Iceland.

old and new. In the beginning of his book he wrote principally about the first settlements in Iceland, the laws and government, and next of the lagmen [law-speakers],[1] and how long each had administered the law; and he reckoned the years at first, until the time when Christianity was introduced into Iceland, and afterwards reckoned from that to his own times. To this he added many other subjects, such as the lives and times of kings of Norway and Denmark, and also of England; besides accounts of great events which have taken place in this country itself. His narratives are considered by many men of knowledge to be the most remarkable of all; because he was a man of good understanding, and so old that his birth was as far back as the year after Harald Sigurdson's fall.[2] He wrote, as he himself says, the lives and times of the kings of Norway from the report of Odd Kolsson, a grandson of Hall of Sida. Odd again took his information from Thorgeir Afradskoll, who was an intelligent man, and so old that when Earl Hakon the Great was killed (995) he was dwelling at Nidaros[3]—the same place at which King Olaf Trygvesson afterwards laid the foundation of the merchant town of Drontheim which is now there.

The priest Are came, when seven years old, to Haukadal[4] to Hall Thorarinson, and was there fourteen years. Hall was a man of great knowledge and of excellent memory; and he could even remember being baptised, when he was three years old, by the priest Thangbrand, the year before Christianity was established by law in Iceland. Are was twelve years of age when Bishop Isleiv[5] died, and at his death eighty years had elapsed since the fall of Olaf Trygvesson. Hall died nine years later than Bishop Isleiv, and had attained nearly the age of ninety-four years. Hall had traded between the two countries, and had been in partnership in trading concerns with King Olaf the Saint, by which his circumstances had been greatly improved, and he had become well acquainted with the kingdom of Norway. He had fixed his residence in Haukadal when he was thirty years of age, and he had dwelt there nearly sixty-four years, as Are tells us. Teit, a son of Bishop Isleiv, was fostered in the house of Hall of Haukadal, and afterwards dwelt

---

[1] The law-speaker was the highest officer of the Icelandic Commonwealth and president of the Althing. In each of his three years of office he recited one-third of the laws at the Althing.

[2] Harald was killed in 1066.

[3] Nidaros, Drontheim, Trondhjem, all the same place.

[4] In the South of Iceland.

[5] Isleiv was the first native bishop in Iceland; he had studied at Hervorden (Westphalia); consecrated 1056 (or '57), died 1080.

there himself. He taught Are the priest, and gave him information about many circumstances which Are afterwards wrote
down. Are also got many a piece of information from Thurid,
a daughter of the gode[1] Snorri.[2] Thurid was wise and intelligent, and remembered her father Snorri, who was nearly thirty-
five years of age when Christianity was introduced into Iceland,
and died a year after King Olaf the Saint's fall.[3] So it is not
wonderful that Are the priest had good information about
ancient events both here in Iceland, and abroad, being a man
anxious for information, intelligent, and of excellent memory,
and having besides learned much from old intelligent persons.

But the poems seem to me least corrupt, if the metrical rules
are observed in them and if they are sensibly interpreted.

[1] The word *gode* was the title given to the local leaders in early Iceland;
they had a kind of political authority and in pagan times were also responsible for the performance of the public sacrifices. In national affairs
they constituted a kind of loose oligarchy, since they were the voting members of the Legislative Court (*lögrétta*) at the Althing. They numbered
thirty-six when the Althing was established, A.D. 930; an additional three
were appointed *c.* 965, and an additional nine *c.* 1005.
[2] Snorri Gode died in 1031, at the age of sixty-seven.
[3] This happened in 1030.

I

THE YNGLINGA SAGA

OR THE STORY OF THE YNGLING FAMILY FROM ODIN TO HALFDAN THE BLACK

CHAPTER I. OF THE SITUATION OF COUNTRIES.—It is said that the earth's circle which the human race inhabits is torn across into many bights, so that great seas run into the land from the out-ocean. Thus it is known that a great sea goes in at Narvesund,[1] and up to the land of Jerusalem. From the same sea a long sea-bight stretches towards the north-east, and is called the Black Sea, and divides the three parts of the earth; of which the eastern part is called Asia, and the western is called by some Europa, by some Enea.[2] Northward of the Black Sea lies Swithiod the Great,[3] or the Cold. The Great Swithiod is reckoned by some as not less than the Great Serkland[4]; others compare it to the Great Blueland.[5] The northern part of Swithiod lies uninhabited on account of frost and cold, as likewise the southern parts of Blueland are waste from the burning of the sun. In Swithiod are many great domains, and many races of men, and many kinds of languages. There are giants, and there are dwarfs, and there are also blue men, and there are many kinds of strange creatures. There are huge wild beasts, and dreadful dragons. On the south side of the mountains which lie outside of all inhabited lands runs a river through Swithiod, which is properly called by the name of Tanais,[6] but was formerly called Tanakvisl, or Vanakvisl, and which falls into the Black Sea. The country of the people on the Vanakvisl was called Vanaland, or Vanaheim; and the river separates the

[1] The Straits of Gibraltar; Narvesund (N(j)örvasund) means "narrow sound."

[2] In ancient days it was a common belief that the Romans, Franks, British, and other peoples, were descended from Æneas and the Trojans.

[3] Swithiod the Great, or the Cold, is the ancient name for Russia (Scythia Major). It is also called Godheim in the mythological sagas, the home of Odin and the other gods. Swithiod the Less is Sweden proper, and is called Mannheim, or the home of the descendants of these gods.

[4] Serkland means North Africa and Spain and the countries of the Saracens in Asia.

[5] Bláland, the country of the blacks in Africa.

[6] The modern river Don.

7

three parts of the world, of which the eastermost part is called Asia, and the westermost Europe.

CHAPTER II. OF THE PEOPLE OF ASIA.—The country east of the Tanakvisl in Asia was called Asaland, or Asaheim, and the chief city in that land was called Asgaard.[1] In that city was a chief called Odin, and it was a great place for sacrifice. It was the custom there that twelve temple priests should both direct the sacrifices, and also judge the people. They were called Diar,[2] or Drotner,[3] and all the people served and obeyed them. Odin was a great and very far-travelled warrior, who conquered many kingdoms, and so successful was he that in every battle the victory was on his side. It was the belief of his people that victory belonged to him in every battle. It was his custom when he sent his men into battle, or on any expedition, that he first laid his hand upon their heads, and called down a blessing upon them; and then they believed their undertaking would be successful. His people also were accustomed, whenever they fell into danger by land or sea, to call upon his name; and they thought that always they got comfort and aid by it, for where he was they thought help was near. Often he went away so far that he passed many seasons on his journeys.

CHAPTER III. OF ODIN'S BROTHERS.—Odin had two brothers, the one called Ve, the other Vilje, and they governed the kingdom when he was absent. It happened once when Odin had gone to a great distance, and had been so long away that the people of Asa doubted if he would ever return home, that his two brothers took it upon themselves to divide his estate; but both of them took his wife Frigg to themselves. Odin soon after returned home, and took his wife back.

CHAPTER IV. OF ODIN'S WAR WITH THE PEOPLE OF VANALAND. —Odin went out with a great army against the Vanaland people; but they were well prepared, and defended their land, so that victory was changeable, and they ravaged the lands of each other, and did great damage. They tired of this at last, and on both sides appointed a meeting for establishing peace, made a truce, and exchanged hostages. The Vanaland people sent their best men, Njord the Rich, and his son Frey. The

---

[1] The old gods were called Æsir (sing. Áss) and Snorri derives the name from Asia.

[2] Diar is a rare name of the old gods and is supposed to be a term imported from the Irish in the ninth or tenth century.

[3] Dróttinn, sing., lord. The word does not seem to have been applied directly to the heathen gods, but it was later common for God and Christ.

people of Asaland sent a man called Höne, whom they thought
well suited to be a chief,[1] as he was a stout and very handsome
man; and with him they sent a man of great understanding
called Mime. On the other side, the Vanaland people sent the
wisest man in their community, who was called Kvase. Now,
when Höne came to Vanaheim he was immediately made a
chief, and Mime came to him with good counsel on all occasions.
But when Höne stood in the Things or other meetings, if Mime
was not near him, and any difficult matter was laid before him,
he always answered in one way—"Now let others give their
advice"; so that the Vanaland people got a suspicion that the
Asaland people had deceived them in the exchange of men.
They took Mime, therefore, and beheaded him, and sent his
head to the Asaland people. Odin took the head, smeared it
with herbs so that it should not rot, and sang incantations
over it. Thereby he gave it the power that it spoke to him,
and discovered to him many secrets. Odin placed Njord and
Frey as priests of the sacrifices, and they became Diar of
the Asaland people. Njord's daughter Freya was priestess of
the sacrifices, and first taught the Asaland people the magic
art, as it was in use and fashion among the Vanaland people.
While Njord was with the Vanaland people he had taken
his own sister in marriage, for that was allowed by their law;
and their children were Frey and Freya. But among the
Asaland people it was forbidden to intermarry with such near
relations.

CHAPTER V. ODIN DIVIDES HIS KINGDOM: ALSO CONCERNING
GEFION.—There goes a great mountain barrier [2] from north-east
to south-west, which divides the Greater Swithiod from other
kingdoms. South of this mountain ridge it is not far to Turkland,[3] where Odin had great possessions. In those times the
Roman chiefs went wide around in the world, subduing to themselves all people; and on this account many chiefs fled from
their domains. But Odin having foreknowledge, and magic-
sight, knew that his posterity would come to settle and dwell
in the northern half of the world. He therefore set his brothers
Ve and Vilje over Asgaard; and he himself, with all the gods
and a great many other people, wandered out, first westward

[1] These exchanges appear not to have been of hostages, but of chiefs
to be incorporated with the people to whom they were sent, and thus
to preserve peace.
[2] The Caucasus, which really runs from S.E. to N.W.
[3] Turkey, i.e. Asia Minor and vicinity. The Turks were then regarded,
from the similarity of names, as the Teucrians or Trojans.

to Gardarike,[1] and then south to Saxland.[2] He had many
sons; and after having subdued an extensive kingdom in Saxland, he set his sons to rule the country. He himself went
northwards to the sea, and took up his abode in an island which
is called Odinsö in Fyen. Then he sent Gefion across the sound
to the north [north-east] to discover new countries; and she
came to King Gylve,[3] who gave her a ploughgate of land. Then
she went to Jotunheim,[4] and bore four sons to a giant, and
transformed them into a yoke of oxen. She yoked them to a
plough, and broke out the land into the ocean right opposite
to Odinsö. This land was called Sealand,[5] and there she afterwards settled and dwelt. Skjold, a son of Odin, married her,
and they dwelt at Leidre.[6] Where the ploughed land was is a
lake or sea called Laage.[7] In the Swedish land the fjords of
Laage correspond to the nesses in Sealand. Brage the Old
sings thus of it:

> Gefion from Gylve drove away,
> To add new land to Denmark's sway—
> Blythe Gefion ploughing in the smoke
> That steamed up from her oxen-yoke:
> Four heads, eight forehead stars had they,
> Bright gleaming, as she ploughed away;
> Dragging new lands from the deep main
> To join them to the sweet isle's plain.

Now when Odin heard that things were in a prosperous
condition in the land to the east beside Gylve, he went thither,
and Gylve made a peace with him, for Gylve thought he had no
strength to oppose the people of Asaland. Odin and Gylve had
many tricks and enchantments against each other; but the Asaland people had always the superiority. Odin took up his
residence at the Mælare lake, at the place now called Old
Sigtun.[8] There he erected a large temple, where there were
sacrifices according to the customs of the Asaland people. He
appropriated to himself the whole of that district, and called
it Sigtun. To the temple priests he gave also domains. Njord
dwelt in Noatun, Frey in Upsal, Heimdal in the Himinbergs,

[1] Gardarike is Russia.
[2] Saxland is North Germany.
[3] Snorri had previously written about King Gylve in Sweden in his *Prose
Edda* (trans. J. Young, 1954, p. 27 ff.).
[4] According to Snorri, Jotunheim lay in the north or north-east of
Sweden.
[5] Modern Sjælland (Zeeland), the largest of the Danish islands.
[6] Near Roskilde in Sjælland. Skjold was the progenitor of the great
Danish dynasty, the Skjoldungs.
[7] The great lake Mälaren in Sweden.
[8] Old Sigtun was near the present Sigtuna on the Uppsalafjord.

Thor in Thrudvang, Balder in Breidablik; to all of them he gave good estates.[1]

CHAPTER VI. OF ODIN'S ACCOMPLISHMENTS.—When Odin of Asaland came to the north, and the Diar with him, they introduced and taught to others the arts which the people long afterwards have practised. Odin was the cleverest of all, and from him all the others learned their arts and accomplishments; and he knew them first, and knew many more than other people. But now, to tell why he is held in such high respect, we must mention various causes that contributed to it. When sitting among his friends his countenance was so beautiful and dignified, that the spirits of all were exhilarated by it; but when he was in war he appeared dreadful to his foes. This arose from his being able to change his skin and form in any way he liked. Another cause was, that he conversed so cleverly and smoothly, that all who heard believed him. He spoke everything in rhyme, such as now composed, which we call scald-craft. He and his temple priests were called song-smiths, for from them came that art of song into the northern countries. Odin could make his enemies in battle blind, or deaf, or terror-struck, and their weapons so blunt that they could no more cut than a willow wand; on the other hand, his men rushed forwards without armour, were as mad as dogs or wolves, bit their shields, and were strong as bears or wild bulls, and killed people at a blow, but neither fire nor iron told upon themselves. This was called the Berserk fury.[2]

CHAPTER VII. OF ODIN'S FEATS.—Odin could transform his shape: his body would lie as if dead, or asleep; but then he would be in shape of a fish, or worm, or bird, or beast, and be off in a twinkling to distant lands upon his own or other people's business. With words alone he could quench fire, still the ocean in tempest, and turn the wind to any quarter he pleased. Odin had a ship which was called Skidbladnir, in which he sailed over wide seas, and which he could roll up like a cloth. Odin carried with him Mime's head, which told him all the

[1] These are the names of the habitations of the gods, culled from the mythology, and not real place-names.
[2] Berserk: a man capable of fits of frenzy, sometimes self-induced (possibly by drugs), which increased his strength and made him regardless of pain; such men were often considered to have magical powers. The name is thought to mean "bear-shirt," probably because they looked on the bear as a kind of totem animal and dressed themselves in bear-skins. On p. 64 the term "wolf-skin-clad" is also used to describe berserks. It is thought that such men were probably paranoic, or perhaps sometimes epileptic, types.

news of other countries. Sometimes even he called the dead out of the earth, or set himself beside the hanged men; whence he was called the ghost-sovereign, and lord of the hanged. He had two ravens,[1] to whom he had taught the speech of man; and they flew far and wide through the land, and brought him the news. Because of all this he was pre-eminently wise. He taught all these arts in Runes, and songs which are called incantations, and therefore the Asaland people are called incantation-smiths. Odin understood also the art in which the greatest power is lodged, and which he himself practised; namely, what is called magic. By means of this he could know beforehand the predestined fate [2] of men, or their not yet completed lot; and also bring on the death, ill-luck, or bad health of people, and take the strength or wit from one person and give it to another. But after such witchcraft followed such weakness and anxiety, that it was not thought respectable for men to practise it; and therefore the priestesses were brought up in this art. Odin knew finely where all hidden treasure was concealed under the earth, and understood the songs by which the earth, the hills, the stones, and mounds were opened to him; and he bound those who dwell in them by the power of his word, and went in and took what he pleased. From these arts he became very celebrated. His enemies dreaded him; his friends put their trust in him, and relied on his power and on himself. He taught the most of his arts to his priests of the sacrifices, and they came nearest to himself in all wisdom and witch-knowledge. Many others, however, occupied themselves much with it; and from that time witchcraft spread far and wide, and continued long. People sacrificed to Odin and the twelve chiefs from Asaland, and called them their gods, and believed in them long after. From Odin's name came the name Audun,[3] which people gave their sons; and from Thor's name come Thore, also Thorarinn; and also it is sometimes compounded with other names, as Steinthor, or Havthor, or even altered in other ways.

CHAPTER VIII. OF ODIN'S LAWGIVING.—Odin established the same law in his land that had been in force in Asaland. Thus he established by law that all dead men should be burned, and

---

[1] Huginn and Muninn, Thought and Memory.
[2] It was believed that the gods too were subject to fate and were destined to perish in a great cataclysmic battle against the evil powers, *ragnarök*, the doom of the gods.
[3] Snorri mistakes here. Audun does not come from Odin, but from audr (riches) and vinr (friend).

their belongings laid with them upon the pile, and the ashes be cast into the sea or buried in the earth. Thus, said he, every one will come to Valhalla [1] with the riches he had with him upon the pile; and he would also enjoy whatever he himself had buried in the earth. For men of consequence a mound should be raised to their memory, and for all other warriors who had been distinguished for manhood a standing stone; which custom remained long after Odin's time. On winter day [2] there should be blood-sacrifice for a good year, and in the middle of winter for a good crop; and the third sacrifice should be on summer day, for victory in battle. Over all Swithiod the people paid Odin a scatt or tax—so much on each head; but he had to defend the country from enemy or disturbance, and pay the expense of the sacrifice feasts for a good year.

CHAPTER IX. OF NJORD'S MARRIAGE.—Njord took a wife called Skade; but she would not live with him and married afterwards Odin, and had many sons by him, of whom one was called Sæming; and about him Eyvind Skaldaspiller sings thus:

> To Asa's son Queen Skade bore
> Sæming, who dyed his shield in gore,—
> The giant-queen of rock and snow,
> Who loves to dwell on earth below,
> The iron pine-tree's daughter, she
> Sprung from the rocks that rib the sea,
> To Odin bore full many a son,
> Heroes of many a battle won.

To Sæming Earl Hakon the Great reckoned back his pedigree. This Swithiod they called Mannheim, but the Great Swithiod they called Godheim; and of Godheim great wonders and novelties were related.

CHAPTER X. OF ODIN'S DEATH.—Odin died in his bed in Swithiod; and when he was near his death he made himself be marked with the point of a spear,[3] and said he was going to Godheim, and would give a welcome there to all his friends, and all dead in battle should be dedicated to him; and the Swedes believed that he was gone to the ancient Asgaard, and would live there eternally. Then began the belief in Odin, and the calling upon him. The Swedes believed that he often showed

---

[1] Odin's hall (in heaven) where fallen heroes went after death.

[2] Winter day was in the middle of October (later 14 October) and summer day in mid-April (later 14 April).

[3] In the *Gautreks Saga* a sacrifice to Odin is described, in which the victim is to be hanged and stabbed with a spear; in the mystic verses of the *Hávamál* Odin is made to describe how he hung on a tree, wounded by a spear, a sacrifice to himself, in order to obtain magic power. The spear is Odin's typical weapon.

himself to them before any great battle. To some he gave
victory; others he invited to himself; and they reckoned both
of these to be fortunate. Odin was burnt, and at his pile there
was great splendour. It was their faith that the higher the
smoke arose in the air, the higher he would be raised whose pile
it was; and the richer he would be, the more property that
was consumed with him.

CHAPTER XI. OF NJORD.—Njord of Noatun was then the
sole sovereign of the Swedes; and he continued the sacrifices,
and was called the drottinn, or lord, by the Swedes, and he
received scatt and gifts from them. In his days were peace
and plenty, and such good years, in all respects, that the Swedes
believed Njord ruled over the growth of seasons and the prosperity of the people. In his time all the diar or gods died, and
blood-sacrifices were made for them. Njord died on a bed of
sickness, and before he died made himself be marked for Odin
with the spear-point. The Swedes burned him, and all wept
over his grave-mound.

CHAPTER XII. FREY'S DEATH.—Frey took the kingdom after
Njord, and was called lord of the Swedes, and they paid
taxes to him. He was, like his father, fortunate in friends and
in good seasons. Frey built a great temple at Upsal, made it
his chief seat, and gave it all his taxes, his land, and goods.
Then began the Upsal domains,[1] which have remained ever
since. Then began in his days the Frode-peace[2]; and then
there were good seasons in all the land, which the Swedes
ascribed to Frey, so that he was more worshipped than the
other gods, as the people became much richer in his days by
reason of the peace and good seasons. His wife was called
Gerd, daughter of Gymir, and their son was called Fjölne.
Frey was called by another name, Yngve; and this name Yngve
was considered long after in his race as a name of honour, so
that his descendants have since been called Ynglings. Frey
fell into a sickness; and as his illness took the upper hand, his
men took the plan of letting few approach him. In the mean-

[1] The Upsal domains were certain estates for the support of the sovereign
and of the temple and rites of worship; after the introduction of Christianity
they remained with the Crown and constituted an important part of its
property. Cf. Snorri's account of the provinces of Sweden in the *Olaf
Sagas*, pp. 184-6.

[2] Snorri is referring to what he says in the *Prose Edda*: "Frode took the
kingdom [Denmark] after his father Fridleiv at the time when the Emperor
Augustus made peace over the whole world. Then Christ was born. But
because Frode was the mightiest king in the North lands, the Northmen
ascribed the peace to him and called it the Frode-peace."

time they raised a great mound, in which they placed a door with three holes in it. Now when Frey died they bore him secretly into the mound, but told the Swedes he was alive; and they kept watch over him for three years. They brought all the taxes into the mound, and through the one hole they put in the gold, through the other the silver, and through the third the copper money that was paid. Peace and good seasons continued.

CHAPTER XIII. OF FREYA AND HER DAUGHTERS.—Freya alone remained of the gods, and she became on this account so celebrated that all women of distinction were called by her name, whence they now have the title Frue; so that every woman is called frue, or mistress over her property, and the wife is called the house-frue. Freya continued the blood-sacrifices. Freya was a rather fickle woman. Her husband was called Od, and her daughters Hnoss and Gerseme.[1] They were so very beautiful, that afterwards the most precious jewels were called by their names.

When it became known to the Swedes that Frey was dead, and yet peace and good seasons continued, they believed that it must be so as long as Frey remained in Sweden; and therefore they would not burn his remains, but called him the god of this world, and afterwards offered continually blood-sacrifices to him, principally for peace and good seasons.

CHAPTER XIV. OF KING FJOLNE'S DEATH. Fjolne, Yngve Frey's son, ruled thereafter over the Swedes and the Upsal domains. He was powerful, and lucky in seasons and in holding the peace. Fredfrode ruled then in Leidre, and between them there was great friendship and visiting. Once when Fjolne went to Frode in Sealand, a great feast was prepared for him, and invitations to it were sent all over the country. Frode had a large house, in which there was a great vessel many ells high, and put together of great pieces of timber; and this vessel stood in a lower room. Above it was a loft, in the floor of which was an opening through which liquor was poured into this vessel. The vessel was full of mead, which was excessively strong. In the evening Fjolne, with his attendants, was taken into the adjoining loft to sleep. In the night he went out to the gallery to seek a certain place, and he was very sleepy and exceedingly drunk. As he came back to his room he went

---

[1] In the *Prose Edda* Snorri says merely: "The daughter of Freya and Od is Hnoss. She is so fair that from her name everything is called *hnoss* which is beautiful and precious." *hnoss* means a jewel, and *gerseme* a precious or superb article.

along the gallery to the door of another loft, went into it, and his foot slipping, he fell into the vessel of mead and was drowned. So says Thjodolf of Kvine:

> In Frode's hall the fearful word,
> The death-foreboding sound was heard:
> The cry of fey [1] denouncing doom,
> Was heard at night in Frode's home.
> And when brave Frode came, he found
> Swithiod's dark chief, Fjolne, drowned.
> In Frode's mansion drowned was he,
> Drowned in a waveless, windless sea.

CHAPTER XV. OF SWEGDE.—Swegde took the kingdom after his father, and he made a solemn vow to seek Godheim and Odin. He went with twelve men through the world, and came to Turkland, and the Great Swithiod, where he found many of his connections. He was five years on this journey; and when he returned home to Sweden he remained there for some time. He had got a wife in Vanaheim, who was called Vana, and their son was Vanlande. Swegde went out afterwards to seek again for Godheim, and came to a mansion on the east side of Swithiod called Stein, where there was a stone as big as a large house. In the evening after sunset, as Swegde was going from the drinking-table to his sleeping-room, he cast his eye upon the stone, and saw that a dwarf was sitting under it. Swegde and his man were very drunk, and they ran towards the stone. The dwarf stood in the door, and called to Swegde, and told him to come in, and he should see Odin. Swegde ran into the stone, which instantly closed behind him, and Swegde never came back. Thjodolf of Kvine tells of this:

> By Durnir's [2] elfin race,
> Who haunt the cliffs and shun day's face,
> The valiant Swegde was deceived,
> The elf's false words the king believed.
> The dauntless hero rushing on,
> Passed through the yawning mouth of stone:
> It yawned—it shut—the hero fell,
> In Sökmime's [3] hall, where giants dwell.

CHAPTER XVI. OF VANLANDE, SWEGDE'S SON.—Vanlande, Swegde's son, succeeded his father, and ruled over the Upsal

[1] Fey, *feigr*, is used in the same sense in the northern languages as in Scotland, denoting the acts or words or sounds preceding, and supposed to be portending, a sudden death.

[2] Durnir, a dwarf's name, which is thought to mean "door-keeper."

[3] Sökmime, a giant's name; both the dwarfs and the giants were thought of as mountain-dwellers.

domain. He was a great warrior, and went far around in different lands. Once he took up his winter abode in Finland with Snæ [1] the Old, and got his daughter Driva in marriage; but in spring he set out leaving Driva behind, and although he had promised to return within three years he did not come back for ten. Then Driva sent a message to the witch Huld; and sent Visbur, her son by Vanlande, to Sweden. Driva bribed the witch-wife Huld, either that she should bewitch Vanlande to return to Finland, or kill him. When this witch-work was going on Vanlande was at Upsal, and a great desire came over him to go to Finland; but his friends and counsellors advised him against it, and said the witchcraft of the Finn people showed itself in this desire of his to go there. He then became very drowsy, and laid himself down to sleep; but when he had slept but a little while he cried out, saying that the Mara [2] was treading upon him. His men hastened to him to help him; but when they took hold of his head she trod on his legs, and when they laid hold of his legs she pressed upon his head; and it was his death. The Swedes took his body and burnt it at a river called Skytaa,[3] where standing stones were raised over him. Thus says Thjodolf:

> And Vanlande, in a fatal hour,
> Was dragg'd by Grimhild's daughter's power,
> The witch-wife's, to the dwelling-place
> Where men meet Odin face to face.
> Trampled to death, to Skytaa's shore
> The corpse his faithful followers bore;
> And there they burnt, with heavy hearts,
> The good chief killed by witchcraft's arts.

CHAPTER XVII. OF VISBUR, VANLANDE'S SON.—Visbur succeeded his father Vanlande. He married the daughter of Aude the Rich, and gave her as her bride-gift three large farms, and a gold ornament. They had two sons, Gisl and Ondur; but Visbur left her and took another wife, whereupon she went home to her father with her two sons. Visbur had a son who was called Domald, and his stepmother used witchcraft to give him ill-luck. Now, when Visbur's sons were the one twelve, the other thirteen years of age, they went to their father's place, and desired to have their mother's dower; but he would not deliver it to them. Then they said that the gold ornament should be the death of the best man in all his race, and they

---

[1] Snæ, snow and Driva, snowdrift. This story has certain analogies with the wooing of the Northern princess by the Finnish hero of *Kalevala*.

[2] Mara, the nightmare. The Norse witch or female ghost (Succubus) often chose this way of haunting male victims.

[3] This river and place are not now known; but see below, p. 20, Skjotan's Ford.

returned home. Then they began again with enchantments and witchcraft, to try if they could destroy their father. The sorceress Huld said that by witchcraft she could bring it about by this means, that a murderer of his own kin should never be wanting in the Yngling race; and they agreed to have it so. Thereafter they collected men, came unexpectedly in the night on Visbur, and burned him in his house. So sings Thjodolf:

> Have the fire-dogs' fierce tongues yelling
> Lapt Visbur's blood on his own hearth?
> Have the flames consumed the dwelling
> Of the hero's soul on earth?
> Madly ye acted, who set free
> The forest foe, red fire, night thief,
> Fell brother of the raging sea,
> Against your father and your chief.[1]

CHAPTER XVIII. OF DOMALD, VISBUR'S SON.—Domald took the heritage after his father Visbur, and ruled over the land. As in his time there was great famine and distress, the Swedes made great offerings of sacrifice at Upsal. The first autumn they sacrificed oxen, but the succeeding season was not improved thereby. The following autumn they sacrificed men, but the succeeding year was rather worse. The third autumn, when the offer of sacrifices should begin, a great multitude of Swedes came to Upsal; and now the chiefs held consultations with each other, and all agreed that the times of scarcity were on account of their king Domald, and they resolved to offer him for good seasons, and to assault and kill him, and sprinkle the stalls [2] of the gods with his blood. And they did so. Thjodolf tells of this:

> It has happened oft ere now,
> That foeman's weapon has laid low
> The crowned head, where battle plain
> Was miry red with the blood-rain.
> But Domald dies by bloody arms,
> Raised not by foes in war's alarms—
> Raised by his Swedish liegemen's hand,
> To bring good seasons to the land.

CHAPTER XIX. OF DOMAR, DOMALD'S SON.—Domald's son, called Domar, next ruled over the land. He reigned long, and in his days were good seasons and peace. Nothing is told of him but that he died in his bed in Upsal, and was transported

---

[1] A literal version of the stanza reads thus (the *kennings* are in quotation marks): And the "kinsman of the sea" [fire] swallowed the "citadel of the will" [body] of Visbur, when the "defenders of the kingship" [princes] incited the "harmful thief of the forest" [fire] against their father, and the "hound of embers" [fire] crackling bit the all-powerful one in the "ship of the fireplace" [house].

[2] The stalls apparently resembled altars.

to the Fyrisvold,[1] where his body was burned on the river bank, and where his standing stones still remain. So says Thjodolf:

> I have asked wise men to tell
> Where Domar rests, and they knew well.
> Domar, on Fyrie's wide-spread ground,
> Was burned, and laid on Yngve's mound.

CHAPTER XX. OF DYGVE, DOMAR'S SON.—Dygve was the name of his son, who succeeded him in ruling the land; and about him nothing is said but that he died in his bed. Thjodolf tells of it thus:

> Dygve the Brave, the mighty king,
> It is no hidden secret thing,
> Has gone to meet a royal mate,
> Riding upon the horse of Fate.
> For Loke's daughter [2] in her house
> Of Yngve's race would have a spouse;
> Therefore the fell-one snatched away
> Brave Dygve from the light of day.

Dygve's mother was Drott, a daughter of King Danp, the son of Rig, who was first called "king" in the Danish tongue. His descendants always afterwards considered the title of king the title of highest dignity. Dygve was the first of his family to be called king, for his predecessors had been called *Drottnar*, and their wives *Drottningar*, and their court *Drott*. Each of their race was called Yngve, or Yngune, and the whole race together Ynglinger. The Queen Drott was a sister of King Dan Mikillati, from whom Denmark took its name.

CHAPTER XXI. OF DAG THE WISE.—King Dygve's son, called Dag, succeeded to him, and was so wise a man that he understood the language of birds. He had a sparrow which told him much news, and flew to different countries. Once the sparrow flew to Reidgotaland,[3] to a farm called Varva, where he flew into a peasant's corn-field and took his grain. The peasant came up, took a stone, and killed the sparrow. King Dag was ill-pleased that the sparrow did not come home; [4]

---

[1] The plains along the banks of the river Fyris, between Old Uppsala and the present Uppsala.

[2] Hel was the daughter of Loke and she was set to rule over the under-world to which those men who did not die in battle were consigned; see the *Prose Edda*, trans. J. Young, 1954, p. 56.

[3] In the *Prose Edda* Snorri says that "the whole mainland was called Reidgotaland, and all the islands Eygotaland. Now the former is called the dominion of the Danes, the latter the dominion of the Swedes." Originally Reidgotaland seems to have meant Gothic dominions on the south-east Baltic coast. See G. Turville-Petre, *Hervarar Saga* (Viking Society, 1956), p. 77, note to 27/6.

[4] Dag resembles the god Odin in having special birds to bring him news.

and as he, in a sacrifice of expiation, inquired after the sparrow, he got the answer that it was killed at Varva. Thereupon he ordered a great army, and went to Gotland; and when he came to Varva he landed with his men and plundered, and the people fled away before him. King Dag returned in the evening to his ships, after having killed many people and taken many prisoners. As they were going across a river at a place called Skjotan's [Projectiles] Ford, a labouring thrall came running to the river-side, and threw a hay-fork into their troop. It struck the king on the head, so that he fell instantly from his horse and died. In those times the chief who ravaged a country was called Gram,[1] and the men-at-arms under him Gramer. Thjodolf sings of it thus:

> What news is this that the king's men,
> Flying eastward through the glen,
> Report? That Dag the Brave, whose name
> Is sounded far and wide by Fame—
> That Dag, who knew so well to wield
> The battle-axe in bloody field,
> Where brave men meet, no more will head
> The brave—that mighty Dag is dead!

> Varva was wasted with the sword,
> And vengeance taken for the bird—
> The little bird that used to bring
> News to the ear of the great king.
> Varva was ravaged, and the strife
> Was ended, when the monarch's life.
> Was ended too—the great Dag fell
> By the hay-fork of a base thrall!

CHAPTER XXII. OF AGNE, DAG'S SON.—Agne was the name of Dag's son, who was king after him—a powerful and celebrated man, expert, and exercised in all feats. It happened one summer that King Agne went with his army to Finland, and landed and marauded. The Finland people gathered a large army, and proceeded to the strife under a chief called Froste. There was a great battle, in which King Agne gained the victory, and Froste fell there with a great many of his people. King Agne proceeded with armed hand through Finland, subdued it, and made enormous booty. He took Froste's daughter Skjalv, and her brother Loge, and carried them along with him. When he sailed from the east he came to land at Stoksund,[2] and put up his tent on the flat side of the river, where then there was a wood. King Agne had at the time the gold ornament which had

---

[1] Gram is equivalent to grim, fierce.
[2] Stoksund is the sound Norrström at Stockholm, between Mälaren and the Baltic.

belonged to Visbur. He now married Skjalv and she begged him
to make burial feast in honour of her father. He invited a great
many guests, and made a great feast. He had become very celebrated by his expedition, and there was a great drinking match.
Now when King Agne had got drunk, Skjalv bade him take care of
his gold ornament which he had about his neck; therefore he
took hold of the ornament, and bound it fast about his neck
before he went to sleep. The land-tent stood at the wood side,
and a high tree over the tent protected it against the heat of
the sun. Now when King Agne was asleep, Skjalv took a noose,
and fastened it under the ornament. Thereupon her men threw
down the tent-poles, cast the loop of the noose up in the branches
of the tree, and hauled upon it, so that the king was hanged
close under the branches and died; and Skjalv with her men
ran down to their ships, and rowed away. King Agne was
burned upon the spot, which was afterwards called Agnefet [1];
and it lies on the east side of the Tauren, and west [2] of Stoksund. Thjodolf speaks of it thus:

> How do ye like the high-souled maid,
> Who, with the grim Fate-goddess' aid,
> Avenged her sire?—made Swithiod's king
> Through air in golden halter swing?
> How do ye like her, Agne's men?
> Think ye that any chief again
> Will court the fate your chief befell,
> To ride on wooden horse to hell?

CHAPTER XXIII. OF ALRIC AND ERIC.—The sons of Agne
were called Alric and Eric, and were kings together after him.
They were powerful men, great warriors, and expert at all feats
of arms. It was their custom to ride and break in horses both
to walk and to gallop, which nobody understood so well as they;
and they vied with each other who could ride best, and keep
the best horses. It happened one day that both the brothers
rode out together alone, and at a distance from their followers,
with their best horses, and rode on to a field; but never came
back. The people at last went out to look after them, and
they were both found dead with their heads crushed. As they
had no weapons, except it might be their horses' bridles, people
believed that they had killed each other with these. So says
Thjodolf:

> Alric fell, by Eric slain,
> Eric's life-blood dyed the plain.
> Brother fell by brother's hand;
> And they tell it in the land,

---

[1] Agne-fet—Agne-meadow, to the south of the modern Stockholm.
[2] It was really to the south of Stoksund.

> That they worked the wicked deed
> With the sharp bits that guide the steed.
> Shall it be said of Frey's brave sons,
> The kingly race, the noble ones,
> That they have fought in deadly battle
> With the head-gear of their cattle?

CHAPTER XXIV. OF YNGVE AND ALF.—Alric's sons, Yngve and Alf, then succeeded to the kingly power in Sweden. Yngve was a great warrior, always victorious; handsome, expert in all exercises, strong and very sharp in battle, generous and full of mirth; so that he was both renowned and beloved. Alf was a silent, harsh, unfriendly man, and sat at home in the land, and never went out on war expeditions. His mother was called Dageid, a daughter of King Dag the Great, from whom the Dagling family is descended. King Alf had a wife named Bera, who was the most agreeable of women, very brisk and gay. One autumn Yngve, Alric's son, had arrived at Upsal from a viking cruise by which he was become very celebrated. He often sat long in the evening at the drinking-table; but Alf went willingly to bed very early. Queen Bera sat often till late in the evening, and she and Yngve conversed together for their amusement; but Alf soon told her that she should not sit up so late in the evening, but should go first to bed, so as not to waken him. She replied, that happy would be the woman who had Yngve instead of Alf for her husband; and as she often repeated the same, he became very angry. One evening Alf went into the hall, where Yngve and Bera sat on the high seat speaking to each other. Yngve had a short sword upon his knees, and the guests were so drunk that they did not observe the king coming in. King Alf went straight to the high seat, drew a sword from under his cloak, and pierced his brother Yngve through and through. Yngve leaped up, drew his short sword, and gave Alf his death-wound; so that both fell dead on the floor. Alf and Yngve were buried under mounds in Fyrisvold. Thus tells Thjodolf of it:

> I tell you of a horrid thing,
> A deed of dreadful note I sing—
> How by false Bera, wicked queen,
> The murderous brother-hands were seen
> Each raised against a brother's life;
> How wretched Alf with bloody knife
> Gored Yngve's heart, and Yngve's blade
> Alf on the bloody threshold laid.
> Can men resist Fate's iron laws?
> They slew each other without cause.

CHAPTER XXV. OF HUGLEIK.—Hugleik was the name of

King Alf's son, who succeeded the two brothers in the kingdom of the Swedes, the sons of Yngve being still children.[1] King Hugleik was no warrior, but sat quietly at home in his country. He was very rich, but had still more the reputation of being very greedy. He had at his court all sorts of players, who played on harps, fiddles, and viols; and had with him magicians, and all sorts of witches. Hake and Hagbard were two brothers, very celebrated as sea-kings, who had a great force of men-at-arms. Sometimes they cruised in company, sometimes each for himself, and many warriors followed them both. King Hake came with his troops to Sweden against King Hugleik, who, on his side, collected a great army to oppose him. Two brothers came to his assistance, Svipdag and Geigad, both very celebrated men, and powerful combatants. King Hake had about him twelve champions, and among them Starkad the Old; and King Hake himself was a murderous combatant. They met on Fyrisvold, and there was a great battle, in which King Hugleik's army was soon defeated. Then the combatants, Svipdag and Geigad, pressed forward manfully; but Hake's champions went six against one, and they were both taken prisoners. Then King Hake penetrated within the shield-circle around King Hugleik, and killed him and two of his sons within it. After this the Swedes fled; and King Hake subdued the country, and became king of Sweden. He then sat quietly at home for three years, but during that time his combatants went abroad on viking expeditions, and gathered property for themselves.

CHAPTER XXVI. KING GUDLÖG'S DEATH.—Jorund and Eric, the sons of Yngve Alricsson, lay all this time in their warships, and were great warriors. One summer they marauded in Denmark, where they met a King Gudlög from Halogaland, and had a battle with him, which ended in their clearing Gudlög's ship and taking him prisoner. They carried him to the land at Strömönes,[2] and hanged him there, and afterwards his men raised a mound over him. So says Eyvind Skaldaspiller:

> By the fierce East-kings [3] cruel pride,
> Gudlög must on the wild horse ride—
> The wildest horse you e'er did see:
> 'Tis Sigur's steed—the gallows tree.

---

[1] This episode, with the same characters Hugleik, Svipdag, Geigad and Starkad, is closely paralleled by Saxo, see O. Elton, *The First Nine Books of the Danish History of Saxo Grammaticus*, 1894, pp. 228–9.

[2] Place name unknown.

[3] The Swedish kings Jorund and Eric, of Yngve's race, are said to be of the East—as relative to Norway, from which Gudlög came.

At Strömönes the tree did grow,
Where Gudlög's corpse waves on the bough.
A high stone stands on Strömö's heath,
To tell the gallant hero's death.

CHAPTER XXVII. OF KING HAKE.—The brothers Eric and
Jorund became more celebrated by this deed, and appeared to
be much greater men than before. When they heard that King
Hake in Sweden had sent from him his champions, they steered
towards Sweden, and gathered together a strong force. As
soon as the Swedes heard that the Yngling brothers were come
to them, they flocked to them in multitudes. The brothers
proceeded up the Mælare lake, and advanced towards Upsal
against King Hake, who came out against them on the Fyrisvold with far fewer people. There was a great battle, in which
King Hake went forward so bravely that he killed all who
were nearest to him, and at last killed King Eric, and cut down
the banner of the two brothers. King Jorund with all his men
fled to their ships. King Hake had been so grievously wounded
that he saw his days could not be long; so he ordered a warship
which he had to be loaded with his dead men and their weapons,
and to be taken out to the sea; the tiller to be shipped, and the
sails hoisted. Then he set fire to some tar-wood, and ordered
a pile to be made over it in the ship. Hake was almost if not
quite dead, when he was laid upon this pile of his. The wind
was blowing off the land—the ship flew, burning in clear flame,
out between the islets, and into the ocean. Great was the
fame of this deed in after times.

CHAPTER XXVIII. JORUND, YNGVE'S SON.—Jorund, King
Yngve's son, remained king at Upsal. He ruled the country;
but was often in summer out on war expeditions. One summer
he went with his forces to Denmark; and having plundered all
around in Jutland, he went into Lymfjord in autumn, and
marauded there also. While he was thus lying in Oddesund
with his people, King Gylög of Halogaland, a son of King
Gudlög, of whom mention is made before, came up with a
great force, and gave battle to Jorund. When the country
people saw this they swarmed from all parts towards the battle,
in great ships and small; and Jorund was overpowered by the
multitude, and his ships cleared of their men. He sprang
overboard, but was made prisoner and carried to the land.
Gylög ordered a gallows to be erected, led Jorund to it, and
had him hanged there. So ended his life. Thjodolf talks of
this event thus:

Jorund has travelled far and wide,
But the same horse he must bestride
On which he made brave Gudlög ride.
He too must for a necklace wear
Hagbert's [1] fell noose in middle air.
The army leader thus must ride
On Horva's [2] horse, at Lymfjord's side.

CHAPTER XXIX. OF KING ON, JORUND'S SON.—On or Ane
was the name of Jorund's son, who became king of the Swedes
after his father. He was a wise man, who made great sacrifices
to the gods; but being no warrior, he lived quietly at home.
In the time when the kings we have been speaking of were in
Upsal, Denmark had been ruled over by Dan Mikellati, who
lived to a very great age; then by his son, Frode Mikellati, or
the Peace-loving, who was succeeded by his sons Halfdan and
Fridleif, who were great warriors. Halfdan was older than his
brother, and above him in all things. He went with his army
against King On to Sweden, and was always victorious. At
last King On fled to Wester Gotland when he had been king
in Upsal about twenty-five years, and was in Gotland twenty-
five years, while Halfdan remained king in Upsal. King Halfdan died in his bed at Upsal, and was buried there in a mound;
and King On returned to Upsal when he was sixty years of age.
He made a great sacrifice, and in it offered up his son to Odin.
On got an answer from Odin, that he should live sixty years
longer; and he was afterwards king in Upsal for twenty-five
years. Now came Ole the Bold, a son of King Fridleif, with
his army to Sweden, against King On, and they had several
battles with each other; but Ole was always the victor. Then
On fled a second time to Gotland; and for twenty-five years
Ole reigned in Upsal, until he was killed by Starkad the Old.
After Ole's fall, On returned to Upsal, and ruled the kingdom
for twenty-five years. Then he made a great sacrifice again
for long life, in which he sacrificed his second son, and received
the answer from Odin, that he should live as long as he gave
him one of his sons every tenth year, and also that he should
name one of the districts of his country after the number of sons
he should offer to Odin. When he had sacrificed the seventh
of his sons he continued to live; but so that he could not walk,
but was carried on a chair. Then he sacrificed his eighth son,
and lived thereafter ten years, lying in his bed. Now he

---

[1] Hagbert's noose—the gallows rope by which Hagbert was hanged.
[2] This word is not a personification as suggested in the verse, but means
"cords of flax," whose "horse" or support is the gallows.

sacrificed his ninth son, and lived ten years more; but so that he drank out of a horn like a weaned infant. He had now only one son remaining, whom he also wanted to sacrifice, and to give Odin Upsal and the domains thereunto belonging, under the name of the Ten Lands,[1] but the Swedes would not allow it; so there was no sacrifice, and King On died, and was buried in a mound at Upsal. Since that time it is called On's sickness when a man dies, without pain, of extreme old age. Thjodolf tells of this:

> In Upsal's town the cruel king
> Slaughtered his sons at Odin's shrine—
> Slaughtered his sons with cruel knife,
> To get from Odin length of life.
> He lived until he had to turn
> His toothless mouth to the deer's horn;
> And he who shed his children's blood
> Sucked through the ox's horn his food.
> At length fell Death has tracked him down,
> Slowly, but sure, in Upsal's town.

CHAPTER XXX. OF EGIL AND TUNNE.—Egil was the name of On the Old's son, who succeeded as king in Sweden after his father's death. He was no warrior, but sat quietly at home. Tunne was the name of a slave who had been the counsellor and treasurer of On the Old; and when On died Tunne took much treasure and buried it in the earth. Now when Egil became king he put Tunne among the other slaves, which he took very ill and ran away with others of the slaves. They dug up the treasures which Tunne had concealed, and he gave them to his men, and was made their chief. Afterwards many malefactors flocked to him; and they lay out in the woods, but sometimes fell upon the domains, pillaging and killing the people. When King Egil heard this he went out with his forces to pursue them; but one night when he had taken up his night quarters, Tunne came there with his men, fell on the king's men unexpectedly, and killed many of them. As soon as King Egil perceived the tumult, he prepared for defence, and set up his banner; but many people deserted him, because Tunne and his men attacked them so boldly, and King Egil saw that nothing was left but to fly. Tunne pursued the fugitives into the forest, and then returned to the inhabited land, ravaging and plundering without resistance. All the goods that fell into Tunne's hands he gave to his people, and thus became popular and strong in men. King Egil assembled an army again, and hastened to give battle to Tunne. But

[1] Tiundaland: which really means the Ten-hundreds (circuits) land.

Tunne was again victorious, and King Egil fled with the loss of many people. Egil and Tunne had eight battles with each other, and Tunne always gained the victory. Then King Egil fled out of the country, and went to Sealand in Denmark, to Frode the Bold, and promised him a scatt[1] from the Swedes to obtain help. Frode gave him an army, and also his champions, with which force King Egil repaired to Sweden. When Tunne heard this he came out to meet him; and there was a great battle, in which Tunne fell, and King Egil recovered his kingdom, and the Danes returned home. King Egil sent King Frode great and good presents every year, but he paid no scatt to the Danes; but notwithstanding, the friendship between Egil and Frode continued without interruption. After Tunne's fall, Egil ruled the kingdom for three years. It happened in Sweden that an old bull, which was destined for sacrifice, was fed so high that he became dangerous to people; and when they were going to lay hold of him he escaped into the woods, became furious, and was long in the forest committing great damage to the country. King Egil was a great hunter, and often rode into the forest to chase wild animals. Once he rode out with his men to hunt in the forest. The king had traced an animal a long while, and followed it in the forest, separated from all his men. He observed at last that it was the bull, and rode up to it to kill it. The bull turned round suddenly, and the king struck him with his spear; but it tore itself out of the wound. The bull now struck his horn in the side of the horse, so that he instantly fell flat on the earth with the king. The king sprang up, and was drawing his sword, when the bull struck his horns right into the king's breast. The king's men then came up and killed the bull. The king lived but a short time, and was buried in a mound at Upsal. Thjodolf sings of it thus:

> The fair-haired son of Odin's race,
> Who fled before fierce Tunne's face,
> Has perished by the demon-beast
> Who roams the forests of the East.
> The hero's breast met the full brunt
> Of the wild bull's shaggy front;
> The hero's heart's asunder torn
> By the fell Jotun's spear-like horn.

CHAPTER XXXI. OF KING OTTAR.—Ottar was the name of King Egil's son who succeeded to the domains and kingdom

[1] Scatt is tax or tribute. In the *Skjoldunga Saga* it says that Frode defeated King Jorund (*see* p. 24) and claimed tribute from him.

after him. He did not continue friendly with King Frode, and therefore King Frode sent messengers to King Ottar to demand the scatt which Egil had promised him. Ottar replied, that the Swedes had never paid scatt to the Danes, neither would he; and the messengers had to depart with this answer. Frode was a great warrior; and he came one summer with his army to Sweden, and landed and ravaged the country. He killed many people, took some prisoners, burned all around in the inhabited parts, made a great booty, and made great devastation. The next summer King Frode made an expedition to the eastward[1]; and when King Ottar heard that Frode was not at home in his own country, he went on board his own ships, sailed over to Denmark, and ravaged there without opposition. As he heard that a great many people were collected at Sealand, he proceeds westward[2] to the Sound, and sails north[3] about to Jutland; lands at Lymfjord; plunders the Vend district[4]; burns, and lays waste, and makes desolate the country he goes over with his army. Vött and Faste were the names of the earls whom Frode had appointed to defend the country in Denmark while he was abroad. When the earls heard that the Swedish king was laying Denmark waste, they collected an army, hastened on board their ships, and sailed by the south[5] side to Lymfjord. They came unexpectedly upon Ottar, and the battle began immediately. The Swedes gave them a good reception, and many people fell on both sides; but as soon as men fell in the Danish army other men hastened from the country to fill their places, and also all the vessels in the neighbourhood joined them. The battle ended with the fall of Ottar and the greater part of his people. The Danes took his body, carried it to the land, laid it upon a mound of earth, and let the wild beasts and ravens tear it to pieces. Thereafter they made a figure of a crow out of wood, sent it to Sweden, and sent word with it that their king, Ottar, was no better than it; and from this he was called Ottar Vendelcrow. Thjodolf tells so of it:

> By Danish arms the hero bold,
> Ottar the Brave, lies stiff and cold.
> To Vendel's plain the corpse was borne;
> By eagles' claws the corpse is torn,

---

[1] An expedition to the east meant going on a viking cruise to the Baltic lands.
[2] Really northward.
[3] An error for the original's "south."
[4] Vendel, the part of Jutland north of Lymfjord, now called Vendsyssel.
[5] By the south side: the original has merely "south."

Spattered by ravens' bloody feet,
The wild bird's prey, the wild wolf's meat.
The Swedes have vowed revenge to take
On Frode's earls, for Ottar's sake;
Like dogs to kill them in their land,
In their own homes, by Swedish hand.

CHAPTER XXXII. OF KING ADILS' MARRIAGE.—Adils was
the name of King Ottar's son and successor. He was a long
time king, became very rich, and went also for several summers
on viking expeditions. On one of these he came to Saxland [1]
with his troops. There a king was reigning called Geirthjof,
and his wife was called Alof the Great; but nothing is told of
their children. The king was not at home, and Adils and his
men ran up to the king's house and plundered it, while others
drove a herd of cattle down to the strand. [2] The herd was
attended by slave-people, churls, and girls, and they took all of
them together. Among them was a remarkably beautiful girl
called Yrsa. Adils returned home with this plunder. Yrsa
was not one of the slave girls, and it was soon observed that
she was intelligent, spoke well, and in all respects was well
behaved. All people thought well of her, and particularly the
king; and at last it came to this that the king celebrated his
wedding with her, and Yrsa became queen of Sweden, and was
considered an excellent woman.

CHAPTER XXXIII. OF KING ADILS' DEATH.—King Halfdan's son Helge ruled at that time over Leidre. He came to
Sweden with so great an army, that King Adils saw no other
way than to fly at once. King Helge landed with his army,
plundered, and made a great booty. He took Queen Yrsa
prisoner, carried her with him to Leidre, took her to wife, and
had a son by her called Rolf Krake. When Rolf was three
years old, Queen Alof came to Denmark, and told Queen Yrsa
that her husband, King Helge, was her own father, and that
she, Alof, was her mother. Thereupon Yrsa went back to
Sweden to King Adils, and was queen there as long as she
lived. King Helge fell in a war expedition; and Rolf Krake,

---

[1] Here = the coast of Holstein on the Baltic.
[2] The ordinary way, with the vikings, of victualling their ships was to
drive cattle down to the strand and kill them, without regard to the
property of friends or enemies; and this was so established a practice that
it was expressed in a single word, *strandhögg*. On p. 68 it is told how
Rolf Ganger, the son of Earl Rognvald, made a *strandhögg* in the Vik.
King Harald the Fairhaired had expressly forbidden the practice in his own
dominions by his own subjects, and in consequence of this breach he
banished Rolf. The hunger of Rolf's men for beef in Norway thus led
ultimately to the foundation of the duchy of Normandy.

who was then eight years old, was taken to be king in Leidre. King Adils had many disputes with a king called Ole of the Uplands; and these kings had a battle on the ice of the Väner lake, in which King Ole fell, and King Adils won the battle. There is a long account of this battle in the Skjoldunga Saga,[1] and also about Rolf Krake's coming to Adils, and sowing gold upon the Fyrisvold. King Adils was a great lover of good horses, and had the best horses of these times. One of his horses was called Slöngve, and another Raven. This horse he had taken from Ole on his death, and bred from him a horse, also called Raven, which the king sent in a present to King Godgest in Halogaland. When Godgest mounted the horse he was not able to manage him, and fell off and was killed. This accident happened at Omd in Halogaland.[2] King Adils was at a Disa[3] sacrifice; and as he rode around the Disa hall his horse Raven stumbled and fell, and the king was thrown forward upon his head, and his skull was split, and his brains dashed out against a stone. Adils died at Upsal, and was buried there in a mound. The Swedes called him a great king. Thjodolf speaks thus of him:

> Witch-demons, I have heard men say,
> Have taken Adils' life away.
> The son of kings of Frey's great race,
> First in the fray, the fight, the chase,
> Fell from his steed—his clotted brains
> Lie mixed with mire on Upsal's plains.
> Such death (grim Fate has willed it so)
> Has struck down Ole's deadly foe.

CHAPTER XXXIV. ROLF KRAKE'S DEATH.—Eystein, King Adils' son, ruled next over Sweden, and in his lifetime Rolf Krake of Leidre fell. In those days many kings, both Danes and Northmen, ravaged the Swedish dominions; for there were many sea-kings who ruled over many people, but had no lands, and he might well be called a sea-king who never slept beneath sooty roof-timbers.

CHAPTER XXXV. OF EYSTEIN AND THE JUTLAND KING SOLVE. —There was a sea-king called Solve, a son of Hogne of Njardö,[4] who at that time plundered in the Baltic, but had his dominion

---

[1] See Introduction, p. xiii.

[2] Halogaland is the province of Norway now called Nordland, extending from the Namsen river north to Vestfjord, where it joins the province of Finmark.

[3] The Dísir were female divinities connected especially with fertility rites celebrated in autumn. In Sweden the sacral kingship was closely connected with the "Disa sacrifice." The "Disa hall" was probably the temple of Freya, the chief of the Dísir.

[4] Njardö, an island in North Trondhjem district, now called Nærö.

in Jutland. He came with his forces to Sweden, just as King Eystein was at a feast in a district called Lofund.[1] Solve came unexpectedly in the night on Eystein, surrounded the house in which the king was, and burned him and all his court. Then Solve went to Sigtun, and desired that the Swedes should receive him, and give him the title of king; but they collected an army, and tried to defend the country against him, on which there was a great battle, that lasted, according to report, eleven days. There King Solve was victorious, and was afterwards king of the Swedish dominions for a long time, until at last the Swedes betrayed him, and he was killed. Thjodolf tells of it thus:

> For a long time none could tell
> How Eystein died—but now I know
> That at Lofönd the hero fell;
> The branch of Odin was laid low,
> Was burnt by Solve's Jutland men.
> The raging tree-devourer fire
> Rushed on the monarch in its ire;
> First fell the castle timbers, then
> The roof-beams—Eystein's funeral pyre.

CHAPTER XXXVI. OF YNGVAR'S FALL.—Yngvar, who was King Eystein's son, then became king of Sweden. He was a great warrior, and often lay out with his warships; for the Swedish dominions were much ravaged then by Danes and East-country men.[2] King Yngvar made a peace with the Danes; but betook himself to ravaging the East country in return. One summer he went with his forces to Estland, and plundered at a place called Stein. The men of Estland came down from the interior with a great army, and there was a battle; but the army of the country was so great that the Swedes could not withstand them, and King Yngvar fell, and his people fled. He was buried close to the seashore under a mound in Estland; and after this defeat the Swedes returned home. Thjodolf sings of it thus:

> Certain it is the Estland foe
> The fair-haired Swedish king laid low.
> On Estland's strand, o'er Swedish graves,
> The East Sea sings her song of waves;
> King Yngvar's dirge is ocean's roar
> Resounding on the rock-ribbed shore.

CHAPTER XXXVII. OF ONUND THE LAND-CLEARER.—Onund was the name of Yngvar's son who succeeded him. In his

[1] Lofund, possibly Laghunda in Fjadrundaland, where there was an ancient royal residence.
[2] Men from the Baltic lands.

days there was peace in Sweden, and he became rich in valuable goods. King Onund went with his army to Estland to avenge his father, and landed and ravaged the country round far and wide, and returned with a great booty in autumn to Sweden. In his time there were fruitful seasons in Sweden, so that he was one of the most popular of kings. Sweden is a great forest land, and there are such great uninhabited forests in it that it is a journey of many days to cross them. Onund bestowed great diligence and expense on opening the woods and cultivating the cleared land. He made roads through the desert forests; and clear land was found in many places in the forest country, and great districts were settled. In this way extensive tracts of land were brought into cultivation, for there were country people enough to cultivate the land. Onund had roads made through all Sweden, both through forests and morasses, and also over mountains; and he was therefore called Onund Roadmaker. He had a house built for himself in every district of Sweden, and went over the whole country in guest-quarters.[1]

CHAPTER XXXVIII. OF INGJALD THE BAD.—Onund had a son called Ingjald, and at that time Yngvar was king of the district of Fjadryndaland.[2] Yngvar had two sons by his wife —the one called Alf, the other Agnar—who were about the same age as Ingjald. Onund's district-kings were at that time spread widely over Sweden, and Svipdag the Blind ruled over Tiundaland, in which Upsal lies, where the assemblies of all the Swedes are held. There also were held the mid-winter sacrifices, at which many kings attended. One year at mid-winter [3] there was a great assembly of people at Upsal, and King Yngvar had also come there with his sons. Alf, King Yngvar's son, and Ingjald, King Onund's son, were there— both about six years old. They amused themselves with child's play, in which each should be leading on his army. In their play Ingjald found himself not so strong as Alf, and was so vexed that he almost cried. His foster-brother Gautvid came up, led him to his foster-father Svipdag the Blind, and told him how ill it appeared that he was weaker and less manly

---

[1] This continued to be the ordinary way of subsisting the kings and court in Norway for many generations. In Sweden the kings appear to have had a fixed residence at Upsal, and in Denmark at Leidre and Odinsö; while in Norway they appear to have lived always in royal progresses through the districts in turns, without any palace, castle, or fixed abode.
[2] Fjadryndaland was the most westerly district in Upland.
[3] i.e. in the middle of January, when the pagan Yule feast was observed.

than Alf, King Yngvar's son. Svipdag replied that it was a
great shame. The day after Svipdag took the heart of a wolf,
roasted it on a stick, and gave it to the king's son Ingjald
to eat, and from that time he became a most ferocious person,
and of the worst disposition. When Ingjald was grown up,
Onund applied for him to King Algaut for his daughter Gauthild.
Algaut was a son of Gautrek the Mild, and grandson of Gaut;
and from them Gotland [1] (Gautland) took its name. King
Algaut thought his daughter would be well married if she got
King Onund's son, and if he had his father's disposition; so
the girl was sent to Sweden, and King Ingjald celebrated his
wedding with her in due time.

CHAPTER XXXIX. OF KING ONUND'S DEATH.—King Onund
one autumn, travelling between his mansion-houses, came over
a road called Heavenheath,[2] where there are some narrow
mountain valleys, with high mountains on both sides. There
was heavy rain at the time, and before there had been snow on
the mountains. A landslip of clay and stones came down upon
King Onund and his people, and there he met his death, and
many with him. So says Thjodolf, namely:

> We all have heard how Jonkur's [3] sons,
> Whom weapons could not touch, with stones
> Were stoned to death—in open day,
> King Onund died in the same way.
> Or else perhaps the wood-grown land,
> Which long had felt his conquering hand,
> Uprose at length in deadly strife,
> And pressed out Onund's hated life.

CHAPTER XL. THE BURNING IN UPSAL.—Then Ingjald, King
Onund's son, came to the kingdom. The Upsal kings were the
highest in Sweden among the many district-kings who had been
since the time that Odin was chief. The kings who resided at
Upsal had been the supreme chiefs over the whole Swedish
dominions until the death of Agne, when, as before related
[p. 21], the kingdom came to be divided between brothers.
After that time the dominions and kingly powers were spread
among the branches of the family as these increased; but some

[1] Gotland, Gautland, i.e. Väster- and Öster-Götland, inhabited by the
Gautar, whose name is related to that of the Goths (etymology uncertain,
probably related to the verb gjóta, to pour, mould, give birth (of animals);
perhaps means "the fertile, the virile"). These districts remained
independent, to a greater or lesser degree, of the central Swedish monarchy
until a much later period.

[2] Himinheiðr, probably Snorri's construction from the words und Himin-
fjöllum in the following verse; probably not a real place-name.

[3] Jonakr, father of Hamdir and Sörle, who were stoned to death because
steel weapons could not harm them; see the Lay of Hamdir (Hamðismál) in
The Poetic Edda (trans. H. A. Bellows; The American-Scandinavian
Foundation, New York, 1923).

kings cleared great tracts of forest-land, and settled them, and thereby increased their domains. Now when Ingjald took the dominions and the kingdom of his father, there were, as before said [p. 32,] many district-kings. King Ingjald ordered a great feast to be prepared in Upsal, and intended at that feast to enter on his heritage after King Onund his father. He had a large hall made ready for the occasion—one not less, nor less sumptuous, than that of Upsal; and this hall was called the Seven Kings Hall, and in it were seven high seats for kings. Then King Ingjald sent men all through Sweden, and invited to his feast kings, earls, and other men of consequence. To this heirship-feast came King Algaut, his father-in-law; Yngvar king of Fjadryndaland, with his two sons, Alf and Agnar; King Sporsnjall of Nerike; King Sighvat of Aattundaland: but Granmar king of Södermanland did not come. Six kings were placed in the seats in the new hall; but one of the high seats which Ingjald had prepared was empty. All the persons who had come got places in the new hall; but to his own court, and the rest of his people, he had appointed places at Upsal. It was the custom at that time that he who gave an heirship-feast after kings or earls, and entered upon the heritage, should sit upon the footstool in front of the high seat, until the full bowl, which was called the Brage-beaker,[1] was brought in. Then he should stand up, take the Brage-beaker, make solemn vows to be after-wards fulfilled, and thereupon empty the beaker. Then he should ascend the high seat which his father had occupied; and thus he came to the full heritage after his father. Now it was done so on this occasion. When the full Brage-beaker came in, King Ingjald stood up, grasped a large bull's horn, and made a solemn vow to enlarge his dominions by one half, towards all the four corners of the world, or die; and thereupon he emptied the beaker at a single draught. Now when the guests had become drunk towards evening King Ingjald told Svipdag's sons, Folkvid and Hulvid, to arm themselves and their men, as had before been settled; and accordingly they went out, and came up to the new hall, and set fire to it. The hall was soon in a blaze, and the six kings, with all their people, were burned in it. Those who tried to come out were killed. Then King Ingjald laid all the dominions these kings had possessed under himself, and took scatt from them.

---

[1] *Bragafull*, here taken to mean "the cup of Brage," the god of poetry. The usual and more authentic form is *bragarfull*, "the chieftain's toast," the most important toast and one connected with a solemn vow.

CHAPTER XLI. OF HJORVARD'S MARRIAGE. — When King Granmar heard the news of this treachery, he thought the same lot awaited him if he did not take care. The same summer King Hjorvard, who was called Ylfing, came with his fleet to Sweden, and went into a fjord called Myrkva-fjord.[1] When King Granmar heard this he sent a messenger to him to invite him and all his men to a feast. He accepted it willingly; for he had never committed waste in King Granmar's dominions. When he came to the feast he was gladly welcomed. In the evening, when the full bowls went round, as was the custom of kings when they were at home, or in the feasts they ordered to be made, they sat and drank together, a man and woman with each other in pairs, and the rest of the company sat and drank all together. But it was the law among the vikings that all who were at the entertainment should drink together in one company all round. King Hjorvard's high seat was placed right opposite to King Granmar's high seat, and on the same bench sat all his men. King Granmar told his daughter Hildigunn, who was a remarkably beautiful girl, to make ready to carry ale to the vikings. Thereupon she took a silver goblet, filled it, bowed before King Hjorvard, and said, "Success to all Ylfinger: this cup to the memory of Rolf Krake"—drank out the half, and handed the cup to King Hjorvard. He took the cup, and took her hand, and said she must sit beside him. She says that is not viking fashion to drink two and two with women. Hjorvard replies that it were better for him to make a change, and leave the viking law, and drink in company with her. Then Hildigunn sat down beside him, and both drank together, and spoke a great deal with each other during the evening. The next day, when King Granmar and Hjorvard met, Hjorvard spoke of his courtship, and asked to have Hildigunn in marriage. King Granmar laid this proposal before his wife Hilda, and before people of consequence, saying they would have great help and trust in Hjorvard; and all approved of it highly, and thought it very advisable. And the end was, that Hildigunn was promised to Hjorvard, and the wedding followed soon after; and King Hjorvard stayed with King Granmar, who had no sons, to help him to defend his dominions.

CHAPTER XLII. WAR BETWEEN INGJALD AND GRANMAR AND HJORVARD.—The same autumn King Ingjald collected a warforce, with which he intended to fall upon Granmar and Hjorvard; but when they heard it they also collected a force, and Hogne,

[1] Now Mörköfjord in Södermanland province.

who ruled over East Gotland, together with his son Hildir, came to their assistance. Hogne was father of Hilda, who was married to King Granmar. King Ingjald landed with his army, which was by far the most numerous. A battle began, which was very sharp; but after it had lasted a short time, the chiefs who ruled over Fjadryndaland, West Gotland, Nerike, and Aattundaland, took to flight with all the men from those countries, and hastened to their ships. This placed King Ingjald in great danger, and he received many wounds, but escaped by flight to his ships. Svipdag the Blind, Ingjald's foster-father, together with his sons, Gautvid and Hulvid, fell. Ingjald returned to Upsal, very ill-satisfied with his expedition; and he thought the army levied from those countries he had acquired by conquest would be unfaithful to him. There was great hostility afterwards between King Ingjald and King Granmar, and his son-in-law King Hjorvard; and after this had continued a long time the friends of both parties brought about a reconciliation. The king appointed a meeting, and concluded a peace. This peace was to endure as long as the three kings lived, and this was confirmed by oath and promises of fidelity. The spring after, King Granmar went to Upsal to make offering, as usual, for a steady peace. Then the fore-boding [1] turned out for him so that it did not promise him long life, and he returned to his dominions.

CHAPTER XLIII. DEATH OF THE KINGS GRANMAR AND HJORVARD.—The autumn after, King Granmar and his son-in-law Hjorvard went to a feast at one of their farms in the island Sile. [2] When they were at the entertainment, King Ingjald came there in the night with his troops, surrounded the house, and burnt them in it, with all their men. Then he took to himself all the country these kings had possessed, and placed chiefs over it. King Hogne and his son Hildir often made inroads on horseback into the Swedish dominions, and killed King Ingjald's men, whom he had placed over the kingdom which had belonged to their relation Granmar. This strife between King Ingjald and King Hogne continued for a long time; but King Hogne defended his kingdom against King Ingjald to his dying day. King Ingjald had two children by his wife—the eldest called Aasa, the other Olaf. Gauthild, the wife of Ingjald, sent the boy to his foster-father Bove, in West

[1] In connection with such sacrifices it was usual to scatter chips or strips of wood, perhaps with runes on them, and to read from the arrangement of these what was likely to happen soon by the will of the gods.
[2] Now the island Sela, in Mälaren.

Gotland, where he was brought up along with Saxe, Bove's son, who had the surname of Flette. It was a common saying that King Ingjald had killed twelve kings, and deceived them all under pretence of peace; therefore he was called Ingjald the Evil-worker. He was king over the greater part of Sweden. He married his daughter Aasa to Gudrod king of Skaane; and she was like her father in disposition. Aasa brought it about that Gudrod killed his brother Halfdan, father of Ivar Vidfavne; and also she brought about the death of her husband Gudrod, and then fled to her father; and she thus got the name also of Aasa the Evil-worker.

CHAPTER XLIV. OF INGJALD'S DEATH.—Ivar Vidfavne came to Skaane after the fall of his uncle Gudrod, and collected an army in all haste, and moved with it into Sweden. Aasa had gone to her father before. King Ingjald was at a feast in Ræning,[1] when he heard that King Ivar's army was in the neighbourhood. Ingjald thought he had not strength to go into battle against Ivar, and he saw well that if he betook himself to flight his enemies would swarm around him from all corners. He and Aasa took a resolution which has become celebrated. They drank until all their people were dead drunk, and then put fire to the hall; and it was consumed, with all who were in it, including themselves, King Ingjald, and Aasa. Thus says Thjodolf:

> With fiery feet devouring flame
> Has hunted down a royal game
> At Ræning, where King Ingjald gave
> To all his men one glowing grave.
> On his own hearth the fire he raised,
> A deed his foemen even praised;
> By his own hand he perished so,
> And life for freedom did forego.

CHAPTER XLV. OF IVAR.—Ivar Vidfavne subdued the whole of Sweden. He brought in subjection to himself all the Danish dominions, a great deal of Saxland, all the East Country,[2] and a fifth part of England.[3] From his race the kings of Sweden and Denmark who have had the supreme authority in those countries, are descended. After Ingjald the Evil-worker the Upsal dominion fell from the Yngling race, notwithstanding

---

[1] Ræning: it is not known for certain where this farm was; it is possibly to be identified with Rällinge on the island Fogd in Mälaren, or possibly its site was on Toster in the same inland sea.

[2] East country, i.e. Russia or its Baltic provinces. In the ninth century the Swedes first obtained supremacy in Russia.

[3] By this is meant Northumberland which was, however, first taken by Danish vikings in 866.

the length of time they could reckon up the series of their forefathers.

CHAPTER XLVI. OF OLAF THE TREE-FELLER.—When Olaf, King Ingjald's son, heard of his father's end, he went with the men who chose to follow him to Nerike; for all the Swedish community rose with one accord to drive out Ingjald's family and all his friends. Now, when the Swedes got intelligence of him he could not remain there, but went on westwards, through the forest, to a river which comes from the north and falls into the Vänern lake, and is called Klar river.[1] There they sat themselves down, turned to and cleared the woods, burnt, and then settled there. Soon there were great districts, which altogether were called Vermeland; and a good living was to be made there. Now when it was told of Olaf, in Sweden, that he was clearing the forests, they laughed at his proceedings, and called him the Tree-feller. Olaf got a wife called Solva, or Solveig, a daughter of Halfdan Guldtand, westward in Soleyar.[2] Halfdan was a son of Solve Solvarson, who was a son of Solve the Old, who first settled on these islands. Olaf Tree-feller's mother was called Gauthild, and her mother was Alov, daughter of Olaf the Sharp-sighted, king in Nerike. Olaf and Solva had two sons, Ingjald and Halfdan. Halfdan was brought up in Soleyar, in the house of his mother's brother Solve, and was called Halfdan Hvitbein.

CHAPTER XLVII. OLAF THE TREE-FELLER'S DEATH.—There were a great many people who fled the country from Sweden, on account of King Ivar; and when they heard that King Olaf had got good lands in Vermeland, so great a number came there to him that the land could not support them. Then there came dear times and famine, which they ascribed to their king; as the Swedes used always to reckon good or bad crops for or against their kings. The Swedes took it amiss that Olaf was sparing in his sacrifices, and believed the dear times must proceed from this cause. The Swedes therefore gathered together troops, made an expedition against King Olaf, surrounded his house and burnt him in it, giving him to Odin as a sacrifice for good crops. This happened at the Vänern lake. Thus tells Thjodolf of it:

> The temple wolf,[3] by the lake shores,
> The corpse of Olaf now devours.

---

[1] Göta river.
[2] Soleyar was a district comprehending some of the continent, as well as the group of islands now called Solöer.
[3] The temple wolf—the fire which devoured the body of Olaf.

The clearer of the forests died
At Odin's shrine by the lake side.
The glowing flames stripped to the skin
The royal robes from the Swedes' king.
Thus Olaf, famed in days of yore,
Vanished from earth at Venner's shore.

CHAPTER XLVIII. HALFDAN HVITBEIN [1] MADE KING.—Those
of the Swedes who had more understanding found that the
dear times proceeded from there being a greater number of
people on the land than it could support, and that the king
could not be blamed for this. They took the resolution, therefore, to cross the Eida forest [2] with all their men, and came
quite unexpectedly into Soleyar, where they put to death King
Solve, and took Halfdan Hvitbein prisoner, and made him their
chief, and gave him the title of king. Thereupon he subdued
Soleyar, and proceeding with his army into Raumarike,[3] plundered there, and laid that district also in subjection by force
of arms.

CHAPTER XLIX. OF HALFDAN HVITBEIN.—Halfdan Hvitbein became a great king. He was married to Aasa, a daughter
of Eystein the Severe, who was king of the Upland people, and
ruled over Hedemark. Halfdan and Aasa had two sons,
Eystein and Gudrod. Halfdan subdued a great part of Hedemark, Toten, Hadeland, and much of Westfold.[4] He lived to
be an old man, and died in his bed at Toten, from whence his
body was transported to Westfold, and was buried under a mound
at a place called Skæreid, at Skiringsale.[5] So says Thjodolf:

Halfdan, esteemed by friends and foes,
Receives at last life's deep repose:
The aged man at last, though late,
Yielded in Toten to stern fate.
At Skiringsale hangs o'er his grave
A rock, that seems to mourn the brave.
Halfdan, to chiefs and people dear,
Received from all a silent tear.

---

[1] Halfdan Whiteleg.

[2] Eydiskogr, a great uninhabited forest, which then, and to a late
period, covered the frontier of Norway towards Sweden on the south.

[3] Romerike in Akershus province in Norway.

[4] Hedemark, Toten, Hadeland, Westfold, are all districts in Central
or Southern Norway; the Uplands or Highlands, is the region to the south
of Dovrefjeld.

[5] Skiringsale: in Tjölling parish between Larvik and Sandefjord on the
west of the Oslofjord. It was a port and market town in the ninth century,
when it was visited by Ohtere, whose voyage from Halogaland to the Baltic
is described on the basis of Ohtere's own account in an addition made by
King Alfred in his translation of Orosius. It is only some ten miles from
the site of the Gokstad ship-burial (cf. p. 42, note 2, and p. 43, Chronological Note).

CHAPTER L. OF INGJALD, BROTHER OF HALFDAN.—Ingjald, Halfdan's brother, was king of Vermeland; but after his death King Halfdan took possession of Vermeland, raised scatt from it, and placed earls over it as long as he lived.

CHAPTER LI. OF KING EYSTEIN'S DEATH.—Eystein, Halfdan Hvitbein's son, was king after him in Raumarike and Westfold. He was married to Hild, a daughter of Eric Agnarsson, who was king in Westfold. Agnar, Eric's father, was a son of Sigtryg, king in the Vendel domain. King Eric had no son, and died while King Halfdan Hvitbein was still in life. The father and son, Halfdan and Eystein, then took possession of the whole of Westfold, which Eystein ruled over as long as he lived. At that time there lived at Varna [1] a king called Skjold, who was a great warlock. King Eystein went with some ships of war to Varna, plundered there, and carried away all he could find of clothes or other valuables, and of peasants' stock, and killed cattle on the strand for provision, and then went off. King Skjold came to the strand with his army, just as Eystein was at such a distance over the fjord that King Skjold could only see his sails. Then he took his cloak, waved it, and blew into it. King Eystein was sitting at the helm as they sailed in past Jarlsö, and another ship was sailing at the side of his, when there came a stroke of a wave, by which the boom of the other ship struck the king and threw him overboard, which proved his death. His men fished up his body, and it was carried into Borre, where a mound was thrown up over it, out towards the sea at Raden, near Vadla. [2] So says Thjodolf:

> King Eystein sat upon the poop
> Of his good ship: with sudden swoop
> The swinging boom dashed him to hell,
> And fathoms deep the hero fell
> Beneath the brine.   The fury whirl
> Of Loke, Tempest's brother's girl,
> Grim Hel, clutched his soul away;
> And now where Vadla's ocean bay
> Receives the ice-cold stream, the grave
> Of Eystein stands—the good, the brave!

CHAPTER LII. OF HALFDAN THE MILD.—Halfdan was the name of King Eystein's son who succeeded him. He was

---

[1] Varna, now Rygge in Smaalenene. The great farm Værne became a royal dwelling until about the year 1200, when it became a hospital for old soldiers of the king's bodyguard.

[2] Vadla seems to·have been taken by Snorri as the name of a river, although there is none flowing into the Oslofjord in this locality.

called Halfdan the Mild, but the Bad Entertainer; that is to say, he was reported to be generous, and to give his men as much gold as other kings gave of silver, but he starved them in their diet. He was a great warrior, who had been long on viking cruises, and had collected great property. He was married to Liv, a daughter of King Dag of Westmare.[1] Holtar, in Westfold, was his chief house; and he died there on the bed of sickness, and was buried at.Borre under a mound. So says Thjodolf:

> By Hel's summons, a great king
> Was called away to Odin's Thing:
> King Halfdan, he who dwelt of late
> At Holtar, must obey grim Fate.
> At Borre, in the royal mound,
> They laid the hero in the ground.

CHAPTER LIII. OF GUDROD THE HUNTER.—Gudrod, Halfdan's son, succeeded. He was called Gudrod the Magnificent, and also Gudrod the Hunter. He was married to Alfhild, a daughter of King Alfarin of Alfheim, and got with her half the district of Vingulmark.[2] Their son Olaf was afterwards called Geirstad-Alf. Alfheim, at that time, was the name of the land between the Glommen and Gotha rivers. Now when Alfhild died, King Gudrod sent his men west to Agder to the king who ruled there, and who was called Harald Redbeard. They were to make proposals to his daughter Aasa upon the king's account; but Harald declined the match, and the ambassadors returned to the king, and told him the result of their errand. Soon after King Gudrod hove down his ships into the water, and proceeded with a great force in them to Agder. He immediately landed, and came altogether unexpectedly at night to King Harald's house. When Harald was aware that an army was at hand, he went out with the men he had about him, and there was a great battle, although he wanted men so much. King Harald and his son Gyrd fell, and King Gudrod took a great booty. He carried away with him Aasa, King Harald's daughter, and had a wedding with her. They had a son by their marriage called Halfdan; and the autumn that Halfdan was a year old Gudrod went upon a round of feasts. He lay with his ship in Stiflesund,[3] where they had been drinking hard, so that the king was very tipsy. In the evening, about dark, the king left the ship; and when he had got to the end of

---

[1] The district round Langesund fjord.
[2] The present Oslo and surrounding district.
[3] Place unknown.

the gangway from the ship to the shore,[1] a man ran against him, thrust a spear through him, and killed him. The man was instantly put to death, and in the morning when it was light the man was discovered to be Aasa's page-boy: nor did she conceal that it was done by her orders. Thus tells Thjodolf of it:

> Gudrod is gone to his long rest,
> Despite of all his haughty pride—
> A traitor's spear has pierced his side:
> For Aasa cherished in her breast
> Revenge; and as, by wine opprest,
> The hero staggered from his ship,
> The cruel queen her thrall let slip
> To do the deed of which I sing:
> And now the far-descended king,
> At Stiflesund, in the old bed
> Of the old Gudrod race, lies dead.

CHAPTER LIV. OF KING OLAF'S DEATH.—Olaf came to the kingdom after his father. He was a great warrior, and an able man; and was besides remarkably handsome, very strong and large of growth. He had Westfold; for King Alfgeir took all Vingulmark to himself, and placed his son Gandalf over it. Both father and son made war on Raumarike, and subdued the greater part of that land and district. Hogne was the name of a son of the Upland king, Eystein the Great, who subdued for himself the whole of Hedemark, Toten, and Hadeland. Then Vermeland fell off from Gudrod's sons, and turned itself, with its payment of scatt, to the Swedish king. Olaf was about twenty years old when Gudrod died; and as his brother Halfdan now had the kingdom with him, they divided it between them; so that Olaf got the eastern and Halfdan the southern part. King Olaf had his main residence at Geirstad.[2] There he died of a disease in his leg, and was laid under a mound at Geirstad. So sings Thjodolf:

> Long while this branch of Odin's stem
> Was the stout prop of Norway's realm;
> Long while King Olaf with just pride
> Ruled over Westfold [3] far and wide.
> At length by cruel gout oppressed,
> The good King Olaf sank to rest:
> His body now lies under ground,
> Buried at Geirstad, in the mound.

---

[1] The ships appear generally to have been laid all night close to or at the shore, with a gangway to land by; and the crew appear to have had tents on shore to pass the night in.

[2] This ancient seat of petty royalty is now supposed to have been a farm called Gjerstad, in the parish Tjölling, of which Skiringsale also formed part.

[3] The present Oslo fjord and district.

CHAPTER LV. OF ROGNVALD THE MOUNTAIN-HIGH.—Rognvald was the name of Olaf's son who was king of Westfold after his father. He was called "Mountain-high," [1] and Thjodolf of Kvine composed for him the "Ynglinga-tal," [2] in which he says:

> Under the heaven's blue dome, a name
> I never knew more true to fame
> Than Rognvald bore; whose skilful hand
> Could tame the scorners of the land,—
> Rognvald, who knew so well to guide
> The wild sea-horses [3] through the tide:
> The "Mountain-high" was the proud name
> By which the king was known to fame.

---

[1] The word is *heiðumhæri* here, *heiðumhár* in the verse, and most probably means "the highly honoured."

[2] Ynglinga-tal: "enumeration of the Ynglings," a poetic catalogue of the dynasty.

[3] Sea-horse, a common type of *kenning* for ship.

A CHRONOLOGICAL NOTE

External references enable us to fix some chronological points in this early period. Ottar and Adils (pp. 27–9) are equated with the Ohterc and Eadgils of the Old English *Beowulf*. In this poem it is said that Ottar's father fell in battle against Hygelac, who is an historical figure, reported by Gregory of Tours (died 594) to have been killed in an attack on Frisian territory in 516. Ottar was presumably king at this time, and it is estimated that his death occurred in the second quarter of the sixth century, and that of his son Adils some time towards the end of the century. These dates agree quite well with the archaeological dating of the three royal grave-mounds near Uppsala, where Snorri says On (p. 25), Egil (p. 26), and Adils (p. 29) were buried. The earliest is dated *c.* 500 (at the latest), the second early in the sixth century, the third to the end of the sixth century. A fourth mound at Husby in Vendel parish north of Uppsala was known until post-Reformation times as "Ottar's mound"; it is dated archaeologically to the early part of the sixth century and may well have been the resting-place of King Ottar.

A terminus is set, of course, by the composition of the poem *Ynglingatal*, probably within the period 880–900. The great ship-burials of Oseberg and Gokstad on the west coast of the Oslofjord are plausibly identified as the graves of Queen Aasa (p. 41) and her stepson Olaf (p. 42); they are dated archaeologically to the earlier and later part of the second half of the ninth century respectively.

A plausible case has also been made for identifying this Olaf Gudrodsson with the man of the same name who was king in Dublin from 853 to 871.

II

HALFDAN THE BLACK [1]

CHAPTER I. HALFDAN FIGHTS WITH GANDALF AND SIGTRYG.—
Halfdan was a year old when his father Gudrod [2] was killed,
and his mother Aasa set off immediately with him westwards
to Agder, and set herself there in the kingdom which her father
Harald had possessed. Halfdan grew up there, and soon became
stout and strong; and, by reason of his black hair, was called
Halfdan the Black. When he was eighteen years old he took
his kingdom in Agder, and went immediately to Westfold,
where he divided that kingdom, as before related, with his
brother Olaf. The same autumn he went with an army to
Vingulmark against King Gandalf. They had many battles,
and sometimes one, sometimes the other gained the victory;
but at last they agreed that Halfdan should have half of Vingulmark, as his father Gudrod had had it before. Then King
Halfdan proceeded to Raumarike, and subdued it. King
Sigtryg, son of King Eystein, who then had his residence in
Hedemark, and who had subdued Raumarike before, having
heard of this, came out with his army against King Halfdan,
and there was a great battle, in which King Halfdan was
victorious; and just as King Sigtryg and his troops were turning
about to fly, an arrow struck him under the left arm, and he
fell dead. Halfdan then laid the whole of Raumarike under
his power. King Eystein's second son, King Sigtryg's brother,
was also called Eystein, and was then king in Hedemark. As

[1] The chronology of Halfdan the Black's reign is far from clear, and it is
unlikely that much reliance can be placed on the precise figures given by
Snorri for Halfdan's age at his succession and death (eighteen and forty,
see above and p. 49). If Olaf Gudrodsson is to be identified with the
Norse king of Dublin, 853–71 (cf. note p. 43), he must have been born not
later than c. 830 and been about forty when his father died, not twenty as is
said on p. 42 above. Halfdan was his younger half-brother and may have
been born c. 840–50; he shared the kingdom with Olaf after the death of
their father Gudrod, and Olaf does not seem to have lived long after this.
Halfdan's son, Harald the Fairhaired, was probably born c. 865–70, and
Halfdan himself probably died c. 880. Harald's decisive battle at Hafrsfjord (see p. 63) was probably fought round about 890.
[2] King Gudrod, Halfdan's son, p. 41.

44

soon as Halfdan had returned to Westfold, King Eystein went out with his army to Raumarike, and laid the whole country in subjection to him.

CHAPTER II. BATTLE BETWEEN HALFDAN AND EYSTEIN.— When King Halfdan heard of these disturbances in Raumarike, he again gathered his army together, and went out against King Eystein. A battle took place between them, and Halfdan gained the victory, and Eystein fled up to Hedemark, pursued by Halfdan. Another battle took place, in which Halfdan was again victorious; and Eystein fled northwards, up the Dales [1] to the Herse [2] Gudbrand. There he was strengthened with new people, and in winter he went towards Hedemark, and met Halfdan the Black upon a large island [3] which lies in the Mjösen lake. There a great battle was fought, and many people on both sides were slain, but Halfdan won the victory. There fell Guttorm, the son of the Herse Gudbrand, who was one of the finest men in the Uplands. Then Eystein fled north up the Dales, and sent his relation Halvard Skalk to King Halfdan to beg for peace. On consideration of their relationship, King Halfdan gave King Eystein half of Hedemark, which he and his relations had held before; but kept to himself Toten and the district called Land. He likewise appropriated to himself Hadeland; and he plundered far and wide around, and was become a mighty king.

CHAPTER III. HALFDAN'S MARRIAGE.—Halfdan the Black got a wife called Ragnhild, a daughter of Harald Goldbeard, who was a king in Sogn. They had a son, to whom Harald gave his own name; and the boy was brought up in Sogn, by his mother's father, King Harald. Now when this Harald had lived out his days nearly, and was become weak, having no son, he gave his dominions to his daughter's son Harald, and gave him his title of king; and he died soon after. The same winter his daughter Ragnhild died; and the following spring the young Harald fell sick, and died at ten years of age. As soon as Halfdan the Black heard of his son's death, he took the road northwards to Sogn with a great force, and was well received. He claimed the heritage and dominion after his son; and no opposition being made, he took the whole kingdom. Earl Atle the Slender, who was a friend of King Harald, came

---

[1] Now Gudbrandsdal and lateral valleys.

[2] Herse, *hersir*, the title of local leaders in some parts of Norway. They held hereditary office. The title is related to *herr*, host, army, and probably originally implied military command. Their social position was between that of the *höldr*, landed yeoman, and the *jarl*, earl.

[3] Helgöen.

to him from Gaular[1]; and the king set him over the Sogn district, to judge in the country according to the country's laws, and collect scatt upon the king's account. Thereafter King Halfdan proceeded to his kingdom in the Uplands.

CHAPTER IV. HALFDAN'S STRIFE WITH GANDALF'S SONS.— In autumn, King Halfdan proceeded to Vingulmark. One night when he was there in guest quarters, it happened that about midnight a man came to him who had been on the watch on horseback, and told him a war force was come near to the house. The king instantly got up, ordered his men to arm themselves, and went out of the house and drew them up in battle order. At the same moment Gandalf's sons, Hysing and Helsing, made their appearance with a large army. There was a great battle; but Halfdan being overpowered by the numbers of people, fled to the forest, leaving many of his men on this spot. His foster-father, Olve the Wise, fell here. The people now came in swarms to King Halfdan, and he advanced to seek Gandalf's sons. They met on the neck of land at Öieren,[2] and fought there. Hysing and Helsing fell, and their brother Hake saved himself ·by flight. King Halfdan then took possession of the whole of Vingulmark, and Hake fled to Alfheim.

CHAPTER V. KING HALFDAN'S LAST MARRIAGE WITH SIGURD HJORT'S DAUGHTER.—Sigurd Hjort was the name of a king in Ringerike, who was stouter and stronger than any other man, and his equal could not be seen for a handsome appearance. His father was Helge the Sharp; and his mother was Aslaug, a daughter of Sigurd the Snake-eyed. It is told of Sigurd, that when he was only twelve years old he killed in single combat the Berserk Hildebrand, and eleven others of his comrades; and many are the deeds of manhood told of him in a long saga about his feats.[3] Sigurd had two children, one of whom was a daughter, called Ragnhild, then twenty years of age, and an excellent brisk girl. Her brother Guttorm was a youth. It is related that Sigurd had a custom of riding out quite alone in the uninhabited forest to hunt the wild beasts that are hurtful to man, and he was always very eager at this sport. One day he rode out into the forest as usual, and when he had ridden a long way he came out at a piece of cleared land near to Hadeland. There the Berserk Hake came against him with thirty

[1] In Sunnfjord.
[2] The present Askim and part of Trögstad in Smaalenene.
[3] Perhaps part of the *Skjoldunga Saga*, cf. Introduction, p. xiii.

men, and they fought. Sigurd Hjort fell there, after killing
twelve of Hake's men; and Hake himself lost one hand, and
had three other wounds. Then Hake and his men rode to
Sigurd's house, where they took his daughter Ragnhild and her
brother Guttorm, and carried them, with much property and
valuables, home to Hadeland, where Hake had many great
farms. He ordered a feast to be prepared, intending to hold
his wedding with Ragnhild; but the time passed on account of
his wounds, which healed slowly; and the Berserk Hake of
Hadeland had to keep his bed, on account of his wounds, all the
autumn and beginning of winter. Now King Halfdan was in
Hedemark at the Yule entertainments when he heard this
news; and one morning early, when the king was dressed, he
called to him Haarek Gand, and told him to go over to Hadeland, and bring him Ragnhild, Sigurd Hjort's daughter. Haarek
got ready with a hundred men, and made his journey so that
they came over the lake to Hake's house in the grey of the
morning, and beset all the doors and stairs of the house in which
the men were sleeping. Then they broke into the sleeping-
room where Hake slept, took Ragnhild, with her brother
Guttorm, and all the goods that were there, and set fire to the
hall where they slept, and burnt all the people in it. Then
they covered over a magnificent wagon, placed Ragnhild and
Guttorm in it, and drove down upon the ice. Hake got up and
went after them a while; but when he came to the ice on the
lake, he turned his sword-hilt to the ground and let himself
fall upon the point, so that the sword went through him. He
was buried under a mound on the banks of the lake. When
King Halfdan, who was very quick of sight, saw the party
returning over the frozen lake, and with a covered wagon, he
knew that their errand was accomplished according to his
desire. Thereupon he ordered the tables to be set out, and
sent people all round in the neighbourhood to invite plenty of
guests; and the same day there was a good feast which was also
Halfdan's marriage-feast with Ragnhild, who became a great
queen. Ragnhild's mother was Tyrne, a daughter of Harald
Klak, king in Jutland, and a sister of Tyre Dannebod, who
was married to the Danish king, Gorm the Old, who then
ruled over the Danish dominions.

CHAPTER VI. OF RAGNHILD'S DREAM.—Ragnhild, who was
wise and intelligent, dreamt great dreams. She dreamt, for
one, that she was standing out in her herb-garden, and she
took a thorn out of her shift; but while she was holding the

thorn in her hand it grew so that it became a great tree, one end of which struck itself down into the earth, and it became firmly rooted; and the other end of the tree raised itself so high in the air that she could scarcely see over it, and it became also wonderfully thick. The under part of the tree was red like blood, but the stem upwards was beautifully green, and the branches white as snow. There were many and great limbs to the tree, some high up, others low down; and so vast was the tree's foliage that it seemed to her to cover all Norway, and even much more.[1]

CHAPTER VII. OF HALFDAN'S DREAM.—King Halfdan never had dreams, which appeared to him an extraordinary circumstance; and he told it to a man called Torleiv the Wise, and asked him what his advice was about it. Torleiv said that what he himself did, when he wanted to have any revelation by dream, was to take his sleep in a swine-stye, and then it never failed that he had dreams. The king did so, and the following dream was revealed to him. He thought he had the most beautiful hair, which was all in ringlets; some so long as to fall upon the ground, some reaching to the middle of his legs, some to his knees, some to his loins or the middle of his sides, some to his neck, and some were only as knots springing from his head. These ringlets were of various colours; but one ringlet surpassed all the others in beauty, lustre, and size. This dream he told to Torleiv, who interpreted it thus: There should be a great posterity from him, and his descendants should rule over countries with great, but not all with equally great, honour; but one of his race should be more celebrated than all the others. It is the opinion of people that this ringlet betokened King Olaf the Saint.

King Halfdan was a wise man, a man of truth and uprightness —who made laws,[2] observed them himself, and obliged others to observe them. And that violence should not come in place of the laws, he himself fixed the number of criminal acts in law, and the compensations, mulcts, or penalties, for each case, according to every one's birth and dignity.[3]

Queen Ragnhild gave birth to a son, and water was poured

---

[1] Cf. Harald the Fairhaired's Saga, p. 83.
[2] Cf. Hakon the Good's Saga, p. 91.
[3] The exaction of vengeance or atonement was a family matter, and the early laws lay down precisely the atonement payable for injury and the way in which such atonement shall be shared amongst the members of the injured party's family and the expense borne by the members of the injurer's family. Fines were also payable to the king for offences done, and the atonement varied according to the status of the person injured.

over him, and the name of Harald given him, and he soon grew stout and remarkably handsome. As he grew up he became very expert at all feats, and showed also a good understanding. He was much beloved by his mother, but less so by his father.

CHAPTER VIII. HALFDAN'S MEAT VANISHES AT A FEAST.— King Halfdan was at a Yule-feast in Hadeland, where a wonderful thing happened one Yule[1] evening. When the great number of guests assembled were going to sit down to table, all the meat and all liquors disappeared from the table. The king sat alone very confused in mind; all the others set off, each to his home, in consternation. That the king might come to some certainty about what had occasioned this event, he ordered a Laplander to be seized who was particularly knowing, and tried to force him to disclose the truth; but however much he tortured the man, he got nothing out of him. The Laplander sought help particularly from Harald, the king's son; and Harald begged for mercy for him, but in vain. Then Harald let him escape against the king's will, and accompanied the man himself. On their journey they came to a place where the man's chief had a great feast, and it appears they were well received there. When they had been there until spring, the chief said, "Thy father took it much amiss that in winter I took some provisions from him—now I will repay it to thee by a joyful piece of news: thy father is dead; and now thou shalt return home, and take possession of the whole kingdom which he had, and with it thou shalt lay the whole kingdom of Norway under thee."

CHAPTER IX. HALFDAN'S DEATH.—Halfdan the Black was driving from a feast in Hadeland, and it so happened that his road lay over the lake called Rand.[2] It was in spring, and there was a great thaw. They drove across the bight called Rökensvik, where in winter there had been a hole broken in the ice for cattle to drink at, and where the dung had fallen upon the ice the thaw had eaten it into holes. Now as the king drove over it the ice broke, and King Halfdan and many with him perished. He was then forty years old. He had been one of the most fortunate kings in respect of good seasons. The people thought so much of him, that when his death was

[1] The pagan midwinter festival was called Yule (Jól). The meaning of the root from which it is derived is uncertain (the chief suggestions connect it with the turn of the year or a sense of joyous festival). Little is known of its pagan celebration, but it appears to have been closely connected with cults of the dead and of fertility spirits.

[2] The Rands-fjord; and the bight called Rökensvik is at a farm called Röken.

known, and his body was carried to Ringerike to bury it there, the people of most consequence from Raumarike, Westfold, and Hedemark, came to meet it. All desired to take the body with them to bury it in their own district, and they thought that those who got it would have good crops to expect. At last it was agreed to divide the body into four parts. The head was laid in a mound at Stein [1] in Ringerike, and each of the others took his part home and laid it in a mound; and these have since been called Halfdan's Mounds.

[1] The farm of Stein in Hole.

III

HARALD THE FAIRHAIRED [1]

CHAPTER I. HARALD'S STRIFE WITH HAKE AND HIS FATHER GANDALF.—Harald was but ten years old when he succeeded his father, Halfdan the Black. He became a stout, strong, and comely man, and withal prudent and manly. His mother's brother, Guttorm, was regent over the realm, captain of the king's body-guard, and commander of the army.[2] After Halfdan the Black's death, many chiefs coveted the dominions he had left. Among these King Gandalf was the first; then Hogne and Frode, sons of Eystein, king of Hedemark; and also Hogne Kaarason ravaged in Ringerike. Hake, the son of Gandalf, began with an expedition of three hundred men against Westfold, marched round the head of and over some valleys, and expected to come suddenly upon King Harald; while his father Gandalf sat at home with his army, and prepared to cross over the fjord into Westfold. When Guttorm heard of this he gathered an army, and marched up the country with King Harald against Hake. They met in a valley, in which they fought a great battle, and King Harald was victorious; and there fell King Hake and most of his people. The place has since been called Hakedal.[3] Then King Harald and Guttorm turned back, but they found King Gandalf had come to Westfold. The two armies marched against each other, and met, and had a great battle; and it ended in King Gandalf flying, after leaving most of his men dead on the spot, and so he came back to his kingdom. Now when the sons of King Eystein in Hedemark heard the news, they expected the war would come

[1] This saga brings us into the realm of history, although much of the chronology remains obscure; cf. p. 44, note 1.

[2] About the king's person were men-at-arms of the court, kept in pay, and holding guard by night. In later times the Norwegian kings and other great leaders had a regular household organization. The king's immediate retainers were *hirdmen*, members of his *hird* (a loan-word from Old English) or "familia"; they paid him personal homage and formed his bodyguard. A second class of retainers were the Guests; cf. p. 325, note 1.

[3] About fifteen English miles north of Oslo.

upon them, and they sent a message to Hogne Kaarason and to Herse Gudbrand, and appointed a meeting with them at Ringsaker [1] in Hedemark.

CHAPTER II. KING HARALD OVERCOMES FIVE KINGS.—After these battles King Harald and Guttorm turned back, and went with all the men they could gather through the forests towards the Uplands. They found out where the Upland kings had appointed their meeting-place, and came there about the time of midnight, without the watchmen observing them until their army was before the door of the house in which Hogne Kaarason was, as well as that in which Gudbrand slept. They set fire to both houses; but King Eystein's two sons slipped out with their men, and fought for a while, until both Hogne and Frode fell. After the fall of these four chiefs, King Harald, by his relation Guttorm's success and power, subdued Hedemark, Ringerike, Gudbrandsdal, Hadeland, Toten, Raumarike, and the whole northern part of Vingulmark. King Harald and Guttorm had thereafter war with King Gandalf, and fought several battles with him; and in the last of them King Gandalf was slain, and King Harald took the whole of his kingdom as far south as the Glommen.

CHAPTER III. OF GYDA, DAUGHTER OF ERIC.—King Harald sent his men to a girl called Gyda, a daughter of King Eric of Hordaland, who was brought up as foster-child in the house of a great bonde [2] in Valders. The king wanted her for his concubine; for she was a remarkably handsome girl, but of high spirit withal. Now when the messengers came there, and delivered their errand to the girl, she answered, that she would not throw herself away even to take a king for her husband, who had no greater kingdom to rule over than a few fylker. [3] "And methinks," said she, "it is wonderful that no king here in Norway will make the whole country subject to him, in the same way as Gorm the Old did in Denmark, or Eric at Upsal." The messengers thought her answer was dreadfully haughty, and asked what she thought would come of such an answer; for Harald was so mighty a man, that his invitation was good enough for her. But although she had replied to their errand differently from what they wished, they saw no chance on this occasion of taking her with them against her will, so they pre-

---

[1] On the east side of Lake Mjösen.

[2] Bonde (*sing*.), bonder (*pl*.). The bonder were freeholders, freeborn proprietors.

[3] In Snorri's own day there were twenty-six fylker in Norway, but there was no nation-wide fylke organization in the time of Harald the Fairhaired.

pared to return. When they were ready, and the people followed them out, Gyda said to the messengers, "Now tell to King Harald these my words—I will only agree to be his lawful wife upon the condition that he shall first, for my sake, subject to himself the whole of Norway, so that he may rule over that kingdom as freely and fully as King Eric over the Swedish dominions, or King Gorm over Denmark; for only then, methinks, can he be called the king of a nation."

CHAPTER IV. KING HARALD'S VOW.—Now came the messengers back to King Harald, bringing him the words of the girl, and saying she was so bold and foolish that she well deserved that the king should send a greater troop of people for her, and inflict on her some disgrace. Then answered the king, "This girl has not spoken or done so much amiss that she should be punished, but rather she should be thanked for her words. She has reminded me," said he, "of something which it appears to me wonderful I did not think of before. And now," added he, "I make the solemn vow, and take God to witness, who made me,[1] and rules over all things, that never shall I clip or comb my hair until I have subdued the whole of Norway, with scatt,[2] and duties, and domains; or if not, have died in the attempt." Guttorm thanked the king warmly for his vow; adding, that it was royal work to fulfil royal words.

CHAPTER V. THE BATTLE IN ORKEDAL.—After this the two relations gather together a great force, and prepare for an expedition to the Uplands, and northwards up the valley (Gudbrandsdal), and north over Dovrefjeld; and when the king came down to the inhabited land[3] he ordered all the men to be killed, and everything far and wide to be delivered to the flames. And when the people came to know this, they fled every one where he could; some down the country to Orkedal, some to Guldal, some to the forests. But some begged for grace,[4] and obtained it on condition of joining the king and becoming his men. He met no opposition until he came to Orkedal. There a crowd of people had assembled, and he had his first battle with a king called Gryting. Harald won the victory, and King Gryting was made prisoner, and most of his

[1] Great men of the pagan period were sometimes felt to have had sense enough to see through the polytheism of the pagan religion, which may account for Harald's anachronistic oath here.

[2] In Orkney, though the land in general was feudalized by the annexation to the Scottish crown in 1463, the old udal tax survived until the passing of the Crofters' Acts in the last quarter of the nineteenth century.

[3] Opdal.

[4] Grace = *grid*, quarter, truce, safe-conduct.

people killed. He took service himself under the king, and swore fidelity to him. Thereafter all the people in Orkedal district went under King Harald, and became his men.

CHAPTER VI. OF KING HARALD'S LAWS FOR LAND PROPERTY. —King Harald made this law over all the lands he conquered, that all the udal [1] property should belong to him; and that the bonder, both great and small, should pay him land dues for their possessions.[2] Over every district he set an earl to judge according to the law of the land and to justice, and also to collect the land dues and the fines; and for this each earl received a third part of the dues, and services, and fines, for the support of his table and other expenses. Each earl had under him four or more herser, each of whom had an estate of twenty merks yearly income bestowed on him and was bound to support twenty men-at-arms, and the earl sixty men, at their own expenses. The king had increased the land dues and burdens so much, that each of his earls had greater power and income than the kings had before; and when that became known in Drontheim,[3] many great men joined the king, and took his service.

CHAPTER VII. BATTLE IN GULDAL.—It is told that Earl Hakon Grjotgardsson came to King Harald from Yrjar,[4] and brought a great crowd of men to his service. Then King Harald went into Guldal, and had a great battle, in which he slew two kings, and conquered their dominions; and these were Guldal and Strind fylker. He gave Earl Hakon Strind fylke to rule over as earl. King Harald then proceeded to Stjordal, and had a third battle, in which he gained the victory, and took that district also. The people of inner Drontheim assembled, and four kings met together with their troops. The one ruled over Værdal,[5] the second over Skogn, the third over Sparbu, and the fourth over Inderöen; and this latter had also Eyna fylke. These four kings marched with their men against King Harald, but he won the battle; and some of these kings fell, and some fled. In all, King Harald fought at the least eight battles, and slew eight kings, in the land of Drontheim, and laid the whole of it under him.

[1] Udal or odel, absolute proprietorship of land.
[2] This feudal system hardly answers to tenth-century facts.
[3] The German name Drontheim grates on modern ears. It is used for the old regional name Thrandheim (modern Tröndelag) and the old town name Nidaros (modern Trondhjem, -heim, the forms used in the notes).
[4] Now Örland, on the north side of the entrance to Trondheimsfjord.
[5] Værdal, Skogn, Sparbu, Inderöen, are small districts or parishes on the side of the Trondhjem fjord.

CHAPTER VIII. KING HARALD SEIZES ALL NAUMADAL DISTRICT.
—North in Naumadal were two brothers, kings—Herlaug and
Rollaug; and they had been for three summers raising a mound
or tomb of stone and lime and of wood. Just as the work was
finished, the brothers got the news that King Harald was
coming upon them with his army. Then King Herlaug had a
great quantity of meat and drink brought into the mound, and
went into it himself, with eleven companions, and ordered the
mound to be covered up.[1] King Rollaug, on the contrary,
went upon the summit of the mound, on which the kings were
wont to sit, and made a throne to be erected, upon which he
seated himself. Then he ordered feather-beds to be laid upon
the bench below, on which the earls were wont to be seated,
and threw himself down from his high seat or throne into the
earls' seat, giving himself the title of earl. Now Rollaug went
to meet King Harald, gave up to him his whole kingdom,
offered to enter into his service, and told him his whole proceeding. Then took King Harald a sword, fastened it to
Rollaug's belt, bound a shield to his neck, and made him thereupon an earl, and led him to his earl's seat; and therewith gave
him the district of Naumadal, and set him as earl over it.[2]

CHAPTER IX. KING HARALD'S HOME AFFAIRS.—King Harald
then returned to Drontheim, where he dwelt during the winter,
and always afterwards called it his home. He fixed here his
head residence, which is called Lade.[3] This winter he took to
wife Aasa, a daughter of Earl Hakon Grjotgardsson, who then
stood in great favour and honour with the king. In spring the
king fitted out his ships. In winter he had caused a great
dragon-ship to be built, and had it fitted out in the most
splendid way, and brought his house-troops and his berserks
on board. The forecastle men were picked men, for they had
the king's banner. From the stem to the mid-hold was called

[1] There is a similar briefer account in the *Egils Saga Skalla-Grimssonar*,
ch. 3. A story is also told in the *Agrip*, ch. 15 (cf. Introduction, p. xvii), of
a king of Namdal called Herse; he is said to have been a forefather of Earl
Hakon Sigurdsson (see pp. 118 ff.). Herse wished to commit suicide
after the death of his wife, but could find no precedent for a king's death in
this way, although men with the title of earl had killed themselves. "He
then went on to a certain mound and rolled himself down and said he had
rolled himself out of his title of king, and afterwards he hanged himself
under the title of earl; and his descendants afterwards would never accept
the title of king." This pleasant story attempts, of course, to explain the
absence of the kingly title in the great dynasty of the earls of Lade.

[2] Originally the title of earl was that of an independent chieftain, whose
position in no way differed from that of a king in one of Norway's petty
states. The investiture described here is doubtless an anachronism.

[3] Lade, a large farm on a peninsula, two English miles to the north of
Trondheim.

rausn,[1] or the fore-defence; and there were the berserks.[2] Such
men only were received into King Harald's house-troop as were
remarkable for strength, courage, and all kinds of dexterity;
and they alone got place in his ship, for he had a good choice of
house-troops from the best men of every district.   King Harald
had a great army, many large ships, and many men of might
followed him.   Hornklove, in his poem called *Glymdraapa*, tells
of this; and also that King Harald had a battle with the people
of Orkedal, at Opdal forest, before he went upon this expedition.

> O'er the broad heath the bowstrings twang,
> While high in air the arrows sang;
> The iron shower drives to flight
> The foemen from the bloody fight.
> The warder of great Odin's shrine,
> The fair-haired son of Odin's line,
> Raises the voice which gives the cheer,
> First in the track of wolf or bear.
> His master voice drives them along
> To Hell—a destined, trembling throng;
> And Nokve's ship, with glancing sides,
> Must fly to the wild ocean's tides—
> Must fly before the king who leads
> Norse axe-men on their ocean-steeds.

CHAPTER X. BATTLE AT SOLSKJEL.—King Harald moved out
with his army from Drontheim, and went southwards to Möre.[3]
Hunthjof was the name of the king who ruled over the Möre
fylke.   Solve Klove was the name of his son, and both were
great warriors.   King Nokve, who ruled over Raumsdal,[4] was
the father of Solve's mother.   Those chiefs gathered a great
force when they heard of King Harald, and came against him.
They met at Solskjel,[5] and there was a great battle, which was
gained by King Harald.   Hornklove tells of this battle:

> Thus did the hero known to fame,
> The leader of the shields, whose name
> Strikes every heart with dire dismay,
> Launch forth his war-ships to the fray.
> Two kings he fought; but little strife
> Was needed to cut short their life.
> A clang of arms by the sea-shore—
> And the shields' sound was heard no more.

---

[1] *Rausn*, the forecastle-deck. The term translated "mid-hold" is
austrúm, literally "baling-station."
[2] Cf. p. 11, note 2.
[3] Möre is a name cognate with English moor, morass, mere, and related
to Norse *marr*, sea (cf. Latin *mare*). The reference here is to the southern
part of the fylke of Nordmöre, which extends along the coast north and
south of the mouth of Trondheimsfjord.   Sunnmöre lies further south along
the coast, separated from Nordmöre by Romsdal.
[4] Raumsdal is the present Romsdal.
[5] Solskjel is an island in the parish of Ædö in Nordmöre.

The two kings were slain, but Solve escaped by flight; and King Harald laid both fylker under his power. He stayed here long in summer to establish law and order for the country people, and set men to rule them, and keep them faithful to him; and in autumn he prepared to return northwards to Drontheim. Rognvald Earl of Möre, a son of Eystein Glumra, had the summer before become one of Harald's men; and the king set him as chief over these two fylker, North Möre and Raumsdal; strengthened him both with men of might and bonder, and gave him the help of ships to defend the coast against enemies. He was called Rognvald the Mighty, or the Wise; and people say both names suited well. King Harald came back to Drontheim to winter.

CHAPTER XI. FALL OF THE KINGS ARNVID AND AUDBJORN. —The following spring, King Harald raised a great force in Drontheim, and gave out that he would proceed to South Möre. Solve Klove had passed the winter in his ships of war, plundering in North Möre, and had killed many of King Harald's men; pillaging some places, burning others, and making great ravage: but sometimes he had been, during the winter, with a kinsman, King Arnvid, in South Möre. Now when he heard that King Harald was come with ships and a great army, he gathered people, and was strong in men-at-arms; for many thought they had to take vengeance of King Harald. Solve Klove went southwards to the Fjords,[1] which King Audbjorn ruled over, to ask him to help, and join his force to King Arnvid's and his own. "For," said he, "it is now clear that we all have but one course to take; and that is to rise, all as one man, against King Harald, for we have strength enough, and fate must decide the victory: for as to the other condition of becoming his servants, that is no condition for us, who are not less noble than Harald. My father thought it better to fall in battle for his kingdom, than to go willingly into King Harald's service, or not to abide the chance of weapons like the Naumadal kings." King Solve's speech was such that King Audbjorn promised his help, and gathered a great force together, and went with it to King Arnvid, and they had a great army. Now, they got news that King Harald was come from the north, and they met within Solskjel. And it was the custom to lash the ships together, stem to stem; so it was done now. King Harald laid his ship against King Arnvid's, and there was the sharpest fight, and many men fell on both sides. At last King Harald

---

[1] The Fjords, or Firdafylke, now Sunnfjord and Nordfjord.

was raging with anger, and went forward to the fore-deck, and
slew so dreadfully that all the forecastle men of Arnvid's ship
were driven aft to the mast, and some fell. Thereupon Harald
boarded the ship, and King Arnvid's men tried to save themselves by flight, and he himself was slain in his ship. King
Audbjorn also fell; but Solve fled. So says Hornklove:

> Against the hero's shield in vain
> The arrow-storm fierce pours its rain.
> The king stands on the blood-stained deck,
> Trampling on many a stout foe's neck;
> And high above the dinning stound
> Of helm and axe, and ringing sound
> Of blade and shield, and raven's cry,
> Is heard his shout of "Victory!"

Of King Harald's men, fell his earls Asgaut and Asbjorn,
together with his brothers-in-law Grjotgard and Herlaug, the
sons of Earl Hakon of Lade. Solve became afterwards a great
viking, and often did great damage in King Harald's domains.

CHAPTER XII. KING VEMUND BURNT TO DEATH.—After this
battle King Harald subdued South Möre; but Vemund, King
Audbjorn's brother, still had power in Firdafylke. It was now
late in harvest, and King Harald's men gave him the counsel
not to proceed southwards round Stad.[1] Then King Harald
set Earl Rognvald over South and North Möre and also Raumsdal, and he had many people about him. King Harald returned
to Drontheim. The same winter Rognvald went over the
inner neck of land, and southwards in the Fjords. There he
heard news of King Vemund, and came by night to a place
called Naustdal,[2] where King Vemund was living in guest-
quarters. Earl Rognvald surrounded the house in which they
were quartered, and burnt the king in it, together with
ninety men. Then came Kaare of Berdla[3] to Earl Rognvald
with a completely armed long-ship, and they both returned to
Möre. The earl took all the ships Vemund had, and all the
goods he could get hold of. Berdla-Kaare proceeded north to
Drontheim to King Harald, and became his man; and a dreadful
berserk he was.

CHAPTER XIII. DEATH OF EARL HAKON AND OF EARL ATLE
THE SLENDER.—The following spring King Harald went south-

---

[1] Stad is often mentioned in the sagas, being the most westerly and
exposed part of the mainland of Norway; and vessels coasting along from
the north or south had to steer a new course along the coast after passing
Stad. It is now called Stadtland.

[2] In Nordfjord.

[3] Now Berle in Nordfjord.

wards with his fleet along the coast, and subdued the Firdafylke. Then he sailed eastward along the land until he came
to Viken[1]; but he left Earl Hakon Grjotgardsson behind, and
set him over Firdafylke. Earl Hakon sent word to Earl Atle
the Slender that he should leave Sogne district, and be earl
over Gaular district, as he had been before, alleging that King
Harald had given Sogne district to him. Earl Atle sent word
back that he would keep both Sogne district and Gaular district,
until he met King Harald. The two earls quarrelled about this
so long, that both gathered troops. They met at Fjaler, in
Stavenesvaag,[2] and had a great battle, in which Earl Hakon
fell, and Earl Atle got a mortal wound, and his men carried
him to the island of Atle,[3] where he died. So says Eyvind
Skaldaspiller:

> He who stood a rooted oak,
> Unshaken by the swordsman's stroke,
> Amidst the whiz of arrows slain,
> Has fallen upon Fjaler's plain.
> There, by the ocean's rocky shore,
> The waves are stained with the red gore
> Of stout Earl Hakon Grjotgard's son,
> And of brave warriors many a one.

CHAPTER XIV. OF KING HARALD AND THE SWEDISH KING
ERIC.—King Harald came with his fleet eastward to Viken,
and landed at Tunsberg, which was then a trading town. He
had then been four years in Drontheim, and in all that time
had not been in Viken. Here he heard the news that Eric
Eymundson, king of Sweden, had laid under him Vermeland,
and was taking scatt or land-tax from all the forest settlers;
and also that he called the whole country north to Svinesund,
and west along the sea, Westgotland; which altogether he
reckoned to his kingdom, and took land-tax from it. Over
this country he had set an earl, by name Rane the Gotlander,
who had the earldom between Svinesund and the Gotha river,
and was a mighty earl. And it was told to King Harald that
the Swedish king said he would not rest until he had as great
a kingdom in Viken as Sigurd Ring, or his son Ragnar Lodbrok,
had possessed; and that was Raumarike and Westfold, all the
way to the isle Grenmar, and also Vingulmark, and all that

[1] Viken = the Creek; district on both sides of the Oslo fjord.
[2] Now Staangfjord immediately to the south of Stavenes, the extreme
point on the south side of the Förde fjord.
[3] Atle-isle in Fjaler, now included in Sunnfjord, lies immediately south of
Stavenes. Snorri seems to imply that Earl Atle was the island's eponym.

lay south of it. In these fylker many chiefs, and many other people, had given obedience to the Swedish king. King Harald was very angry at this, and summoned the bonder to a Thing in Folden,[1] where he laid an accusation[2] against them for treason towards him. Some bonder defended themselves from the accusation, some paid fines, some were punished. He went thus through the whole fylke during the summer, and in harvest he did the same in Raumarike. Towards winter he heard that Eric king of Sweden was, with his court, going about in Vermeland in guest-quarters.

CHAPTER XV.—KING HARALD AT A FEAST OF THE PEASANT AAKE, AND THE MURDER OF AAKE.—King Harald takes his way across the Eida forest eastward, and comes out in Vermeland, where he also orders feasts to be prepared for himself. There was a man, by name Aake, who was the greatest of the bonder of Vermeland, very rich, and at that time very aged. He sent men to King Harald, and invited him to a feast, and the king promised to come on the day appointed. Aake invited also King Eric to a feast, and appointed the same day. Aake had a great feasting hall, but it was old; and he made a new hall, not less than the old one, and had it ornamented in the most splendid way. The new hall he had hung with new hangings, but the old had only its old ornaments. Now when the kings came to the feast, King Eric with his court was taken into the old hall; but Harald with his followers into the new. The same difference was in all the table furniture, and King Eric and his men had the old-fashioned vessels and horns, but all gilded and splendid; while King Harald and his men had entirely new vessels and horns adorned with gold, all with carved figures, and shining like glass: and both companies had the best of liquor. Aake the bonde had formerly been King Halfdan the Black's man. Now when the day came on which the feasting was to end, and the kings made themselves ready for their journey, and the horses were saddled, came Aake before King Harald, leading in his hand his son Obbe, a boy of twelve years of age, and said, "If the goodwill I have shown to thee, sire, in my feast, be worth thy friendship, show it hereafter to my son. I give him to thee now for thy service." The king thanked him with many agreeable words for his friendly entertainment, and promised him his full friendship in return. Then

---

[1] Folden, the present Oslo fjord district.

[2] A reference to a Thing, and an accusation before it, appears to have been a necessary mode of proceeding, even to authorise the king to punish the udal landholders for treason.

Aake brought out great presents, which he gave to the king, and they gave each other thereafter the parting kiss. Aake went next to the Swedish king, who was dressed and ready for the road, but not in the best humour. Aake gave to him also good and valuable gifts; but the king answered only with few words, and mounted his horse. Aake followed the king on the road, and talked with him. The road led through a wood which was near to the house; and when Aake came to the wood, the king said to him, "How was it that thou madest such a difference between me and King Harald as to give him the best of everything, although thou knowest thou art my man?" "I think," answered Aake, "that there failed in it nothing, king, either to you or to your attendants, in friendly entertainment at this feast. But that all the utensils for your drinking were old, was because you are now old; but King Harald is in the bloom of youth, and therefore I gave him the new things. And as to my being thy man, thou art just as much my man." On this the king out with his sword, and gave Aake his death-wound. King Harald was ready now also to mount his horse, and desired that Aake should be called. The people went to seek him; and some ran up the road that King Eric had taken, and found Aake there dead. They came back, and told the news to King Harald, and he bids his men to be up, and avenge Aake the bonde. And away he rode he and his men the way King Eric had taken, until they came in sight of each other. Each for himself rode as hard as he could, until Eric came into the wood which divided Gotland and Verme-land. There King Harald wheels about, and returns to Verme-land, and lays the country under him, and kills King Eric's men wheresoever he can find them. In winter King Harald returned to Raumarike, and dwelt there a while.

CHAPTER XVI. KING HARALD'S JOURNEY TO TUNSBERG.—
King Harald went out in winter to his ships at Tunsberg, rigged them, and sailed away eastward over the Fjord, and subjected all Vingulmark to his dominion. All winter he was out with his ships, and marauded in Ranrike[1]; so says Thorbjorn Hornklove:

> The Norseman's king is on the sea,
> Tho' bitter wintry cold it be—
> On the wild waves his Yule keeps he.
> When our brisk king can get his way,
> He'll no more by the fireside stay

---

[1] Ranrike was the province between the Gotha and Glommen river-mouths.

> Than the young sun: he makes us play
> The game of the bright sun-god Frey.
> But the soft Swede loves well the fire,
> The well-stuffed couch, the downy glove,
> And from the hearth-seat will not move.

The Gotlanders gathered people together all over the country to oppose him.

CHAPTER XVII. THE BATTLE IN GOTLAND.—In spring, when the ice was breaking up, they drove stakes into the Gotha river to hinder King Harald with his ships from coming to the land. But King Harald laid his ships alongside the stakes, and plundered the country, and burnt all around; so says Hornklove:

> The king, who finds a dainty feast
> For battle-bird and prowling beast,
> Has won in war the southern land
> That lies along the ocean's strand.
> The leader of the helmets, he
> Who leads his ships o'er the dark sea,
> Harald, whose high-rigged masts appear
> Like antlered fronts of the wild deer,
> Has laid his ships close alongside
> Of the foe's piles with daring pride.

Afterwards the Gotlanders came down to the strand with a great army, and gave battle to King Harald, and great was the fall of men. But it was King Harald who gained the day. Thus says Hornklove:

> Whistles the battle-axe in its swing,
> O'er head the whizzing javelins sing,
> Helmet and shield and hauberk ring;
> The air-song of the lance is loud,
> The arrows pipe in darkening cloud;
> Through helm and mail the foemen feel
> The blue edge of our king's good steel.
> Who can withstand our gallant king?
> The Gotland men their flight must wing.

CHAPTER XVIII. RANE THE GOTLANDER'S DEATH.—King Harald went far and wide through Gotland, and many were the battles he fought there, and in general he was victorious. In one of these battles fell Rane the Gotlander; and then the king took his whole land north of the Gotha river and west of the Vänern, and all Vermeland. And after he turned back therefrom, he set Guttorm as chief to defend the country, and left a great force with him. King Harald himself went first to the Uplands, where he remained a while, and then proceeded northwards over the Dovrefjeld to Drontheim, where he dwelt for a long time. Harald began to have children. By Aasa he had four sons. The eldest was Guttorm.[1] Halfdan the Black and Halfdan the White were twins. Sigfröd was the fourth. They were all brought up in Drontheim with all honour.

CHAPTER XIX. BATTLE IN HAFRSFJORD.—News came in from the south land that the people of Hordaland and Rogaland, Agder and Thelemark, were gathering, and bringing together ships and weapons, and a great body of men. The leaders of this were Eric king of Hordaland; Sulke king of Rogaland, and his brother Earl Sote; Kjotve the Rich, king of Agder, and his son Tore Haklang; and from Thelemark two brothers, Roald Rygg and Hadd the Hard. Now when Harald got certain news of this, he assembled his forces, set his ships on the water, made himself ready with his men, and set out southwards along the coast, gathering many people from every district. King Eric heard of this when he came south of Stad; and having assembled all the men he could expect, he proceeded southwards to meet the force which he knew was coming to his help from the east. The whole met together north of Jæderen, and went into Hafrsfjord, where King Harald was waiting with his forces. A great battle began, which was both hard and long; but at last King Harald gained the day. There King Eric fell, and King Sulke, with his brother Earl Sote. Tore Haklang, who was a great berserk, had laid his ship against King Harald's, and there was above all measure a desperate attack, until Tore Haklang fell, and his whole ship was cleared of men. Then King Kjotve fled to a little isle outside, on which there was a good place of strength. Thereafter all his men fled, some to their ships, some up to the land; and the latter ran southwards over the country of Jæderen. So says Hornklove, viz.:

> Has the news reached you?—have you heard
> Of the great fight at Hafrsfjord,[2]
> Between our noble king brave Harald
> And King Kjotve rich in gold?
> The foemen came from out the East.
> Keen for the fray as for a feast.
> A gallant sight it was to see
> Their fleet sweep o'er the dark-blue sea;
> Each war-ship, with its threatening throat

---

[1] This is the only place where Guttorm is said to be Aasa's son.
[2] Now Havsfjord, just west of Stavanger.

Of dragon fierce or ravenous brute [1]
Grim gaping from the prow; its wales
Glittering with burnished shields,[2] like scales;
Its crew of udal men of war,
Whose snow-white targets shone from far;
And many a mailed spearman stout
From the West countries round about,
English and Scotch, a foreign host,
And swordsmen from the far French coast.[3]
And as the foemen's ships drew near,
The dreadful din you well might hear;
Savage berserker roaring mad,
And champions fierce in wolf-skins clad,[4]
Howling like wolves; and clanking jar
Of many a mail-clad man of war.
Thus the foe came; but our brave king
Taught them to fly as fast again.
For when he saw their force come o'er,
He launched his warships from the shore;
On the deep sea he launched his fleet,
And boldly rowed the foe to meet.
Fierce was the shock, and loud the clang
Of shields, until the fierce Haklang,
The foemen's famous berserk, fell.
Then from our men burst forth the yell
Of victory; and the King of Gold
Could not withstand our Harald bold,
But fled before his flaky locks
For shelter to the island rocks.
All in the bottom of the ships
The wounded lay, in ghastly heaps;
Backs up and faces down they lay,
Under the row-seats stowed away;
And many a warrior's shield, I ween,
Might on the warrior's back be seen,
To shield him as he fled amain
From the fierce stone-storm's pelting rain.
The mountain-folk, as I've heard say,
Ne'er stopped as they ran from the fray,
Till they had crossed the Jæderen sea,
And reached their homes—so keen each soul
To drown his fright in the mead bowl.

CHAPTER XX. KING HARALD THE SUPREME SOVEREIGN IN
NORWAY. OF THE SETTLEMENT OF DISTANT LANDS.—After
this battle King Harald met no opposition in Norway, for all
his opponents and greatest enemies were cut off. But some,
and they were a great multitude, fled out of the country, and
thereby great uninhabited districts were peopled. Jemteland

[1] The warships were called dragons, from being decorated with the
head of a dragon, serpent, or other wild animal; and the word "draco"
was adopted in the Latin of the Middle Ages to denote a ship of war of
the larger class. The snekke was the cutter or smaller warship.
[2] The shields were hung over the side rails of the ships.
[3] Faulty translation. The poem refers to Norse vikings from the British
Isles and to weapons of French manufacture.
[4] *Úlfheðnar*, "the wolf-skin-clad ones," another term for berserks.

and Helsingeland were peopled then, although some Norwegians had already set up their habitation there. In the discontent when King Harald seized on the lands of Norway,[1] the out-countries of Iceland and the Faroe Isles were discovered and peopled. The Northmen had also a great resort to Shetland, and many men left Norway, flying the country on account of King Harald, and went on viking cruises into the West sea. In winter they were in the Orkney Islands and Hebrides; but marauded in summer in Norway, and did great damage. Many, however, were the mighty men who took service under King Harald, and became his men, and dwelt in the land with him.

When King Harald had now become sole king over all Norway, he remembered what the proud girl Gyda had said to him (p. 53); so he sent men to her, and had her brought to him, and married her. And these were their children: Aalaf —she was the eldest; then was their son Rörek; then Sigtryg, Frode, and Torgils. King Harald had many wives [2] and many children. Among them he had one wife, who was called Ragnhild the Mighty, a daughter of King Eric, from Jutland; and by her he had a son, Eric Bloody-axe. He was also married to Swanhild, a daughter of Earl Eystein; and their sons were Olaf Geirstadaelf, Bjorn, and Ragnar Rykkel. Lastly, King Harald married Aashild, a daughter of Ring Dagsson, up in Ringerike; and their children were Dag, Ring, Gudrod Skerja, and Ingigerd. It is told that King Harald put away nine wives when he married Ragnhild the Mighty. So says Hornklove:

> Harald, of noblest race the head,
> A Danish wife took to his bed;
> And out of doors nine wives he thrust—
> The mothers of the princes first,
> Who of Holmryger [3] hold command,
> And those who rule in Hordaland.
> And then he packed from out the place
> The children born of Holge's race.[4]

---

[1] i.e. when he forced the rulers of the petty Norwegian states to acknow-ledge his sovereignty.

[2] Concubines were commonly held by kings and men of wealth in early Scandinavia. There was no rule of primogeniture in the succession to the kingdom and illegitimate as well as legitimate sons were regarded as having similar claims. Under this system internal strife was frequent and inevitable, and many of the sagas in the *Heimskringla* would have been as short as that of Olaf the Quiet (pp. 242–9) if things had been different. It was not until 1163–4 that the succession was properly regulated, with age and legitimacy preferred, in connection with the coronation of Magnus Erlingsson (pp. 408–9), although the successful upstart Sverre, who defeated and succeeded Magnus, based his claim on the old practice.

[3] Inhabitants of the islands in the Stavanger-fjord.

[4] The verse means that he rejected the women of Rogaland, Hedemark, Hordaland and Halogaland (all Norway in effect) and preferred a Dane.

CHAPTER XXI. OF KING HARALD'S CHILDREN AND MAR-
RIAGES.—King Harald's children were all fostered and brought
up by their relations on the mother's side. Guttorm the Duke
had poured water over King Harald's eldest son,[1] and had given
him his own name. He set the child upon his knee,[2] and was
his foster-father, and took him with himself eastward to Viken,
and there he was brought up in the house of Guttorm. Guttorm
ruled the whole land in Viken, and the Uplands, when King
Harald was absent.

CHAPTER XXII. KING HARALD'S VOYAGE TO THE WEST.—
King Harald heard that the vikings, who fared to the West [3]
in winter, plundered far and wide in the middle part [4] of Norway; and therefore every summer he made an expedition to
search the isles and out-skerries [5] on the coast. Wheresoever
the vikings heard of him they all took to flight, and most of them
out into the open ocean. At last the king grew weary of this
work, and therefore one summer he sailed with his fleet right
out into the West sea. First he came to Shetland, and he slew
all the vikings who could not save themselves by flight. Then
King Harald sailed southwards, to the Orkney Islands, and
cleared them all of vikings. Thereafter he proceeded to the
Hebrides, plundered there, and slew many vikings who formerly
had had men-at-arms under them. Many a battle was fought,
and King Harald was usually victorious. He then plundered
far and wide in Scotland itself, and had battles there. When
he was come westward as far as the Isle of Man, the report of
his exploits on the land had gone before him; for all the inhabitants had fled over to Scotland, and the island was left
entirely bare both of people and goods, so that King Harald
and his men made no booty when they landed. So says
Hornklove:

> The wise, the noble king, great Harald,
> Whose hand so freely scatters gold,
> Led many a northern shield to war
> Against the town upon the shore.
> The wolves soon gathered on the sand
> Of that sea-shore; for Harald's hand
> The Scottish army drove away,
> And on the coast left wolves a prey.

---

[1] This pagan ceremony is comparable with Christian baptism. After the
child was born it was presented to the father and, if he accepted it, immediately sprinkled with water and given a name.
[2] This appears to have been a common symbol of adoption; cf. the story
of Hakon and Athelstan, p. 81.
[3] West, i.e. over the North Sea to the British Isles.
[4] Used here and elsewhere of Western Norway.
[5] Skerries are the uninhabited dry or half-tide rocks of a coast.

In this war fell Ivar, a son of Rognvald, Earl of Möre; and King Harald gave Rognvald, as a compensation for the loss, the Orkney and Shetland Isles, when he sailed from the West; but Rognvald immediately gave both these countries to his brother Sigurd, who remained behind them; and King Harald, before sailing eastward, gave Sigurd the earldom of them. Thorstein the Red, son of Olaf the White [1] and Aud the Deep-minded, entered into partnership with him; and after plundering in Scotland, they subdued Caithness and Sutherland, as far as Ekkjalsbakke. [2] Earl Sigurd killed Melbridge-Tooth, a Scotch earl, and hung his head to his stirrup-leather; but the calf of his leg was scratched by the teeth, which were sticking out from the head, and the wound caused inflammation in his leg, of which the earl died, and he was laid in a mound at Ekkjalsbakke. His son Guttorm ruled over these countries for about a year thereafter, and died without children. Many vikings, both Danes and Northmen, set themselves down then in those countries.

CHAPTER XXIII. KING HARALD HAS HIS HAIR CLIPPED.— After King Harald had subdued the whole land, he was one day at a feast in Möre, given by Earl Rognvald. Then King Harald went into a bath, and had his hair dressed. Earl Rognvald now cut his hair, which had been uncut and un-combed for ten years; and therefore the king had been called Harald Luva. [3] But then Earl Rognvald gave him the dis-tinguishing name—Harald Haarfager [4]; and all who saw him agreed that there was the greatest truth in that surname, for he had the most beautiful and abundant head of hair.

CHAPTER XXIV. ROLF GANGER IS DRIVEN INTO BANISHMENT. —Earl Rognvald was King Harald's dearest friend, and the king had the greatest regard for him. He was married to Hild, a daughter of Rolf Nefja, and their sons were Rolf and Tore. Earl Rognvald had also three sons by concubines—the one called Hallad, the second Einar, the third Rollaug; and all three were grown men when their brothers born in marriage were still children. Rolf became a great viking, and was of so stout a growth that no horse could carry him, and wheresoever he went he must go on foot; and therefore he was called Gange-

[1] In other Icelandic sources Olaf is said to be a great-grandson of King Olaf Gudrodsson (see p. 42), but this is impossible. His wife Aud was a famous settler in Iceland, see especially the *Laxdæla Saga*.
[2] Ekkjal was the Norse name for Oykel, a river flowing into Dornoch Firth; Ekkjalsbakke is Strath Oykel; "those countries" means Suther-land, Caithness, Ross, and Cromarty.
[3] Of the Matted Hair.
[4] Of the Fair Hair.

Rolf.[1] He plundered much in the East sea.[2] One summer, as
he was coming from the eastward on a viking's expedition to
the coast of Viken, he landed there and had a strandhögg.
As King Harald happened, just at that time, to be in Viken,
he heard of it, and was in a great rage; for he had forbidden,
by the greatest punishment, any plundering within the bounds
of the country. The king assembled a Thing, and had Rolf
declared an outlaw over all Norway. When Rolf's mother,
Hild, heard of it she hastened to the king, and entreated peace
for Rolf; but the king was so enraged that her entreaty was of
no avail. Then Hild spake these lines:

> Think'st thou, King Harald, in thy anger,
> To drive away my brave Rolf Ganger,
> Like a mad wolf, from out the land?
> Why, Harald, raise thy mighty hand?
> Why banish Nefja's gallant name-son,
> The brother of brave udal-men?
> Why is thy cruelty so fell?
> Bethink thee, monarch, it is ill
> With such a wolf at wolf to play,
> Who, driven to the wild woods away,
> May make the king's best deer his prey.

Gange-Rolf went afterwards over sea to the West to the
Hebrides, or Sudreyar[3]; and at last farther west to Valland,[4]
where he plundered and subdued for himself a great earldom,
which he peopled with Northmen, from which that land is
called Normandy. Gange-Rolf's son was William, father to
Richard, and grandfather to another Richard, who was the
father of Robert Longspear,[5] and grandfather of William the
Bastard, from whom all the succeeding English kings are
descended. From Gange-Rolf also are descended the earls in
Normandy.[6] Queen Ragnhild the Mighty lived three years after

[1] Gange-Rolf, Rolf Ganger, Rolf the Walker, is usually identified with the
Rollo who in 911 took Normandy in fief from the Frankish emperor. The
settlement in Normandy was, however, predominantly Danish, and there
has been much controversy over Rollo's nationality.

[2] *Austrvegr*, the Baltic and Baltic lands.

[3] *Suðreyjar*, the southern isles, is the name given to the Hebrides by the
Norsemen sailing south from Shetland and Orkney.

[4] Valland was the name applied to France, especially its northern parts.
The inhabitants were called Valir, and the adjective denoting origin from
France is *valskr*. This last is the same as the English word Welsh, which
originally meant "foreign," and in early sources the Norse word may also
sometimes have this less specific sense.

[5] Should be Long-sword and properly attached to William Rolfsson.

[6] Gange-Rolf probably left Norway between 890 and 900. Rollo took
Normandy in 911, was baptized in 912, and died in 931.

she came to Norway; and after her death, Eric her son and King Harald's was taken to Tore Roaldson, and Eric was fostered by him.

CHAPTER XXV. OF THE LAPLANDER SVASE AND KING HARALD.—King Harald, one winter, went about in guest-quarters in Upland, and had ordered a Christmas feast to be prepared for him at the farm Toftar.[1] On Christmas eve came Svase to the door, just as the king sat at table, and sent a message to the king to say that he should go out to him. The king was angry at such a message, and the man who had brought it in took out with him a reply of the king's displeasure. But Svase, notwithstanding, desired that his message should be delivered a second time; adding to it, that he was the Laplander whose hut the king had permitted him to set up on a site on the other side of the ridge. Now the king went out, and promised to follow him, and went over the ridge to his hut, although some of his men dissuaded him. There stood Snæfrid, the daughter of Svase, a most beautiful girl, and she filled a cup of mead for the king. But he took hold both of the cup and of her hand. Immediately it was as if a hot fire went through his body; and he wanted that very night to take her to his bed. But Svase said that should not be unless by main force, if he did not first make her his lawful wife. Now King Harald made Snæfrid his lawful wife, and loved her so passionately that he forgot his kingdom, and all that belonged to his high dignity. They had four sons: the one was Sigurd Rise; the others Halfdan Haaleg, Gudrod Ljome, and Rognvald Rettilbein. Thereafter Snæfrid died; but her corpse never changed, but was as fresh and red as when she lived. The king sat always beside her, and thought she would come to life again. And so it went on for three years that he was sorrowing over her death, and the people over his delusion. At last Torleiv the Wise succeeded, by his prudence, in curing him of his delusion by accosting him thus: "It is nowise wonderful, king, that thou grievest over so beautiful and noble a wife, and bestowest costly coverlets and beds of down on her corpse, as she desired; but these honours fall short of what is due, as she still lies in the same clothes. It would be more suitable to raise her, and change her dress." As soon as the body was raised in the bed all sorts of corruption and foul smells came from it, and it was necessary in all haste to gather a pile of wood and burn it; but before this could be done the body

[1] Now Tofte, in Dovre, near the head of Gudbrandsdal.

turned blue, and worms, toads, newts, paddocks, and all sorts of ugly reptiles came out of it, and it sank into ashes. Now the king came to his understanding again, threw the madness out of his mind, and after that day ruled his kingdom as before. He was strengthened and made joyful by his subjects, and his subjects by him, and the country by both.

CHAPTER XXVI. OF THJODOLF OF HVINE, THE SCALD.— After King Harald had experienced the cunning of the Lap-lander, he was so angry that he drove from him the sons he had with her, and would not suffer them before his eyes. But one of them, Gudrod Ljome, went to his foster-father Thjodolf, and asked him to go to the king, who was then in the Uplands; for Thjodolf was a great friend of the king. And so they went, and came to the king's house late in the evening, and sat down together unnoticed near the door. The king walked up and down the floor casting his eye along the benches; for he had a feast in the house, and the mead was just mixed. The king then murmured out these lines:

> Tell me, ye aged grey-haired heroes,
> Who have come here to seek repose,
> Wherefore must I so many keep
> Of such a set, who, one and all,
> Right dearly love their souls to steep,
> From morn till night, in the mead-bowl?

Then Thjodolf replies:

> A certain wealthy chief, I think,
> Would gladly have had more to drink
> With him, upon one bloody day,
> When crowns were cracked in our sword-play.

Thjodolf then took off his hat, and the king recognised him, and gave him a friendly reception. Thjodolf then begged the king not to cast off his sons; "for they would with great pleasure have taken a better family descent upon the mother's side, if the king had given it to them." The king assented, and told him to take Gudrod with him as formerly; and he sent Halfdan and Sigurd to Ringerike, and Rognvald to Hadeland, and all was done as the king ordered. They grew up to be very clever men, very expert in all exercises. In these times King Harald sat in peace in the land, and the land enjoyed quietness and good crops.

CHAPTER XXVII. OF EARL TORF-EINAR'S OBTAINING ORK-NEY.—When Earl Rognvald in Möre heard of the death of his brother Earl Sigurd, and that the vikings were in possession of

the country, he sent his son Hallad westward, who took the title
of earl to begin with, and had many men-at-arms with him
When he arrived at the Orkney Islands, he established himself
in the country; but both in harvest, winter, and spring, the
vikings cruised about the isles, plundering the headlands, and
committing depredations on the coast. Then Earl Hallad grew
tired of the business, resigned his earldom, took up again his
rights as höld,[1] and afterwards returned eastward into Norway.
When Earl Rognvald heard of this he was ill-pleased with
Hallad, and said his sons were very unlike their ancestors.
Then said Einar, "I have enjoyed but little honour among you,
and have little affection here to lose: now if you will give me
force enough, I will go West to the islands, and promise you
what at any rate will please you—that I shall not return to
Norway." Earl Rognvald replied, that he would be glad if he
never came back; "for there is little hope," said he, "that
thou wilt ever be an honour to thy family, as all thy kin on
the mother's side are born slaves." Earl Rognvald gave Einar
a vessel completely equipped, and he sailed with it into the
West sea in harvest. When he came to the Orkney Isles, two
vikings, Tore Træskjæg, and Kalf Skurfa, were in his way with
two vessels. He attacked them instantly, gained the battle,
and slew the two vikings. He was called Torf-Einar, because
he cut peat (torf) for fuel, there being no fire-wood, as in
Orkney there are no woods. He afterwards was earl over the
islands, and was a mighty man. He was ugly, and blind of an
eye, yet very sharp-sighted withal.

CHAPTER XXVIII. KING ERIC EMUNDSSON'S DEATH.—
Duke Guttorm[2] dwelt principally at Tunsberg, and governed
the whole of Viken when the king was not there. He defended
the land, which at that time was much plundered by the
vikings. There were disturbances also up in Gotland as long
as King Eric Emundsson lived; but he died when King Harald
Fairhair had been ten years king of all Norway.

CHAPTER XXIX. GUTTORM'S DEATH IN TUNSBERG.—After
Eric, his son Bjorn was king of Sweden for fifty years. He
was father of Eric the Victorious, and of Olaf the father of
Styrbjorn. Guttorm died on a bed of sickness at Tunsberg,

---

[1] This condition which Hallad resumed on resigning the earldom is
explained as that of a holder of inherited udal-land, not purchased but
received by hereditary right. In the eyes of the law the *höld* was worth
twice an ordinary yeoman and half as much as a lenderman (who in turn
was worth half as much as an earl).

[2] Guttorm, Harald the Fairhaired's uncle.

and King Harald gave his son Guttorm the government of that part of his dominions, and made him chief of it.

CHAPTER XXX. EARL ROGNVALD BURNT IN HIS HOUSE.— When King Harald was forty years of age many of his sons were well advanced, and indeed they all came early to strength and manhood. And now they began to take it ill that the king would not give them any part of the kingdom, but put earls into every district; for they thought earls were of inferior birth to them. Then Halfdan Haaleg and Gudrod Ljome set off one spring with a great force, and came suddenly upon Earl Rognvald, earl of Möre, and surrounded the house in which he was, and burnt him and sixty men in it. Thereafter Halfdan took three long-ships, and fitted them out, and sailed into the West sea; but Gudrod set himself down in the land which Rognvald formerly had. Now when King Harald heard this he set out with a great force against Gudrod, who had no other way left but to surrender, and he was sent to Agder. King Harald then set Earl Rognvald's son Tore over Möre, and gave him his daughter Aalof Aarbot in marriage. Tore, called the Silent, got the same territory his father Rognvald had possessed.

CHAPTER XXXI. HALFDAN HAALEG'S DEATH. — Halfdan Haaleg came very unexpectedly to Orkney, and Earl Einar immediately fled; but came back soon after, about harvest-time, unnoticed by Halfdan. They met, and after a short battle Halfdan fled in the evening. Einar and his men lay all night without tents, and when it was light in the morning they searched the whole island, and killed every man they could lay hold of. Then Einar said, "What is that I see upon the isle of Rinansö[1]? Is it a man or a bird? Sometimes it raises itself up, and sometimes lies down again." They went to it, and found it was Halfdan Haaleg, and took him prisoner.

Earl Einar sang the following song the evening before he went into this battle:

> Where is the spear of Rollaug[2]? where
> Is stout Rolf Ganger's bloody spear?
> I see them not; yet never fear,
> For Einar will not vengeance spare
> Against his father's murderers, though
> Rollaug and Rolf are somewhat slow,
> And silent Tore sits and dreams
> At home, beside the mead-bowl's streams.

---

[1] Now North Ronaldshay, one of the Orkney Isles.

[2] Rollaug, Rolf Ganger, Tore the Silent, and Einar were all sons of that Earl Rognvald whom Harald Fairhair's sons, and among them Halfdan, had surprised and burnt in his house. They ought, according to the opinion of the times, to have taken vengeance as well as Einar on the murderers.

Thereafter Earl Einar went up to Halfdan, and cut a spread eagle upon his back,[1] by striking his sword through his back into his belly, dividing his ribs from the backbone down to his loins, and tearing out his lungs; and so Halfdan was killed. Einar then sang:

> For Rognvald's death my sword is red:
> Of vengeance it cannot be said
> That Einar's share is left unsped.
> So now, brave boys, let's raise a mound—
> Heap stones and gravel on the ground
> O'er Halfdan's corpse: this is the way
> We Norsemen our scatt duties pay.

Then Earl Einar took possession of the Orkney Isles as before. Now when these tidings came to Norway, Halfdan's brothers took it much to heart, and thought that his death demanded vengeance; and many were of the same opinion. When Einar heard this, he sang:

> Many a stout udal-man, I know,
> Has cause to wish my head laid low;
> And many an angry udal knife
> Would gladly drink of Einar's life.
> But ere they lay Earl Einar low—
> Ere this stout heart betrays its cause,
> Full many a heart will writhe, we know,
> In the wolf's fangs, or eagle's claws.

CHAPTER XXXII. KING HARALD AND EARL EINAR RECONCILED.—King Harald now ordered a levy, and gathered a great force, with which he proceeded westward to Orkney; and when Earl Einar heard that King Harald was come, he fled over to Caithness. He made the following verses on this occasion:

> Many a bearded man must roam,
> An exile from his house and home,
> For cow or horse; but Halfdan's gore
> Is red on Rinansö's wild shore.
> A nobler deed—on Harald's shield
> The arm of one who ne'er will yield
> Has left a scar. Let peasants dread
> The vengeance of the Norsemen's head;
> I reck not of his wrath, but sing,
> "Do thy worst!—I defy thee, king!"

Men and messages, however, passed between the king and the earl, and at last it came to a conference; and when they met the earl submitted the case altogether to the king's decision, and the king condemned the earl and the Orkney people to pay a fine of sixty marks of gold. As the bonder thought this was too heavy for them to pay, the earl offered to pay the whole

---

[1] This punishment was called *at rista blóðörn*, to cut a blood-eagle.

if they would surrender their udal lands to him. This they all agreed to do: the poor because they had but little pieces of land; the rich because they thought to redeem their udal rights when they liked. Thus the earl paid the whole fine to the king, who returned in harvest to Norway. The earls for a long time afterwards possessed all the udal lands in Orkney, until Sigurd Lodvison [1] gave back the udal rights. [2]

CHAPTER XXXIII. DEATHS OF GUTTORM AND OF HALFDAN THE WHITE. — While King Harald's son Guttorm had the defence of Viken, he sailed outside of the islands on the coast, and came in by one of the mouths of the Gotha river. When he lay there Solve Klove came upon him, and immediately gave him battle, and Guttorm fell. Halfdan the White and Halfdan the Black went out on an expedition, and plundered in the East sea, [3] and had a battle in Estland, [4] where Halfdan the White fell.

CHAPTER XXXIV. MARRIAGE OF ERIC, THE SON OF KING HARALD.—Eric, Harald's son, was fostered in the house of the herse Tore, son of Roald, in the Fjords district. He was the most beloved and honoured by King Harald of all his sons. When Eric was twelve years old, [5] King Harald gave him five long-ships, with which he went on an expedition—first in the Baltic; then southwards to Denmark, Friesland, [6] and Saxland; on which expedition he passed four years. He then sailed out into the West sea, and plundered in Scotland, Bretland, [7] Ireland, and Valland, and passed four years more in this way. Then he sailed north to Finmark, [8] and all the way to Bjarmeland, [9] where he fought a great battle and won the victory. When he came back to Finmark, his men found a girl in a

[1] He ruled from *c.* 980 until 1014, when he fell in the battle of Clontarf. He was one of the greatest of the Orkney earls.

[2] There are still a few udal properties in Orkney, and many which are described in feudal charters as having been udal lands of old. Snorri tells the story differently in St. Olaf's Saga (see the *Olaf Sagas*, pp. 218–19).

[3] Baltic.

[4] Estland is Esthonia.

[5] In those days a boy came of age at twelve.

[6] Friesland appears to have been the name given to the whole coast from the Eyder in Schleswig to North Holland.

[7] *Bretar* is the Norse word for Britons, and *Bretland* is the country of the Britons. This is most often used of Wales and south-western England (*Kornbretaland* is found for Cornwall), sometimes for Brittany. The last is also distinguished as *syðra* (southern) *Bretland*.

[8] Finmark is the country we call Lapland in the north of Norway, Sweden, Finland, and Russia.

[9] Bjarmeland is the coast of the White Sea about the mouth of the Dvina.

Lapland hut, whose equal for beauty they never had seen.
She said her name was Gunhild, and that her father dwelt in
Halogaland, and was called Ossur Tote. "I am here," she
said, "to learn Lapland-art,[1] from two of the most knowing
Laplanders in all Finmark, who are now out hunting. They
both want me in marriage. They are so skilful that they can
hunt out traces either upon the frozen or the thawed earth,
like dogs; and they can run so swiftly on ski, that neither man
nor beast can escape from their chase. They hit whatever
they take aim at, and thus kill every man who comes near them.
When they are angry the very earth turns away in terror, and
whatever living thing they look upon then falls dead. Now
you must not come in their way; but I will hide you here in the
hut, and you must try to get them killed." They agreed to it,
and she hid them, and then took a linen bag, in which they
thought there were ashes which she took in her hand, and
strewed both outside and inside of the hut. Shortly after the
Laplanders came home, and asked who had been there; and she
answered, "Nobody has been here." "That is wonderful,"
said they; "we followed the traces close to the hut, and can
find none after that." Then they kindled a fire, and made
ready their meat, and Gunhild prepared her bed. It had so
happened that Gunhild had slept the three nights before, but
the Laplanders had watched the one upon the other, being
jealous of each other. "Now," she said to the Laplanders,
"come here, and lie down one on each side of me." On which
they were very glad to do so. She laid an arm round the neck
of each, and they went to sleep directly. She roused them up;
but they fell to sleep again instantly, and so soundly that she
scarcely could waken them. She even raised them up in the
bed, and still they slept. Thereupon she took two great seal-
skin bags, and put their heads in them,[2] and tied them fast
under their arms; and then she gave a hint to the king's men.
They run forth with their weapons, kill the two Laplanders,
and drag them out of the hut. That same night came such a
dreadful thunderstorm that they could not stir. Next morning
they came to the ship, taking Gunhild with them, and presented
her to Eric. Eric and his followers then sailed southwards to
Halogaland; and he sent word to Ossur Tote, the girl's father,
to meet him. Eric said he would take his daughter in marriage,
to which Ossur Tote consented; and Eric took Gunhild, and
went southwards with her.

[1] Witchcraft.
[2] She blindfolded them to render their evil eye powerless.

CHAPTER XXXV. HARALD DIVIDES HIS KINGDOM AMONG HIS SONS.—When King Harald was fifty years of age many of his sons were grown up, and some were dead. Many of them committed acts of great violence in the country, and were in discord among themselves. They drove some of the king's earls out of their properties, and even killed some of them. Then the king called together a numerous Thing [1] in the south part of the country, and summoned to it all the people of the Uplands. At this Thing he gave to all his sons the title of king, and made a law that his descendants in the male line should each succeed to the kingly title and dignity; but his descendants by the female side only to that of earl. And he divided the country among them thus: Vingulmark, Raumarike, Westfold, and Thelemark, he bestowed on Olaf, Bjorn, Sigtryg, Frode, and Torgils. Hedemark and Gudbrandsdal he gave to Dag, Ring, and Ragnar. To Snæfrid's sons he gave Ringerike, Hadeland, Toten, and the lands thereto belonging. His son Guttorm, as before mentioned, he had set over the country from Svinesund to the Gotha river, and to defend the country eastwards. King Harald himself generally dwelt in the middle of the country, and Rörek and Gudrod were generally with his court, and had great estates in Hordaland and in Sogn. King Eric was also with his father King Harald; and the king loved and regarded him the most of all his sons, and gave him Halogaland, and North Möre, and Raumsdal. North in Drontheim he gave Halfdan the Black, Halfdan the White, and Sigröd land to rule over. In each of these districts he gave his sons the one half of his revenues, together with the right to sit on a high seat—a step higher than earls, but a step lower than his own high seat. His king's seat each of his sons wanted for himself after his death, but he himself destined it for Eric. The Drontheim people wanted Halfdan the Black to succeed to it. The people of Viken, and the Uplands, wanted those under whom they lived. And thereupon new quarrels arose among the brothers; and because they thought their dominions too little, they drove about in piratical expeditions. In this way, as before related, Guttorm fell at the Gotha estuary, slain by Solve Klove; upon which Oláf took the kingdom he had possessed. Halfdan the White fell in Estland, Halfdan Haaleg in Orkney. King Harald gave ships of war to Torgils and Frode, with which they went westward on a viking cruise, and

[1] Perhaps the Eidsiva Thing, whose original meeting-place was probably near Hamar; it was moved south to Eidsvoll in the eleventh century.

plundered in Scotland, Ireland, and Bretland. They were the
first of the Northmen who took Dublin. It is said that Frode
got poisoned drink there; but Torgils[1] was a long time king over
Dublin, until he fell into a snare of the Irish, and was killed.

CHAPTER XXXVI. DEATH OF ROGNVALD RETTILBEIN.—
Eric Bloodyaxe expected to be head king over all his brothers,
and King Harald intended he should be so; and the father and
son lived long together. Rognvald Rettilbein governed Hadeland, and allowed himself to be instructed in the arts of witchcraft, and became a great warlock. Now King Harald was a
hater of all witchcraft. There was a warlock in Hordaland
called Vitgeir; and when the king sent a message to him that he
should give up his art of witchcraft, he replied in this verse:

> The danger surely is not great
> From wizards born of mean estate,
> When Harald's son in Hadeland,
> King Rognvald, to the art lays hand

But when King Harald heard this, King Eric Bloodyaxe went
by his orders to the Uplands, and burned his brother Rognvald
in a house, along with eighty other warlocks; which work was
much praised.

CHAPTER XXXVII. OF GUDROD LJOME.—Gudrod Ljome
was in winter on a friendly visit to his foster-father Thjodolf
in Kvine, and had a well-manned ship, with which he wanted
to go north to Rogaland. It was blowing a heavy storm at the
time; but Gudrod was bent on sailing, and would not consent
to wait. Thjodolf sang thus:

> Wait, Gudrod, till the storm is past —
> Loose not thy long-ship while the blast
> Howls overhead so furiously—
> Trust not thy long-ship to the sea—
> Loose not thy long-ship from the shore:
> Hark to the ocean's angry roar!
> See how the very stones are tost,
> By raging waves high on the coast!
> Stay, Gudrod, till the tempest's o'er—
> Deep runs the sea off Jædern's shore.

Gudrod set off in spite of what Thjodolf could say; and
when they came off Jæderen the vessel sank with them, and all
on board were lost.

CHAPTER XXXVIII. KING BJORN THE MERCHANT'S DEATH.
—King Harald's son, Bjorn, ruled over Westfold at that time,
and generally lived at Tunsberg, and went but little on war

[1] Nothing is known of this Thorgils and Frode in Irish sources. Thorgils's kingship might perhaps reflect the reign of the great Turgeis (probably
Norse Thorgest), who ruled in Ireland a century earlier (killed 845 or 846).
On Turgeis see W. E. D. Allen, *The Poet and the Spae-wife* (1960), pp. 29–
35, 55–65.

expeditions. Tunsberg at that time was much frequented by merchant vessels, both from Viken and the north country, and also from the south, from Denmark, and Saxland. King Bjorn had also merchant ships on voyages to other lands, by which he procured for himself costly articles, and such things as he thought needful; and therefore his brothers called him the Farman,[1] and the Merchant. Bjorn was a man of sense and understanding, and promised to become a good ruler. He made a good and suitable marriage, and had a son by his wife, who was named Gudrod. Eric Bloodyaxe came from his Baltic cruise with ships of war, and a great force, and required his brother Bjorn to deliver to him King Harald's share of the scatt and incomes of Westfold. But it had always been the custom before, that Bjorn himself either delivered the money into the king's hands, or sent men of his own with it; and therefore he would continue with the old custom, and would not deliver the money. Eric again wanted provisions, tents, and liquor. The brothers quarrelled about this; but Eric got nothing, and left the town. Bjorn went also out of the town towards evening up to Sæim. In the night Eric came back after Bjorn, and came to Sæim just as Bjorn and his men were seated at table drinking. Eric surrounded the house in which they were; but Bjorn with his men went out and fought. Bjorn, and many men with him, fell. Eric, on the other hand, got a great booty, and proceeded northwards. But this work was taken very ill by the people of Viken, and Eric was much disliked for it; and the report went that King Olaf would avenge his brother Bjorn, whenever opportunity offered. King Bjorn lies in the Farman's mound at Sæim.[2]

CHAPTER XXXIX. OF THE RECONCILIATION OF THE KINGS. —King Eric went in winter northwards to Möre, and was at a feast in Solva, within the point Agdanes[3]; and when Halfdan heard of it he set out with his men, and surrounded the house in which they were. Eric slept in a room which stood detached by itself, and he escaped into the forest with four others; but Halfdan and his men burnt the main house, with all the people who were in it. With this news Eric came to King Harald, who was very wroth at it, and assembled a great force against

[1] Farman, i.e. seaman or skipper.
[2] Sæim, called afterwards Sem, the present Jarlsberg, about two miles from the town of Tunsberg. The Farman's mound is still to be seen about a quarter of a mile south of Jarlsberg.
[3] Agdanes is the south point of land at the entrance of the Trondhjem fjord, and Solva, now Selven, is about three miles to the east of Agdanes.

the Drontheim people. When Halfdan the Black heard this he levied. ships and men, so that he had a great force, and proceeded with it to Stad,[1] within Thorsberg. King Harald lay with his men at Reinsletta. Now people went between them, and among others a noble man called Guttorm Sindre, who was then in Halfdan's army, but had been formerly in the service of King Harald, and was a great friend of both. Guttorm was a great scald, and had once composed a song both about the father and the son, for which they had offered him a reward. But he would take nothing; but only asked that, some day or other, they should grant him any request he should make, which they promised to do. Now he presented himself to King Harald—brought words of peace between them, and made the request to them both that they should be reconciled. So highly did the kings esteem him, that in consequence of his request they were reconciled. Many other able men promoted this business as well as he; and it was so settled that Halfdan should retain the whole of his kingdom as he had it before, and should let his brother Eric sit in peace.

CHAPTER XL. BIRTH OF HAKON THE GOOD.—Earl Hakon Grjotgardsson of Lade had the whole rule over Drontheim when King Harald was anywhere away in the country; and Hakon stood higher with the king than any in the country of Drontheim. After Hakon's death his son Sigurd succeeded to his power in Drontheim, and was the earl, and had his mansion at Lade. King Harald's sons, Halfdan the Black, and Sigröd, who had been before in the house of his father Earl Hakon, continued to be brought up in his house. The sons of Harald and Sigurd were about the same age. Earl Sigurd was one of the wisest men of his time, and married Bergljot, a daughter of Earl Tore the Silent; and her mother was Aalof Aarbot, a daughter of Harald Fairhair. When King Harald began to grow old he generally dwelt on some of his great farms in Hordaland; namely, Alrekstad,[2] or Sæim,[3] Fitjar,[4] Utstein,[5] or Augvaldsness in the island Kormt.[6] When Harald was seventy years of age he begat a son with a girl called Tora Mosterstang, because her family came from Moster.[7] She was descended

[1] Stad, Thorsberg, and Reinsletta are all on the north side of the Trondhjem fjord.
[2] Aalrekstad, now Aarstad, at the foot of Ulrikken, near Bergen.
[3] Now Seim, in Alversund, Nordhordland.
[4] Now Fitje, on the north of Stordö in Sunnhordland.
[5] Now Utstens Abbey, on the island of that name in Ryfylke.
[6] Now Avaldsnes, on the north-east of the Karm isle (Kormt).
[7] Now Mosterö, in the south of Sunnhordland.

from good people, being connected with Horda-Kaare; and was moreover a fine woman and a remarkably handsome one. She was called the king's serving-woman; for at that time many were subject to service to the king who were of good birth, both men and women. Then it was the custom, with people of consideration, to choose with great care the man who should pour water over their children, and give them a name. Now when the time came that Tora, who was then at Moster, expected her confinement, she would go to King Harald, who was then living at Sæim; and she went northwards in a ship belonging to Earl Sigurd. They lay at night close to the land; and there Tora brought forth a child on the land, up among the rocks,[1] close to the ship's gangway, and it was a man child. Earl Sigurd poured water over him, and called him Hakon, after his own father, Hakon earl of Lade. The boy soon grew handsome, large in size, and very like his father King Harald. King Harald let him be with his mother, and they were both in the king's farms as long as he was an infant.

CHAPTER XLI. KING ATHELSTAN'S MESSAGE.—At this time a king called Athelstan [2] had taken the kingdom of England. He was called the Victorious and the Faithful. He sent men to Norway to King Harald, with the errand that the messengers should present him with a sword, with the hilt and handle gilt, and also the whole sheath adorned with gold and silver, and set with precious jewels. The ambassadors presented the sword-hilt to the king, saying, "Here is a sword which King Athelstan sends thee, with the request that thou wilt accept it." The king took the sword by the handle; whereupon the ambassadors said, "Now thou hast taken the sword according to our king's desire, and therefore art thou his subject, as thou hast taken his sword." King Harald saw now that this was a jest, for he would be subject to no man. But he remembered it was his rule, whenever anything raised his anger, to collect himself, and let his passion run off, and then take the matter into consideration coolly. Now he did so, and consulted his friends, who all gave him the advice to let the ambassadors, in the first place, go home in safety.

CHAPTER XLII. HAUK'S JOURNEY TO ENGLAND.—The following summer King Harald sent a ship westward to England, and

---

[1] Hellen, some six miles south-west of Bergen. Here King Hakon also died, see p. 109.
[2] Ruled from 925 to 939. Grandson of Alfred the Great.

gave the command of it to Hauk Haabrok.[1] He was a great
warrior, and very dear to the king. Into his hands he gave
his son Hakon. Hauk proceeded westward to England, and
found the king in London, where there was just at the time a
great feast and entertainment. When they came to the hall,
Hauk told his men how they should conduct themselves;
namely, that he who went first in should go last out, and all
should stand in a row at the table, at equal distance from each
other; and each should have his sword at his left side, but
should fasten his cloak so that his sword should not be seen.
Then they went into the hall, thirty in number. Hauk went
up to the king and saluted him, and the king bade him welcome.
Then Hauk took the child Hakon, and set it on the king's knee.[2]
The king looks at the boy, and asks Hauk what the meaning
of this is. Hauk replies, "Harald the king bids thee foster his
serving-woman's child." The king was in great anger, and
seized a sword which lay beside him, and drew it, as if he was
going to kill the child. Hauk says, "Thou hast borne him on
thy knee, and thou canst murder him if thou wilt; but thou
wilt not make an end of all King Harald's sons by so doing."
On that Hauk went out with all his men, and took the way
direct to his ship, and put to sea—for they were ready—and
came back to King Harald. The king was highly pleased with
this; for it is the common observation of all people, that the
man who fosters another's children is of less consideration than
the other. From these transactions between the two kings, it
appears that each wanted to be held greater than the other;
but in truth there was no injury to the dignity of either, for
each was the upper king in his own kingdom till his dying day.

CHAPTER XLIII. HAKON, THE FOSTER-SON OF ATHELSTAN,
IS BAPTISED.—King Athelstan had Hakon baptised, and brought
up in the right faith, and in good habits, and all sorts of
exercises; he loved Hakon above all his relations. Hakon was
called Athelstan's foster-son. He was popular, a man of sense
and eloquence, and also a good Christian. King Athelstan gave
Hakon a sword, of which the hilt and handle were gold, and the
blade still better; for with it Hakon cut down a millstone to
the centre eye, and the sword thereafter was called the Quernbiter. Better sword never came into Norway, and Hakon carried
it to his dying day.

[1] High-breeches, long-legged.
[2] There is no other evidence to show that the custom of "knee-sitting"
was known to the English. But the implications of foster-fatherhood
certainly were so.

CHAPTER XLIV. ERIC IS BROUGHT TO THE SOVEREIGNTY.—
When King Harald was eighty years of age he became very
heavy, and unable to travel through the country, or do the
business of a king. Then he brought his son Eric to his high
seat, and gave him the power and command over the whole
land. Now when King Harald's other sons heard this, King
Halfdan the Black also took a king's high seat, and took all
Drontheim land, with the consent of all the people, under his
rule as upper king. After the death of Bjorn the Merchant, his
brother Olaf took the command over Westfold, and took Bjorn's
son, Gudrod, as his foster-child. Olaf's son was called Trygve;
and the two foster-brothers were about the same age, and were
hopeful and clever. Trygve, especially, was remarkable as a
stout and strong man. Now when the people of Viken heard
that the Hordlanders had taken Eric as upper king, they did
the same, and made Olaf the upper king in Viken, which
kingdom he retained. Eric did not like this at all. Two years
after this, Halfdan the Black died suddenly at a feast in Drontheim, and the general report was, that Gunhild had bribed a
witch to give him a death-drink. Thereafter the Drontheim
people took Sigröd to be their king.

CHAPTER XLV. KING HARALD'S DEATH.—King Harald lived
three years after he gave Eric the supreme authority over his
kingdom, and lived mostly on his great farms which he possessed,
some in Rogaland, and some in Hordaland. Eric and Gunhild
had a son, on whom King Harald poured water, and gave him
his own name, and the promise that he should be king after
his father Eric. King Harald married most of his daughters
within the country to his earls, and from them many great
families are descended. King Harald died on a bed of sickness
in Rogaland, and was buried under a mound at Haugar in Kormsund. In Haugesund is a church, now standing; and not far
from the churchyard, at the north-west side, is King Harald
Fairhair's mound; but his gravestone stands west of the church,
and is thirteen feet and a half high, and two ells broad.
The grave, mound, and stone, are there to the present day.[1]
Harald Fairhair was, according to the report of men of knowledge, of remarkably handsome appearance, great and strong,
and very generous and affable to his men. He was a great

[1] The stone and some remains of the mound are still to be seen at Gar,
or the Gaard, the principal farm-house in the parish of Kormsund. The
church referred to was taken down in the sixteenth century, and on its
site in 1872 was erected a Harald monument, into which has been set
the old flat gravestone, measuring exactly 11 ft. 8 in. × 4 ft. 1 in.

warrior in his youth; and people think that this was foretold by his mother's dream before his birth, as the lowest part of the tree she dreamt of was red as blood. The stem again was green and beautiful, which betokened his flourishing kingdom; and that the tree was white at the top showed that he should reach a grey-haired old age. The branches and twigs showed forth his posterity, spread over the whole land: for of his race, ever since, Norway has always had kings.[1]

CHAPTER XLVI. THE DEATH OF OLAF AND OF SIGRÖD.—
King Eric took all the revenues which the king had in the middle of the country, the next winter after King Harald's decease. But Olaf took all the revenues eastward in Viken, and their brother Sigröd all that of the Drontheim country. Eric was very ill-pleased with this; and the report went that he would attempt with force to get the sole sovereignty over the country, in the same way as his father had given it to him. Now when Olaf and Sigröd heard this, messengers passed between them; and after appointing a meeting place, Sigröd went eastward in spring to Viken, and he and his brother Olaf met at Tunsberg, and remained there a while. The same spring King Eric levied a great force, and ships, and steered towards Viken. He got such a strong steady gale that he sailed night and day, and came faster than the news of him. When he came to Tunsberg, Olaf and Sigröd, with their forces, went out of the town a little eastward to a ridge,[2] where they drew up their men in battle order; but as Eric had many more men, he won the battle. Both brothers, Olaf and Sigröd, fell there; and both their grave-mounds are upon the ridge where they fell. Then King Eric went through Viken, and subdued it, and remained far into summer. Gudrod and Trygve fled to the Uplands. Eric was a stout handsome man, strong, and very manly—a great and fortunate man of war; but hot-headed, harsh, unfriendly, and silent. Gunhild, his wife, was the most beautiful of women—clever, with much knowledge, and lively; but a very false person, and very cruel in disposition. The children of King Eric and Gunhild were Gamle, the oldest; then Guttorm, Harald, Ragnfrid, Ragnhild, Erling, Gudrod, and Sigurd Sleva. All were handsome, and of manly promise.

[1] Harald the Fairhaired probably died soon after 940, perhaps in 942. Hakon, his son, probably returned from England in 946. King Athelstan had died in 939.
[2] Bakken, the ridge, now Möllebakken, in the east end of Tönsberg. The two large tumuli there are supposed to be the graves of Olaf and Sigröd.

IV

HAKON THE GOOD

CHAPTER I. HAKON CHOSEN KING.—Hakon, Athelstan's foster-son, was in England at the time he heard of his father King Harald's death, and he immediately made himself ready to depart. King Athelstan gave him men, and a choice of good ships, and fitted him out for his journey most excellently. In harvest time he came to Norway, where he heard of the death of his brothers, and that King Eric was then in Viken. Then Hakon sailed northwards to Drontheim, where he went to Sigurd, earl of Lade, who was the ablest man in Norway. He gave Hakon a good reception; and they made a league with each other, by which Hakon promised great power to Sigurd if he was made king. They assembled then a numerous Thing, and Sigurd the earl recommended Hakon's cause to the Thing,[1] and proposed him to the bonder as king. Then Hakon himself stood up and spoke; and the people said to each other, two and two, as they heard him, "Harald Haarfager is come again, and grown young." The beginning of Hakon's speech was, that he offered himself to the bonder as king, and desired from them the title of king, and aid and forces to defend the kingdom. He promised, on the other hand, to make all the bonder udal-holders, and to give every man udal rights to the land he lived on. This speech met such joyful applause, that the whole public cried and shouted that they would take him to be king. And the Drontheim people took Hakon, then fifteen years old, as king over the whole land; and he took a hird or body-guard, and servants, and proceeded through the country. The news reached the Uplands that the people in Drontheim had taken to themselves a king, who in every respect was like King Harald Fairhair—with the difference,

[1] Succession to the throne depended on a combination of hereditary and elective principles: the king had to be a member of the royal dynasty, but also had to be accepted by the people at the Things.

that Harald had made all the people of the land vassals,[1] and unfree; but this Hakon wished well to every man, and offered the bonder to give them their udal rights again, which Harald had taken from them. All were rejoiced at this news, and it passed from mouth to mouth—it flew, like fire in dry grass, through the whole land, and eastward to the land's end. Many bonder came from the Uplands to meet King Hakon. Some sent messages, some tokens[2]; and all to the same effect—that his men they would be: and the king received all thankfully.

CHAPTER II. KING HAKON'S PROGRESS THROUGH THE COUNTRY.—Early in winter, the king went to the Uplands, and summoned the people to a Thing; and there streamed all to him who could come. He was proclaimed king at every Thing; and then he proceeded eastward to Viken, where his brother's sons, Trygve and Gudrod, and many others, came unto him, and complained of the sorrow and evil his brother Eric had wrought. The hatred to King Eric grew more and more, the more liking all men took to King Hakon; and they got more boldness to say what they thought. King Hakon gave Trygve and Gudrod the title of kings, and the dominions which King Harald had bestowed on their fathers.[3] Trygve got Ranrike and Vingulmark, and Gudrod got Westfold; but as they were young, and in the years of childhood, he appointed able men to rule the land for them. He gave them the country on the same conditions as it had been given before—that they should have half of the scatt and revenues with him. Towards spring King Hakon returned north, over the Uplands, to Drontheim.

CHAPTER III. ERIC'S DEPARTURE FROM THE COUNTRY.— King Hakon, early in spring, collected a great army at Drontheim, and fitted out ships. The people of Viken had also a great force on foot, and intended to join Hakon. King Eric also levied people in the middle of the country; but it went badly with him to gather people, for many great men left him, and went over to Hakon. As he saw himself not nearly strong enough to oppose Hakon, he sailed out to the West with such men as would follow him. He first sailed to Orkney, and took many people with him from that country; and then went south towards England, plundering in Scotland, and in the north

---

[1] It is unlikely that the administration introduced under Harald the Fairhaired was nearly so centralized and feudal as the system attributed to him here by Snorri. Cf. the Introduction, p. xxv.

[2] *Jartegnir*, i.e. tokens or vouchers sent with messengers to prove the authenticity of their messages.

[3] Trygve and Gudrod were grandsons of Harald the Fairhaired.

parts of England, wherever he could land. Athelstan, the king of England, sent a message to Eric, offering him dominions under him in England; saying that King Harald his father was a good friend of King Athelstan, and therefore he would do kindly towards his son. Messengers passed between the two kings; and it came to an agreement that King Eric should take Northumberland as a fief from King Athelstan, and this land he should defend against the Danes or other vikings. Eric should let himself be baptised, together with his wife and children, and all the people who had followed him. Eric accepted this offer, and was baptised, and adopted the right faith. Northumberland is called a fifth part of England. Eric had his residence at York, where Lodbrok's sons,[1] it is said, had formerly been, and Northumberland was principally inhabited by Northmen, after Lodbrok's sons had taken the country. Danes and Northmen often plundered there, when the power of the land was out of their hands. Many names of places in the country are Norwegian; as Grimsby, Hauksfljot,[2] and many others.

CHAPTER IV. ERIC'S DEATH.—King Eric had many people about him, for he kept many Northmen who had come with him from the East; and also many of his friends had joined him from Norway. But as he had little land, he went on a cruise every summer, and plundered in Scotland, the Hebrides, Ireland, and Bretland, by which he gathered property. King Athelstan died on a sick bed, after a reign of fourteen years, eight weeks, and three days.[3] After him his brother Edmund [4] was king of England, and he was no friend to the Northmen. King Eric, also, was in no great favour with him; and the word went about that King Edmund would set another chief over Northumberland. Now when King Eric heard this, he set off on a viking cruise to the westward; and from the Orkneys took with him the Earls Arnkel and Erlend, the sons of Earl Torf-Einar. Then he sailed to the Hebrides, where there were many vikings and troop-kings, who joined their men to his. With

[1] Ingvar, Ubbe and Halfdan, who were among the chiefs in the "great army" of Danes who came to England in 865 and conquered York in 866. Halfdan became king of Northumberland in 875, but was deposed in 880 by his own men. Northumberland was regained by the English in 926.

[2] Hauksfljot has not yet been located.

[3] Athelstan died in 939, after a reign of fourteen years and ten weeks. The most famous event in his reign was the decisive battle of Brunanburh (perhaps Bromborough in the Wirral), when he defeated the allied forces of the Norse king of Dublin and the kings of Scotland and Strathclyde.

[4] Edmund ruled from 939 to 946. He established English rule over York, the Five Boroughs of the Danelaw, and Strathclyde.

all this force he steered to Ireland first, where he took with
him all the men he could, and then to Bretland,[1] and plundered;
and sailed around the south of England, and marauded there
as elsewhere. The people fled before him wherever he appeared.
As King Eric was a bold warrior, and had a great force, he
trusted so much to his people that he penetrated far inland
in the country, following and plundering the fugitives. King
Edmund had set a king, who was called Olaf, to defend the land;
and he gathered an innumerable mass of people, with whom
he marched against King Eric. A dreadful battle [2] ensued, in
which many Englishmen fell; but for one who fell came three
in his place out of the country behind, and when evening came
on the loss of men turned on the side of the Northmen, and
many people fell. Towards the end of the day, King Eric and
five kings with him fell. Three of them were Guttorm and his
two sons, Ivar and Haarek: there fell, also, Sigurd and Ragnvald; and with them Torf-Einar's two sons, Arnkel and Erlend.
Besides these, there was a great slaughter of Northmen; and
those who escaped went to Northumberland, and brought the
news to Gunhild and her sons.

CHAPTER V. GUNHILD AND HER SONS.—When Gunhild and
her sons knew for certain that King Eric had fallen, after having
plundered the land of the King of England, they thought there
was no peace to be expected for them; and they made themselves ready to depart from Northumberland, with all the ships
King Eric had left, and all the men who would follow them.
They took also all the loose property, and goods which they
had gathered partly as taxes in England, partly as booty on
their expeditions. With their army they first steered northward to Orkney, where Torfin Hausakljuf was earl, a son of
Torf-Einar, and took up their station there for a time. Eric's
sons subdued these islands and Shetland, took scatt for themselves, and stayed there all the winter; but went on viking
cruises in summer to the West, and plundered in Scotland and
Ireland. About this Glum Geirason [3] sings:

> The hero who knows well to ride
> The sea-horse [4] o'er the foaming tide—

---

[1] Bretland must mean Wales here.

[2] The Old English Chronicle says only that the Northumbrians expelled
Eric in 954. Twelfth-century northern English traditions say that Eric
was afterwards killed by a certain Maccus (= Magnus), son of Olaf, on
Stainmore.

[3] An Icelander, one of Harald Greycloak's scalds; cf. p. 112.

[4] The sea-horse, ocean-steed, etc., are common *kennings* for ship in Norse
poetry.

He who in boyhood wild rode o'er
The seaman's horse to Scania's shore,
And showed the Danes his galley's bow,
Right nobly scours the ocean now.
On Scotland's coast he lights the brand
Of flaming war; with conquering hand
Drives many a Scottish warrior tall
To the bright seats in Odin's hall.
The fire-spark, by the fiend of war
Fanned to a flame, soon spreads afar.
Crowds trembling fly—the southern foes
Fall thick beneath the hero's blows:
The hero's blade drips red with gore,
Staining the green sward on the shore.

CHAPTER VI. BATTLE IN JUTLAND.—When King Eric had left the country, King Hakon, Athelstan's foster-son, subdued the whole of Norway. The first winter he visited the western parts, and then went north, and settled in Drontheim. But as no peace could be reasonably looked for so long as King Eric with his forces could come to Norway from the westward, he set himself with his men-at-arms in the middle of the country—in Firdafylke, or in Sogn, or Hordaland, or Rogaland. Hakon placed Sigurd, earl of Lade, over the whole Drontheim district, as he and his father had before had it under Harald Fairhair. When King Hakon heard of his brother Eric's death, and also that his sons had no footing in England, he thought there was not much to fear from them, and he went with his troops one summer eastward to Viken. At that time the Danes plundered often in Viken, and wrought much evil there; but when they heard that King Hakon was come with a great army, they got out of the way—some to Sealand, or to Halland[1]; and those who were nearest to King Hakon went out to sea, and over to Jutland. When the king heard of this, he sailed after them with all his army. On arriving at Jutland he plundered all round; and when the country people heard of it, they assembled in a great body, and determined to defend their land, and fight. There was a great battle; and King Hakon fought so boldly, that he went forward before his banner without helmet or coat of mail. King Hakon won the victory, and drove the fugitives far up the country. So says Guttorm Sindre, in his song of Hakon:[2]

Furrowing the deep-blue sea with oars,
The king pursues to Jutland's shores.

---

[1] Halland, the coastal province south of Gothenburg. With Skaane and Bleking in the southern tip of Sweden it formed part of the Danish dominions until a late period.

[2] *Hákonardrápa.*

They met; and in the battle storm
Of clashing shields, full many a form
Of goodly warrior on the plain,
Full many a corpse by Hakon slain,
Glutted the ravens, who from far,
Scenting the banquet-feast of war,
Came in black flocks to Jutland's plains
To drink the blood-wine from the veins.

CHAPTER VII. BATTLE IN THE SOUND.—Then Hakon steered
north-east with his fleet to seek the vikings, and so on to
Sealand.[1] He rowed with two cutters into Öresund, where he
found eleven viking ships, and instantly attacked them. It
ended in his gaining the victory, and clearing the viking ships
of all their men. So says Guttorm Sindre:

Hakon the Brave, whose skill all know
To bend in battle storm the bow,
Rushed o'er the waves to Sealand's tongue,
His two war-ships with gilt shields hung,
And cleared the decks with his blue sword
That rules the fate of war, on board
Eleven ships of the Vendland men—
Famous is Hakon's name since then.

CHAPTER VIII. KING HAKON'S EXPEDITION IN DENMARK.—
Thereafter King Hakon carried war far and wide in Sealand;
plundering some, slaying others, taking some prisoners of war,
taking ransom from others—and all without opposition. Then
Hakon proceeded along the coast of Skaane, pillaging everywhere, levying taxes and ransoms from the country, and killing
all vikings, both Danes and Vends.[2] He then went eastwards
round the coast of Gautland, raided there, and took great
ransoms from the country. So says Guttorm Sindre:

Hakon, who midst the battle shock
Stands like a firmly-rooted oak,
Subdued all Sealand with the sword;
From Vendland vikings the sea-board
Of Scania swept; and, with the shield
Of Odin clad, made Gotland yield
A ransom of the ruddy gold,
Which Hakon to his war-men bold
Gave with free hand, who in his feud
Against the arrow-storm had stood.

[1] Sjælland (Zeeland), the largest of the Danish islands.
[2] Vendland and the Vends were the country and people living along the
Baltic coast from Saxland and Holstein eastwards, including the regions of
Mecklenburg, Pomerania, and Prussia.

King Hakon returned home in autumn with his army and an immense booty; and remained all the winter in Viken to defend it against the Danes and the Gauts, if they should attack it.

CHAPTER IX. OF KING TRYGVE.—In the same autumn King Trygve Olafsson returned from a viking cruise in the West sea, having before ravaged in Scotland and Ireland. In spring King Hakon went north, and set his brother's son, King Trygve, over Viken [1] to defend that country against enemies. He gave him also in property all that he could reconquer of the country in Denmark,[2] which the summer before King Hakon had subjected to payment of scatt to him. So says Guttorm:

> King Hakon, whose sharp sword dyes red
> The bright steel cap on many a head,
> Has set a warrior brave and stout
> The foreign foeman to keep out—
> To keep that green land safe from war
> Which black Night bore to dwarf Onar.[3]
> For many a carle whose trade's to wield
> The battle-axe, and swing the shield,
> On the swan's ocean-skates [4] has come,
> In white-winged ships, across the foam—
> Across the sea, from far Ireland,
> To war against the Norseman's land.

CHAPTER X. OF GUNHILD'S SONS.—King Harald Gormson ruled over Denmark [936–86] at that time. He took it much amiss that King Hakon had made war in his dominions, and the report went that he would have revenge; but this did not take place so soon. When Gunhild and her sons heard there was enmity between Denmark and Norway, they began to turn their course from the West. They married King Eric's daughter, Ragnhild, to Arnfin, a son of Torfin Hausakljuf; and as soon as Eric's sons went away, Torfin took the earldom again over the Orkney Islands. Gamle Ericson was somewhat older than the other brothers, but still he was not a grown man. When Gunhild and her sons came from the westward to Denmark, they were well received by King Harald. He gave them great fiefs in his kingdom, so that they could maintain themselves and their men very well. He also took Harald Ericson

---

[1] Viken, the country north of the Gotha river, forming the great bight (Vik) on the coast of Norway, the Oslo fjord.

[2] Cf. p. 88, note 1.

[3] The dwarf Onar (or Anar) was the husband of Night, and Earth was their daughter; cf. the *Prose Edda*, trans. J. Young, 1954, p. 37.

[4] Figurative expression for ship. The original's *kenning* is "Ski of the swan-field."

to be his foster-son, set him on his knee,[1] and thereafter he was brought up at the Danish king's court. Some of Eric's sons went out on viking expeditions as soon as they were old enough, and gathered property, ravaging all around in the East sea. They grew up quickly to be handsome men, and far beyond their years in strength and perfection. Glum Geirason tells of one of them in the Graafelds-draapa [2]:

> I've heard that, on the Eastland coast,
> Great victories were won and lost.
> The king, whose hand is ever graced
> With gift to scald, his banner placed
> On, and still on; while, midst the play
> Of swords, sung sharp his good sword's sway.
> As strong in arm as free of gold,
> He thinn'd the ranks of warriors bold.

Then Eric's son turned northwards with their troops to Viken; but King Trygve kept troops on foot with which he met them, and they had many a battle, in which the victory was sometimes on one side, and sometimes on the other. Sometimes Eric's sons plundered in Viken, and sometimes Trygve in Sealand and Halland.

CHAPTER XI. KING HAKON'S DISPOSITION AND GOVERNMENT. —As long as Hakon was king in Norway, there was good peace between the bonder and merchants; so that none did harm either to the life or goods of the other. Good seasons also there were, both by sea and land. King Hakon was of a remarkably cheerful disposition, clever in words, and very condescending. He was a man of great understanding also, and bestowed attention on lawgiving. He gave out the Gula Thing's laws on the advice of Torleiv the Wise; also the Frosta Thing's laws on the advice of Earl Sigurd, and of other Drontheim men of wisdom. Eidsiva Thing laws were first established in the country by Halfdan the Black, the father of Harald Fairhair, as has formerly been written.[3]

CHAPTER XII. THE BIRTH OF EARL HAKON THE GREAT.— King Hakon kept Yule at Drontheim, and Earl Sigurd had

[1] Setting the child on the knee of the foster-father seems to have been a common symbol of adoption, cf. pp. 66, 81.

[2] Poem on Harald Greycloak, cf. p. 115.

[3] The eight fylker of Inner and Outer Tröndelag first had a central Thing, the Öre Thing, at Trondheim; when Namdal, Nordmöre, and Romsdal joined them, the central Thing was held at Frosta on the Trondheimsfjord. The fylker in the Gula Thing region were Firdafylke, Sogn, and Hordaland (later also Rogaland and Agder). The "Eidsiva Thing laws" were originally *Heiðsævislög*, Heidsævi being an ancient name for Lake Mjösen and the country around it (cf. p. 76, note 1); later the districts round the head of the Oslofjord also belonged to it. On the laws of Halfdan the Black see p. 48.

made a feast for him at Lade. The night of the first day of Yule the earl's wife, Bergljot, was brought to bed of a boy-child, which afterwards King Hakon poured water over, and gave him his own name. The boy grew up, and became in his day a mighty and able man, and was earl after his father, who was King Hakon's dearest friend.

CHAPTER XIII. OF EYSTEIN THE BAD.—Eystein, a king of the Uplands, whom some called the Great, and some the Bad, once on a time made war in Drontheim, and subdued Eyna district and Sparbu district, and set his own son Onund over them; but the Drontheim people killed him. Then King Eystein made another inroad into Drontheim, and ravaged the land far and wide, and subdued it. He then offered the people either his slave, who was called Tore Faxe, or his dog, whose name was Saur, to be their king. They preferred the dog, as they thought they would be the more independent. Now the dog was, by witchcraft, gifted with three men's wisdom; and when he barked, he spoke one word and barked two. A collar and chain of gold and silver were made for him, and his courtiers carried him on their shoulders when weather or ways were foul. A throne was erected for him, and he sat upon a high place, as kings are used to sit. He dwelt in Inderöen, and had his mansion in a place now called Saurshoug.[1] It is told that the occasion of his death was that the wolves one day broke into his fold, and his courtiers stirred him up to defend his cattle; but when he ran down from his mound, and attacked the wolves, they tore him to pieces. Many other extraordinary things were done by this King Eystein against the Drontheim people, and in consequence of this persecution and trouble, many chiefs and people fled and left their udal properties.

CHAPTER XIV. THE COLONISING OF JEMTELAND AND HEL-SINGELAND.—Ketil Jemte, a son of Earl Onund of Sparbu, went eastward across the mountain ridge,[2] and with him a great multitude, who took all their farm-stock and goods with them. They cleared the woods, and established large farms, and settled the country afterwards called Jemteland. Tore Helsing, Ketil's grandson, on account of a murder, ran away from Jemteland, and fled eastward through the forest, and settled down. Many people followed; and that country which, extends

---

[1] The scene of this irrelevant story has been placed here in order to explain the name Saurshoug, now Saxhaug in Inderöen. .
[2] Kjölen, the Keel, the range of mountains forming the march between Norway and Sweden.

eastward down to the sea-coast, was called Helsingeland; and its eastern parts are inhabited by Swedes. Now when Harald Fairhair took possession of the whole country many people fled before him, both people of Drontheim and of Naumadal districts; and thus new settlers came to Jemteland, and some all the way to Helsingeland. The Helsingeland people travelled into Sweden for their merchandise, and thus became altogether subjects of that country. The Jemteland people, again, were in a manner between the two countries; and nobody cared about them, until Hakon entered into friendly intercourse with Jemteland, and made friends of the more powerful people. Then they resorted to him, and promised him obedience and payment of taxes, and became his subjects; for they saw nothing but what was good in him, and being of Norwegian race they would rather stand under his royal authority than under the king of Sweden: and he gave them laws, and rights to their land. All the people of Helsingeland did the same—that is, all who were of Norwegian race, from the other side of Kjölen.

CHAPTER XV. KING HAKON UPHOLDS AND SPREADS CHRISTIANITY.—King Hakon was a good Christian when he came to Norway; but as the whole country was heathen, with much heathenish sacrifice, and as many great people, as well as the favour of the common people, were to be conciliated, he resolved to practise his Christianity in private. But he kept Sundays, and the Friday fasts, and some token of the great holydays. He made a law that the festival of Yule should begin at the same time as the Christmas of the Church, and that every man, under penalty, should brew a meal [1] of malt into ale, and therewith keep the Yule holy as long as it lasted. Before him, the beginning of Yule, or the slaughter night,[2] was the night of mid-winter, and Yule was kept for three days thereafter. It was his intent, as soon as he had set himself fast in the land, and had subjected the whole to his power, to introduce Christianity. He went to work first by enticing to Christianity the men who were dearest to him; and many, out of friendship to him, allowed themselves to be baptised, and

[1] A maling, or meal, is a measure of grain varying in size in different parts of the country. It is still used in Orkney.

[2] The word translated here as "slaughter night" is *höggunótt*, a less authentic variant of the original's *hökunótt*. The meaning of this is uncertain; one conjecture is that it refers to the particularly large hack (*haka*) cut in the calendar-staff to mark midwinter's day. In pagan times midwinter's day fell on 12 January.

some laid aside sacrifices. He dwelt long in the Drontheim district, for the strength of the country lay there; and when he thought that, by the support of some powerful people there, he could set up Christianity, he sent a message to England for a bishop and other clerics; and when they arrived in Norway, Hakon made it known that he would proclaim Christianity over all the land. The people of Möre and Raumsdal referred the matter to the people of Drontheim. King Hakon then had several churches consecrated, and put priests into them; and when he came to Drontheim he summoned the bonder to a Thing, and invited them to accept Christianity. They gave an answer to the effect that they would defer the matter until the Frosta Thing, at which there would be men from every district of the Drontheim country, and then they would give their determination upon this difficult matter.

CHAPTER XVI. ABOUT SACRIFICES.—Sigurd, earl of Lade, was one of the greatest men for sacrifices, and so had Hakon his father been; and Sigurd always presided on behalf of the king at all the festivals of sacrifice in the Drontheim country. It was an old custom, that when there was to be sacrifice all the bonder should come to the spot where the temple stood, and bring with them all that they required while the festival of the sacrifice lasted. To this festival all the men brought ale with them; and all kinds of cattle, as well as horses, were slaughtered, and all the blood that came from them was called *laut,* and the vessels in which it was collected were called laut-vessels. Laut-staves were made, like sprinkling brushes, with which the whole of the altars and the temple walls, both outside and inside, were sprinkled over, and also the people were sprinkled with the blood; but the flesh was boiled for the delectation of the company. The fire was in the middle of the floor of the temple, and over it hung the kettles, and the full goblets were handed across the fire; and he who made the feast, and was a chief, blessed the full goblets, and all the meat of the sacrifice. And first Odin's goblet was emptied for victory and power to his king; thereafter, Njord's and Freya's goblets for peace and a good season. Then it was the custom of many to empty the Brage-beaker [1]; and then the guests emptied a goblet to the memory of departed kinsmen, called the remembrance-goblet. Sigurd the earl was an open-handed man, who did what was very much celebrated; namely, he made a great sacrifice festival at Lade, of which he paid all the expenses. Kormak Ogmund-

[1] The bragging-cup, over which boastful vows were made. *Vide* p. 34.

son [1] sings of it in his ballad of Sigurd:

> Of cup or platter need has none
> The guest who seeks the generous one—
> Sigurd the Generous, who can trace
> His lineage from the giant race [2];
> For Sigurd's hand is bounteous, free—
> The guardian of the temples he.
> He loves the gods—his liberal hand
> Scatters his sword's gains o'er the land.

CHAPTER XVII. THE THING AT FROSTA.—King Hakon came to the Frosta Thing, at which a vast multitude of people were assembled. And when the Thing was seated, the king spoke to the people, and began his speech with saying—it was his message and entreaty to the bonder and householding men, both great and small, and to the whole public in general, young and old, rich and poor, women as well as men, that they should all allow themselves to be baptised, and should believe in one God, and in Christ the son of Mary; and refrain from all sacrifices and heathen gods; and should keep holy the seventh day, and abstain from all work on it, and keep a fast on the seventh day. As soon as the king had proposed this to the bonder, great was the murmur and noise among the crowd. They complained that the king wanted to take their labour and their old faith from them, and the land could not be cultivated in that way. The labouring men and slaves thought that they could not work if they did not get meat; and they said it was the character of King Hakon, and his father, and all the family, to be generous enough with their money, but sparing with their diet. Asbjorn of Medalhus in the Guldal stood up, and answered thus to the king's proposal:

"We bonder, King Hakon, when we elected thee to be our king, and got back our udal rights at the Thing held in Drontheim, thought we had got into heaven; but now we don't know whether we have really got back our freedom, or whether thou wishest to make vassals of us again by this extraordinary proposal—that we should abandon the ancient faith which our fathers and forefathers have held from the oldest times, in the times when the dead were burnt,[3] as well as since that they are laid under mounds, and which, although they were braver than the people of our days, has served us as a faith to the present time. We have also held thee so dear, that we have

---

[1] The hero of the *Kormáks Saga*. He is also said to have composed a poem in honour of Harald Greycloak. He died in Scotland, probably *c.* 970.

[2] He claimed descent from the giantess Skade, cf. p. 13.

[3] *Vide* p. 4.

allowed thee to rule and give law and right to all the country.
And even now we bonder will unanimously hold by the law
which thou gavest us here in the Frosta Thing, and to which
we have also given our assent[1]; and we will follow thee, and
have thee for our king, as long as there is a living man among
us bonder here in this Thing assembled. But thou, king, must
use some moderation towards us, and only require from us such
things as we can obey thee in, and are not impossible for us.
If, however, thou wilt take up this matter with a high hand,
and wilt try thy power and strength against us, we bonder
have resolved among ourselves to part with thee, and to
take to ourselves some other chief, who will so conduct
himself towards us that we can freely and safely enjoy that
faith that suits our own inclinations. Now, king, thou must
choose one or other of these conditions before the Thing
is ended."

The bonder gave loud applause to this speech, and said it
expressed their will, and they would stand or fall by what had
been spoken. When silence was again restored, Earl Sigurd
said, "It is King Hakon's will to give way to you, the bonder,
and never to separate himself from your friendship." The
bonder replied, that it was their desire that the king should
offer a sacrifice for peace and a good year, as his father was
wont to do; and thereupon the noise and tumult ceased, and
the Thing was concluded. Earl Sigurd spoke to the king afterwards, and advised him not to refuse altogether to do as the
people desired, saying there was nothing else for it but to give
way to the will of the bonder; "for it is, as thou hast heard
thyself, the will and earnest desire of the head-people, as well
as of the multitude. Hereafter we may find a good way to
manage it." And in this resolution the king and earl agreed.

CHAPTER XVIII. THE PEASANTS FORCE KING HAKON TO
OFFER SACRIFICES.—The harvest thereafter, towards the winter
season, there was a festival of sacrifice at Lade, and the king
came to it. It had always been his custom before, when he
was present at a place where there was sacrifice, to take his
meals in a little house by himself, or with some few of his men;
but the bonder grumbled that he did not seat himself on his
throne at these the most joyous of the meetings of the people.

---

[1] Our yea. The assent of the people in old times to the laws and
the power of the Frosta Thing, are as well defined as in our Parliament
in this speech.

The earl said that the king should do so this time. The king accordingly sat upon his throne. Now when the first full goblet was filled, Earl Sigurd spoke some words over it, blessed it in Odin's name, and drank to the king out of the horn; and the king then took it, and made the sign of the cross over it. Then said Kaar of Gryting,[1] "What does the king mean by doing so? Will he not sacrifice?" Earl Sigurd replies, "The king is doing what all of you do, who trust to your power and strength. He is blessing the full goblet in the name of Thor, by making the sign of his hammer over it before he drinks it." On this there was quietness for the evening. The next day, when the people sat down to table, the bonder pressed the king strongly to eat of horse-flesh[2]; and as he would on no account do so, they wanted him to drink of the soup; and as he would not do this, they insisted he should at least taste the grease; and on his refusal they were going to lay hands on him. Earl Sigurd came and made peace among them, by asking the king to hold his mouth over the handle of the kettle, upon which the fat smoke of the boiled horse-flesh had settled itself; and the king first laid a linen cloth over the handle, and then gaped over it, and returned to the throne; but neither party was satisfied with this.

CHAPTER XIX. FEAST OF THE SACRIFICE AT MÆRE.—The winter thereafter the king prepared a Yule feast in Mære,[3] and eight chiefs resolved with each other to meet at it. Four of them were from the outer Drontheim district—namely, Kaar of Gryting, Asbjorn of Medalhus, Torberg of Varnæs, and Orm from Ljoxa; and four from the Drontheim district itself, viz. Blotolf of Olvishaug, Narve of Stav in Værdal, Trond Hake from Egge, and Tore Skjeg from Husebö in Inderöen. These eight men bound themselves, the four first to root out Christianity in Norway, and the four others to oblige the king to offer sacrifice to the gods. The four first went in four ships

---

[1] The old name of the parsonage in the present parish of Orkedal.

[2] The horse was probably the commonest sacred animal amongst Indo-European peoples. (In Norse sources it is particularly associated with the god Frey.) Horse-racing and horse-fighting were associated with pagan festivals, and horse-flesh was an important constituent of the ritual meal that followed the sacrifice. The eating of horse-flesh was in consequence resolutely opposed by Christian missionaries. When Christianity was adopted in Iceland in 1000 men were permitted to go on eating horse-flesh, probably because it formed an important element in the ordinary diet. This permission was soon withdrawn, and in all the Christian laws of Iceland and Norway the consumption of horse-flesh is forbidden, penalties for the crime ranging from fines to banishment.

[3] In the parish of Mæren in Sparbu.

southwards to Möre, and killed three priests, and burnt three churches, and then they returned. Now, when King Hakon and Earl Sigurd came to Möre with their court, the bonder assembled in great numbers; and immediately, on the first day of the feast, the bonder insisted hard with the king that he should offer sacrifice, and threatened him with violence if he refused. Earl Sigurd tried to make peace between them, and brought it so far that the king took some bits of horse-liver, and emptied all the goblets the bonder filled for him; but as soon as the feast was over, the king and the earl returned to Lade. The king was very ill-pleased, and made himself ready to leave Drontheim forthwith with all his people; saying that the next time he came to Drontheim, he would come with such strength of men-at-arms that he would repay the bonder for their enmity towards him. Earl Sigurd entreated the king not to take it amiss of the bonder; adding, that it was not wise to threaten them, or to make war upon the people within the country, and especially in the Drontheim district where the strength of the land lay; but the king was so enraged that he would not listen to a word from anybody. He went out from Drontheim, and proceeded south to Möre where he remained the rest of the winter, and on to the spring season; and when summer came he assembled men, and the report was that he intended with this army to attack the Drontheim people.

CHAPTER XX. BATTLE AT AUGVALDSNES.—But just as the king had embarked with a great force of troops, the news was brought him from the south of the country, that King Eric's sons had come from Denmark to Viken, and had driven King Trygve Olafsson from his ships at Sotenes,[1] and then had plundered far and wide around in Viken, and that many had submitted to them. Now when King Hakon heard this news, he thought that help was needed; and he sent word to Earl Sigurd, and to the other chiefs from whom he could expect help, to hasten to his assistance. Sigurd the earl came accordingly with a great body of men, among whom were all the Drontheim people who had set upon him the hardest to offer sacrifice; and all made their peace with the king, by the earl's persuasion. Now King Hakon sailed south along the coast; and when he came south as far as Stad, he heard that Eric's sons were come to North Agder. Then they advanced against each other, and met at Kormt. Both parties left their ships there, and gave battle at Augvaldsnes. Both parties had a great force, and it

[1] Sotenes, a peninsula in Ranrike (cf. note, p. 61), west of Aabyfjord.

was a great battle. King Hakon went forward bravely, and King Guttorm Ericson met him with his troop, and they exchanged blows with each other. Guttorm fell, and his standard was cut down. Many people fell around him. The army of Eric's sons then took flight to their ships, and rowed way with the loss of many a man. So says Guttorm Sindre:

> The king's voice waked the silent host
> Who slept beside the wild sea-coast,
> And bade the song of spear and sword
> Over the battle plain be heard.
> Where heroes' shields the loudest rang,
> Where loudest was the sword-blade's clang,
> By the sea-shore at Kormt Sound,
> Hakon felled Guttorm to the ground.

Now King Hakon returned to his ships, and pursued Gunhild's sons. And both parties sailed all they could sail, until they came to East Agder,[1] from whence Eric's sons set out to sea, and southwards for Jutland. Guttorm Sindre speaks of it in his song:

> And Guttorm's brothers too, who know
> So skilfully to bend the bow,
> The conquering hand must also feel
> Of Hakon, god of the bright steel—
> The sun-god, whose bright rays, that dart
> Flame-like, are swords that pierce the heart.
> Well I remember how the King
> Hakon, the battle's life and spring,
> O'er the wide ocean cleared away
> Eric's brave sons. They durst not stay,
> But round their ships' sides hung their shields,
> And fled across the blue sea-fields.

King Hakon returned then northwards to Norway, but Eric's sons remained a long time in Denmark.

CHAPTER XXI. KING HAKON'S LAWS.—King Hakon after this battle made a law, that all inhabited land over the whole country along the sea-coast, and as far back from it as the salmon swims up in the rivers, should be divided into ship-raths according to the districts; and it was fixed by law how many ships there should be from each district, and how great each should be, when the whole people were called out on service. For this outfit the whole inhabitants should be bound, whenever a foreign army came to the country. With this came also the order that beacons should be erected upon the hills,

---

[1] East Agder stretched from a little north of Risör south to about Kristiansand, and West (or North) Agder from there to about Flekkefjord.

so that every man could see from the one to the other; and it is told that a war-signal could thus be given in seven days, from the most southerly beacon to the most northerly Thing-seat in Halogaland.

CHAPTER XXII. CONCERNING ERIC'S SONS.—Eric's sons plundered much on the Baltic coasts, and sometimes, as before related, in Norway; but so long as Hakon ruled over Norway there was in general good peace, and good seasons, and he was the most beloved of kings. When Hakon had reigned about twenty years in Norway, Eric's sons came from Denmark with a powerful army, of which a great part consisted of the people who had followed them on their expeditions; but a still greater army of Danes had been placed at their disposal by King Harald Gormson. They sailed with a fair wind from Vende-syssel,[1] and came to Agder; and then sailed northwards, night and day, along the coast. But the beacons were not fired; and besides King Hakon had set heavy penalties for giving false alarm, by lighting the beacons without occasion. The reason of this was, that ships of war and vikings cruised about and plundered among the outlying islands, and the country people took them for Eric's sons, and lighted the beacons, and set the whole country in trouble and dread of war. Sometimes, no doubt, the sons of Eric were there; but having only their own troop, and no Danish army with them, they returned to Denmark; and sometimes these were only small vikings. King Hakon was very angry at this, because it cost both trouble and money to no purpose. The bonder also suffered by these false alarms when they were given use-lessly; and thus it happened that no news of this expedition of Eric's sons circulated through the land until they had come as far north as Ulvesund,[2] where they lay for seven days. Then spies set off across the upper neck of land and northwards to Möre. King Hakon was at that time in the island Fræde, in North Möre, at a place called Birkestrand, where he had a dwelling-house, and had no troops with him, only his body-guard or hird, and the neighbouring bonder he had invited to his house.

CHAPTER XXIII. OF EGIL ULDSÆRK.—The spies came to King Hakon, and told him that Eric's sons, with a great army, lay just to the south of Stad. Then he called together the

---

[1] The end of Jutland, to the north of Lymfjord.
[2] The sound between Vaagsöen and the mainland near Moldöen to the north of Nordfjord.

most understanding of the men about him, and asked their opinion, whether he should fight with Eric's sons, although they had such a great multitude with them, or should set off northwards to gather together more men. Now there was a bonde there, by name Egil Uldsærk, who was a very old man, but in former days had been strong and stout beyond most men, and a hardy man-at-arms withal, having long carried King Harald's banner. Egil answered thus to the king's speech— "I was in several battles with thy father Harald the king, and he gave battle sometimes with many, sometimes with few people; but he always came off with victory. Never did I hear him ask counsel of his friends whether he should fly—and neither shalt thou get any such counsel from us, king; but as we know we have a brave leader, thou shalt get a trusty following from us." Many others agreed with this speech, and the king himself declared he was most inclined to fight with such strength as they could gather. It was so determined. The king split up a war-arrow, which he sent off in all directions, and by that token a number of men was collected in all haste. Then said Egil Uldsærk—"At one time the peace had lasted so long I was afraid I might come to die of old age, within doors upon a bed of straw, although I would rather fall in battle following my chief. And now it may so turn out in the end as I wished it to be."

CHAPTER XXIV. BATTLE AT FRÆDEBERG. — Eric's sons sailed northwards around Stad, as soon as the wind suited; and when they had passed it, and heard where King Hakon was they sailed to meet him. King Hakon had nine ships, with which he lay under Frædeberg [2] in Fæösund; and Eric's sons had over twenty ships, which they brought up on the south side of the same cape, in Fæö Sound. King Hakon sent them a message, asking them to go upon the land; and telling them that he had hedged in with hazel boughs a place of combat at Rastarkalv,[3] where there is a flat large field, at the foot of a long and rather low ridge. Then Eric's sons left their ships, and went northwards over the neck of land within Frædeberg, and onward to Rastarkalv. Then Egil asked King Hakon to

---

[1] This was commonly regarded as an inglorious end for any great warrior. Cf. the adjective *strádauða*, "straw-dead," dead from sickness.

[2] Snorri wrongly says that the island of Fræde, now Fredö, is in South Möre instead of North Möre, and thus makes it only a short distance from Stad. (North Möre, on p. 100, is the translator's correction.)

[3] Rastarkalv is the plain east of Freihaugen. It slopes from Freines westward up to Frei Church and Skrubhaugen.

give him ten men with ten banners, and the king did so. Then
Egil went with his men under the ridge; but King Hakon went
out upon the open field with his army, and set up his banner,
and drew up his army, saying, "Let us draw up in a long line,
that they may not surround us, as they have the most men."
And so it was done; and there was a severe battle, and a very
sharp attack. Then Egil Uldsærk set up the ten banners he
had with him, and placed the men who carried them so that
they should go as near the summit of the ridge as possible,
leaving a space between each of them. They went so near
the summit that the banners could be seen over it, and moved
on as if they were coming behind the army of Eric's sons. Now
when the men who stood uppermost in the line of the troops
of Eric's sons saw so many flying banners advancing high over
the edge of the ridge, they supposed a great force must be
following, who would come behind their army; and between
them and their ships. They made each other acquainted with
what was going on in a loud shout, and the whole took to flight;
and when the kings saw it, they fled with the rest. King
Hakon now pushed on briskly with his people, pursuing the
flying, and killing many.

CHAPTER XXV. OF KING GAMLE, THE SON OF ERIC.—When
Gamle Ericsson came up the ridge of the hill he turned round,
and he observed that not more people were following than his
men had been engaged with already, and he saw it was but a
stratagem of war; so he ordered the war-horns to be blown, his
banner to be set up, and he put his men in battle order. On
this, all his Northmen stood, and turned with him, but the
Danes fled to the ships; and when King Hakon and his men
came thither, there was again a sharp conflict; but now Hakon
had most people. At last the Eric's sons' force fled, and took
the road south about the hill; but a part of their army retreated
upon the hill southwards, followed by King Hakon. There is
a flat field east of the ridge which runs westward along the
range of hills, and is bounded on its west side by a steep
ridge. Gamle's men retreated towards this ground; but Hakon
followed so closely that he killed some, and others ran west
over the ridge, and were killed on that side of it. King
Hakon did not part with them till the last man of them was
killed.

CHAPTER XXVI. KING GAMLE AND ULDSÆRK FALL.—Gamle
Ericsson fled from the ridge down upon the plain to the south
of the hill. There he turned himself again, and fought until

more people gathered to him. All his brothers, and many troops of their men, assembled there. Egil Uldsærk was in front, and in advance of Hakon's men, and made a stout attack. He and King Gamle exchanged blows with each other, and King Gamle got grievous wounds; but Egil fell, and many people with him. Then came Hakon the king with the troops which had followed him, and a new battle began. King Hakon pushed on, cutting down men on both sides of him, and killing the one upon the top of the other. So sings Guttorm Sindre:

> Scared by the sharp sword's singing sound,
> Brandished in air, the foe gave ground.
> The boldest warrior cannot stand
> Before King Hakon's conquering hand;
> And the king's banner ever flies
> Where the spear-forests thickest rise.
> Altho' the king had gained of old
> Enough of Freya's tears of gold,[1]
> He spared himself no more than tho'
> He'd had no well-filled purse to show.

When Eric's sons saw their men falling all round, they turned and fled to their ships; but those who had sought the ships before had pushed off some of them from the land, while some of them were still hauled up and on the strand. Now the sons of Eric and their men plunged into the sea, and betook themselves to swimming. Gamle Ericsson was drowned; but the other sons of Eric reached their ships, and set sail with what men remained. They steered southwards to Denmark, where they stopped a while, very ill satisfied with their expedition.

CHAPTER XXVII. EGIL ULDSÆRK'S BURIAL-MOUND.—King Hakon took all the ships of the sons of Eric that had been left upon the strand, and had them drawn quite up, and brought on the land. Then he ordered that Egil Uldsærk, and all the men of his army who had fallen, should be laid in the ships, and covered entirely over with earth and stones.[2] King Hakon had many of the ships drawn up and placed the slain in them, and the hillocks over them are to be seen to the present day a little to the south of Frædeberg. At the time when King Hakon was killed, when Glum Geirason, in his song, boasted of

---

[1] Freya's husband was Od; and her tears, when she wept at the long absence of her husband, were tears of gold. "Od's wife's tears" thus becomes a *kenning* for gold. See the *Prose Edda*, trans. J. Young, 1954, p. 59.

[2] On and near the shore at Rastarkalv (the name has not in fact survived to modern times) are numerous burial-mounds and long-shaped heaps of stones, but no standing stones are now found there. Snorri's description is not exact, but his errors may be explained by assuming that he had only observed this coastal topography from the sea.

King Hakon's fall, Eyvind Skaldaspiller composed these verses
on this battle:

> Our dauntless king with Gamle's gore
> Sprinkled his bright sword o'er and o'er;
> Sprinkled the gag that holds the mouth
> Of the fell demon Fenri's wolf.[1]
> Proud swelled our warriors' hearts when he
> Drove Eric's sons out to the sea,
> With all their Gotland host: but now
> Our warriors weep—Hakon lies low!

High standing stones mark Egil Uldsærk's grave.[2]

CHAPTER XXVIII. NEWS OF WAR COMES TO KING HAKON.—
When King Hakon, Athelstan's foster-son, had been king for
twenty-six years after his brother Eric had left the country,
it happened that he was at a feast at Fitjar, an estate on Stord,
and he had with him at the feast his court and many of the
peasants. And just as the king was seated at the morning-
meal, his watchmen who were outside observed many ships
coming sailing along from the south, and not very far from the
island. Now, said the one to the other, they should inform
the king that they thought an armed force was coming against
them; but none thought it advisable to be the bearer of an
alarm of war to the king, as he had set heavy penalties on those
who raised such alarms falsely, yet they thought it unsuitable
that the king should remain in ignorance of what they saw.[3]
Then one of them went into the room and asked Eyvind Finsson
to come out as fast as possible, for it was very needful. Eyvind
immediately came out, and went to where he could see the
ships, and saw directly that a great army was on the way; and
he returned in all haste into the room, and, placing himself
before the king, said, "Short is the hour for acting, and long

---

[1] The wolf Fenrir, one of Loke's evil children, was fettered and chained
to a rock, with a sword jammed between his upper and lower jaws. The
"wolf's gag" is thus a *kenning* for sword. See *The Prose Edda*, trans. J.
Young, 1954, pp. 55-9.

[2] Ship-formed graves, where the grave is surrounded by stones forming
the outline of a ship, are known in Scandinavia from the late Bronze Age
onwards. The earliest graves known where the corpse was interred in a
boat or ship date from c. 500; they reached their greatest popularity from
c. 800 onwards. The most famous ship-burials excavated in Norway are
those of Oseberg and Gokstad (cf. note, p. 43). The original intention was
to provide transport for the dead man on his journey to the next world.
On the standing stones cf. p. 4, note 3.

[3] A curious instance of the discipline and deference for the king of these
Northmen, in contrast with what follows—the reference by the king to his
men for approving his plan of giving battle. This strict discipline and
freedom united accounts for the success of their predatory expeditions.

the hour for feasting." The king cast his eyes upon him, and said, "What now is in the way?" Eyvind said:

> Up, king! the avengers are at hand!
> Eric's bold sons approach the land!
> The judgment of the sword they crave
> Against their foe. Thy wrath I brave;
> Tho' well I know 'tis no light thing
> To bring war-tidings to the king,
> And tell him 'tis no time to rest.
> Up! gird your armour to your breast:
> Thy honour's dearer than my life;
> Therefore I say, up to the strife!

Then said the king, "Thou art too brave a fellow, Eyvind, to bring us any false alarm of war." The others all said it was a true report. The king ordered the tables to be removed, and then he went out to look at the ships; and when it could be clearly seen that these were ships of war, the king asked his men what resolution they should take—whether to give battle with the men they had, or go on board ship and sail away northwards along the land. "For it is easy to see," said he, "that we must now fight against a much greater force than we ever had against us before; although we have often thought the same before joining battle with Gunhild's sons." No one was in a hurry to give an answer to the king; but at last Eyvind replied to the king's speech:

> Thou who in the battle-plain
> Hast often poured the sharp spear-rain!
> Ill it beseems our warriors brave
> To fly upon the ocean wave:
> To fly upon the blue wave north,
> When Harald from the south comes forth,
> With many a ship riding in pride
> Upon the foaming ocean-tide;
> With many a ship and southern viking—
> Let us take shield in hand, brave king!

The king replied, "Thy counsel, Eyvind, is manly, and after my own heart; but I will hear the opinion of others upon this matter." Now as the king's men thought they discerned what way the king was inclined to take, they answered that they would rather fall bravely and like men, than fly before the Danes; adding, that they had often gained the victory against greater odds of numbers. The king thanked them for their resolution, and bade them arm themselves; and all the men did so. The king put on his armour, and girded on his sword Quernbiter, and put a gilt helmet upon his head, and took a spear in his hand, and a shield by his side. He then drew up his hird-men and the bonder in one body, and set up his banner.

CHAPTER XXIX. THE ARMAMENT OF ERIC'S SONS.—After Gamle's death King Harald, Eric's son, was the chief of the brothers, and he had a great army with him from Denmark. In their army were also their mother's brothers—Eyvind Skreya, and Alv Askmand, both strong and able men, and great man-slayers. The sons of Eric brought up with their ships off the island, and it is said that their force was not less than six to one—so much stronger in men were Eric's sons.

CHAPTER XXX. KING HAKON'S BATTLE ARRAY. — When King Hakon had drawn up his men, it is told of him that he threw off his armour before the battle began.   So sings Eyvind Skaldaspiller:

> They found Bjorne's brother [1] bold
> Under his banner as of old,
> Ready for battle.   Foes advance—
> The front rank raise the shining lance;
> And now begins the bloody fray!
> Now! now begins Hildur's wild play [2]!
> Our noble king, whose name strikes fear
> Into each Danish heart—whose spear
> Has single-handed spilt the blood
> Of many a Danish noble—stood
> Beneath his helmet's eagle wing [3]
> Amidst his guards; but the brave king
> Scorned to wear armour, while his men
> Bared naked breasts against the rain
> Of spear and arrow.   Off he flung
> His coat of mail, his breast-plate rung
> Against the stones; and, blithe and gay,
> He rushed into the thickest fray.
> With golden helm, and naked breast,
> Brave Hakon played at slaughter's feast.

King Hakon selected willingly such men for his guard or hird-men as were distinguished for their strength and bravery, as his father King Harald also used to do; and among these was Toralf Skolmson the Strong,[4] who went on one side of the king. He had helmet and shield, spear and sword; and his sword was called by the name of Footbreadth. It was said that Toralf and King Hakon were equal in strength.   Thord

---

[1] King Hakon.
[2] Hildur's play was battle.
[3] The helmet was perhaps adorned with the figure of an eagle; the original can also be read as meaning "helmet of bronze."
[4] He was an Icelander, and is said to have been eighteen when he took part in this battle. He is mentioned in a number of sources.

Sjaarekson speaks of it in the poem he composed concerning Toralf:

> The king's men went with merry words
> To the sharp clash of shields and swords,
> When these wild rovers of the sea
> At Fitjar fought. Stout Toralf he
> Next to the Northmen's hero came,
> Scattering wide round the battle flame,
> For in the storm of shields not one
> Ventured like him with brave Hakon.

When both lines met there was a hard combat, and much bloodshed. The combatants threw their spears, and then drew their swords. Then King Hakon, and Toralf with him, went in advance of the banner, cutting down on both sides of them. So says Eyvind Skaldaspiller:

> The body-coats of linked steel,
> The woven iron coats of mail,
> Like water fly before the swing
> Of Hakon's sword—the champion-king.
> About each Gotland war-man's head
> Helm splits, like ice beneath the tread,
> Cloven by the axe or sharp sword-blade.
> The brave king, foremost in the fight,
> Dyes crimson-red the spotless white
> Of his bright shield with foemen's gore—
> Amidst the battle wild uproar,
> Wild pealing round from shore to shore.

CHAPTER XXXI. THE FALL OF EYVIND SKREYA AND OF ALV ASKMAND.—King Hakon was conspicuous, bigger than other men, and also when the sun shone his helmet glanced, and thereby many weapons were directed at him. Then Eyvind Finnson took a hat and put it over the king's helmet. Now Eyvind Skreya called out, "Does the king of the Norsemen hide himself, or has he fled? Where is now the golden helmet?" Then Eyvind, and his brother Alv with him, pushed on like fools or madmen. The king said, "Come on as ye are coming, and ye will find the king of the Norsemen." So says Eyvind Skaldaspiller:

> The raiser of the storm of shields,
> The conqueror in battle-fields—
> Hakon the brave, the warrior's friend,
> Who scatters gold with liberal hand,
> Heard Skreya's taunt, and saw him rush
> Amidst the sharp spears' thickest push,
> And loudly shouted in reply—
> "If thou wilt for the victory try,
> The Norsemen's king thou soon shalt find!
> Hold onwards, friend! Hast thou a mind?"

It was also but a short space of time before Eyvind did come up swinging his sword, and made a cut at the king; but Toralf thrust his shield so hard against Eyvind that he tottered with the shock. Now the king takes his sword Quernbiter with both hands, and hewed Eyvind through helm and head, and clove him down to the shoulders. Toralf also slew Alv Askmand. So says Eyvind Skaldaspiller:

> With both his hands the gallant king
> Swung round his sword, and to the chin
> Clove Eyvind down: his faithless mail
> Against it could no more avail,
> Than the thin plank against the shock
> When the ship's side beats on the rock.
> By his bright sword with golden haft
> Thro' helm, and head, and hair, was cleft
> The Danish champion; and amain,
> With terror smitten, fled his men.

After this fall of the two brothers, King Hakon pressed on so hard that all men gave way before his assault. Now fear came over the army of Eric's sons, and the men began to fly; and King Hakon, who was at the head of his men, pressed on the flying, and hewed down oft and hard. Then flew an arrow, one of the kind called flein,[1] into Hakon's arm, into the muscles below the shoulder; and it is said by many people that Gunhild's shoe-boy, whose name was Kisping, ran out and forwards amidst the confusion of arms, and called out, "Make room for the king-killer." Others again say that nobody could tell who shot the king, which is indeed the most likely; for spears, arrows, and all kinds of missiles flew as thick as a snow-drift. Many of the people of Eric's sons were killed, both on the field of battle and on the way to the ships, and also on the strand, and many threw themselves into the water. Many also, among whom were Eric's sons, got on board their ships, and rowed away as fast as they could, and Hakon's men after them. So says Thord Sjaarekson:

> The wolf, the murderer, and the thief,
> Fled from before the people's chief:
> Few breakers of the peace grew old
> Under the Northmen's king so bold.
> When gallant Hakon lost his life
> Black was the day, and dire the strife.
> It was bad work for Gunhild's sons,
> Leading their pack of hungry Danes
> From out the south, to have to fly,
> And many a bonder leave to die,
> Leaning his heavy wounded head

---

[1] Flein was an arrow with hooks like anchor flukes.

> On the oar-bench for feather-bed.
> Toralf was nearest to the side
> Of gallant Hakon in the tide
> Of battle; his the sword that best
> Carved out the raven's bloody feast:
> Amidst the heaps of foemen slain,
> He was named bravest on the plain.

CHAPTER XXXII. HAKON'S DEATH. — When King Hakon came out to his ship he had his wound bound up; but the blood ran from it so much and so constantly, that it could not be stopped; and when the day was drawing to an end his strength began to leave him. Then he told his men that he wanted to go northwards to his house at Alrekstad[1]; but when he came north, as far as Hakon's Rock,[2] they put in towards the land, for by this time the king was almost lifeless. Then he called his friends around him, and told them what he wished to be done with regard to his kingdom. He had only one child, a daughter, called Tora, and had no son. Now he told them to send a message to Eric's sons, that they should be kings over the country; but asked them to hold his friends in respect and honour. "And if fate," added he, "should prolong my life, I will, at any rate, leave the country, and go to a Christian land, and do penance for what I have done against God; but should I die in heathen land, give me any burial you think fit." Shortly afterwards Hakon expired on the flat rocks on the shore-side at which he was born. So great was the sorrow over Hakon's death, that he was lamented both by friends and enemies; and they said that never again would Norway see such a king. His friends removed his body to Sæim,[3] in North Hordaland, and made a great mound, in which they laid the king in full armour and in his best clothes, but with no other goods. They spoke over his grave, as heathen people are used to do, and wished him in Valhalla. Eyvind Skaldaspiller composed a poem on the death of King Hakon, and on how well he was received in Valhalla. The poem is called Hakonarmal:

> In Odin's hall an empty place
> Stands for a king of Yngve's race;
> "Go, my valkyries," Odin said,
> "Go forth, my angels of the dead,

---

[1] Alrekstad is now called Aarstad, in the neighbourhood of Bergen.
[2] Cf. p. 80, note 1.
[3] At Sæim (now Sem, north of Bergen) there is a mound still called Hakon's Mound, although it is not certain that it is his burial-place.

Gondul and Skögul, to the plain
Drenched with the battle's bloody rain,
And to the dying Hakon tell,
Here in Valhalla he shall dwell."

At Stord, so late a lonely shore,
Was heard the battle's wild uproar;
The lightning of the flashing sword
Burned fiercely at the shore of Stord.
From levelled halberd and spear-head
Life-blood was dropping fast and red;
And the keen arrows' biting sleet
Upon the shore at Stord fast beat.

Upon the thundering cloud of shield
Flashed bright the sword-storm o'er the field;
And on the plate-mail rattled loud
The arrow-shower's rushing cloud,
In Odin's tempest-weather, there
Swift whistling through the angry air;
And the spear-torrent swept away
Ranks of brave men from light of day.

With batter'd shield, and blood-smear'd sword,
Sits one beside the shore at Stord,
With armour crushed and gashed sits he,
A grim and ghastly sight to see;
And round about in sorrow stand
The warriors of his gallant band:
Because the king of Döglin's race
In Odin's hall must fill a place.

Then up spake Gondul, standing near,
Resting upon her long ash spear—
"Hakon! the gods' cause prospers well,
And thou in Odin's halls shalt dwell!"
The king beside the shore of Stord
The speech of the valkyrie heard,
Who sat there on her coal-black steed,
With shield on arm and helm on head.

Thoughtful, said Hakon, "Tell me why,
Ruler of battles, victory
Is so dealt out on Stord's red plain?
Have we not well deserved to gain?"
"And is it not as well dealt out?"
Said Gondul.   "Hearest thou not the shout?
The field is cleared—the foemen run—
The days is ours—the battle won!"

Then Skögul said, "My coal-black steed,
Home to the gods I now must speed,
To their green home, to tell the tiding
That Hakon's self is thither riding."
To Hermod and to Braga then
Said Odin, "Here, the first of men,
Brave Hakon comes, the Norsemen's king—
Go forth, my welcome to him bring."

Fresh from the battle-field came in,
Dripping with blood, the Norsemen's king.
"Methinks," said he, "great Odin's will
Is harsh, and bodes me further ill:
Thy son from off the field to-day
From victory to snatch away!"
But Odin said, "Be thine the joy
Valhalla gives, my own brave boy!"

And Braga said, "Eight brothers here
Welcome thee to Valhalla's cheer,
To drain the cup, or fights repeat
Where Hakon Eric's earls beat."
Quoth the stout king, "And shall my gear,
Helm, sword, and mail-coat, axe and spear,
Be still at hand? 'Tis good to hold
Fast by our trusty friends of old."

Well was it seen that Hakon still
Had saved the temples from all ill [1];
For the whole council of the gods
Welcomed the king to their abodes.
Happy the day when men are born
Like Hakon, who all base things scorn—
Win from the brave an honoured name,
And die amidst an endless fame.

Sooner shall Fenri's wolf devour
The race of man from shore to shore,
Than such a grace to kingly crown
As gallant Hakon want renown.
Life, land, friends, riches, all will fly,
And we in slavery shall sigh. [2]
But Hakon in the blessed abodes
For ever lives with the bright gods.

---

[1] Despite Hakon's Christianity he is praised for having spared or protected the pagan sanctuaries. His Christianity is clearly recognized by the poet, however, for in the last stanza he says that Hakon has gone amongst the *heathen* gods (this is completely lost in the translation above). His earlier praise is consequently to be regarded as commendation of Hakon as an inactive missionary, not as a pious heathen.

[2] Eyvind Skaldaspiller was not well disposed to the sons of Eric, who succeeded Hakon; cf. pp. 112–14.

V

THE SONS OF ERIC

CHAPTER I. ON THE SONS OF ERIC; AND EYVIND SKALDASPILLER [961].—When King Hakon was killed, the sons of Eric took the sovereignty of Norway. Harald, who was the oldest of the living brothers,[1] was over them ·in dignity. Their mother Gunhild, who was called the King-mother, mixed herself much in the affairs of the country. There were many chiefs in the land at that time. There was Trygve Olafsson[2] in the Eastland, Gudrod Bjornson[2] in the Westfold, Sigurd earl of Lade in the Drontheim land; but Gunhild's sons held the middle of the country the first winter. There went messages and ambassadors between Gunhild's sons and Trygve and Gudrod, and all was settled upon the footing that they should hold from Gunhild's sons the same part of the country which they formerly had held under King Hakon. A man called Glum Geirason, who was King Harald's scald, and was a very brave man, made this song upon King Hakon's death:

> Gamle is avenged by Harald!
> Great is thy deed, thou champion bold!
> The rumour of it came to me
> In distant lands beyond the sea,
> How Harald gave King Hakon's blood
> To Odin's ravens for their food.

This song was much favoured. When Eyvind Finnson heard of it he composed the song which was given before (p. 104), viz.:

> Our dauntless king with Gamle's gore
> Sprinkled his bright sword o'er and o'er, etc.

This song also was much favoured, and was spread widely abroad; and when King Harald came to hear of it, he laid a charge against Eyvind affecting his life; but friends made up the quarrel, on the condition that Eyvind should in future be Harald's scald, as he had formerly been King Hakon's. There

---

[1] The following text down to p. 126 is usually known as the saga of Harald Greycloak. On the dates here and in the following pages cf. Chronological Note, p. 117

[2] Grandsons of Harald Fairhair, cf. p. 82.

was also some relationship between them, as Gunhild, Eyvind's
mother, was a daughter of Earl Halfdan, and her mother was
a daughter of Harald Fairhair. Thereafter Eyvind made a
song about King Harald:

> Guardian of Norway, well we know
> Thy heart failed not when from the bow
> The piercing arrow-hail sharp rang
> On shield and breast-plate, and the clang
> Of sword resounded in the press
> Of battle, like the splitting ice;
> For Harald, wild wolf of the wood,
> Must drink his fill of foemen's blood.

Gunhild's sons resided mostly in the middle of the country,
for they did not think it safe for them to dwell among the
people of Drontheim or of Viken, where King Hakon's best
friends lived; and also in both places there were many powerful
men. Proposals of agreement then passed between Gunhild's
sons and Earl Sigurd, for they got no scatt from the Drontheim
country; and at last an agreement was concluded between the
kings and the earl, and confirmed by oath. Earl Sigurd was
to get the same power in the Drontheim land which he had
possessed under King Hakon, and on that they considered
themselves at peace. All Gunhild's sons had the character of
being penurious; and it was said they hid their money in the
ground. Eyvind Skaldaspiller made a song about this:

> Main-mast of battle! Harald bold!
> In Hakon's days the scald wore gold
> Upon his falcon's seat [1]; he wore
> Rolf Krake's seed,[2] the yellow ore,
> Sown by him as he fled away,
> The avenger Adils' speed to stay.
> The gold crop grows upon the plain;
> But Frode's girls so gay [3] in vain
> Grind out the golden meal, while those
> Who rule o'er Norway's realm like foes,
> In mother earth's old bosom hide
> The wealth which Hakon far and wide
> Scattered with generous hand: the sun
> Shone in the days of that great one,
> On the gold band of Fulla's brow,[4]

---

[1] A *kenning* for hand.

[2] According to the legend, Rolf Krake scattered gold in his flight on the
plains of Fyris in order to divert the pursuit of Adils and his men; see *The
Prose Edda*, trans. J. Young, 1954, pp. 119–21.

[3] Menia and Fenia were strong girls of the giant race, whom Frode bought
in Sweden to grind gold and good luck to him; and their meal means
gold. Cf. *The Prose Edda*, ed. cit., p. 118.

[4] This last sentence is properly construed: "The sun of Fulla's brow
shone on the poets' arms in Hakon's days." Fulla is described as a goddess
who wore a gold head-band, so the "sun of her brow" is a *kenning* for gold.

On gold-ringed hands that bend the bow,
On the scald's hand; but of the ray
Of bright gold, glancing like the spray
Of sun-lit waves, no scald now sings—
Buried are golden chains and rings.

Now when King Harald heard this song, he sent a message
to Eyvind to come to him, and when Eyvind came made a
charge against him of being unfaithful. "And it ill becomes
thee," said the king, "to be my enemy, as thou hast entered
into my service." Eyvind then made these verses:

One lord I had before thee, Harald!
One dear-loved lord! Now am I old,
And do not wish to change again.—
To that loved lord, through strife and pain,
Faithful I stood; still true to Hakon—
To my good king, and him alone.
But now I'm old and useless grown,
My hands are empty, wealth is flown;
I am but fit for a short space
In thy court-hall to fill a place.

But King Harald forced Eyvind to submit himself to his
clemency. Eyvind had a great gold ring, which was called
Molde, that had been dug up out of the earth long since. This
ring the king said he must have as the mulct for the offence;
and there was no help for it. Then Eyvind sang:

I go across the ocean-foam,
Swift skating to my Iceland home
Upon the ocean-skates, fast driven
By gales by Thurse's witch-wife given.
For from the falcon-bearing hand
Harald has plucked the gold snake-band
My father wore—by lawless might
Has taken what is mine by right.

Eyvind went home; but it is not told that he ever came near
the king again.

CHAPTER II. OF THE CHRISTIANITY OF GUNHILD'S SONS —
Gunhild's sons embraced Christianity in England, as told before
(p. 86); but when they came to rule over Norway they made
no progress in spreading Christianity—only they pulled down
the temples of the idols, and cast away the sacrifices where
they had it in their power, and raised great animosity by doing
so. The good crops of the country were soon wasted in their
days, because there were many kings, and each had his hird
about him. They had therefore great expenses, and were very
greedy. Besides, they only observed those laws of King Hakon
which suited themselves. They were, however, all of them

remarkably handsome men—stout, strong, and expert in all exercises. So says Glum Geirason, in the verses he composed about Harald, Gunhild's son:

> The foeman's terror, Harald bold,
> Had gained enough of yellow gold;
> Had Heimdal's teeth [1] enough in store,
> And understood twelve arts or more.

The brothers sometimes went out on expeditions together, and sometimes each on his own account. They were fierce, but brave and active; and great warriors, and very successful.

CHAPTER III. OF THE COUNCILS HELD BY GUNHILD AND HER SONS.—Gunhild the King-mother, and her sons, often met, and talked together upon the government of the country. Once Gunhild asked her sons what they intended to do with their kingdom of Drontheim. "Ye have the title of king, as your forefathers had before you; but you have little land or people, and there are many to divide with. In the East, as Viken, there are Trygve and Gudrod; and they have some right by their descent to their governments. There is besides Earl Sigurd ruling over the whole Drontheim country; and no reason can I see why ye let so large a kingdom be ruled by an earl, and not by yourselves. It appears wonderful to me that ye go every summer upon viking cruises against other lands, and allow an earl within the country to take your father's heritage from you. Your grandfather, whose name you bear, King Harald, thought it but a small matter to take an earl's life and land when he subdued all Norway, and held it under him to old age."

Harald replied, "It is not so easy, mother, to cut off Earl Sigurd as to slay a kid or a calf. Earl Sigurd is of high birth, powerful in relations, popular, and prudent; and I think if the Drontheim people knew for certain there was enmity between us, they would all take his side, and we could expect only evil from them. I don't think it would be safe for any of us brothers to fall into the hands of the Drontheim people."

Then said Gunhild, "We shall go to work another way, and not put ourselves forward. Harald and Erling shall come in harvest to Nordmöre, and there I shall meet you, and we shall consult together what is to be done." And so they did.

---

[1] Heimdal was one of the gods; he kept watch against the giants. One of his names was Gold-toothed. "Heimdal's teeth" is thus a *kenning* for gold. See further *The Prose Edda*, trans. J. Young, 1954, p. 54.

CHAPTER IV. THE PLANS OF GUNHILD'S SONS AND GRJOT-GAARD.—Earl Sigurd had a brother called Grjotgaard, who was much younger, and much less respected, having no title of distinction. He had many people, however, about him, and in summer went on viking cruises, and gathered to himself property. Now King Harald sent messengers to Drontheim with offers of friendship, and with presents. The messengers declared that King Harald was willing to be on the same friendly terms with the earl that King Hakon had been: adding, that they wished the earl to come to King Harald, that their friendship might be put on a firm footing. The Earl Sigurd received well the king's messengers and friendly message, but said that on account of his many affairs he could not come to the king. He sent many friendly gifts, and many glad and grateful words to the king, in return for his friendship. With this reply the messengers set off, and went to Grjotgaard, for whom they had the same message, and brought him good presents, and offered him King Harald's friendship, and invited him to visit the king. Grjotgaard promised to come; and at the appointed time he paid a visit to King Harald and Gunhild, and was received in the most friendly manner. They treated him on the most intimate footing, so that Grjotgaard had access to their private consultations and secret councils. At last the conversation, by an understanding between the king and queen, was turned upon Earl Sigurd; and they spoke to Grjotgaard about the earl having kept him so long in obscurity, and asked him if he would not join the king's brothers in an attack on the earl. If he would join with them, the king promised Grjotgaard that he should be his earl, and have the same government that Sigurd had. It came so far that a secret agreement was made between them, that Grjotgaard should spy out the most favourable opportunity of attacking by surprise Earl Sigurd, and should give King Harald notice of it. After this agreement Grjotgaard returned home with many good presents from the king.

CHAPTER V. EARL SIGURD BURNT IN A HOUSE IN STJORDAL.—Earl Sigurd went in harvest into Stjordal to guest-quarters, and from thence went to Oglo to a feast. The earl usually had many people about him, for he did not trust the king; but now, after friendly messages had passed between the king and him, he had no great following of people with him. Then Grjotgaard sent word to the king that he could never expect a better opportunity to fall upon Earl Sigurd; and immediately, that very evening, Harald and Erling sailed into Drontheim fjord and had four ships and many people. They sailed all night by starlight, and Grjotgaard came out to meet them. Late in the night they came to Oglo,[1] where Earl Sigurd was at the feast, and set fire to the house; and burnt the house, the earl, and all his men. As soon as it was daylight they set out through the fjord, and south to Möre, where they remained a long time.

[1] Oglo is the later Skatval in Nedre Stjördal, about thirty miles up the fjord from Trondheim.

A Chronological Note

The dates given in this section and in the following (to p. 126) are by no means certain. The death of Hakon Athelstan's foster-son can only be approximately established between the probable limits of 961 and 966. The next certain date is 974, when it is known that Earl Hakon was ruling in Norway under the suzerainty of King Harald Gormsson of Denmark. The dates given above depend on the assignment of Hakon's death to 961 and on the accuracy of Snorri's chronology in reckoning Earl Sigurd's death two years after Hakon's and then three years of strife followed by three years of friendship between Earl Hakon and the sons of Eric. This eight years allotted to the rule of the sons of Eric may well be too much.

VI

EARL HAKON

CHAPTER I. OF EARL HAKON, SIGURD'S SON [963].—Hakon, the son of Earl Sigurd, was up in the interior of the Drontheim country [1] when he heard this news. Great was the tumult through all the Drontheim land, and every vessel that could float was put into the water; and as soon as the people were gathered together they took Earl Sigurd's son Hakon to be their earl and the leader of the troops, and the whole body steered out of Drontheim fjord. When Gunhild's sons heard of this, they set off southwards to Raumsdal and South Möre; and both parties kept eye on each other by their spies. Earl Sigurd was killed two years after the fall of King Hakon. So says Eyvind Skaldaspiller in the "Haleygja-tal":

> At Oglo, as I've heard, Earl Sigurd
> Was burnt to death by Norway's lord—
> Sigurd, who once on Hadding's grave
> A feast to Odin's ravens gave.
> In Oglo's hall, amidst the feast,
> When bowls went round and ale flow'd fast,
> He perished: Harald lit the fire
> Which burnt to death the son of Tyr. [2]

Earl Hakon, with the help of his friends, maintained himself in the Drontheim country for three years [963-5]; and during that time Gunhild's sons got no revenues from it. Hakon had several battles with Gunhild's sons, and many a man lost his life on both sides. Of this Einar Skalaglam [3] speaks in his lay called "Vellekla," which he composed about Earl Hakon:

> The sharp bow-shooter on the sea
> Spread wide his fleet, for well loved he
> The battle storm; well loved the earl
> His battle-banner to unfurl.
> O'er the well-trampled battle-field
> He raised the red moon of his shield;
> And often dared King Eric's son
> To try the fray with the Earl Hakon.

---

[1] i.e. in Innherad.
[2] Tyr was one of the gods.
[3] An Icelander. The title of his poem means "gold-dearth.'

And he also says:

> Who is the man who'll dare to say
> That Sigurd's son avoids the fray?
> He gluts the raven—he ne'er fears
> The arrow's song or flight of spears.
> With thundering sword he storms in war,
> As Odin dreadful; or from far
> He makes the arrow-shower fly
> To swell the sail of victory.
> The victory was dearly bought,
> And many a viking-fight was fought
> Before the swinger of the sword
> Was of the eastern country lord.

And Einar tells also how Earl Hakon avenged his father's murder:

> I praise the man, my hero he,
> Who in his good ship roves the sea,
> Like bird of prey, intent to win
> Red vengeance for his slaughtered kin.
> From his blue sword the iron rain
> That freezes life poured down amain
> On him who took his father's life,
> On him and his men in the strife.
> To Odin many a soul was driven—
> To Odin many a rich gift given.
> Loud raged the storm on battle-field—
> Axe rang on helm, and sword on shield.

The friends on both sides at last laid themselves between, and brought proposals of peace; for the bonder suffered by this strife and war in the land. At last it was brought to this, by the advice of mighty men, that Earl Hakon should have the same power in the Drontheim land which his father Earl Sigurd had enjoyed; and the kings, on the other hand, should have the same dominion as King Hakon had; and this agreement was settled with the fullest promises of fidelity to it. Afterwards a great friendship arose between Earl Hakon and Gunhild, although they sometimes attempted to deceive each other. And thus matters stood for three years longer [966–8], in which time Earl Hakon sat quietly in his dominions.

CHAPTER II. OF HARALD GREYCLOAK.—King Harald had generally his seat in Hordaland and Rogaland, and so had his brothers; and very often then they stayed in Hardanger. One summer it happened that a vessel came from Iceland belonging to Icelanders, with woven cloaks as merchandise. They sailed to Hardanger, where they heard that a great number of people were assembled; but when the folks came to deal with them, nobody would buy their wares. Then the skipper went to King Harald, whom he had been acquainted with before, and complained of his ill luck. The king promised to visit him, and did so. King Harald was very condescending, and full of fun. He came with a fully-manned boat, looked at the goods, and then said to the skipper, "Wilt thou give me a present of one of these grey cloaks?"[1] "Willingly," said the steersman, "if it were ever so many." On this the king wrapped himself up in one of them, and went back to his boat; but before they rowed away from the ship, every man in his suite bought just such a grey cloak as the king wore for himself. In a few days so many men came to buy cloaks, that not half of them could be served with what they wanted; and thereafter the king was called Harald Greycloak.

CHAPTER III. EARL ERIC'S BIRTH.—Earl Hakon came one winter to the Uplands to a feast, and it so happened that he had intercourse with a girl of mean birth. Some time after the girl had to prepare for her confinement; and she bore a child, a boy, who had water poured on him, and was named Eric. The mother carried the boy to Earl Hakon, and said that he was the father. The earl placed him to be brought up with a man called Torleiv the Wise, who dwelt in Medaldal,[2] and was a rich and powerful man, and a great friend of the earl. Eric gave hopes very early that he would become an able man, was handsome in countenance, and stout and strong for a child; but the earl did not pay much attention to him. The earl himself was one of the handsomest men in countenance—not tall, but very strong, and well practised in all kinds of exercises; and withal prudent, of good understanding, and a deadly man at arms.

CHAPTER IV. KING TRYGVE OLAFSON'S MURDER.—It happened one harvest that Earl Hakon, on a journey in the Uplands, came to Hedemark; and King Trygve Olafson and King Gudrod Björnson met him there, and Dale-Gudbrand also came to the meeting. They had agreed to meet, and they as usual talked together long by themselves; but so much only was known of their business, that they were to be friends of each other. They parted, and each went home to his own kingdom. Gunhild and her sons came to hear of this meeting, and they suspected it must have been to lay a treasonable plot against the kings; and they often talked of this among themselves. When spring began to set in, King Harald and his brother King

---

[1] These cloaks were made from cloth that had bunches of woollen strands knotted into it; on the outside they thus resembled fleeces.
[2] Now Meldal in Orkedalen.

Gudrod proclaimed that they were to make a viking cruise as usual, either in the West sea, or the Baltic. The people accordingly assembled, launched the ships into the sea, and made themselves ready to sail. When they were drinking the farewell ale—and they drank bravely—much and many things were talked over at the drink-table, and, among other things, were comparisons between different men, and at last between the kings themselves. One said that King Harald excelled his brothers by far, and in every way. On this King Gudrod was very angry, and said that he was in no respect behind Harald, and was ready to prove it. Instantly both parties were so inflamed that they challenged each other to battle, and ran to their arms. But some of the guests who were less drunk, and had more understanding, came between them, and quieted them; and each went to his ship, but nobody expected that they would all sail together. Gudrod sailed eastward along the land, and Harald went out to sea, saying he would go to the westward; but when he came outside of the islands he steered east along the coast, outside of the rocks and isles. Gudrod, again, sailed inside, through the usual channel, to Viken, and eastwards to Folden. He then sent a message to King Trygve to meet him, that they might make a cruise together in summer in the Baltic to plunder. Trygve accepted the invitation willingly, and as a friend; and as he heard King Gudrod had but few people with him, he came to meet him with a single boat. They met at Vegger, to the east of Sotenes[1]; but just as they were come to the meeting place, Gudrod's men ran up and killed King Trygve and twelve men. He lies buried at a place called Trygve's Cairn.[2]

CHAPTER V. KING GUDROD'S FALL.—King Harald sailed far outside of the rocks and isles; but set his course to Viken, and came in the night time to Tunsberg, and heard that Gudrod Björnson was at a feast a little way up the country. Then King Harald set out immediately with his followers, came in the night, and surrounded the house. King Gudrod Björnson went out with his people; but after a short resistance he fell, and many men with him. Then King Harald joined his brother King Gudrod, and they subdued all Viken.

CHAPTER VI. OF HARALD GRENSKE.—King Gudrod Björnson had made a good and suitable marriage, and had by his

[1] The peninsula between Aabyfjord and Sotefjord, in Bohuslen. Vegger is Wægga on the Sotenes.
[2] At Tryggöen on the west side of the Sotenes peninsula.

wife a son called Harald, who had been sent to be fostered to Grenland [1] to a lenderman called Roe the White. Roe's son, called Rane the Far-travelled, was Harald's foster-brother, and about the same age. After his father Gudrod's fall, Harald, who was called Grenske, fled to the Uplands, and with him his foster-brother Rane, and a few people. Harald stayed a while there among his relations; but as Eric's sons sought after every man who interfered with them, and especially those who might oppose them, Harald Grenske's friends and relations advised him to leave the country. Harald therefore went eastward into Sweden, and sought shipmates, that he might enter into company with those who went out a-cruising to gather property. Harald became in this way a remarkably able man. There was a man in Sweden at that time called Toste, one of the most powerful and noble in the land among those who had no high name or dignity; and he was a great warrior, who had been often in battle, and was therefore called Skögul Toste. [2] Harald Grenske came into his company, and cruised with Toste in summer; and wherever Harald came he was well thought of by everyone. In the winter Harald, after passing two years in the Uplands, took up his abode with Toste, and lived five years with him. Toste had a daughter, who was both young and handsome, but she was proud and high-minded. She was called Sigrid, and was afterwards married to the Swedish king, Eric the Successful, and had a son by him, called Olaf the Swede, who was afterwards King of Sweden. King Eric died in a sick-bed at Upsal, ten years after the death of Styrbjorn.

CHAPTER VII. EARL HAKON'S FEUDS [968].—Gunhild's sons levied a great army in Viken, and sailed along the land northwards, collecting people and ships on the way out of every district. They then made known their intent, to proceed northwards with their army against Earl Hakon in Drontheim. When Earl Hakon heard this news, he also collected men, and fitted out ships; and when he heard what an overwhelming force Gunhild's sons had with them, he steered south with his fleet to Möre, pillaging wherever he came, and killing many people, both rich and poor. He then sent the whole of the bonder army back to Drontheim; but he himself, with his men-at-arms, proceeded by both the districts of Möre and Raumsdal, and had his spies out to the south of Stad to spy the army of Gun-

---

[1] Grenland, the district between Vestfold and East Agder (cf. p. 99, note 1).
[2] i.e. warlike Toste. Skögul is a valkyrie's name.

hild's sons; and when he heard they were come into the Fjords, and were waiting for a fair wind to sail northwards round Stad, Earl Hakon set out to sea from the north side of Stad, so far that his sails could not be seen from the land, and then sailed eastward on a line with the coast, and came to Denmark, from whence he sailed into the Baltic, and pillaged there during the summer. Gunhild's sons conducted their army north to Drontheim, and remained there the whole summer collecting the scatt and duties. But when summer was advanced they left Sigurd Sleva and Gudrod behind; and the other brothers returned eastward with the levied army they had taken up in summer.

CHAPTER VIII. OF EARL HAKON AND GUNHILD'S SONS.— Earl Hakon, towards harvest, sailed into the Bothnian Gulf to Helsingeland, drew his ships up there on the beach, and took the land-ways through Helsingeland and Jemteland, and so westwards round the dividing ridge (Kjölen, the keel of the country), and down into the Drontheim district. Many people streamed towards him, and he fitted out ships. When the sons of Gunhild heard of this, they got on board their ships, and sailed out of the fjord; and Earl Hakon came to his seat at Lade, and remained there all winter. The sons of Gunhild, on the other hand, occupied Möre; and they and the earl attacked each other in turns, killing each other's people. Earl Hakon kept his dominions of Drontheim, and was there generally in the winter; but in summer he sometimes went to Helsingeland, where he went on board of his ships and sailed with them down into the Baltic, and plundered there; and sometimes he remained in Drontheim, and kept an army on foot, so that Gunhild's sons could get no hold northwards of Stad.

CHAPTER IX. SIGURD SLEVA'S MURDER.—One summer Harald Greycloak and his troops went north to Bjarmeland,[1] where he forayed, and fought a great battle with the inhabitants on the banks of the Dvina. King Harald gained the victory, killed many people, plundered and wasted and burned far and wide in the land, and made enormous booty. Glum Geirason tells of it thus:

> I saw the hero Harald chase
> With bloody sword Bjarme's race:
> They fly before him through the night,
> All by their burning city's light
> On Dvina's bank, at Harald's word,
> Arose the storm of spear and sword.
> In such a wild war-cruise as this,
> Great would he be who could bring peace.

---

[1] The coast of the White Sea. This name is supposed to be still retained in the name Permia given to the Kola peninsula.

King Sigurd Sleva came to Herse [1] Klypp's house. Klypp was a son of Tord, and a grandson of Horda-Kaare, and was a man of power and great family. He was not at home; but his wife Aalof gave a good reception to the king, and made a great feast at which there was much drinking. Aalof was a daughter of Asbjorn, and sister to Jernskjægge,[2] north in Yrjar. Asbjorn's brother was called Reidar, who was father to Styrkar, whose son was Eindride, father of Einar Tambarskjelve. In the night the king went to bed to Aalof against her will, and then set out on his journey. The harvest thereafter, King Harald and his brother King Sigurd Sleva went to Voss, and summoned the bonder to a Thing. There the bonder fell on them, and would have killed them, but they escaped and took different roads. King Harald went to Hardanger, but King Sigurd to Alrekstad. Now when Herse Klypp heard of this, he and his relations assembled to attack Sigurd; and Vemund Volubrjot was chief of their troop. And when they came to the house they attacked the king, and Herse Klypp, it is said, ran him through with his sword and killed him; but instantly Klypp was killed on the spot by Erling Gamle.

CHAPTER X. GRJOTGAARD'S FALL.—King Harald Greycloak and his brother King Gudrod gathered together a great army in the east country, with which they set out northwards to Drontheim. When Earl Hakon heard of it he collected men, and set out to Möre, where he plundered. There his father's brother, Grjotgaard, had the command and defence of the country on behalf of Gunhild's sons, and he assembled an army by order of the kings. Earl Hakon advanced to meet him, and gave him battle; and there fell Grjotgaard and two other earls, and many a man besides. So says Einar Skalaglam:

> The helm-crown'd Hakon, brave as stout,
> Again has put his foes to rout.
> The bowl runs o'er with Odin's mead,[3]
> That fires the scald when mighty deed
> Has to be sung. Earl Hakon's sword,
> In single combat, as I've heard,
> Three sons of earls from this one fray
> To dwell with Odin drove away.[4]

Thereafter Earl Hakon went out to sea, and sailed outside the coast, and came to Denmark. He went to the Danish

[1] Cf. p. 45, note 2.
[2] Jernskjægge—iron-beard.
[3] Odin's mead, i.e. poetry. How Odin gained the mead of poetry is told in *The Prose Edda*, trans. J. Young, 1954, pp. 100–3.
[4] To dwell with Odin—viz. slew them.

king, Harald Gormson, and was well received by him, and stayed with him all winter. At that time there was also with the Danish king a man called Harald, a son of Knut Gormson, and a brother's son of King Harald. He was lately come home from a long viking cruise, on which he had gathered great riches, and therefore he was called Gold Harald. He seemed to stand a good chance of coming to the Danish kingdom.

CHAPTER XI. KING ERLING'S FALL.—King Harald Greycloak and his brothers proceeded northwards to Drontheim, where they met no opposition. They levied the scatt duties, and all other revenues, and laid heavy penalties upon the bonder; for the kings had for a long time received but little income from Drontheim, because Earl Hakon was there with many troops, and was at variance with these kings. In autumn King Harald went south with the greater part of the men-at-arms, but King Erling remained behind with his men. He raised great contributions from the bonder, and pressed severely on them; at which the bonder murmured greatly, and submitted to their losses with impatience. In winter they gathered together in a great force to go against King Erling, just as he was at a feast; and they gave battle to him, and he with the most of his men fell.

CHAPTER XII. OF THE SEASONS IN NORWAY AT THIS TIME.— While Gunhild's sons reigned in Norway the seasons were always bad, and the longer they reigned the worse were the crops; and the bonder laid the blame on them. They were very greedy, and used the bonder harshly. It came at length to be so bad that fish, as well as corn, were wanting. In Halogaland there was the greatest famine and distress; for scarcely any corn grew, and even snow was lying, and the cattle were bound in the farm-byres all over the country until midsummer. Eyvind Skaldaspiller describes it in his poem, as he came outside of his house and found a thick snow-drift at that season:

> 'Tis midsummer, yet deep snows rest
> On Odin's spouse's frozen breast [1]:
> Like Laplanders, our cattle-kind
> In stall or stable we must bind.

CHAPTER XIII. OF THE ICELANDERS AND EYVIND SKALDA-SPILLER.—Eyvind composed a poem about the people of Iceland, for which they rewarded him by each bonde giving him three

---

[1] Jörd (Earth) was said to have been Odin's daughter and wife.

silver pennies, of full weight and white in the fracture. And when the silver was brought together at the General Thing, the people resolved to have it purified, and made into a shoulder-pin, and after the workmanship of the silver was paid, the shoulder-pin weighed some fifty marks.[1] This they sent to Eyvind; but Eyvind had the shoulder-pin broken into pieces, and with the silver he bought a farmstead for himself. But the same spring a shoal of herrings set in upon the fishing ground beyond the coast-side; and Eyvind manned a ship's boat with his house servants and cottars, and rowed to where the herrings were come, and sang:

> Now let the steed of ocean bound
> O'er the North Sea with dashing sound;
> Let nimble tern and screaming gull
> Fly round and round—our net is full.
> Fain would I know if Fortune sends
> A like provision to my friends.
> Welcome provision 'tis, I wot,
> That the whale drives to our cook's pot.

So entirely were his movable goods exhausted, that he was obliged to sell his arrows to buy herrings, and he spoke this verse:

> Our arms and ornaments of gold
> To buy us food we gladly sold:
> The arrows of the bow gave we
> For the bright arrows of the sea.[2]

---

[1] The shoulder-pin was used to secure a cloak. One weighing 50 marks (25 lb.) was obviously better spent on a farm.
[2] Herrings, from their swift darting along, are called the arrows of the sea.

VII.   KING OLAF TRYGVESSON.

(See *Vol.* 717, *Everyman's Library*.)

VIII.   KING OLAF THE SAINT.

(See *Vol.* 717, *Everyman's Library*.)

IX

MAGNUS THE GOOD

[1035-47]

CHAPTER I. MAGNUS OLAFSON'S JOURNEY FROM THE EAST.—
After Yule Magnus Olafson began his journey from the East
from Novgorod to Ladoga, where he rigged out his ships as
soon as the ice was loosened in spring. Arnor, the earls' scald,
tells of this in the poem on Magnus:

> It is no loose report that he,
> Who will command on land and sea,
> In blood will make his foemen feel
> Olaf's sword Hneiter's sharp blue steel.
> This generous youth, who scatters gold,
> Norway's brave son, but ten years old,
> Is rigging ships in Russia's lake,
> His crown, with friends' support, to take.

In spring Magnus sailed from the East to Sweden. So
says Arnor:

> The young sword-stainer called a Thing,
> Where all his men should meet their king:
> Heroes who find the eagle food
> Before their lord in arms stood.
> And now the curved plank of the bow
> Cleaves the blue sea; the ocean-plough,
> By grey winds driven across the main,
> Reaches Sigtuna's grassy plain.

Here it is related that when King Magnus and his fellow-
travellers sailed from the East to Sweden, they brought up at
Sigtuna. Onund Olafson was then king in Sweden. Queen
Astrid, who had been married to King Olaf the Saint, was also
there. She received very gladly and well her stepson[1] King
Magnus, and summoned immediately a numerous Thing of
Swedes at a place called Hangrar.[2] At the Thing Queen Astrid
spoke these words: "Here is come to us a son of Olaf the Saint,
called Magnus, who intends to make an expedition to Norway
to seek his father's heritage. It is my great duty to give him
aid towards this expedition; for he is my stepson, as is known
to all, both Swedes and Norwegians. Neither shall he want

[1] See p. 132, chapter vii.
[2] An unknown place near Sigtuna. The Thing place of Aattundaland
was in Lunda parish in Seminghundra, and at a later date was called
Folklands Thing.

men or money, in so far as I can procure them or have influence, in order that his strength may be as great as possible; and all the men who will support this cause of his shall have my fullest friendship; and I would have it known that I intend myself to go with him on this attempt, that all may see I will spare nothing that is in my power to help him." She spoke long and cleverly in this strain; but when she had ended many replied thus: "The Swedes made no honourable progress in Norway when they followed King Olaf his father, and now no better success is to be expected, as this man is but in years of boyhood; and therefore we have little inclination for this expedition." Astrid replies: "All men who wish to be thought of true courage must not be deterred by such considerations. If any have lost connections at the side of King Olaf, or been themselves wounded, now is the time to show a man's heart and courage, and go to Norway to take vengeance." Astrid succeeded so far with words and encouragement that many men determined to go with her, and follow King Magnus to Norway. Sigvat the scald speaks of this:

> Now Astrid, Olaf's widowed queen—
> She who so many a change had seen—
> Took all the gifts of happier days,
> Jewels and rings, all she could raise,
> And at a Thing at Hangrar, where
> The Swedes were numerous, did declare
> What Olaf's son proposed to do,
> And brought her gifts—their pay—in view.

> And with the Swedes no wiser plan,
> To bring out every brave bold man,
> Could have been found, had Magnus been
> The son himself of the good queen.
> With help of Christ, she hoped to bring
> Magnus to be the land's sole king,
> As Harald was, who in his day
> Obtained o'er all the upper sway.

> And glad are we so well she sped—
> The people's friend is now their head;
> And good King Magnus always shows
> How much he to Queen Astrid owes.
> Such stepmothers as this good queen
> In truth are very rarely seen;
> And to this noble woman's praise
> The scald with joy his song will raise.

Thjodolf the scald also says in his song of Magnus:

> When thy brave ship left the land,
> The bending yard could scarce withstand
> The fury of the whistling gale,
> That split thy many-coloured sail;

> And many a stout ship, tempest-tost,
> Was in that howling storm lost
> That brought thee safe to Sigtun's shore,
> Far from the sound of ocean's roar.

CHAPTER II. MAGNUS'S EXPEDITION FROM SWEDEN.—King Magnus set out on his journey from Sigtuna with a great force, which he had gathered in Sweden. They proceeded through Sweden on foot to Helsingeland. So says Arnor, the earls' scald:

> And many a dark-red Swedish shield
> Marched with thee from the Swedish field.
> The country people crowded in,
> To help Saint Olaf's son to win;
> And chosen men by thee were led,
> Men who have stained the wolf's tongue red.
> Each milk-white shield and polished spear
> Came to a splendid gathering there.

Magnus Olafson went from the East through Jemteland over the keel-ridge of the country, and came down upon the Drontheim district, where all men welcomed the king with joy. But no sooner did the men of King Svein[1], the son of Alfiva, hear that King Magnus Olafson was come to the country, than they fled on all sides and made themselves safe, so that no opposition was made to King Magnus; for King Svein was in the south part of the country. So says Arnor, the earls' scald:

> He who the eagle's talons stains
> Rushed from the East on Drontheim's plains;
> The terror of his plumed helm
> Drove his pale foemen from the realm.
> The lightning of thy eye so near,
> Great king! thy foemen could not bear.
> Scattered they fled—their only care
> If thou their wretched lives wilt spare.

CHAPTER III. MAGNUS MADE KING. — Magnus Olafson advanced to Kaupangen, where he was joyfully received. He then summoned the people to the Eyra-Thing[2]; and when the bonder met at the Thing, Magnus was taken to be king over the whole land, as far as his father Olaf had possessed it. Then

---

[1] The eldest son of Canute the Great by an English lady, Aelfgifu of Northampton. Canute's other son by her was Harald I, King of England, 1035–40, called "Harefoot" (cf. pp. 131, 141). Hardacanute, on the other hand, was Canute's son by Queen Emma. These illegitimate sons of a monarch were thought to have a fair claim to the throne, cf. p. 65, note 2.

[2] Eyra Thing (Öre Thing) was held on the spit of land dividing the fjord and the estuary just outside the original township of Trondheim. It was at first the central thing-place for the whole of the Trondheim district (cf. p. 91, note 3), later particularly for Trondheim and the districts in its immediate vicinity. On its importance cf. p. 295.

the king selected a court, and named lendermen, and placed bailiffs and officers in all domains and offices. Immediately after harvest King Magnus ordered a levy through all Drontheim land, and he collected men readily; and thereafter he proceeded southwards along the coast.

CHAPTER IV. KING SVEIN'S FLIGHT.—King Svein Alfivason was staying in South Hordaland when he heard this news of war. He immediately sent out war-tokens to four different quarters, summoned the bonder to him, and made it known to all that they should join him with men and ships to defend the country. All the men who were in the neighbourhood of the king presented themselves; and the king formed a Thing, at which in a speech he set forth his business, and said he would advance against Magnus Olafson and have a battle with him, if the bonder would aid his cause. The king's speech was not very long, and was not received with much approbation by the bonder. Afterwards the Danish chiefs who were about the king made long and clever speeches; but the bonder then took up the word, and answered them; and although many said they would follow Svein, and fight on his side, some refused to do so bluntly, some were altogether silent, and some declared they would join King Magnus as soon as they had an opportunity. Then King Svein says: "Methinks very few of the bonder to whom we sent a message have appeared here; and of those who have come, and tell us to our face that they will join King Magnus as soon as they can, we shall have as little benefit as of those who say they will sit at home quietly. It is the same with those who say nothing at all. But as to those who promise to help us, every second man, or more, will prove to be missing when we go into battle against King Magnus. It is my counsel, therefore, that we do not trust to these bonder; but let us rather go to the land where all the people are sure and true to us, and where we will obtain forces to conquer this country again." As soon as the king had made known this resolution all his men followed it, turned their ships' bows, and hoisted sail. King Svein sailed eastward along the land, and then set right over to Denmark without delay, and Hardacanute received his brother Svein very kindly. At their first meeting Hardacanute offered King Svein to divide the kingdom of Denmark with him, which offer King Svein accepted.

In autumn King Magnus proceeded eastward to the end of the country, and was received as king throughout the whole land, and the country people were rejoiced at his arrival.

CHAPTER V. DEATH OF KING CANUTE THE GREAT AND HIS
SON SVEIN [1035].—King Svein, Canute's son, went to Denmark as before related, and took part in the government with
his brother Hardacanute. In the same autumn King Canute
the Great died in England,[1] 13 November, forty years old, and
was buried at Winchester. He had been King of Denmark
for twenty-seven years, and over Denmark and England together
twenty-four years,[2] and also over Norway for seven years. King
Canute's son Harald was then made king in England. The
same winter King Svein, Alfiva's son, died in Denmark. Thjodolf
the scald made these lines concerning King Magnus:

> Through Sweden's dirty roads the throng
> Followed the king in spearmen strong.
> Svein now flies, in truth afraid,
> And partly by his men betrayed:
> Flying to Denmark o'er the sea,
> He leaves the land quite clear to thee.

Bjorn Gulbraascald composed the following lines concerning
Kalv Arneson:

> By thee the kings got each his own,—
> Magnus by thee got Norway's throne;
> And Svein in Denmark got a seat,
> When out of Norway he was beat.
> Kalv! it was you who showed the way
> To our young king, the battle-lover,—
> From Russia to his father's sway
> You showed the way, and brought him over.

King Magnus ruled over Norway this winter, and Hardacanute over Denmark.

CHAPTER VI. FEALTY BETWEEN KING HARDACANUTE AND
KING MAGNUS [1036].—The following spring the kings on both
sides ordered out a levy, and the news was that they would
have a battle at the Gotha river; but when the two armies
approached each other, the lendermen in the one army sent
messengers to their connections and friends in the other; and
it came to a proposal for a reconciliation between the two kings,
especially as, from both kings being but young and childish,
some powerful men, who had been chosen in each of the
countries for that purpose, had the rule of the country on their
account. It thus was brought about that there was a friendly

---

[1] Canute ruled England from November 1016 and died on 12 November
1035. He was buried in the cathedral of St. Peter in Winchester.
[2] The figures should be 16 and 19 respectively; for Canute became king
in England in 1016 and in Denmark in 1019. Snorri has reckoned from
the death of Svein Forkbeard, which he incorrectly sets in 1008.

meeting between the kings, and in this meeting a peace was proposed; and the peace was to be a brotherly union under oath to keep the peace towards each other to the end of their lives; and if one of them should die without leaving a son, the longest liver should succeed to the whole land and people. Twelve principal men in each kingdom took oaths with the kings that this treaty should be observed, so long as any one of them was in life. Then the kings separated, and each returned home to his kingdom; and the treaty was kept as long as both lived.

CHAPTER VII. OF QUEEN ASTRID.—Queen Astrid, who had been married to King Olaf the Saint, came to Norway with King Magnus her stepson, as before related, and was held by him deservedly in great honour and esteem. Then came also Alvhild, King Magnus's mother, to the court, and the king received her with the greatest affection, and showed her great respect. But it went with Alvhild, as it does with many who come to power and honour, that pride keeps pace with promotion. She was ill pleased that Queen Astrid was treated with more respect, had a higher seat, and more attention. Alvhild wanted to have a seat next to the king, but Astrid called Alvhild her slave-woman, as indeed she had formerly been when Astrid was Queen of Norway and King Olaf ruled the land, and therefore would on no account let her have a seat beside her, and they could not lodge in the same house.

CHAPTER VIII. OF SIGVAT THE SCALD.—Sigvat the scald had got leave from King Olaf to go home when the king went to Russia. The summer after, Sigvat left the country, and went south to Rome, where he was at the time of the battle of Stiklestad. He made these verses then:

> Tired of war, I left my home,
> And took the saving road to Rome;
> No more the wild wolf's jaws to fill,
> No more the blood of man to spill.
> The gold-entwined sword I left,
> The blue steel sword—the king's own gift;
> And with the pilgrim's staff in hand,
> I took my way through many a land.

In autumn, as Sigvat was on his way back from the South, he heard the tidings of King Olaf's fall, which gave him great grief. He then sang these lines:

> One morning early on a hill,
> The misty towns asleep and still,
> Wandering I thought upon the fields,
> Strewed o'er with broken mail and shields,

Where our king fell—our kind good king,
Where now his happy youthful spring?
My father too!—for Thord [1] was then
One of the good king's chosen men.

One day Sigvat went through a village, and heard a husband
lamenting grievously over the loss of his wife, striking his
breast, tearing his clothes, weeping bitterly, and saying he
wanted to die; and Sigvat sang these lines:

This poor man mourns a much-loved wife,
Gladly would he be quit of life.
Must love be paid for by our grief?
The price seems great for joy so brief.
But the brave man who knows no fear
Drops for his king a silent tear,
And feels, perhaps, his loss as deep
As those who clamour when they weep.

Sigvat came home to Norway to the Drontheim country,
where he had a farm and children. He came from the South
along the coast in a merchant vessel, and as they lay in Hillar [2]
sound they saw a great many ravens flying about. Then
Sigvat said:

I see here many a croaking raven
Flying about the well-known haven:
When Olaf's ship was floating here,
They knew that food for them was near;
When Olaf's ship lay here wind-bound,
Oft screamed the erne o'er Hillar sound,
Impatient for the expected prey,
And wont to follow to the fray.

When Sigvat came north to Kaupangen, King Svein was
there before him. He invited Sigvat to stay with him, as
Sigvat had formerly been with his father King Canute the
Great; but Sigvat said he would first go home to his farm.
One day, as Sigvat was walking in the street, he saw the king's
men at play, and he sang:

One day before I passed this way,
When the king's guards were at their play,
Something there was—I need not tell—
That made me pale, and feel unwell.
Perhaps it was I thought, just then,
How noble Olaf with his men,
In former days, I oft have seen
In manly games upon this green.

Sigvat then went to his farm; and as he heard that many

[1] Thord Sigvaldescald, *Olaf Sagas*, p. 147.
[2] The Sound between Hillö and the mainland south-west of Mandal.

men upbraided him with having deserted King Olaf, he made these verses:

> May Christ condemn me still to burn
> In quenchless fire, if I did turn,
> And leave King Olaf in his need—
> My soul is free from such base deed.
> I was at Rome, as men know well
> Who saw me there, and who can tell
> That there in danger I was then [1]:
> The truth I need not hide from men.

Sigvat was ill at ease in his home. One day he went out and sang:

> While Olaf lived, how smiled the land!—
> Mountain and cliff, and pebbly strand.
> All Norway then, so fresh, so gay,
> On land or sea, where oft I lay.
> But now to me all seems so dreary,
> All black and dull—of life I'm weary:
> Cheerless to-day, cheerless to-morrow—
> Here in the North we have great sorrow.

Early this winter [1031] Sigvat went eastward over the ridge of the country to Jemteland, and onwards to Helsingeland, and came to Sweden. He went immediately to Queen Astrid, and was with her a long time, and was a welcome guest. He was also with her brother King Onund, and received from him ten marks of proved silver, as is related in the song of Canute. Sigvat always inquired of the merchants who traded to Novgorod if they could tell him any news of Magnus Olafson. Sigvat composed these lines at that time:

> I ask the merchant oft who drives
> His trade to Russia, "How he thrives,
> Our noble prince? How lives he there?"
> And still good news—his praise—I hear.
> To little birds, which wing their way
> Between the lands, I fain would say
> How much we long our prince to see;
> They seem to bear a wish from me.

CHAPTER IX. OF KING MAGNUS'S FIRST ARRIVAL IN SWEDEN. —Immediately after Magnus Olafson came to Sweden from Russia, Sigvat met him at Queen Astrid's house, and glad they all were at meeting. Sigvat then sang:

> Thou art come here, prince, young and bold!
> Thou art come home! With joy behold
> Thy land and people. From this hour
> I join myself to thy young power.

---

[1] Sigvat had gone to Rome because of a mortal sin he had committed; and his journey was a pilgrimage of penance.

> I could not o'er to Russia hie—
> Thy mother's guardian here was I.
> It was my punishment for giving [1]
> Magnus his name, while scarcely living.

Afterwards Sigvat travelled with Queen Astrid, and followed Magnus to Norway. Sigvat sang thus:

> To the crowds streaming to the Thing,
> To see and hear Magnus their king,
> Loudly, young king, I'll speak my mind—
> "God to His people has been kind."
> If He, to whom be all the praise,
> Give us a son in all his ways
> Like to his sire, no folk on earth
> Will bless so much a royal birth.

Now when Magnus became king of Norway Sigvat attended him, and was his dearest friend. Once it happened that Queen Astrid and Alvhild the king's mother had exchanged some sharp words with each other, and Sigvat said:

> Alvhilda! though it was God's will
> To raise thee—yet remember still
> The queen-born Astrid should not be
> Kept out of due respect by thee.

Chapter X. King Olaf's Shrine.—King Magnus had a shrine made and mounted with gold and silver, and studded with jewels. This shrine was made so that in shape and size it was like a coffin. Under it was an arched way, and above was a raised roof, with a head and a roof-ridge. Behind were plaited hangings; and before were gratings with padlocks, which could be locked with a key. In this shrine King Magnus had the holy remains of King Olaf deposited, and many were the miracles there wrought. Of this Sigvat speaks:

> For him a golden shrine is made,
> For him whose heart was ne'er afraid
> Of mortal man—the holy king,
> Whom the Lord God to heaven did bring.
> Here many a man shall feel his way,
> Stone-blind, unconscious of the day,
> And at the shrine where Olaf lies
> Give songs of praise for opened eyes.

It was also appointed by law that King Olaf's holy day should be held holy over all Norway, and that day was at once celebrated as one of the greatest church days. Sigvat speaks of it:

> To Olaf, Magnus' father, raise,
> Within my house, the song of praise!
> With joy, yet grief, we'll keep the day
> Olaf to heaven was called away.

---

[1] Sigvat often refers to the circumstance of his having been the godfather of King Magnus, and having given him his name in baptism. See the *Olaf Sagas*, p. 258.

Well may I keep within my breast
A day for him in holy rest—
My upraised hands a golden ring
On every branch [1] bear from that king.

CHAPTER XI. OF TORE HUND.—Tore Hund left the country
immediately after King Olaf's fall. He went all the way to
Jerusalem, and many people say he never came back. Tore
Hund had a son called Sigurd, father of Ranveig who was
married to John, a son of Arne Arneson. Their children were
Vidkun of Bjarkö, Sigurd Hund, Erling, and Jardtrud.

CHAPTER XII. OF THE MURDER OF HAREK OF THJOTTA.—
Harek of Thjotta sat at home in his farm, till King Magnus
Olafson came to the country and was made king. Then Harek
went south to Drontheim to King Magnus. At that time
Asmund Grankelsson [2] was in the king's house. When
Harek came to Nidaros, and landed out of the ship, Asmund
was standing with the king in the balcony outside the loft, and
both the king and Asmund knew Harek when they saw him.
"Now," says Asmund to the king, "I will pay Harek for my
father's murder." He had in his hand a little thin hatchet.
The king looked at him, and said, "Rather take this axe of
mine." It was thick, and made like a club. "Thou must
know, Asmund," added he, "that there are hard bones in the
old fellow." Asmund took the axe, went down, and through
the house, and when he came down to the cross-road [3] Harek
and his men coming up met him. Asmund struck Harek on
the head, so that the axe penetrated to the brains; and that
was Harek's death-wound. Asmund turned back directly to
the king's house, and the whole edge of the axe was turned with
the blow. Then said the king, "What would thy axe have done,
for even this one, I think, is spoilt?" King Magnus afterwards
gave him a fief and office in Halogaland, and many are the
tales about the strife between Asmund and Harek's sons.

CHAPTER XIII. OF TORGEIR FLEK.—Kalv Arneson had at
first, for some time, the greatest share of the government of the
country under King Magnus; but afterwards there were people
who reminded the king of the part Kalv had taken at Stiklestad,
and then it became difficult for Kalv to give the king satisfaction in anything. Once it happened there were many men
with the king bringing their affairs before him; and Torgeir

---

[1] The fingers, the branches of the hand, bore golden fruits from the
generosity of the king.
[2] See *Olaf Sagas*, pp. 232, 259–60, 291–2.
[3] i.e. the common leading from the river (Skipakroken) to the main street.

Flek from Suul in Værdal, of whom mention is made before in the history of King Olaf the Saint [p. 354], came to him about some needful business. The king paid no attention to his words, but was listening to people who stood near him. Then Torgeir said to the king, so loud that all who were around him could hear:

> Listen, my lord,
> To my plain word.
> I too was there,
> And had to bear
> A bloody head
> From Stiklested:
> For I was then
> With Olaf's men.
> Listen to me:
> Well did I see
> The men you're trusting
> The dead corpse thrusting
> Out of their way,
> As dead it lay;
> And striding o'er
> Your father's gore.

There was instantly a great uproar, and some told Torgeir to go out; but the king called him, and not only despatched his business to his satisfaction, but promised him favour and friendship.

CHAPTER XIV. KALV ARNESON FLIES THE COUNTRY.—Soon after this the king was at a feast at the farm of Haug in Værdal, and at the dinner-table Kalv Arneson sat upon one side of him, and Einar Tambarskelve on the other. It was already come so far that the king took little notice of Kalv, but paid most attention to Einar. The king said to Einar, "Let us ride to-day to Stiklestad. I should like to see the memorials of the things which took place there." Einar replies, "I can tell thee nothing about it; but take thy foster-father Kalv with thee: he can give thee information about all that took place." When the tables were removed, the king made himself ready, and said to Kalv, "Thou must go with me to Stiklestad."

Kalv replied, "That is really not my duty."

Then the king stood up in a passion, and said, "Go thou shalt, Kalv!" and thereupon he went out.

Kalv put on his riding clothes in all haste, and said to his foot-boy, "Thou must ride directly to Egge, and order my house-servants to ship all my property on board my ship before sunset."

King Magnus now rides to Stiklestad, and Kalv with him. They alighted from horseback, and went to the place where the battle had been. Then said the king to Kalv, "Where is the spot at which the king fell?"

Kalv stretched out his spear-shaft, and said, "There he lay when he fell."

The king: "And where wast thou, Kalv?"

Kalv: "Here where I am now standing."

The king turned red as blood in the face, and said, "Then thy axe could well have reached him."

Kalv replied, "My axe did not come near him"; and immediately went to his horse, sprang on its back, and rode away with all his men; and the king rode back to Haug. Kalv did not stop until he got home in the evening to Egge. There his ship lay ready at the shore side, and all his effects were on board, and the vessel manned with his house-servants. They set off immediately by night down the fjord, and afterwards proceeded day and night, when the wind suited. He sailed out into the West sea, and was there a long time plundering in Ireland, Scotland, and the Hebrides. Bjorn Gulbraascald tells of this in the song about Kalv:

> Brother of Thorberg,[1] who still stood
> Well with the king! in angry mood
> He is the first to break with thee,
> Who well deserves esteemed to be:
> He is the first who friendship broke,
> For envious men the falsehood spoke;
> And he will be the first to rue
> The breach of friendship 'twixt you two.

CHAPTER XV. OF THE THREATS OF THE PEASANTS.—King Magnus added to his property Viggia,[2] which Rut had been owner of, and Kviststad,[3] which had belonged to Torgeir, and also Egge, with all the goods which Kalv had left behind him; and thus he confiscated to the king's estate many great farms, which had belonged to those of the bonder-army who had fallen at Stiklestad. In like manner, he laid heavy punishments upon many men who fought there in opposition to King Olaf. He drove some out of the country, took large sums of money from others, and had the cattle of others slaughtered for his use. Then the bonder began to murmur, and to say among themselves, "Will he go on in the same way as his father and other chiefs, whom we made an end of when their pride and lawless proceedings became insupportable?" This discontent spread widely through the country. The

---

[1] Thorberg was a brother of Kalv Arneson.
[2] Vide *Olaf Sagas*, p. 361.   [3] Vide *Olaf Sagas*, p. 371.

people of Sogn gathered men, and, it was said, were determined to give battle to King Magnus, if he came into the Fjords district. King Magnus was then in Hordaland, where he had remained a long time with a numerous retinue, and was now come to the resolution to proceed north to Sogn. When the king's friends observed this, twelve men had a meeting, and resolved to determine by casting lots which of them should inform the king of the discontent of the people; and it so happened that the lot fell upon Sigvat.

CHAPTER XVI. OF THE FREE-SPEAKING SONG, AND OF THE LAW-BOOK.—Sigvat accordingly composed a poem, which he called the Free-speaking Song, which begins with saying the king had delayed too long to pacify the people, who were threatening to rise in tumult against him. He said:

> Here in the South, from Sogn is spread
> The news that strife draws to a head:
> The bonder will the king oppose—
> Kings and their folk should ne'er be foes.
> Let us take arms, and briskly go
> To battle, if it must be so;
> Defend our king—but still deplore
> His land plunged in such strife once more.

In this song are also these verses:

> Hakon,[1] who at Fitjar died—
> Hakon the Good, could not abide
> The viking rule, or robber train,
> And all men's love he thus did gain.
> The people since have still in mind
> The laws of Hakon, just and kind;
> And men will never see the day
> When Hakon's laws have passed away.
>
> The bonder ask but what is fair:
> The Olafs[2] and the Earls, when there
> Where Magnus sits, confirmed to all
> Their lands and gear—to great and small.
> Bold Trygve's son, and Harald's heir,
> The Olafs, while on earth they were,
> Observed the laws themselves had made,
> And none was for his own afraid.
>
> Let not thy counsellors stir thy wrath
> Against the man who speaks the truth:
> Thy honour lies in thy good sword,
> But still more in thy royal word;
> And, if the people do not lie,
> The new laws turn out not nigh

---

[1] See pp. 106–9, and on the laws ascribed to King Hakon see p. 91. Some of the dissatisfaction felt by the people seems to have been because Magnus kept various taxes imposed by Svein and Alfiva.

[2] Olaf Trygvesson, and Olaf the Saint, Harald's son.

So just and mild, as the laws given
At Ulvesund in face of heaven.

Dread king! who urges thee to break
Thy pledged word, and back to take
Thy promise given?   Thou warrior bold!
With thy own people word to hold,
Thy promise fully to maintain,
Is to thyself the greatest gain:
The battle-storm raiser he
Must by his own men trusted be.

Who urges thee, who seek'st renown,
The bonder cattle to cut down?
No king before e'er took in hand
Such viking-work in his own land.
Such rapine men will not long bear,
And the king's counsellors will but share
In their ill-will: when once inflamed,
The king himself for all is blamed.

Be cautious, with this news of treason
Flying about—give them no reason.
We hang the thief, but then we use
Consideration of the excuse.
I think, great king (who wilt rejoice
Eagle and wolf with battle voice),
It would be wise not to oppose
Thy bonder, and make them thy foes.

A dangerous sign it is, I fear,
That old grey-bearded men appear
In corners whispering at the Thing,
As if they had bad news to bring.
The young sit still—no laugh, or shout—
More looks than words passing about;
And groups of whispering heads are seen,
On buttoned breasts, with lowering mien.

Among the udalmen, they say
The king, if he could have his way,
Would seize the bonder's udal land,
And free-born men must this withstand.
In truth the man whose udal field,
By any doom that law can yield
From him adjudged the king would take,
Could the king's throne and power shake.

This verse is the last:

A holy bond between us still [1]
Makes me wish speedy end to ill:
The sluggard waits till afternoon—
At once, great Magnus! grant our boon.
Thee we will serve with heart and hand,
With thee we'll fight by sea or land:
With Olaf's sword take Olaf's mind,
And to thy bonder be more kind.

---

[1] The bond of godfather at his baptism, to which Sigvat often alludes.

In this song the king was exhorted to observe the laws which his father had established. This exhortation had a good effect on the king, for many others held the same language to him. So at last the king consulted the most prudent men, and they decided what the law should be. Thereafter King Magnus had the law-book composed in writing which is still in use in the Drontheim district, and is called Grey-Goose.[1] King Magnus afterwards became very popular, and was beloved by all the country people, and therefore he was called Magnus the Good.

CHAPTER XVII. OF THE ENGLISH KINGS [1040].—The king of the English, King Harald, died [2] five years after his father King Canute, and was buried beside his father at Winchester. After his death his brother Hardacanute, the second son of the old King Canute, was king of England, and was thus king both of Denmark and England. He ruled these kingdoms two years, and then died of sickness in England [1042],[3] leaving no children. He was buried at Winchester beside his father. After his death Edward the Good, a son of the English king Ethelred, and Emma a daughter of Richard earl of Rouen, was chosen king in England. King Edward the Good was, on his mother's side, a brother of Harald[4] and Hardacanute, the sons of Canute the Great; and the daughter of Canute and Queen Emma was Gunhild, who was married to the Emperor[5] Henry of Germany, who was called Henry the Mild. Gunhild was three years in Germany when she fell sick, and she died two years after the death of her father King Canute the Great.[6]

CHAPTER XVIII. OF KING MAGNUS OLAFSON [1042].—When King Magnus Olafson heard of Hardacanute's death, he imme-

---

[1] Another reference to this law-book called Grey-Goose is found in the *Sverris Saga*, chap. 117, where it says: "At this time [1190] many differences arose between King Sverre and the Archbishop. In his causes the King always referred to the law of the land established by King Olaf the Saint and to the law-book of the Trondheim people called Grey-Goose, which had been written at the instance of King Magnus the Good, son of Olaf. The Archbishop had the book called Gold-Feather produced, which had been written under Archbishop Eystein, and he brought forward Roman canonical law, and as authority for some things he had letters bearing the papal seal." Neither Grey-Goose nor Gold-Feather is now known, but material from the former must doubtless be contained in the extant Frostathings Law, a thirteenth-century version of the laws of the Trondheim district. The law-code of the medieval Icelandic Commonwealth is also known by the name Grey-Goose, although this designation can only be traced as far back as 1546.

[2] 17 March, 1040.   [3] 8 June, 1042.

[4] Not really; see p. 129, note 1.

[5] More correctly—king; for Henry did not become emperor until 1047.

[6] Gunhild died three years after her father, 18 July, 1038, and she had been married for only two years.

diately sent people south to Denmark, with a message to the men who had bound themselves by oath to the peace and agreement which was made between King Magnus and Hardacanute, and reminded them of their pledge. He added, as a conclusion, that in summer he would come with his army to Denmark to take possession of his Danish dominions, in terms of the agreement, or to fall in the field with his army. So says Arnor, the earls' scald:

> Wise were the words, exceeding wise,
> Of him who stills the hungriest cries
> Of beasts of prey—the earls' lord;
> And soon fulfilled will be his word:
> "With his good sword he'll Denmark gain,
> Or fall upon a bloody plain;
> And rather than give up his cause,
> Will leave his corpse to ravens' claws."

CHAPTER XIX. KING MAGNUS'S ARMAMENT. — Thereafter King Magnus gathered together a great army, and summoned to him all lendermen and powerful bonder, and collected warships. When the army was assembled it was very handsome, and well fitted out. He had seventy large vessels when he sailed from Norway. So says Thjodolf the scald:

> Brave king! the terror of the foe,
> With thee will many a long-ship go.
> Full seventy sail are gathered here,
> Eastward with their great king to steer.
> And southward now the bright keel glides;
> O'er the white waves the Bison rides.
> Sails swell, yards crack, the highest mast
> O'er the wide sea scarce seen at last.

Here it is related that King Magnus had the great Bison,[1] which his father King Olaf had built. It had more than thirty benches of rowers; and forward on the bow was a great buffalo head, and aft on the stern-post was its tail. Both the head and the tail, and both necks [2] of the ship, were gilded over. Of this speaks Arnor, the earls' scald:

> The white foam lashing o'er the deck
> Oft made the gilded head to shake:
> The helm down, the vessel's heel
> Oft showed her stem's bright glancing steel.
> Around Stavanger-point careering,
> Through the wild sea's white flames steering,
> Tackle loud singing to the strain,
> The storm-horse flies to Denmark's plain.

---

[1] Vide *Olaf Sagas*, p. 302.   [2] Vide *Olaf Sagas*, p. 71 note.

King Magnus set out to sea from Agder, and sailed over to Jutland. So says Arnor:

> I can relate how through the gale
> The gallant Bison carried sail,
> With her lee gunwale in the wave,
> The king on board, Magnus the brave!
> The iron-clad Thingmen's chief to see
> On Jutland's coast right glad were we—
> Right glad our men to see a king
> Who in the fight his sword could swing.

CHAPTER XX. KING MAGNUS COMES TO DENMARK.—When King Magnus came to Denmark he was joyfully received. He appointed a Thing without delay, to which he summoned the people of the country, and desired they would take him as king, according to the agreement which had been entered into. As the highest of the chiefs of the country were bound by oath to King Magnus, and were desirous of keeping their word and oath, they endeavoured zealously to promote the cause with the people. It contributed also that King Canute the Great, and all his descendants, were dead; and a third assistance was, that his father King Olaf's sanctity and miracles were become celebrated in all countries.

CHAPTER XXI. KING MAGNUS CHOSEN KING OF DENMARK. —King Magnus afterwards ordered the people to be summoned to Viborg[1] to a Thing. Both in older and later times, the Danes elected their kings at the Viborg Thing. At this Thing the Danes chose Magnus Olafson to be king of all the Danish dominions. King Magnus remained long in Denmark during the summer; and wherever he came the people received him joyfully, and obeyed him willingly. He divided the country into baronies and districts, and gave fiefs to men of power in the land. Late in autumn he returned with his fleet to Norway, but lay for some time at the river Gotha.

CHAPTER XXII. OF SVEIN ULVSON.—There was a man, by name Svein, a son of Earl Ulv, and grandson of Torgils Sprakaleg. Svein's mother was Astrid, a daughter of King Svein of England. She was a sister of Canute the Great by the father's side, and of the Swedish King Olaf Ericson by the mother's side; for her mother was Queen Sigrid the Haughty, a daughter of Skögul Toste. Svein Ulvson had been a long time living with his kinsmen, the Swedish kings, ever since King Canute had ordered his father Ulv to be killed, as is related in the story of old King Canute[2]—that he had his brother-in-law, Earl

---

[1] See p. 182, note 1.   [2] Vide *Olaf Sagas*, p. 312.

Ulv, murdered in Roskilde; and on which account Svein had not since been in Denmark. Svein Ulvson was one of the handsomest men that could be seen; he was very stout and strong, and very expert in all exercises, and a well-spoken man withal. Every one who knew him said he had every quality which became a good chief. Svein Ulvson waited upon King Magnus while he lay in the Gotha river, as before mentioned, and the king received him kindly, as he was by many advised to do; for Svein was a particularly popular man. He could also speak for himself to the king well and cleverly; so that it came at last to Svein entering into King Magnus's service, and becoming his man. They often talked together afterwards in private concerning many affairs.

CHAPTER XXIII. SVEIN ULVSON CREATED AN EARL.—One day, as King Magnus sat in his high seat and many people were around him, Svein Ulvson sat upon a footstool before the king. The king then made a speech: "Be it known to you, chiefs, and the people in general, that I have taken the following resolution. Here is a distinguished man, both for family and for his own merits, Svein Ulvson, who has entered into my service, and given me promise of fidelity. Now, as ye know, the Danes have this summer become my men, so that when I am absent from the country it is without a head; and it is not unknown to you how it is ravaged by the people of Vendland, Kurland, and others from the Baltic, as well as by Saxons. Therefore I promised them a chief who could defend and rule their land; and I know no man better fitted, in all respects, for this than Svein Ulvson, who is of birth to be chief of the country. I will therefore make him my earl, and give him the government of my Danish dominions while I am in Norway; just as King Canute the Great set his father, Earl Ulv, over Denmark while he was in England."

Then Einar Tambarskelve said, "Too great an earl—too great an earl, my foster-son!"

The king replied in a passion, "Ye have a poor opinion of my judgment. It seems to me that ye think some are over-mighty earls and others ye think are fit for nothing."

Then the king stood up, took a sword, and girt it on the earl's loins, and took a shield and fastened it on his shoulders, put a helmet upon his head, and gave him the title of earl, with the same fiefs in Denmark which his father Earl Ulv had formerly held. Afterwards a shrine was brought forth containing holy relics, and Svein laid his hand thereon, and swore

the oath of fidelity to King Magnus; upon which the king led
the earl to the high seat by his side. So says Thjodolf:

> 'Twas at the Gotha river's shore,
> With hand on shrine Svein Ulvson swore,
> King Magnus first said o'er the oath,
> With which Svein Ulvson pledged his troth.
> The vows by Svein solemnly given,
> On holy bones of saints in heaven,
> To Magnus seemed both fair and fast:
> He found they were too fair to last.

Earl Svein went thereafter to Denmark, and the whole nation
received him well. He established a hird about him, and soon
became a great man. In winter he went much about the
country, and made friends among the powerful chiefs; and,
indeed, he was beloved by all the people of the land.

CHAPTER XXIV. KING MAGNUS'S FORAY [1043]. — King
Magnus proceeded northward to Norway with his fleet, and
wintered there; but when the spring set in he gathered a large
force, with which he sailed south to Denmark, having heard the
news from Vendland that the Vendland people in Jomsborg
had withdrawn from their submission to him. The Danish
kings had formerly had a very large earldom there, and they
first founded Jomsborg; and now the place was become a very
strong fortress. When King Magnus heard of this, he ordered
a large fleet and army to be levied in Denmark and sailed in
summer to Vendland with all his forces, which made a very
large army altogether. Arnor, the earls' scald, tells of it thus:

> Now in this strophe, royal youth!
> I tell no more than the plain truth.
> Thy armed outfit from the strand
> Left many a keel-trace on the sand,
> And never did a king before
> So many ships to any shore
> Lead on, as thou to Vendland's isle:
> The Vendland men in fright recoil.

Now when King Magnus came to Vendland he attacked
Jomsborg, and soon took the fortress, killing many people,
burning and destroying both in the town and in the country
all around, and making the greatest havoc. So says Arnor,
the earls' scald:

> The robbers, hemmed 'twixt death and fire,
> Knew not how to escape thy ire;
> O'er Jomsborg castle's highest towers
> Thy wrath the whirlwind-fire pours.
> The heathen on his false gods calls,
> And trembles even in their halls;
> And by the light from its own flame
> The king this viking-hold o'ercame.

Many people in Vendland submitted to King Magnus, but many more got out of the way and fled. King Magnus returned to Denmark, and prepared to take his winter abode there, and sent away the Danish, and also a great many of the Norwegian people he had brought with him.

CHAPTER XXV. SVEIN RECEIVES THE TITLE OF KING.—The same winter in which Svein Ulvson was raised to the government of the whole Danish dominions, and had made friends of a great number of the principal chiefs in Denmark, and obtained the affections of the people, he assumed, by the advice of many of the chiefs, the title of king. But when in the spring thereafter he heard that King Magnus had come from the north with a great army, Svein went over to Skaane, from thence up to Gotland, and so on to Sweden to his relation King Onund, where he remained all summer, and sent spies out to Denmark, to inquire about the king's proceedings and the number of his men. Now when Svein heard that King Magnus had let a great part of his army go away, and also that he was south [west] in Jutland, he rode from Sweden with a great body of people which the Swedish king had given him. When Svein came to Skaane the people of that country received him well, treated him as their king, and men joined him in crowds. He then went on to Sealand, where he was also well received, and the whole country joined him. He then went to Fyen, and laid all the islands under his power; and as the people also joined him, he collected a great army, and many ships of war. King Magnus married his sister Ulvhild, Olaf's daughter, to Otto duke of Saxony. They had a son who was called Magnus, from whom a great family has descended. The dukes who rule over Brunswick reckon their descent from King Olaf the Saint.

CHAPTER XXVI. OF KING MAGNUS'S MILITARY FORCE.— King Magnus heard this news, and at the same time that the people of Vendland had a large force on foot. He summoned people therefore to come to him, and drew together a great army in Jutland. Otto [1] also, the duke of Brunswick, who had married Ulvhild, King Olaf the Saint's daughter, and the sister of King Magnus, came to him with a great troop. The Danish chiefs pressed King Magnus to advance against the Vendland army, and not to allow pagans to march over and lay waste the country; so it was resolved that the king with his army

[1] He was called Ordulf, not Otto, and was a son of Duke Bernhard of Saxony. He came to the throne in 1059.

should proceed south to Heidaby.[1] While King Magnus lay at Skotburg river, on Lyrskog Heath, he got intelligence concerning the Vendland army, and that it was so numerous it could not be counted; whereas King Magnus had so few, that there seemed no chance for him but to fly. The king, however, determined on fighting, if there was any possibility of gaining the victory; but the most dissuaded him from venturing on an engagement, and all, as one man, said that the Vendland people had undoubtedly a prodigious force. Duke Otto, however, pressed much to go to battle. Then the king ordered the whole army to be gathered by the war trumpets into battle array, and ordered all the men to arm, and to lie down for the night under their shields; for he was told the enemy's army had come to the neighbourhood. The king was very thoughtful; for he was vexed that he should be obliged to fly, which fate he had never experienced before. He slept but little all night, and chanted his prayers.

CHAPTER XXVII. OF KING OLAF'S MIRACLE.—The following day was Michaelmas eve [28 September]. Towards dawn the king slumbered, and dreamt that his father King Olaf the Saint appeared to him, and said, "Art thou so melancholy and afraid, because the Vendland people come against thee with a great army? Be not afraid of heathens, although they be many; for I shall be with thee in the battle. Prepare, therefore, to give battle to the Vendlanders, when thou hearest my trumpet." When the king awoke he told his dream to his men, and the day was then dawning. At that moment all the people heard a ringing of bells in the air; and those among King Magnus's men who had been in Nidaros thought that it was the ringing of the bell called Glad, which King Olaf had presented to the church of Saint Clement in Kaupangen.

CHAPTER XXVIII. BATTLE OF LYRSKOG HEATH. — Then King Magnus stood up, and ordered the war trumpets to sound, and at that moment the Vendland army advanced from the south across the river against him; on which the whole of the king's army stood up, and advanced against the heathens. King Magnus threw off from him his coat of ring-mail, and had a red silk shirt outside over his clothes, and had in his

---

[1] It lay near the present Schleswig, some twenty miles north-west of Kiel, and was the most important trading town in Scandinavia from the ninth to eleventh century. Lyrskog Heath lies west of the town, but the Skotburg river is identified with the Kongeaa, which flows into the North Sea north of Ribe, and this is some sixty miles north of Lyrskog Heath.

hands the battle-axe called Hel [1] which had belonged to King
Olaf. King Magnus ran on before all his men to the enemy's
army, and instantly hewed down with both hands every man
who came against him. So says Arnor, the earls' scald:

> His armour on the ground he flung,
> His broad axe round his head he swung;
> And Norway's king strode on in might,
> Through ringing swords, to the wild fight.
> His broad axe Hel with both hands wielding,
> Shields, helms, and skulls before it yielding,
> He seemed with Fate the world to share,
> And life or death to deal out there.

This battle was not very long; for the king's men were very
fiery, and where they came the Vendland men fell as thick as
sand heaped up by the waves on the strand. They who stood
behind betook themselves to flight, and were hewed down like
cattle at a slaughter. The king himself drove the fugitives
eastward over the heath, and people fell all over the moor.
So says Thjodolf:

> And foremost he pursued,
> And the flying foe down hewed;
> An eagle's feast each stroke,
> As the Vendland helms he broke.
> He drove them o'er the heath,
> And they fly from bloody death;
> But the moor, a mile or more,
> With the dead was studded o'er.

It is a common saying, that there never was so great a slaughter
of men in the northern lands, since the time of Christianity, as
took place among the Vendland people on Lyrskog Heath. On
the other side, not many of King Magnus's people were killed,
although many were wounded. It is told in the Bremen Book,[2]
that the Danes had killed Rettebur, a Vendland king; and that
he had eight sons, who sought to avenge their father, and laid
waste a great part of Denmark, as far north as Ribe; but they
all fell on Lyrskog Heath before King Magnus, and fifteen
thousand men with them. After the battle, the king ordered
the wounds of his men to be bound; but there were not so
many doctors in the army as were necessary, so the king
himself went round, and felt the hands of those he thought
best suited for the business; and when he had thus stroked
their palms he named twelve men, who, he thought, had the
softest hands, and told them to bind the wounds of the people:

---

[1] Hel = Death, the goddess of Death.
[2] *Gesta Hammaburgensis Ecclesiae Pontificum*, lib. ii, cap. 78. The author,
Adam of Bremen, wrote only about thirty years after the battle.

and although none of them had ever tried it before, they all became afterwards the best of doctors. There were two Iceland men among them: the one was Torkel, a son of Geire, from Lyngar; the other was Atle, father of Baard Swart of Selardal,[1] from whom many good doctors are descended. After this battle, the report of the miracle which King Olaf the Saint had worked was spread widely through the country; and it was the common saying of the people, that no man could venture to fight against King Magnus Olafson, for his father Saint Olaf stood so near to him that his enemies, on that account, could never withstand him.

CHAPTER XXIX. BATTLE AT RE.—King Magnus immediately turned round with his army against Svein, whom he called his earl, although the Danes called him their king; and he collected ships, and a great force, and on both sides a great strength was assembled. In Svein's army were many chiefs from Skaane, Halland, Sealand, and Fyen; while King Magnus, on the other hand, had mostly Norway and Jutland men, and with that war-force he hastened to meet Svein. They met at Re,[2] on the west side of the isle of Rügen; and there was a great battle, which ended in King Magnus gaining the victory, and Svein taking flight. After losing many people, Svein fled back to Skaane, and from thence to Gotland, which was a safe refuge if he needed it, and stood open to him. King Magnus returned to Jutland, where he remained all winter with many people, and had a guard to watch his ships. Arnor, the earls' scald, speaks of this:

> At Re our battle-loving lord
> In bloody meeting stained his sword—
> At Re, upon the western shore,
> In Westland warriors' blood once more.

CHAPTER XXX. BATTLE AT AARHUS, IN JUTLAND.—Svein Ulvson went directly to his ships as soon as he heard that King Magnus had left his fleet. He drew to him all the men he could, and went round in winter among the islands, Sealand, Fyen, and others. Towards Yule he sailed to Jutland, and went into Lymfjord, where many people submitted to him. He imposed scatt upon some, but some joined King Magnus. Now when King Magnus heard what Svein was doing, he betook himself to his ships with all the Northmen then in Denmark,

---

[1] His grandson was Hrafn Sveinbjarnarson, died 1213, a famous physician.
[2] Snorri has thought that Re was somewhere among the Danish isles; but it is really Rö, the old name of Rügen.

and a part of the Danish troops, and steered north along the
land. Svein was then in Aarhus with a great force; and when
he heard of King Magnus he laid his vessels without the town,
and prepared for battle. When King Magnus heard for certain
where Svein was, and that the distance between them was but
short, he held a House-thing, and addressed his people thus:
"It is reported to me that the earl and his fleet are lying not
far from us, and that he has many people. Now I would let
you know that I intend to go out against the earl and fight for
it, although we have fewer people. We will, as formerly, put
our trust in God, and Saint Olaf my father, who has given us
victory sometimes when we fought, even though we had fewer
men than the enemy. Now I would have you get ready to
seek out the enemy, and give battle the moment we find him
by rowing all to the attack, and being all ready for battle."
Thereupon the men put on their weapons, each man making
himself and his place ready; and then they stretched themselves
to their oars. When they saw the earl's ships they rowed towards
them, and made ready to attack. When Svein's men saw the
forces they armed themselves, bound their ships together, and
then began one of the sharpest of battles. So says Thjodolf
the scald:

> Shield against shield, the earl and king
> Made shields and swords together ring.
> The gold-decked heroes made a play
> Which Hilda's iron-shirt men say
> They never saw before or since
> On battle-deck: the brave might wince,
> As spear and arrow whistling flew,
> Point blank, death-bringing, quick and tru

They fought at the bows, so that the men only on the bows
could strike; the men on the forecastle thrust with spears;
and all who were farther off shot with light spears or javelins,
or war-arrows. Some fought with stones, or short stakes; and
those who were aft of the mast shot with the bow. So says
Thjodolf:

> Steel-pointed spear, and sharpened stake,
> Made the broad shield on arm shake:
> The eagle, hovering in the air,
> Screamed o'er the prey preparing there.
> And stones and arrows thickly flew,
> And many a warrior bold they slew.
> The bowman never twanged his bow
> And drew his shaft so oft as now;
> And Drontheim's bowmen on that day
> Were not first tired of this play:
> Arrows and darts so quickly fly,
> You could not follow with the eye.

Here it appears how hot the battle was with casting weapons.
King Magnus stood in the beginning of the battle within a
shield-rampart; but as it appeared to him that matters were
going too slowly, he leaped over the shields, and rushed forward
in the ship, encouraging his men with a loud cheer, and springing
to the bows, where the battle was going on hand to hand. When
his men saw this they urged each other on with mutual cheering,
and there was one great hurrah through all the ships. So
says Thjodolf:

> "On with our ships! on to the foe!"
> Cry Magnus' men—on, on they go.
> Spears against shields in fury rattle—
> Was never seen so fierce a battle.

And now the battle was exceedingly sharp; and in the assault
Svein's ship was cleared of all her forecastle men upon and on
both sides of the forecastle. Then Magnus boarded Svein's
ship, followed by his men; and one after the other came up,
and made so stout an assault that Svein's men gave way, and
King Magnus first cleared that ship, and then the rest, one
after the other. Svein fled, with a great part of his people; but
many fell, and many got life and grace. Thjodolf tells of this:

> Brave Magnus, from the stern springing
> On to the stem, where swords were ringing,
> From his sea-raven's beak of gold
> Deals death around—the brave! the bold!
> The earl's housemen now begin
> To shrink and fall: their ranks grow thin—
> The king's luck thrives—their decks are cleared,
> Of fighting men no more appeared.
> The earl's ships are driven to flight,
> Before the king would stop the fight:
> The gold-distributor first then
> Gave quarters to the vanquished men.

This battle was fought on the last Sunday before Yule
[18 December, 1043]. So says Thjodolf:

> 'Twas on a Sunday morning bright,
> Fell out this great and bloody fight,
> When men were arming, fighting, dying,
> Or on the red decks wounded lying.
> And many a man, foredoomed to die,
> To save his life o'erboard did fly,
> But sank; for swimming could not save,
> And dead men rolled in every wave.

Magnus took seven ships from Svein's people. So says
Thjodolf:

> Thick Olaf's son seven vessels cleared,
> And with his fleet the prizes steered.
> The Norway girls will not be sad
> To hear such news—each from her lad.

He also sings:

> The captured men will grieve the most
> Svein and their comrades to have lost;
> For it went ill with those who fled,
> Their wounded had no easy bed.
> A heavy storm that very night
> O'ertook them flying from the fight;
> And skulls and bones are tumbling round,
> Under the sea, on sandy ground.

Svein fled immediately by night to Sealand, with the men who had escaped and were inclined to follow him; but King Magnus brought his ships to the shore, and sent his men up the country in the night-time, and early in the morning they came down to the strand with a great booty in cattle. Thjodolf tells about it:

> But yesterday with heavy stones
> We crushed their skulls, and broke their bones,
> And thinned their ranks; and now to-day
> Up through their land we've ta'en our way,
> And driven their cattle to the shore,
> And filled our ships with food in store.
> To save his land from our quick swords,
> Svein will need something more than words.

CHAPTER XXXI. SVEIN'S FLIGHT.—King Magnus sailed with his fleet from the south after Svein to Sealand; but as soon as the king came there Svein fled up the country with his men, and Magnus followed them, and pursued the fugitives, killing all that were laid hold of. So says Thjodolf:

> The Sealand girl asks with fear,
> "Whose blood-bespattered shield and spear—
> The earl's or king's—up from the shore
> Moved on with many a warrior more?"
> We scoured through all their muddy lanes,
> Woodlands, and fields, and miry plains.
> Their hasty footmarks in the clay
> Showed that to Ringsted [1] led their way.

> Spattered with mud from heel to head,
> Our gallant lord his true men led.
> Will Lund's [2] earl halt his hasty flight,
> And try on land another fight?
> His banner yesterday was seen,
> The sand-hills and green trees between,
> Through moss and mire to the strand,
> In arrow flight, leaving the land.

Then Svein fled over to Fyen Island, and King Magnus carried fire and sword through Sealand, burning the farms of

---

[1] Now Ringsted in the centre of Sealand, the king's seat.
[2] Lund in Skaane.

many of the men who had joined Svein's troop in autumn.   So
says Thjodolf:

> As Svein in winter had destroyed
> The royal house, the king employed
> No little force to guard the land,
> And the earl's forays to withstand.
> An armed band one morn he found,
> And so beset them round and round,
> That Canute's nephew quickly fled,
> Or he would have been captive led.
>
> Our Drontheim king in his just ire
> Laid waste the land with sword and fire,
> Burnt every house, and over all
> Struck terror into great and small.
> To the earl's friends he well repaid
> Their deadly hate—such wild work made
> On them and theirs, that from his fury,
> Flying for life, away they hurry.

CHAPTER XXXII. BURNING IN FYEN.—As soon as King
Magnus heard that Svein with his troops had gone across to
Fyen, he sailed after them; and when Svein heard this news he
went on board ship and sailed to Skaane, and from thence to
Gotland, and at last to the Swedish king.   King Magnus landed
in Fyen, and plundered and burned over all; and all of Svein's
men who were there fled far enough.   Thjodolf speaks of
it thus:

> Fiona [1] Isle, once green and fair,
> Lies black and reeking through the air:
> The red fog rises, thick and hot,
> From burning farm and smouldering cot.
> The gaping thralls in terror gaze
> On the broad upward-spiring blaze,
> From thatched roofs and oak-built walls,
> Their murdered masters' stately halls.
>
> Svein's men, my girl, will not forget
> That thrice they have the Norsemen met—
> By sea, by land, with steel, with fire,
> Thrice have they felt the Norse king's ire.
> Fiona's maids are slim and fair,
> The lovely prizes, lads, we'll share:
> Some stand to arms in rank and row,
> Some seize, bring off, and fend with blow.

After this the people of Denmark submitted to King Magnus,
and during the rest of the winter there was peace.   King
Magnus then appointed some of his men to govern Denmark;
and when spring was advanced he sailed northwards with
his fleet to Norway, where he remained a great part of the
summer [1044].

[1] Fyen, Fünen, the second largest island in Denmark.

CHAPTER XXXIII. BATTLE AT HELGANES.—Now when
Svein heard that King Magnus had gone to Norway he rode
straight down, and had many people out of Sweden with him.
The people of Skaane received him well, and he again collected
an army, with which he first crossed over into Sealand, and
seized upon it and Fyen, and all the other isles. When King
Magnus heard of this he gathered together men and ships, and
sailed to Denmark; and as soon as he knew where Svein was
lying with his ships, King Magnus sailed to meet him. They
met at a place called Helganes,[1] and the battle began about
the fall of day. King Magnus had fewer men, but larger and
better equipt vessels. So says Arnor, the earls' scald:

> At Helganes—so goes the tale—
> The brave wolf-feeder, under sail,
> Made many an ocean-elk [2] his prey,
> Seized many a ship ere break of day.
> When twilight fell he urged the fight,
> Close combat—man to man—all night;
> Through a long harvest night's dark hours,
> Down poured the battle's iron showers.

The battle was very hot, and as night advanced the fall of
men was great. King Magnus, during the whole night, threw
hand-spears. Thjodolf speaks of this:

> And there at Helganes sank down,
> Sore wounded, men of great renown;
> And Svein's retainers lost all heart,
> Ducking before the flying dart.
> The Norsemen's king let fly his spears,
> His death-wounds adding to their fears;
> For each spear-blade was wet all o'er,
> Up to the shaft in their life-gore.

To make a short tale, King Magnus won the victory in this
battle, and Svein fled. His ship was cleared of men from stem
to stern; and it went so on board all the rest of his ships. So
says Thjodolf:

> Earl Svein fled from the empty deck,
> His lonely ship an unmann'd wreck;
> Magnus the Good, the people's friend,
> Pressed to the death on the false Svein.
> Neite,[3] the sword his father bore,
> Was, edge and point, stained red with gore:
> Swords sprinkle blood o'er armour bright,
> When kings for land and power fight.

---

[1] Helganes is eastward of the town Aarhus, in North Jutland, in the
parish of Helganes, barony of Mots.
[2] Ship.
[3] Taken to mean St. Olaf's sword, but the verse is mistranslated.

Arnor also says:

> The cutters of Bjorne's brother [1]
> Soon changed their owner for another;
> The king took them and all their gear:
> The crews, however, got off clear.

A great number of Svein's men fell, and King Magnus and his men had a vast booty to divide. So says Thjodolf:

> Where the Norsemen the Danish slew,
> A Gotland shield and breast-plate true
> Fell to my share of spoil by lot;
> And something more i' the south I got:
> (There all the summer swords were ringing:)
> A helm, gay arms, and gear worth bringing,
> Home to my quiet lovely one
> I sent—with news how we had won.

Svein fled up to Skaane with all the men who escaped with him; and King Magnus and his people drove the fugitives up through the country, without meeting any opposition either from Svein's men or the bonder. So says Thjodolf:

> Olaf's brave son then gave command,
> All his ships' crews should quickly land:
> King Magnus, marching at their head,
> A noble band of warriors led.
> A foray through the land he makes;
> Denmark in every quarter shakes.
> Up hill and down the horses scour,
> Carrying the Danes from Norsemen's power.

King Magnus drove with fire and sword through the land. So says Thjodolf:

> And now the Norsemen storm along,
> Following their banner in a throng:
> King Magnus' banner flames on high,
> A star to guide our roaming by.
> To Lund, o'er Scania's peaceful field,
> My shoulder bore my useless shield:
> A fairer land, a better road,
> As friend or foe, I never trod.

They began to burn the habitations all around, and the people fled on every side. So says Thjodolf:

> Our ice-cold iron in great store,
> Our arms, beside the king we bore:
> The Scanian rogues fly at the view
> Of men and steel all sharp and true.
> Their timbered houses flame on high,
> Red flashing over half the sky;
> The blazing town flings forth its light,
> Lighting the cowards on their flight.

---

[1] Svein Ulvson had a brother called Björn, or by the English chroniclers Esbern.

And he also sang:

> The king o'er all the Danish land
> Roams, with his fire-bringing band:
> The house, the hut, the farm, the town,
> All where men dwelt is burned down.
> O'er Denmark's plains and corn-fields,
> Meadows and moors, are seen our shields:
> Victorious over all, we chase
> Svein's wounded men from place to place.
>
> Across Fiona's moor again,
> The paths late trodden by our men
> We tread once more, until quite near,
> Through morning mist, the foes appear.
> Then up our numerous banners flare
> In the cold early morning air;
> And they from Magnus' power who fly
> Cann>t his quick war-work deny.

Then Svein fled eastwards along Skaane, and King Magnus returned to his ships, and steered eastwards also along the Scanian coast, having got ready with the greatest haste to sail. Thjodolf sings thus about it:

> No drink but the salt sea
> On board our ships had we,
> When, following our king,
> On board our ships we spring.
> Hard work on the salt sea,
> Off Scania's coast, had we;
> But we laboured for the king,
> To his foemen death to bring.

Svein fled to Gotland, and then sought refuge with the Swedish king, with whom he remained all winter, and was treated with great respect.

CHAPTER XXXIV. OF KING MAGNUS'S CAMPAIGN.—When King Magnus had subdued Scania he turned about, and first went to Falster,[1] where he landed, plundered, and killed many people who had before submitted to Svein. Arnor speaks of this:

> A bloody vengeance for their guile
> King Magnus takes on Falster Isle;
> The treacherous Danes his fury feel,
> And fall before his purpled steel.
> The battle-field is covered o'er
> With eagles' prey from shore to shore;
> And the king's birdmen were the first
> To quench with blood the ravens' thirst.

Thereafter Magnus with his fleet proceeded to the isle of

[1] A Danish island in the Baltic, south of Sealand.

Fyen, went on land, plundered, and made great devastation. So says Arnor, the earls' scald:

> To fair Fiona's grassy shore
> His banner now again he bore;
> He who the mail-shirt's linked chains
> Severs, and all its lustre stains—
> He will be long remembered there,
> The warrior in his twentieth year,
> Whom their black ravens from afar
> Saluted as he went to war.

CHAPTER XXXV. OF KING MAGNUS'S BATTLES [1044-5].— King Magnus remained in Denmark all that winter, and sat in peace. He had held many battles, and had gained the victory in all. So says Odd Kikinescald:

> 'Fore Michaelmas was struck the blow
> That laid the Vendland vikings low;
> And people learned with joy to hear
> The clang of arms, and leaders' cheer.
> Short before Yule fell out the day,
> Southward of Aarhus, where the fray,
> Though not enough the foe to quell,
> Was of the bloodiest men can tell.

And Arnor says:

> Olaf's avenger who can sing?
> The scald cannot o'ertake the king,
> Who makes the war-bird daily drain
> The corpse-blood of his foemen slain.
> Four battles won within a year—
> Breaker of shields! with sword and spear,
> And hand to hand, exalt thy fame
> Above the kings of greatest name.

King Magnus had three battles with Svein Ulvson. So says Thjodolf:

> To our brave Drontheim sovereign's praise
> The scald may all his scaldcraft raise;
> For fortune, and for daring deed,
> His song will not the truth exceed.
> After three battles to regain
> What was his own, unjustly ta'en,
> Unjustly kept, and dues denied,
> He levied dues in red blood dyed.

While King Magnus the Good, a son of King Olaf the Saint, ruled over Norway, as before related, the Earl Rognvald Bruseson lived with him. Earl Torfinn Sigurdson, the uncle of Rognvald, ruled then over Orkney. King Magnus sent Rognvald west to Orkney, and ordered that Torfinn should let him have his father's heritage. Torfinn let Rognvald have a third part of the land along with him; for so had Bruse, the father of

Rognvald, had it at his dying day. Earl Torfinn was married to Ingeborg, the earl-mother, who was a daughter of Finn Arneson. Earl Rognvald thought he should have two-thirds of the land, as Olaf the Saint had promised to his father Bruse, and as Bruse had enjoyed as long as Olaf lived. This was the origin of a great strife between these relations, concerning which we have a long saga.[1] They had a great battle in Pentland Firth, in which Kalv Arneson was with Earl Torfinn. So says Bjorn Gulbraascald:

> Thy cutters, dashing through the tide,
> Brought aid to Earl Torfinn's side,
> Finn's son-in-law, and people say
> Thy aid made Bruse's son give way.
> Kalv, thou art fond of warlike toil,
> Gay in the strife and bloody broil;
> But here 'twas hate made thee contend
> Against Earl Rognvald, the king's friend.

CHAPTER XXXVI. OF KING MAGNUS'S LETTERS. — King Magnus ruled then both over Denmark and Norway; and when he had got possession of the Danish dominions he sent ambassadors over to England to King Edward, who brought to him King Magnus's letter and seal.[2] And in this letter there stood, along with a salutation from King Magnus, these words: "Ye must have heard of the agreement which I and Hardacanute made—that he of us two who survived the other should have all the land and people which the deceased had possessed. Now it has so turned out, as ye have no doubt heard, that I have taken the Danish dominions as my heritage after Hardacanute. But before he departed this life he had England as well as Denmark; therefore I consider myself now, in consequence of my rights by this agreement, to own England also. Now I will therefore that thou deliver to me the kingdom; otherwise I will seek to take it by arms, both from Denmark and Norway: and let him rule the land to whom fate gives the victory."

CHAPTER XXXVII. KING EDWARD'S ANSWER TO KING MAGNUS'S LETTER.—Now when King Edward had read this letter, he replied thus: "It is known to all men in this country that King Ethelred, my father, was udal-born to this kingdom, both after the old and new law of inheritance. We were four sons after him; and when he by death left the throne, my brother Edmund took the government and kingdom; for he was the oldest of us brothers, and I was well satisfied that it was

---

[1] Orkneyingasaga.
[2] A letter with the seal on it unbroken.

so. And after him my stepfather, Canute the Great, took the kingdom, and while he lived it was hard to lay claim to it. After him my brother [1] Harald was king as long as he lived; and after him my brother Hardacanute took the kingdoms both of Denmark and England; for he thought that a just brotherly division that he should have both England and Denmark, and that I should have no kingdom at all. Now he died, and then it was the resolution of all the people of the country to take me for king here in England. So long as I had no kingly title I served my superiors, in all respects, like those who had no claims by birth to land or kingdom. Now, however, I have received the kingly title, and am consecrated king. I have established my royal dignity and authority, as my father before me; and while I live I will not renounce my title. If King Magnus come here with an army, I will gather no army against him; but he shall only get the opportunity of taking England when he has taken my life. Tell him these words of mine." The ambassadors went back to King Magnus, and told him the answer to their message. King Magnus reflected a while, and answered thus: "I think that it is most just and fitting to let King Edward have his kingdom in peace for me, and that I keep the kingdoms God has put into my hands."

[1] Half-brother, cf. p. 129, note 1, and p. 141. The treaty between Magnus and Hardacanute was made in 1038 or 1939. Hardacanute died on 8 June, 1042, and Magnus invaded Denmark. He also claimed the English throne, and until his death in 1046 the English were in constant fear of a Norwegian attack. Strangely enough, Queen Emma, mother of Edward the Confessor, appears to have favoured Magnus's claim, and it was probably because of this that the king confiscated her property in 1043. She could have had little support in England generally, where the leaders found it better policy to favour Svein Ulvsson's cause in Denmark and use him as their first defence against Magnus. Magnus's successor, Harald the Stern, thought he fell heir to Magnus's claims to the Danish and English thrones, and it was this that brought him to England in 1066.

X

HARALD THE STERN[1]

[1030–66]

CHAPTER I. HARALD ESCAPES FROM THE BATTLE OF STIKLESTAD [1030].—Harald, son of Sigurd Syr, brother of Olaf the Saint by the same mother, was at the battle of Stiklestad, and was fifteen years old when King Olaf the Saint fell, as before related. Harald was wounded, and escaped with other fugitives. Of this Thjodolf the scald makes mention in the poem he composed about King Harald, which he called "Sexstefia":

> At Haug[2] the fire-sparks from his shield
> Flew round the king's head on the field,
> As blow for blow, for Olaf's sake,
> His sword and shield would give and take.
> Bulgaria's conqueror,[3] I ween,
> Had scarcely fifteen winters seen,
> When from his murdered brother's side
> His unhelmed head he had to hide.

Rognvald Bruseson[4] led Harald from the battle, and the night after the fray took him to a bonde who dwelt in the forest far from other people. The peasant received Harald, and kept him concealed; and Harald was waited upon until he was quite cured of his wounds. Then the bonde's son attended him on the way east over Kjölen, and they went by all the forest paths they could, avoiding the common road. The bonde's son did not know who it was he was attending; and as they were riding together through the uninhabited forests, Harald made these verses:

> My wounds were bleeding as I rode;
> And down below the bonder strode,
> Killing the wounded with the sword,
> The followers of their rightful lord.
> From wood to wood I crept along,
> Unnoticed by the bonder-throng;
> "Who knows," I thought, "a day may come
> My name will yet be great at home."

---

[1] Harald Hardrade (the Stern) was born in 1015 and reigned from about 1046 to 1066.
[2] Haug is a farm near Stiklestad in Værdal, where the battle was fought.
[3] An allusion to Harald's exploits in the East with the Væringer, when he helped to subdue the rebel Bulgarians in 1041.
[4] Vide *Olaf Sagas*, p. 378.

He went eastward over the ridge through Jemteland and Helsingeland, and came to Sweden, where he found Rognvald Bruseson, and many others of King Olaf's men who had fled from the battle at Stiklestad, and they remained there till winter was over.

CHAPTER II. HARALD'S JOURNEY TO CONSTANTINOPLE [1031]. —The spring after, Harald and Rognvald got ships, and went east in summer to Russia to King Jarisleif, and were with him all the following winter. So says the scald Bolverk, in the poem he composed about King Harald:

> The king's sharp sword lies clean and bright,
> Prepared in foreign lands to fight:
> Our ravens croak to have their fill,
> The wolf howls from the distant hill.
> Our brave king is to Russia gone—
> Braver than he on earth there's none:
> His sharp sword will carve many a feast
> To wolf and raven in the East.

King Jarisleif gave Harald and Rognvald a kind reception, and made Harald and Eilif, the son of Earl Rognvald,[1] chiefs over the land-defence[2] men of the king. So says Thjodolf:

> Where Eilif was, one heart and hand
> The two chiefs had in their command;
> In wedge or line their battle order
> Was ranged by both without disorder.
> The eastern Vendland[3] men they drove
> Into a corner; and they move
> The Lesians,[4] although ill at ease,
> To take the laws their conquerors please.

Arnor, the earls' scald, related that Rognvald Bruseson was for a long time land-defence man in Russia, and fought many battles there:

> In Russia, though now grown old,
> The battle-loving earl, the bold,
> Of Gondul[5] favoured, in the field
> Raised in ten fights his battered shield

---

[1] See *Olaf Sagas*, p. 210.

[2] *Landvarnarmenn konungs*, the king's land-defence-men, chiefly responsible for protecting the frontiers and garrisoning the march fortresses. Cf. German *Landwehr*.

[3] Jarisleif (Yaroslav) the Wise, Grand Duke of Novgorod from 1016 to 1019, became Prince of Kiev in 1019, and ruled until 1054. He was married to Ingegerd, daughter of King Olaf. In 1031 he invaded his Vendish and Polish neighbours, and Harald and Eilif probably took part in this campaign.

[4] Lesians were most probably the Poles. Lazzi, Lezilii, are similar names in the early history of Poland.

[5] Gondul, one of the valkyries, who selected the slain for Odin's hall.

Harald remained several years in Russia, and travelled far
and wide in the Eastern land. Then he began his expedition
out to Greece, and had a great suite of men with him; and on
he went to Constantinople.[1] So says Bolverk:

> Before the cold sea-curling blast
> The cutter from the land flew past,
> Her black yards swinging to and fro,
> Her shield-hung gunwale dipping low.
> The king saw glancing o'er the bow
> Constantinople's metal glow
> From tower and roof, and painted sails
> Gliding past towns and wooded vales.

CHAPTER III. OF HARALD.—At that time the Greek empire
was ruled by the empress Zoe the Great,[2] and with her Michael
Catalactus. Now when Harald came to Constantinople he presented himself to the empress, and went into her pay; and
immediately, in autumn, went on board the galleys manned
with troops which went out to the Greek sea.[3] Harald had his
own men along with him. Now Harald had been but a short
time in the army before all the Væringer [4] flocked to him, and
they all joined together when there was a battle. It thus came
to pass that Harald was made chief of the Væringer. There
was a chief over all the troops who was called Gyrge,[5] and who
was a relation of the empress. Gyrge and Harald went round
among all the Greek islands, and fought much against the
corsairs.

CHAPTER IV. OF HARALD AND GYRGE CASTING LOTS.—It
happened once that Gyrge and the Væringer were going through

---

[1] Miklegarth is the regular Norse name for Byzantium (Constantinople).
-garth is the second element in names such as Novgorod.
[2] She reigned from 1028 to 1052, wife of three emperors in succession.
[3] The Eastern Mediterranean, south and east of Greece.
[4] The Varangians have become famous as a picked body of Norse mercenary soldiers in the service of the Byzantine emperors. The name
Væringjar has been interpreted in various ways. The best explanation is
that it originally meant "men who bind themselves together by pledges,"
and was used of themselves by the companies of traders from Sweden who
penetrated through Russia following the course of the great rivers. (This
commercial expansion had already begun by about 800 and was followed
by the establishment of principalities under Swedish leadership, first
centred on Novgorod, later on Kiev as well.) When the word first came
into Greek it was used to mean Norseman. and it was only after the Norsemen became well known as fighting men that it acquired the special sense
of "mercenary soldier of Norse origin." It was finally used of all mercenary soldiers from the Germanic countries (Englishmen formed the chief
element in the Varangian troops *c.* 1100). Harald Sigurdsson served with
the Varangians *c.* 1034-42.
[5] Georgios Maniakes, who was the brave leader of the Greeks in the
Euphrates regions 1033-5, and in Sicily 1038-40.

the country, and they resolved to take their night quarters by a wood; and as the Væringer came first to the ground, they chose the place which was best for pitching their tents upon, which was the highest ground; for it is the nature of the land there to be soft when rain falls, and therefore it is bad to choose a low situation for tents. Now when Gyrge, the chief of the army, came up, and saw where the Væringer had set up their tents, he told them to remove, and pitch their tents elsewhere, saying he would himself pitch his tents on their ground. Harald replies, "If you come first to the night quarter, you take up your ground, and we must go pitch our tents at some other place where we best can. Now do you so, in the same way, and find a place where you will. It is, I think, the privilege of us Væringer here in the dominions of the Greek emperor to be free, and independent of all but their own commanders, and bound only to serve the emperor and empress." They disputed long and hotly about this, and both sides armed themselves, and were on the way to fight for it; but men of understanding came between and separated them. They said it would be better to come to an agreement about such questions, so that in future no dispute could arise. It came thus to an arbitration between them, at which the best and most sagacious men should give their judgment in the case. At this arbitration it was determined, with the consent of all parties, that lots should be thrown into a box, and the Greeks and Væringer should draw which was first to ride, or to row, or to take place in a harbour, or to choose tent ground; and each side should be satisfied with what the drawing of the lots gave them. Accordingly the lots were made, and marked. Harald said to Gyrge, "Let me see what mark thou hast put upon thy lot, that we may not both mark our lots in the same way." He did so. Then Harald marked his lot, and put it into the box along with the other. The man who was to draw out the lots then took up one of the lots between his fingers, held it up in the air, and said, "This lot shall be the first to ride, and to row, and to take place in harbour and on the tent field." Harald seized his hand, snatched the die, and threw it into the sea, and called out, "That was our lot!" Gyrge said, "Why did you not let other people see it?" Harald replies, "Look at the one remaining in the box—there you see your own mark upon it." Accordingly the lot which was left behind was examined, and all men saw that Gyrge's mark was upon it, and accordingly the judgment was given that the Væringer had gained the first choice in all they had been quarrelling about. There were many things they quarrelled about, but the end always was that Harald got his own way.

CHAPTER V. HARALD'S EXPEDITION IN THE LAND OF THE SARACENS.—They went out all on a campaign in summer. When the whole army was thus assembled Harald kept his men out of the battle, or wherever he saw the least danger, under pretext of saving his men; but where he was alone with his own men only, he fought so desperately that they must either come off victorious or die. It thus happened often that when he commanded the army he gained victories, while Gyrge could do nothing. The troops observed this, and insisted they would be more successful if Harald alone was chief of the whole army, and upbraided the general with never effecting anything, neither himself, nor his people. Gyrge again said that the Væringer would give him no assistance, and ordered Harald to go with his men somewhere else, and he, with the rest of his army, would win what they could. Harald accordingly left the army with the Væringer and the Latin men,[1] and Gyrge on his side went off with the Greek troops. Then it was seen what each could do. Harald always gained victories and booty; but the Greeks went home to Constantinople with their army, all except the young men, who, to gain booty and money, joined themselves to Harald, and took him for their leader. He then went with his troops westward to Africa, which the Væringer call Saracen's land,[2] where he was strengthened with many men. In the Saracen's land he took eighty castles, some of which surrendered, and others were stormed. He then went to Sicily. So says Thjodolf:

> The serpent's bed of glowing gold
> He hates [3]—the generous king, the bold!
> He who four score towers laid low,
> Ta'en from the Saracenic foe.
> Before upon Sicilian plains,
> Shield joined to shield, the fight he gains,
> The victory at Hilda's game,[4]
> And now the heathens dread his name.

---

[1] Soldiers from the Latin lands, France or Italy.

[2] Serkland in Asia may be here confounded with Africa, for Harald in the years 1035-7 was engaged in wars in Syria and Armenia before he went to Sicily in 1038.

[3] The hater of the serpent's bed is the figurative expression of the scald for the generous man. Serpents were legendarily the guardians of gold; and its hater is the man who parts with it as a thing he hates—the generous giver.

[4] Hilda's game—the game of war.

So says also Illuge Bryndæla-scald [1]:

> For Michael's empire Harald fought,
> And southern lands to Michael brought;
> So Budle's son his friendship showed
> When he brought friends to his abode. [2]

Here it is said that Michael was king of the Greeks at that time. Harald remained many years in Africa, where he gathered great wealth in gold, jewels, and all sorts of precious things; and all the wealth he gathered there which he did not need for his expenses, he sent with trusty men of his own north to Novgorod to King Jarisleif's care and keeping. He gathered together there extraordinary treasure, as is reasonable to suppose; for he had the plundering of the part of the world richest in gold and valuable things, and he had done such great deeds as with truth are related, such as taking eighty strongholds by his valour.

CHAPTER VI. BATTLE IN SICILY.—Now when Harald came to Sicily he plundered there also, and sat down with his army before a strong and populous castle. He surrounded the castle; but the walls were so thick there was no possibility of breaking into it, and the people of the castle had enough of provisions, and all that was necessary for defence. Then Harald hit upon an expedient. He made his bird-catchers catch the small birds which had their nests within the castle, but flew into the woods by day to get food for their young. He had small splinters of tarred wood bound upon the backs of the birds, smeared these over with wax and sulphur, and set fire to them. As soon as the birds were let loose they all flew at once to the castle to their young, and to their nests, which they had under the house roofs that were covered with reeds or straw. [3] The fire from the birds seized upon the house roofs; and although each bird could only carry a small burden of fire, yet all at once there was a mighty flame, caused by so many birds carrying fire with them and spreading it widely among the house roofs. Thus one house after the other was set on fire, until the castle itself was in flames. Then the people came out of the castle and begged for mercy; the same men who for many days had set at defiance the

---

[1] i.e. probably from Brynjudal in the south-west of Iceland.

[2] These last two lines form a refrain, which apparently has no reference to those preceding. The allusion is to Atle, Budle's son, who invited his brothers-in-law, Gunnar and Högne, to his home and then killed them. See the Lay of Atle (*Atlakviða*) in *The Poetic Edda*.

[3] The same unlikely stratagem is attributed to various other commanders in medieval sources.

Greek army and its leader. Harald granted life and safety
to all who asked quarter, and made himself master of the
place.

CHAPTER VII. BATTLE AT ANOTHER CASTLE.—There was
another castle before which Harald had come with his army.
This castle was both full of people and so strong that there
was no hope of breaking into it. The castle stood upon a
flat hard plain. Then Harald undertook to dig a passage from
a place where a stream ran in a bed so deep that it could not
be seen from the castle. They threw out all the earth into
the stream, to be carried away by the water. At this work
they laboured day and night, and relieved each other in gangs;
while the rest of the army went the whole day against the
castle, where the castle people shot through their loopholes.
They shot at each other all day in this way, and at night they
slept on both sides. Now when Harald perceived that his
underground passage was so long that it must be within the
castle walls, he ordered his people to arm themselves. It was
towards daybreak that they went into the passage. When they
got to the end of it they dug over their heads until they came
upon stones laid in lime, which was the floor of a stone hall.
They broke open the floor, and rose into the hall. There sat
many of the castle-men eating and drinking, and not in the
least expecting such uninvited wolves; for the Væringer instantly
attacked them sword in hand, and killed some, and those who
could get away fled. The Væringer pursued them; and some
seized the castle gate, and opened it, so that the whole body of
the army got in. The people of the castle fled; but many
asked quarter from the troops, which was granted to all who
surrendered. In this way Harald got possession of the place,
and found an immense booty in it.

CHAPTER VIII. BATTLE AT A THIRD CASTLE.—They came to
a third castle, the greatest and strongest of them all, and also
the richest in property and fullest of people. Around this
castle there were great ditches, so that it evidently could not
be taken by the same device as the former; and they lay a
long time before it without doing anything. When the castle-
men saw this they became bolder, drew up their array on the
castle walls, threw open the castle gates, and shouted to the
Væringer, urging them, and jeering at them, and telling them
to come into the castle, and that they were no more fit for
battle than so many poultry. Harald told his men to make as
if they did not know what to do, or did not understand what

was said. "For," said he, "if we do make an assault we can effect nothing, as they can throw their weapons under their feet among us; and if we get into the castle with a party of our people, they have it in their power to shut them in, and shut out the others; for they have all the castle gates beset with men. We shall therefore show them the same scorn they show us, and let them see we do not fear them. Our men shall go out upon the plain nearest to the castle; taking care, however, to keep out of bow-shot. All our men shall be unarmed, and be playing with each other, so that the castle-men may see we do not regard them or their array." Thus it went on for some days, without anything being done.

CHAPTER IX. OF ULV AND HALDOR.—Two Iceland men were then with Harald: the one was Haldor, a son of the gode Snorre, who brought this account to Iceland; the other was Ulv Ospakson, a grandson of Osviver Spake. Both were very strong men, bold under arms, and Harald's best friends; and both were in this play. Now when some days were passed the castle people showed more courage, and would go without weapons upon the castle wall, while the castle gates were standing open. The Væringer observing this, went one day to their sports with the sword under their cloaks, and the helmet under their hats. After playing a while they observed that the castle people were off their guard; and instantly seizing their weapons, they made a rush at the castle gates. When the men of the castle saw this they went against them armed completely, and a battle began in the castle gates. The Væringer had no shields, but wrapped their cloaks round their left arms. Some of them were wounded, some killed, and all stood in great danger. Now came Harald, with the men who had remained in the camp, to the assistance of his people; and the castle-men had now got out upon the walls, from which they shot and threw stones down upon them; so that there was a severe battle, and those who were in the castle gates thought that help was brought them slower than they could have wished. When Harald came to the castle gates his standard-bearer fell, and Harald said to Haldor, "Do thou take up the banner now." Haldor took up the banner, and said foolishly, "Who will carry the banner before thee, if thou followest it so timidly as thou hast done for a while?" But these were words more of anger than of truth; for Harald was one of the boldest of men under arms. Then they pressed in, and had a hard battle in the castle; and the end was that Harald gained the victory, and took the castle. Haldor was much wounded in the face, and he wore great scars as long as he lived.[1]

CHAPTER X. BATTLE AT A FOURTH CASTLE.—The fourth castle which Harald came to was the greatest of all we have been speaking about. It was so strong that there was no possibility of breaking into it. They surrounded the castle, so that no supplies could get into it. When they had remained here a short time Harald fell sick, and he betook himself to his bed. He had his tent put up a little from the camp, for he found quietness and rest out of the clamour and clang of armed men. His men went usually in companies to or from him to hear his orders; and the castle people observing there was something new among the Væringer, sent out spies to discover what this might mean. When the spies came back to the castle they had to tell of the illness of the commander of the Væringer, and that no assault on that account had been made on the castle. A while after this Harald's strength began to fail, at which his men were very melancholy and cast down; all which was news to the castle-men. At last Harald's sickness increased so rapidly that his death was made known among all the army. Thereafter the Væringer went to the castle-men; told them, in a parley, of the death of their commander; and begged of the priests to grant him burial in the castle. When the castle people heard this news, there were many among them who ruled over cloisters or other great establishments within the place, and who were very eager to get the corpse for their church, knowing that upon that there would follow very rich presents. A great many priests, therefore, clothed themselves in all their robes, and went out of the castle with cross, and shrine, and relics, and formed a beautiful procession. The Væringer also made a great burial. The coffin was borne high in the air, and over it was a tent of costly linen, and before it were carried many banners. Now when the corpse was brought within the castle gates the Væringer set down the coffin right across the entry, fixed a bar to keep the gates open, and sounded to battle with all their trumpets, and drew their swords. The whole army of the Væringer, fully armed, rushed from the camp to the assault of the castle with shout and cry; and the monks and other priests who had gone to meet the corpse, and had striven with each other who should be the first to come out and take the offering at the burial, were now striving much more

[1] Snorri Sturluson, author of the *Heimskringla*, was descended from Haldor in the fifth generation.

who should first get away from the Væringer; for they killed
before their feet every one who was nearest, whether clerk or
unconsecrated. The Væringer rummaged so well this castle,
that they killed all the men, pillaged everything, and made an
enormous booty.

CHAPTER XI. OF HARALD.—Harald was many years in these
campaigns, both in Saracen land and in Sicily. Then he came
back to Constantinople with his troops, and stayed there but a
little time before he began his expedition to Jerusalem.[1] There
he left the pay he had received from the Greek emperor, and
all the Væringer who accompanied him did the same. It is
said that on all these expeditions Harald had fought eighteen
regular battles. So says Thjodolf:

> Harald the Stern ne'er allowed
> Peace to his foemen, false and proud:
> In eighteen battles, fought and won,
> The valour of the Norseman shone.
> The king, before his home return,
> Oft dyed the bald head of the erne
> With bloody specks, and o'er the waste
> The sharp-claw'd wolf his footsteps traced.

CHAPTER XII. HARALD'S EXPEDITION TO PALESTINE.—
Harald went with his men to Palestine, and then up to the
city of Jerusalem, and wheresoever he came in the land all the
towns and strongholds were given up to him. So says the scald
Stuv, who had heard the king himself relate these tidings:

> He went, the warrior bold and brave,
> Jerusalem, the holy grave,
> And the interior of the land,
> To bring under the Greeks' command;
> And by the terror of his name
> Under his power the country came,
> Nor needed wasting fire and sword
> To yield obedience to his word.

Here it is told that this land came without fire and sword
under Harald's command. He then went out to Jordan, and
bathed therein, according to the custom of other palmers.[2]
Harald gave great gifts to our Lord's grave, to the Holy Cross,
and other holy relics in Palestine. He also cleared the whole

---

[1] The Greek emperor, Michael, had in 1036 made peace with the
Egyptian caliph, who permitted the emperor to build the church over
the grave of Jesus Christ. The emperor sent artisans thither, and in the
guard detailed to protect them Harald was one of the leaders.

[2] i.e. pilgrims who on the way home from Jerusalem were wont to carry
palm branches to testify where they had been.

road all the way out to Jordan, by killing the robbers and other disturbers of the peace. So says the scald Stuv:

> The Agder king cleared far and wide
> Jordan's fair banks on either side;
> The robber-bands before him fled,
> And his great name was widely spread.
> The wicked people of the land
> Were punished here by his dread hand,
> And they hereafter will not miss
> Much worse from Jesus Christ than this.

CHAPTER XIII. HARALD PUT IN PRISON.—Thereafter he went back to Constantinople. When Harald returned to Constantinople from Jerusalem he longed to return to the North to his native land; and when he heard that Magnus Olafson, his brother's son, had become king both of Norway and Denmark, he gave up his command in the Greek service. And when the empress Zoe heard of this she became angry, and raised an accusation against Harald, that he had misapplied the property of the Greek emperor which he had received in the campaigns in which he was commander of the army. There was a young and beautiful girl called Maria, a brother's daughter of the empress Zoe,[1] and Harald had paid his addresses to her; but the empress had given him a refusal. The Væringer, who were then in pay in Constantinople, have told here in the North that there went a report among well-informed people that the empress Zoe herself wanted Harald for her husband, and that she chiefly blamed Harald for his determination to leave Constantinople, although another reason was given out to the public. Constantinus Monomachus [2] was at that time emperor of the Greeks, and ruled along with Zoe. On this account the Greek emperor had Harald made prisoner, and carried to prison.[3]

CHAPTER XIV. KING OLAF'S MIRACLE, AND PUTTING OUT THE EYES OF THE GREEK EMPEROR.—When Harald drew near to the prison King Olaf the Saint stood before him, and said he would assist him. On that spot of the street a chapel [4] has since been built, and consecrated to Saint Olaf, and that chapel has stood there ever since. The prison was so constructed

---

[1] Zoe had no brother—the relationship is incorrect, and the lady unknown to history.

[2] Constantine IX Monomachus married Zoe on 11 June, 1042, and was crowned emperor at the same time (reigned till 1055). His predecessor, Michael Calaphates, was blinded and put in a monastery on 21 April, 1042.

[3] This imprisonment is mentioned by William of Malmesbury, who says that Harald was thrown to a lion, which he strangled.

[4] Such a chapel is not known in Constantinople.

that there was a high tower open above, but a door below to
go into it from the street. Through it Harald was thrust in,
along with Haldor and Ulv. Next night a lady of distinction
with two servants came, by the help of ladders, to the top of
the tower, let down a rope into the prison, and hauled them
up. Saint Olaf had formerly cured this lady of a sickness, and
he had appeared to her in a vision, and told her to deliver his
brother. Harald went immediately to the Væringer, who all
rose from their seats when he came in, and received him with
joy. The men armed themselves forthwith, and went to where
the emperor slept. They took the emperor prisoner, and put
out both the eyes of him. So says Thorarin Skjeggeson in his
poem:

> Of glowing gold that decks the hand
> The king got plenty in this land;
> But its great emperor in the strife
> Was made stone-blind for all his life.

So says Thjodolf the scald also:

> He who the hungry wolf's wild yell
> Quiets with prey, the stern, the fell,
> Midst the uproar of shriek and shout
> Stung the Greek emperor's eyes both out:
> The Norse king's mark will not adorn,
> The Norse king's mark gives cause to mourn;
> His mark the Eastern king must bear,
> Groping his sightless way in fear.

In these two songs, and many others, it is told that Harald
himself blinded the Greek emperor; and they would surely
have named some duke, count, or other great man, if they had
not known this to be the true account; and King Harald himself, and other men who were with him, spread this account.[1]

CHAPTER XV. HARALD'S JOURNEY FROM CONSTANTINOPLE.—
The same night King Harald and his men went to the house
where Maria slept, and carried her away by force. Then they
went down to where the galleys of the Væringer lay, took two
of them, and rowed out into Sævids sound.[2] When they came
to the place where the iron chain is drawn across the sound,
Harald told his men to stretch out at their oars in both galleys,
but the men who were not rowing to run all to the stern of the
galley, each with his luggage in his hand. The galleys thus

---

[1] Michael Calaphates, not Constantine Monomachus, was blinded.
Harald perhaps saw to the execution of the order, which was given by the
city governor.

[2] Sævids sound, the Golden Horn, the sound between Constantinople
proper and Galata. Across its mouth an iron chain resting on wooden
floats could be fixed.

ran up, and lay on the iron chain. As soon as they stood fast on it, and would advance no farther, Harald ordered all the men to run forward into the bow. Then the galley in which Harald was balanced forwards, and swung down over the chain; but the other, which remained fast athwart the chain, split in two, by which many men were lost; but some were taken up out of the sound. Thus Harald escaped out of Constantinople, and sailed thence into the Black Sea; but before he left the land he put the lady ashore, and sent her back with a good escort to Constantinople, and bade her tell her relation, the empress Zoe, how little power she had over Harald, and how little the empress could have hindered him from taking the lady. Harald then sailed northwards in the Ellepallta,[1] and then all round the Eastern empire.[2] On this voyage Harald composed sixteen songs for amusement, and all ending with the same words. This is one of them:

> Past Sicily's wide plains we flew,
> A dauntless, never-wearied crew;
> Our viking steed rushed through the sea,
> As viking-like fast, fast sailed we.
> Never, I think, along this shore
> Did Norseman ever sail before;
> Yet to the Russian queen, I fear,
> My gold-adorned, I am not dear.

With this he meant Ellesiv, daughter of King Jarisleif in Novgorod.

CHAPTER XVI. OF KING HARALD.—When Harald came to Novgorod, King Jarisleif received him in the most friendly way, and he remained there all winter. Then he took into his own keeping all the gold, and the many kinds of precious things which he had sent there from Constantinople, and which together made up so vast a treasure, that no man in the northern lands ever saw the like of it in one man's possession. Harald had been three times in the Polota-svarv [3] while he was in Constantinople. It is the custom, namely, there, that every time one of the Greek emperors dies, the Væringer are allowed polota-svarv; that is, they may go through all the emperor's

---

[1] Thought to be compounded of Greek *hele* and Latin *paludes* (*plur.*), each meaning swamp; here it appears to mean the estuary of the Dnieper.

[2] The Eastern Empire is a general name for the lands east and south-east of the Baltic, including the principalities of Novgorod and Kiev.

[3] This is usually taken to mean "palace-rifling," but it is unlikely that the emperor's palace was thrown open to the soldiery on his death. Another explanation is that *pólúta* here is not derived from *palatium* but from Russian *pol'udije*, tax-gathering circuit, reinforced by Norse *svarf*, also meaning circuit. These were profitable excursions.

palaces where his treasures are, and each may take and keep
what he can lay hold of while he is going through them.

CHAPTER XVII. KING HARALD'S MARRIAGE.—This winter
King Jarisleif gave Harald his daughter Elizabeth in marriage.
She is called by the Northmen Ellesiv. This is related by
Stuv the Blind, thus:

> Agder's chief now got the queen
> Who long his secret love had been.
> Of gold, no doubt, a mighty store
> The princess to her husband bore.

In spring [1045] he began his journey from Novgorod, and
came to Aldeigjaborg,[1] where he took shipping, and sailed from
the East in summer. He turned first to Sweden, and came to
Sigtuna. So says Valgard of Völl[2]:

> The fairest cargo ship e'er bore,
> From Russia's distant eastern shore
> The gallant Harald homeward brings—
> Gold, and a fame that scald still sings.
> The ship through dashing foam he steers,
> Through the sea-rain to Sweden veers,
> And at Sigtuna's grassy shores
> His gallant vessel safely moors.

CHAPTER XVIII. THE LEAGUE BETWEEN KING HARALD
AND SVEIN ULVSON.—Harald found there before him Svein
Ulvson, who the autumn before had fled from King Magnus
at Helganes; and when they met they were very friendly on
both sides. The Swedish king, Olaf the Swede, was father of
the mother of Ellesiv, Harald's wife; and Astrid, the mother of
Svein, was King Olaf's sister. Harald and Svein entered into
friendship with each other, and confirmed it by oath. All the
Swedes were friendly to Svein, because he belonged to the
greatest family in the country; and thus all the Swedes were
Harald's friends and helpers also, for many great men were
connected with him by marriage-ties. So says Thjodolf:

> 'Cross the East sea the vessel flew—
> Her oak-keel a white furrow drew
> From Russia's coast to Swedish land,
> Where Harald can great help command.
> The heavy vessel's leeward side
> Was hid beneath the rushing tide;
> While the broad sail and gold-tipped mast
> Swung to and fro in the hard blast.

CHAPTER XIX. KING HARALD'S FORAY.—Then Harald and
Svein fitted out ships, and gathered together a great force;

---

[1] Old Ladoga, on Lake Ladoga, not far from present Leningrad.
[2] A farm in the parish of Hvoll, Rangárvallasýsla, south Iceland.

and when the troops were ready they sailed from the East towards Denmark. So says Valgard:

> Brave Yngve! to the land decreed
> To thee by fate, with tempest speed
> The winds fly with thee o'er the sea—
> To thy own udal land with thee.
> As past the Scanian plains they fly,
> The gay ships glance 'twixt sea and sky,
> And Scanian brides look out, and fear
> Some ill to those they hold most dear.

They landed first in Sealand with their men, and herried[1] and burned in the land far and wide. Then they went to Fyen, where they also landed and laid waste. So says Valgard:

> Harald! thou hast the isle laid waste,
> The Sealand men away hast chased,
> And the wild wolf by daylight roams
> Through their deserted silent homes.
> Fiona too could not withstand
> The fury of thy wasting hand.
> Helms burst, shields broke—Fiona's bounds
> Were filled with death's terrific sounds.

> Red flashing in the southern sky,
> The clear flame sweeping broad and high,
> From fair Roskilde's lofty towers,
> On lowly huts its fire-rain pours;
> And shows the housemates' silent train
> In terror scouring o'er the plain,
> Seeking the forest's deepest glen,
> To house with wolves, and 'scape from men.

> Few were they of escape to tell,
> For, sorrow-worn, the people fell:
> The only captives from the fray
> Were lovely maidens led away.
> And in wild terror to the strand,
> Down to the ships, the linked band
> Of fair-haired girls is roughly driven,
> Their soft skins by the irons riven.

CHAPTER XX. KING MAGNUS'S LEVY [1044].—King Magnus Olafson sailed north to Norway after the battle at Helganes.[2] There he hears the news that Harald Sigurdson, his relation, was come to Sweden; and moreover that Svein Ulvson and Harald had entered into a friendly bond with each other, and gathered together a great force, intending first to subdue Den-

---

[1] Laing prefers this "old North-country word . . . revived by Sir Walter Scott" to the usual English "harry." The Norse verb is *herja*, cognate with Old English *hergian*, both with the same sense.

[2] See p. 154, note 1.

mark, and then Norway. King Magnus then ordered a general
levy over all Norway, and he soon collected a great army. He
hears then that Harald and Svein were come to Denmark
[1046], and were burning and laying waste the land, and that
the country people were everywhere submitting to them. It
was also told that King Harald was stronger and stouter than
other men, and so wise withal that nothing was impossible to
him, and he had always the victory when he fought a battle;
and he was also so rich in gold that no man could compare
with him in wealth. Thjodolf speaks thus of it:

> Norsemen, who stand the sword of foe
> Like forest-stems, unmoved by blow!
> My hopes are fled, no peace is near—
> People fly here and there in fear.
> On either side of Sealand's coast
> A fleet appears—a white-winged host:
> Magnus from Norway takes his course,
> Harald from Sweden leads his force.

CHAPTER XXI. TREATY BETWEEN HARALD AND MAGNUS.—
Those of Magnus's men who were in his counsel said that it
would be a great misfortune if relations like Harald and Magnus
should fight, and throw a death-spear against each other; and
therefore many offered to attempt bringing about some agreement between them, and the king, by their persuasion, agreed
to it. Thereupon some men were sent off in a light boat, in
which they sailed south in all haste to Denmark, and got some
Danish men, who were proven friends of King Magnus, to
propose this matter to Harald. This affair was conducted very
secretly. Now when Harald heard that his relation King
Magnus would offer him a league and partition, so that Harald
should have half of Norway with King Magnus, and that they
should divide all their movable property into two equal parts,
he accepted the proposal, and the people went back to King
Magnus with this answer.

CHAPTER XXII. TREATY BETWEEN HARALD AND SVEIN
BROKEN.—A little after this it happened that Harald and
Svein one evening were sitting at table drinking and talking
together, and Svein asked Harald what valuable piece of all
his property he esteemed the most.

He answered, it was his banner Land-ravager.

Svein asked what was there remarkable about it, that he
valued it so highly.

Harald replied, it was a common saying that he must gain

the victory before whom that banner is borne, and it had turned out so ever since he had owned it.

Svein replies, "I will begin to believe there is such virtue in the banner when thou hast held three battles with thy relation Magnus, and hast gained them all."

Then answered Harald with an angry voice, "I know my relationship to King Magnus, without thy reminding me of it; and although we are now going in arms against him, yet other meetings between us may be of a better sort."

Svein changed colour, and said, "There are people, Harald, who say that thou hast done as much before as only to hold that part of an agreement which appears to suit thy own interest best."

Harald answers, "It becomes thee ill to say that I have not stood by an agreement, when I know what King Magnus could tell of thy proceedings with him."

Thereupon each went his own way. At night, when Harald went to sleep within the bulwarks of his vessel, he said to his footboy, "I will not sleep in my bed to-night, for I suspect there may be treachery abroad. I observed this evening that my friend Svein was very angry at my free discourse. Thou shalt keep watch, therefore, in case anything happen in the night." Harald then went away to sleep somewhere else, and laid a billet of wood in his place. At midnight a boat rowed alongside to the ship's bulwark; a man went on board, lifted up the cloth of the tent over the bulwarks, went up, and struck in Harald's bed with a great axe, so that it stood fast in the lump of wood. The man instantly ran back to his boat again, and rowed away in the dark night, for the moon was set; but the axe remained sticking in the piece of wood as an evidence. Thereupon Harald waked his men, and let them know the treachery intended. "We can now see sufficiently," said he, "that we could never match Svein, if he practises such deliberate treachery against us; so it will be best for us to get away from this place while we can. Let us cast loose our vessels and row away as quickly as possible." They did so, and rowed during the night northwards along the land; and then proceeded night and day until they came to King Magnus, where he lay with his army. Harald went to his relation Magnus, and there was a joyful meeting betwixt them. So says Thjodolf:

> The far-known king the order gave,
> In silence o'er the swelling wave,
> With noiseless oars, his vessels gay
> From Denmark west to row away;

And Olaf's son, with justice rare,
Offers with him the realm to share.
People, no doubt, rejoiced to find
The kings had met in peaceful mind.

Afterwards the two relatives conversed with each other, and all was settled by peaceful agreement.

CHAPTER XXIII. KING MAGNUS GIVES HARALD HALF OF NORWAY.—King Magnus lay at the shore, and had set up tents upon the land. There he invited his relation King Harald to be his guest at table; and Harald went to the entertainment with sixty of his men, and was feasted excellently. Towards the end of the day King Magnus went into the tent where Harald sat, and with him went men carrying parcels consisting of clothes and arms. Then the king went to the man who sat lowest, and gave him a good sword, to the next a shield, to the next a kirtle, and so on—clothes, or weapons, or gold; to all he gave one or the other valuable gift, and the more costly to the more distinguished men among them. Then he placed himself before his relation Harald, holding two sticks in his hand, and said, "Which of these two sticks wilt thou have, my kinsman?"

Harald replies, "The one nearest me."

"Then," said King Magnus, "with this stick I give thee half of the Norwegian power, with all the scatt and duties, and all the domains thereunto belonging, with the condition that everywhere thou shalt be as lawful king in Norway as I am myself; but when we are both together in one place, I shall be the first man in seat, service, and salutation; and if there be three of us together of equal dignity, that I shall sit in the middle, and shall have the royal tent-ground, and the royal landing-place. Thou shalt strengthen and advance our kingdom, in return for making thee that man in Norway whom we never expected any man should be so long as our head was above ground."

Then Harald stood up, and thanked him for the high title and dignity. Thereupon they both sat down, and were very merry together. The same evening Harald and his men returned to their ships.

CHAPTER XXIV. HARALD GIVES KING MAGNUS THE HALF OF HIS TREASURES.—The following morning King Magnus ordered the trumpets to sound to a General Thing of the people; and when it was opened, he made known to the whole army the gift he had given to his relation Harald. Tore of Steig [1] gave

---

[1] Son of Thord Guttormsson of Steig, see *Olaf Sagas*, pp. 265–6.

Harald the title of king there at the Thing; and the same day King Harald invited King Magnus to table with him, and he went with sixty men to King Harald's land-tent, where he had prepared a feast. The two kings sat together on a high seat, and the feast was splendid; everything went on with magnificence, and the kings were merry and glad. Towards the close of the day King Harald ordered many caskets to be brought into the tent, and in like manner people bore in weapons, clothes, and other sorts of valuables; and all these King Harald divided among King Magnus's men who were at the feast. Then he had the caskets opened, and said to King Magnus, "Yesterday you gave us a large kingdom, which your hand won from your and our enemies, and took us in partnership with you, which was well done; and this has cost you much. Now we on our side have been in foreign parts, and oft in peril of life, to gather the gold which you here see. Now, King Magnus, I will divide this with you. We shall both own this movable property, and each have his equal share of it, as each has his equal half share of Norway. I know that our dispositions are different, as thou art more liberal than I am; therefore let us divide this property equally between us, so that each may have his share free to do with as he will." Then Harald had a large ox-hide spread out, and turned the gold out of the caskets upon it. Then scales and weights were taken, and the gold separated, and divided by weight into equal parts; and all people wondered exceedingly that so much gold should have come together in one place in the northern countries. But it was understood that it was the Greek emperor's property and wealth; for, as all people say, there are whole houses there full of red gold. The kings were now very merry. Then there appeared an ingot among the rest as big as a man's head. Harald took it in his hands, and said, "Where is the gold, kinsman Magnus, that thou canst show against this piece?"

King Magnus replied, "So many disturbances and levies have been in the country, that almost all the gold and silver I could lay up is gone. I have no more gold in my possession than this ring." And he took the ring off his hand, and gave it to Harald.

Harald looked at it, and said, "That is but little gold, nephew, for the king who owns two kingdoms; and yet some may doubt whether thou art rightful owner of even this ring."

Then King Magnus replied, after a little reflection, "If I be not rightful owner of this ring, then I know not what I have

got any right to; for my father King Olaf the Saint gave me
this ring at our last parting."

Then said King Harald, laughing, "It is true, King Magnus,
what thou sayest. Thy father gave thee this ring, but he took
the ring ·from my father for some trifling cause; and in truth
it was not a good time for small kings in Norway when thy
father was in full power."

King Harald gave Tore of Steig at that feast a bowl of
hollowed wood, that was encircled with a silver ring and had
a silver handle, both which parts were gilt; and the bowl was
filled with money of pure silver. With that came also two
gold rings, which together weighed one mark. He gave him
also his cloak of dark purple lined with white skins within, and
promised him besides his friendship and great dignity. Torgils
Snorreson,[1] an intelligent man, says he has seen an altar-cloth
that was made of this cloak; and Gudrid, a daughter of Guttorm
the son of Tore of Steig, said, according to Torgils' account,
that she had seen this bowl in her father Guttorm's possession.
Bolverk also tells of these matters:

> Thou, generous king, I have been told,
> For the green land hast given gold;
> And Magnus got a mighty treasure,
> That thou one half might'st rule at pleasure.
> The people gained a blessed peace,
> Which 'twixt the kings did never cease;
> While Svein, disturbed with war's alarms,
> Had his folk always under arms.

CHAPTER XXV. OF KING MAGNUS.—The kings Magnus and
Harald both ruled in Norway the winter after their agreement,
and each had his court. In winter they went around the
Upland country in guest-quarters; and sometimes they were
both together, sometimes each was for himself. They went
all the way north to Drontheim, to the town of Nidaros. King
Magnus had taken special care of the holy remains of King
Olaf after he came to the country; had the hair and nails clipped
every twelve-month, and kept himself the keys that opened
the shrine. Many miracles were worked by King Olaf's holy
remains. It was not long before there was a breach in the
good understanding between the two kings, as many were so
mischievous as to promote discord between them.

CHAPTER XXVI. OF SVEIN ULVSON.—Svein Ulvson remained
behind still sleeping after Harald had gone away, and inquired

---

[1] Son of the law-speaker Snorri Hunbogason (died 1170). Torgils was a
priest and lived at Skard on the Breidefjord in the west of Iceland; he died
in 1201.

about his proceedings. When he heard at last of Magnus and
Harald having agreed and joined their forces, he steered with
his forces eastward along Skaane, and remained there until
towards winter, when he heard that King Magnus and King
Harald had gone northwards to Norway. Then Svein, with
his troops, came south to Denmark, and took all the royal
income that winter.

CHAPTER XXVII. OF THE LEVY OF THE TWO KINGS [1047].
—Towards spring King Magnus and his relation King Harald
ordered a levy in Norway. It happened once that the kings
lay all night in the same harbour, and next day, King Harald
being first ready, made sail. Towards evening he brought up
in the harbour in which Magnus and his retinue had intended
to pass the night. Harald laid his vessel in the royal ground,
and there set up his tents. King Magnus got under sail later
in the day, and came into the harbour just as King Harald had
done pitching his tents. They saw then that King Harald had
taken up the king's ground, and intended to lie there. After
King Magnus had ordered the sails to be taken in, he said,
"The men will now get ready along both sides of the vessel to
lay out their oars, and some will open the hatches and bring
up the arms and arm themselves; for if they will not make way
for us, we will fight them." Now when King Harald sees that
King Magnus will give him battle, he says to his men, "Cut
our land-fastenings, and back the ship out of the ground, for
friend Magnus is in a passion." They did so, and laid the
vessel out of the ground, and King Magnus laid his vessel in it.
When they were now ready on both sides with their business,
King Harald went with a few men on board of King Magnus's
ship. King Magnus received him in a friendly way, and bade
him welcome. King Harald answered, "I thought we were
come among friends; but just now I was in doubt if ye would
have it so. But it is a truth that childhood is hasty, and I
will only consider it as a childish freak." Then said King
Magnus, "It is no childish whim, but a trait of my family, that
I never forget what I have given, or what I have not given. If
this trifle had been settled against my will, there would soon
have followed some other discord like it. In all particulars I
will hold the agreement between us; but in the same way we
will have all that belongs to us by that right." King Harald
coolly replied, that it is an old custom for the wisest to give
way; and returned to his ship. From such circumstances it
was found difficult to preserve good understanding between the

kings. King Magnus's men said he was in the right; but others, less wise, thought there was some slight put upon Harald in the business. King Harald's men, besides, insisted that the agreement was only that King Magnus should have the preference of the harbour-ground when they arrived together, but that King Harald was not bound to draw out of his place when he came first. They observed, also, that King Harald had conducted himself well and wisely in the matter. Those who viewed the business in the worst light insisted that King Magnus wanted to break the agreement, and that he had done King Harald injustice, and put an affront on him. Such disputes were talked over so long among foolish people, that the spirit of disagreeing affected the kings themselves. Many other things also occurred, in which the kings appeared determined to have each his own way; but of these little will be set down here.

CHAPTER XXVIII. KING MAGNUS THE GOOD'S DEATH.—The kings Magnus and Harald sailed with their fleet south to Denmark; and when Svein heard of their approach, he fled away east to Skaane. Magnus and Harald remained in Denmark late in summer, and subdued the whole country. In autumn they were in Jutland. One night, as King Magnus lay in his bed, it appeared to him in a dream that he was in the same place as his father Saint Olaf, and that he spoke to him thus: "Wilt thou choose, my son, to follow me, or to become a mighty king, and have long life; but to commit a crime which thou wilt never be able to expiate?" He thought he made the answer, "Do thou, father, choose for me." Then the king thought the answer was, "Thou shalt follow me." King Magnus told his men this dream. Soon after he fell sick, and lay at a place called Sudathorp.[1] When he was near his death he sent his brother [2] Tore with tokens to Svein Ulvson, with the request to give Tore the aid he might require. In this message King Magnus also gave the Danish dominions to Svein after his death; and said it was just that Harald should rule over Norway, and Svein over Denmark. Then King Magnus the Good died, and great was the sorrow of all the people at his death. So says Odd Kikinescald:

> The tears o'er good King Magnus' bier,
> The people's tears, were all sincere:
> Even they to whom he riches gave
> Carried him heavily to the grave.

---

[1] Svein Ulvsson died at Sudathorp in 1076, but Magnus Olafsson probably died in Zeeland (some sources say he was drowned).
[2] i.e. half-brother, the son of Alvhild, not of Olaf.

All hearts were struck at the king's end;
His house-thralls wept as for a friend;
His hird-men oft alone would muse,
As pondering o'er unthought-of news.

CHAPTER XXIX. KING MAGNUS'S FUNERAL. — After this
event King Harald held a Thing of his men-at-arms, and told
them his intention to go with the army to Viborg [1] Thing, and
make himself be proclaimed king over the whole Danish
dominions, to which, he said, he had hereditary right after
his relation Magnus, as well as to Norway. He therefore asked
his men for their aid, and said he thought the Norsemen would
always be the superiors of the Danes. Then Einar Tambarskelve replies, that he considered it a greater duty to bring
his foster-son King Magnus's corpse to the grave, and lay it
beside his father King Olaf north in Drontheim town, than
to be fighting abroad, and taking another king's dominions and
property. He ended his speech with saying that he would
rather follow King Magnus dead than any other king alive.
Thereupon he had the body adorned in the most honourable
way, so that the adorned coffin was visible on board the king's
ship. Then all the Drontheim people and all the Northmen
made themselves ready to return home with the king's body,
and so the army was broken up. King Harald saw then that
it was better for him to return to Norway to secure that kingdom first, and to assemble men anew; and so King Harald
returned to Norway with all his army. As soon as he came
to Norway he held a Thing with the people of the country,
and had himself proclaimed king everywhere. He proceeded
thus from the East through Viken, and in every district in
Norway he was named king.

Einar Tambarskelve, and with him all the Drontheim troops,
went with King Magnus's body, and transported it to the town
of Nidaros, where it was buried in Saint Clement's church,
where also was the shrine of King Olaf the Saint. King Magnus
was of the middle size, of long and clear-complexioned countenance, and light hair, eloquent and decisive, was brisk in his
actions, and extremely generous. He was a great warrior, and
remarkably bold in arms. He was the most popular of kings,
prized even by enemies as well as friends.

CHAPTER XXX. OF SVEIN ULVSON.—Svein Ulvson remained
that autumn in Skaane, and was making ready to travel east-

---

[1] Viborg, an ancient town in north Jutland. The Thing at Viborg is said
to have been the proper place for the conferment of sovereign power in
Denmark; cf. p. 143.

ward to Sweden, with the intention of renouncing the title of
king he had assumed in Denmark; but just as he was mounting
his horse, some men came riding to him with the first news
that King Magnus was dead, and all the Northmen had left
Denmark. Svein answered in haste, "I call God to witness
that I shall never again fly from the Danish dominions as long
as I live." Then he got on his horse, and rode south into
Skaane, where immediately many people crowded to him. That
winter he brought under his power all the Danish dominions,
and all the Danes took him for their king. Tore, King Magnus's
brother, came to Svein in autumn with the message of King
Magnus, as before related, and was well received; and Tore
remained long with Svein, and was well taken care of.

CHAPTER XXXI. OF KING HARALD SIGURDSON. — King
Harald Sigurdson took the royal power over all Norway after
the death of King Magnus Olafson; and when he had reigned
over Norway one winter, and spring was come, he ordered a
levy through all the land of one half of all men and ships, and
went south to Jutland. He herried and burned all summer
wide around in the land, and came into Godnar fjord,[1] where
King Harald made these verses:

> While wives of husbands fondly dream,
> Here let us anchor in the stream,
> In Godnar fjord; we'll safely moor
> Our sea-homes, and sleep quite secure.

Then he spoke to Thjodolf the scald, and asked him to add
to it what it wanted; and he sang:

> In the next summer, I foresee,
> Our anchorage in the South will be;
> To hold our sea-homes on the ground,
> More cold-tongued anchors will be found.

To this Bolverk alludes in his song also, that Harald went
to Denmark the summer after King Magnus's death. Bolverk
sings thus:

> Next summer thou the levy raised,
> And seawards all the people gazed,
> Where thy sea-steeds in sunshine glancing
> Over the waves were gaily prancing;
> While the deep ships that plunder bore
> Seemed black specks from the distant shore.
> The Danes, from banks or hillocks green,
> Looked with dismay upon the scene.

CHAPTER XXXII. OF GEYSA'S DAUGHTERS. — Then they
burned the house of Torkel Geysa, who was a great lord, and

[1] Godnar fjord is supposed to be the present Randers fjord, in North
Jutland, into which a river runs called Guden-aa.

his daughters they carried off bound to their ships. They had made a great mockery the winter before of King Harald's coming with warships against Denmark; and they cut their cheese into the shape of anchors, and said such anchors might hold all the ships of the Norway king. Then this was composed:

> The island-girls, we were told,
> Made anchors all our fleet to hold:
> Their Danish jest cut out in cheese
> Did not our stern king's fancy please.
> Now many a maiden fair, maybe,
> Sees iron anchors splash the sea,
> Who will not wake a maid next morn
> To laugh at Norway's ships in scorn.

It is said that a spy who had seen the fleet of King Harald said to Torkel Geysa's daughters, "Ye said, Geysa's daughters, that King Harald dared not come to Denmark." Dotta, Torkel's daughter, replied, "That was yesterday." Torkel had to ransom his daughters with a great sum. So says Grane:

> The gold-adorned girl's eye
> Through Hornskog wood was never dry,
> As down towards the sandy shore
> The men their lovely prizes bore.
> The Norway leader kept at bay
> The foe who would contest the way,
> And Dotta's father had to bring
> Treasure to satisfy the king.

King Harald plundered in Denmark all that summer, and made immense booty; but he had not any footing in the land that summer in Denmark. He went to Norway again in autumn, and remained there all winter.

CHAPTER XXXIII. OF THE MARRIAGES AND CHILDREN OF KING HARALD THE STERN [1048].—The winter after King Magnus the Good died, King Harald wed Tora, daughter of Torberg Arneson, and they had two sons; the oldest called Magnus, and the other Olaf. King Harald and Queen Ellesiv had two daughters; the one Maria, the other Ingigerd. The spring after the foray which has just been related [p. 182] King Harald ordered the people out, and went with them to Denmark, and herried there, and did so summer after summer thereafter. So says Stuv the scald:

> Falster lay waste, as people tell—
> The raven in other isles fared well.
> The Danes were everywhere in fear,
> For the dread foray every year.

CHAPTER XXXIV. OF THE ARMAMENTS OF KING SVEIN AND KING HARALD.—King Svein ruled over all the Danish dominions

after King Magnus's death. He sat quiet all the winter; but in
summer he lay out in his ships with all his people, and it was
said he would go north to Norway with the Danish army, and
make not less havoc there than King Harald had made in
Denmark. King Svein proposed to King Harald in winter to
meet him the following summer at the Gotha river, and fight
until in the battle-field their differences were ended, or they
were settled peacefully. They made ready on both sides all
winter with their ships, and called out in summer one half of
all the fighting men. The same summer came Torleik the Fair
out of Iceland [1049], and composed a poem about King Svein
Ulvson. He heard, when he arrived in Norway, that King
Harald had sailed south to the Gotha river against King Svein.
Then Torleik sang this:

> The wily Svein, I think, will meet
> These inland Norsemen fleet to fleet:
> The arrow-storm, and heaving sea,
> His vantage-fight and field will be.
> God only knows the end of strife,
> Or which shall have his land and life:
> This strife must come to such an end,
> For terms will never bind King Svein.

He also sang these verses:

> Harald, whose red shield oft has shone
> O'er harried coasts, and fields hard won,
> Rides in hot wrath, and eager speeds
> O'er the blue waves his ocean-steeds.
> Svein, who in blood his arrows stains,
> Brings o'er the ocean's heaving plains
> His gold-beaked ships, which come in view
> Out from the Sound with many a hue.

King Harald came with his forces to the appointed meeting-
place; but there he heard that King Svein was lying with his
fleet to the southward off Sealand. Then King Harald divided
his forces; let the greater part of the bonder-troops return
home; and took with him nis hird-men, his lendermen, the
best men-at-arms, and all the bonder-troops who lived nearest
to the Danish land. They sailed over to Jutland to the south
of Vendelskage,[1] and so south to Thjoda [2]; and over all they
carried fire and sword. So says Stuv the scald:

> In haste the men of Tyland fly
> From the great monarch's threat'ning eye:
> At the stern Harald's angry look,
> The boldest hearts in Denmark shook.

---

[1] Vendelskage, now Vendsyssel, is the northern district of Jutland, in
which the Scaw Point is situated.
[2] Thjoda is now Tyland in Jutland. It is on the north-west of Jutland,
although Snorri thought it lay on the east.

They went forward all the way south to Heidaby, took the merchant town, and burnt it. Then one of Harald's men made the following verses:

> All Heidaby is burned down!
> Strangers will ask where stood the town.
> In our wild humour up it blazed,
> And Svein looks round him all amazed.
> All Heidaby is burned down!
> From a far corner of the town
> I saw, before the peep of morning,
> Roofs, walls, and all in flame high burning.

To this also Torleik alludes in his verses, when he heard there had been no battle at the Gotha river:

> The stranger-warrior may inquire
> Of Harald's men, why in his ire
> On Heidaby his wrath he turns,
> And the fair town to ashes burns?
> Would that the day had never come
> When Harald's ships returned home
> From the East sea, since now the town,
> Without his gain, is burned down!

CHAPTER XXXV. HARALD'S ESCAPE INTO THE JUTLAND SEA.—Then King Harald sailed north, and had sixty ships, and the most of them large and heavily laden with the booty taken in summer; and as they sailed north past Thjoda, came King Svein down from the land with a great force, and he challenged King Harald to land and fight. King Harald had rather less than half the force of King Svein, and therefore he challenged Svein to fight at sea. So says Torleik the Fair:

> Svein, who of all men under heaven
> Has had the luckiest birth-hour given,
> Invites his foemen to the field,
> There to contest with blood-stained shield.
> The king, impatient of delay,
> Harald, will with his sea-hawks stay;
> On board will fight, and fate decide
> If Svein shall by his land abide.

After that King Harald sailed north along Vendelskage; and the wind then came against them, and they brought up under Lessö, where they lay all night. A thick fog lay upon the sea; and when the morning came, and the sun rose, they saw upon the other side of the sea as if there were fires burning. This was told to King Harald; and he looked at it, and said immediately, "Strike the tents down on the ships, and take to the oars. The Danish forces are coming upon us; and the fog there where they are must have cleared off, and the sun shines

upon the dragon-heads of their ships, which are gilded, and that
is what we see." It was so as he had said. Svein had come
there with a prodigious armed force. They rowed now on
both sides all they could. The Danish ships flew lighter before
the oars; for the Northmen's ships were both soaked with
water and heavily laden, so that the Danes approached nearer
and nearer. Then Harald, whose own dragon-ship was the
last of the fleet, saw that he could not get away; so he ordered
his men to throw overboard some wood, and lay upon it clothes
and other good and valuable articles; and it was so perfectly
calm, that these drove about with the tide. Now when the
Danes saw their own goods driving about on the sea, they who
were in advance turned about to save them; for they thought
it was easier to take what was floating freely about, than to
go on board the Northmen to take it. They dropped rowing,
and lost ground. Now when King Svein came up to them with
his ship, he urged them on; saying it would be a great shame
if they, with so great a force, could not overtake and master
so small a number. The Danes then began again to stretch
out lustily at their oars. When King Harald saw that the
Danish ships went faster, he ordered his men to lighten their
ships, and cast overboard malt, wheat, bacon, and to let their
liquor run out, which helped a little. Then Harald ordered the
bulwark-screens, the empty casks and puncheons, and the
prisoners to be thrown overboard; and when all these were
driving about on the sea, Svein ordered help to be given to save
the men. This was done; but so much time was lost, that
they separated from each other. The Danes turned back,
and the Northmen proceeded on their way. So says Torleik
the Fair:

> Svein drove his foes from Jutland coast—
> The Norsemen's ships would have been lost.
> But Harald all his vessels saves,
> Throwing his booty on the waves.
> The Jutlanders saw, as he threw,
> Their own goods floating in their view:
> His lighten'd ships fly o'er the main,
> While they pick up their own again.

King Svein returned southwards with his ships to Lessö,
where he found seven ships of the Northmen, with bonder and
men of the levy. When King Svein came to them they begged
for mercy, and offered ransom for themselves. So says Torleik
the Fair:

> The stern king's men good offers make,
> If Svein will ransom for them take;

Too few to fight, they boldly say
Unequal force makes them give way.
The hasty bonder for a word
Would have betaken them to the sword,
And have prolonged a bloody strife—
Such men can give no price for life.

CHAPTER XXXVI. OF HARALD AND HALDOR SNORRESON.—
King Harald was a great man, who ruled his kingdom well in
home concerns. Very prudent was he, of good understanding;
and it is the universal opinion that no chief ever was in northern
lands of such deep judgment and ready counsel as Harald. He
was a great warrior; bold in arms; strong and expert in the use
of his weapons beyond any others, as has been before related
[p. 167], although many of the feats of his manhood are not
here written down. This is owing partly to our uncertainty
about them, partly to our wish not to put stories into this book
for which there is no testimony. Although we have heard
many things talked about, and even circumstantially related,
yet we think it better that something may be added to, than
that it should be necessary to take something away from, our
relation. A great part of his history is put in verse by Iceland
men, which poems they presented to him or his sons, and for
which reason he was their great friend. He was, indeed, a
great friend to all the people of that country; and once, when
a very dear time set in, he allowed four ships to transport meal
to Iceland, and fixed that the shippund should not be dearer
than 120 ells of wadmal.[1] He permitted also all poor people,
who could find provisions to keep them on the voyage across
the sea, to emigrate from Iceland to Norway; and from that
time there was better subsistence in the country, and the
seasons also turned out better. King Harald also sent from
Norway a bell for the church of which Olaf the Saint had sent
the timbers to Iceland, and which was erected on the Thing-
plain. Such remembrances of King Harald are found here in
the country,[2] besides many great gifts which he presented to
those who visited him.

Haldor Snorreson and Ulv Ospakson, as before related [p. 167],
came to Norway with King Harald. They were, in many
respects, of different dispositions. Haldor was very stout and
strong, and remarkably handsome in appearance. King Harald

---

[1] Wadmal was homespun cloth which in early Iceland formed with silver
the chief staple of exchange. In the eleventh century 1 oz. of refined silver
was worth approx. 24 yards of yard-wide wadmal. The weight of the
skippund is uncertain, cf. p. 285, note 1.
[2] Viz. in Iceland, where Snorri was writing.

gave him this testimony, that he, among all his men, cared least about doubtful circumstances, whether they betokened danger or pleasure; for, whatever turned up, he was never in higher nor in lower spirits, never slept less nor more on account of them, nor ate or drank but according to his custom. Haldor was not a man of many words, but short in conversation, told his opinion bluntly, and was obstinate and hard; and this could not please the king, who had many high-born men about him zealous in his service. Haldor remained a short time with the king; and then came to Iceland, where he took up his abode in Hjardarholt,[1] and dwelt in that farm to a very advanced age.

CHAPTER XXXVII. OF ULV OSPAKSON.—Ulv Ospakson stood in great esteem with King Harald; for he was a man of great understanding, clever in conversation, active and brave, and withal true and sincere. King Harald made Ulv his marshal, and married him to Jorun, Torberg's daughter, a sister of Harald's wife Tora. Ulv and Jorun's children were Joan Sterke of Rosvold,[2] and Brigita mother of Sauda Ulv, who was father of Peter Byrde-Svein,[3] grandfather of Svein and Ulv Fly. Joan Sterke's son was Erlend Himalde, father of Archbishop Eystein [4] and his brothers. King Harald gave Ulv the marshal the rights of a lenderman, and a fief of twelve marks income, besides a half-fylke in the Drontheim land. Of this Stein Herdisarson speaks in his song about Ulv.

CHAPTER XXXVIII. OF THE BUILDING OF CHURCHES AND HOUSES.—King Magnus Olafson built Olaf's church in Kaupangen, on the spot where Olaf's body was set down for the night, and which, at that time, was above the town.[5] He also had the king's house built there. The church was not quite finished when the king died; but King Harald had what was wanting completed. There, beside the house, he began to construct a stone hall, but it was not finished when he died. King Harald had the church called Maria Kirke built from the foundations up, at the sand-hill close to the spot where the king's holy remains were concealed in the earth the first winter after his fall. It was a large minster, and so strongly built with lime that it was difficult to break it when the archbishop

---

[1] In Laxárdal in Dalasýsla, western Iceland.
[2] In Værdalen in the north of the shire of Trondhjem.
[3] Not a proper name but a nickname, meaning porter, see p. 352.
[4] Archbishop from 1161 to 1188.
[5] The ruins of Olaf's church were found under the present Council Chamber in King Street.

Eystein had it pulled down.[1] Olaf's holy remains [2] were kept in Olaf's church while Maria Kirke was building. King Harald had the king's house erected below Maria Kirke, at the side of the river, where it now is; and he had the house in which he had made the great hall consecrated, and called Gregorius Church.

CHAPTER XXXIX. BEGINNING OF HAKON IVARSON'S STORY. —There was a man called Ivar the White, who was a noble lenderman dwelling in the Uplands, and was a daughter's son of Earl Hakon the Great. Ivar was the handsomest man that could be seen. Ivar's son was called Hakon; and of him it was said that he was distinguished above all men then in Norway for bravery, strength, and all accomplishments. In his very youth he had been sent out on war expeditions, where he acquired great honour and consideration, and became afterwards one of the most celebrated men.

CHAPTER XL. OF EINAR TAMBARSKELVE.—Einar Tambarskelve was the most powerful lenderman [3] in the Drontheim land. There was but little friendship between him and King Harald, although Einar retained all the fiefs he had held while Magnus the Good lived. Einar had many large estates, and was married to Bergljot, a daughter of Earl Hakon, as related above. Their son Eindride was grown up, and married to Sigrid, the daughter of Ketel Calf and Gunhild, King Harald's sister's daughter. Eindride had inherited the beauty of his mother's father Earl Hakon, and his sons; and in size and strength he took after his father Einar, and also in all bodily perfections by which Einar had been distinguished above other men. He was also, as well as his father, the most popular of men, which the sagas, indeed, show sufficiently.

CHAPTER XLI. OF EARL ORM.—Orm was at that time earl in the Uplands. His mother was Ragnhild, a daughter of Earl Hakon the Great,[4] and Orm was a remarkably clever man.

---

[1] Archbishop Eystein removed the Maria Kirke over to Elgesæter and converted it into an Abbey Church about 1178.

[2] i.e. they were removed thither from the Clement church.

[3] The fiefs of these feudatories not being hereditary, nor conveying the feudal baronial privileges and powers over the sub-vassals belonging to the fiefs in feudally constituted countries, and being in reality only life-rent tacks of Crown lands, or collectorships of Crown rents and taxes in certain districts, the original word Lendermen (Lendr Madr) is preferred, in this translation, to the word Baron, which denotes feudal rights and powers which the lendermen had not. The King's Sheriffs might, perhaps, express this condition and class better.

[4] On pp. 343, 357 (cf. Appendix iv, p. 437) Orm is called son of Eiliv. Ragnhild was probably the daughter of Earl Hakon who married Skopte Skageson (Olaf Sagas, p. 19); Eiliv was presumably her second husband.

Aslak Erlingson was then in Jæderen at Sole, and was married to Sigrid, a daughter of Earl Svein Hakonson. Gunhild, Earl Svein's other daughter, was married to the Danish king Svein Ulvson. These were the descendants of Earl Hakon at that time in Norway, besides many other distinguished people; and the whole race was remarkable for their very beautiful appearance, and the most of them were gifted with great bodily perfection, and were all distinguished and important men.

CHAPTER XLII. HARALD'S PRIDE.—King Harald was very proud, and his pride increased after he was established in the country; and it came so far that at last it was not good to speak against him, or to propose anything different from what he desired. So says Thjodolf the scald:

> In arms 'tis right the common man
> Should follow orders, one by one—
> Should stoop or rise, or run or stand,
> As his war-leader may command;
> But now to the king who feeds the ravens
> The people bend like heartless cravens—
> Nothing is left them, but consent
> To what the king calls his intent.

CHAPTER XLIII. OF THE QUARREL OF KING HARALD AND EINAR TAMBARSKELVE.—Einar Tambarskelve was the principal man among the bonder all about Drontheim, and answered for them at the Things even against the king's men. Einar knew well the law, and did not want boldness to bring forward his opinion at Things, even if the king was present; and all the bonder stood by him. The king was very angry at this, and it came so far that they disputed eagerly against each other. Einar said that the bonder would not put up with any unlawful proceedings from him if he broke through the law of the land; and this occurred several times between them. Einar then began to keep people about him at home, and he had many more when he came into the town if the king was there. It once happened that Einar came to the town with a great many men and ships; he had with him eight or nine great warships, and nearly five hundred men. When he came to the town he went up from the strand with his attendants. King Harald was then in his house, standing out in the balcony of the loft; and when he saw Einar's people going on shore, it is said Harald composed these verses:

> I see great Tambarskelve go,
> With mighty pomp, and pride, and show,
> Across the ebb-shore up the land—
> Before, behind, an armed band.

This bonder-leader thinks to rule,
And fill himself the royal stool.
A goodly earl I have known
With fewer followers of his own.
He who strikes fire from the shield,
Einar, may some day make us yield,
Unless our axe-edge quickly ends,
With sudden kiss, what he intends.

Einar remained several days in the town.

CHAPTER XLIV. THE FALL OF EINAR AND EINDRIDE.—One day there was a Thing-meeting held in the town, at which the king himself was present. A thief had been taken in the town, and he was brought before the Thing. The man had before been in the service of Einar, who had been very well satisfied with him. This was told to Einar, and he well knew the king would not let the man off, and the more because he took an interest in the matter. Einar, therefore, let his men get under arms, went to the Thing, and took the man by force. The friends on both sides then came between, and endeavoured to effect a reconciliation; and they succeeded so far that a meeting-place was appointed, to which both should come. There was an audience-room in the king's house [1] at the river Nid, and the king went into it with a few men, while the most of his people were out in the yard. The king ordered the shutters of the loft-opening to be turned, so that there was but a little space left clear. When Einar came into the yard with his people, he told his son Eindride to remain outside with the men, "for then I shall be in no danger." Eindride remained standing outside at the room-door. When Einar came into the room, he said, "It is dark in the king's audience-room." At that moment some men ran against him, and assaulted him, some with spears, some with swords. When Eindride heard this he drew his sword, and rushed into the room; but he was instantly killed along with his father. The king's men then ran up and placed themselves before the door, and the bonder lost courage, having no leader. They urged each other on, indeed, and said it was a shame they should not avenge their chief; but it came to nothing with their attack. The king went out to his men, arrayed them in battle order, and set up his standard; but the bonder did not venture to assault. Then the king went with all his men on board of his ships, rowed down the river, and then took his way out of the fjord. When Einar's wife Bergljot, who was in the house which Einar had possessed

[1] i.e. the new palace which Harald built down by the river to the east of the Maria Kirke.

in the town, heard of Einar's fall, she went immediately to the king's house where the bonder army was, and urged them to the attack; but at the same moment the king was rowing out of the river. Then said Bergljot, "Now we want here my relation Hakon Ivarson: Eindride's slayer would not be rowing out of the river if Ivar stood here on the river-bank." Then Bergljot adorned Einar's and Eindride's corpses, and buried them in Olaf's church, beside King Magnus Olafson's grave.[1] After Einar's murder, the king was so much disliked for that deed, that there was nothing that prevented the lendermen and bonder from attacking the king, and giving him battle, but the want of some leader to raise the banner in the bonder army.

CHAPTER XLV. OF KING HARALD AND FINN ARNESON.— Finn Arneson dwelt at Austratt in Yrjar, and was King Harald's lenderman there. Finn was married to Bergljot, a daughter of Halfdan, who was a son of Sigurd Syr, and brother of Olaf the Saint and of King Harald. Tora, King Harald's wife, was Finn Arneson's brother's daughter; and Finn and all his brothers were the king's dearest friends. Finn Arneson had been for some summers on a viking cruise in the West sea; and Finn, Guttorm Gunhildson,[2] and Hakon Ivarson had all been together on that cruise. King Harald now proceeded out of Drontheim fjord to Austratt, where he was well received. Afterwards the king and Finn conversed with each other about this new event of Einar's and his son's death, and of the murmuring and threatening which the Drontheim people made against the king.

Finn took up the conversation briskly, and said, "Thou art managing ill in two ways: first in doing all manner of mischief; and next in being so afraid that thou knowest not what to do."

The king replied, laughing, "I will send thee, cousin, into the town to bring about a reconciliation with the bonder; and if that will not do, thou must go to the Uplands, and bring matters to such an understanding with Hakon Ivarson that he shall not be my opponent."

Finn replies, "And how wilt thou reward me if I undertake this dangerous errand; for both the people of Drontheim and the people of Upland are so great enemies to thee, that it would not be safe for any of thy messengers to come among them, unless he were one who would be spared for his own sake?"

The king replies, "Go thou on this embassy, for I know

[1] On p. 182 it is said that Magnus was buried in Saint Clement's church, but his body was, along with that of Saint Olaf, temporarily removed to Olaf's church, vide p. 190.
[2] Son of Ketel Calf and Gunhild (see p. 190).

thou wilt succeed in it if any man can, and bring about a reconciliation; and then choose whatever favour from us thou wilt."

Finn says, "Hold thou thy word, king, and I will choose my petition. I will desire to have peace and safe residence in the country for my brother Kalv, and all his estates restored; and also that he receive all the dignity and power he had when he .left the country."

The king assented to all that Finn laid down, and it was confirmed by witnesses and shake of hand.

Then said Finn, "What shall I offer Hakon, who rules most among his relations in the land, to induce him to agree to a treaty and reconciliation with thee?"

The king replies, "Thou shalt first hear what Hakon on his part requires for making an agreement; then promote my interest as thou art best able; and deny him nothing in the end short of the kingdom."

Then King Harald proceeded southwards to Möre, and drew together men in considerable numbers.

CHAPTER XLVI. OF FINN ARNESON'S JOURNEY.—Finn Arneson proceeded to the town, and had with him his house-servants, nearly eighty men. When he came into the town he held a Thing with the town's people. Finn spoke long and ably at the Thing; and told the town's people, and bonder, above all things not to have a hatred against their king, or to drive him away. He reminded them of how much evil they had suffered by acting thus against King Olaf the Saint; and added, that the king was willing to pay penalty for this murder, according to the judgment of understanding and good men. The effect of Finn's speech was, that the bonder promised to wait quietly until the messengers came back whom Bergljot had sent to the Uplands to her relative Hakon Ivarson. Finn then went out to Orkedal with the men who had accompanied him to the town. From thence he went up to the Dovrefjeld, and eastwards [south] over the Fjelds. He went first to his son-in-law Earl Orm, who was married to Sigrid, Finn's daughter, and told him his business.

CHAPTER XLVII. OF FINN AND HAKON IVARSON.—Then Finn and Earl Orm appointed a meeting with Hakon Ivarson [1]; and when they met Finn explained his errand to Hakon, and the offer which King Harald made him. It was soon seen,

[1] He lived somewhere in Romerike, a long day's ride from Oslo (vide p. 212).

from Hakon's speech, that he considered it to be his great
duty to avenge the death of his relative Eindride; and added,
that word was come to him from Drontheim, from which he
might expect help in making head against the king.   Then
Finn represented to Hakon how much better it would be for
him to accept of as high a dignity from the king as he himself
could desire, rather than to attempt raising a strife against the
king to whom he was owing service and duty.   He said if he
came out of the conflict without victory, he forfeited life and
property: "And even if thou hast the victory, thou wilt still be
called a traitor to thy sovereign."   Earl Orm also supported
Finn's speech.   After Hakon had reflected upon this he disclosed what lay on his mind, and said, "I will be reconciled with
King Harald if he will give me in marriage his relation Ragnhild, King Magnus Olafson's daughter, with such dower as is
suitable to her and she will be content with."   Finn said he
would agree to this on the king's part; and thus it was settled
among them.   Finn then returned to Drontheim, and the
disturbance and enmity were quashed, so that the king could
retain his kingdom in peace at home; and the league was
broken which Eindride's relations had made among themselves
for opposing King Harald.

CHAPTER XLVIII. OF THE COURTSHIP OF HAKON IVARSON.—
When the day arrived for the meeting at which this agreement
with Harald should be finally concluded, Hakon went to King
Harald; and in their conference the king said that he, for his
part, would adhere to all that was settled in their agreement.
"Thou, Hakon," says he, "must thyself settle that which concerns Ragnhild, as to her accepting thee in marriage; for it
would not be advisable for thee, or for any one, to marry
Ragnhild, without her consent."   Then Hakon went to Ragnhild
and paid his addresses to her.   She answered him thus: "I
have often to feel that my father King Magnus is dead and
gone from me, since I must marry a bonde; although I acknow-
ledge thou art a handsome man, expert in all exercises.   But if
King Magnus had lived he would not have married me to
any man less than a king; so it is not to be expected that I
will take a man who has no dignity or title."   Then Hakon
went to King Harald, and told him his conversation with
Ragnhild, and also repeated the agreement which was made
between him and Finn, who was with him, together with many
others of the persons who had been present at the conversation
between him and Finn.   Hakon takes them all to witness that

such was the agreement that the king should give Ragnhild the dower she might desire. "And now since she will have no man who has not a high dignity, thou must give me such a title of honour; and, according to the opinion of the people, I am of birth, family, and other qualifications, to be called earl."

The king replies, "When my brother King Olaf and his son King Magnus ruled the kingdom, they allowed only one earl at a time to be in the country, and I have done the same since I came to the kingly title; and I will not take away from Orm the title of honour I had before given him."

Hakon saw now that his business had not advanced, and was very ill pleased; and Finn was outrageously angry. They said the king had broken his word; and thus they all separated.

Hakon then went out of the country with a well-manned ship. When he came to Denmark he went immediately to his relative King Svein,[1] who received him honourably, and gave him great fiefs. Hakon became King Svein's commander of the coast defence against the vikings—the Vendland people, Kurland people, and others from the East countries—who infested the Danish dominions; and he lay out with his ships of war both winter and summer.

CHAPTER XLIX. MURDER OF ASMUND.—There was a man called Asmund, who is said to have been King Svein's sister's son,[2] and his foster-son. This Asmund was distinguished among all by his boldness, and was made much of by the king. When Asmund came to years, and to age of discretion, he became an ungovernable person given to murder and manslaughter. The king was ill pleased at this, and sent him away, giving him a good fief, which might keep him and his followers well. As soon as Asmund had got this property from the king, he drew together a large troop of people; and as the estate he had got from the king was not sufficient for his expenses, he took as his own much more which belonged to the king. When the king heard this he summoned Asmund to him, and when they met the king said that Asmund should remain with the hird without keeping any retinue of his own; and this took place as the king desired. But when Asmund had been a little time in the king's court he grew weary of being there, and escaped in the night, returned to his former companions, and did more mischief than ever. Now when the king was riding through the

---

[1] He was married to Hakon's relative, the daughter of Earl Svein (p. 191).
[2] Not sister's but brother's son. Asmund's father was Björn Ulvsson (died 1049).

country, he came to the neighbourhood where Asmund was, and he sent out men-at-arms to seize him. The king then had him laid in irons, and kept him so for some time in hope he would reform; but no sooner did Asmund get rid of his chains than he absconded again, gathered together people and war-vessels, and betook himself to plunder, both abroad and at home. Thus he made great forays, killing and plundering all around. When the people who suffered under these disturbances came to the king, and complained to him of their losses, he replied, "Why do ye tell me of this? Why don't you go to Hakon Ivarson, who is my officer for the land-defence, placed on purpose to keep the peace for you peasants, and to hold the vikings in check? I was told that Hakon was a gallant and brave man, but I think he is rather shy when any danger of life is in the way." These words of the king were brought to Hakon, with many additions   Then Hakon went with his men in search of Asmund, and when their ships met Hakon gave battle immediately; and the conflict was sharp, and many men were killed. Hakon boarded Asmund's ship, and cut down the men before his feet. At last he and Asmund met, and exchanged blows until Asmund fell. Hakon cut off his head, went in all haste to King Svein, and found him just sitting down to the dinner-table. Hakon presented himself before the table, laid Asmund's head upon the table before the king, and asked if he knew it. The king made no reply, but became as red as blood in the face. Soon after the king sent him a message, ordering him to leave his service immediately. "Tell him that I will do him no harm; but I cannot keep watch over all our relations."[1]

CHAPTER L. HAKON IVARSON'S MARRIAGE.—Hakon then left Denmark, and came north to his estates in Norway. His relation Earl Orm was dead. Hakon's relations and friends were glad to see Hakon, and many gallant men gave themselves much trouble to bring about a reconciliation between King Harald and Hakon. It was at last settled in this way, that Hakon got Ragnhild, the king's daughter, and that King Harald gave Hakon the earldom, with the same power Earl Orm had possessed. Hakon swore to King Harald an oath of fidelity to all the services he was liable to fulfil.

CHAPTER LI. RECONCILIATION OF KING HARALD AND KALV. —Kalv Arneson had been on a viking cruise to the Western

[1] This incident shows how strong, in these ages, was the tie of relationship, and the point of honour of avenging its injuries—the clanship spirit.

countries ever since he had left Norway; but in winter he was often in the Orkney Islands with his relative Earl Torfinn. Finn Arneson sent a message to his brother Kalv, and told him the agreement which he had made with King Harald, that Kalv should enjoy safety in Norway, and his estates, and all the fiefs he had held from King Magnus. When this message came to Kalv he immediately got ready for his voyage, and went east to Norway to his brother Finn. Then Finn obtained the king's peace for Kalv, and when Kalv and the king met they went into the agreement which Finn and the king had settled upon before. Kalv bound himself to the king in the same way as he had bound himself to serve King Magnus, according to which Kalv should do all that the king desired and considered of advantage to his realm. Thereupon Kalv received all the estates and fiefs he had before.

CHAPTER LII. FALL OF KALV ARNESON.—The summer following King Harald ordered out a levy, and went to Denmark, where he plundered during the summer; but when he came south to Fyen he found a great force assembled against him. Then the king prepared to land his men from the ships, and to engage in a land-fight. He drew up his men on board in order of battle; set Kalv Arneson at the head of one division; ordered him to make the first attack, and told him where they should direct their assault, promising that he would soon make a landing with the others, and come to their assistance. When Kalv came to the land with his men a force came down immediately to oppose them, and Kalv without delay engaged in battle, which, however, did not last long; for Kalv was immediately overpowered by numbers, and betook himself to flight with his men. The Danes pursued them vigorously, and many of the Northmen fell, and among them Kalv Arneson. Now King Harald landed with his array; and they soon came on their way to the field of battle, where they found Kalv's body, and bore it down to the ships. But the king penetrated into the country, killing many people, and destroying much. So says Arnor:

> His shining sword with blood he stains,
> Upon Fiona's grassy plains;
> And in the midst of fire and smoke,
> The King Fiona's forces broke.

CHAPTER LIII. FINN ARNESON'S EXPEDITION OUT OF THE COUNTRY.—After this Finn Arneson thought he had cause to be an enemy of the king upon account of his brother Kalv's death; and said the king had betrayed Kalv to his fall, and had also deceived him by making him entice his brother Kalv to come over from the West and trust to King Harald's faith. When these speeches came out among people, many said that it was very foolish in Finn to have ever supposed that Kalv could obtain the king's sincere friendship and favour; for they thought the king was the man to seek revenge for smaller offences than Kalv had committed against the king. The king let every one say what he chose, and he himself neither said yes nor no about the affair; but people perceived that the king was very well pleased with what had happened. King Harald once made these verses:

> I have, in all, the death-stroke given
> To foes of mine at least eleven;
> Two more, perhaps, if I remember,
> May yet be added to this number.
> I prize myself upon these deeds,
> My people such examples needs.
> Bright gold itself they would despise,
> Or healing leek-herb [1] underprize,
> If not still brought before their eyes.

Finn Arneson took the business so much to heart that he left the country, and went to Denmark to King Svein, where he met a friendly reception. They spoke together in private for a long time; and the end of the business was that Finn went into King Svein's service, and became his man. King Svein then gave Finn an earldom, and placed him in Halland, where he was long earl, and defended the country against the Northmen.

CHAPTER LIV. OF GUTTORM GUNHILDSON.—Ketel Calf and Gunhild of Ringaness had a son called Guttorm, and he was a sister's son to King Olaf and Harald Sigurdson. Guttorm was a gallant man, early advanced to manhood. He was often with King Harald, who loved him much, and asked his advice; for he was of good understanding, and very popular. Guttorm had also been engaged early in forays, and had marauded much in the Western countries with a large force. Ireland was for him a land of peace; and he had his winter quarters often in Dublin, and was in great friendship with King Margad.[2]

---

[1] The second half of this verse is much paraphrased. The original says: "Men still repay treacherous deceit with hostility. They say it does not take much to make a leek grow big." This last sentence seems to contain a proverb, and means that the king's enemies would soon grow powerful if he did not take ruthless measures against them.

[2] Margad (Irish—Eachmargach), Ragnvald's son, was king in Dublin, 1035-8 and 1046-52.

CHAPTER LV. GUTTORM'S JUNCTION WITH THE IRISH KING MARGAD.—The summer after King Margad, and Guttorm with him, went out on an expedition against Bretland [Wales], where they made immense booty. Then they put in at Anglesey; and there they were to divide the spoil. But when the king saw the quantity of silver which was gathered he wanted to have the whole booty, and regarded little his friendship for Guttorm. Guttorm was ill pleased that he and his men should be robbed of their share; but the king said, "Thou must choose one of two things—either to be content with what we determine, or to fight; and they shall have the booty who gain the victory: and likewise thou must give up thy ships, for them I will have." Guttorm thought there were great difficulties on both sides; for it was disgraceful to give up ships and goods without a stroke, and yet it was highly dangerous to fight the king and his force, the king having sixteen ships and Guttorm only five. Then Guttorm desired three days' time to consider the matter with his people, thinking in that time to pacify the king, and come to a better understanding with him through the mediation of others; but he could not obtain from the king what he desired. This was the day before Saint Olaf's day [28 July, 1052]. Guttorm chose the condition that they would rather die or conquer like men, than suffer disgrace, contempt, and scorn, by submitting to so great a loss. He called upon God, and his uncle Saint Olaf, and entreated their help and aid; promising to give to the holy man's house the tenth of all the booty that fell to their share, if they gained the victory. Then he arranged his men, placed them in battle-order against the great force, prepared for battle, and gave the assault. By the help of God, and the holy Saint Olaf, Guttorm won the battle. King Margad fell, and every man, old and young, who followed him; and after that great victory, Guttorm and all his people returned home joyfully with all the booty they had gained by the battle. Every tenth penny of the booty they had made was set aside, according to the vow they had made to Saint Olaf; and there was so much silver that Guttorm had a crucifix made of it, the height of it being modelled after his own or his forecastle-man's; and the figure was seven ells high. The rood thus produced was given by Guttorm to King Olaf the Saint's church, where it has since remained [1] as a memorial of Guttorm's victory and King Olaf the Saint's miracle.

CHAPTER LVI. MIRACLE OF KING OLAF IN DENMARK.—There

[1] In the cathedral.

was a wicked, evil-minded count in Denmark, who had a Norwegian servant-girl whose family belonged to Drontheim district. She worshipped King Olaf the Saint, and believed firmly in his sanctity. But the above-mentioned count doubted of all that was told of the holy man's miracles, insisted that it was nothing but nonsense and idle talk, and made a joke and scorn of the esteem and honour which all the country people showed the good king. Now when the holyday came, on which the mild monarch ended his life, and which all Northmen kept sacred, this unreasonable count would not observe it, but ordered his servant-girl to bake and put fire in the oven that day. She knew well the count's mad passion, and that he would revenge himself severely on her if she refused doing as he ordered. She went, therefore, of necessity, and baked in the oven, but wept much at her work; and she threatened King Olaf that she never would believe in him, if he did not avenge this misdeed by some mischance or other. And now shall ye come to hear a well-deserved vengeance, and a true miracle. It happened, namely, in the same hour, that the count became blind of both eyes, and the bread which she had shoved into the oven was turned into stone! Of these stones some are now in Saint Olaf's church, and in other places; and since that time Olafsmas has been always held holy in Denmark.

CHAPTER LVII. KING OLAF'S MIRACLE ON A CRIPPLE.— West in Valland,[1] a man had such bad health that he became a cripple, and went on knees and knuckles. One day he was upon the road, and had fallen asleep. He dreamt that a gallant man came up to him, and asked him where he was going. When he named the neighbouring town, the man said to him, "Go to Saint Olaf's church that stands in London, and there thou shalt be cured." Thereupon he awoke, and went straightway to inquire the road to Olaf's church in London. At last he came to London's port, and asked the men of the burgh if they could tell him where Olaf's church was; but they replied, there were so many churches that they could not tell to whom each of them was consecrated. Soon after a man came up, and asked him where he wanted to go, and he answered to Olaf's church. Then said the man, "We shall both go together to Olaf's church for I know the way to it." Thereupon they went over the jetty to the street where Olaf's church was; and when they came to the gates of the churchyard the man mounted over the half-door that was in the gate, but the cripple rolled himself

[1] The west coast of France.

in, and rose up immediately sound and strong: when he looked about him his conductor had vanished.

CHAPTER LVIII. KING HARALD'S FORAY IN DENMARK.— King Harald had built a merchant town in the East at Oslo,[1] where he often resided; for there was good supply from the extensive cultivated district wide around. There also he had a convenient station to defend the country against the Danes, or to make an attack upon Denmark, which he was in the custom of doing often, although he kept no great force on foot. One summer King Harald went from thence with a few light ships and a few men. He steered southwards out from Viken, and, when the wind served, stood over to Jutland, and marauded; but the country people collected and defended the country. Then King Harald steered to Lymfjord, and went into the fjord. Lymfjord is so formed that its entrance is like a narrow river; but when one gets farther into the fjord, it spreads out into a wide sea. King Harald marauded on both sides of the land; and when the Danes gathered together on every side to oppose him, he lay at a small island which was uncultivated. They wanted drink on board his ships, and went up into the island to seek water; but finding none, they reported it to the king. He ordered them to look for some long earth-worms on the island, and when they found them they brought them to the king. He ordered the people to bring the worms to a fire, and bake them before it, so that they should be thirsty. Then he ordered a thread to be tied round the tails of the worms, and to let them loose. The worms crept away immediately, while the threads were wound off from the clew as the worms took them away; and the people followed the worms until they sought downwards in the earth. There the king ordered them to dig for water, which they did, and found so much water that they had no want of it. King Harald now heard from his spies that King Svein was come with a large armament to the mouth of the fjord; but it took a long time for him to come into it, as only one ship at a time can come in. King Harald then steered with his fleet in through the fjord to where it was broadest, to a place called Lygsbreid.[2] In the inmost bight, there is but a narrow neck of land dividing the fjord from the

[1] In 1624 the town was rebuilt by King Christian IV and was thereafter called Christiania. At the beginning of 1925 the name Christiania was changed back again to Oslo, a name which the diocese had never lost.

[2] Lusbreid in the Icelandic. Now Livö Bredning (Livö, earlier Lyg). It is the widest part of the Limfjord.

sea.[1] Thither King Harald rowed with his men towards
èvening; and at night when it was dark he unloaded his ships,
drew them over the neck of land into the West sea, loaded
them again, and was ready with all this before day. He then
steered northwards along the Jutland coast. People then said
that Harald had escaped from the hands of the Danes. Harald
said that he would come to Denmark next time with more
people and larger vessels. King Harald then proceeded north
to Drontheim.

CHAPTER LIX. KING HARALD HAD A SHIP BUILT. — King
Harald remained all winter at Nidaros, and had a vessel built
out upon the strand, and it was a buss.[2] The ship was built
of the same size as the Long Serpent, and every part of her
was finished with the greatest care. On the stem was a dragon-
head, and on the stern a dragon-tail, and the sides of the bows
of the ship were gilt. The vessel had thirty-five rowers' benches,
and was large for that size, and was remarkably handsome; for
the king had everything belonging to the ship's equipment of
the best, both sails and rigging, anchors and cables.

King Harald sent a message in winter south to Denmark to
King Svein, that he should come northwards in spring; that
they should meet at the Gotha river and fight, and so settle
the division of the countries that the one who gained the victory
should have both kingdoms.

CHAPTER LX. KING HARALD'S CHALLENGE.—King Harald
during this winter called out a general levy of all the people
of Norway, and assembled a great force towards spring. Then
Harald had his great ship drawn down and put into the river
Nid, and set up the dragon's head on her. Thjodolf the scald
sang about it thus:

> My lovely girl! the sight was grand
> When the great war-ship down the strand
> Into the river gently slid,
> And all below her sides was hid.
> Come, lovely girl, and see the show!—
> Her sides that on the water glow,
> Her serpent-head with golden mane,
> All shining back from the Nid again.

Then King Harald rigged out his ship, got ready for sea, and

---

[1] Magnus seems to have drawn his ships over a coastal strip about three
miles wide due north of the middle of the Limfjord, reaching the North Sea
somewhere near the headland Bulbjærg, going via the Lund Fjord, where
some other portage may have been necessary.

[2] Not much is known of this type of ship except that it was large and
used both as a merchantman and as a warship. The word is from medieval
Latin *buza*, used of both galleys and transport vessels.

when he had all in order went out of the river.   His men rowed
very skilfully and beautifully.   So says Thjodolf:

> It was upon a Saturday,
> Ship-tilts were struck and stowed away,
> And past the town our dragon glides,
> That girls might see our glancing sides.
> Out from the Nid brave Harald steers;
> Westward at first the dragon veers;
> Our lads together down with oars,
> The splash is echoed round the shores.
>
> Their oars our king's men handle well,
> One stroke is all the eye can tell:
> All level o'er the water rise;
> The girls look on in sweet surprise.
> Such things, they think, can ne'er give way;
> They little know the battle-day.
> The Danish girls, who dread our shout,
> Might wish our ship-gear not so stout.
>
> 'Tis in the fight, not on the wave,
> That oars may break and fail the brave.
> At sea, beneath the ice-cold sky,
> Safely our oars o'er ocean ply;
> And when at Drontheim's holy stream
> Our seventy oars in distance gleam,
> We seem, while rowing from the sea,
> An erne with iron wings to be.

King Harald sailed south along the land, and called out the
levy everywhere of men and ships.   When they came south
to Viken they got a strong wind against them, and the forces
lay dispersed in sheltered places: some in the isles outside,
and some in the fjords.   So says Thjodolf:

> The cutters' sea-bleached bows scarce find
> A shelter from the furious wind
> Under the inland forests' side,
> Where the fjord runs its farthest tide.
> In all the isles and creeks around
> The bonder ships lie on the ground,
> And ships with gunwales hung with shields
> Seek the lee-side of the green fields.

In the heavy storm that raged for some time the great ship
had need of good ground tackle.   So says Thjodolf:

> With lofty bow above the seas,
> Which curl and fly before the breeze,
> The gallant vessel rides and reels,
> And every plunge her cable feels.
> The storm that tries the spar and mast
> Tries the main-anchor at the last:
> The storm above, below the rock,
> Chafe the thick cable with each shock.

When the weather became favourable King Harald sailed

eastwards to the Gotha river with his fleet, and arrived there
in the evening. So says Thjodolf:

> The gallant Harald now has come
> To Gotha, half-way from his home,
> And on the river frontier stands,
> To fight with Svein for life and lands.
> The night passed o'er, the gallant king
> Next day at Tumle [1] calls a Thing,
> Where Svein is challenged to appear—
> A day which ravens wish were near.

CHAPTER LXI. OF KING HARALD'S FLEET.—When the Danes
heard that the Northmen's army was come to the Gotha river,[2]
they all fled who had opportunity to get away.   The Northmen
heard that the Danish king had also called out his forces, and
lay in the south, partly at Fyen and partly about Sealand.
When King Harald found that King Svein would not hold a
meeting with him, or a fight, according to what had been agreed
upon between them, he took the same course as before—letting
the bonder troops return home, but manning 150 [180] ships,
with which he sailed southwards along Halland, where he
herried all round, and then brought up with his fleet in Love
fjord,[3] and laid waste the country. A little afterwards King
Svein came upon them with all the Danish fleet, consisting of
300 [4] [360] ships. When the Northmen saw them, King Harald
ordered a general meeting of the fleet to be called by sound of
trumpet; and many there said it was better to fly, as it was
not now advisable to fight. The king replied, "Sooner shall all
lie dead one upon another than fly." Stein Herdisarson says:

> With falcon eye, and courage bright,
> Our king saw glory in the fight;
> To fly, he saw, would ruin bring
> On them and him—the folk and king.
> "Hand up the arms to one and all,"
> Cries out the king; "we'll win or fall!
> Sooner than fly, heaped on each other
> Each man shall fall across his brother!"

Then King Harald drew up his ships to attack, and brought
forward his great dragon in the middle of his fleet. So says
Thjodolf:

> The brave king through his vessels' throng
> His dragon war-ship moves along;
> He runs her gaily to the front,
> To meet the coming battle's brunt.

---

[1] Now Tumlehed on Hisingen.
[2] The country round the river Gotha, as well as Skaane on the north side
of Öresund, was part of the kingdom of Denmark.
[3] i.e. in Laholms bay.
[4] The big hundreds, as usual; therefore 360.

The ship was remarkably well equipt, and fully manned. So says Thjodolf:

> The king had got a chosen crew—
> He told his brave lads to stand true.
> The ring of shields seemed to enclose
> The ship's deck from the boarding foes.
> The dragon, on the Nissaa flood,
> Beset with men, who thickly stood,
> Shield touching shield, was something rare,
> That seemed all force of man to dare.

Ulv the marshal laid his ship by the side of the king's, and ordered his men to bring her well forward. Stein Herdisarson was himself in Ulv's ship and sings of it thus:

> Our oars were stowed, our lances high,
> As the ship moved swung in the sky.
> The marshal Ulv went through our ranks,
> Drawn up beside the rowers' banks:
> The brave friend of our gallant king
> Told us our ship well on to bring,
> And fight like Norsemen in the cause—
> Our Norsemen answered with huzzas.

Hakon Ivarson lay outside on the other wing, and had many ships with him, all well equipped. At the extremity of the other side lay the Drontheim chiefs, who had also a great and strong force.

CHAPTER LXII. OF KING SVEIN'S ARMAMENT.—Svein the Danish king also drew up his fleet, and laid his ship forward in the centre against King Harald's ship, and Finn Arneson laid his ship next; and then the Danes laid their ships, according as they were bold or well equipped. Then, on both sides, they bound the ships together all through the middle of the fleets; but as the fleets were so large, very many ships remained loose, and each laid his ship forward according to his courage, and that was very unequal. Although the size of their armies differed much, altogether there was a very great force on both sides. King Svein had six earls among the people following him. So says Stein Herdisarson:

> Danger our chief would never shun,
> With eight score ships he would not run:
> The Danish fleet he would abide,
> And give close battle side by side.
> From Leidre's [1] coast the Danish king
> Three hundred ocean steeds could bring,
> And o'er the sea-weed plain in haste
> Thought Harald's vessels would be chased.

CHAPTER LXIII. BEGINNING OF THE BATTLE OF NISSAA.—As soon as King Harald was ready with his fleet, he orders the

[1] Near Roskilde in Zeeland.

war-blast to sound, and the men to row forward to the attack.
So says Stein Herdisarson:

> Harald and Svein first met as foes,
> Where Nissaa in the ocean flows;
> For Svein would not for peace entreat,
> But, strong in ships, would Harald meet.
> The Norsemen prove, with sword in hand,
> That numbers cannot skill withstand.
> Off Halland's coast the blood of Danes
> The blue sea's calm smooth surface stains.

Soon the battle began, and became very sharp; both kings
urging on their men. So says Stein Herdisarson:

> Our king, his broad shield disregarding,
> More keen for striking than for warding,
> Now tells his lads their spears to throw—
> Now shows them where to strike a blow.
> From fleet to fleet so short the way,
> That stones and arrows have full play;
> And from the keen sword dropped the blood
> Of short-lived seamen in the flood.

It was late in the day when the battle began, and it continued the whole night. King Harald shot for a long time
with his bow. So says Thjodolf:

> The Upland king was all the night
> Speeding the arrows' deadly flight.
> All in the dark his bow-string's twang
> Was answered; for some white shield rang,
> Or yelling shriek gave certain note
> The shaft had pierced some ring-mail coat.
> The foemen's shields and bulwarks bore
> A Lapland arrow-scatt [1] or more.

Earl Hakon, and the people who followed him, did not make
fast their ships in the fleet, but rowed against the Danish ships
that were loose, and slew the men of all the ships they came up
with. When the Danes observed this, each drew his ship out
of the way of the earl; but he set upon those who were trying
to escape, and they were nearly driven to flight. Then a boat
came rowing to the earl's ship, and hailed him, and said that
the other wing of King Harald's fleet was giving way, and
many of their people had fallen. Then the earl rowed thither,
and gave so severe an assault that the Danes had to retreat
before him. The earl went on in this way all the night, coming
forward where he was most wanted, and wheresoever he came
none could stand against him. Hakon rowed outside around

---

[1] Lapland arrow-scatt, i.e. arrows. In the saga of Arrow-Odd (*Örvar-Odds Saga*) reference is made to the magic arrows of Gusir, king of the Finns. They were taken from him and finally came into Odd's possession.

the battle. Towards the end of the night the greatest part of the Danish fleet broke into flight, for then King Harald with his men boarded the vessel of King Svein; and it was so completely cleared that all the crew fell in the ship, except those who sprang overboard. So says Arnor, the earls' scald:

> Brave Svein did not his vessel leave
> Without good cause, as I believe:
> Oft on his casque the sword-blade rang,
> Before into the sea he sprang.
> Upon the wave his vessel drives;
> All his brave crew had lost their lives.
> O'er dead courtmen into the sea
> The Jutland king had now to flee.

And when King Svein's banner was cut down, and his ship cleared of its crew, all his forces took to flight, and some were killed. The ships which were bound together could not be cast loose, so the people who were in them sprang overboard, and some got to the other ships that were loose; and all King Svein's men who could get off rowed away, but a great many of them were slain. Where the kings themselves lay the ships were mostly bound together, and there were more than seventy left behind of King Svein's vessels. So says Thjodolf:

> Svein's ships rode proudly o'er the deep,
> When, by a single sudden sweep,
> Full seventy sail, as we are told,
> Were seized by Norway's monarch bold.

King Harald rowed after the Danes, and pursued them; but that was not easy, for the ships lay so thick together that they scarcely could move. Earl Finn Arneson would not flee; and being also short-sighted, was taken prisoner. So says Thjodolf:

> To the six Danish earls who came
> To aid his force, and raise his name,
> No mighty thanks King Svein is owing
> For mighty actions of their doing.
> Finn Arneson, in battle known,
> With a stout Norse heart of his own,
> Would not take flight his life to gain,
> And in the foremost ranks was ta'en.

CHAPTER LXIV. KING SVEIN'S FLIGHT.—Earl Hakon lay behind with his ships, while the king and the rest of the forces were pursuing the fugitives; for the earl's ships could not get forward on account of the ships which lay in the way before him. Then a man came rowing in a boat to the earl's ship, and lay at the bulwarks. The man was stout, and had on a broad hat. He hailed the ship. "Where is the earl?" said he.

The earl was in the fore-hold, stopping a man's blood. The earl cast a look at the man in the hat, and asked what his name was. He answered, "Here is Vandraad[1]: speak to me, earl."

The earl leant over the ship's side to him. Then the man in the boat said, "Earl, I will accept of my life from thee, if thou wilt give it."

Then the earl raised himself up, called two men who were friends dear to him, and said to them, "Go into the boat; take Vandraad to the land; attend him to my friend's Karl the bonde; and tell Karl, as a token that these words come from me, that he let Vandraad have the horse which I gave to him yesterday, and also his saddle, and his son to attend him."

Thereupon they went into the boat, and took the oars in hand, while Vandraad steered. This took place just about daybreak, while the vessels were in movement, some rowing towards the land, some towards the sea, both small and great. Vandraad steered where he thought there was most room between the vessels; and when they came near to Norway ships the earl's men gave their names, and then they all allowed them to go where they pleased. Vandraad steered along the shore, and only set in towards the land when they had come past the crowd of ships. They then went up to Karl the bonde's farm, and it was then beginning to be light. They went into the room where Karl had just put on his clothes. The earl's men told him their message, and Karl said they must take some food; and he set a table before them, and gave them water to wash with.

Then came the housewife into the room, and said, "I wonder why we could get no peace or rest all night with the shouting and screaming."

Karl replies, "Dost thou not know that the kings were fighting all night?"

She asked which had the best of it.

Karl answered, "The Northmen gained."

"Then," said she, "our king will have taken flight again."

"Nobody knows," says Karl, "whether he has fled or is fallen."

She says, "What a useless sort of king we have! He is both slow and frightened."

[1] The one who has difficulty in deciding for himself, who is embarrassed or perplexed.

Then said Vandraad, "Frightened he is not; but he is not lucky."

Then Vandraad washed his hands; but he took the towel and dried them right in the middle of the cloth. The housewife snatched the towel from him, and said, "Thou hast been taught little good; it is cottar's [1] way to wet the whole cloth at one time."

Vandraad replies, "I may yet come so far forward in the world as to be able to dry myself with the middle of the towel."

Thereupon Karl set a table before them, and Vandraad sat down between them. They ate for a while, and then went out. The horse was saddled, and Karl's son ready to follow him with another horse. They rode away to the forest; and the earl's men returned to the boat, rowed to the earl's ship, and told the success of their expedition.

CHAPTER LXV. OF KING HARALD.—King Harald and his men followed the fugitives only a short way, and rowed back to the place where the deserted ships lay. Then the battle-place was ransacked, and in King Svein's ship was found a heap of dead men; but the king's body was not found, although people believed for certain that he had fallen. Then King Harald had the greatest attention paid to the dead of his men, and had the wounds of the living bound up. The dead bodies of Svein's men were brought to the land, and he sent a message to the peasants to come and bury them. Then he let the booty be divided, and this took up some time. The news came now that King Svein had come to Sealand, and that all who had escaped from the battle had joined him, along with many more, and that he had a great force.

CHAPTER LXVI. FINN ARNESON GETS QUARTER.—Earl Finn Arneson was taken prisoner in the battle, as before related; and when he was led before King Harald, the king was very merry, and said, "Finn, we meet here now, and we met last in Norway. The Danish court has not stood very firmly by thee; and it will be a troublesome business for Northmen to drag thee, a blind old man, with them, and preserve thy life."

The earl replies, "The Northmen are obliged to do many bad things, yet the worst things they have to do are the things you order."

Then said King Harald, "Wilt thou accept of life and grace, although thou hast not deserved it?"

---

[1] Torpere, i.e. cottars, really smallholders, who live together in a hamlet (thorp).

The earl replies, "Not from thee, thou dog."

The king: "Wilt thou, then, if thy relation Magnus gives thee quarter?"

Magnus, King Harald's son, was then steering the ship.

The earl replies, "Can the whelp rule over life and grace?"

The king laughed, as if he found amusement in vexing him.— "Wilt thou accept thy life, then, from thy relative Tora?"

The earl: "Is she here?"

"She is here," said the king.

Then Earl Finn broke out with the ugly expressions which since have been preserved, as a proof that he was so mad with rage that he could not govern his tongue: "No wonder thou hast bit so strongly, if the mare [1] was with thee."

Earl Finn got life and grace, and the king kept him a while about him. But Finn was rather melancholy, and obstinate in conversation; and King Harald said, "I see, Finn, that thou dost not live willingly in company with me and thy relations; now I will give thee leave to go to Svein, thy king."

The earl said, "I accept of the offer willingly, and the more gratefully the sooner I get away from hence."

The king afterwards let Earl Finn be landed, and the traders going to Halland received him well. King Harald sailed from thence to Norway with his fleet; and went first to Oslo, where he gave all his people leave to go home who wished to do so.

CHAPTER LXVII. OF KING SVEIN.—King Svein, it is told, sat in Denmark all that winter, and had his kingdom as formerly. In winter he sent men north to Halland for Karl the bonde and his wife. When Karl came the king called him to him, and asked him if he knew him, or thought he had ever seen him before.

Karl replies, "I know thee, sire, and knew thee before, the moment I saw thee; and God be praised if the small help I could give was of any use to thee."

The king replies, "I have to reward thee for all the days I have to live. And now, in the first place, I will give thee any farm in Sealand thou wouldst desire to have; and, in the next place, will make thee a great man, if thou knowest how to conduct thyself."

Karl thanked the king for his promise, and said he had now but one thing to ask.

The king asked what that was.

Karl said that he would ask to take his wife with him.

---

[1] In equine fights the mares stand by and look on whilst the stallions bite their rivals. Horse fights were a favourite "sport" in saga times.

The king said, "I will not let thee do that; but I will provide thee a far better and more sensible wife. But thy wife can keep the bonde-farm you had before, and she will have her living from it."

The king gave Karl a great and valuable farm, and provided him a good marriage; and he became a considerable man. This was reported far and wide, and much praised; and thus it came to be told here north in Norway.

CHAPTER LXVIII. OF THE TALK OF THE COURT-MEN.—King Harald stayed in Oslo the winter after the battle at Nissaa. In autumn, when the men came from the south, there was much talk and many stories about the battle which they had fought at Nissaa, and every one who had been there thought he could tell something about it. Once some of them sat in a house and drank, and were very merry and talkative. They talked about the Nissaa battle, and who had earned the greatest praise and renown. They all agreed that no man there had been at all equal to Earl Hakon. He was the boldest in arms, the quickest, and the most lucky: what he did was of the greatest help, and he won the battle. King Harald, in the mean time, was out in the yard, and spoke with some people. He went then to the room-door, and said, "Every one here would now willingly be called Hakon"; and then went his way.

CHAPTER LXIX. OF THE ATTEMPT TO TAKE EARL HAKON.— Earl Hakon went in winter to the Uplands, and was all winter in his domains. He was much beloved by all the Uplanders. It happened, towards spring, that some men were sitting drinking in the town, and the conversation turned, as usual, on the Nissaa battle; and some praised Earl Hakon, and some thought others as deserving of praise as he. When they had thus disputed a while, one of them said, "It is possible that others fought as bravely as the earl at Nissaa; but none, I think, has had such luck with him as he."

The others replied, that his best luck was his driving so many Danes to flight along with other men.

The same man replied, "It was a greater luck that he gave King Svein quarter."

One of the company said to him, "Thou dost not know what thou art saying."

He replied, "I know it for certain, for the man told me himself who brought the king to the land."

It went according to the old proverb, that the king has many ears. This was told the king, and he immediately ordered horses to be gathered, and rode away directly with 200 [240] men. He rode all that night, and the following day. Then some men met them, who were riding to Oslo with mead and malt. In the king's retinue was a man called Gamal, who rode to one of these bonder who was an acquaintance of his, and spoke to him privately. "I will pay thee," said he, "to ride with the greatest speed, by the shortest private paths that thou knowest, to Earl Hakon, and tell him the king will kill him; for the king has got to the knowledge that Earl Hakon set King Svein on shore at Nissaa." They agreed on the payment. The bonde rode, and came to the earl just as he was sitting drinking, and had not yet gone to bed. When the bonde told his errand, the earl immediately stood up with all his men, had all his loose property removed from the farm to the forest, and all the people left the house in the night. When the king came he halted there all night; but Hakon rode away, and came east to Sweden to King Steinkel,[1] and stayed with him all summer. King Harald returned to the town, travelled northwards to Drontheim district, and remained there all summer; but in autumn he returned eastwards to Viken.

CHAPTER LXX. OF EARL HAKON.—As soon as Earl Hakon heard the king had gone north, he returned immediately in summer to the Uplands, and remained there until the king had returned from the north. Then the earl went east into Vermeland, where he remained during the winter, and where the Swedish king gave him fiefs. For a short time in winter he went west to Raumarike with a great troop of men from Gotland and Vermeland, and received the scatt and duties from the Upland people which belonged to him, and then returned to Gotland, and remained there till spring [1064]. King Harald had his seat in Oslo all winter, and sent his men to the Uplands to demand the scatt, together with the king's land dues, and the mulcts of court; but the Uplanders said they would pay all the scatt and dues which they had to pay, to Earl Hakon as long as he was in life, and had not forfeited his life or his fief; and the king got no land dues that winter.

CHAPTER LXXI. AGREEMENT BETWEEN KING HARALD AND KING SVEIN.—This winter messengers and ambassadors went between Norway and Denmark, whose errand was that both Northmen and Danes should make peace, and a league with each other, and to ask the kings to agree to it. These messages gave favourable hopes of a peace; and the matter proceeded

[1] He was king in Sweden c. 1056–66.

so far, that a meeting for peace was appointed at the Gotha river between King Harald and King Svein. When spring approached [1064], both kings assembled many ships and people for this meeting. So says a scald in a poem on this expedition of the kings, which begins thus:

> The king, who from the northern sound
> His land with war-ships girds around,
> The raven-feeder, filled the coast
> With his proud ships, a gallant host!
> The gold-tipped stems dash through the foam
> That shakes the seamen's planked home;
> The high wave breaks up to the mast,
> As west of Halland on they passed.

> Harald, whose word is fixed and sure,
> Whose ships his land from foes secure,
> And Svein, whose isles maintain his fleet,
> Hasten as friends again to meet;
> And every creek with vessels teems,—
> All Denmark men and shipping seems;
> And all rejoice that strife will cease,
> And men meet now but to make peace.

Here it is told that the two kings held the meeting that was agreed upon between them, and both came to the frontiers of their kingdoms. As it here says:

> To meet (since peace the Dane now craves)
> On to the south upon the waves
> Sailed forth our gallant northern king,
> Peace to the Danes with him to bring.
> Svein northward to his frontier hies
> To get the peace his people prize,
> And meet King Harald, whom he finds
> On land, hard used by stormy winds.

When the kings found each other, people began at once to talk of their being reconciled. But as soon as peace was proposed, many began to complain of the damage they had sustained by herrying, robbing, and killing men; and for a long time it did not look very like peace. It is here related:

> Before this meeting of the kings
> Each bonde his own losses brings,
> And loudly claims some recompense
> From his king's foes, at their expense.
> It is not easy to make peace,
> Where noise and talking never cease:
> The bonder warmth may quickly spread,
> And kings be by the people led.

> When kings are moved, no peace is sure;
> For that peace only is secure
> Which they who make it fairly make,—
> To each side give, from each side take.

The kings will often rule but ill
Who listen to the people's will:
The people often have no view
But their own interests to pursue.

At last the best men, and those who were the wisest, came
between the kings, and settled the peace thus: that Harald
should have Norway, and Svein Denmark, according to the
boundaries of old established between Denmark and Norway;
neither of them should pay to the other for any damage sustained; the war should cease as it now stood, each retaining
what he had got; and this peace should endure as long as they
were kings. This peace was confirmed by oath. Then the
kings parted, having given each other hostages, as is here
related:

And I have heard that to set fast
The peace God brought about at last,
Svein and stern Harald pledges sent,
Who witnessed to their sworn intent;
And much I wish that they and all
In no such perjury may fall
That this peace ever should be broken,
And oaths should fail before God spoken.

King Harald with his people sailed northwards to Norway,
and King Svein southwards to Denmark.

CHAPTER LXXII. KING HARALD'S QUARREL WITH EARL
HAKON.—King Harald was in Viken in the summer, and he
sent his men to the Uplands after the scatt and duty which
belonged to him; but the bonder paid no attention to the
demand, but said they would hold all for Earl Hakon until
he came for it. Earl Hakon was then up in Gotland with a
large armed force. When summer was past King Harald went
south to Konghelle. Then he took all the light sailing vessels
he could get hold of, and steered up the river. He had the
vessels drawn past all the waterfalls, and brought them thus
into Lake Vänern. Then he rowed eastward across the lake
to where he heard Earl Hakon was; but when the earl got
news of the king's expedition he advanced down the country,
and would not let the king plunder the land. Earl Hakon had
a large armed force which the Gotland people had raised for
him. King Harald lay with his ships up in a river, and made
a foray on land, but left some of his men behind to protect the
ships. The king himself rode with a part of the men, but the
greater part were on foot. They had to cross a forest, then came
a bush-grown bogland, and close to it a wood; and when they
reached the wood they saw the earl's men, but the mire

was between them. They drew up their people now on both sides. Then King Harald ordered his men to sit down on the hill-side. "We will first see if they will attack us. Earl Hakon does not usually wait to talk." It was frosty weather, with some snow-drift, and Harald's men sat down under their shields; but it was cold for the Gotlanders, who had but little clothing with them. The earl told them to wait until King Harald came nearer, so that all would stand equally high on the ground. Earl Hakon had the same banner which had belonged to King Magnus Olafson.

The lagman of the Gotland people, Torvid, sat upon a horse, and the bridle was fastened to a stake that stood in the mire. He broke out with these words: "God knows we have many brave and handsome fellows here; let not King Steinkel hear that we did not stand by the good earl bravely. I am sure of one thing: we shall behave gallantly against these Northmen, if they attack us; but if our young people give way, and should not stand to it, let us not run farther than to that stream; but if they should give way farther, which I am sure they will not do, let it not be farther than to that hill." At that instant the Northmen sprang up, raised the war-cry, and struck on their shields; and the Gotland army began also to shout. The lagman's horse got shy with the war-cry, and backed so hard that the stake flew up and struck the lagman on the head. He said, "Ill luck to thee, Northman, for that arrow!" and away fled the lagman. King Harald had told his people, "If we do make a clash with the weapons, we shall not, however, go down from the hill until they come nearer to us"; and they did so. When the war-cry was raised the earl let his banner advance; but when they came under the hill the king's army rushed down upon them, and killed some of the earl's people, and the rest fled. The Northmen did not pursue the fugitives long, for it was the fall of day; but they took Earl Hakon's banner, and all the arms and clothes they could get hold of. King Harald had both the banners carried before him as they marched away. They spoke among themselves debating whether Hakon was dead. As they were riding through the forest they could only ride singly, one following the other. Suddenly a man came full gallop across the path, struck his spear through him who was carrying the earl's banner, seized the banner-staff, and rode into the forest on the other side with the banner. When this was told the king he said, "Bring me my armour, for the earl is alive." Then the king rode to his

ships in the night; and many said that the earl had now taken
his revenge. But Thjodolf sang thus:

> Steinkel's troops, who were so bold,
> Who the Earl Hakon would uphold,
> Were driven by our horsemen's power
> To Hel, death goddess, in an hour;
> And the great earl, so men say
> Who won't admit he ran away,
> Because his men fled from the ground,
> Retired, and cannot now. be found.

CHAPTER LXXIII. DEATH OF HALL, THE MURDERER OF
KODRAN.—The rest of the night Harald passed in his ships;
but in the morning, when it was daylight, it was found that so
thick ice had gathered about the vessels that one could walk
around them. The king ordered his men to cut the ice from
the ships all the way out to the clear water; on which they all
went to break the ice. King Harald's son Magnus steered the
vessel that lay lowest down the river and nearest the water.
When the people had cleared the ice away almost entirely, a
man ran out to the ice, and began hewing away at it like a
madman. Then said one of the men, "It is going now as usual,
that none can do so much as Hall who killed Kodran, when
once he lays himself to the work. See how he is hewing away
at the ice." There was a man in the crew of Magnus the king's
son who was called Tormod Eindrideson; and when he heard
the name of Kodran's murderer he ran up to Hall, and gave
him a death-wound. Kodran was a son of Gudmund Eyolf-
son [1]; and Valgerd, who was a sister of Gudmund, was the
mother of Jorun, and the grandmother by the mother's side
of this Tormod. Tormod was a year old when Kodran was
killed, and had never seen Hall Otrygson until now. When
the ice was broken all the way out to the water, Magnus drew
his ship out, set sail directly, and sailed westward across the
lake; but the king's ship, which lay farthest up the river, came
out the last. Hall had been in the king's retinue, and was
very dear to him; so that the king was enraged at his death.
The king came the last into the harbour, and Magnus had let
the murderer escape into the forest, and offered to pay the
mulct for him; and the king had very nearly attacked Magnus
and his crew, but their friends came up and reconciled them.

CHAPTER LXXIV. OF KING HARALD.—That winter King
Harald went up to Raumarike, and had many people with him;

[1] Gudmund the Mighty of Mödruvellir in the north of Iceland, died 1024.
See *Olaf Sagas*, p. 198.

and he accused the bonder there of having kept from him his scatt and duties, and of having aided his enemies to raise disturbance against him. He seized on the bonder, and maimed some, killed others, and robbed many of all their property. They who could do it fled from him. He burned everything in the districts, and laid them altogether waste. So says Thjodolf:

> He who the island-people drove,
> When they against his power strove,
> Now bridles Raumarike's men,
> Marching his forces through their glen.
> To punish them the fire he lights
> That shines afar off in dark nights
> From house and yard, and, as he says,
> Will warn the man who disobeys.

Thereafter the king went up to Hedemark, burnt the dwellings, and made no less waste and havoc there than in Raumarike. From thence he went to Hadeland and Ringerike, burning and ravaging all the land. So says Thjodolf:

> The bonder household goods are seen
> Before his door upon the green,
> Smoking and singed; and sparks red hot
> Glow in the thatched roof of his cot.
> In Hedemark the bonder pray
> The king his crushing hand to stay;
> In Ringerike and Hadeland,
> None 'gainst his fiery wrath can stand.

Then the bonder left all to the king's mercy. After the death of King Magnus fifteen years had passed when the battle at Nissaa took place, and afterwards two years elapsed before Harald and Svein made peace. So says Thjodolf:

> The Horder's king under the land
> At anchor lay close to the strand,
> At Hvarv, prepared with shield and spear;
> But peace was settled the third year.

After this peace the disturbances with the people of the Upland districts lasted a year and a half. So says Thjodolf:

> No easy task it is to say
> How the king brought beneath his sway
> The Upland bonder, and would give
> Nought but their ploughs from which to live.
> The king in eighteen months brought down
> Their peasant power, and raised his own,
> And the great honour he has gained
> Will still in memory be retained.

CHAPTER LXXV. OF THE KINGS OF ENGLAND.—Edward, Ethelred's son, was king of England after his brother Harda-

canute. He was called Edward the Good; and so he was.
King Edward's mother was Queen Emma, daughter of Richard
earl of Rouen. Her brother [1] was Earl Robert, whose son was
William the Bastard, who at that time was duke at Rouen in
Normandy. King Edward's queen was Gyda,[2] a daughter of
Earl Godwin the son of Ulfnad.[3] Gyda's brothers were, Earl
Toste,[4] the eldest; Earl Mauro-kaare [5] the next; Earl Walter [6]
the third; Earl Svein the fourth; and the fifth was Harald,
who was the youngest, and he was brought up at King Edward's
court, and was his foster-son. The king loved him very much,
and kept him as his own son [7]; for he had no children.

CHAPTER LXXVI. OF HARALD GODWINSON. — One summer
it happened that Harald, the son of Godwin, made an expedition to Bretland [8] with his ships; but when they got to sea
they met a contrary wind, and were driven off into the ocean.
They landed west in Normandy, after suffering from a dangerous
storm. They brought up at Rouen, where they met Earl
William, who received Harald and his company gladly. Harald
remained there late in harvest, and was hospitably entertained;
for the stormy weather continued, and there was no getting to
sea, and this continued until winter set in; so the earl and
Harald agreed that he should remain there all winter. Harald
sat on the high seat on one side of the earl; and on the other
side sat the earl's wife,[9] one of the most beautiful women that
could be seen. They often talked together for amusement at
the drinking-table; and the earl went generally to bed, but
Harald and the earl's wife sat long in the evenings talking
together, and so it went on for a great part of the winter. In
one of their conversations she said to Harald, "The earl has

[1] Really nephew; cf. p. 233, note 1.
[2] She is called Githa and Eadgitha by English writers. Her mother's
name was Gyda.
[3] Earl Godwin was the son of Wulfnoth (= Ulfnad).
[4] Harald, and not Toste, was the eldest son of Earl Godwin; but the
enmity of Toste and others at his assuming the royal title is better ac-
counted for by supposing he was the youngest, and the foster-son of King
Edward.
[5] Earl Morcar, as he is called in English history, was not Harald's brother,
but the brother of his wife. He was a son of Ælfgar of Mercia, and after
1065 Earl of Northumberland.
[6] Godwin had no son Walter. Waltheof, son of Siward Earl of Northumberland (d. 1055), is meant.
[7] This does not agree with the account of the English historians, who say
that King Edward favoured Edgar, grandson of his brother Edmund, who
was brought up in Hungary.
[8] Wales.
[9] Her name was Matilda, and she was a daughter of Count Baldwin of
Flanders, not, as far as is known, famed for her beauty.

asked me what it is we have to talk about so much, for he is angry at it." Harald replies, "We shall then at once let him know all our conversation." The following day, Harald asked the earl to a conference, and they went together into the conference-chamber; where the earl's wife was, and some of the councillors. Then Harald began thus: "I have to inform you, earl, that there lies more in my visit here than I have let you know. I would ask your daughter in marriage, and have often spoken over this matter with her mother, and she has promised to support my suit with you." As soon as Harald had made known this proposal of his, it was well received by all who were present. They urged his suit before the earl; and at last it came so far, that the girl was contracted to Harald; but as she was very young, it was resolved that the wedding should be deferred for some years.

CHAPTER LXXVII. KING EDWARD'S DEATH, AND THE SUCCESSION.—When spring came Harald rigged his ships, and set off; and he and the earl parted with great friendship. Harald sailed over to England to King Edward, but did not return to Valland to fulfil the marriage agreement. Edward was king over England for twenty-three years, and died [1] on a bed of sickness in London on 5 January, and was buried in Paul's church. Englishmen call him a saint.

The sons of Earl Godwin were the most powerful men in England. Toste was made chief of the English king's army, and was his land-defence man when the king began to grow old; and he was also placed above all the other earls. His brother Harald was always with the hird itself, and nearest to the king in all service, and had the charge of the king's treasure-chamber. [2] It is said that when the king was approaching his last hour, Harald and a few others were with him. Harald first leant down over the king, and then said, "I take you all to witness that the king has now given me the kingdom, and all the realm of England": and then the king was taken dead out of the bed. The same day there was a meeting of the chiefs, at which there was some talk of choosing a king; and then Harald brought forward his witnesses that King Edward had given him the kingdom on his dying day. The meeting ended by choosing

[1] Succeeded to the throne 1042, crowned 3 April, 1043, died 5 January, 1066, at Westminster.
[2] This is unhistoric. Toste was earl in Northumberland after 1055, but was expelled by the Northumbrians in 1065. He fled to Flanders and was away at Edward's death. Harald was earl in Wessex and the strongest man in the country.

Harald as king, and he was consecrated and crowned the 13th day of Yule [6 January], in Paul's church. Then all the chiefs and all the people submitted to him. Now when his brother Earl Toste heard of this he took it very ill, as he thought himself quite as well entitled to be king. "I want," said he, "that the principal men of the country choose him whom they think best fitted for it." And sharp words passed between the brothers. King Harald says he will not give up his kingly dignity, for he is seated on the throne which kings sat upon, and is anointed and consecrated a king. On his side also was the strength of the people, for he had the king's whole treasure.

CHAPTER LXXVIII. EARL TOSTE'S EXPEDITION TO DENMARK.—Now when King Harald perceived that his brother Toste wanted to have him deprived of the kingdom, he did not trust him; for Toste was a clever man, and a great warrior, and was in friendship with the principal men of the country.[1] He therefore took the command of the army from Toste, and also all the power he had beyond that of the other earls of the country. Earl Toste, again, would not submit to be his own brother's serving-man; therefore he went with his people over the sea to Flanders, and stayed there a while, then went to Friesland, and from thence to Denmark to his relation King Svein. Earl Ulv, King Svein's father, and Gyda, Earl Toste's mother, were brother's and sister's children. The earl now asked King Svein for support and help of men; and King Svein invited him to stay with him, with the promise that he should get so large an earldom in Denmark that he would be an important chief.

The earl replies, "My inclination is to go back to my domain in England; but if I cannot get help from you for that purpose, I will agree to help you with all the power I can command in England, if you will go there with the Danish army, and win the country, as Canute your mother's brother did."

The king replied, "So much smaller a man am I than Canute the Great, that I can with difficulty defend my own Danish dominions against the Northmen. King Canute, on the other hand, got the Danish kingdom in heritage, took England by slash and blow, and sometimes was near losing his life in the contest; and Norway he took without slash or blow. Now it suits me much better to be guided by my own slender ability, than to imitate my relation King Canute's achievements."

[1] Toste was very unpopular in Northumbria and had little support elsewhere in England.

Then Earl Toste said, "The result of my errand here is less fortunate than I expected of thee who art so gallant a man, seeing that thy relative is in so great need. It may be that I will seek friendly help where it is less fitting to do so; and that I may find a chief who is less afraid, king, than thou art of a great enterprise."

Then the king and the earl parted, not just the best friends.

CHAPTER LXXIX. EARL TOSTE'S EXPEDITION TO NORWAY. —Earl Toste turned away then, and went to Norway, where he presented himself to King Harald, who was at that time in Viken. When they met the earl explained his errand to the king. He told him all his proceedings since he left England, and asked his aid to recover his dominions in England.

The king replied, that the Northmen had no great desire for a campaign in England, and to have an Englishman over them there. "People say," added he, "that the English are not to be trusted."

The earl replied, "Is it true what I have heard people tell in England, that thy relative King Magnus sent men to King Edward with the message that King Magnus had right to England as well as to Denmark, and had got that heritage after Hardacanute, in consequence of a regular agreement?"

The king replied, "How came it that he did not get it, if he had right to it?"

"Why," replied the earl, "hast thou not Denmark, as King Magnus thy predecessor had it?"

The king replies, "The Danes have nothing to brag of over us Northmen; for many a place have we laid in ashes to thy relations."

Then said the earl, "If thou wilt not tell me, I will tell thee. Magnus subdued Denmark, because all the chiefs of the country helped him; and thou hast not done it, because all the people of the country were against thee. Therefore, also, King Magnus did not strive for England, because all the nation would have Edward for king. Wilt thou take England now? I will bring the matter so far that most of the principal men in England shall be thy friends, and assist thee; for nothing is wanting to place me at the side of my brother Harald but the king's name. All men allow that there never was such a warrior in the northern lands as thou art; and it appears to me extraordinary that thou hast been fighting for fifteen years for Denmark, and wilt not take England that lies open to thee."

King Harald weighed carefully the earl's words, and per-

ceived at once that there was truth in much of what he said;
and he himself had also a great desire to acquire that land.
Then King Harald and the earl talked long and frequently
together; and at last he took the resolution to proceed in
summer to England, and conquer the country. King Harald
sent a message-token through all Norway, and ordered out a
levy of one half of all the men in Norway able to carry arms.
When this became generally known, there were many guesses
about what might be the end of this expedition. Some reckoned
up King Harald's great achievements, and thought he was also
the man who could accomplish this. Others, again, said that
England was difficult to attack; that it was very full of people;
and the men-at-arms, who were called Thing-men, were so
brave, that one of them was better than two of Harald's best
men. Then said Ulv the marshal:

> I am still ready gold to gain;
> But truly it would be in vain,
> And the king's marshal in the hall
> Might leave his good post once for all,
> If two of us in any strife
> Must from one Thing-man fly for life.
> My lovely Norse maid, in my youth
> We thought the opposite the truth.

Ulv the marshal died that spring. King Harald stood over
his grave, and said, as he was leaving it, "There lies now the
truest of men, and the most devoted to his king."

Earl Toste sailed in spring [1] west to Flanders, to meet the
people who had left England with him, and others besides who
had gathered to him both out of England and Flanders.

CHAPTER LXXX. GYRD'S DREAM.—King Harald's fleet assembled in Solunder.[2] When King Harald was ready to leave
Nidaros he went to King Olaf's shrine, unlocked it, clipped his
hair and nails, and locked the shrine again, and threw the keys
into the Nid. Some say he threw them overboard outside of
Agdaness; and since then the shrine of Saint Olaf the king has
never been opened. Thirty-five [3] years had passed since he
was slain; and he lived thirty-five years here on earth. King
Harald sailed with the ships he had about him to the south to
meet his people, and a great fleet was collected; so that, according to the people's reckoning, King Harald had nearly 200
[240] ships, besides provision-ships and small craft.

[1] In May, 1066, Toste made an attack on the Sussex coast. He then sailed
northwards and met defeat in Lincolnshire, whence he retired to Scotland
before combining with King Harald for the attack on Yorkshire.

[2] Solunder, the Sulen Isles, at the mouth of Sogne fjord.

[3] It was really thirty-six.

While they lay in Solunder a man called Gyrd, on board the king's ship, had a dream. He thought he was on the king's ship, and saw a great witch-wife standing on the island, with a knife in one hand and a dish in the other. He thought also that he saw over all the fleet, and that a fowl was sitting upon every ship's stern, and that these fowls were all ravens or ernes; and the witch-wife sang this song:

> From the east I'll 'tice the king,
> To the west the king I'll bring;
> Many a noble bone will be
> In battle left for me.
> Ravens o'er prince's ship are flitting,
> Eyeing the prey they think most fitting.
> Upon the stem I'll sail with them!
> Upon the stem I'll sail with them!

CHAPTER LXXXI. TORD'S DREAM.—There was also a man called Tord, in a ship which lay not far from the king's. He dreamt one night that he saw King Harald's fleet coming to land, and he knew the land to be England. He saw a great battle-array on the land; and he thought both sides began to fight, and had many banners flapping in the air. And before the army of the people of the country was riding a huge witch-wife upon a wolf; and the wolf had a man's carcass in his mouth, and the blood was dropping from his jaws; and when he had eaten up one body she threw another into his mouth, and so one after another, and he swallowed them all. And she sang thus:

> Skade's eagle eyes
> The king's ill luck espies;
> Though glancing shields
> Hide the green fields,
> The king's ill luck she spies.
> To bode the doom of this great king,
> The flesh of bleeding men I fling
> To hairy jaw and hungry maw!
> To hairy jaw and hungry maw!

CHAPTER LXXXII. KING HARALD'S DREAM.—King Harald also dreamt one night that he was in Nidaros, and met his brother King Olaf, who sáng to him these verses:

> In many a fight
> My name was bright;
> Men weep, and tell
> How Olaf fell.
> Thy death is near;
> Thy corpse, I fear,
> The crow will feed,
> The witch-wife's steed.

Many other dreams and forebodings were then told of, and most of them gloomy. Before King Harald left Drontheim, he let his son Magnus be proclaimed king, and set him as king over Norway while he was absent. Tora, the daughter of Torberg, also remained behind; but he took with him Queen Ellesiv and her two daughters, Maria and Ingigerd. Olaf, King Harald's son, also accompanied his father abroad.

CHAPTER LXXXIII. BATTLE AT SCARBOROUGH.—When King Harald was clear for sea, and the wind became favourable, he sailed out into the ocean; and he himself landed in Shetland, but a part of his fleet in the Orkney Islands. King Harald stopped but a short time in Shetland before sailing to Orkney, from whence he took with him a great armed force, and the earls Paul and Erlend, the sons of Earl Torfinn; but he left behind him here the Queen Ellesiv, and her daughters Maria and Ingigerd. Then he sailed, leaving Scotland and England westward of him, and landed at a place called Kliflönd.[1] There he went on shore and plundered, and brought the country in subjection to him without opposition. Then he brought up at Skardaborg,[2] and fought with the people of the place. He went up a hill which is there, and made a great pile upon it, which he set on fire; and when the pile was in clear flame, his men took large forks and pitched the burning wood down into the town, so that one house caught fire after the other, and the town surrendered. The Northmen killed many people there, and took all the booty they could lay hold of. There was nothing left for the Englishmen now, if they would preserve their lives, but to submit to King Harald; and thus he subdued the country wherever he came. Then the king proceeded south along the land, and brought up at Hellorness,[3] where there came a force that had been assembled to oppose him, with which he had a battle, and gained the victory.

CHAPTER LXXXIV. OF HARALD'S ORDER OF BATTLE.— Thereafter the king sailed to the Humber, and up along the river, and then he landed. Up in Jorvik [4] were two earls, Earl Mauro-kaare,[5] and his brother Earl Walter of Hundatunir,[6] and they had an immense army. While the army of the earls was coming down from the upper part of the country, King Harald lay in the Usa [Ouse]. King Harald now went on the

---

[1] Cleveland in Yorkshire.   [2] Scarborough.   [3] Holderness.   [4] York.
[5] Morcar, or Morcad, in our histories. The brother who accompanied him was not Walter but Edwin.
[6] Huntingdon.

land, and drew up his men.[1] The one arm of his line stood at
the outer edge of the river, the other turned up towards the
land along a ditch; and there was also a morass, deep, broad,
and full of water. The earls let their army proceed slowly
down along the river, with all their troops in line. The king's
banner was next the river, where the line was thickest. It was
thinnest at the ditch, where also the weakest of the men were.
When the earls advanced downwards along the ditch, the arm
of the Northmen's line which was at the ditch gave way; and the
Englishmen followed, thinking the Northmen would fly. The
banner of Earl Mauro-kaare advanced then bravely.

CHAPTER LXXXV. THE BATTLE AT THE HUMBER.—When
King Harald saw that the English array had come to the ditch
against him, he ordered the charge to be sounded, and urged
on his men. He ordered the banner which was called the Land-
ravager to be carried before him, and made so severe an assault
that all had to give way before it; and there was a great loss
among the men of the earls, and they soon broke into flight,
some running up the river, some down, and the most leaping
into the ditch, which was so filled with dead that the Norsemen
could go dry-foot over the fen. There Earl Mauro-kaare fell.
So says Stein Herdisarson:

> The gallant Harald drove along,
> Flying but fighting, the whole throng.
> At last, confused, they could not fight,
> And the whole body took to flight.
> Up from the river's silent stream
> At once rose desperate splash and scream;
> But they who stood like men this fray
> Round Mauro-kaare's [2] body lay.

This song was made by Stein Herdisarson about Olaf, son
of King Harald; and he speaks of Olaf being in this battle with
King Harald his father. These things are also spoken of in the
song called "Harald's Stave":

> Earl Walter's men
> Lay in the fen,
> By sword down hewed,
> So thickly strewed,
> That Norsemen say
> They paved a way
> Across the fen
> For the brave Norsemen.

---

[1] At Gate Fulford, to the south-east of York.
[2] Earl Morcar did not fall in the battle; but in the original the verse does
not certainly imply that he did.

Earl Walter, and the people who escaped, fled up to the castle in York; and there the greatest loss of men had been. This battle took place upon the Wednesday next Mathias' day.[1]

CHAPTER LXXXVI. OF EARL TOSTE.—Earl Toste had come from Flanders to King Harald as soon as he arrived in England, and the earl was present at all these battles. It happened, as he had foretold the king at their first meeting, that in England many people would flock to them, as being friends and relations of Earl Toste, and thus the king's forces were much strengthened. After the battle now told of, all people in the nearest districts submitted to Harald, but some fled. Then the king advanced to take the castle, and laid his army at Stafnfurdo-bryggia[2]; and as King Harald had gained so great a victory against so great chiefs and so great an army, the people were dismayed, and doubted if they could make any opposition. The men of the castle therefore determined, in a council, to send a message to King Harald, and deliver up the castle into his power. All this was soon settled; so that on Sunday [24 September, 1066] the king proceeded with the whole army to the castle, and appointed a Thing of the people without the castle, at which the people of the castle were to be present. At this Thing all the people accepted the condition of submitting to Harald, and gave him, as hostages, the children of the most considerable persons; for Earl Toste was well acquainted with all the people of that town. In the evening the king returned down to his ships, after they had achieved this bloodless victory, and was very merry. A Thing was appointed within the castle [3] early on Monday morning, and then King Harald was to name officers to rule over the town, to give out laws, and bestow fiefs. The same evening, after sunset, King Harald Godwinsson came from the south to the castle with a numerous army, and rode into the city with the good-will and consent of the people of the castle. All the gates and walls were beset so that the Northmen could receive no intelligence, and the army remained all night in the town.

CHAPTER LXXXVII. OF KING HARALD'S LANDING.—On Monday [25 September, 1066], when King Harald Sigurdson had taken breakfast, he ordered the trumpets to sound for going on shore. The army accordingly got ready, and he

---

[1] Wednesday before St. Matthew's Day; 20 September, 1066.
[2] Stamford Bridge, which is really some eight miles from York.
[3] This is incorrect. The Thing was to be held at Stamford and hostages were to be given from the whole of Yorkshire, and so the battle took place there.

divided the men into the parties who should go, and who should stay behind. In every division he allowed two men to land, and one to remain behind. Earl Toste and his retinue prepared to land with King Harald; and, for watching the ships, remained behind the king's son Olaf; the earls of Orkney, Paul and Erlend; and also Eystein Orre, a son of Torberg Arneson, who was the most able and best beloved by the king of all the lendermen, and to whom the king had promised his daughter Maria. The weather was uncommonly fine, and it was hot sunshine. The men therefore laid aside their armour, and went on the land only with their shields, helmets, and spears, and girt with swords; and many had also arrows and bows, and all were very merry. Now as they came near the castle a great army seemed coming against them, and they saw a cloud of dust as from horses' feet, and under it shining shields and bright armour. The king halted his people, and called to him Earl Toste, and asked him what army this could be. The earl replied, that he thought it most likely to be a hostile army; but possibly it might be some of his relations who were seeking for mercy and friendship, in order to obtain certain peace and safety from the king. Then the king said, "We must all halt, to discover what kind of a force this is." They did so; and the nearer this force came the greater it appeared, and their shining arms were to the sight like glancing ice.

CHAPTER LXXXVIII. OF EARL TOSTE'S COUNSEL.—Then said King Harald, "Let us now fall upon some good sensible counsel; for it is not to be concealed that this is an hostile army, and the king himself without doubt is here."

Then said the earl, "The first counsel is to turn about as fast as we can to our ships to get our men and our weapons, and then we will make a defence according to our ability; or otherwise let our ships defend us, for there these horsemen have no power over us."

Then King Harald said, "I have another counsel. Put three of our best horses under three of our briskest lads, and let them ride with all speed to tell our people to come quickly to our relief. The Englishmen shall have a hard fray of it before we give ourselves up for lost."

The earl said the king must order in this, as in all things, as he thought best; adding, at the same time, it was by no means his wish to fly. Then King Harald ordered his banner Landravager to be set up; and Fridrek was the name of him who bore the banner.

CHAPTER LXXXIX. OF KING HARALD'S ARRAY.—Then King Harald arranged his army, and made the line of battle long, but not deep. He bent both wings of it back, so that they met together; and formed a wide ring equally thick all round, shield to shield, both in the front and rear ranks. The king himself and his retinue were not in the circle; with him was the banner, and a body of chosen men. Earl Toste, with his retinue, was at another place, and had a different banner. The army was arranged in this way, because the king knew that horsemen [1] were accustomed to ride forwards with great vigour, but to turn back immediately. Now the king ordered that his own and the earl's attendants should ride forwards where it was most required. "And our bowmen," said he, "shall be near to us; and they who stand in the first rank shall set the spear-shaft on the ground, and the spear-point against the horseman's breast, if he rides at them; and those who stand in the second rank shall set the spear-point against the horse's breast."

CHAPTER XC. OF KING HARALD GODWINSSON.—King Harald Godwinsson had come with an immense army, both of cavalry and infantry. Now King Harald Sigurdson rode around his array, to see how every part was drawn up. He was upon a black horse, and the horse stumbled under him, so that the king fell off. He got up in haste, and said, "A fall is lucky for a traveller."

The English king Harald said to the Northmen who were with him, "Do ye know the stout man who fell from his horse, with the blue kirtle and the beautiful helmet?"

"That is the king himself," said they.

The English king said, "A great man, and of stately appearance is he; but I think his luck has left him."

CHAPTER XCI. OF THE TROOP OF THE NOBILITY.—Twenty horsemen rode forward from the Thing-men's troops against the Northmen's array; and all of them, and likewise their horses, were clothed in armour.

One of the horsemen said, "Is Earl Toste in this army?"

The earl answered, "It is not to be denied that ye will find him here."

The horseman says, "Thy brother King Harald sends thee salutation, with the message that thou shalt have the whole of

---

[1] Here and in what follows, traditions have been introduced from the Battle of Hastings, 14 Oct., 1066. It was the Normans who there fought on horseback and used against the English the stratagem of pretending to flee. These had no cavalry.

Northumberland; and rather than thou shouldst not submit to him, he will give thee the third part of his kingdom to rule over along with himself."

The earl replies, "This is something different from the enmity and scorn he offered last winter; and if this had been offered then it would have saved many a man's life who now is dead and it would have been better for the kingdom of England. But if I accept of this offer, what will he give King Harald Sigurdson for his trouble?"

The horseman replied, "He has also spoken of this; and will give him seven feet of English ground, or as much more as he may be taller than other men."

"Then," said the earl, "go now and tell King Harald to get ready for battle; for never shall the Northmen say with truth that Earl Toste left King Harald Sigurdson to join his enemy's troops, when he came to fight west here in England. We shall rather all take the resolution to die with honour, or to gain England by a victory."

Then the horsemen rode back.

King Harald Sigurdson said to the earl, "Who was the man who spoke so well?"

The earl replied, "That was King Harald Godwinsson."

Then said King Harald Sigurdson, "That was by far too long concealed from me; for they had come so near to our army, that this Harald should never have carried back the tidings of our men's slaughter."

Then said the earl, "It was certainly imprudent for such chiefs, and it may be as you say; but I saw he was going to offer me peace and a great dominion, and that, on the other hand, I would be his murderer if I betrayed him; and I would rather he should be my murderer than I his, if one of us two be to die."

King Harald Sigurdson observed to his men, "That was but a little man, yet he sat firmly in his stirrups."

It is said that Harald made these verses at this time:

> Advance! advance!
> No helmets glance,
> But blue swords play
> In our array.
> Advance! advance!
> No mail-coats glance,
> But hearts are here
> That ne'er knew fear.

His coat of mail was called Emma; and it was so long that

it reached almost to the middle of his leg, and so strong that no weapon ever pierced it. Then said King Harald Sigurdson, "These verses are but ill composed; I must try to make better"; and he composed the following:

> In battle-storm we seek no lee,
> With skulking head, and bending knee,
> Behind the hollow shield.
> With eye and hand we fend the head;
> Courage and skill stand in the stead
> Of panzer, helm, and shield,
> In Hilda's bloody field.

Thereupon Thjodolf sang:

> And should our king in battle fall,—
> A fate that God may give to all,—
> His sons will vengeance take;
> And never shone the sun upon
> Two nobler eaglets in his run,
> And them we'll ne'er forsake.

CHAPTER XCII. OF THE BATTLE AND KING HARALD'S FALL. —Now the battle began. The Englishmen made a hot assault upon the Northmen, who sustained it bravely. It was no easy matter for the English to ride against the Northmen on account of their missiles; and so they rode in a circle around them. And the fight at first was but loose and light, as long as the Northmen kept their order of battle; for although the English rode hard against the Northmen, they gave way again immediately, as they could do nothing against them. Now when the Northmen thought they perceived that the enemy were making but weak assaults, they set after them, and would drive them into flight; but when they had broken their shield-rampart the Englishmen rode up from all sides, and threw arrows and spears on them. Now when King Harald Sigurdson saw this, he went into the fray where the greatest crash of weapons was; and there was a sharp conflict, in which many people fell on both sides. King Harald then was in a rage, and ran out in front of the array, and hewed down with both hands; so that neither helmet nor armour could withstand him, and all who were nearest gave way before him. It was then very near with the English that they had taken to flight. So says Arnor, the earls' scald:

> Where battle-storm was ringing,
> Where arrow-cloud was singing,
> Harald stood there,
> Of armour bare,
> His deadly sword still swinging.

> The foemen feel its bite;
> His Norsemen rush to fight,
>   Danger to share
>   With Harald there,
> Where steel on steel was ringing.

King Harald Sigurdson was hit by an arrow in the windpipe, and that was his death-wound. He fell, and all who had advanced with him, except those who retired with the banner. There was afterwards the warmest conflict, and Earl Toste had taken charge of the king's banner. They began on both sides to form their array again, and for a long time there was a pause in fighting. Then Thjodolf sang these verses:

> The army stands in hushed dismay;
> Stilled is the clamour of the fray.
> Harald is dead, and with him goes
> The spirit to withstand our foes.
> A bloody scatt the folk must pay
> For their king's folly on this day.
> He fell; and now, without disguise,
> We say this business was not wise.

But before the battle began again Harald Godwinsson offered his brother Earl Toste peace, and also quarter to the Northmen who were still alive; but the Northmen called out all of them together that they would rather fall, one across the other, than accept of quarter from the Englishmen. Then each side set up a war-shout, and the battle began again. So says Arnor, the earls' scald:

> The king, whose name would ill-doers scare,
> The gold-tipped arrow would not spare.
> Unhelmed, unpanzered, without shield,
> He fell among us in the field.
> The gallant men who saw him fall
> Would take no quarter; one and all
> Resolved to die with their loved king,
> Around his corpse in a corpse-ring.

CHAPTER XCIII. SKIRMISH OF ORRE.—Eystein Orre came up at this moment from the ships with the men who followed him, and all were clad in armour. Then Eystein got King Harald's banner Land-ravager; and now was, for the third time, one of the sharpest of conflicts, in which many Englishmen fell, and they were near to taking flight. This conflict is called Orre's storm. Eystein and his men had hastened so fast from the ships that they were quite exhausted, and scarcely fit to fight before they came into the battle; but afterwards they became so furious, that they did not guard themselves with their shields as long as they could stand upright. At last they threw off their coats of ring-mail, and then the Englishmen could easily lay their blows at them; and many fell from weariness, and died without a wound. Thus almost all the chief men fell among the Norway people. This happened towards evening; and then it went, as one might expect, that all had not the same fate, for many fled, and were lucky enough to escape in various ways; and darkness fell before the slaughter was altogether ended.

CHAPTER XCIV. OF STYRKAR THE MARSHAL.—Styrkar, King Harald Sigurdson's marshal, a gallant man, escaped upon a horse, on which he rode away in the evening. It was blowing a cold wind, and Styrkar had not much other clothing upon him but his shirt, and had a helmet on his head, and a drawn sword in his hand. As soon as his weariness was over, he began to feel cold. A wagoner met him in a lined skin-coat. Styrkar asks him, "Wilt thou sell thy coat, friend?"

"Not to thee," says the peasant: "thou art a Northman; that I can hear by thy tongue."

Styrkar replies, "If I were a Northman, what wouldst thou do?"

"I would kill thee," replied the peasant; "but as ill luck would have it, I have no weapon just now by me that would do it."

Then Styrkar says, "As you can't kill me, friend, I shall try if I can't kill you." And with that he swung his sword, and struck him on the neck, so that his head came off. He then took the skin-coat, sprang on his horse, and rode down to the strand.

Olaf Haraldson had not gone on land with the others, and when he heard of his father's fall he made ready to sail away with the men who remained.

CHAPTER XCV. OF WILLIAM THE BASTARD.—When the Earl of Rouen, William the Bastard, heard of his relative King Edward's death, and also that Harald Godwinsson was chosen, crowned, and consecrated king of England, it appeared to him that he had a better right to the kingdom of England than Harald, by reason of the relationship between him and King Edward.[1] He thought, also, that he had grounds for avenging

---

[1] The relationship between Edward and William was, according to Snorri, that of first cousins, since he counts Emma, the wife of Ethelred and mother of Edward, as the sister of Robert, William's father (see p. 219). The reckoning is out by one generation, however, for Emma was really the sister of Richard, William's grandfather.

the affront that Harald had put upon him with respect to his daughter. From all these grounds William gathered together a great army in Normandy, and had many men, and sufficient transport-shipping. The day that he rode out of the castle to his ships, and had mounted his horse, his wife came to him, and wanted to speak with him; but when he saw her he struck at her with his heel, and set his spurs so deep into her breast that she fell down dead [1]; and the earl rode on to his ships, and went with his ships over to England. His brother, Bishop Otto,[2] was with him; and when the earl came to England he began to plunder, and take possession of the land as he came along. Earl William was stouter and stronger than other men; a great horseman and warrior, but somewhat stern; and a very sensible man, but not considered a man to be relied on.

CHAPTER XCVI. FALL OF KING HARALD GODWINSSON.—King Harald Godwinsson gave King Harald Sigurdson's son Olaf leave to go away, with the men who had followed him and had not fallen in battle; but he himself turned round with his army to go south, for he had heard that William the Bastard was overwhelming the south of England with a vast army, and was subduing the country for himself. With King Harald went his brothers Svein [3] and Gyrd, and Earl Walter.[4] King Harald and Earl William met each other south in England at Helsingja-port.[5] There was a great battle, in which King Harald and his brother Earl Gyrd and a great part of his men fell. This was the nineteenth day [i.e. 14 October, 1066] after the fall of King Harald Sigurdson. Harald's brother, Earl Walter, escaped by flight, and towards evening fell in with a division of William's people, consisting of a hundred men; and when they saw Earl Walter's troop they fled to a wood. Earl Walter set fire to the wood, and they were all burnt. So says Torkel Skallason in Walthjof's ballad:

> Earl of Walthjof the brave
> His foes a warming gave:
> Within the blazing grove
> A hundred men he drove.

---

[1] This story is false, or relates to some concubine; for William's queen, Matilda, was crowned in London and lived till 1083.
[2] William's half-brother, Odo, Bishop of Bayeux, *ob.* 1097.
[3] He had been killed in 1052. Leofwine is meant.
[4] *Vide* p. 219.
[5] Helsingja-port—Hastings.

The wolf will soon return,
And the witch's horse will burn
Her sharp claws in the ash,
To taste the Frenchman's flesh.

CHAPTER XCVII (*a*). EARL WALTER'S DEATH.—William was proclaimed king of England. He sent a message to Earl Walter that they should be reconciled, and gave him assurance of safety to come to the place of meeting. The earl set out with a few men; but when he came to a heath north of Kastalabryggia,[1] there met him two officers of King William, with many followers, who took him prisoner, put him in fetters, and afterwards he was beheaded; and the English call him a saint. Torkel tells of this:

William came o'er the sea,
With bloody sword came he:
Cold heart and bloody hand
Now rule the English land.
Earl Walter he slew,—
Walter the brave and true.
Cold heart and bloody hand
Now rule the English land.

William was after this king of England for twenty-one years [1066–87], and his descendants have been so ever since.[2] William died in his bed in Normandy, and after him his son William the Red was king there for fourteen years. Then Henry his brother took the kingdom. He was a son of William the First.

[3] [CHAPTER XCVII (*b*). FAMILY REGISTER.—William's father was Robert Longspear; his father was Richard son of Richard, who was son of William the son of Rolf Ganger, who first conquered Normandy. All these, one after the other, were Rouen earls; that is, counts of Rothemage [4] in Normandy. Rolf Ganger

---

[1] Possibly Castleford on the Aire, ten miles south-east of Leeds. Earl Walter (Waltheof) appears to have submitted to William soon after the battle of Hastings, and after some difficulties he won William's favour so far as to have the king's niece given him in marriage; in 1072 he was made earl of Northumbria. In 1075 he became involved in a conspiracy, but confessed the plot to William; he was imprisoned for his pains and finally executed in 1076. He seems to have been popular amongst the English, who regarded his death as martyrdom. Miracles took place at his tomb in Crowland Abbey.

[2] The male line died out in 1135.

[3] This genealogical section is derived from Peder Claussøn's work through the medium of Peringskiöld's edition of the *Heimskringla*, see the Introduction, pp. xxix–xxxi. The opening material is paralleled in genealogies found in *Fagrskinna*, ed. Finnur Jónsson, 1902–3, pp. 296–8.

[4] Rothemagi, Rothemadun are names given to Rouen and its territory

was a son of Rognvald, earl of Möre in Norway, a brother of
Earl Tore the Silent, and of Torf Einar the earl of Orkney who
killed Halfdan Haaleg because he had killed his father Rognvald earl of Möre, as is related in the Saga of Harald Fairhair.
King Ethelred of England was married to Queen Emma, a
sister of William the Bastard of Normandy, and had two sons
by her, Edward and Edmund,[1] who after him were kings of
England, but afterwards were driven out by Canute the Great
of Denmark; and Jatward, or Edward the Saint,[2] was king of
England after Hardacanute. Canute the Great married Emma
after the death of Ethelred, and had by her Harald[3] and Hardacanute, or Hardaknut. King Edward was married to Gyda,
daughter of Earl Godwin, and a grand-daughter of Torgils
Sprakaleg, and sister's daughter to the Danish king Svein
Ulvson. As she and King Edward had no children, her brother
Harald took the kingdom after King Edward, and thus came
England out of the family of Ethelred the Good. Harald Godwinsson had been king of England nine months and a half [4]
when he fell, and there was none remaining of Earl Godwin's
descendants but Earl Toste's sons Ketel and Skule, and Gyda
the daughter of Harald. She was married to Valdemar king
of Novgorod, a son of Jarisleif and Queen Ingigerd, who was
a daughter of King Olaf the Swede. By her he had King
Harald who was married to Christina, a daughter of King Inge
Steinkelsson of Sweden. Their daughters were Malfrid and
Ingeborg. Sigurd the Crusader married Malfrid, and afterwards she married King Eric Eimune of Denmark. Duke
Canute Lavard married Ingeborg, Harald's daughter; and their
children were the Danish king Valdemar, Christina, Katrina,
and Margaret. King Valdemar married Sophia, a daughter of
Valader king of Poland by Queen Rikize. The children of

Normandy, first received in fief by Rollo in 911 (see pp. 67–8). Rúða
and Rúðuborg are the Norse names for Rouen, and the ruling dynasty
there are referred to as Rúðujarlar. The true succession of William the
Conqueror's genealogy is: Rognvald, earl of Möre; Rolf Ganger; William
Longsword; Richard I; Richard II, brother of Queen Emma; Robert;
William the Conqueror (usually called the Bastard in Norse sources—he
was an illegitimate son). It will be clear that the genealogies in the text
given above are not to be taken too seriously.
    [1] This is King Edmund Ironside who for a few months strongly resisted
Canute, from his accession in April to his death in November 1016.
    [2] This is Edward the Confessor, not St. Edward, son of Edgar, who was
killed in 979.
    [3] Harald was not a son of Emma, but of Aelfgifu, a former wife or con-
cubine of Canute; cf. p. 129, note 1.
    [4] He had ruled from 6 January, 1066, and fell at Hastings, 14 October, 1066.

Valdemar and Sophia were King Valdemar and King Canute and Queen Rikize. Margaret was the daughter of Canute Lavard and she married Stig Hvitaleder; their children were Nicolas and Christina. Christina was married to King Karl Sörkveson of Sweden, and their son was King Sörkve, the father of King Jon. King Karl Sörkveson's mother was Queen Ulvhild, a daughter of Hakon the son of Finn, who was the son of Harek of Thjotta (cf. p. 136). Ulvhild was first married to the Danish king Nicolas, and afterwards she was married to King Inge Hallsteinsson of Sweden. Lastly she was married to King Sörkve, son of King Kol, of Sweden. Queen Rikize, daughter of Valdemar, was married to Eric, who was king of Sweden and son of Canute.]

CHAPTER XCVIII. OF OLAF HARALDSSON'S EXPEDITION TO NORWAY.—Olaf, the son of King Harald Sigurdson, sailed with his fleet from England from Rafnseyre, and came in autumn to the Orkney Isles, where the event had happened that Maria, a daughter of Harald Sigurdson, died a sudden death the very day and hour her father King Harald fell. Olaf remained there all winter; but the summer after [1067] he proceeded east to Norway, where he was proclaimed king along with his brother Magnus. Queen Ellesiv came from the West, along with her stepson Olaf and her daughter Ingigerd. There came also with Olaf over the West sea Skule, a son of Earl Toste,[1] and who since has been called the king's foster-son, and his brother Ketel Krok. Both were gallant men, of high family in England, and both were very intelligent; and the brothers were much beloved by King Olaf. Ketel Krok went north to Halogaland, where King Olaf procured him a good marriage, and from him are descended many great people. Skule, the king's foster-son, was a very clever man, and the handsomest man that could be seen. He was the commander of King Olaf's hird-men, spoke at the Things, and took part in all the country affairs with the king. The king offered to give Skule whatever district in Norway he liked, with all the income and duties that belonged to the king in it. Skule thanked him very much for the offer, but said he would rather have something else from him. "For

---

[1] The description of Skule (the king's foster-father, not foster-son as in the translation *passim*) as a son of Toste is not in the *Heimskringla*, though it occurs in *Morkinskinna* and *Fagrskinna* (on these see the Introduction, pp. xvii–xviii). The great Duke Skule (died 1240), Snorri's patron in Norway, reckoned his descent from this Skule, and Snorri may have omitted Toste's name on the duke's information.

if there came a shift of kings," said he, "the gift might come
to nothing. I would rather take some properties lying near to
the merchant towns, where you, sire, usually take up your
abode, and then I would enjoy your Yule-feasts." The king
agreed to this, and conferred on him lands eastward at Konghelle, Oslo, Tunsberg, Sarpsborg, Bergen, and north at Nidaros.
These were nearly the best properties at each place, and have
since descended to the family branches which came from Skule.
King Olaf gave Skule his female relative Gudrun, the daughter
of Nevstein, in marriage. Her mother was Ingerid, a
daughter of Sigurd Syr and Aasta, King Olaf the Saint's mother.
Ingerid was a sister of King Olaf the Saint and of King Harald. Skule's
and Gudrun's son was Asolf of Reine, who married Tora, a
daughter of Skopte Ogmundsson; and this Skopte was a grandson of Torberg Arneson. Skule's and Gudrun's daughter was
Ragnhild, who was married to Orm Kyrping; and his daughter
was Aasa, mother of Bjorn Buck. Asolf and Tora's son was
Guttorm of Rein, father of Baard, and grandfather of King Inge
and of Duke Skule.[1] [Aasolf and Tora's daughter was Sigrid,
who was married to Halkel Huk; and their son was John, father
of Halkel, Rognvald, and Gregorius. Guttorm of Rein married
Elrida, sister of Halkel Huk; and their daughters were Rangrid,
Ingrid, and Gudrud. Rangrid was married to Bjorn Byrdar-
svend; and their daughters were Elrid and Ingeborg. Elrid
was married to King Magnus; and they had a daughter, Christine,
married to Reidar Sendeman. Tore Skirfell had been married
before to Elrid, and had two sons by her, Kiniad and Torgrim
Klove; and after King Magnus Haraldson's death [2] she, Elrid,
married the lagman in Gotland, and had a son called Harald.
Among Ingeborg's sons was Torstein Skolm-Olld. Rangrid
was afterwards married to Frederic Köna, and their daughter
was called Astrid. Ingrid, a daughter of Guttorm of Rein,
was married to Guttorm Ostmansson of Jemteland. Guttorm
of Rein afterwards married Bergljot, and their son was called
Asulf, whose daughter Torbjorg was married to Eric Griffel;
and they had also a son called Asulf. Torbjorg afterwards was
married to the king's relative Reida. Guttorm of Rein married
afterwards Sigrid, a daughter of Thorkel and Halkatla. Halkatla was a daughter of Svein Bryniulfsson and Ingerid, a

---

[1] The following is derived from the same source as the genealogies, pp.
235-7 above, cf. p. 235, note 3. It is paralleled by material in a manuscript
of *Fagrskinna*, ed. cit. (p. 235, note 3), p. 388.
[2] Should be King Magnus Erlingsson.

sister of Canute the Great[1]; and Svein was a brother of Sörkve
in Sogn. Guttorm's and Sigrid's son was Baard Guttormsson;
first married with Ulvhild, a daughter of Paul the bishop,
afterwards with Cecilia, a daughter of King Sigurd Haraldson;
and their children were King Inge,[2] Duke Skule,[3] Guttorm,
and a daughter Sigrid.]

CHAPTER XCIX. OF KING HARALD SIGURDSON [1067].—One
year after King Harald's fall his body was transported from
England north to Nidaros, and was buried in Maria Kirke
which he had built. It was a common observation, that King
Harald distinguished himself above all other men by wisdom
and resources of mind; whether he had to take a resolution
suddenly for himself and others, or after long deliberation.
He was also, above all other men, bold, brave, and lucky, until
his dying day, as above related; and bravery is half victory.
So says Thjodolf:

> Harald, who till his dying day
> Came off the best in many a fray,
> Had one good rule in battle-plain,
> In Sealand and elsewhere, to gain—
> That, be his foes' strength more or less,
> Courage is always half success.

King Harald was a handsome man, of noble appearance; his
hair and beard yellow. He had a short beard, and long mous-
taches. The one eyebrow was somewhat higher than the other.
He had large hands and feet; but these were well made. His
height was five ells.[4] He was stern and severe to his enemies,
and avenged cruelly all opposition or misdeed. So says Thjodolf:

> Severe alike to friends or foes,
> Who dared his royal will oppose;
> Severe in discipline to hold
> His men-at-arms wild and bold;

---

[1] This is St Canute, son of Svein, who died in 1086. The cognomen "the
Great" appears to be an error for "the Saint."

[2] King, 1204-17.   [3] Duke, 1237-40, Snorri's patron.

[4] The original says "his measure is five ells high," and this presumably
refers to the marks measured on the wall of St. Mary's Church, Trondheim,
described on p. 269. From this it appears that Harald was taller than
his son Olaf the Quiet, who in turn was taller than his son Magnus Bareleg.
Magnus is said, however, to have been distinguished by his tall stature.
Early skeletal remains from Iceland and Denmark show a mean stature
for males of about 5 feet 8 inches, and it was doubtless much the same
in Norway. The early standard ell in Norway and Iceland was about
18½ inches. Harald may not have been 7 feet 6 inches tall, but if he was
say 6 feet 6 inches it was still possible for Magnus his grandson to be
shorter than he and yet a good deal taller than most men. It may be noted
that the laws reckon the average height of men as 3½ ells.

> Severe the bonder to repress;
> Severe to punish all excess;
> Severe was Harald—but we call
> That just which was alike to all.

King Harald was most greedy of power, and of all distinction and honour. He was bountiful to the friends who suited him. So says Thjodolf:

> I got from him, in sea-fight strong,
> A mark of gold for my ship-song.
> Merit in any way
> He generously would pay.

King Harald was fifty years old when he fell. We have no particular account of his youth before he was fifteen years old, when he was with his brother King Olaf at the battle of Stiklestad. He lived thirty-five years after that, and in all that time was never free from care and war. King Harald never fled from battle, but often tried cunning ways to escape when he had to do with great superiority of forces. All the men who followed King Harald in battle or skirmish said that when he stood in great danger, or anything came suddenly upon him, he always took that course which all afterwards saw gave the best hope of a fortunate issue.

CHAPTER C. KING HARALD AND KING OLAF COMPARED.— When Haldor, a son of Bryniulf Ulvalde [1] the Old, who was a sensible man and a great chief, heard people talk of how unlike the brothers Saint Olaf and King Harald were in disposition, he used to say, "I was in great friendship with both the brothers, and knew intimately the dispositions of both, and never did I know two men more like in disposition. Both were of the highest understanding, and bold in arms, and greedy of power and property; of great courage, but not acquainted with the way of winning the favour of the people; zealous in governing, and severe in their revenge. King Olaf forced the people into Christianity and good customs, and punished cruelly those who disobeyed. This just and rightful severity the chiefs of the country could not bear, but raised an army against him, and killed him in his own kingdom; and therefore he is held to be a saint. King Harald, again, marauded to obtain glory and power, forced all the people he could under his power, and died in another king's dominions. Both brothers, in daily life, were of a worthy and considerate manner of living: they were of great experience, and very laborious, and were known and celebrated far and wide for these qualities."

[1] v. *Olaf Sagas*, p. 163.

CHAPTER CI. KING MAGNUS'S DEATH.—King Magnus Haraldson ruled over Norway the first winter after King Harald's death, and afterwards two years along with his brother King Olaf. Thus there were two kings of Norway at that time; and Magnus had the northern and Olaf the eastern part of the country. King Magnus had a son called Hakon, who was fostered by Tore of Steig in Gudbrandsdal, who was a brother of King Magnus by the mother's side; and Hakon was a most promising man.

After King Harald Sigurdson's death the Danish king Svein let it be known that the peace between the Northmen and the Danes was at an end, and insisted that the league between Harald and Svein was not for longer time than their lives. There was a levy in both kingdoms. Harald's sons called out the whole people in Norway for procuring men and ships, and Svein set out from the South with the Danish army. Messengers then went between with proposals for a peace; and the Northmen said they would either have the same league as was concluded between King Harald and Svein, or otherwise give battle instantly on the spot. Verses were made on this occasion, viz.:

> Ready for war or peace,
> King Olaf will not cease
> From foeman's hand
> To guard his land.

So says also Stein Herdisarson in his song of Olaf:

> From Drontheim town, where in repose
> The holy king defies his foes,
> Another Olaf will defend
> His kingdom from the greedy Svein.
> King Olaf has both power and right,
> And the Saint's favour in the fight.
> The Saint will ne'er his kin forsake,
> And let Svein Ulvson Norway take.

And by the intervention of good men a meeting was agreed upon between the kings, and that it should be at Konghelle. At this meeting friendship was concluded between the kings, and peace · between the countries. The agreement was confirmed by Olaf taking in marriage Ingerid, King Svein's daughter; and this peace endured long, and Olaf reigned in quietness unknown before in Norway. King Magnus fell ill, and died of the ringworm [1069] disease,[1] after being ill for some time. He died and was buried at Nidaros. He was an amiable king, and bewailed by the people.

[1] This disease was probably the acute form of ergotism, caused by eating meal ground from corn affected by a fungus disease. Chronic ergotism was widespread in Europe in the Middle Ages.

XI

OLAF THE QUIET

[1069–93]

CHAPTER I. OLAF'S PERSONAL APPEARANCE.—Olaf remained
sole king of Norway after the death of his brother King Magnus.
Olaf was a stout man, well grown in limbs; and every one said
a handsomer man could not be seen, nor of a nobler appearance.
His hair was yellow as silk, and became him well; his skin was
white and fine over all his body; his eyes beautiful, and his
limbs well proportioned. He was rather silent in general, and
did not speak much even at Things; but he was merry in
drinking parties. He loved drinking much, and was talkative
enough then; but quite peaceful. He was cheerful in conversation, peacefully inclined during all his reign, and loving gentleness and moderation in all things. Stein Herdisarson says
this of him:

> Our Drontheim king is brave and wise,
> His love of peace our bonder prize;
> By friendly word and ready hand
> He holds good peace through every land.
> He is for all a lucky star;
> England he frightens from a war;
> The stiff-necked Danes he drives to peace;
> Troubles by his good influence cease.

CHAPTER II. OF KING OLAF'S MANNER OF LIVING.—It was
the fashion in Norway in old times for the king's high seat to
be on the middle of a long bench, and the ale was handed across
the fire[1]; but King Olaf had his high seat made on a high bench
across the room; he also first had chimney-places in the rooms,
and the floors strewed[2] both summer and winter. In King

---

[1] We may understand the arrangement by supposing the fire in the
middle of the room, the smoke escaping by a hole in the roof, and a long
bench on each side of the fire; one bench occupied by the high seat of
the king and great guests, the other by the rest of the guests; and the
cup handed across the fire, which appears to have had a religious meaning
previous to the introduction of Christianity.

[2] Floors were usually only of bare stamped earth or clay and they were
often strewn with straw or rushes; fresh juniper-tops have been used in
Norway for the same purpose.

Olaf's time many merchant towns arose in Norway, and many new ones were founded. Thus King Olaf founded a merchant town at Bergen, where very soon many wealthy people settled themselves, and it was regularly frequented by merchants from foreign lands. He had the foundations laid for the large Christ church,[1] which was to be a stone church; but in his time there was little done to it. Besides, he completed the old Christ church,[2] which was of wood. King Olaf also had a great feasting-house built in Nidaros, and in many other merchant towns, where before there were only private feasts; and in his time no one could drink in Norway but in these houses, adorned for the purpose with branches and leaves, and which stood under the king's protection. The great guild-bell[3] in Drontheim, which was called the "Town's Salvation," tolled to call together to these guilds. The guild-brethen built Margaret's church in Nidaros of stone. In King Olaf's time there were public drinking houses, and lyke-wake festivals.[4] At this time also much unusual splendour and foreign customs and fashions in the cut of clothes were introduced; as, for instance, costly hose plaited about the legs. Some had gold rings about the legs, and also used coats which had lists down the sides, and arms five ells long, and so narrow that they must be drawn up with ties, and lay in folds all the way up to the shoulders. The shoes were high, and all edged with silk, or even with gold. Many other kinds of wonderful fashions were in use at that time.

CHAPTER III. FASHION OF KING OLAF'S COURT.—King Olaf used the fashion, which was introduced from the courts of foreign kings, of letting his grand-butler stand in front of the table, and fill the table-cups for himself and the other distinguished guests who sat at the table. He had also torch-bearers, who held as many candles at the table as there were guests of distinction present. There was also a marshal's bench

[1] The *great* Christ church, at the point now called Bergenhus, was not quite completed until about 1160.
[2] The little Christ church, temporary cathedral till the other was ready.
[3] The bell hung in the tower of St. Margaret's church.
[4] The Icelandic has *leizludrykkjur*, which seems to mean "lyke-wake drinkings." It probably refers to funeral feasts held for dead guild-brothers which members of the guild were obliged to attend. The guilds were primarily organized as mutual insurance societies, fire and shipwreck being the chief contingencies covered by their insurance regulations. Members were required to help one another in various other ways—seeking vengeance for a slain member and helping his dependants, for example. An essential feature of the societies was the common banquet (*convivium* is the Latin word used for guild).

beyond the serving-table,[1] where the marshal and other persons of distinction sat with their faces towards the high seat. King Harald, and the kings before him, used to drink out of a deer-horn; and the ale was handed from the high seat to the other side over the fire, and he drank to the memory of any one he thought of. So says Stuv the scald:

> He who in battle is the first,
> And now in peace is best to trust,
> A welcome, hearty and sincere,
> Gave to me on my coming here.
> He whom the ravens watch with care,
> He who the gold rings does not spare,
> A golden horn full to the brink
> Gave me himself at Haug [2] to drink.

CHAPTER IV. ARRANGEMENT OF KING OLAF'S COURT.—King Olaf had 120 courtmen-at-arms, and 60 pursuivants, besides 60 house-servants, who provided what was wanted for the king's house wherever it might be, or did other work required for the king. When the bonder asked why he kept a greater retinue than the law allowed, or former kings kept when they went in guest-quarters or feasts which the bonder had to provide for them, the king answered, "It does not happen that I rule the kingdom better, or produce greater respect for me than ye had for my father, although I have one half more people than he had. I do not by any means do it merely to plague you, or to make your condition harder than formerly."

CHAPTER V. KING SVEIN ULVSON'S DEATH [1076].—King Svein Ulvson died ten years after the fall of both the Haralds.[3] After him his son, Harald Hein,[4] was king for four years; then Canute the Holy for eight years; afterwards Olaf, King Svein's third son, for eight years, then Eric the Good, a fourth son of Svein, also for eight years. Olaf the king of Norway was married to Ingigerd, a daughter of Svein the Danish king; and Olaf the Danish King Svein's son married Ingerid, a daughter of King Harald, and sister of King Olaf of Norway. King

---

[1] *Trapiza*, a word borrowed ultimately from Greek. Under the old arrangements the hall had benches down each wall, with the high seat in the middle of one set of benches. Now they were set across the room, separated by side serving-tables. The newfangled ovens, probably placed in the corner, made the rearrangement possible.

[2] The name of the king's farm in Værdal.

[3] The Norwegian King Harald, and the English King Harald God-winsson.

[4] There is confusion regarding the reigns of these kings—the chronology seems properly to be Harald Hein 1076–80, Canute 1080–86, Svein 1086–95, Eric 1095–1103.

Olaf Haraldson was called by some Olaf Kyrre,[1] but by many Olaf the Bonde, because he sat in peace, without strife within or without the country, and gave no reasonable cause for others to plunder in his dominions. He had a son by Tora, Joan's daughter, who was called Magnus, and was one of the handsomest lads that could be seen, and was promising in every respect. He was brought up in the king's hird.

CHAPTER VI. MIRACLES OF KING OLAF THE SAINT.—Olaf Kyrre had a minster of stone built in Nidaros, on the spot where King Olaf's shrine was removed to it, and was placed above placed directly over the spot where the king's grave had been. This church was consecrated, and called Christ church; and King Olaf's shrine was removed to it, and was placed before the altar, and many miracles took place there. The following summer, on the same day of the year as the church was consecrated, which was the day before Olafsmass, there was a great assemblage of people, and then a blind man was restored to sight.[3] And on the mass-day itself, when the shrine and the holy relics were taken out and carried, and the shrine itself, according to custom, was taken and set down in the churchyard, a man who had long been dumb recovered his speech again, and sang with flowing tongue praise-hymns to God, and to the honour of King Olaf the Saint. The third miracle was of a woman who had come from Sweden, and had suffered much distress on this pilgrimage from her blindness; but, trusting in God's mercy, had come travelling to this solemnity. She was led blind into the church to hear mass this day; but before the service was ended she saw with both eyes, and got her sight fully and clearly, although she had been blind fourteen years. She returned with great joy, praising God and King Olaf the Saint.

CHAPTER VII. OF THE SHRINE OF KING OLAF THE SAINT.— There happened a circumstance in Nidaros, when King Olaf's coffin was being carried through Lower Long Street, that it became so heavy that the bearers could not lift it from the spot. Now when the coffin was set down, the street was broken up to see what was under it at that spot, and the body of a child was found which had been murdered and concealed there. The body was carried away, the street put in order

---

[1] Kyrre means "the calm" or "quiet."
[2] Vide *Olaf Sagas*, p. 389.
[3] The following miracles Snorri has incorrectly referred to Olaf Kyrre's time. According to the old legend they should be placed in the year 1153.

again as it had been before, and the shrine carried on according
to custom.

[1] [CHAPTER VIII. MEETING OF OLAF KYRRE AND CANUTE THE
HOLY, AND THEIR PREPARATIONS AGAINST ENGLAND.—King
Olaf Kyrre was a great friend of his brother-in-law the Danish
king, Canute the Holy. They appointed a meeting, and met
at the Gotha river at Konghelle,[2] where the kings used to have
their meetings. There King Canute made the proposal that
they should send an army westward to England on account of
the revenge they had to take there; first and foremost King
Olaf himself, and also the Danish king. "Do one of two
things," said King Canute—"either take sixty ships, which I
will furnish thee with, and be thou the leader; or give me sixty
ships, and I shall be the leader." Then said King Olaf, "This
speech of thine, King Canute, is altogether according to my
mind; but there is this great difference between us: your family
has had more luck in conquering England with great glory, and,
among others, King Canute the Great; and it is likely that this
good fortune follows your race. On the other hand, when King
Harald my father went westward to England, he got his death
there; and at that time the best men in Norway followed him.
But Norway was so emptied then of chosen men, that such
men are not since to be found in the country; nor, especially,
such a leader as King Harald was for wisdom and bravery.
For that expedition there was the most excellent outfit, and
you know what was the end of it. Now I know my own
capacity, and how little I am suited to be the leader; so I would
rather you should go, with my help and assistance."

So King Olaf gave Canute sixty large ships, with excellent
equipment and faithful men, and set his lendermen as chiefs
over them; and all must allow that this armament was admirably equipped. It is also told in the saga about Canute,
that the Northmen alone did not break the levy when the army
was assembled, for they were obedient to the king; but as the
Danes would not obey their king's orders, the Northmen also
returned to Norway, with the king's leave and consent. This
King Canute acknowledged, and gave them, on their way home,
leave to trade in merchandise where they pleased through his
country, and in his rivers, and at the same time sent the king
of Norway costly presents for his assistance. On the other

---

[1] Chapters viii and ix are not in the *Heimskringla*; here they are ultimately
derived from *Morkinskinna*, cf. Introduction, p. xxx.

[2] Near Kungälv, about twelve miles from Gothenburg.

hand, he was enraged against the Danes, and laid heavy fines
upon them when he returned home to Denmark. This strife
between them was carried so far that the Danes themselves
killed King Canute, rather than submit to his just judgment
against them.

CHAPTER IX. OF OLAF KYRRE AND A PEASANT WHO UNDER-
STOOD THE LANGUAGE OF BIRDS.—One summer, when King
Olaf's men had gone round the country collecting his income
and land dues, it happened that the king, on their return home,
asked them where on their expedition they had been best
entertained. They said it was in the house of a bonde, in a
district in the province of Lister. "There is an old bonde there
who knows many things before they happen. We asked him
about many things, which he explained to us; and we never
asked him anything but he was sure to know all about it; nay,
we even believe that he understands perfectly the language of
birds." The king replies, "How can ye believe such nonsense?"
and insisted that it was wrong to put confidence in such things.
It happened soon after that the king was sailing along the
coast; and as they sailed through several Sounds the king
said, "What is that township up in the country?"

They replied, "That is the district, sire, where we told you
we were best entertained."

Then said the king, "What house is that which stands up
there, not far from the Sound?"

They replied, "That house belongs to the wise old man we
told you of, sire."

They saw now a horse standing close to the house. Then
said the king, "Go there, and take that horse, and kill him."

They replied, "We would not like to do him such harm."

The king: "I will command. Cut off the horse's head; but
take care of yourselves that ye let no blood come to the ground,
and bear the horse out to my ship. Go then and bring to me
the old man; but tell him nothing of what has happened, as
ye shall answer for it with your lives."

They did as they were ordered, and then came to the old
man, and told him the king's message. When he came before
the king, the king asked him, "Who owns the house thou art
dwelling in?"

He replies, "Sire, you own it, and take rent for it."

The king: "Show us the way round the ness, for here thou
must be a good pilot."

The old man went into his boat, and rowed before the king's

ship; and when he had rowed a little way a crow came flying over the ship, and croaking hideously. The peasant listens to the crow. The king said, "Do you think, bonde, that betokens anything?"

"Sire, that is certain," said he.

Then another crow flies over the ship, and screeches dreadfully. The bonde was so ill hearing this that he could not row, and the oars hung loose in his hands.

Then said the king, "Thy mind is turned much to these crows, bonde, and to what they say."

The bonde replies, "Now I suspect it is true what they say."

The third time the crow came flying screeching at its very worst, and almost settling on the ship. Now the bonde threw down his oars, regarded them no more, and stood up before the king.

Then the king said, "Thou art taking this much to heart, bonde; what is it they say?"

The peasant: "It is likely that either they or I have misunderstood——"

"Say on," replied the king.

The bonde replied in a song:

> The "one-year old"
> Mere nonsense told;
> The two-years' chatter
> Seemed senseless matter;
> The three-years' croak
> Of wonders spoke.
> The foul bird said
> My old mare's dead
> I row along;
> And, in her song,
> She said the thief
> Was the land's chief

"The three-year-old crow says that you bid me row here before your ship, and yet have taken my property from me."

The king said, "What is this, bonde! Wilt thou call me a thief? That is not judging well of me."

"It is true, sire," said the bonde, "that would not be well said, neither do I think you the thief; and there has been some joke played on me, for the crow said my horse is on board the ship."

After some conversation between the king and the bonde, the king gave him good presents, and remitted the land-rent of the place he lived on; and gave him the farm to be his own property for ever, besides other considerable gifts.

King Olaf was not niggardly in giving presents to his men, and gave all kinds of valuable articles. So says Stuv the scald:

> The pillar of our royal race
> Stands forth adorned with every grace.
> What king before e'er took such pride
> To scatter bounty far and wide?
> To one he gives the ship of war,
> Hung round with shields that gleam afar;
> The merchant ship on one bestows,
> With painted streaks in glowing rows.
>
> The man-at-arms a golden ring
> Boasts as the present of his king;
> At the king's table sits the guest,
> By the king's bounty richly drest.
> King Olaf, Norway's royal son,
> Who from the English glory won,
> Pours out with ready-giving hand
> His wealth on children of the land.
>
> Brave clothes to servants he awards,
> Helms and ring-mail coats grace his guards;
> Or axe and sword Haar's [1] warriors gain,
> And heavy armour for the plain.
> Gold, too, for service duly paid,
> Red gold all pure, and duly weighed,
> King Olaf gives—he loves to pay
> All service in a royal way.]

CHAPTER X. OF KING OLAF KYRRE'S DEATH.—King Olaf lived principally in his domains on his large farms. Once when he was east in Ranrike, on his estate of Haukaby,[2] he took the disease which ended in his death. He had then been king of Norway for twenty-six years; for he was made king of Norway the year after King Harald's death. King Olaf's body was taken north to Nidaros, and buried in Christ church, which he himself had built there. He was the most amiable king of his time, and Norway was much improved in riches and cultivation during his reign.

---

[1] *Háarr*, one of Odin's names. The original has "the heavy equipment of Haar," a *kenning* for armour. These verses are properly to be attributed to Stein Herdisarson, not Stuv the scald.

[2] Now Haakeby in the north of Bohuslen.

XII

MAGNUS BAREFOOT

[1093-1103]

CHAPTER I. BEGINNING OF THE REIGN OF KING MAGNUS AND HIS COUSIN HAKON.—Magnus, King Olaf's son, was, immediately after King Olaf's death, proclaimed at Viken king of all Norway; but the Upland people, on hearing of King Olaf's death, chose Hakon, Tore's foster-son, a cousin [1] of King Magnus, as king. Thereupon Hakon and Tore went north to the Drontheim country, and when they came to Nidaros they summoned a Thing at Öre; and at that Thing Hakon desired the bonder to give him the kingly title, which was agreed to, and the Drontheim people proclaimed him king of half of Norway, as his father King Magnus had been before. Hakon relieved the Drontheim people of all tolls on ships, and gave them many other privileges. He did away with Yule-gifts, and gained by this the good-will of all the Drontheim people. Thereafter Hakon formed a hird, and then proceeded to the Uplands, where he gave the Upland people the same privileges as the Drontheim people; so that they also were perfectly well affected to him, and were his friends. The people in Drontheim sang this ballad about him:

> Young Hakon was the Norseman's pride,
> And Steige-Thor was on his side.
> Young Hakon from the Upland came,
> With royal birth, and blood, and name.
> Young Hakon from the king demands
> His royal birthright, half the lands;
> Magnus will not the kingdom break—
> The whole or nothing he will take.

CHAPTER II. HAKON'S DEATH. — King Magnus proceeded north to the merchant town [Kaupangen],[2] and on his arrival went straight to the king's house, and there took up his abode. He remained here the first part of the winter, and kept seven long-ships in the open water of the river Nid, abreast of the

---

[1] Hakon was a son of Magnus, Harald the Stern's son; and Magnus was a son of Olaf Kyrre, Harald's son also.
[2] i.e. Nidaros.

king's house. Now when King Hakon heard that King Magnus
was come to Drontheim, he came from the East [1] over the
Dovrefjeld, and thence down upon Drontheim to Kaupangen,
where he settled in the house called Skulegarth, down below
Clement's church, which had formerly been the king's house.[2]
King Magnus was ill pleased with the great gifts which Hakon
had given to the bonder to gain their favour, and thought it was
so much given out of his own property. This irritated his
mind; and he thought he had suffered injustice from his relative
in this respect, that he must now put up with less income than
his father and his predecessors before him had enjoyed; and
he gave Tore the blame. When King Hakon and Tore observed
this, they were alarmed for what Magnus might do; and they
thought it suspicious that Magnus kept long-ships afloat rigged
out, and with tents. The following spring, about Candlemas
[2 February, 1094], King Magnus left the town in the night
with his ships; the tents up, and lights burning in the tents.
They brought up at Hevring,[3] remained there all night, and
lit large fires on the land. Then Hakon and the men in the
town thought some treachery was on foot, and he let the
trumpets call all the men together out on the Öre, where the
whole people of the town came to him, and the people were
assembled together the whole night. When it was light in the
morning, King Magnus saw the people from all districts gathered
together on the Öre; and he sailed out of the fjord, and proceeded south to where the Gulathing is held. Hakon thanked
the people for their support which they had given him and
got ready to travel east to Viken. But he first held a mot [4]
in the town, where, in a speech, he asked the people for their
friendship, promising them his; and added, that he had some
suspicions of his relation King Magnus's intentions. Then
King Hakon mounted his horse, and was ready to travel. All
men promised him their good-will and support whenever he
required them, and the people followed him out to the foot of
the Steinberg.[5] From thence King Hakon proceeded up the
Dovrefjeld; but as he was going over the Fjelds he rode by day
after a ptarmigan, which flew up beside him, and in this chase
a sickness overfell him, which ended in his death; and he died
on the mountain. His body was carried north, and came to

---

[1] i.e. from the eastern districts; by compass he came north.
[2] The one which St. Olaf built by St. Clement's Church.
[3] Now Hövringen, off Ilsviken, to the west of Trondhjem.
[4] A Thing-meeting in a town.
[5] Now Stenberget, where from ancient times the road went and still goes.

Kaupangen just half a month after he left it. The whole townspeople went to meet the body, sorrowing, and the most of them weeping; for all people loved him with sincere affection. King Hakon's body was interred in Christ church, and Hakon and Magnus had ruled the country for two years. Hakon was a man full twenty-five years old, and was one of the chiefs the most beloved by all the people. He had made a journey to Bjarmeland, where he had given battle and gained a victory.

CHAPTER III. OF A FORAY IN HALLAND. — King Magnus sailed in autumn eastward to Viken; but when spring approached he went southwards to Halland,[1] and plundered far and wide. He laid waste Viskedal and many other districts, and returned with a great booty back to his own kingdom. So says Bjorn Cripplehand [2] in his song on Magnus:

> Through Halland wide around
> The clang and shriek resound;
>   The houses burn,
>   The people mourn,
> Through Halland wide around.
>
> The Norse king strides in flame,
> Through Viskedal he came;
>   The fire sweeps,
>   The widow weeps,
> The Norse king strides in flame.

Here it is told that King Magnus made the greatest devastation through Halland.

CHAPTER IV. OF TORE OF STEIGE.—There was a man called Svein, a son of Harald Flett. He was a Danish man by family, a great viking and champion, and a very strong man, and of high birth in his own country. He had been some time with King Hakon Magnusson, and was very dear to him; but after King Hakon's decease Tore of Steig, his foster-father, had no great confidence in any treaty or friendship with King Magnus, if the whole country came into his power, on account of the position in which Tore had stood to King Magnus, and the opposition he had made to him. Thereupon Tore and Svein took counsel with each other, which they afterwards carried into effect—to raise, with Tore's assistance, and his men, a troop against Magnus. But as Tore was old and heavy, Svein took the command, and name of leader of the troop. In this

---

[1] Halland was the coastal district south of the river Gotha, now Swedish territory but formerly Danish.
[2] Rather, Knitted Nieve or Clench-hand.

design several chiefs took part, among whom the principal was
Egil Aslaksson of Forland.[1] Egil was a lenderman, and married
to Ingeborg, a daughter of Ogmund Torbergsson, a sister of
Skopte of Giske. The rich and powerful man Skjalg Erlingsson
from Jæderen also joined their party. Torkel Hammerscald
speaks of this in his ballad of Magnus:

> Tore and Egil were not wise—
> They aimed too high to win a prize:
> There was no reason in their plan,
> And it hurt many a udalman.
> The stone, too great for them to throw,
> Fell back, and hurt them with the blow;
> And now the udalmen must rue
> That to their friends they were so true.

Tore and Svein collected a troop in the Uplands, and went
down through Raumsdal into Sunnmöre, and there collected
vessels, with which they afterwards sailed north to Drontheim.

CHAPTER V. OF TORE'S ADVENTURES.—The lenderman
Sigurd Ullstreng, a son of Loden Viggeskalle,[2] collected men by
sending round the war-token, as soon as he heard of Tore and
the troop which followed him, and had a rendezvous with all
the men he could raise at Vigg. Svein and Tore also met there
with their people, fought with Sigurd, and gained the victory
after giving him a great defeat; and Sigurd fled, and joined
King Magnus. Tore and his followers proceeded to the town
[Kaupangen], and remained there some time in the fjord, where
many people joined them. King Magnus hearing this news
immediately collected an army, and proceeded north to Drontheim. And when he came into the fjord Tore and his party
heard of it while they lay at Hevring, and they were ready to
leave the fjord; and they rowed their ships to the strand at
Vagnvik,[3] and left them, and came into Texdal in Seliuverf,[4]
and Tore was carried in a litter over the Fjelds. Then they
got hold of ships, and sailed north to Halogaland. As soon as
King Magnus was ready for sea, he sailed from Drontheim in
pursuit of them. Tore and his party went north all the way
to Bjarkö; and Jon, with his son Vidkunn, fled from thence.
Tore and his men robbed all the movable goods, and burnt
the house, and a good long-ship that belonged to Vidkunn.
While the hull was burning the vessel heeled to one side, and

---

[1] Now Folland, a large farm on Averö, Nordmöre.
[2] Viggeskalle, i.e. the farmer of Viggen on the Orkedals fjord.
[3] Vagnvik in Strinden.
[4] Now Jössund in South Trondhjem.

Tore called out, "Hard to starboard, Vidkunn!" Some verses were made about this burning in Bjarkö:

> The sweetest farm that I have seen
> Stood on Bjarkö's island green;
> And now, where once this farm-house stood,
> Fire crackles through a pile of wood;
> And the clear red flame, burning high,
> Flashes across the dark night-sky.
> Jon and Vidkunn on this dark night,
> Will not be wandering without light.

CHAPTER VI. DEATH OF TORE AND EGIL.—Jon and Vidkunn travelled day and night till they met King Magnus. Svein and Tore proceeded southwards with their men, and plundered far and wide in Halogaland. But while they lay in a fjord called Harm,[1] Tore and his party saw King Magnus coming under sail towards them; and thinking they had not men enough to fight him, they rowed away and fled. Tore and Egil brought up at Hesiutun[2]; but Svein rowed out to sea, and some of their people rowed into the fjords. King Magnus pursued Tore, and the vessels struck together while they were landing. Tore stood in the forecastle of his ship, and Sigurd Ullstreng called out to him, and asked, "Art thou well, Tore?" Tore replied, "I am well in hands, but ill on my feet." And some one made these verses:

> The vessels struck, and swords were out,
> When Ullstreng calls out with a shout,
> "Old Tore, how d'ye do?"
> The grey old warrior, firm and true
> To his own cause, cries "How d'ye do?
> When loving friends, such as we two,
> Happen in bloody fray to meet,
> I'm brisk in hands, but slow in feet."

Then said Sigurd Ullstreng, "Thou art pretty fat, Tore." He replied, "My meat and my ale make me so." Then all his men leaped ashore and fled, and Tore was taken prisoner. Egil was also taken prisoner, for he would not leave his wife. King Magnus then ordered both of them to be taken out to Vambar Holm[3]; and when they were leading Tore from the ship he tottered on his legs. Then Vidkunn called out, "More to larboard, Tore!" When he was being led to the gallows he sang:

> We were four comrades gay—
> Let one by the helm stay.

---

[1] Now Velfjorden in South Helgeland.   [2] Now Hestun on Havnöen.
[3] Now Vomba off Havnöen.

When he came to the gallows he said, "Bad counsel comes to a bad end." Then Tore was hanged; but when he was hoisted up the gallows-tree he was so heavy that his neck gave way, and the body fell down to the ground; for Tore was a man exceedingly stout, both high of stature and thick. Egil was also led to the gallows; and when the king's thralls were about hanging him he said, "Ye should not hang me, for in truth each of you deserves much more to be hanged." People sang these verses about it:

> I hear, my girl, that Egil said,
> When to the gallows he was led,
> That the king's thralls far more than he
> Deserved to hang on gallows-tree.
> It might be so; but, death in view,
> A man should to himself be true—
> End a stout life by death as stout,
> Showing no fear, or care, or doubt.

King Magnus sat near while they were being hanged, and was in such a rage that none of his men was so bold as to ask mercy for them. The king said, when Egil was hanging on the gallows, "Thy great kinsmen help thee but poorly in time of need." From this people supposed that the king only wanted to have been entreated to have spared Egil's life. Bjorn the Cripplehand speaks of these things:

> King Magnus in the robbers' gore
> Dyed red his sword; and round the shore
> The wolves howled out their wild delight,
> At corpses swinging in their sight.
> Have ye not heard how the king's sword
> Punished the traitors to their lord?
> How the king's thralls hung on the gallows
> Old Tore and his traitor-fellows?

CHAPTER VII. OF THE PUNISHMENT OF THE DRONTHEIM PEOPLE.—After this King Magnus sailed south to Drontheim, and brought up in the fjord, and punished severely all who had been guilty of treason towards him; killing some, and burning the houses of others. So says Bjorn Cripplehand:

> He who despises fence of shields
> Drove terror through the Drontheim fields,
> When all the land through which he came
> Was swimming in a flood of flame.
> The raven-feeder, well I know,
> Cut off two chieftains at a blow;
> The wolf could scarcely ravenous be,
> The ernes flew round the gallows-tree.

Svein, Harald Flett's son, fled out to sea first, and sailed then to Denmark, and remained there; and at last came into great favour with King Eystein, the son of King Magnus, who took so great a liking to Svein that he made him his dish-bearer,[1] and held him in great respect. King Magnus had now alone the whole kingdom, and he kept good peace in the land, and rooted out all vikings and lawless men. He was a man quick, warlike, and able, and more like in all things to his grandfather King Harald in disposition and talents than to his father.

[2][CHAPTER VIII. OF THE PEASANT SVEINKE, THE RIVER BOR-DERER, AND SIGURD ULLSTRENG. — There was a man called Sveinke Steinarsson, who was very wealthy, and dwelt in Viken at the Gotha river. He had brought up Hakon Magnusson before Tore of Steige took him. Sveinke had not yet sub-mitted to King Magnus. King Magnus ordered Sigurd Ull-streng to be called, and told him he would send him to Sveinke with the command that he should quit the king's land and domain. "He has not yet submitted to us, or shown us due honour." He added, that there were some lendermen east in Viken, namely, Svein Bryggefod, Dag Eilivsson, or Kolbjorn Klakka, who could bring this matter into right bearing. Then Sigurd said, "I did not know there was the man in Norway against whom three lendermen besides myself were needful." The king replied, "Thou needst not take this help, unless it be necessary." Now Sigurd made himself ready for the journey with a ship, sailed east to Viken, and there summoned the lendermen to him. Then a Thing was appointed in Viken, to which the people were called who dwelt on the East river, besides others; so that it was a numerous assembly. When the Thing was formed they had to wait for Sveinke. They soon after saw a troop of men coming along, so well furnished with weapons that they looked like pieces of shining ice; and now came Sveinke and his people to the Thing, and set themselves down in a circle. All were clad in iron, with glowing arms, and five hundred in number. Then Sigurd stood up, and spoke. "My master, King Magnus, sends God's salutations and his own to all friends, lendermen and others, his subjects in the kingdom; also to the powerful bonder, and the people in general, with kind words and offers of friendship; and to all who will obey him he offers his friendship and good-will. Now the king will, with all cheerfulness and peace, show himself a gracious

---

[1] According to the later Court Regulations (*Hirðskrá*), the dish-bearer (*skutilsveinn*) came next to the king's standard-bearer in dignity.
[2] This chapter is not in the *Heimskringla*, cf. Introduction, p. xxx.

master to all who submit to him, and to all in his dominions. He will be the leader and defender of all the men of Norway; and it will be good for you to accept his gracious speech, and this offer."

Then stood up a man in the troop of the river-borderers, who was of great stature and grim countenance, clad in a leather cloak, with a halberd on his shoulder, and a great steel hat upon his head. He looked sternly, and said, "Here is no need of wheels, says the fox, when he draws the trap over the ice." He said nothing more, but sat down again.

Soon after Sigurd Ullstreng stood up again, and spoke thus: "But little concern or help have we for the king's affairs from you river-borderers, and but little friendship; yet by such means every man shows how much he respects himself. But now I shall produce more clearly the king's errand." Thereupon he demanded land-dues and levy-dues, together with all other rights of the king, from the great bonder. He bade each of them to consider with himself how they had conducted themselves in these matters; and that they should now promote their own honour, and do the king justice, if they had come short hitherto in doing so. And then he sat down.

Then the same man got up in the troop of river-borderers who had spoken before, lifted his hat a little up, and said, "The lads run well, say the Laplanders, who have skis for nothing." Then he sat himself down again.

Soon after Sigurd arose, after speaking with the lendermen, and said that so weighty a message as the king's ought not to be treated lightly as a jest. He was now somewhat angry; and added, that they ought not to receive the king's message and errand so scornfully, for it was not decent. He was dressed in a red or scarlet coat, and had a blue coat over it. He cast off his upper coat, and said, "Now it is come so far that every one must look to himself, and not loiter and jest with others; for by so doing every man will show what he is. We do not require now to be taught by others; for now we can see ourselves how much we are regarded. But this may be borne with; but not that ye treat so scornfully the king's message. Thereby every one shows how highly he considers himself. There is one man called Sveinke Steinarsson, who lives east at the river; and from him the king will have his just land-dues, together with his own land, or will banish him from the country. It is of no use here to seek excuses, or to answer with sharp words; for people are to be found who are his equals in power, although he now receives our speech so unworthily; and it is better now than afterwards to return to the right way, and do himself honour, rather than await disgrace for his obstinacy." He then sat down.

Sveinke then got up, threw back his steel-hat, and gave Sigurd many scornful words, and said, "Tut! tut! 'tis a shame for the dogs, says the proverb, when the fox is allowed to piss in the peasant's well. Here will be a miracle! Thou useless fellow! with a coat without arms, and a kirtle with skirts, wilt thou drive me out of the country? Thy relation Sigurd Wool-sack was sent before on this errand, and one called Gille the Backthief, and one who had still a worse name. They were a night in every house, and stole wherever they came. Wilt thou drive me out of the country? Formerly thou wast not so mighty, and thy pride was less when King Hakon, my foster-son, was in life. Then thou wert as frightened for him when he met thee on the road as a mouse in a mouse-trap, and hid thyself under a heap of clothes, like a dog on board a ship. Thou wast thrust into a leather-bag like corn in a sack; and driven from house and farm like a year-old colt from the mares; and dost thou dare to drive me from the land? Thou shouldst rather think thyself lucky to escape from hence with life. Let us stand up and attack him."

Then all his men stood up, and made a great clash with their weapons. Then Svein Bryggefod and the other lendermen saw there was no other chance for Sigurd but to get him on horse-back, which was done, and he rode off into the forest. The end was that Sveinke returned home to his farm, and Sigurd Ullstreng came, with great difficulty, by land north to Drontheim to King Magnus, and told the result of his errand. "Did I not say," said the king, "that the help of my lendermen would be needed?" Sigurd was ill pleased with his journey; insisted that he would be revenged, cost what it will; and urged the king much. The king ordered five ships to be fitted out; and as soon as they were ready for sea he sailed south along the land, and then east to Viken, where he was entertained in excellent guest-quarters by his lendermen. The king told them he would seek out Sveinke. "For I will not conceal my sus-picion that he thinks to make himself king of Norway." They said that Sveinke was both a powerful and an ungovernable man. Now the king went from Viken until he came to Sveinke's farm. Then the lendermen desired that they might be put on shore to see how matters stood; and when they came to the land they saw that Sveinke had already come down from the farm, and was on the road with a number of well armed men. The lendermen held up a white shield in the air, as a peace-token; and when Sveinke saw it he halted his men, and they approached each other. Then said Kolbjorn Klakka, "King Magnus sends thee God's salutation and his own, and bids thee consider what becomes thee, and do him obedience, and not prepare thyself to give him battle." Kolbjorn offered to mediate peace between them, if he could, and told him to halt his troops.

Sveinke said he would wait for them where he was. "We came out to meet him," he said, "that ye might not tread down our corn-fields."

The lendermen returned to the king, and told him all was now at his pleasure.

The king said, "My doom is soon delivered. He shall fly the country, and never come back to Norway as long as the kingdom is mine; and he shall leave all his goods behind."

"But will it not be more for thy honour," said Kolbjorn, "and give thee a higher reputation among other kings, if, in banishing him from the country, thou shouldst allow him to keep his property, and show himself among other people? And we shall take care that he never comes back while we live. Consider of this, sire, by yourself, and have respect for our assurance."

The king replied, "Let him then go forth immediately."

They went back, therefore, to Sveinke, and told him the king's words; and also that the king had ordered him out of the country, and he should show his obedience, since he had forgotten himself towards the king. "It is for the honour of both that thou shouldst show obedience to the king."

Then Sveinke said, "There must be some great change if the king speaks agreeably to me; but why should I fly the country and my properties? Listen now to what I say. It appears to me better to die upon my property than to fly from my udal estates. Tell the king that I will not stir from them even an arrow-flight."

Kolbjorn replied, "This is scarcely prudent, or right; for it is better for one's own honour to give way to the best chief, than to make opposition to one's own loss. A gallant man succeeds wheresoever he goes; and thou wilt be the more respected wheresoever thou art, with men of power, just because thou hast made head so boldly against so powerful a chief.

Hear our promises, and pay some attention to our errand. We offer thee to manage thy estates, and take them faithfully under our protection; and also never, against thy will, to pay scatt for thy land until thou comest back. We will pledge our lives and properties upon this. Do not throw away good counsel from thee, and avoid thus the ill fortune of other good men."

Then Sveinke was silent for a short time, and said at last, "Your endeavours are wise; but I have my suspicions that ye are changing a little the king's message. In consideration, however, of the great good-will that ye show me, I will hold your advice in such respect that I will go out of the country for the whole winter, if, according to your promises, I can then retain my estates in peace. Tell the king, also, these my words —that I do this on your account, not on his."

Thereupon they returned to the king, and said that Sveinke left all in the king's hands. "But he entreats you to have respect to his honour. He will be away for three years, and then come back, if it be the king's pleasure. Do this; let all things be done according to what is suitable for the royal dignity, and according to our entreaty, now that the matter is entirely in thy power, and we shall do all we can to prevent his returning against thy will."

The king replied, "Ye treat this matter like men, and, for your sakes, shall all things be as ye desire. Tell him so."

They thanked the king, and then went to Sveinke, and told him the king's gracious intentions. "We will be glad," said they, "if ye can be reconciled. The king requires, indeed, that thy absence shall be for three years; but, if we know the truth rightly, we expect that before that time he will find he cannot do without thee here in this part of the country. It will be to thy own future honour, therefore, to agree to this."

Sveinke replies, "What condition is better than this? Tell the king that I shall not vex him longer with my presence here, and accept of my goods and estates on this condition."

Thereupon he went home with his men, and set off directly; for he had prepared everything beforehand. Kolbjorn remains behind, and makes ready a feast for King Magnus, which also was thought of and prepared. Sveinke, on the other hand, rides up to Gotland with all the men he thought proper to take with him. The king let himself be entertained in guest-quarters at his house, returned to Viken, and Sveinke's estates were nominally the king's, but Kolbjorn had them under his charge.

The king received guest-quarters in Viken, proceeded from thence northwards, and there was peace for a while; but now that the river-borderers were without a chief, marauding gangs infested them, and the king saw that this eastern part of the kingdom would be laid waste. It appeared to him, therefore, most suitable and advisable to make Sveinke himself oppose the stream, and twice he sent messages to him. But he did not stir until King Magnus himself was south in Denmark, when Sveinke and the king met, and made a full reconciliation; on which Sveinke returned home to his house and estates, and was afterwards King Magnus's best and trustiest friend, who strengthened his kingdom on the eastern border; and their friendship continued as long as they lived.]

CHAPTER IX. KING MAGNUS MAKES WAR ON THE SOUTHERN HEBUDES [1098].—King Magnus undertook an expedition out of the country, with many fine men and a good assortment of shipping. With this armament he sailed out into the West sea, and first came to the Orkney Islands. There he took the two earls, Paul and Erlend, prisoners, and sent them east to Norway, and placed his son Sigurd as chief over the islands, leaving some counsellors to assist him. From thence King Magnus, with his followers, proceeded to the Southern Hebudes,[1] and when he came there began to burn and lay waste the inhabited places, killing the people, and plundering wherever he came with his men; and the country people fled in all directions, some into the Scottish firths, some down to Kintire, or out to Ireland: some obtained life and safety by entering into his service. So says Bjorn Cripplehand:

> In Lewis Isle with fearful blaze
> The house-destroying fire plays;
> To hills and rocks the people fly,
> Fearing all shelter but the sky.
> In Uist the king deep crimson made
> The lightning of his glancing blade;
> The peasant lost his land and life
> Who dared to bide the Norseman's strife.

---

[1] The Hebridean isles mentioned in the saga are: Liodhus (Lewis), Ivist (Uist, north and south), Skid (Skye), Myl (Mull), Tyrvist (Tiree), Eyin helga ("the holy isle," Iona), Il (Islay), Mön (Isle of Man), Sa(l)tiri (Kintyre). The Hebrides and Man were sold in 1266 to the Scottish crown by King Magnus the Law-Mender for 4,000 marks sterling, and 100 marks yearly as feu duty. The diocese of the Hebrides and Man remained under the metropolitan see of Nidaros (Trondheim) until c. 1350; c. 1400 the diocese was split and in 1472 the Hebrides were attached to the province of St. Andrews. The two are now reunited as the diocese of Sodor and Man.

> The hungry battle-birds were filled
> In Skye with blood of foemen killed,
> And wolves on Tiree's lonely shore
> Dyed red their hairy jaws in gore.
> The men of Mull were tired of flight;
> The Scottish foemen would not fight,
> And many an island-girl's wail
> Was heard as through the isles we sail.

Chapter X. Of Lagmadr, King Gudrod's Son.—King
Magnus came with his forces to the Holy Island [Iona], and
gave peace and safety to all men there. It is told that the
king opened the door of the little Columb's Kirk [now St.
Oran's Chapel] there, but did not go in, but instantly locked
the door again, and said that no man should be so bold as to
go into that church hereafter; which has been the case ever
since. From thence King Magnus sailed to Islay, where he
plundered and burnt; and when he had taken that country he
proceeded south around Kintire, marauding on both sides in
Scotland and Ireland, and advanced with his foray to Man,
where he plundered. So says Bjorn Cripplehand:

> On Sanda's [1] plain our shields they spy:
> From Islay smoke rose heaven-high,
> Whirling up from the flashing blaze
> The king's men o'er the island raise.
> South of Kintire the people fled,
> Scared by our swords in blood dyed red,
> And our brave champion onward goes
> To meet in Man the Norsemen's foes.

Lagmadr [Lawman] was the name of the son of Gudrod king
of the Hebudes. Lawman was sent to defend the most northerly
islands [2]; but when King Magnus and his army came to the
Hebudes, Lawman fled here and there about the isles, and at
last King Magnus's men took him and his ship's crew as he
was flying over to Ireland. The king put him in irons to secure
him. So says Bjorn Cripplehand:

> To Gudrod's son no rock or cave,
> Shore-side or hill, a refuge gave;
> Hunted around from isle to isle,
> This Lawman found no safe asyle.
> From isle to isle, o'er firth and sound,
> Close on his track his foe he found.
> At Ness [3] the Agder chief at length
> Seized him, and iron-chained his strength.

---

[1] Probably the small isle Sanda, off the Mull of Kintire.
[2] Snorri did not know that King Gudrod had died in 1095 and that
Lagmadr was his successor as king over the Sudreys and Man.
[3] The original has "outside the nesses," i.e. at sea.

CHAPTER XI. OF THE FALL OF EARL HUGO THE BRAVE.—
Afterwards King Magnus sailed to Wales [1]; and when he came
to the sound of Anglesey there came against him an army
from Wales, which was led by two earls [2]—Hugo the Brave,
and Hugo the Stout. They began immediately to give battle,
and there was a severe conflict. King Magnus shot with the
bow; but Hugo the Brave was all over in armour, so that
nothing was bare about him excepting his eyes. King Magnus
let fly an arrow at him, as also did a Halogaland man who was
beside the king. They both shot at once. The one shaft hit
the nose-screen of the helmet, and so was deflected to one side,
but the other arrow hit the earl's eye, and went through his
head; and that arrow was attributed to the king. Earl Hugo
fell, and the Britons fled with the loss of many people. So
says Bjorn Cripplehand:

> The swinger of the sword
> Stood by Anglesey's ford;
> His quick shaft flew,
> And Hugo slew.
> His sword gleamed a while
> O'er Anglesey Isle,
> And his Norsemen's band
> Scoured the Anglesey land.

There was also sung the following verse about it:

> On the panzers arrows rattle,
> Where our Norse king stands in battle;
> From the helmets blood-streams flow,
> Where our Norse king draws his bow:
> His bowstring twangs—its biting hail
> Rattles against the ring-linked mail.
> Up in the land in deadly strife
> Our Norse king took Earl Hugo's life.

King Magnus gained the victory in this battle, and then took
Anglesey Isle, which was the farthest south the Norway kings
of former days had ever extended their rule. Anglesey is a
third part of Wales. After this battle King Magnus turned
back with his fleet, and came first to Scotland. Then men

---

[1] Bretland, which is used in Norse sources for Wales and sometimes for
other Celtic parts in the west of England and for Brittany.
[2] In 1098 the earls of Chester and Shrewsbury, Hugh of Avranches and
Hugh Montgomery, were attempting to recover fortresses in north Wales.
Their success was cut short by Magnus's attack on them in Anglesey, in
which Hugh, earl of Shrewsbury (Hugo the Brave above), was killed. It
is unlikely that Magnus laid any claim to permanent rule in Anglesey after
this.

went between the Scottish king Melkolm [1] and King Magnus, and a peace was made between them; so that all the islands lying west of Scotland, between which and the mainland he could pass in a vessel with her rudder shipped, should be held to belong to the king of Norway. Now when King Magnus came north to Kintire, he had a skiff drawn over the neck at Kintire,[2] and shipped the rudder of it. The king himself sat in the stern-sheets, and held the tiller; and thus he appropriated to himself the land that lay on the larboard side. Kintire is a great district, better than the best of the southern isles of the Hebudes, excepting Man; and there is a small neck of land between it and the mainland of Scotland, over which long-ships are often drawn.

CHAPTER XII. DEATH OF THE EARLS OF ORKNEY.—King Magnus was all the winter in the southern isles, and his men went over all the fjords of Scotland, rowing within all the inhabited and uninhabited isles, and took possession for the king of Norway of all the islands west of Scotland. King Magnus contracted in marriage his son Sigurd to Biadmynia, King Moriartak's daughter. Moriartak was a son of the Irish king Thiolve, and ruled over Connaught. Magnus gave his son the title of king, and set him over the Orkneys and Hebudes; and gave him in charge of his relative Hakon Paulson. The summer after, King Magnus, with his fleet, returned east to Norway. Earl Erlend [3] died of sickness at Nidaros, and is buried there; and Earl Paul [3] died in Bergen.

Skofte Ogmundsson, a grandson of Torberg, was a gallant lenderman, who dwelt at Giske in Sunnmöre, and was married to Gudrun, a daughter of Thord Folason, who carried King Olaf's banner at Stiklestad when he fell. Their children were Ogmund, Finn, Tord, and Tora, who was married to Aasolf Skuleson. Skofte's and Gudrun's sons were the most promising and popular men in their youth.

CHAPTER XIII. QUARRELS OF KING MAGNUS AND KING INGE.—Steinkel the Swedish king died about the same time as the two Haralds [4] fell, and the king who came after him in Sweden was called Hakon. Afterwards Inge, a son of Steinkel, was king, and was a good and powerful king, strong and stout

---

[1] King Malcolm had died in 1093, but his son Eadgar was king in 1098, and it was he who made peace with Magnus.

[2] The narrow strip between the two lochs, East Tarbert and West Tarbert.

[3] The two Earls of Orkney, Erlend and Paul.

[4] The two Haralds meant are Harald the Stern of Norway, and the English king Harald Godwinsson, who fell at Hastings.

beyond most men; and he was king of Sweden when King Magnus was king of Norway. King Magnus insisted that the boundaries of the countries in old times had been so, that the Gotha river divided the kingdoms of the Swedish and Norwegian kings, but afterwards the Lake Vänern up to Værmeland. Thus King Magnus insisted that he was owner of all the places lying west of the Vänern Lake up to Værmeland, which are the districts of Sundal, Nordal, Vear,[1] and Vardyniar,[2] with all the woods [3] belonging thereto. But these had for a long time been under the Swedish dominion, and with respect to scatt were joined to West Gotland; and, besides, the forest-settlers [4] preferred being under the Swedish king. King Magnus rode from Viken up to Gotland with a great and fine army, and when he came to the forest-settlements he plundered and burnt all round; on which the people submitted, and took the oath of fidelity to him. When he came to the Vänern Lake, when autumn was advanced, he went out to the island Kvaldinsey,[5] and made a stronghold of turf and wood, and dug a ditch around it. When the work was finished, provisions and other necessaries that might be required were brought to it. The king left in it 300 [360] men, who were the chosen of his forces, and Finn Skoftesson and Sigurd Ullstreng as their commanders. The king himself returned to Viken.

CHAPTER XIV. OF THE NORTHMEN.—When the Swedish king heard this he drew together people, and the report came that he would ride against these Northmen; but there was delay about his riding, and the Northmen made these lines:

> The fat-hipped king, with heavy sides,
> Finds he must mount before he rides.

But when the ice set in upon the Vänern Lake, King Inge rode down, and had near 3,000 [3,600] men with him. He sent a message to the Northmen who sat in the burgh that they might retire with all the booty they had taken, and go to Norway. When the messengers brought this message, Sigurd Ullstreng replied to it, saying that King Inge must take some other action than to dismiss them on their way like sheep to pasture, and said he must come nearer if he wished them to remove. The messengers returned with this answer to the king, who then rode out with all his army to the island, and again sent a

---

[1] Now Vedbo.   [2] Now Valbo.   [3] Nordmarka in Vermeland.
[4] The inhabitants of the districts just specified.
[5] Now Kaallandsö on the south side of the lake Vänern.

message to the Northmen that they might go away, taking with them their weapons, clothes, and horses; but must leave behind all their booty. This they refused. The king made an assault upon them, and they shot at each other. Then the king ordered timber and stones to be collected, and he filled up the ditch; and then he fastened anchors to long spars which were brought up to the timber-walls, and, by the strength of many hands, the walls were broken down. Thereafter a large pile of wood was set on fire, and the lighted brands were flung in among them. Then the Northmen asked for quarter. The king ordered them to go out without weapons or cloaks. As they went out each of them received a stroke with a whip, and then they set off for Norway, and all the forest-men submitted again to King Inge. Sigurd and his people went to King Magnus, and told him their misfortune.

CHAPTER XV. BATTLE AT FOXERNE [1100].—The spring after, as soon as the ice broke up, King Magnus, with a great army, sailed eastwards to the Gotha river, and went up the southern arm of it, laying waste all that belonged to the Swedish dominions. When they came to Foxerne [1] they landed from their vessels; but as they came over a river on their way an army of Gotland people came against them, and there was immediately a great battle, in which the Northmen were overwhelmed by numbers, driven to flight, and many of them killed near to a waterfall.[2] King Magnus fled, and the Gotlanders pursued, and killed those they could get near. King Magnus was easily known. He was a very large man, and had a red short cloak over him, and bright yellow hair like silk that fell over his shoulders. Ogmund Skoftesson, who was a tall and handsome man, rode on one side of the king. He said, "Sire, give me that cloak."

The king said, "What would you do with it?"

"I would like to have it," said Ogmund; "and you have given me greater gifts, sire."

The road was such that there were great and wide plains, so that the Gotlanders and Northmen were always in sight of each other, unless where rocky outcrops and bushes concealed them from each other now and then. The king gave Ogmund the cloak, and he put it on. When they came out again upon the plain ground, Ogmund and his people rode off right across the road. The Gotlanders, supposing this must be the king,

[1] Now Fuxerna at Lille Edet, on the east of the Gotha.
[2] Supposed to be at Fors church.

rode all after him, and the king proceeded to the ships. Ogmund escaped with great difficulty; however he reached the ships at last in safety. King Magnus then sailed down the river, and proceeded north to Viken.

[1] [CHAPTER XVI. MAGNUS'S SECOND BATTLE WITH INGE AT FOXERNE. — When King Magnus was east in Viken, there came to him a foreigner called Gifford. He gave himself out for a good knight, and offered his services to King Magnus; for he understood that in the king's dominions there was something to be done. The king received him well. At that time the king was preparing to go to Gotland, on which country the king had pretensions; and besides he would repay the Gotland people the disgrace they had occasioned him in spring, when he was obliged to fly from them. He had then a great force in arms, and the West Gotlanders in the northern districts submitted to him. He set up his camp on the borders, intending to make a foray from thence. When King Inge heard of this he collected troops, and hastened to oppose King Magnus; and when King Magnus heard of this expedition, many of the chiefs of the people urged him to turn back: but this the king would not listen to, but in the night-time went unsuspectedly against the Swedish king. They met at Foxerne; and when he was drawing up his men in battle order he asked, "Where is Gifford?" but he was not to be found. Then the king made these verses:

> Cannot the foreign knight abide
> Our rough array?—where does he hide?

Then a scald who followed the king replied:

> The king asks where the foreign knight
> In our array rides to the fight:
> Gifford the knight rode quite away
> When our men joined in bloody fray.
> When swords were wet the knight was slow
> With his bay horse in front to go:
> The foreign knight could not abide
> Our rough array, and went to hide.

There was a great slaughter, and after the battle the field was covered with the Swedes slain, and King Inge escaped by flight. King Magnus gained a great victory. Then came Gifford riding down from the country, and people did not speak well of him for not being in the fight. He went away, and proceeded westward to England; and the voyage was stormy, and Gifford lay in bed. There was an Iceland man called

[1] This chapter is not in the *Heimskringla*, cf. Introduction, p. xxx.

Elldiarn, who went to bale out the water in the ship's hold, and when he saw where Gifford was lying he made this verse:

> Does it beseem a hirdman bold
> Here to be dozing in the hold?
> The bearded knight should danger face:
> The leak gains on our ship apace.
> Here, ply this bucket! bale who can;
> We need the work of every man.
> Our sea-horse stands full to the breast—
> Sluggards and cowards must not rest.

When they came west to England, Gifford said the Northmen had slandered him. A meeting was appointed, and a count came to it, and the case was brought before him for trial. He said he was not much acquainted with law cases, as he was but young, and had only been a short time in office; and also, of all things, he said what he least understood to judge about was poetry. "But let us hear what it was." Then Elldiarn sang:

> I heard that in the bloody fight
> Gifford drove all our foes to flight:
> Brave Gifford would the foe abide,
> While all our men ran off to hide.
> At Foxerne the fight was won
> By Gifford's valour all alone:
> Where Gifford fought, alone was he;
> Not one survived to fight or flee.

Then said the count, "Although I know but little about scald-craft, I can hear that this is no slander, but rather the highest praise and honour." Gifford could say nothing against it, yet he felt it was a mockery.]

CHAPTER XVII. MEETING OF THE KINGS AT THE GOTHA RIVER [1101].—The following summer a meeting of the kings was agreed upon at Konghelle on the Gotha river; and King Magnus, the Swedish king Inge, and the Danish king Eric Sveinson all met there, after giving each other safe conduct to the meeting. Now when the Thing had sat down the kings went forward upon the plain, apart from the rest of the people, and they talked with each other a little while. Then they returned to their people, and a treaty was brought about, by which each should possess the dominions his forefathers had held before him; but each should make good to his own men the waste and manslaughter suffered by them, and then they should agree between themselves about settling this with each other. King Magnus should marry King Inge's daughter Margaret, who afterwards was called Fred-kolla.[1] This was

---

[1] Peace-lady.

proclaimed to the people; and thus, within a little hour, the greatest enemies were made the best of friends.

It was observed by the people that none had ever seen men with more of the air of chiefs than these had. King Inge was the largest and stoutest, and, from his age, of the most dignified appearance. King Magnus appeared the most gallant and brisk, and King Eric the most handsome. But they were all handsome men; stout, gallant, and ready in speech. After this was settled they parted.

CHAPTER XVIII. KING MAGNUS'S MARRIAGE.—King Magnus got Margaret, King Inge's daughter, as above related; and she was sent from Sweden to Norway with an honourable retinue. King Magnus had some children before, whose names shall here be given. The one of his sons who was of a mean mother was called Eystein; the other, who was a year younger, was called Sigurd, and his mother's name was Tora. Olaf was the name of a third son, who was much younger than the two first mentioned, and whose mother was Sigrid, a daughter of Saxe of Vik,[1] who was a respectable man in the Drontheim country; she was the king's concubine. People say that when King Magnus came home from his viking cruise to the Western countries,[2] he and many of his people brought with them a great deal of the habits and fashion of clothing of those western parts. They went about on the streets with bare legs, and had short kirtles and over-cloaks[3]; and therefore his men called him Magnus Barefoot or Bareleg. Some called him Magnus the Tall, others Magnus the Strife-lover. He was distinguished among other men by his tall stature. The mark of his height is put down in Maria Kirke, in Kaupangen, which King Harald built. In the northern door there were cut into the wall three crosses— one for Harald's stature, one for Olaf's, and one for Magnus's; and marked where each of them could with the greatest ease kiss. The upper was Harald's mark; the lowest was Magnus's; and Olaf's was in the middle, about equally distant from both.

It is said that Magnus composed the following verses about the emperor's daughter:

> The ring of arms where blue swords gleam,
> The battle-shout, the eagle's scream,
> The joy of war, no more can please:

---

[1] Now Saxvik at Strinden, east of Trondhjem.
[2] i.e. Scotland and Ireland.
[3] Despite Snorri's explanation of Magnus's nickname, it is not certain that the kilt was worn in Ireland and the Hebrides at this time.

Matilda [1] is far o'er the seas.
My sword may break, my shield be cleft,
Of land or life I may be reft;
Yet I could sleep, but for one care—
One, o'er the seas, with light-brown hair.

He also composed the following:

The time that breeds delay feels long,
The scald feels weary of his song;
What sweetens, brightens, eases life?
'Tis a sweet-smiling lovely wife.
My time feels long in Thing affairs,
In Things my loved one ne'er appears.
The folk full-dressed, while I am sad,
Talk and oppose—can I be glad?

When King Magnus heard the friendly words the emperor's daughter had spoken about him—that she had said such a man as King Magnus was appeared to her an excellent man, he composed the following:

The lover hears—across the sea,
A favouring word was breathed to me.
The lovely one with light-brown hair
May trust her thoughts to senseless air:
Her thoughts will find like thoughts in me;
And though my love I cannot see,
Affection's thoughts fly in the wind,
And meet each other, true and kind.

CHAPTER XIX. OF THE QUARREL OF KING MAGNUS AND SKOFTE OGMUNDSSON.—Skofte Ogmundsson came into variance with King Magnus, and they quarrelled about the inheritance of a deceased person which Skofte retained; but the king demanded it with so much earnestness, that it had a dangerous appearance. Many meetings were held about the affair, and Skofte took the resolution that he and his sons should never put themselves into the king's power at the same time; and all would be well if this were followed. When Skofte was with the king he represented to him that there was relationship between the king and him; and also that he, Skofte, had always been the king's friend, and his father's likewise, and that their friendship had never been shaken. He added, "People might know that I have sense enough not to hold a strife, sire, with you, if I was wrong in what I asked; but it is inherited from my ancestors to defend my rights against any man, without distinction of persons." The king was just the same on this point, and his resolution was by no means softened by such a speech. Then Skofte went home.

[1] This may have been the daughter of King Malcolm of Scotland, Mathilda (Edith); she married Henry I of England in 1100.

CHAPTER XX. FINN SKOFTESSON'S PROCEEDINGS. — Then Finn Skoftesson went to the king, spoke with him, and entreated him to render justice to the father and son in this business. The king answers angrily and sharply. Then said Finn, "I expected something else, sire, from you, than that you would use the law's vexations against me when I took my seat in Kvaldinsey [1] Island, which few of your other friends would do; as they said, what was true, that those who were left there were deserted and doomed to death, if King Inge had not shown greater generosity to us than you did; although many consider that we brought shame and disgrace only from thence." The king was not to be moved by this speech, and Finn returned home.

CHAPTER XXI. OGMUND SKOFTESSON'S PROCEEDINGS.— Then came Ogmund Skoftesson to the king; and when he came before him he produced his errand, and begged the king to do what was right and proper towards him and his father. The king insisted that the right was on his side, and said they were "particularly impudent."

Then said Ogmund, "It is a very easy thing for thee, having the power, to do me and my father injustice; and I must say the old proverb is true, that one whose life you save gives none, or a very bad return. This I shall add, that never again shall I come into thy service; nor my father, if I can help it." Then Ogmund went home, and they never saw each other again.

CHAPTER XXII. SKOFTE OGMUNDSSON'S VOYAGE ABROAD [1102].—The spring after, Skofte Ogmundsson made ready to travel out of the country. They had five long-ships all well equipped. His sons, Ogmund, Finn, and Thord, accompanied him on this journey. It was very late before they were ready, and in autumn they went over to Flanders, and wintered there. Early in spring they sailed westward to Valland, and stayed there all summer [1103]. Then they sailed farther, and through Nörvesund; and came in autumn to Rome, where Skofte died. All, both father and sons, died on this journey. Thord, who died in Sicily, lived the longest. It is a common saying among the people, that Skofte was the first Northman who sailed through Nörvesund; and this voyage was much celebrated.

CHAPTER XXIII. MIRACLE OF KING OLAF THE SAINT AT A FIRE.—It happened once in Kaupangen, where King Olaf

[1] See p. 265, note 5.

reposes, that there broke out a fire in the town which spread around. Then Olaf's shrine was taken out of the church, and set up opposite the fire. Thereupon came a crazy foolish man, struck the shrine, threatened the holy saint, and said all must be consumed by the flames, both churches and other houses, if he did not save them by his prayers. Now the church was saved from burning by the help of Almighty God; but the insane man got sore eyes on the following night, and he lay there until King Olaf entreated God Almighty to be merciful to him; after which he recovered in the same church.

CHAPTER XXIV. MIRACLE OF KING OLAF THE SAINT ON A LAME WOMAN.—It happened also in the merchant town that a woman was brought to the place where the holy King Olaf reposes. She was miserably shaped, and she was altogether crumpled up; so that both her feet were bent back against her loins. But as she was diligent in her prayers, often weeping and making vows to King Olaf, he cured her great infirmities; so that feet, legs, and other limbs straightened, and every limb and part came to the right use for which they were made. Formerly she could not creep there, and now she went away active and brisk to her family and home.

CHAPTER XXV. WAR IN IRELAND [1102].—When King Magnus had been nine years king of Norway, he equipped himself to go out of the country with a great force. He sailed out into the West sea with the finest men who could be got in Norway. All the powerful men of the country followed him; such as Sigurd Ranesson and his brother Ulv, Vidkunn Jonsson, Dag Eilivsson, Serk of Sogn, Eyvind Olboge the king's marshal, and many other great men. With all this armament the king sailed west to the Orkney Islands, from whence he took with him Earl Erlend's sons, Magnus and Erling, and then sailed to the southern Hebudes. But as he lay under the Scotch land, Magnus Erlendsson [1] swam ashore, in the night from the king's ship, and, escaped into the woods, and came at last to the Scotch king's court. King Magnus sailed to Ireland with his fleet, and plundered there. King Moriartak came to his assistance, and they conquered a great part of the country, both Dublin [2] and Dyflinarskiri [Dublin shire]. King Magnus was in winter up in Connaught with King Moriartak, but set

[1] This was Saint Magnus, Earl of Orkney, to whom the cathedral of Kirkwall is dedicated, and whose miracles are equal to Saint Olaf's.
[2] This is incorrect, for Moriartak had ruled in Dublin since 1094; but it is likely that he had had to hand over Dublin to Magnus.

men to defend the country he had taken. Towards spring both kings went westward with their army all the way to Ulster [1103], where they had many battles, subdued the country, and had conquered the greatest part of Ulster when Moriartak returned home to Connaught.

CHAPTER XXVI. KING MAGNUS'S FORAY ON THE LAND.— King Magnus rigged his ships, and intended returning to Norway, but set his men to defend the country of Dublin. He lay at Ulster ready for sea with his whole fleet. As they thought they needed cattle for ship-provision, King Magnus sent a message to King Moriartak, telling him to send some cattle for slaughter; and appointed the day before Bartholomew's day [23 August] as the day they should arrive, if the messengers reached him in safety; but the cattle had not made their appearance the evening before Bartholomew's mass. On the mass-day [24 August] itself, when the sun rose in the sky, King Magnus went on shore himself with the greater part of his men, to look after his people, and to carry off cattle from the coast. The weather was calm, the sun shone, and the road lay through mires and mosses, and there were paths cut through; but there was brushwood on each side of the road. When they came somewhat farther, they reached a height from which they had a wide view. They saw from it a great dust rising up the country, as of horsemen, and they said to each other, "That must be the Irish army," but others said, "It was their own men coming with the cattle." They halted there; and Eyvind Olboge said, "How, sire, do you intend to direct the march? The men think we are advancing imprudently. You know the Irish are treacherous; think, therefore, of a good counsel for your men." Then the king said, "Let us draw up our men, and be ready, if there be treachery." This was done, and the king and Eyvind went before the line. King Magnus had a helmet on his head; a red shield, in which was inlaid a gilded lion; and was girt with the sword Legbiter, of which the hilt was of tooth [ivory], and the hand-grip wound about with gold thread; and the sword was extremely sharp. In his hand he had a short spear, and a red silk short cloak over his coat, on which, both before and behind, was embroidered a lion in yellow silk; and all men acknowledged that they never had seen a brisker, statelier man. Eyvind had also a red silk cloak like the king's; and he also was a stout, handsome, warlike man.

CHAPTER XXVII. FALL OF KING MAGNUS.—When the dust·

cloud approached nearer they knew their own men, who were driving the cattle. The Irish king had been faithful to the promises he had given the king, and had sent them. Thereupon they all turned towards the ships, and it was mid-day. When they came to the mires they went but slowly over the boggy places; and then the Irish started up on every side against them from every bushy point of land, and the battle began instantly. The Northmen were going divided in various heaps, so that many of them fell.

Then said Eyvind to the king, "Unfortunate is this march to our people, and we must instantly hit upon some good plan."

The king answered, "Call all the men together with the war-horns under the banner, and the men who are here shall make a rampart with their shields, and thus we will retreat backwards out of the mires; and we will clear ourselves fast enough when we get upon firm ground."

The Irish shot boldly; and although they fell in crowds, there came always others to fill the gaps. Now when the king had come to the last of the ditches there was a difficult crossing, and few places were passable; so that many Northmen fell there. Then the king called to his lenderman Torgrim Skindhue, who was an Upland man, and ordered him to go over the ditch with his division. "We shall defend you," said he, "in the mean time, so that no harm shall come to you. Go out then to those holms, and shoot at them from thence; for ye are good bowmen."

When Torgrim and his men came over the ditch they cast their shields behind their backs, and set off to the ships.

When the king saw this, he said, "Thou art deserting thy king in an unmanly way. I was foolish in making thee a lenderman, and driving Sigurd Hund[1] out of the country; for never would he have behaved so."

King Magnus received a wound, being pierced by a spear through both thighs above the knees. The king laid hold of the shaft between his legs, broke the spear in two, and said, "Thus we break spear-shafts, my lads; let us go briskly on. Nothing hurts me." A little after King Magnus was struck in the neck with an Irish axe, and this was his death-wound. Then those who were behind fled. Vidkunn Jonsson instantly killed the man who had given the king his death-wound, and fled,

[1] Sigurd Hund was brother of Vidkunn Jonsson at Bjarkö. The sur-name Hund (dog-hound) he had inherited from his great-grandfather Tore Hund.

after having received three wounds; but brought the king's banner and the sword Legbiter to the ships. Vidkunn was the last man who fled; there were two others who stayed to the last, Sigurd Ranesson and Dag Eilivsson. There fell with King Magnus, Eyvind Olboge, Ulv Ranesson, and many other great people. Many of the Northmen fell, but many more of the Irish. The Northmen who escaped sailed away immediately in autumn. Erling, Earl Erlend's [1] son, fell with King Magnus in Ireland; but the men who fled from Ireland came to the Orkney Islands. Now when King Sigurd heard that his father had fallen, he set off immediately, leaving the Irish king's daughter behind, and proceeded in autumn with the whole fleet directly to Norway.

CHAPTER XXVIII. OF KING MAGNUS AND VIDKUNN JONSSON. — King Magnus was ten years king of Norway [1094–1103], and in his days there was good peace kept within the country; but the people were sorely oppressed with levies. King Magnus was beloved by his men, but the bonder thought him harsh. The words have been transmitted from him that he said when his friends observed that he proceeded incautiously when he was on his expeditions abroad—"that kings are made for honour, not for long life." King Magnus was nearly thirty years of age when he fell. Vidkunn did not fly until he had killed the man who gave the king his mortal wound, and for this cause King Magnus's sons had him in the most affectionate regard.

[1] Earl Erlend of Orkney, who was taken in the former expedition and died in Trondheim.

XIII

THE SONS OF MAGNUS

[1103–30]

CHAPTER I. BEGINNING OF THE REIGN OF KING MAGNUS'S SONS.—After King Magnus Barefoot's fall, his sons, Eystein, Sigurd, and Olaf, took the kingdom of Norway. Eystein got the northern, and Sigurd the southern part of the country. King Olaf was then four or five years old, and the third part of the country which he had was under the management of his two brothers. King Sigurd was chosen king when he was thirteen or fourteen years old, and Eystein was a year older. When King Magnus's sons were chosen kings, the men who had followed Skofte Ogmundsson returned home. Some had been to Jerusalem, some to Constantinople; and there they had made themselves renowned, and they had many kinds of novelties to talk about. By these extraordinary tidings many men in Norway were incited to the same expedition; and it was also told that the Northmen who liked to go into the military service at Constantinople found many opportunities of getting property. Then these Northmen desired much that one of the two kings, either Eystein or Sigurd, should go as commander of the troop which was preparing for this expedition. The kings agreed to this, and carried on the equipment at their common expense. Many great men, both of the lendermen and bonder, took part in this enterprise; and when all was ready for the journey it was determined that Sigurd should go, and Eystein, in the meantime, should rule the kingdom upon their joint account.

CHAPTER II. OF THE EARLS OF ORKNEY [1105].—A year or two after King Magnus's fall, Hakon, a son of Earl Paul, came from Orkney. The kings gave him the earldom and government of the Orkney Islands, as the earls before him, his father Paul or his uncle Erlend, had possessed it; and Earl Hakon then sailed back immediately to Orkney.

CHAPTER III. KING SIGURD'S JOURNEY OUT OF THE COUNTRY. —Four years after the fall of King Magnus,[1] King Sigurd

---

[1] i.e. in 1107 by Snorri's reckoning; the real date was 1108.

sailed with his people from Norway. He had then sixty ships.
So says Thorarin Stuttfeld:

> A young king just and kind,
> People of loyal mind:
> Such brave men soon agree—
> To distant lands they sail with glee.
> To the distant Holy Land
> A brave and pious band,
> Magnificent and gay,
> In sixty long-ships glide away.

King Sigurd sailed in autumn to England, where Henry,[1] son
of William the Bastard, was then king, and Sigurd remained
with him all winter. So says Einar Skuleson:

> The king is on the waves!
> The storm he boldly braves.
>   His ocean-steed,
>   With winged speed,
> O'er the white-flashing surges,
> To England's coast he urges;
> And there he stays the winter o'er:
> More gallant king ne'er trod that shore.

CHAPTER IV. OF KING SIGURD'S JOURNEY [1109].—In spring
King Sigurd and his fleet sailed westward to Valland, and in
autumn came to Galicia,[2] where he stayed the second winter.
So says Einar Skuleson:

> Our king, whose land so wide
> No kingdom stands beside,
> In Jacob's land [3] next winter spent,
> On holy things intent;
> And I have heard the royal youth
> Cut off an earl who swerved from truth.
> Our brave king will endure no ill—
> The hawks with him will get their fill.

It went thus: The earl who ruled over the land made an
agreement with King Sigurd, that he should provide King
Sigurd and his men a market at which they could purchase
victuals all the winter; but this he did not fulfil longer than to
about Yule. It began then to be difficult to get food and
necessaries, for it is a poor barren land. Then King Sigurd
with a great body of men went against a castle which belonged
to the earl; and the earl fled from it, having but few people.
King Sigurd took there a great deal of victuals and of other

---

[1] Henry I, 1100–35.
[2] In the north-west of Spain.
[3] Jacob's land. Galicia is called Jacob's land by the scald, from Saint
James of Compostella. Ferdinand I (1035–65) had united Galicia with
Castille and Leon. Portugal was founded as a vassal county in 1095 and
became an independent kingdom in 1143.

booty, which he put on board of his ships, and then made ready and proceeded west around Spain [1] [1110]. It so fell out, as the king was sailing past Spain, that some vikings who were cruising for plunder met him with a fleet of galleys, and King Sigurd attacked them. This was his first battle with heathen men; and he won it, and took eight galleys from them. So says Halldor Skvalldre:

> Bold vikings, not slow
> To the death-fray to go,
> Meet our Norse king by chance,
> And their galleys advance.
> The bold vikings lost
> Many a man of their host,
> And eight galleys too,
> With cargo and crew.

Thereafter King Sigurd sailed against a castle called Cintre,[2] and fought another battle. This castle is in Spain, and was occupied by many heathens, who from thence plundered Christian people. King Sigurd took the castle, and killed every man in it, because they refused to be baptised; and he got there an immense booty. So says Halldor Skvalldre:

> From Spain I have much news to tell
> Of what our generous king befell.
> And first he routs the viking crew,
> At Cintra next the heathens slew;
> The men he treated as God's foes,
> Who dared the true faith to oppose.
> No man he spared who would not take
> The Christian faith for Jesus' sake.

CHAPTER V. LISBON TAKEN.—After this King Sigurd sailed with his fleet to Lisbon, which is a great city in Spain, half Christian and half heathen; for there lies the division between Christian Spain and heathen Spain,[3] and all the districts which lie west of the city are occupied by heathens. There King Sigurd had his third battle with the heathens, and gained the victory, and with it a great booty. So says Halldor Skvalldre:

> The son of kings on Lisbon's plains
> A third and bloody battle gains.
> He and his Norsemen boldly land,
> Running their stout ships on the strand.

Then King Sigurd sailed westwards along the heathen Spain,

[1] Here Portugal, really southward.
[2] Cintra, in Portugal.
[3] i.e. the western wards and suburbs of the city were Muslim. The boundary in the country generally ran eastwards from Lisbon on the coast, with the Christian lands to the north. Other sources show the year to have been 1110, when Sigurd aided Count Henry in an unsuccessful attempt to take Lisbon from the Moors. Henry of Burgundy, first independent count of Portugal, reigned 1095–1112, being son-in-law to the king of Leon.

and brought up at a town called Alkassi[1]; and here he had his fourth battle with the heathens, and took the town, and killed so many people that the town was left empty. They got there also immense booty. So says Halldor Skvalldre:

> A fourth great battle, I am told,
> Our Norse king and his people hold
> At Alkassi; and here again
> The victory fell to our Norsemen.

And also this verse:

> I heard that through the town he went,
> And heathen widows' wild lament
> Resounded in the empty halls;
> For every townsman flies or falls.

CHAPTER VI. BATTLE IN ISLAND FORMENTARA.[2]—King Sigurd then proceeded on his voyage, and came to Nörvesund; and in the sound he was met by a large viking force, and the king gave them battle: and this was his fifth engagement with heathens since the time he left Norway. He gained the victory here also. So says Halldor Skvalldre:

> Ye moistened your dry swords with blood,
> As through Niorfa sound ye stood:
> The screaming raven got a feast,
> As ye sailed onward to the East.

King Sigurd then sailed eastward along the coast of Serkland, and came to an island there called Formentara. There a great many heathen Moors had taken up their dwelling in a cave, and had built a strong stone wall before its mouth. It was high up to climb to the wall, so that whoever attempted to ascend was driven back with stones or missile weapons. They herried the country all round, and carried all their booty to their cave. King Sigurd landed on this island, and went to the cave; but it lay in a precipice, and there was a high winding path to the stone wall, and the precipice above projected over it. The heathens defended the stone wall, and were not afraid of the Northmen's arms; for they could throw stones, or shoot down upon the Northmen under their feet: neither did the Northmen, under such circumstances, dare to mount

---

[1] There is some difficulty in finding a town corresponding to this Alkassi. It cannot be Alkassir in Fez in Africa, as some have supposed, because the context does not agree with it; nor with Algeciras, which lies within the Straits of Gibraltar and would doubtless have been so described. (So Laing in 1844. The place is now generally held to have been Alcacer do Sal on the river Sado, south of Setubal. It has also been pointed out that Arabic *al-kasr* need mean no more than a fortress.)

[2] One of the Balearic isles.

up. The heathens took their clothes and other valuable things, carried them out upon the wall, spread them out before the Northmen, shouted, and defied them, and upbraided them as cowards. Then Sigurd fell upon this plan. He had two ships' boats, such as we call barks, drawn up the precipice right above the mouth of the cave; and had thick ropes fastened around the stem, stern, and hull of each. In these boats as many men went as could find room, and then the boats were lowered by the ropes down in front of the mouth of the cave; and the men in the boats shot with stones and missiles into the cave, and the heathens were thus driven from the stone wall. Then Sigurd with his troops climbed up the precipice to the foot of the stone wall, which they succeeded in breaking down, so that they came into the cave. Now the heathens fled within the stone wall that was built across the cave; on which the king ordered large trees to be brought to the cave, made a great pile in the mouth of it, and set fire to the wood. When the fire and smoke got the upper hand, some of the heathens lost their lives in it; some fled; some fell by the hands of the Northmen; and part were killed, part burned; and the Northmen made the greatest booty they had got in all their expedition. So says Halldor Skvalldre:

> Formentara lay
> In the victor's way;
> His ships' stems fly
> To victory.
> The bluemen there
> Must fire bear,
> And Norsemen's steel
> At their hearts feel.

And also thus:

> 'Twas a feat of renown—
> The boat lowered down,
> With a boat's crew brave,
> In front of the cave;
> While up the rock scaling,
> And comrades up trailing,
> The Norsemen gain,
> And the bluemen are slain.

And also Thorarin Stuttfeld says:

> The king's men up on the mountain's side
> Drag two boats from the ocean's tide:
> The two boats lay,
> Like hill-wolves grey.
> Now o'er the rock in ropes they're swinging,
> Well manned, and death to bluemen bringing:
> They hang before
> The robbers' door.

CHAPTER VII. OF THE BATTLES AT IVIZA AND MINORCA.—
Thereafter King Sigurd proceeded on his expedition, and came
to an island called Iviza, and had there his seventh battle, and
gained a victory. So says Halldor Skvalldre:

> His ships at Iviza now ride,
> The king's, whose fame spreads far and wide;
> And here the bearers of the shield
> Their arms again in battle wield.

Thereafter King Sigurd came to an island called Minorca, and
held there his eighth battle with heathen men, and gained the
victory. So says Halldor Skvalldre:

> On green Minorca's plains
> The eighth battle now he gains:
> Again the heathen foe
> Falls at the Norse king's blow.

CHAPTER VIII. EARL ROGER MADE A KING.—In spring King
Sigurd came to Sicily, and remained a long time there. There
was then a Duke Roger in Sicily, who received the king kindly,
and invited him to a feast. King Sigurd came to it with a
great retinue, and was splendidly entertained. Every day
Duke Roger stood at the company's table, doing service to the
king; but the seventh day of the feast, when the people had
come to table, and had wiped their hands, King Sigurd took the
duke by the hand, led him up to the high seat, and saluted
him with the title of king; and gave the right that he should be
permanently king over the dominion of Sicily, although before
there had only been earls or dukes over that country.[1]

CHAPTER IX. OF KING ROGER.—It is written in the chronicles,
that Earl Roger let himself first be called king of Sicily in the
year of our Lord 1102, having before contented himself with
the title of earl only of Sicily, although he was duke of Calabria
and Apulia, and was called Roger the Great; and when he
afterwards made the king of Tunet or Tunis tributary to him,
he had these words engraved on his sword:

Apulus et Calaber, Siculus mihi servit et Afer.

King Roger of Sicily was a very great king. He won and
subdued all Apulia, and many large islands besides in the Greek
sea; and therefore he was called Roger the Great. His son was
William king of Sicily, who for a long time had great hostility

---

[1] Presumably Roger II, then a child, son of Roger I, son of Tancred of
Hauteville. Roger II (born 1095) succeeded as count in 1105, took the
title of duke of Cyprus in 1127 and the title of king in 1130. He died in
1154. His court is famous in the "renaissance of the twelfth century" as
a meeting place of oriental and western culture.

with the emperor of Constantinople. King William had three
daughters, but no son. One of his daughters he married to the
Emperor Henry, a son of the Emperor Frederic; and their son
was Frederic, who in recent times has been emperor of Rome.
His second daughter was married to the Duke of Kypur.[1] The
third daughter was married to Margrit, the commander of
the fleet; but the Emperor Henry killed both these brothers-
in-law. The daughter of Roger the Great, king of Sicily, was
married to the Emperor Manuel of Constantinople; and their
son was the Emperor Kirialax.[2]

CHAPTER X. KING SIGURD'S EXPEDITION TO PALESTINE.—
In summer King Sigurd sailed across the Greek sea to Palestine,[3]
and came to Acre,[4] where he landed, and went by land to
Jerusalem. [5][Now when Baldwin, king of Palestine, heard that
King Sigurd would visit the city, he let valuable clothes be
brought and spread upon the road, and the nearer to the city
the more valuable; and said, "Now ye must know that a celebrated king from the northern part of the earth is come to
visit us; and many are the gallant deeds and celebrated actions
told of him, therefore we shall receive him well; and in doing
so we shall also know his magnificence and power. If he ride
straight on to the city, taking little notice of these splendid
preparations, I will conclude that he 'has enough of such things
in his own kingdom; but, on the other hand, if he rides off the
road, I shall not think so highly of his royal dignity at home."
Now King Sigurd rides to the city with great state; and when
he saw this magnificence, he rode straight forward over the
clothes, and told all his men to do the same.] King Baldwin
received him particularly well, and rode with him all the way
to the river Jordan, and then back to the city of Jerusalem.
Einar Skuleson speaks thus of it:

> Good reason has the scald to sing
> The generous temper of the king,
> Whose sea-cold keel from northern waves
> Ploughs the blue sea that green isles laves.
> At Acre scarce were we made fast,
> In holy ground our anchors cast,
> When the king made a joyful morn
> To all who toil with him had borne.

---

[1] i.e. Cyprus.   The emperor ruling "recently" was Frederick II, 1220–50.
[2] Kirialax is Alexios II Comnenos, emperor 1180–3.   His mother was not a
Sicilian princess but the daughter of Prince Raymond of Antioch.
[3] Jorsalaland = Palestine; the land of Jerusalem.
[4] Acre. He landed not at Acre but at Joppa.
[5] The passages in brackets are not in the *Heimskringla*.

And again he made these lines:

> To Jerusalem he came,
> He who loves war's noble game,
> (The scald no greater monarch finds
> Beneath the heaven's wide hall of winds)
> All sin and evil from him flings
> In Jordan's wave: he pardon wins
> (Which all must praise) for all his sins.

King Sigurd stayed a long time in the land of Jerusalem in autumn, and in the beginning of winter.

CHAPTER XI. SIDON TAKEN.—King Baldwin made a magnificent feast for King Sigurd and many of his people, and gave him many holy relics. By the orders of King Baldwin and the patriarch, there was taken a splinter off the holy cross; and on this holy relic both made oath, that this wood was of the holy cross upon which God himself had been tortured. Then this holy relic was given to King Sigurd; with the condition that he, and twelve other men with him, should swear to promote Christianity with all his power, and erect an archbishop's seat in Norway if he could; and also that the cross should be kept where the holy King Olaf reposed, and that he should introduce tithes, and also pay them himself. After this King Sigurd returned to his ships at Acre; and then King Baldwin prepared to go to Syria, to a town called Saet, which some think had been Sidon. This castle, which belonged to the heathens, he wished to conquer, and lay under the Christians. On this expedition King Sigurd accompanied him with all his men, and sixty ships; and after the kings had besieged the town some time it surrendered, and they took possession of it [on 19 December, 1110]. The kings took the city itself and the troops all the other booty. King Sigurd made a present of his share to King Baldwin. So says Halldor Skvalldre:

> He who for wolves provides the feast
> Seized on the city in the East,
> The heathen nest; and honour drew,
> And gold to give, from those he slew.

Einar Skuleson also tells of it:

> The Norsemen's king, the scalds relate,
> Has ta'en the heathen town of Saet:
> The slinging engine with dread noise
> Gables and roofs with stones destroys.
> The town wall totters too—it falls;
> The Norsemen mount the blackened walls.
> He who stains red the raven's bill
> Has won—the town lies at his will.

Thereafter King Sigurd went to his ships, and made ready to leave Palestine. They sailed north to the island Cyprus; and King Sigurd stayed there a while, and then went to the Greek country, and came to the land with all his fleet at Engilsness.[1] Here he lay still for a fortnight, although every day it blew a breeze for going before the wind to the north; but Sigurd would wait a side wind, so that the sails might stretch fore and aft in the ship: for in all his sails there was silk joined in, before and behind in the sail, and neither those before nor those behind the ships could see the slightest appearance of this, if the vessel was before the wind; so they would rather wait a side wind.

CHAPTER XII. KING SIGURD'S EXPEDITION TO CONSTANTINOPLE.—When King Sigurd sailed into Constantinople, he steered near the land. Over all the land there are burghs, castles, country towns, the one upon the other without interval. There from the land one could see into the bights of the sails; and the sails stood so close beside each other, that they seemed to form one enclosure. All the people turned out to see King Sigurd sailing past. The Emperor Kirialax had also heard of King Sigurd's expedition, and ordered the city port of Constantinople to be opened, which is called the Golden Port, through which the emperor rides when he has been long absent from Constantinople, or has made a campaign in which he has been victorious. The emperor had precious cloths spread out from the Golden Port to Laktiarner, where is situated the emperor's most splendid hall.[2] King Sigurd ordered his men to ride in great state into the city, and not to regard all the new things they might see; and this they did. The emperor sent singers and stringed instruments to meet them; and with this great splendour King Sigurd and his followers were received into Constantinople. It is told that King Sigurd had his horse shod with golden shoes before he rode into the city, and managed so that one of the shoes came off in the street, but that none of his men should regard it. When King Sigurd came to the magnificent hall, everything was in the grandest style; and when King Sigurd's men had come to their seats, and were ready to drink, the emperor's messengers came into the hall, bearing between them purses of gold and silver, which they said the

---

[1] Engilsness—supposed to be the cape at the river Ægos, called Ægisnes in the Orkeyinga Saga, within the Dardanelles. Perhaps Cape Saint Angelo in the Morea, or Malea on the south coast of Greece.
[2] The palace Blachernæ in the north of the town.

emperor had sent to King Sigurd: but the king did not look upon it, but told his men to divide it among themselves. When the messengers returned to the emperor, and told him this, he said, "This king must be very powerful and rich not to care for such things, or even give a word of thanks for them"; and ordered them to return with great chests filled with gold. They come again to King Sigurd, and say, "These gifts and presents are sent thee from the emperor." King Sigurd said, "This is a great and handsome treasure, my men; divide it among you." The messengers return, and tell this to the emperor. He replies, "This king must either exceed other kings in power and wealth, or he has not so much understanding as a king ought to have. Go thou now the third time, and carry him the costliest purple, and these chests with ornaments of gold": to which he added two gold rings. Now the messengers went again to King Sigurd, and told him the emperor had sent him this great treasure. Then he stood up, and took the rings, and put them on his hand; and the king made a beautiful oration in Greek, in which he thanked the emperor in many fine expressions for all this honour and magnificence, but divided the treasure again very equitably among his men. King Sigurd remained here some time. The Emperor Kirialax sent his men to him to ask if he would rather accept from the emperor six skippund [1] of gold, or would have the emperor give the games in his honour which the emperor was used to have played at the Padreimr.[2] King Sigurd preferred the games, and the messengers said the spectacle would not cost the emperor less than the money offered. Then the emperor prepared for the games, which were held in the usual way: but this day everything went on better for the king than for the queen; for the queen has always the half part in the games, and their men, therefore, always strive against each other in all games. The Greeks accordingly think that when the king's men win more games at the Padreimr than the queen's, the king will gain the victory when he goes into battle. [People who have been in Constantinople tell that the Padreimr is thus constructed: A high wall surrounds a flat plain, which may be compared to a round bare Thing-place, with earthen banks all around at the stone wall, on which banks the spectators sit; but the games themselves are in the

[1] The weight of a skippund varied in the different parts of Norway from about 290 to about 360 lb.
[2] *Padreimr*, derived from Greek *hippodromos*, the hippodrome where the great spectacles were given.

flat plain. There are many sorts of old events represented concerning the Æser, Volsunger, and Giukunger, in these games [1]; and all the figures are cast in copper, or metal, with so great art that they appear to be living things; and to the people it appears as if they were really present in the games. The games themselves are so artfully and cleverly managed, that people appear to be riding in the air; and at them also are used shot-fire,[2] and all kinds of harp-playing, singing, and music instruments.

CHAPTER XIII. KING SIGURD MAKES A GREAT FEAST FOR THE EMPEROR OF CONSTANTINOPLE.—It is related that King Sigurd one day was to give the emperor a feast, and he ordered his men to provide sumptuously all that was necessary for the entertainment; and when all things were provided which are suitable for an entertainment given by a great personage to persons of high dignity, King Sigurd ordered his men to go to the street in the city where fire-wood was sold, as they would require a great quantity to prepare the feast. They said the king need not be afraid of wanting fire-wood, for every day many loads were brought into the town. When it was necessary, however, to have fire-wood, it was found that it was all sold, which they told the king. He replied, "Go and try if you can get walnuts. They will answer as well as wood for fuel." They went and got as many as they needed. Now came the emperor, and his grandees and court, and sat down to table. All was very splendid; and King Sigurd received the emperor with great state, and entertained him magnificently. When the queen and the emperor found that nothing was a-wanting, she sent some persons to inquire what they had used for fire-wood; and they came to a house filled with walnuts, and they came back and told the queen. "Truly," said she, "this is a magnificent king, who spares no expense where his honour is concerned." She had contrived this to try what they would do when they could get no fire-wood to dress their feast with.]

CHAPTER XIV. KING SIGURD THE CRUSADER'S RETURN HOME.—King Sigurd soon after prepared for his return home. He gave the emperor all his ships; and the valuable figure-heads which were on the king's ship were set up in Peter's

---

[1] It is not likely that the feats of the Aser, Volsunger, and Giukunger were represented in the games of the Hippodrome at Constantinople; but very likely that the Væringer, and other Northmen there, would apply the names of their own mythology to the representations taken from the Greek mythology.

[2] Fireworks, or the Greek fire, probably were used.

church,[1] where they have since been to be seen. The emperor
gave the king many horses and guides to conduct him through
all his dominions, and appointed markets for him in his terri-
tories at which he could buy food and drink. Then King Sigurd
left Constantinople; but a great many Northmen remained, and
went into the emperor's pay. Then King Sigurd travelled
from Bulgaria,[2] and through Hungary, Pannonia, Suabia, and
Bavaria. In Suabia he met the Emperor Lotharius,[3] who
received him in the most friendly way, gave him guides through
his dominions, and had markets established for him at
which he could purchase all he required. When King Sigurd
came to Slesvig in Denmark, Earl Eiliv made a sumptuous
feast for him; and it was then midsummer [1110].—In Heidaby [4]
he met the Danish king Nicolas,[5] who received him in the most
friendly way, made a great entertainment for him, accompanied him north to Jutland, and gave him a ship provided
with everything needful. From thence the king returned to
Norway, and was joyfully welcomed on his return to his kingdom. It was the common talk among the people, that none
had ever made so honourable a journey from Norway as this
of King Sigurd. He was twenty years of age, and had been
three years on these travels. His brother Olaf was then twelve
years old.

CHAPTER XV. KING EYSTEIN'S DOINGS AT HOME IN THE
MEANTIME. — King Eystein had also effected much in the
country that was useful while King Sigurd was on his journey.
He had a large hall built in Bergen, which was the greatest
and most celebrated lodging-inn in Norway. He also established a monastery at Nordness in Bergen, and endowed it with
much property. He also built Michael's church, which is a
very splendid stone minster. In the king's house there he also
built the Church of the Apostles, and the great hall, which is
the most magnificent wooden structure that was ever built in
Norway.[6] He also built a church at Agdaness with a parapet;
and a harbour, where formerly there had been a barren spot
only. In Nidaros he built in the King's garth the church

---

[1] William of Malmesbury says that Sigurd set up his ship in the Church
of Sophia.
[2] Then a Greek province.
[3] At this time he was Duke of Saxony. It was not till 1125 that he
became Emperor, namely after Henry V's death.
[4] See p. 147, note 1.
[5] Danish king, 1104–34.
[6] This oldest king's hall in Bergen was situated where the commandant's
residence at Bergenhus now is.

of Saint Nicolas, which was particularly ornamented with carved work, and all in wood. He also built a church north in Vaagan in Lofoten, and endowed it with property and revenues.

CHAPTER XVI. OF KING EYSTEIN.—King Eystein sent a verbal message to the most intelligent and powerful of the men of Jemteland, and invited them to him; received them all as they came, with great kindness; accompanied them part of the way home, and gave them presents, and thus enticed them into a friendship with him. Now as many of them became accustomed to visit him and receive gifts from him, and he also sent gifts to some who did not come themselves, he soon gained the favour of all the people who had most influence in the country. Then he spoke to the Jemteland people, and told them they had done ill in turning away from the kings of Norway, and withdrawing from them their taxes and allegiance. He represented to them how many useful things they could get from Norway, and how inconvenient it was for them to apply to the Swedish king for what they needed.[1] By these speeches he brought matters so far, that the Jemteland people of their own accord offered to be subject to him, which they said was useful and necessary for them; and thus, on both sides, it was agreed that the Jemtelanders should put their whole country under King Eystein. The first beginning was with the men of consequence, who persuaded the people to take an oath of fidelity to King Eystein; and then they went to King Eystein, and confirmed the country to him by oath; and this arrangement has since continued for a long time. King Eystein thus conquered Jemteland by his wisdom, and not by hostile inroads as some of his forefathers had done.

CHAPTER XVII. OF KING EYSTEIN'S PERFECTIONS OF BODY AND MIND.—King Eystein was the handsomest man that could be seen. He had blue open eyes; his hair yellow and curling; his stature not tall, but of the middle size. He was wise, intelligent, and acquainted with the laws and history. He had much knowledge of mankind, was quick in counsel, prudent in words, and very eloquent and very generous. He was very merry, yet modest; and was liked and beloved, indeed, by all the people. He was married to Ingeborg, a daughter of Guttorm son of Tore of Steig; and their daughter was Maria, who afterwards married Gudbrand Skafhoggson.

[1] The dried fish of Norway are a necessary article of food to the people of this district, which they cannot get from the Baltic coast of Sweden.

[King Eystein had in many ways improved the laws and privileges of the country people, and kept strictly to the laws; and he made himself acquainted with all the laws of Norway, and showed in everything great prudence and understanding. From this it could be easily seen what a valuable man King Eystein was, how full of friendship, and how much he turned his mind to examining and avoiding everything that could be of disadvantage to his friends.

There was an Iceland man in the king's house called Ivar Ingemundson. The man was witty, of great family, and also a poet; and the king was particularly kind to him, which will be seen from what we are now going to relate. Ivar was one day out of spirits; and when the king perceived it he called Ivar to him, entered into conversation with him, and asked him why he was so melancholy. "Before, when thou wast with us, we had much amusement with thy conversation. Art thou no longer satisfied to be with us?"

Ivar replied, it was not the case.

The king: "I do not ask thee on this account; for I know thou art a man of too good an understanding to believe that I would do anything against thee. Tell me, then, what it is."

He replied, "I cannot tell thee what it is."

Then said the king, "I will try to guess what it is. Is there any man who displeases thee?"

To this he replied, "No."

"Dost thou think thou art held in less esteem by me than thou wouldst like to be?"

To this he also replied, "No."

"Hast thou observed anything whatever that has made an impression on thee at which thou art ill pleased?"

He replied, it was not this either.

The king: "It is difficult now to guess. Is there any girl here, or in any other country, to whom thy affections are engaged?"

He said it was so.

The king said, "Do not be melancholy on that account. Go to Iceland when spring sets in, and I shall give thee money, and presents, and with these my letters and seal to the men who have the principal sway there; and I know no man there who will not obey my persuasions or threats."

Ivar replied, "My fate is heavier, sire; for my own brother has the girl."

Then said the king, "Throw it out of thy mind; and I know

a counsel against this. After Yule I will travel in guest-quarters. Thou shalt come along with me, and thou wilt have an opportunity of seeing many beautiful girls; and, provided they are not of the royal stock, I will get thee one of them in marriage."

Ivar replies, "Sire, my fate is still the heavier; for as oft as I see beautiful and excellent girls I only remember the more that girl, and they increase my misery."

The king: "Then I will give thee property to manage, and estates for thy amusement."

He replied, "For that I have no desire."

The king: "Then I will give thee money, that thou mayst travel in other countries."

He said he did not wish this.

Then said the king, "It is difficult for me to seek farther, for I have proposed everything that occurs to me. There is but one thing else; and that is but little compared to what I have offered thee. Come to me every day after the tables are removed, and, if I am not sitting upon important business, I shall talk with thee about the girl in every way that I can think of; and I shall do so at leisure. It sometimes happens that sorrow is lightened by being brought out openly; and thou shalt never go away without some gift."

He replied, "This I will do, sire, and return thanks for this inquiry."

And now they did so constantly; and when the king was not occupied with weightier affairs he talked with him, and his sorrow by degrees wore away, and he was again in good spirits.]

CHAPTER XVIII. OF KING SIGURD.—King Sigurd was a stout and strong man, with brown hair; of a manly appearance, but not handsome; well grown; of little speech, and often not friendly, but good to his friends, and faithful; not very eloquent, but moral and polite. King Sigurd was self-willed, and severe in his revenge; strict in observing the law; was generous; and withal an able, powerful king. His brother Olaf was a tall, thin man; handsome in countenance; lively, modest, and popular. When all these brothers, Eystein, Sigurd, and Olaf, were kings of Norway, they did away with many burdens which the Danes had laid upon the people in the time that Svein Alfivason ruled Norway; and on this account they were much beloved, both by the people and the great men of the country.

[CHAPTER XIX. OF KING SIGURD'S DREAM.—Once King

Sigurd fell into low spirits, so that few could get him to con-
verse, and he sat but a short time at the drinking-table. This
was heavy on his counsellors, friends, and hird; and they begged
King Eystein to consider how they could discover the cause
why the people who came to the king could get no reply to
what they laid before him. King Eystein answered them, that
it was difficult to speak with the king about this; but at last,
on the entreaty of many, he promised to do it. Once, when
they were both together, King Eystein brought the matter
before his brother, and asked the cause of his melancholy. "It
is a great grief, sire, to many to see thee so melancholy; and we
would like to know what has occasioned it, or if perchance thou
hast heard any news of great weight?"

King Sigurd replies, that it was not so.

"Is it then, brother," says King Eystein, "that thou wouldst
like to travel out of the country, and augment thy dominions
as our father did?"

He answered, that it was not that either.

"Is it, then, that any man here in the country has offended?"
To this also the king said "No."

"Then I would like to know if thou hast dreamt anything
that has occasioned this depression of mind?"

The king answered, that it was so.

"Tell me then, brother, thy dream."

King Sigurd said, " I will not tell it, unless thou interpretest it
as it may turn out; and I shall be quick at perceiving if thy
interpretation be right or not."

King Eystein replies, "This is a very difficult matter, sire,
on both sides; as I am exposed to thy anger if I cannot interpret
it, and to the blame of the public if I can do nothing in the
matter; but I will rather fall under thy displeasure, even if
my interpretation should not be agreeable."

King Sigurd replies, "It appeared to me, in a dream, as if
we brothers were all sitting on a bench in front of Christ church
in Drontheim; and it appeared to me as if our relative King
Olaf the Saint came out of the church adorned with the royal
raiment glancing and splendid, and with the most delightful
and joyful countenance. He went to our brother King Olaf,
took him by the hand, and said cheerfully to him, 'Come with
me, friend.' On which he appeared to stand up and go into
the church. Soon after King Olaf the Saint came out of the
church, but not so gay and brilliant as before. Now he went
to thee, brother, and said to thee that thou shouldst go with

him; on which he led thee with him, and ye went into the church. Then I thought, and waited for it, that he would come to me, and meet me; but it was not so. Then I was seized with great sorrow, and great dread and anxiety fell upon me, so that I was altogether without strength; and then I awoke."

King Eystein replies, "Thus I interpret your dream, sire— That the bench betokens the kingdom we brothers have; and as you thought King Olaf came with so glad a countenance to our brother King Olaf, he will likely live the shortest time of us brothers, and have all good to expect hereafter; for he is amiable, young in years, and has gone but little into excess, and King Olaf the Saint must help him. But as you thought he came towards me, but not with so much joy, I may possibly live a few years longer, but not become old, and I trust his providence will stand over me; but that he did not come to me with the same splendour and glory as to our brother Olaf, that will be because, in many ways, I have sinned and transgressed his command. If he delayed coming to thee, I think that in no way betokens thy death, but rather a long life: but it may be that some heavy accident may occur to thee, as there was an unaccountable dread overpowering thee; but I foretell that thou wilt be the oldest of us, and wilt rule the kingdom longest."

Then said Sigurd, "This is well and intelligibly interpreted, and it is likely it will be so." And now the king began to be cheerful again.]

CHAPTER XX. OF KING SIGURD'S MARRIAGE.—King Sigurd married Malmfrid, a daughter of King Harald Valdemarson [1] eastward in Novgorod. Valdemar was a son of Jarisleiv the Old and Ingigerd, daughter of the Swedish king Olaf the Swede. King Harald Valdemarson's mother was Queen Gyda the Old, a daughter of the English king Harald Godwinson. Queen Malmfrid's mother was Queen Christina, a daughter of the Swedish king Inge Steinkelson. Harald Valdemarson's other daughter, sister to Malmfrid, was Ingeborg, who was married to Canute Lavard, a son of the Danish king Eric the Good, and grandson of King Svein Ulvson. Canute's and Ingeborg's children were, the Danish king Valdemar [2] [ob. 1182], who came to the Danish kingdom after Svein Ericsson; and daughters Margaret, Christina, and Catherine. Margaret was married to Stig Hvitaleder; and their daughter was Christina, married to the Swedish king Karl Sörkvison,[3] King Jon's father. Christina,

---

[1] Harald, son of Vladimir Monomach, the Russian Grand Prince, 1125-32.
[2] Valdemar the Great, king, 1157-82.   [3] Karl, Swedish king, 1161-7.

who was married to Earl Erling Skakke, was a daughter of King
Sigurd and Malmfrid.

[CHAPTER XXI. HERE BEGINS THE ACCOUNT OF THE CASES
BEFORE THE THING.—The king's relative, Sigurd Raneson, came
into strife with King Sigurd; he was married to Skjaldvor, a
sister of King Magnus Barefoot by the mother's side. He had
had the Lapland collectorship[1] on the king's account, because
of their relationship and long friendship, and also of the many
services Sigurd Raneson had done to the kings; for he was a
very distinguished, popular man. But it happened to him, as
it often does to others, that persons more wicked and jealous
than upright slandered him to King Sigurd, and whispered in
the king's ear that he took more of the Laplanders' tribute to
himself than was proper. They spoke so long about this, that
King Sigurd conceived a dislike and anger to him, and sent a
message to him. When he appeared before the king, the king
carried these feelings with him, and said, "I did not expect
that thou shouldst have repaid me for thy great fiefs and other
dignities by taking the king's property, and abstracting a
greater portion of it than is allowable."

Sigurd Raneson replies, "It is not true that has been told
you; for I have only taken such portion as I had your permission to take."

King Sigurd replies, "Thou shalt not slip away with this;
but the matter shall be seriously treated before it comes to an
end." With that they parted.

Soon after, by the advice of his friends, the king laid an
action against Sigurd Raneson at the Thing-meeting in Bergen,
and would have him made an outlaw. Now when the business
took this turn, and appeared so dangerous, Sigurd Raneson went
to King Eystein, and told him what mischief King Sigurd
intended to do him, and entreated his assistance. King Eystein
replied, "This is a difficult matter that you propose to me, to
speak against my brother; and there is a great difference between
defending a cause and pursuing it in law": and added, that
this was a matter which concerned him and Sigurd equally.
"But for thy distress, and our relationship, I shall bring in a
word for thee."

Soon after Eystein visited King Sigurd, and entreated him to
spare the man, reminding him of the relationship between

[1] The journey to Lapland to collect the taxes, with which a profitable
trade in furs was connected, was, even in the earliest times, one of the
greatest offices the king had to confer in respect of gain. Furs were
always at a high value in the Middle Ages for ornamental purposes.

them and Sigurd Raneson, who was married to their aunt Skjaldvor; and said he would pay the penalty for the crime committed against the king, although he could not with truth impute any blame to him in the matter.   Besides, he reminded the king of the long friendship with Sigurd Raneson.   King Sigurd replied, that it was better government to punish such acts.   Then King Eystein replied, "If thou, brother, wilt follow the law, and punish such acts according to the country's privileges, then it would be most correct that Sigurd Raneson produce his witnesses, and that the case be judged at the Thing, but not at a meeting; for the case comes under the law of the land, not under Bjarkö law." [1]   Then said Sigurd, "It may possibly be so that the case belongs to it, as thou sayest, King Eystein; and if it be against law what has hitherto been done in this case, then we shall bring it before the Thing."   Then the kings parted, and each seemed determined to take his own way.   King Sigurd summoned the parties in the case before the Arnarness Thing, and intended to pursue it there.   King Eystein came also to the Thing-place; and when the case was brought forward for judgment, King Eystein went to the Thing before judgment was given upon Sigurd Raneson.   Now King Sigurd told the lagmen to pronounce the judgment; but King Eystein replied thus: "I trust there are here men acquainted sufficiently with the laws of Norway, to know that they cannot condemn a lenderman to be outlawed at this Thing." [2]   And he then explained how the law was, so that every man clearly understood it.   Then said King Sigurd, "Thou art taking up this matter very warmly, King Eystein, and it is likely the case will cost more trouble before it comes to an end than we intended; but nevertheless we shall follow it out.   I will have him condemned to be outlawed in his native place."   Then said King Eystein, "There are certainly not many things which do not succeed with thee, and especially when there are but few and small folks to oppose one who has carried through such great things."   And thus they parted, without anything being concluded in the case.   Thereafter King Sigurd called together a Gula Thing, went himself there, and summoned to

---

[1] The Bjarkö law was the special code of law governing commercial and mercantile affairs; in its oldest forms it was accepted as a kind of international law.   The "meeting" referred to is the town-moot in Bergen, where apparently the Bjarkö laws applied.

[2] The site of this Thing is not known, but the name may be a fiction.   In the longer version of this story the corresponding Thing is on Kefsisey in Lofoten, a district-thing not competent to judge a lenderman's case.

him many high chiefs. King Eystein came there also with his suite; and many meetings and conferences were held among people of understanding concerning this case, and it was tried and examined before the lagmen. Now King Eystein objected that all the parties summoned in any cases tried here belonged to the Thing-district; but in this case the deed and the parties belonged to Halogaland. The Thing accordingly ended in doing nothing, as King Eystein had thus made it incompetent. The kings parted in great wrath; and King Eystein went north to Drontheim. King Sigurd, on the other hand, summoned to him all lendermen, and also the house-servants of the lendermen, and named out of every district a number of the bonder from the south parts of the country, so that he had collected a large army about him; and proceeded with all this crowd northwards along the coast to Halogaland, and intended to use all his power to make Sigurd Raneson an outlaw among his own relations. For this purpose he summoned to him the Halogaland and Naumadal people, and appointed a Thing at Hrafnista.[1] King Eystein prepared himself also, and proceeded with many people from the town of Nidaros to the Thing, where he made Sigurd Raneson, by hand-shake before witnesses, deliver over to him the following and defending this case. At this Thing both the kings spoke, each for his own side. Then King Eystein asks the lagmen, where that law was made in Norway which gave the bonder the right to judge between the kings of the country, when they had pleas with each other. "I shall bring witnesses to prove that Sigurd has given the case into my hands; and it is with me, not with Sigurd Raneson, that King Sigurd has to do in this case." The lagmen said, that disputes between kings must be judged only at the Öre Thing in Nidaros.

King Eystein said, "So I thought that it should be there, and the case must be removed there."

Then King Sigurd said, "The more difficulties and inconvenience thou bringest upon me in this matter, the more I will persevere in it." And with that they parted.

Both kings then went south to Nidaros town, where they summoned a Thing from eight districts.[2] King Eystein was in the town with a great many people, but Sigurd was on board his ships. When the Thing was opened, peace and safe conduct were given to all; and when the people were all collected,

---

[1] Now Ramstad in Namdal.
[2] i.e. the eight *fylker* of the Trondheim district.

and the case should be gone into, Bergthor Bok, a son of Svein Bryggefod, stood up, and gave his evidence that Sigurd Raneson had concealed a part of the Laplanders' taxes.

Then King Eystein stood up and said, "If thy accusation were true, although we do not know what truth there may be in thy testimony, yet this case has already been dismissed from three Things, and a fourth time from a town meeting; and therefore I require that the lagmen acquit Sigurd in this case according to law." And they did so.

Then said King Sigurd, "I see sufficiently, King Eystein, that thou hast carried this case by law-quirks,[1] which I do not understand. But now there remains, King Eystein, a way of determining the case which I am more used to, and which I shall now apply."

He then retired to his ships, had the tents taken down, laid his whole fleet out at the holm, and held a Thing of his people; and told them that early in the morning they should land at Ilevold, and give battle to King Eystein. But in the evening, as King Sigurd sat at his table in his ship taking his repast, before he was aware of it a man cast himself on the floor of the forehold, and at the king's feet. This was Sigurd Raneson, who begged the king to take what course with regard to him the king himself thought proper, for he would not be the cause of any unhappy division between the brothers. Then came Bishop Magne and Queen Malmfrid, and many other great personages, and entreated forgiveness for Sigurd Raneson; and at their entreaty the king raised him up, took him by the hand and placed him among his men, and took him along with himself to the south part of the country. In autumn the king gave Sigurd Raneson leave to go north to his farm, gave him an employment, and was always afterwards his friend. After this day, however, the brothers were never much together, and there was no cordiality or cheerfulness among them.]

CHAPTER XXII. OF KING OLAF'S DEATH.—In the thirteenth year of the government of the brothers, King Olaf Magnusson fell into a sickness which ended in his death. He was buried in Christ church in Nidaros, and many were in great grief at his death. [King Olaf's mother was Sigrid, a daughter of Saxe of Vik, sister of Kare of Ostraat, who was called the king's foster-brother, and who was a great and popular man. Saxe had another daughter called Tora, who had a son called Sigurd

---

[1] These law-quirks show a singularly advanced state of law, and deference to the Law Things, amidst such social disorder and misdeeds.

Slembedegn, who afterwards gave himself out for a son of King Magnus Barefoot. Kare the king's foster-brother was married to Borghild, a daughter of Dag Eilivsson; and their son was Sigurd of Ostraat, a lenderman, father to Jon who was married to Sigrid, a sister of King Inge Baardsson.] After Olaf's death, Eystein and Sigurd ruled the country, the three brothers together having been kings of Norway for twelve years; namely, five years after King Sigurd returned home, and seven years before. King Olaf was seventeen years old when he died, and it happened on the 22nd of December. King Eystein had been about a year in the east part of the country at that time, and King Sigurd was then in the north. King Eystein remained a long time that winter in Sarpsborg.

CHAPTER XXIII. MAGNUS THE BLIND; HIS BIRTH.—There was once a powerful and rich bonde called Olaf of Dal, who dwelt in Mikle Dal in Aamord,[1] and had two children—a son called Hakon Fauk, and a daughter called Borghild, who was a very beautiful girl, and prudent, and well skilled in many things. Olaf and his children were a long time in winter in Sarpsborg, and Borghild conversed very often with King Eystein; so that many reports were spread about their friendship. The following summer King Eystein went north, and King Sigurd came eastward, where he remained all winter, and was long in Konghelle, which town he greatly enlarged and improved. He built there a great castle of turf and stone, dug a great ditch around it, and built a church and several houses within the castle. The holy cross he allowed to remain at Konghelle, and therein did not fulfil the oath he had taken in Palestine; but, on the other hand, he established tithe, and most of the other things to which he had bound himself by oath. The reason of his keeping the cross east at the frontier of the country was, that he thought it would be a protection to all the land; but it proved the greatest misfortune to place this relic within the power of the heathens, as it afterwards turned out.

When Borghild, Olaf's daughter, heard it whispered that people talked ill of her conversations and intimacy with King Eystein, she went to Sarpsborg; and after suitable fasts she took the iron ordeal as a proof of her innocence, and cleared herself thereby fully from all offence. When King Sigurd heard this, he rode one day as far as usually was two days' travelling, and came to Dal to Olaf, where he remained all night, made Borghild his concubine, and took her away with him. They had a son, who was called Magnus, and he was sent immediately to Halogaland, to be fostered at Bjarkö by Vidkunn Jonson; and he was brought up there. Magnus grew up to be the handsomest man that could be seen, and was very soon stout and strong.

CHAPTER XXIV. COMPARISON BETWEEN THE TWO KINGS.— King Eystein and King Sigurd went off one winter to guest-quarters in the Uplands; and each was entertained in a separate house, and the houses were not very distant from each other. The bonder, however, thought it more convenient that both should be entertained together by turns in each house; and thus they were both at first in the house of King Eystein. But in the evening, when the people began to drink, the ale was not good; so that the guests were very quiet and still. Then said King Eystein, "Why are the people so silent? It is more usual in drinking parties that people are merry, so let us fall upon some jest over our ale that will amuse people; for surely, brother Sigurd, everyone will think it fitting that we start some game."

Sigurd replies, bluntly, "Do you talk as much as you please, but give me leave to be silent."

Eystein says, "It is a common custom over the ale-table to compare one person with another, and now let us do so." Then Sigurd was silent.

"I see," says King Eystein, "that I must begin this amusement. Now I will take thee, brother, to compare myself with, and will make it appear so as if we had both equal dignities and property, and that there is no difference in our birth and education."

Then King Sigurd replies, "Do you remember that I was always able to throw you on your back, when I pleased, although you are a year older?"

Then King Eystein replied, "But I remember that you were not so good at the games which require agility."

Sigurd: "Do you remember that I could drag you under water, when we swam together, as often as I pleased?"

Eystein: "But I could swim as far as you, and could dive as well as you; and I could skate so well that nobody could beat me, and you could no more do it than an ox."

Sigurd: "Methinks it is a more useful and suitable accomplishment for a chief to be expert at his bow; and I think you could scarcely draw my bow, even if you took your foot to help."

Eystein: "I am not strong at the bow as you are, but there is less difference between our shooting at a target; and I can run on ski much better than you, and in former times that was held a great accomplishment."

Sigurd: "It appears to me much better for a chief who is to be the superior of other men, that he is conspicuous in a crowd, and strong and powerful in weapons above other men; easily seen, and easily known, where there are many together."

Eystein: "It is not less a distinction and an ornament that a man is of a handsome appearance, so as to be easily known from others on that account; and this appears to me to suit a chief best, because the best clothing suits the best looks. I am moreover more knowing in the law than you, and on every subject my words flow more easily than yours."

Sigurd: "It may be that you know more law-quirks, for I have had something else to do; neither will any deny you a smooth tongue. But there are many who say that your words are not to be trusted; that what you promise is little to be regarded; and that you talk just according to what those who are about you say, which is not kingly."

Eystein: "This is because, when people bring their cases before me, I wish first to give every man that satisfaction in his affair which he desires; but afterwards comes the opposite party, and then there is something to be given or taken away very often, in order to mediate between them, so that both may be satisfied. It often happens too that I promise whatever is desired of me, that all may be joyful about me. It would be an easy matter for me to do as you do—to promise evil to all; and I never hear any complain of your not keeping this promise to them."

Sigurd: "It is the conversation of all that the expedition I made out of the country was a princely expedition, while you in the meantime sat at home like your father's daughter."

Eystein: "Now you betake yourself to your cudgel. I would not have brought up this conversation if I had not known what to reply on this point. I can truly say that I equipped you from home like a sister, before you went upon this expedition."

Sigurd: "You must have heard that on this expedition I was in many a battle in the Saracen's land, and gained the victory in all; and you must have heard of the many valuable articles I acquired, the like of which were never seen before in this country, and I was the most respected wherever the most gallant men were; and, on the other hand, you cannot conceal that you have only a home-bred reputation. I went to Palestine, and I came to Apulia; but I did not see you there, brother.

I gave Roger the Great the title of king; I won seven battles and you were in none of them. I was at our Lord's grave; but did not see you there, my brother. On this expedition I went all the way to Jordan, where our Lord was baptised, and swam across the river; but did not see you there. On the edge of the river-bank there was a bush of willows, and there I twisted a knot of willows which is waiting you there; for I said this knot thou shouldst untie, and fulfil the vow, brother, that is bound up in it."

Eystein: "It is but little I have to set up against this. I have heard that you had several battles abroad, but it was more useful for the country what I was doing in the meantime here at home. In the north at Vaage I built fish-houses, so that all the poor people could earn a livelihood, and support themselves. I built there a priest's house, and endowed a church, where before all the people almost were heathen; and on this account I think all these people will remember that Eystein was once king of Norway. [The road from Drontheim goes over the Dovrefjelds, and many people had to sleep out of doors, and made a very severe journey; but I built hospices, and supported them with money; and all travellers know that Eystein has been king in Norway.] Out at Agdaness was a barren waste, and no harbour, and many a ship was lost there; and now there is a good harbour and ship-station, and a church also built there. Then I raised beacons on all the high fjelds, of which all the people in the interior enjoy the benefit. In Bergen I built a royal hall, and the church of the Apostles, with a stair between the two; so that all the kings who come after me will remember my name. I built Michael's church, and founded a monastery beside it. I settled the laws, brother, so that every man can obtain justice from his fellow-man; and according as these are observed the country will be the better governed. I raised a tower in the sound of Sinsholm.[1] The Jemteland people are again joined to this kingdom, and more by prudence and kind words than by force and war. Now although all this that I have reckoned up be but small doings, yet I am not sure if the people of the country have not been better served by it than by your killing bluemen for the devil in the land of the Saracens, and sending them to hell. Now if you prize yourself on your good deeds, I think the places I

---

[1] This locality is not known, unless it be the sound between Senholm and the mainland in North Bergenhus. The tower was raised to be a landmark or rather seamark.

have raised for chaste people of God will serve me not less for my soul's salvation. So if you tied a knot for me, I will not go to untie it; and if I had been inclined to tie a knot for thee, thou wouldst not have been king of Norway at thy return to this country, when with a single ship thou camest into my fleet. Now let men of understanding judge what thou hast above me, and thou wilt discover that here in Norway there are men equal to thee."

Thereupon both were silent, and there was anger on both sides. More things passed between the brothers, from which it appeared that each of them would be greater than the other; however, peace was preserved between them as long as they lived. [It is told that once when King Sigurd had taken his seat, and Eystein had not arrived, Ingeborg, Guttorm's daughter, the wife of King Eystein, said to Sigurd, "The many great achievements, Sigurd, which you have performed in foreign lands, will long be held in remembrance." He answered her in these verses:

> White was my shield
> When I took the field,
> And red when I came home:
> The brave takes all
> That may befall;
> Fate deals out what's to come.
> My men I taught,
> In the onslaught,
> The blow to give and fend—
> The weal or woe
> Of every blow
> Is just what God may send.]

CHAPTER XXV. OF THE BATH.—It is told that King Sigurd was at a feast in the Uplands, and a bath was made ready for him. When the king came to the bath, and the tent was raised over the bathing-tub, the king thought there was a fish in the tub beside him; and a great laughter came upon him, so that he was beside himself, and was out of his mind, and often afterwards these fits returned.

Magnus Barefoot's daughter, Ragnhild, was married by her brothers to Harald Kesja, a son of the Danish king Eric the Good; and their sons were Magnus, Olaf, Canute, and Harald [ob. 1135].

CHAPTER XXVI. OF KING EYSTEIN'S SHIPBUILDING, AND OF HIS DEATH.—King Eystein built a large ship at Nidaros, which, in size and shape, was like the Long Serpent which King Olaf Trygveson had built. At the head there was a dragon's head, and at the stern a crooked tail, and both were gilded over. The ship was high-sided; but the fore and aft parts appeared less than they should be. He also made in Nidaros many and large dry-docks of the best material, and well timbered, so that they were admired by all who saw them.

Six years after King Olaf's death, it happened that King Eystein, at a feast at Hustad in Stim,[1] was seized with an illness which soon carried him off. He died the 29th of August [1123], and his body was carried north to Nidaros, and buried in Christ church; and jt is generally said that so many mourners never stood over any man's grave in Norway as over King Eystein's, at least since the time Magnus the Good, Saint Olaf's son, died. Eystein had been twenty years king of Norway; and after his decease his brother King Sigurd was the sole king of Norway as long as he lived.

CHAPTER XXVII. — OF THE BAPTISING THE PEOPLE OF SMAALAND.—The Danish king Nicolas, a son of Svein Ulvsòn, married afterwards the Queen Margaret, a daughter of King Inge, who had before been married to King Magnus Barefoot; and their son was called Magnus the Strong. King Nicolas sent a message to King Sigurd the Crusader, and asked him if he would go with him with all his might and help to the east of the Swedish dominion, to Smaaland, to baptise the inhabitants; for the people who dwelt there had no regard for Christianity, although some of them had allowed themselves to be baptised. At that time there were many people all around in the Swedish dominions who were heathens, and many were bad Christians; for there were some of the kings who renounced Christianity, and continued heathen sacrifices, as Blot Svein, and afterwards Eric Aarsal, had done. King Sigurd promised to undertake this journey, and the kings appointed their meeting at Öre Sound.[2] King Sigurd then summoned all people in Norway to a levy, both of men and ships; and when the fleet was assembled he had about 300 [360] ships. King Nicolas came very early to the meeting-place, and stayed there a long time; and the bonder murmured much, and said the Northmen did not intend to come. Thereupon the Danish army dispersed, and the king went away with all his fleet. King Sigurd came there soon afterwards, and was ill pleased; but sailed east to Svimraros,[3]

---

[1] The peninsula between Romsdal and Sundalsfjord, where the mountain Stemhest is. It was here that the king's estate Hustad was situated.
[2] Öresund, the Baltic Straits.
[3] Now Simrishamn in Skaane.

and held a House-Thing, at which Sigurd spoke about King
Nicolas's breach of faith; and the Northmen, on this account,
determined to go marauding in his country.   They first plundered a village called Tumathorp,[1] which is not far from Lund;
and then sailed east to the merchant-town of Calmar, where
they plundered, as well as in Smaaland, and imposed on the
country a tribute of 1500 [1800] cattle for ship provision; and
the people of Smaaland received Christianity.   After this King
Sigurd turned about with his fleet, and came back to his kingdom
with many valuable articles and great booty, which he had
gathered on this expedition; and this levy was called the Calmar
levy.   This was the summer before the great eclipse [11 August,
1124].   This was the only levy King Sigurd carried out as long
as he was king.

[CHAPTER XXVIII. OF THORARIN STUTTFELD.—It happened
once when King Sigurd was going from the drinking-table to
vespers, that his men were very drunk and merry; and many
of them sat outside the church singing the evening song, but
their singing was very irregular.   Then the king said, "Who
is that fellow I see standing at the church with a skin jacket
on?"   They answered, that they did not know.   Then the
king said:

> This skin-clad man, in sorry plight,
> Puts all our wisdom here to flight.

Then the fellow came forward and said:

> I thought that here I might be known,
> Although my dress is scanty grown.
> 'Tis poor, but I must be content:
> Unless, great king, it's thy intent
> To give me better; for I have seen
> When I and rags had strangers been.

The king answered, "Come to me to-morrow when I am at
the drink-table."   The night passed away; and the morning
after, the Icelander, who was afterwards called Thorarin Stuttfeld, went into the drinking-room.   A man stood outside of the
door of the room with a horn in his hand, and said, "Icelander!
the king says that if thou wilt deserve any gift from him thou
shalt compose a song before going in, and make it about a man
whose name is Hakon Serkson, and who is called Mörstrutr[2];
and speak about that surname in thy song."   The man who
spoke to him was called Arne Fjöruskeif.   Then they went

---

[1] Now Tomarp, south of Simrishamn.
[2] Mörstrutr is a short, fat, paunchy fellow.

into the room; and when Thorarin came before the king's seat
he recited these verses:

> Drontheim's warrior-king has said
> The scald shoud be by gifts repaid,
> If he before this meeting gave
> The king's friend Serk a passing stave.
> The generous king has let me know
> My stave, to please, must be framed so
> That my poor verse extol the fame
> Of one called Hakon Lump by name.

Then said the king, "I never said so, and somebody has
been making a mock of thee. Hakon himself shall determine
what punishment thou shalt have. Go into his suite." Hakon
said, "He shall be welcome among us, for I can see where the
joke came from"; and he placed the Icelander at his side next
to himself, and they were very merry. The day was drawing
to a close, and the liquor began to get into their heads, when
Hakon said, "Dost thou not think, Icelander, that thou owest
me some penalty? and dost thou not see that some trick has
been played upon thee?"

Thorarin replies, "It is true, indeed, that I owe thee some
compensation."

Hakon says, "Then we shall be quits, if thou wilt make me
another stave about Arne."

He said he was ready to do so; and they crossed over to the
side of the room where Arne was sitting, and Thorarin gave
these verses:

> Fjöruskeff has often spread,
> With evil heart and idle head,
> The eagle's voidings [1] round the land,
> Lampoons and lies, with ready hand.
> Yet this landlouper we all know,
> In Africa scarce fed a crow.
> Of all his arms used in the field,
> Those in most use were helm and shield.

Arne sprang up instantly, drew his sword, and was going to
fall upon him; but Hakon told him to let it alone and be quiet,
and bade him remember that if it came to a quarrel he would
come off the worst himself.

Thorarin afterwards went up to the king, and said he had
composed a poem which he wished the king to hear. The king

---

[1] This is an allusion to the story of the theft of the mead of poetry.
Odin stole it from its owner Suttung, drinking it in three draughts, and then
flew off in the shape of an eagle, closely pursued by Suttung. Odin spat
the drink out into vessels the gods had ready, but in such haste that some
was spilt—and that is called "the poetasters' share." See *The Prose Edda*,
trans. J. Young, 1954, pp. 102–3.

consented, and the song is known by the name of the Stuttfeld
Poem. The king asked Thorarin what he intended to do. He
replied, it was his intention to go to Rome. Then the king
gave him much money for his pilgrimage, and told him to visit
him on his return, and promised to provide for him. But it
is not related whether they ever met again.

CHAPTER XXIX. OF SIGURD AND OTTAR BIRTING.—It is
the general opinion among the people, that there never was
a king more able to act for himself, or more adapted to govern,
than King Sigurd; but latterly it happened that he could with
difficulty govern his own mind and reason, so that, now and
then, unhappy and heavy occurrences took place; although he
was always respected as a great prince, and stood in great
reputation on account of his foreign expedition. It is told that
King Sigurd, one holiday in Easter, sat at table with many
people, among whom were many of his friends; and when he
came to his high seat, people saw that his countenance was
very wild, and as if he had been weeping, so that people were
afraid of what might follow. The king rolled his eyes, and looked
at those who were seated on the benches; but none of his men
ventured to speak to him. Then he seized the holy book which
he had brought with him from abroad, and which was written
all over with gilded letters; so that never had such a costly
book come to Norway. His queen sat by his side. Then said
King Sigurd, "Many are the changes which may take place
during a man's lifetime. I had two things which were dear to
me above all when I came from abroad, and these were this
book and the queen; and now I think the one is only worse and
more loathsome than the other, and nothing I have belonging
to me that I more detest. The queen does not know herself
how hideous she is; for a goat's horn is standing out on her
head, and the better I liked her before the worse I like her
now; and as to this book, it is good for nothing." Thereupon
he cast the book on the fire which was burning on the hall-
floor, and gave the queen a blow with his fist between the
eyes. The queen wept; but more at the king's illness than at
the blow, or the affront she had suffered.

Then a man stood up before the king: his name was Ottar
Birting; and he was one of the torch-bearers, although a bonde's
son, and was on service that day. He was of small stature,
but of agreeable appearance; lively, bold, and full of fun; black-
haired, and of a dark skin; so that it was a nickname to call
him Birting—or fair. He ran and snatched the book which

the king had cast into the fire, held it out, and said, "Different were the days, sire, when you came with great state and splendour to Norway, and with great fame and honour; for then all your friends came to meet you with joy, and were glad at your coming. All as one man would have you for king, and have you in the highest regard and honour. But now days of sorrow are come over us; for on this holy festival many of your friends have come to you, and cannot be cheerful on account of your melancholy and ill-health. It is much to be desired that you would be merry with them; and do, good king, take this saving advice—make peace first with the queen, and make her joyful, whom you have so highly affronted, with a friendly word; and then all your chiefs, friends, and servants: that is my advice."

Then said King Sigurd, "Dost thou dare to give me advice, thou great lump of a houseman's lad!—thou peasant boy of the meanest, most contemptible race and family!" And he sprang up, drew his sword, and swung it with both hands, as if going to cut him down.

But Ottar stood quiet and upright; did not stir from the spot, nor show the slightest sign of fear; and the king turned round the sword-blade which he had waved over Ottar's head, and gently touched him on the shoulder with it. Then he sat down in silence on his high seat.

All were silent who were in the hall, for nobody dared to say a word. Now the king looked around him, milder than before, and said, "It is difficult to know what there is in people. Here sat my friends, and lendermen, marshals, and shield-bearers, and all the best men in the land; but none did so well against me as this man, who appears to you of little worth compared to any of you, although now I esteem him most. I came here like a madman, and would have destroyed my precious property; but he turned aside my deed, and was not afraid of death for it. Then he made an able speech, ordering his words so that they were honourable to me, and not saying a single word about things which could increase my vexation; but even avoiding what might, with truth, have been said. So excellent was his speech, that no man here, however great his understanding, could have spoken better. Then I sprang up in a pretended rage, and made as if I would have cut him down; but he was as courageous as if he had nothing to fear: and seeing that, I let go my purpose; for he was altogether innocent. Now ye shall know, my friends, how I intend to reward him: he was before my torch-

bearer, and shall now be my lenderman; and there shall follow
what is still more, that he shall be the most distinguished of
my lendermen."

Then the king, in presence of all, thanked the bonde's son for
having appeased his passion by sensible words and steady courage,
and having done what his chief lendermen had not ventured to
do; and then made him one of his principal lendermen.

Often these fits of insanity, and wonderful whims, came over
the king; and when any of his lower servants recalled him to
himself, he listened to them best, and bestowed on them property
and farms. Ottar became one of the most celebrated men in
Norway for various good and praiseworthy deeds.]

CHAPTER XXX. OF KING SIGURD'S DREAM. — In King
Sigurd's latter days he was once at an entertainment at one of
his farms; and in the morning when he was dressed he was
silent and still, so that his friends were afraid he was not able
to govern himself. Now the farm-bailiff, who was a man of
good sense and courage, brought him into conversation, and
asked if he had heard any news of such importance that it
disturbed his mirth; or if the entertainment had not satisfied
him; or if there was anything else that people could remedy.

King Sigurd said, that none of the things he had mentioned
was the cause. "But it is, that I think upon the dream I had
in the night."

"Sire," replied he, "may it prove a lucky dream! I would
gladly hear it."

The king said, "I thought that I was in Jædcren, and looked
out towards the sea; and that I saw something very black
moving itself; and when it came near it appeared to be a large
tree, of which the branches stretched far above the water, and
the roots were down in the sea. Now when the tree came to
the shore it broke in pieces, and drove all about the land, both
the mainland, and the out-islands, rocks, and strands; and it
appeared to me as if I saw over all Norway along the sea-coast,
and saw pieces of that tree, some small and some large, driven
into every bight."

Then said the bailiff, "It is likely that you can best interpret
this dream yourself; and I would willingly hear your interpretation of it."

Then said the king, "This dream appears to me to denote
the arrival in this country of some man who will fix his seat
here, and whose posterity will spread itself over the land; but
with unequal power, as the dream shows."

[CHAPTER XXXI. OF ASLAK HANE.—It so happened once, that King Sigurd sat in a gloomy mood among many worthy men. It was a Friday evening, and the kitchen-master asked what meat should be made ready.

The king replies, "What else but flesh-meat?" And so harsh were his words that nobody dared to contradict him, and all were ill at ease. Now when people prepared to go to table, dishes of warm flesh-meat were carried in; but all were silent, and grieved at the king's illness. Before the blessing was pronounced [1] over the meat, a man called Aslak Hane spoke. He had been a long time with King Sigurd on his journey abroad, and was not a man of any great family; and was small of stature, but fiery. When he perceived how it was, and that none dared to accost the king, he asked, "What is it, sire, that is smoking on the dish before you?"

The king replies, "What do you mean, Aslak? what do you think it is?"

Aslak: "I think it is flesh-meat; and I would it were not so."

The king: "But if it be so, Aslak?"

He replied, "It would be vexatious to know that a gallant king, who has gained so much honour in the world, should so forget himself. When you rose up out of Jordan, after bathing in the same waters as God himself, with palm-leaves in your hands, and the cross upon your breast, it was something else you promised, sire, than to eat flesh-meat on a Friday. If a meaner man were to do so, he would merit a heavy punishment. This royal hall is not so beset as it should be, when it falls upon me, a mean man, to challenge such an act."

The king sat silent, and did not partake of the meat; and when the time for eating was drawing to an end, the king ordered the flesh dishes to be removed, and other food was brought in, such as it is permitted to use. When the meal-time was almost past, the king began to be cheerful, and to drink. People advised Aslak to fly, but he said he would not do so. "I do not see how it could help me; and, to tell the truth, it is as good to die now that I have got my will, and have prevented the king from committing a sin. It is for him to kill me if he likes."

Towards evening the king called him, and said, "Who set thee on, Aslak Hane, to speak such free words to me in the hearing of so many people?"

"No one, sire, but myself."

[1] Or rather signed over the meat; viz. the sign of the cross made over it.

The king: "Thou wouldst like, no doubt, to know what thou art to have for such boldness: what thinkest thou it deserves?"

He replies, "If it be well rewarded, sire, I shall be glad; but should it be otherwise, then it is your concern."

Then the king said, "Smaller is thy reward than thou hast deserved. I give thee three farms. It has turned out, what could not have been expected, that thou hast prevented me from a great crime—thou, and not the lendermen, who are indebted to me for so much good." And so it ended.

One Yule eve the king sat in the hall, and the tables were laid out; and the king said, "Get me flesh-meat."

They answered, "Sire, it is not the custom to eat flesh-meat on Yule eve."

The king said, "If it be not the custom, I will make it the custom."

They went out, and brought him a seal.[1] The king stuck his knife into it, but did not eat of it.]

CHAPTER XXXII. HARALD GILLE COMES TO NORWAY.—Halkel Huk, a son of Jon Smörbalte, who was lenderman in Möre, made a voyage in the West sea, all the way to the South Hebudes. A man came to him out of Ireland called Gille Krist,[2] and gave himself out for a son of King Magnus Barefoot. His mother came with him, and said his other name was Harald. Halkel received the man, brought him to Norway with him, and went immediately to King Sigurd with Harald and his mother. When they had told their story to the king, he talked over the matter with his principal men, and bade them give their opinions upon it. They were of different opinions, and all left it to the king himself, although there were several who opposed this; and the king followed his own counsel. King Sigurd ordered Harald to be called before him, and told him that he would not deny him the proof, by ordeal, of who his father was; but on condition that if he should prove his descent according to his claim, he should not desire the kingdom in the lifetime of King Sigurd, or of King Magnus: and to this he bound himself by oath. King Sigurd said he must tread over hot iron to prove his birth; but this ordeal was thought by many too severe, as he was to undergo it merely to prove

[1] The Icelandic laws say that seal is to be eaten only on days when meat is allowed. The same rule applied in Norway, cf. *The King's Mirror*, trans. L. M. Larson, 1917, p. 140.
[2] Gille-Krist means the servant of Christ and in Norway has been abbreviated to Gille.

his father, and without getting the kingdom; but Harald agreed to it, and prepared himself by a fast: and this ordeal was the greatest ever made in Norway; for nine glowing ploughshares were laid down, and Harald went over them with bare feet, attended by two bishops, and invoking the holy Saint Columb. His bed was ready on the spot.

Then said Magnus, King Sigurd's son, "He does not tread on the irons in a manly way."

The king replies, "Evil and wicked is thy speech; for he has done it admirably."

Thereupon Harald was laid in bed, and three days after the iron trial the ordeal was taken to proof, and the feet were found unburnt. Thereafter King Sigurd acknowledged Harald's relationship; but his son Magnus conceived a great hatred of him, and in this many chiefs followed Magnus. King Sigurd trusted so much to his favour with the whole people of the country, that he desired all men, under oath, to promise to accept King Magnus after him as their king; and all the people took this oath.

CHAPTER XXXIII. OF A RACE BETWEEN MAGNUS AND HARALD GILLE.—Harald Gille was a tall, slender-grown man, of a long neck and face, black eyes, and dark hair, brisk and quick; and wore generally the Irish dress of short light clothes. The Norse language was difficult for Harald, and he brought out words which many laughed at; but King Sigurd did not permit this when he was present. Harald used to attend the king to bed in the evening; but it once happened that Magnus and his people detained him, and they sat late drinking together. Harald spoke with another man about different things in the West in Ireland; and among other things, said that there were men in Ireland so swift of foot that no horse could overtake them in a race. Magnus the king's son heard this, and said, "Now he is lying, as he usually does."

Harald replies, "It is true that there are men in Ireland whom no horse in Norway could overtake." They exchanged some words about this, and both were drunk. Magnus had got a horse he had sent for from Gotland—a beautiful animal, and very swift. Those who were present thought that no horse was so swift, and asked Harald's opinion. Then said Magnus, "Thou shalt make a wager with me, and stake thy head if thou canst not run so fast as I ride upon my horse, and I shall stake my gold ring."

Harald replies, "I did not say that I could run so swiftly;

but I said that men are to be found in Ireland who will run as fast; and on that I would wager."

The king's son Magnus replies, "I will not go to Ireland about it: we are wagering here, and not there."

Harald on this went to bed, and would not speak to him more about it. This was in Oslo. The following morning, when the early mass was over, Magnus rode up the street,[1] and sent a message to Harald to come to him. When Harald came he was dressed thus. He had on a shirt and trousers which were bound with ribands under his foot-soles, a short cloak, an Irish hat on his head, and a spear-shaft in his hand. Magnus set up a mark for the race. Harald said, "Thou hast made the course too long"; but Magnus thought if it were even longer, it would still be too short. There were many spectators. They began the race, and Harald followed always the horse's pace; and when they came to the end of the race-course, Magnus said, "Thou hadst hold of the saddle-girths, and the horse dragged thee along." Magnus had his swift runner, the Gotland horse. They began the race again, and Harald ran the whole race-course before the horse. When they came to the end Harald asked, "Had I hold of the saddle-girths now?"

Magnus replied, "Thou hadst the start at first."

Then Magnus let his horse breathe a while, and when he was ready he put spurs to him, and set off in full gallop. Harald stood still, and Magnus looked back, and called out, "Set off now."

Then Harald ran quickly past the horse, and came to the end of the course so long before him that he lay down, and got up and saluted Magnus as he came in.

Then they went home to the town. In the meantime King Sigurd had been at high mass, and knew nothing of this until after he had dined that day. Then he said to Magnus angrily, "Thou callest Harald useless; but I think thou art a great fool, and knowest nothing of the customs of foreign people. Dost thou not know that men in other countries exercise themselves in other feats than in filling themselves with ale, and making themselves mad, and so unfit for everything that they scarcely know each other? Give Harald his ring, and do not try to make a fool of him again, as long as I am above ground and have the rule here."

CHAPTER XXXIV. OF SIGURD'S SWIMMING.—It happened

---

[1] The present St. Halvard Street.

once that Sigurd was out in his ship, which lay in the harbour; and there lay a merchant ship, which was an Iceland trader, at the side of it. Harald Gille was in the forecastle of the king's ship, and Svein Rimhildson, a son of Knut Sveinson [1] of Jæderen, had his berth the next before him. There was also Sigurd Sigurdson, a gallant lenderman, who himself commanded a ship. It was a day of beautiful weather and warm sunshine, and many went out to swim, both from the long-ship and the merchant vessel. An Iceland man, who was among the swimmers, amused himself by drawing those under water who could not swim so well as himself; and at that the spectators laughed. When King Sigurd saw and heard this, he cast off his clothes, sprang into the water, and swam to the Icelander, seized him, and pressed him under the water, and held him there; and as soon as the Icelander came up the king pressed him down again, and thus the one time after the other.

Then said Sigurd Sigurdson, "Shall we let the king kill this man?"

Somebody said, "No one has any wish to interfere."

Sigurd replies, that "if Dag Eilivson were here, we should not be without one who dared."

Then Sigurd sprang overboard, swam to the king, took hold of him, and said, "Sire, do not kill the man. Everybody sees that you are a much better swimmer."

The king replies, "Let me loose, Sigurd; I shall be his death, for he will destroy our people under water."

Sigurd says, "Let us first amuse ourselves; and, Icelander, do thou set off to the land," which he did. The king now got loose from Sigurd, and swam to his ship, and Sigurd went his way: but the king ordered that Sigurd should not presume to come into his presence; so he went up into the country.

CHAPTER XXXV. OF HARALD AND SVEIN RIMHILDSON.— In the evening, when people were going to bed, some of the ship's men were still at their games up in the country. Harald was with those who played on the land, and told his footboy to go out to the ship, make his bed, and wait for him there. The lad did as he was ordered. The king had gone to sleep; and as the boy thought Harald late, he laid himself in Harald's berth. Svein Rimhildson said, "It is a shame for brave men to be brought from their farms at home, and to have here serving-boys to sleep beside them." The lad said that Harald had ordered him to come there. Svein Rimhildson said, "We

[1] Grandson of Aslak Erlingsson, on whom see p. 191.

do not so much care for Harald himself lying here, without his bringing his slaves and beggars"; and seized a riding-whip, and struck the boy on the head until the blood flowed from him.   The boy ran immediately up to the land, and told Harald what had happened, who went immediately out to the ship, to the aft part of the forecastle, and with a hand-axe struck Svein so that he received a severe wound on his hands; and then Harald went on shore.   Svein ran to the land after him, and, gathering his kinsmen, took Harald prisoner, and they were about hanging him.   But while they were busy about this, Sigurd Sigurdson went out to the king's ship and awoke him. When the king opened his eyes and recognised Sigurd, he said, "For this reason thou shalt die, that thou hast intruded into my presence; for thou knowest that I forbade thee": and with these words the king sprang up.

Sigurd replied, "That is in your power as soon as you please; but other business is more urgent.   Go to the land as quickly as possible to help thy brother; for the Rogaland people are going to hang him."

Then said the king, "God give us luck, Sigurd!   Call my trumpeter, and let him call the people all to land, and to meet me."

The king sprang on the land, and all who knew him followed him to where the gallows was being erected.   The king instantly took Harald to him; and all the people gathered to the king in full armour, as they heard the trumpet.   Then the king ordered that Svein and all his comrades should depart from the country as outlaws; but by the intercession of good men the king was prevailed on to let them remain and hold their properties, but no mulct should be paid for Svein's wound.

Then Sigurd Sigurdson asked if the king wished that he should go forth out of the country.

"That will I not," said the king; "for I can never be without thee."

CHAPTER XXXVI. OF KING OLAF'S MIRACLE ON A MAN WHOSE TONGUE HAD BEEN CUT OUT FROM THE ROOT.—There was a young and poor man called Kolbein; and Tora, King Sigurd the Crusader's mother,[1] had ordered his tongue to be cut out of his mouth, and for no other cause than that this young man had taken a piece of meat out of the king-mother's

---

[1] In the *Oldest Saga of Saint Olaf* (cf. Introduction, p. xv) Tora is said to have been the mother of Sigurd, son of Harald Gille (see pp. 341 ff.); the date of the miracle would then be *c.* 1150.

plate, and he said the cook had given it to him, but the cook did not dare to admit that it was so. This man had long gone about speechless. So says Einar Skuleson in his Olaf's ballad:

> The proud rich dame, for little cause,
> Had the lad's tongue cut from his jaws:
> The helpless man, of speech deprived,
> His dreadful sore wound scarce survived.
> A few weeks since at Lid [1] was seen,
> As well as ever he had been,
> The same poor lad—to speech restored
> By Olaf's power, whom he adored.

Afterwards the young man came to Nidaros, and watched in the Christ church; but at the second mass for Olaf before matins he fell asleep, and thought he saw King Olaf the Saint coming to him; and that Olaf talked to him, and took hold with his hands of the stump of his tongue and pulled it. Now when he awoke he found himself restored, and joyfully did he thank our Lord and the holy Saint Olaf, who had pitied and helped him; for he had come there speechless, and had gone to the holy shrine, and went away cured, and with his speech clear and distinct.

CHAPTER XXXVII. OF KING OLAF'S MIRACLE WITH A PRISONER.—The heathens took prisoner a young man of Danish family, and carried him to Vendland, where he was in fetters along with other prisoners. In the day-time he was alone in irons, without a guard; but at night a peasant's son was beside him in the chain, that he might not escape from them. This poor man never got sleep or rest from vexation and sorrow, and considered in many ways what could help him; for he had a great dread of slavery, and was pining with hunger and torture. He could not again expect to be ransomed by his friends, as they had already restored him twice from heathen lands with their own money; and he well knew that it would be difficult and expensive for them to submit a third time to this burden. It is well with the man who does not undergo so much in the world as this man knew he had suffered. He saw but one way; and that was to get off and escape if he could. He resolved upon this in the night-time, killed the peasant, and cut his foot off after killing him; and set off to the forest with the chain upon his leg. Now when the people knew this, soon after daylight in the morning, they pursued him with two dogs accustomed to trace any one who

---

[1] The farm of Lien in Bratsberg.

escaped, and to find him in the forest however carefully he might be concealed. They got him into their hands, and beat him, and did him all kinds of mischief; and, dragging him home, left him barely alive, and showed him no mercy. They tortured him severely; put him in a dark room, in which there lay already sixteen Christian men; and bound him both with iron and other bonds, as fast as they could. Then he began to think that the misery and pain he had endured before were but shadows to his present sufferings. He saw no man before his eyes in this prison who would beg for mercy for him; no one had compassion on his wretchedness, except the Christian men who lay bound with him, who sorrowed with him, and bemoaned his fate together with their own misfortunes and helplessness. One day they advised him to make a vow to the holy King Olaf, to devote himself to some office in his sacred house, if he, by God's compassion and Saint Olaf's prayers, could get away from this prison. He gladly agreed to this, and made a vow, and promised himself for the situation they mentioned to him. The night after he thought in his sleep that he saw a man, not tall, standing at his side, who spoke to him thus: "Hear, thou wretched man! why dost thou not get up?"

He replied, "Sir, who are you?"

"I am King Olaf, on whom thou hast called."

"Oh, my good lord! gladly would I raise myself; but I lie bound with iron and with chains on my legs, and also the other men who lie here."

Thereupon the king accosts him with the words, "Stand up at once, and be not afraid; for thou art loose."

He awoke immediately, and told his comrades what had appeared to him in this dream. They told him to stand up, and try if it was true. He stood up, and observed that he was loose. Now said his fellow-prisoners this would help him but little, for the door was locked both on the inside and on the outside. Then an old man who sat there in a deplorable condition put in his word, and told him not to doubt the mercy of the man who had loosened his chains: "For he has wrought this miracle on thee that thou shouldst enjoy his mercy, and hereafter be free, without suffering more misery and torture. Make haste, then, and seek the door; and if thou art able to slip out, thou art saved."

He did so, found the door open, slipped out, and away to the forest. As soon as the Vendland people were aware of this they set loose the dogs, and pursued him in great haste; and the poor man lay hid, and saw well where they were following him. But now the hounds lost the trace when they came nearer, and all the eyes that sought him were struck with a blindness, so that nobody could find him, although he lay before their feet; and they all returned home, vexed that they could not find him. King Olaf did not permit this man's destruction after he had reached the forest, and restored him also to his health and hearing; for they had so long tortured and beaten him that he had become deaf. At last he came on board of a ship, with two other Christian men who had been long afflicted in that country. All of them worked zealously in this vessel, and so had a successful flight. Then he repaired to the holy man's house, strong and fit to bear arms. Now he was vexed at his vow, went from his promise to the holy king, ran away one day, and came in the evening to a bonde who gave him lodging for God's sake. Then in the night he saw three girls coming to him; and handsome and nobly dressed were they. They spoke to him directly, and sharply reprimanded him for having been so bold as to run from the good king who had shown so much compassion to him, first in freeing him from his irons, and then from the prison; and yet he had deserted the mild master into whose service he had entered. Then he awoke full of terror, got up early, and told the housefather his dream. The good man said the only thing to do was for him to fare back to the holy place. This miracle was first written down by a man who himself saw the man, and the marks of the chains upon his body.

[CHAPTER XXXVIII. KING SIGURD MARRIES CECILIA.—In the last period of King Sigurd's life, his new and extraordinary resolution was whispered about—that he would be divorced from his queen, and would take Cecilia, who was a great man's daughter, to wife. He ordered accordingly a great feast to be prepared, and intended to hold his wedding with her in Bergen. Now when Bishop Magne heard this, he was very sorry; and one day the bishop goes to the king's hall, and with him a priest called Sigurd, who was afterwards bishop of Bergen. When they came to the king's hall, the bishop sent the king a message that he would like to meet him; and asked the king to come out to him. He did so, and came out with a drawn sword in his hand. He received the bishop kindly, and asked him to go in and sit down to table with him.

The bishop replies, "I have other business now. Is it true,

sire, what is told me, that thou hast the intention of marrying
and of driving away thy queen, and taking another wife?"

The king said it was true.

Then the bishop changed countenance, and angrily replied,
"How can it come into your mind, sire, to do such an act in
our bishopric as to betray God's word and law, and the holy
church? It surprises me that you treat with contempt our
episcopal office, and your own royal office. I will now do
what is my duty; and in the name of God, of the holy King
Olaf, of Peter the apostle, and of the other saints, forbid thee
this wickedness."

While he thus spoke he stood straight up, as if stretching
out his neck to the blow, and as if ready if the king chose to
let the sword fall; and the priest Sigurd, who afterwards was
bishop, has declared that the sky appeared to him no bigger
than a calf's skin, so frightful did the appearance of the king
present itself to him. The king returned to the hall, however,
without saying a word; and the bishop went to his house and
home so cheerful and gay that he laughed, and saluted every
child on his way, and was playing with his fingers. Then the
priest Sigurd asked him the reason; saying, "Why are you so
cheerful, sir? Do you not consider that the king may be
exasperated against you? and would it not be better to get
out of the way?"

Then said the bishop, "It appears to me more likely that he
will not act so; and besides, what death could be better, or more
desirable, than to leave life for the honour of God? or to die
for the holy cause of Christianity and our own office, by pre-
venting that which is not right? I am so cheerful because I
have done what I ought to do."

There was much noise in the town about this. The king
got ready for a journey, and took with him corn, malt, and
honey. He went south to Stavanger, and prepared a feast
there for his marriage with Cecilia. When the bishop [1] who
ruled there heard of this he went to the king, and asked if it
were true that he intended to marry in the lifetime of the queen.

The king said it was so.

The bishop answers, "If it be so, sire, you must know how
much such a thing is forbidden to inferior persons. Now it
appears as if you thought it was allowable for you, because you
have great power, and that it is proper for you, although it is
against right and propriety; but I do not know how you will

[1] Reinald, an Englishman, first bishop of Stavanger, cf. p. 327.

do it in our bishopric, dishonouring thereby God's command, the holy church, and our episcopal authority. But you must bestow a great amount of gifts and estates on this foundation, and thereby pay the mulct due to God and to us for such transgression."

Then said the king, "Take what thou wilt of our possessions. Thou art far more reasonable than Bishop Magne."

Then the king went away, as well pleased with this bishop as ill pleased with him who had laid a prohibition on him. Thereafter the king married the girl, and loved her tenderly.]

CHAPTER XXXIX. IMPROVEMENT OF THE MERCHANT TOWN OF KONGHELLE.—King Sigurd improved the town of Konghelle so much, that there was not a greater town in Norway at the time, and he remained there long for the defence of the frontiers. He built a king's house in the castle, and imposed a duty on all the districts in the neighbourhood of the town, as well as on the townspeople—that every person of nine years of age and upwards should bring to the castle five missile stones for weapons, or as many large stakes sharp at one end and five ells long. In the castle the king built a cross-church of timber, and carefully put together, as far as regards the wood and other materials. This cross-church was consecrated in the twenty-fourth year of King Sigurd's reign [1127]. Here the king deposited the piece of the holy cross, and many other holy relics. It was called the Castle church; and before the high altar he placed the tables he had got made in the Greek country, which were of copper and silver, all gilt, and adorned with enamel and jewels. Here was also the shrine which the Danish king Eric Eimune [1] had sent to King Sigurd; and the altar book, written with gold letters, which the patriarch [in Constantinople] had presented to King Sigurd.

CHAPTER XL. KING SIGURD'S DEATH.—Three years after the consecration of the cross-church, when King Sigurd was stopping at Oslo, he fell sick. [Then his friends entreated him to separate from his wife (Cecilia), which she herself also desired; and she entreated the king that she might be allowed to go away, as it would be most for his advantage. The king said, "Little did I think that thou wouldst leave me like the others"; and turned from her, and became red as blood in the face. She went away nevertheless. His illness now increased, and he died of it; and his body was removed for burial to Oslo.] He died the night after Mary's-mass [26 March, 1130], and was buried in

[1] Danish king, 1134-7.

Halvard's church, where he was laid in the stone wall without the choir on the south side. His son Magnus was in the town at the time, and took possession of the whole of the king's treasury when King Sigurd died. Sigurd had been king of Norway twenty-seven years from the death of his father Magnus Barefoot, and was forty years of age when he died. The time of his reign was good for the country; for there was peace, and crops were good.

XIII

MAGNUS THE BLIND [1] AND HARALD GILLE [2]

CHAPTER I. MAGNUS AND HARALD PROCLAIMED KINGS.—King Sigurd's son Magnus was proclaimed in Oslo king of all the country immediately after his father's death, according to the oath which the whole nation had sworn to King Sigurd; and many went into his service, in addition to the lendermen. Magnus was the handsomest man then in Norway; of a passionate temper, and cruel, but distinguished in bodily·exercises. The favour of the people he owed most to the respect for his father. He was a great drinker, greedy of money, hard, and obstinate.

Harald Gille, on the other hand, was very pleasing in intercourse, gay, mirthful, modest, and so generous that he spared in nothing for the sake of his friends. He willingly listened to good advice, so that he let all who would consult with him and give counsel. With all this he obtained favour and a good repute, and many men attached themselves as much to him as to King Magnus. Harald was in Tunsberg when he heard of his brother King Sigurd's death. He called together his friends to a meeting, and it was resolved to hold the Hauge Thing [3] there in the town. At this Thing, Harald was chosen king of half the country, and it was called a forced oath which had been taken from him to renounce his paternal heritage. Then Harald formed a hird, and appointed lendermen; and very soon he had as many people about him as King Magnus. Then men went between them, and matters stood in this way for seven days; but King Magnus, finding he had fewer people, was obliged to give way, and to divide the kingdom with Harald in two parts. The kingdom accordingly was so divided that each of them should have the half part of the kingdom which King Sigurd had possessed; but that King Magnus alone should inherit the fleet of ships, the table service, the valuable articles, and the movable effects which had belonged to his father King

---

[1] Magnus reigned from 1130 to 1135.
[2] Harald Gille-Christ, from 1130 to 1136.
[3] Hauge Thing means a Thing held at the Haugar, i.e. tumuli or burial mounds at Tunsberg. The spot is now called Möllebakke.

Sigurd. He was notwithstanding the least satisfied with his share. Although they were of such different dispositions, they ruled the country for some time in peace. King Harald had a son called Sigurd, by Tora, a daughter of Guttorm Graabarde. King Harald afterwards married Ingerid, a daughter of Rognvald, who was a son of the Swedish king Inge Steinkelson. King Magnus was married to a daughter of Knut Lavard,[1] and she was sister of the Danish king Valdemar; but King Magnus having no affection for her, sent her back to Denmark; and from that day everything went ill with him, and he brought upon himself the enmity of her family.

CHAPTER II. OF THE FORCES OF HARALD AND MAGNUS [1134].—When the two relatives, Harald and Magnus, had been about three years kings of Norway, they both passed the fourth winter in the town of Nidaros, and invited each other as guests; but their people were always ready for a fight. In spring King Magnus sailed southwards along the land with his fleet, and drew all the men he could obtain out of each district, and sounded his friends if they would strengthen him with their power to take the kingly dignity from Harald, and give him such a portion of the kingdom as might be suitable; representing to them that King Harald had already renounced the kingdom by oath. King Magnus obtained the consent of many powerful men. The same spring Harald went to the Uplands, and by the upper road eastward to Viken; and when he heard what King Magnus was doing, he also drew together men on his side. Wheresoever the two parties went they killed the cattle, or even the people, upon the farms of the adverse party. King Magnus had by far most people, for the main strength of the country lay open to him for collecting men from it. King Harald was in Viken on the east side of the fjord,[2] and collected men, while they were doing each other damage in property and life. King Harald had with him Kriströd, his brother by the mother's side, and many other lendermen; but King Magnus had many more. King Harald was with his forces at a place called Fors[3] in Ranrike, and went from thence towards the sea. The evening before Saint Laurence-day [9 August, 1134] they had their supper at a place called Fyrileiv,[4] while the guard kept a watch on horseback all around the house. The watchmen observed King Magnus's army hastening towards

---

[1] Eric Eiegod's son (died 1131). His daughter was Kristin.
[2] i.e. the Oslofjord.
[3] Now Foss in Tunge, Bohuslen.
[4] Now Färlöf in Tunge.

the house, and consisting of full 6000 [7200] men, while King Harald had but 1500 [1800]. Now come the watchmen who had to bring the news to King Harald of what was going on, and say that King Magnus's army was now very near the house.

The king says, "What will my relative King Magnus Sigurdson have? He wants not surely to fight me?"

Thjostolv Aaleson replies, "You must certainly, sire, make preparation for that, both for yourself and your men. King Magnus has been drawing together an army all the summer for the purpose of giving you battle when he meets you."

Then King Harald stood up, and ordered his men to take their arms. "We shall fight, if our relative King Magnus wants to fight us."

Then the war-horns sounded, and all Harald's men went out from the house to an enclosed field, and set up their banners. King Harald had on two shirts of ring-mail, but his brother Kriströd had no armour on; and a gallant man he was. When King Magnus and his men saw King Harald's troop drew up and made their array, and made their line so long that they could surround the whole of King Harald's troop. So says Halldor Skvalldre:

> King Magnus on the battle-plain
> From his long troop-line had great gain;
> The plain was drenched with warm blood,
> Which lay a red and reeking flood.

CHAPTER III. BATTLE AT FYRILEIV.—King Magnus had the holy cross [1] carried before him in this battle, and the battle was great and severe. The king's brother Kriström had penetrated with his troop into the middle of King Magnus's array, and cut down on each side of him, so that people gave way before him everywhere. But a powerful bonde who was in King Harald's array raised his spear with both hands, and drove it through between Kriström's shoulders, so that it came out at his breast; and thus fell Kriström. Many who were near asked the bonde why he had done so foul a deed.

The bonde replies, "He knows the consequences now of slaughtering my cattle in summer, and taking all that was in my house, and forcing me to follow him here. I determined to give him some return when the opportunity came."

After this King Harald's army took to flight, and he fled himself, with all his men. Many fell: and Ingemar of Ask,[2] a

---

[1] The fragment of the true cross brought home by Sigurd the Crusader from Jerusalem, see p. 283.

[2] Ingemar Sveinsson; Ask is a large farm in Norderhov, Ringerike.

great chief and lenderman, got there his death-wound; and he
sang while dying these verses:

> Some witch-wife's power,
> In evil hour,
> Made me leave home,
> And here to come.
> This shaft, I know,
> Shot from elm bow,
> Will hinder me
> My Ash [1] to see.

There fell nearly sixty of King Harald's hird-men, and he
himself fled eastward to Viken to his ships, and went out of the
country to King Eric in Denmark. So says Halldor Skvalldre:

> Thou who in battle-field hast striven
> Now to thy ocean-steed art driven,
> And o'er the blue field now must ride
> To meet King Eric in his pride.
> The smooth-tongued Jutland king, who reigns
> O'er the brave men of Holstein's plains,
> Will give thee troops again to vie—
> Again with Magnus strength to try.

So says also Einar Skuleson:

> The youth who scatters, frank and free,
> The shining gold—fire of the sea—
> Seeks Scania's sand o'er the blue meads,
> The fields in which the grey fish feeds;
> He who the witches' horses stills,
> Ravens and wolves, and their maws fills,
> To the great King of Denmark hies—
> To get his armed aid he tries. [2]

King Harald sought the Danish king Eric Eimune, to obtain
help and aid from him; and they met in Sealand. King Eric
received him well, and principally because they had sworn to
each other to be as brothers [3]; and gave him Halland as a fief
to rule over, and gave him eight long-ships, but without equipment. Thereafter King Harald went northwards through
Halland, and very many men came to meet him. After this
battle King Magnus subdued the whole country, giving life and
safety to all who were wounded, and had them taken care of
equally with his own men. He then called the whole country
his own, and had a choice of the best men who were in the

[1] i.e. his homestead (Askr).
[2] The whole of this strophe is merely to say that Harald sought refuge
with King Eric.
[3] These brotherhoods, by which one man was bound by oath to aid or
avenge another, were common in the Middle Ages among all ranks. "Sworn
brothers" is still a common expression with us.

country. When they held a council among themselves after-wards, Sigurd Sigurdson, Tore Ingeridsson, and all the men of most understanding, advised that they should keep their forces together in Viken, and remain there, in case Harald should return from the south; but King Magnus would take his own way, and went north to Bergen. There he sat all winter, and allowed his men to leave him; on which the lendermen returned home to their own houses.

CHAPTER IV. DEATH OF ASBJORN AND OF NEREID.—King Harald came to Konghelle with the men who had followed him from Denmark. The lendermen and town's burgesses collected a force against him, which they drew up in a thick array above the town. King Harald landed from his ships, and sent a message to the bonder, desiring that they would not deny him his land, as he wanted no more than what of right belonged to him. Then mediators went between them; and it came to this, that the bonder dismissed their troops, and submitted to him. Thereupon he bestowed fiefs and property on the lendermen, that they might stand by him, and gave to the bonder who joined him a number of advantageous legal reforms. A great body of men attached themselves, therefore, to King Harald; and he proceeded westwards to Viken, where he gave peace to all men, except to King Magnus's people whom he plundered and killed wherever he found them. And when he came west to Sarpsborg, he took prisoners two of King Magnus's lender-men, Asbjorn and his brother Nereid; and gave them the choice that one should be hanged, and the other thrown into the Sarpsborg waterfall, and they might choose as they pleased. Asbjorn chose to be thrown into the cataract, for he was the elder of the two, and this death appeared the most dreadful; and so it was done. Halldor Skvalldre tells of this:

> Asbjorn, who opposed the king,
> O'er the wild cataract they fling:
> Nereid, who opposed the king,
> Must on Hagbart's high tree swing.
> The king gives food in many a way
> To foul-mouthed beasts and birds of prey:
> The generous men who dare oppose
> Are treated as the worst of foes.

Thereafter King Harald proceeded north to Tunsberg, where he was well received, and a large force gathered to him.

CHAPTER V. OF THE COUNSELS PROPOSED.—When King Magnus, who was in Bergen, heard these tidings, he called together all the chiefs who were in the town, and asked them their counsel, and what they should now do. Then Sigurd Sigurdson said, "Here I can give a good advice. Let a ship be manned with good men, and put me, or any other lenderman, to command it; send it to thy relative King Harald, and offer him peace according to the conditions upright men may determine upon, and offer him the half of the kingdom. It appears to me probable that King Harald, by the words and counsel of good men, may accept this offer, and thus there may be a peace established between you."

Then King Magnus replied, "This proposal I will not accept of; for of what advantage would it be, after we have gained the whole kingdom in summer, to give away the half of it now? Give us some other counsel."

Then Sigurd Sigurdson answered, "It appears to me, sire, that your lendermen who in autumn asked your leave to return home will now sit at home, and will not come to you. At that time it was much against my advice that you dispersed so entirely the people we had collected; for I could well suppose that Harald would come back to Viken as soon as he heard that it was without a chief. Now there is still another counsel, and it is but a poor one; but it may turn out useful to us. Send out your pursuivants,[1] and send other people with them, and let them go against the lendermen who will not join you in your necessity, and kill them; and bestow their property on others who will give you help, although they may have been of small importance before. Let them drive together the people, the bad as well as the good; and go with the men you can thus assemble against King Harald, and give him battle."

The king replies, "It would be unpopular to put to death people of distinction, and raise up inferior people who often break faith and law, and the country would be still worse off. I would like to hear some other counsel still."

Sigurd replies, "It is difficult for me now to give advice, as you will neither make peace nor give battle. Let us go north to Drontheim, where the main strength of the country is most inclined to our side; and on the way let us gather all the men we can. It may be that these river-borderers [2] will be tired of such a long stride after us."

The king replies, "We must not fly from those whom we beat in summer. Give some better counsel still."

---

[1] The guests (*gestir*) were a lower class of the king's retainers, receiving half the pay of the hirdmen.

[2] The dwellers by the river Gotha.

Then Sigurd stood up, and said, while he was preparing to go out, "I will now give you the counsel which I see you will take, and which must have its course. Sit here in Bergen until Harald comes with his troops, and then you will either suffer death or disgrace."

And Sigurd remained no longer at that meeting.

CHAPTER VI. OF HARALD'S FORCE.—King Harald came from the East along the coast with a great army, and this winter is called on that account the Crowd-winter. King Harald came to Bergen on Christmas eve, and landed with his fleet at Flore-vaag[1]; but would not fight on account of the sacred season. But King Magnus prepared for defence in the town. He erected a stone-slinging machine out on the holm [now Bergenhus], and had iron chains and wooden booms laid across over the passage from the King's bridge to the North-ness, and to the Monks' bridge. He had caltrops made, and thrown into Saint John's Fields,[2] and did not suspend these works except during the three holy days of Christmas. The last holyday of Yule [7 January, 1135] King Harald ordered his war-horns to sound the gathering of his men for going to the town; and, during the Yule holydays, his army had been increased by about 900 [1080] men.

CHAPTER VII. KING MAGNUS TAKEN PRISONER.—King Harald made a promise to King Olaf the Saint for victory, that he would build an Olaf's church in the town at his own expense. King Magnus drew up his men in the Christ-church yard; but King Harald laid his vessels first at the North-ness. Now when King Magnus and his people saw that, they turned round towards the town, and to the end of the harbour; but as they passed through the street [3] many of the burgesses ran into their houses and homes, and those who went across the St. John's Fields ran upon the caltrops. Then King Magnus and his men perceived that King Harald had rowed with all his men across to Hegravik [now Sand-Viken], and landed there, and had gone from thence the upper road up the hill rising over the town. Now Magnus returned back again through the streets, and then his men fled from him in all directions; some up to the Fjelds [Flöifjeldet], some up to the neighbourhood of the convent of nuns, some to churches, or hid themselves as they best could. King Magnus fled to his ship; but there was no possibility of

---

[1] In Askö, near Bergen.
[2] Now Engen in Bergen.   St. John's Church was hardly built then, 1135.
[3] Now Övregate, opposite Tyskebryggen.

getting away, for the iron chains outside prevented the passage of vessels. He had also but few men with him, and therefore could do nothing. Einar Skuleson tells of this in the song of Harald:

> For a whole week an iron chain
> Cut off all sailing to the main:
> Bergen's blue stable was locked fast—
> Her floating wains could not get past.

Soon after Harald's people came out to the ships, and then King Magnus was made prisoner. He was sitting behind in the forecastle upon the chests of the high seat, and at his side Hakon Fauk, his mother's brother, who was good-looking but was not considered very wise, and Ivar Ossurson. They, and many others of King Magnus's friends, were taken, and some of them killed on the spot.

CHAPTER VIII. KING MAGNUS MUTILATED.—Thereafter King Harald had a meeting of his counsellors, and desired their counsel; and in this meeting the judgment was given that Magnus should be deposed from his dominions, and should no longer be called king. Then he was delivered to the king's slaves, who mutilated him, gouged out both his eyes, cut off one foot, and at last castrated him. Ivar Ossurson was blinded, and Hakon Fauk killed. The whole country then was reduced to obedience under King Harald. Afterwards it was diligently examined who were King Magnus's best friends, or who knew most of his concealments of treasure or valuables. The holy cross King Magnus had kept beside him since the battle of Fyrileiv, but would not tell where it was deposited for preservation. Bishop Reinald of Stavanger, who was an Englishman, was considered very greedy of money. He was a great friend of King Magnus, and it was thought likely that great treasure and valuables had been given into his keeping. Men were sent for him accordingly, and he came to Bergen, where it was insisted against him that he had some knowledge of such treasure; but he denied it altogether, would not admit it, and offered to clear himself by ordeal. King Harald would not have this, but laid on the bishop a money fine of fifteen marks[1] of gold, which he should pay to the king. The bishop declared he would not thus impoverish his bishop's see, but would rather offer his life. On this they hanged the bishop out on the holm, beside the sling machine.[2] As he was going to the gallows he threw the sock from his foot, and said with an oath, "I know no more about King Magnus's treasure than what is in this sock"; and in it there was a gold ring. Bishop Reinald was buried at North-ness in Michael's church, and this deed was much blamed. After this Harald Gille was sole king of Norway as long as he lived.

CHAPTER IX. EXTRAORDINARY OMENS IN KONGHELLE [1135]. —Five years after King Sigurd's death remarkable occurrences took place in Konghelle. Guttorm, a son of Harald Flette, and Sæmund Husfreya, were at that time the king's officers there. Sæmund was married to Ingeborg, a daughter of the priest Andreas Brunson. Their sons were Paul Flip and Gunne Fis. Sæmund's natural son was called Aasmund. Andreas Brunson was a very remarkable man, who carried on divine service in the Cross church. His wife[1] was called Solveig. John Loftson,[2] who was then eleven years old, was in their house to be fostered and educated. The priest Loft Sæmundson, John's father, was also in the town at that time. It happened now in Konghelle, the next Sunday night [14 April] after Easter week, that there was a great noise in the streets through the whole town, as if the king was going through with all his hird-men. The dogs were so affected that nobody could hold them, but they slipped loose; and when they came out they ran mad, biting all that came in their way, people and cattle. All who were bitten by them till the blood came turned raging mad; and pregnant women were taken in labour prematurely, and became mad. From Easter to Ascension-day [16 May], these portentous circumstances took place almost every night. People were dreadfully alarmed at these wonders; and many made themselves ready to remove, sold their houses, and went out to the country districts, or to other towns. The most intelligent men looked upon it as something extremely remarkable; were in dread of it; and said, as it proved to be, that it was an omen of important events which had not yet taken place. And the priest Andreas, on Whit Sunday [26 May], made a long and excellent speech, and turned the conclusion of it to the distressing situation of the townspeople; telling them to muster courage, and not lay waste their excellent town by deserting it, but rather to take the utmost care in all things, and use the greatest foresight against all dangers, as of fire or the enemy, and to pray to God to have mercy on them.

---

[1] The Catholic priests appear to have had wives at that time in Norway, and celibacy to have been confined to the monks.
[2] Snorri was brought up by Jon Loftsson (died 1197).

CHAPTER X. THE RISE OF WAR IN KONGHELLE.—Thirteen
loaded merchant ships made ready to leave the town, intending
to proceed to Bergen; but eleven of them were lost, men and
goods, and all that was in them; the twelfth was lost also, but
the people were saved, although the cargo went to the bottom.
At that time the priest Loft went north to Bergen, with all
that belonged to him, and arrived safely. The merchant vessels
were lost on Saint Laurence eve [10 August]. The Danish
king Eric Eimune, and the Archbishop Ossur,[1] both sent notice
to Konghelle to keep watch on their town; and said the Vendland people had a great force on foot with which they made
war far around on Christian people, and usually gained the
victory. But the townspeople attended very little to this
warning, were indifferent, and forgot more and more the dreadful omens the longer it was since they happened. On the holy
Saint Laurence day, while the words of high mass were spoken,
came the Vendland king Rettibur [2] to Konghelle with six hundred
and sixty Vendland cutters, and in each cutter were forty-four
men and two horses. The king's sister's son Dunimiz, and
Unibur, a chief who ruled over many people, were with him.
These two chiefs rowed at once, with all their troops, up the
east arm of the Gotha river past Hisingen, and thus came down
to the town; but a part of the fleet lay in the western arm, and
came so to the town. They made fast their ships at the piles,
and landed their horses, and rode over the height of Brattaas,
and from thence up around the town. Einar, son-in-law of
priest Andreas, brought these tidings up to the Castle church;
for there the whole inhabitants of the town were gathered to
hear high mass. Einar came just as the priest Andreas was
holding his discourse; and he told the people that an army was
sailing up against the town with a great number of ships of
war, and that some people were riding over Brattaas. Many
said it must be the Danish king Eric, and from him they might
expect peace. The people ran down into the town to their
properties, armed themselves, and went down upon the piers,
whence they immediately saw there was an enemy and an
immense army. Nine East-country [3] trading vessels belonging
to the merchants were afloat in the river at the piers. The
men on board of them armed themselves, and defended them-

---

[1] Ossur (Asger Svensson), bishop of Lund 1089, archbishop of Lund and
metropolitan of Scandinavia 1104, died 1137.

[2] Ratibor, Duke of Forpommern; he became a Christian before his death
in 1152.

[3] Ships trading to the Baltic countries, especially Gotland and Russia.

selves long, well, and manfully.   There was a hard battle, and
resistance, before the merchant vessels were cleared of their
men; and in this conflict the Vendland people lost a hundred
and fifty of their ships, with all the men on board.   When
the battle was sharpest the townsmen stood upon the piers,[1]
and shot at the heathens.   But when the fight slackened the
burgesses fled up to the town, and from thence into the castle;
and the men took with them all their valuable articles, and
such goods as they could carry.   Solveig and her daughters,
with two other women, went on shore, when the Vendlanders
took possession of the merchant vessels.   Now the Vendlanders
landed, and mustered their men, and discovered their loss.
Some of them went up into the town, some on board the
merchant ships, and took all the goods they pleased; and then
they set fire to the town, and burnt it and the ships.   They
hastened then with all their army to assault the castle.

CHAPTER XI. THE SECOND BATTLE.—King Rettibur made
an offer to those who were in the castle that they should go out,
and he would give them their lives, weapons, clothes, silver, and
gold; but all exclaimed against it, and went out on the forti-
fication: some shot, some threw stones, some sharp stakes.   It
was a great battle, in which many fell on both sides, but by far
the most of the Vendlanders.   Solveig came up to a large farm
called Solberg, and brought the news.   A message war-token
was there split, and sent out to Skurbaagar,[2] where there
happened to be a joint ale-drinking feast, and many men
were assembled.   A bonde called Olve Stormund [Big-mouth]
was there, who immediately sprang up, took helmet and shield,
and a great axe in his hand, and said, "Stand up, brave lads,
and take your weapons.   Let us go help the townspeople; for
it would appear shameful to every man who heard of it, if we
sit here sipping our ale, while good men in the town are losing
their lives by our neglect."

Many made an objection, and said they would only be
losing their own lives, without being of any assistance to
the townspeople.

Then said Olve, "Although all of you should hold back,
I will go alone; and one or two heathens, at any rate, shall
fall before I fall."

[1] The piers here spoken of are merely wooden gangways or stages on
piles from the shore to the ship; and every warehouse or dwelling on the
side of a river or harbour has such a pier for itself in Norway.

[2] These farms lay to the north-east of Konghelle, towards where the town
of Kungälv now is.

He ran down to the town, and a few men after him to see what he would do, and also whether they could assist him in any way. When he came near the castle, and the heathens saw him, they sent out eight men fully armed against him; and when they met, the heathen men ran and surrounded him on all sides. Olve lifted his axe, and struck behind him with the extreme point of it, hitting the neck of the man who was coming up behind him, so that his throat and jawbone were cut through, and he fell dead backwards. Then he heaved his axe forwards, and struck the next man in the head, and clove him down to the shoulders. He then fought with the others, and killed two of them; but was much wounded himself. The four who remained took to flight, but Olve ran after them. There was a ditch before them, and two of the heathens jumped into it, and Olve killed them both; but he stuck fast himself in the ditch, so that two of the eight heathens escaped. The men who had followed Olve took him up, and brought him back to Skurbaagar, where his wounds were bound and healed; and it was the talk of the people, that no single man had ever made such a bloody onset. Two lendermen, Sigurd Gyrdson a brother of Philip, and Sigard, came with 600 [720] men to Skurbaagar; on which Sigurd turned back with 400 [480] men. He was but little respected afterwards, and soon died. Sigard, on the other hand, proceeded with 200 [240] men towards the town; and they gave battle to the heathens, and were all slain. While the Vendlanders were storming the castle, their king and his chiefs were out of the battle At one place there was a man among the Vendlanders shooting with a bow, and killing a man for every arrow; and two men stood before him, and covered him with their shields. Then Sæmund Husfreya said to his son Aasmund, that they should both shoot together at this bowman. "But I will shoot at the man who holds the shield before him." He did so, the man holding the shield moved it to protect himself, and in the same instant Aasmund shot between the shields, and the arrow hit the bowman in the forehead, so that it came out at his neck, and he fell down dead. When the Vendlanders saw it they howled like dogs, or like wolves. Then King Rettibur called to them that he would give them safety and life, but they refused terms. The heathens again made a hard assault. One of the heathens in particular fought so bravely, and ventured so near, that he came quite up to the castle gate, and pierced the man who stood outside the gate with his sword; and although they used both arrow and stone against him, and he had neither shield nor helmet, nothing could touch him, for he was so skilled in witchcraft that weapon could not wound him. Then priest Andreas took consecrated fire, signing it with a cross; cut tinder and laid it on the fire; and then laid the tinder on the arrow-point, and gave it to Aasmund. He shot this arrow at the warlock; and the shaft hit so well that it did its business, and the man of witchcraft fell dead. Then the heathens crowded together as before, howling and whining dreadfully; and all gathered about their king, on which the Christians believed that they were holding a council about retreating. The interpreters, who understood the Vendland tongue, heard the chief Unibur make the following speech: "These people are brave, and it is difficult to make anything of them; and even if we took all the goods in their town, we might willingly give as much more that we had never come here, so great has been our loss of men and chiefs. Early in the day, when we began to assault the castle, they defended themselves first with arrows and spears; then they fought against us with stones; and now with sticks and staves, as against dogs. I see from this that they are in want of weapons and means of defence; so we shall make one more hard assault, and try their strength." It was as he said, that they now fought with stakes; because, in the first assault, they had imprudently used up all their missile weapons and stones; and now when the Christians saw the number of their stakes diminishing, they clave each stake in two. The heathens now made a very hot attack, and rested themselves between whiles, and on both sides they were exhausted. During a rest the Vendland king Rettibur again offered terms, and that they should retain the weapons, clothes, and silver they could carry out of the castle. Sæmund Husfreya had fallen, and the men who remained gave the counsel to deliver up the castle and themselves into the power of the heathens: but it was a foolish counsel; for the heathens did not keep their promises, but took all people, men, women, and children, and killed all of them who were wounded or young, or could not easily be carried with them. They took all the goods that were in the castle; went into the Cross church, and plundered it of all its ornaments. The priest Andreas gave King Rettibur a silver-mounted gilt sceptre, and to his sister's son Dunimiz he gave a gold ring. They supposed from this that he was a man of great importance in the town, and held him in higher respect than the others. They took away with them the holy cross, and also the tables which stood before the altar, which Sigurd had got made in the Greek country, and had brought home himself. These they took, and laid flat down on the steps before the altar. Then the heathens went out of the church. Rettibur said, "This house has been adorned with great zeal for the God to whom it is dedicated; but, methinks, he has shown little regard for the town or house: so I see their God has been angry at those who defended them." King Rettibur gave the priest Andreas the church, the shrine, the holy cross, the Bible, the altar-book, and four clerks (prisoners); but the heathens burnt the Castle church, and all the houses that were in the castle. As the fire they had set to the church went out twice, they hewed the church down, and then it burnt like other houses. Then the heathens went to their ships with the booty; but when they mustered their people and saw their loss, they made prisoners of all the people, and divided them among the vessels. Now priest Andreas went on board the king's ship with the holy cross, and there came a great terror over the heathens on account of the portentous circumstance which took place in the king's ship; namely, it became so hot that all thought they were going to be burnt up. The king ordered the interpreter to ask the priest why this happened. He replied, that the Almighty God on whom the Christians believed, sent them a proof of his anger, that they who would not believe in their Creator presumed to lay hands on the emblem of his suffering; and that there lay so much power in the cross, that such, and even clearer miracles, happened to heathen men who had taken the cross in their hands. The king had the priests put into the ship's boat, and the priest Andreas carried the holy cross in his grasp. They led the boat along past the ship's bow, and then aft along the side of the ship, and then shoved it with a boat-hook in beside the pier. Then Andreas went with the cross by night to Solberg, in rain and dreadful weather; but brought it in good preservation.[1]

King Rettibur, and the men he had remaining, went home to Vendland, and many of the people who were taken at Konghelle were long afterwards in slavery in Vendland; and those who were ransomed, and came back to Norway to their udal lands and properties, throve worse than before their capture. The merchant town of Konghelle has never since risen to the importance it had before this event.

CHAPTER XII. OF MAGNUS THE BLIND.—King Magnus, after

[1] He took the cross to Nidaros where it was afterwards preserved.

he was deprived of sight, went north to Nidaros, where he went into the cloister on the holm,[1] and assumed the monk's dress. The cloister received the farm of Great Hernes in Frosta for his support. King Harald alone ruled the country the following winter, gave all men peace and pardon who desired it, and took many of the men who had been with King Magnus into his hird. The priest Einar Skuleson says that King Harald had two battles in Denmark; the one at Hven Isle,[2] and the other at Lessö:

> Unwearied champion! who wast bred
> To stain thy blue-edged weapons red!
> Beneath high Hven's rocky shore,
> The faithless felt thy steel once more.

And again, thus:

> On Lessö's plain the foe must quail
> 'Fore him who dyes their shirts of mail.
> His storm-stretched banner o'er his head
> Flies straight, and fills the foe with dread.

[King Harald was a very generous man. It is told that in his time Magnus Einarsson came from Iceland to be consecrated a bishop,[3] and the king received him well, and showed him much respect. When the bishop was ready to sail for Iceland again, and the ship was rigged out for sea, he went to the hall where the king was drinking, saluted him politely and warmly, and the king received him joyfully. The queen was sitting beside the king.

Then said the king, "Are you ready, bishop, for your voyage?"
He replied that he was.

The king said, "You come to us just now at a bad time; for the tables are just removed, and there is nothing at hand suitable to present to you. What is there to give the bishop?"

The treasurer replies, "Sire, as far as I know, all articles of any value are given away."

The king: "Here is a drinking goblet remaining; take this, bishop, it is not without value."

The bishop expressed his thanks for the honour shown him.

Then said the queen, "Farewell, bishop; and a happy voyage."

The king said to her, "When did you ever hear a noble lady say so to a bishop without giving him something?"

She replies, "Sire, what have I to give him?"

---

[1] The monastery on Nidarholm, an island off Trondheim.
[2] In Öresund.   [3] Bishop of Skálholt, 1134–48.

The king: "Thou hast the cushion under thee."

Thereupon this, which was covered with costly cloth, and was a valuable article, was given to the bishop. When the bishop was going away the king took the cushion from under himself and gave it him, saying, "They have long been together.". When the bishop arrived in Iceland to his bishop's see, it was talked over what should be done with the goblet that would be serviceable for the king; and when the bishop asked the opinion of other people, many thought it should be sold, and the value bestowed on the poor. Then said the bishop, "I will take another plan. I will have a chalice made of it for this church, and consecrate it, so that all the saints of whom there are relics in this church shall let the king have some good for his gift every time a mass is sung over it." This chalice has since belonged to the bishopric of Skalholt; and of the costly cloth with which the cushions given him by the king were covered, were made the choristers' cloaks which are now in Skalholt. From this the generous spirit of King Harald may be seen, as well as from many other things, of which but a few are set down here.

King Harald took Tora, a daughter of Guttorm Graabarde, to be his concubine; and they had a son, who was called Sigurd. He had also a son by Queen Ingerid, who was called Inge. The one of Harald's daughters was called Brigitta, the other Maria. His daughter Brigitta was first married to the Swedish king Inge Halsteinson, then to Magnus Heinrickson, and lastly to Birger Brose.]

CHAPTER XIII. THE BEGINNING OF SIGURD SLEMBEDEGN.— There was a man, by name Sigurd, who was brought up in Norway, and was called priest Adalbrekt's son. Sigurd's mother was Tora, a daughter of Saxe of Vik,[1] a sister of Sigrid, who was mother of King Olaf Magnusson, and of Kaare the king's brother who married Borghild, a daughter of Dag Eilivson. Their sons were Sigurd of Ostraat and Dag. Sigurd of Ostraat's sons were Jon of Ostraat, Torstein, and Andreas the Deaf. Jon was married to Sigrid, a sister of King Inge and of Duke Skule. This Sigurd, in his childhood, was kept at his book, became a clerk, and was consecrated a deacon; but as he ripened in years and strength he became a very clever man, stout, strong, distinguished for all perfections and exercises beyond any of his years—indeed, beyond any man in Norway. Sigurd showed early traces of a haughty ungovernable spirit,

[1] Saxvik at Strinden, near Trondheim.

and was therefore called Slembedegn.[1] He was as handsome a man as could be seen, with rather thin but beautiful hair. When it came to Sigurd's ears that his mother said King Magnus was his father, he laid aside all clerkship; and as soon as he was old enough to be his own master, he left the country. He was a long time on his travels, went to Palestine; was at the Jordan river; and visited many holy places, as palmers usually do. When he came back, he applied himself to trading expeditions. One winter he was in Orkney with Earl Harald,[2] and was with him when Torkel Fostre Summarlideson was killed. Sigurd was also in Scotland with the Scottish king David,[3] and was held in great esteem by him. Thereafter Sigurd went to Denmark; and according to the account of himself and his men, he there submitted to the iron ordeal to confirm his paternal descent, and proved by it, in the presence of five bishops, that he was a son of King Magnus Barefoot. So says Ivar Ingemundson,[4] in Sigurd's song:

> The holiest five
> Of men alive—
> Bishops were they—
> Solemnly say,
> The iron glowing
> Red hot, yet showing
> No scaith on skin,
> Proves cause and kin.

King Harald Gille's friends, however, said this was only a lie, and deceit of the Danes against the people of Norway.

[It is told before of Sigurd that he passed some years in merchant voyages, and he came thus to Iceland one winter, and took up his lodging with Torgils Oddson of Stadarholl in Saurbæ; but very few knew where he was. In autumn, when the sheep were being driven into a fold to be slaughtered, a sheep that was to be caught ran to Sigurd; and as Sigurd thought the sheep ran to him for protection, he stretched out his hands to it, and lifted it over the fold dyke, and let it run to the hills, saying, "There are not many who seek help from me, so I may well help this one." It happened the same winter that a woman had committed a theft, and Torgils, who was angry at her for

---

[1] Slembedegn, Icelandic *slembidjákn* = the obstreperous deacon.
[2] Harald, son of Earl Hakon (p. 276), ruled 1122–8.
[3] David I, reigned 1124–53.
[4] The only poem by Ivar now preserved is the *Sigurðarbálkr*, from which this stanza comes; he is also said to have composed poems in honour of Magnus Barefoot and of Magnus's sons, Eystein and Sigurd. Apart from a reference to an unhappy love-affair (see the interpolation, pp. 289–90), nothing is known of his life and family.

it, was going to punish her; but she ran to Sigurd to ask his
help, and he set her upon the bench by his side. Torgils told
him to give her up, and told him what she had committed; but
Sigurd begged forgiveness for her, since she had come to him
for protection, and that Torgils would dismiss the complaint
against her, but Torgils insisted that she should receive her
punishment. When Sigurd saw that Torgils would not listen
to his entreaty, he started up, drew his sword, and bade him
take her if he dared; and Torgils seeing that Sigurd would
defend the woman by force of arms, and observing his com-
manding mien, guessed who he must be, desisted from pursuing
the woman, and pardoned her.

There were many foreign men there, and Sigurd made the
least appearance among them. One day Sigurd came into the
sitting-room, and a Northman who was splendidly clothed was
playing chess with one of Torgils's house-servants. The Northman called Sigurd, and asked him his advice how to play; but
when Sigurd looked at the board, he saw the game was lost.
The man who was playing against the Northman had a sore
foot, so that one toe was bruised, and matter was coming out
of it. Sigurd, who was sitting on the bench, takes a straw,
and draws it along the floor, so that some young kittens ran
after it. He drew the straw always before them, until they
came near to the house-servant's foot, who, jumping up with
a scream, threw the chessmen in disorder on the board; and
thus it was a dispute how the game had stood. This is given
as a proof of Sigurd's cunning. People did not know that he
was a learned clerk until the Saturday before Easter, when
he consecrated the holy water with chant; and the longer he
stayed there the more he was esteemed. The summer after,
Sigurd told Torgils, before they parted, that he might with all
confidence address his friends to Sigurd Slembedegn. Torgils
asked how nearly he was related to him; on which he replies,
"I am Sigurd Slembedegn, a son of King Magnus Barefoot."
He then left Iceland.

At this time Harald was sole king of Norway, and people
generally said that he was not a man of understanding; but
not so cruel as his relation King Magnus Sigurdson.]

CHAPTER XIV. OF SIGURD SLEMBEDEGN [1136].—When
Harald Gille had been six years King of Norway, Sigurd came
to the country; and many gave him the counsel to go at once
to King Harald, declare his relationship to him, and try how
matters would go. Sigurd accordingly went to his brother

King Harald, and found him in Bergen. He placed himself entirely in the king's hands, disclosed who his father was, and asked him to acknowledge their relationship. The king gave him no hasty or distinct reply; but laid the matter before his friends in a conference at a specially appointed meeting. When the king's counsellors were made acquainted with it, they said that if Sigurd was placed over the kingdom he would become too great, as King Magnus had been: and now they lived in all quietness, and the lendermen alone, in fact, governed the kingdom; and therefore they advised the king to lay a capital accusation against Sigurd, and have him put to death. After this conference it became known that the king laid an accusation against Sigurd, because he had been at the killing of Torkel Fostre in the West. Torkel had accompanied Harald to Norway when he first came to the country, and had been one of Harald's best friends. This case was followed up so severely, that a capital accusation against Sigurd was made, and, by the advice of the lendermen, was carried so far, that some of the king's pursuivants went one evening late to Sigurd, and called him to them. They then took a boat, and rowed away with Sigurd from the town south to North-ness.[1] Sigurd sat on a chest in the stern of the boat, and had his suspicions that foul play was intended. He was clothed in blue trousers, and over his shirt he had a hood tied with ribands, which served him for a cloak. He sat looking down, and holding his hood-strings; and sometimes moved them over his head, sometimes let them fall again before him. Now when they had passed the ness, and had come nearly to Mjolk-a, they were, part of them, drunk and merry, and part were rowing so eagerly that they were not taking notice of anything. Sigurd stood up, and went to the ship's side; but the two men who were placed to guard him stood up also, and followed him to the side of the vessel, holding by his cloak, as is the custom in guarding people of distinction. As he suspected that they were taking hold of more of his clothes, he seized them both, and leaped overboard with them. The boat, in the meantime, had gone on a long way, and it was a long time before those on board could turn the vessel, and long before they could get their own men taken on board again; and Sigurd dived under water, and swam so far away that he reached the land before they could get the boat turned to pursue him. Sigurd, who was very swift of foot, hied up to the Fjelds, and the king's men travelled about the whole

A headland near Bergen, cf. p. 326 and Appendix ii, p. 429.

night seeking him without finding him. He lay down in a cleft of the rocks; and as he was very cold he took off his trousers, cut a hole in the seat of them, and stuck his head through it, and put his arms in the legs of them. He escaped with life this time; and the king's men returned, and could not conceal their unsuccessful adventure.

CHAPTER XV. TREACHERY TOWARDS KING HARALD.—Sigurd thought now that it would be of no use to seek any help from King Harald again; and he kept himself concealed all the autumn and the beginning of winter. He lay hid in Bergen, in the house of a priest. King Harald was also in the town, and many great people with him. Now Sigurd considered how, with his friends' help, he might take the king by surprise, and make an end of him. Many men took part in this design; and among them some who were King Harald's hird-men and chamberlains, but who had formerly been King Magnus's hird-men. They stood in great favour with the king, and some of them sat constantly at the king's table. On St. Lucia's day [13 December], in the evening, when they proposed to execute this treason, two men sat at the king's table talking together; and one of them said to the king, "Sire, we two table-companions submit our dispute to your judgment, having made a wager of a basket of honey to him who guesses right. I say that you will sleep this night with your Queen Ingerid; and he says that you will sleep with Tora, Guttorm's daughter."

The king answered laughing, and without suspecting in the least that there lay treachery under the question—that he who asked had lost his bet.

They knew thus where he was to be found that night; but the main guard was round the house in which most people thought the king would sleep, viz. that which the queen was in.

CHAPTER XVI. MURDER OF KING HARALD.—Sigurd Slembedegn, and some men who were in his design, came in the night to the lodging in which King Harald was sleeping; killed the watchman first; then broke open the door, and went in with drawn swords. Ivar Kolbeinson made the first attack on King Harald; and as the king had been drunk when he went to bed he slept sound, and awoke only when the men were striking at him. Then he said in his sleep, "Thou art treating me hardly, Tora." She sprang up, saying, "They are treating thee hardly who love thee less than I do." Harald was deprived of life [the night of 13 December, 1136]. The men who went in with Sigurd to the king were Ogmund, a son of Thrand Skage,

Kolbein Thorljotson of Batalder, and Erlend, an Icelander. Then Sigurd went out with his helpers, and ordered the men to be called to him who had promised him their support if he should get King Harald taken out of the way. Sigurd and his men then went on, and took a boat, set themselves to the oars, and rowed out in front of the king's house; and then it was just beginning to be daylight. Then Sigurd stood up, spoke to those who were standing on the king's pier, made known to them the murder of King Harald by his hand, and desired that they would take him, and choose him as chief according to his birth. Now came many swarming down to the pier from the king's house; and all with one voice replied, that they would never give obedience or service to a man who had murdered his own brother. "And if thou art not his brother, thou hast no claim from descent to be king." They clashed their weapons together, and adjudged all murderers to be banished and outlawed men. Now the king's horn sounded, and all lendermen and hird-men were called together. Sigurd and his comrades saw it was best for them to get away; and he went northward to North Horda-land, where he held a Thing with the bonder, who submitted to him, and gave him the title of king. From thence he went to Sogn, and held a Thing there with the bonder, and was pro-claimed king. Then he went north and to the Fjords, and most people supported his cause. So says Ivar Ingemundson:

> On Harald's fall
> The bonder all,
> In Hord and Sogn,
> Took Magnus' son.
> The Things swore too
> They would be true
> To this new head,
> In Harald's stead.

King Harald was buried in the old Christ church.[1]

[1] i.e. the little Christ church, *vide* p. 243.

XV

THE SONS OF HARALD

[1136–67]

CHAPTER I. BEGINNING OF THE HISTORY OF THE KINGS SIGURD
AND INGE.—Queen Ingerid, and with her the lendermen and
the hird which had been with King Harald, resolved to send
a fast sailing vessel to Drontheim to make known King Harald's
death, and also to desire the Drontheim people to take King
Harald's son Sigurd for king. He was then in the north, and
was fostered by Gyrd Baardson. Queen Ingerid herself proceeded eastward immediately to Viken. Inge was the name of
her son by King Harald, and he was then fostered by Aamunde
Gyrdson, a grandson of Lagberse. When they came to Viken
a Borgar-thing[1] was immediately called together, at which
Inge, who was in the second year of his age, was chosen king.
This resolution was supported by Aamunde and Thjostolv
Aaleson, together with many other great chiefs. Now when
the tidings came north to Drontheim that King Harald was
murdered, the Drontheim people took Sigurd, King Harald's
son, who was then in his fourth year, to be the king; and at the
Öre-thing this resolution was supported by Ottar Birting, Peter
Saude-Ulvson, the brothers Guttorm of Rein and Ottar Balle
Aasolfsson, and many other great chiefs, and many other
people. Afterwards the whole nation almost submitted to the
brothers, and principally because their father was considered
holy; and the country took the oath to them, that the kingly
power should not go to any other man as long as any of King
Harald's sons was alive.

CHAPTER II. OF SIGURD SLEMBEDEGN.—Sigurd Slembedegn
sailed north around Stad; and when he came to North Möre,
he found that letters and full powers had arrived before him
from the leaders who had given in their allegiance to Harald's
sons; so that there he got no welcome or help. As Sigurd
himself had but few people with him, he resolved to go with
them to Drontheim, and seek out Magnus the Blind; for he
had already sent messages to his own friends and Magnus's

[1] i.e. the Thing at Borg, Sarpsborg, an important place fifty miles south
of Oslo on the east side of the Oslofjord.

At that time King Sigurd Haraldson was in the town, and many great men with him; so it was not easy for Sigurd Slembedegn to come there. He had with him at this time many of Magnus the Blind's friends. Now when they came to the town, they rowed up the river Nid to meet King Magnus, and fastened their land-ropes on the shore at the king's house; but were obliged to set off immediately, for all the people rose against them. They then landed in Munkholm, and took Magnus the Blind out of the cloister against the will of the monks; for he had been consecrated a monk. It is said by some that Magnus willingly went with them; although it was differently reported, in order to make his cause appear better. Sigurd, immediately after Yule [1137], went forth with his suite, expecting aid from his relatives and Magnus's friends, which they also got. Sigurd sailed with his men out of the fjord, and was joined afterwards by Bjorn Egilson, Gunnar of Gimsar, Haldor Sigurdson, Aslak Hakonson, the brothers Benedict and Eric, and also the hird which had before been with King Magnus, and many others. With this troop they went south to Möre, and down to the mouth of Raumsdal fjord. Here Sigurd and Magnus divided their forces, and Sigurd went immediately westwards across the sea. King Magnus again proceeded to the Uplands, where he expected much help and strength, and which he obtained. He remained there the winter and all the summer, and had many people with him; but King Inge proceeded against him with all his forces, and they met at a place called Minne.[1] There was a great battle, at which King Magnus had the most people. It is related that Thjostolv Aaleson carried King Inge in his belt as long as the battle lasted, and stood under the banner; but Thjostolv was hard pressed by fatigue and fighting: and it is commonly said that King Inge there got his ill health which he retained all his life afterward, so that his back was knotted into a hump, and the one leg was shorter than the other; and it was besides so infirm that he could scarcely walk as long as he lived. The defeat began to turn upon Magnus and his men; and in the front rank of his array fell Torkel, Haldor Sigurdson, Bjorn Egilson, Gunnar of Gimsar, and a great number of his men, before he himself would take to his horse and fly. So says Kolle:

Thy arrow-storm on Minna's banks
Fast thinn'd the foemen's strongest ranks;

_____

[1] At the south end of Lake Mjösen.

Thy good sword hewed the raven's feast
On Minna's banks up in the East.
Shield clashed on shield, and bucklers broke
Under thy battle-axe's stroke;
While thou, uncovered, urged the fray,
Thy shield and mail-coat thrown away.

And also this:

The king to heaven belonging [1] fled,
When thou,[2] in war's quick death-game bred,
Unmailed, shieldless, on the plain
His heavy steel-clad guards hadst slain.
The painted shield, and steel-plate mail,
Before thy fierce attack soon fail.
To Magnus, who belongs to heaven,
Was no such fame in battle given.

Magnus fled eastward to Gotland to Earl Karl, who was a
great and ambitious man. Magnus the Blind and his men
said, wherever they happened to meet with chiefs, that Norway
lay quite open to any great chieftain who would attack it; for
it might well be said there was no king in the country, and the
kingdom was only ruled by lendermen, and, among those who
had most sway, there was, from mutual jealousy, most discord.
Now Karl, being ambitious of power, listens willingly to such
speeches; collects men, and rides west to Viken, where many
people, out of fear, submit to him. When Thjostolv Aaleson
and Aamunde heard of this, they went with the men they
could get together, and took King Inge with them. They met
Earl Karl and the Gotland army eastward in Krokaskoven,[3]
where there was a great battle and a great defeat, King Inge
gaining the victory. Munan Ogmundson, Earl Karl's mother's
brother, fell there. Ogmund the father of Munan was a son
of Earl Orm Eilivson [p. 190], and Sigrid a daughter of Earl
Finn Arneson. Astrid, Ogmund's daughter, was the mother of
Earl Karl. Many others of the Gotland people fell at Krokaskoven; and the earl fled eastward through the forest. King
Inge pursued them all the way out of the kingdom; and this
expedition turned out a great disgrace to them. So says Kolle:

I must proclaim how our great lord
Coloured deep red his ice-cold sword;
And ravens played with Gotland bones,
And wolves heard Gotlanders' last groans.

---

[1] Only the first half of this verse is in the *Heimskringla*. The first line is
misinterpreted; it is in fact part of an incomplete refrain.
[2] i.e. King Inge, technically in command though only a child.
[3] In Saurbö (Sörbygden) in Bohuslen.

Their silly jests were well repaid—
In Kroka-skov their laugh was laid:
Thy battle power was then well tried,
And they who won may now deride.

CHAPTER III. KING ERIC'S EXPEDITION TO NORWAY.—
Magnus the Blind then went to Denmark to King Eric Eimune,
where he was well received. He offered to follow the king if
he would invade Norway with a Danish army, and subdue the
country; saying, that if he came to Norway with his army, no
man in Norway would venture to throw a spear against him.
The king allowed himself to be moved by Magnus's persuasions,
ordered a levy, and went north to Norway with 600 [720]
ships; and Magnus and his men were with him on this expedition. When they came to Viken, they proceeded peacefully
and gently on the east side of the fjord; but when the fleet
came westward to Tunsberg, a great number of King Inge's
lendermen came against them. Their leader was Vatn-Orm
Dagson, a brother of Gregorius. The Danes could not land to
get water without many of them being killed; and therefore
they went in through the fjord to Oslo, where Thjostolv Aaleson
opposed them. It is told that some people wanted to carry the
Holy Halvard's coffin [1] out of the town in the evening when the
fleet was first observed, and as many as could took hold of it;
but the coffin became so heavy that they could not carry it over
the church floor. The morning after, however, when they saw
the fleet sailing in past Hovedöen, four men carried the coffin
out of the town, and Thjostolv and all the townspeople followed
it. It was carried to Fors in Raumarike, and was kept there
three months.

CHAPTER IV. THE TOWN OF OSLO BURNT.—King Eric and
his army advanced against the town; and when Thjostolv made
a halt outside, Eric's men hastened after Thjostolv and his
troop; and one of the king's forecastle men, who was called
Askel, was the first in the pursuit. Thjostolv shot an arrow at
him, which hit him under the throat, so that the arrow point
went through his neck; and Thjostolv thought he had never
made a better arrow-shot, for, except the place he hit, there
was nothing bare to be seen. Thjostolv went up to Raumarike,
and collected men during the night, with whom he returned
towards the town in the morning. In the meantime King Eric
set fire to Halvard's church, and to the town, which was entirely
burnt. Thjostolv came soon after to the town with the men

[1] Halvard (ob. 15 May, 1044) was placed in a shrine in the cathedral at
Oslo (Halvard's Kirke).

he had assembled, and Eric sailed off with his fleet; but could not land anywhere on that side of the fjord, on account of the troops of the lendermen who came down against them; and wherever they attempted a landing, they left five or six men or more upon the strand. King Inge, and his foster-father Aamunde Gyrdson, came with a great number of people into Hornboresund,[1] where they fought with King Eric, and killed many of his men; but he fled, and turned about southwards to Denmark again. King Inge pursued him, and took from him all the ships he could get hold of; and it was a common observation among people, that never was so poor an expedition made with so great an armament in another king's dominions. King Eric was ill pleased at it, and thought King Magnus and his men had been making a fool of him by encouraging him to undertake this expedition, and he declared he would never again be such friends with them as before.

CHAPTER V. OF SIGURD SLEMBEDEGN.—Now we shall continue the account of Harald's sons and Sigurd Slembedegn, according to what has been told us by a wise and well-informed man, Eric Oddsson; and this relation was written down from lenderman Hakon Mage, who was present himself, and related these events when they were first taken down. Both he and his sons were in all these expeditions and all these battles, and knew perfectly all about the other expeditions.

Sigurd Slembedegn came that summer from the West sea to Norway, where he heard of his relative King Magnus's unlucky expedition; so he expected no welcome in Norway, but sailed south, outside the skerries, past the land, and set over to Denmark, and went into Öre Sound. He fell in with some Vendland cutters south of Erre,[2] gave them battle, and gained the victory. He cleared eight ships, killing many of the men, and he hanged the others.

[Sigurd fluttered about for some time in the South countries, as he knew there was no help for him in Norway, on account of the people of Drontheim and of Möre. So says Ivar:

> The king from the West
> Was by slander oppress'd:
> In Drontheim and Möre
> His party was bare;
> And the bonder combined,
> From prejudiced mind,
> Against Magnus's son,
> Who all good people won.

---

[1] Either Hamburgsund in Ranrike or Homborsund in East Agder.
[2] Ærö, south of Fyen.

He tells also that when Sigurd withdrew from Norway he came to the Swedish king's dominions:

> On the thundering wave
> The king's men brave
> Stay-ropes make fast,
> 'Gainst the wild sea-blast;
> Close-reef the sail,
> The water bale;
> And brisk the yards swing,
> While sea and sky ring.
>
> By the cold white crest
> Of the waves oppressed,
> The ship scuds fast
> In the wild sea-blast.
> The king's men save
> Their ship from the wave,
> And on Kalmar strand
> Their brave king land.

Then he came to the kingdom of the Danish king, where he made many of the principal people at the court his friends, and the king himself among the first; as is here related:

> He who stains red
> The claw and head
> Of the eagle race,
> Won Eric's grace.]

He also had a battle off Möen with the Vendland men, and gained a victory. He then sailed from the south, and came to the eastern arm of the Gotha river, and took three ships of the fleet of Tore Hvinantorde, and Olaf the son of Harald Kesja, who was Sigurd's own sister's son; for Ragnhild, the mother of Olaf, was a daughter of King Magnus Barefoot. He drove Olaf up the country. So says Ivar:

> King Sigurd sought,
> In fray hard fought
> At Gotha strand,
> His father's land.
> The arrows flew—
> His spearmen slew;
> And many gave way
> On each side that day.

Tore was at this time in Konghelle, and had collected people to defend the country, and Sigurd steered thither with his fleet. They shot at each other, but he could not effect a landing; and, on both sides, many were killed and many wounded. Ulfheden Saxolvsson, Sigurd's forecastle-man, fell there. He was an Icelander, from the north quarter. Sigurd continued his course northwards to Viken, and plundered far and wide around.

Now when Sigurd lay in a harbour called Portyria on Lungard's coast,[1] and watched the ships going to or coming from Viken to plunder them, the Tunsberg men collected an armed force against him, and came unexpectedly upon them while Sigurd and his men were on shore dividing their booty. Some of the men came down from the land, but some of the other party laid themselves with their ships right across the harbour outside of them. Many of Sigurd's men fell there, among whom were Finn Geit and Aslak Smidsson; but Sigurd ran up into his ship, and rowed out against them. Vatn-Orm's ship was the nearest, and he let his ship fall behind the line, and Sigurd rowed clear past, and thus escaped with one ship and the loss of many men. This verse was made upon Vatn-Orm [2]:

The water-serpent, people say,
From Portyria slipped away.

CHAPTER VI. THE MURDER OF BENTEIN [1138].—Sigurd Slembedegn sailed from thence to Denmark; and at that time a man was lost in his ship, whose name was Kolbein Thorljotson of Batalder [3] in Hadaland. He was sitting in a boat which was made fast to the vessel, and upset because she was sailing quickly. When they came south to Denmark, Sigurd's ship itself was cast away; but he got to Aalborg, and was there in winter. The summer after, Magnus and Sigurd sailed together from the south with seven ships, and came unexpectedly in the night to Lister, where they laid their ships on the land. Bentein Kolbeinson, a hird-man of King Inge, and a very brave man, was there. Sigurd and his men jumped on shore at daylight, came unexpectedly on the people, surrounded the house, and were setting fire to the buildings; but Bentein went out to a storehouse with his weapons, well armed, and stood within the door with drawn sword, his shield before him, helmet on, and ready to defend himself. The door was somewhat low. Sigurd asked which of his lads had most desire to go in against Bentein, which he called brave man's work; but none was very hurried to make ready for it. Bentein, who heard what was spoken, said, "Whoever of you comes shall find weapons in his way." It was dark in the store-room, and he stood in the door with

[1] Now Portör, near Kragerö. The coast about Lyngör was called Lungardssida.
[2] His name means Water-Serpent, which could also be used as a *kenning* for ship. In the original, however, the verse says only: "Vatn-Orm did not behave well in the battle at Portyria."
[3] One of those who was at the murder of King Harald Gille. The island, now Batalden, is in Sunnfjord.

drawn sword. Sigurd stood a little way from the door; and observing that nobody was very ready to attack, he took his grey wool coat and wound it around his arm, drew his sword, and went up to the house. He was in his shirt, and had nothing upon his head. He rushed into the house, quick as an arrow, past Bentein. Bentein struck at him, but missed him. Sigurd turned instantly on Bentein; and after exchanging blows Sigurd gave him his death-stroke, and came out presently bearing his head in his hands. [From this it may be seen what a sharp, quick, and brave man he was. Ivar tells of it thus:

> Past Agder steering,
> The East Ness clearing,
> At Lister meet
> Brave Sigurd's fleet.
> His men on shore
> The land drive o'er:
> Where houses stood
> Stands smoking wood.
>
> On the dotted plain
> Lie the owners slain.
> Red is the sky;
> All people fly.
> To the forest side
> Men run to hide;
> But Bentein stood,
> And they spilt his blood.]

They took all the goods that were in the farmhouse, carried the booty to their ships, and sailed away. When King Inge and his friends, and also Kolbein's sons Sigurd and Gyrd the brothers of Bentein, heard of Bentein's murder, the king sent a great force against Sigurd Slembedegn and his followers; and also travelled himself, and took a ship from Hakon Paulson Pungelta, who was a daughter's son of Aslak a son of Erling Skjalgson of Sole, and cousin of Hakon Mage. King Inge drove Hakon and his followers up the country, and took all their gear. Sigurd Stork, a son of Eindride of Gautdal,[1] and his brother Eric Hæl, and Andreas Kelduskit, son of Grim of Ord,[2] all fled away into the fjords. But Sigurd Slembedegn, Magnus the Blind, and Torleiv Skjappa, sailed outside the isles with five ships north to Halogaland; and Magnus was in winter north in Bjarkö with Vidkunn Jonsson. But Sigurd had the stem and stern-post of his ship cut out, made a hole in her, and sank her in the inner part of Egisfjord,[3] and thereafter he

---

[1] Now Guddal in Kvinherred.
[2] Ord, error for Vist (now Viste in north Jæderen).
[3] Now Ögsfjord on the south of Hinnö.

passed the winter at Tjaldasund by Glufrafjord. Far up the fjord there is a cave in the rock: in that place Sigurd sat with his followers, who were above twenty men, secretly, and hung a grey cloth before the mouth of the hole, so that no person could see them from the strand. Torleiv Skjappa and Einar son of Ogmund of Sand, and of Gudrun daughter of Einar Areson of Reykjahol, procured food for Sigurd during the winter. It is said that Sigurd made the Laplanders construct two boats for him during the winter up in the fjord; and they were fastened together with deer sinews, without nails, and with withes of willow instead of knees, and each boat could carry twelve men. Sigurd was with the Laplanders while they were making the boats; and the Laplanders had good ale, with which they entertained Sigurd. Sigurd made these lines on it:

> In the Lapland tent
> Brave days we spent,
> Under the grey birch tree;
> In bed or on bank
> We knew no rank,
> And a merry crew were we.

> Good ale went round
> As we sat on the ground,
> Under the grey birch tree;
> And up with the smoke
> Flew laugh and joke,
> And a merry crew were we.

These boats were so light that no ship could overtake them in the water, according to what was sung at the time [1139]:

> Our skin-sewed Fin-boats lightly swim,
> Over the sea like wind they skim.
> Our ships are built without a nail;
> Few ships like ours can row or sail.

In spring Sigurd and Magnus went south along the coast with the boats which the Laplanders had made; and when they came to Vaagar [1] they killed Svein the priest and his two sons.

CHAPTER VII. OF SIGURD SLEMBEDEGN'S CAMPAIGN.—Thereafter Sigurd came to Vikar,[2] and seized King Sigurd's lenderman, William Skinner, and Toralde Kept and killed them both. Then Sigurd turned southwards along the coast, and met Styrkar Glæserova south of Byrda,[3] as he was coming from the south from Kaupangen, and killed him. Now when Sigurd came south to Valsnes, he met Svinegrim outside of the ness, and cut

---

[1] Now Vaagan in Lofoten. [2] Vik in Brönö, Helgeland.
[3] Börö between Namdalen and Nordmöre.

off his right hand. From thence he went south to Möre, past the mouth of the Drontheim fjord, where they took Heden Haardmaga and Kalf Kringle-Öie. They let Heden escape, but killed Kalf. When King Sigurd, and his foster-father Saade-Gyrd, heard of Sigurd Slembedegn's proceedings, and what he was doing, they sent people to search for him; and their leader was Jon Kada, a son of Kalf Vrange, Bishop Ivar's[1] brother, and besides the priest Jon Smyrel. They went on board the ship Reindeer which had twenty-two rowing-benches, and was one of the swiftest sailing vessels, to seek Sigurd; but as they could not find him, they returned northwards with little glory: for people said that they had got sight of Sigurd and his people, and durst not attack them. Afterwards Sigurd proceeded southwards along the coast, doing much mischief everywhere. He went south to Hordaland, and came to Herdla, where Einar a son of Laxe-Paal had a farm; and he was in Hamar's fjord, at the Gangdage-thing.[2] They took all the goods that were at the farm, and a long-ship of twenty-five benches which belonged to Einar; and also his son, four years old, who was living with one of his labouring people. Some wanted to kill the boy, but others took him and carried him with them. The labouring man said, "It will not be lucky for you to kill the child; and it will be of no use to you to carry him away, for he is my son, and not Einar's." And on his word they let the boy remain, and went away. When Einar came home he gave the labourer money to the value of two öre of gold,[3] thanked him for his clever invention, and promised him his constant friendship. So says Eric Oddsson, who first wrote down this narrative; and he heard himself Einar Paalsson telling these circumstances in Bergen. Sigurd then went southward along the coast all the way east to Viken, and met Finn Saude-Ulvson east at Kvilder,[4] as he was engaged in drawing in King Inge's rents and duties, and hanged him. Then they sailed south to Denmark.

CHAPTER VIII. OF KING INGE'S LETTER TO KING SIGURD.— The people of Viken and of Bergen complained that it was wrong for King Sigurd and his friends to be sitting quietly north in Kaupangen, while his father's murderer was cruising

---

[1] Bishop of Nidaros, 1140–50.
[2] Gangdage-thing—a Thing held in the procession days of the Ascension Week, two weeks before Whitsuntide. In 1139 Ascension Day fell on 1 June.
[3] Two öre (ounces) of gold equalled two marks (one pound) of silver.
[4] Kville in north Bohuslen.

about in the ordinary passage at the mouth of the Drontheim fjord; and King Inge and his people, on the other hand, were in Viken in the midst of the danger, defending the country and fighting many battles. Then King Inge sent a letter north to Kaupangen, in which were these words: "King Inge Haraldsson sends his brother King Sigurd, as also Saade-Gyrd, Ogmund Svifte, Ottar Birting, and all lendermen, hird-men, house-people, and all the public, rich and poor, young and old, his own and God's salutation. The misfortune is known to all men that on account of our childhood—thou being but five, and I but three years of age—we can undertake nothing without the counsel of our friends and other good men. Now I and my men think that we stand nearer to the danger and necessity common to us both, than thou and thy friends; therefore make it so that thou, as soon as possible, come to me, and as strong in troops as possible, that we may be assembled to meet whatever may come. He will be our best friend who does all he can that we may be united, and may take an equal part in all things. But if thou refuse, and wilt not come after this message which I send thee in need, as thou hast done before, then thou must expect that I will come against thee with an armament: and let God decide between us; for we are not in a condition to sit here at so great an expense, and with so numerous a body of troops as are necessary here on account of the enemy, and besides many other pressing charges, while thou hast half the land-tax and other revenues of Norway. Live in the peace of God!"

CHAPTER IX. OTTAR BIRTING'S SPEECH.—Then Ottar Birting stood up in the Thing, and first of all answered thus: "This is King Sigurd's reply to his brother King Inge—that God will reward him for his good salutation, and likewise for the trouble and burden which he and his friends have in this kingdom, and in matters of necessity which affect them both. Although now some think there is something sharp in King Inge's message to his brother Sigurd, yet he has in many respects sufficient cause for it. Now I will make known to you my opinion, and we will hear if King Sigurd and the other people of power will agree to it; and it is, that thou, King Sigurd, make thyself ready, with all the people who will follow thee, to defend thy country; and go as strong in men as possible to thy brother King Inge as soon as thou art prepared, in order to assist each other in all things that are for the common good: and may God Almighty strengthen and assist you both! Now, king, we will have thy words."

Peter, a son of Saude-Ulf, who was afterwards called Peter Byrde-Svein, bore King Sigurd to the Thing. Then the king said, "Ye must know that, if I am to advise, I will go as soon as possible to my brother King Inge." Then others spoke, one after the other; but although each began his speech in his own way, he ended with agreeing to what Ottar Birting had proposed; and it was determined to call together the war forces, and go to the east part of the country. King Sigurd accordingly went with a great armament east to Viken, and there he met his brother King Inge.

CHAPTER X. BATTLE AT HOLMENGRAA.—The same autumn Sigurd Slembedegn and Magnus the Blind came from Denmark with thirty ships, manned both with Danes and Northmen. It was in mid October. When the kings heard of this, they set out with their people eastwards to meet them. They met at the Hvaler, near the Grey Holm,[1] the day after Martinmas, which was a Sunday [12 November, 1139]. King Inge and King Sigurd had twenty ships, which were all large. There was a great battle; but, after the first assault, the Danes fled home to Denmark with eighteen ships. On this Sigurd's and Magnus's ships were cleared; and as the last was almost entirely bare of men, and Magnus was lying in his bed, Reidar Grjotgaardson, who had long followed him, and been his hird-man, took King Magnus in his arms, and tried to run with him on board some other ship. But Reidar was struck by a spear, which went between his shoulders; and people say King Magnus was killed by the same spear. Reidar fell backwards upon the deck, and Magnus upon him; and every man spoke of how honourably he had followed his master and rightful sovereign. Happy are they who have such praise! There fell, on King Magnus's ship, Loden Saupprud of Linusted, Berse Thormodsson, who was forecastle-man to Sigurd Slembedegn, Ivar Kolbeinson and Halvard Fæge, who had been in Sigurd Slembedegn's forehold. This Ivar had been the first who had gone in, in the night, to King Harald, and had laid hands on him. There fell a great number of the men of King Magnus and Sigurd Slembedegn, for Inge's men let not a single one escape if they got hold of him, although I only name a few here. They killed upon a holm more than sixty men, among whom were two Icelanders —the priest Sigurd Bergthorson, a grandson of Maar; the other Clemet, a son of Are Einarsson.

In the battle was Ivar Skrauthank,[2] a son of Kalf Vrange,

---

[1] One of the Hvaler, islands off Smaalenene.   [2] Cf. p. 350, note 1.

and who afterwards was bishop of Drontheim, and was father of the archbishop Eric.[1] Ivar had always followed King Magnus, and he escaped into his brother Jon Kada's ship. Jon was married to Cecilia, a daughter of Gyrd Baardson, and was then in King Inge's and Sigurd's armament. There were three in all who escaped on board of Jon's ship. The second was Arnbjorn Ambe, who afterwards married Torstein's daughter in Audsholt: the third was Ivar Dynte, a son of Starre, but on the mother's side of a Drontheim family—a very agreeable man. When the troops came to know that these three were on board his ship, they took their weapons and assaulted the vessel, and some blows were exchanged, and the whole fleet had nearly come to a fight among themselves; but it came to an agreement, so that Jon ransomed his brother Ivar and Arnbjorn for a fixed sum in ransom, which, however, was afterwards remitted. But Ivar Dynte was taken to the shore, and beheaded; for Sigurd and Gyrd, the sons of Kolbein, would not take any mulct for him, as they knew he had been at their brother Bentein's murder. Ivar the bishop said, that never was there anything that touched him so nearly, as Ivar's going to the shore under the axe, having first kissed them with the wish that they might meet in joy hereafter. Gudrid Birge's daughter, a sister of Archbishop Jon,[2] told Eric Oddsson that she heard Bishop Ivar say this.

CHAPTER XI. SIGURD SLEMBEDEGN TAKEN PRISONER.—A man called Thrand Gjaldkere was master of one of King Inge's ships. It was come so far, that Inge's men were rowing in small boats between the ships after those who were swimming in the water, and killed those they could get hold of. Sigurd Slembedegn threw himself overboard after his ship had lost her crew, stripped off his armour under the water, and then swam with his shield over him. Some men from Thrand's vessel took prisoner a man who was swimming, and were about to kill him; but he begged his life, and offered to tell them where Sigurd Slembedegn was, and they agreed to it. Shields and spears, dead men, weapons, and clothes, were floating all round on the sea about the ships. "Ye can see," said he, "a red shield floating on the water: he is under it." They rowed to it immediately, took him, and brought him on board of Thrand's ship. Thrand then sent a message to Thjostolv, Ottar, Aamunde, and Gyrd. Sigurd Slembedegn had a tinder-box on him,

---

[1] Archbishop, 1188–1205 (*ob.* 1213).
[2] Archbishop, 1152–7; had previously been bishop in Stavanger.

and the tinder was in a walnut-shell, around which there was wax. This is related, because it seems an ingenious way of preserving it from ever getting wet. He swam with a shield over him, because nobody could know one shield from another where so many were floating about; and they would never have hit upon him, if they had not been told where he was. When Thrand came to the land with Sigurd, and it was told to the troops that he was taken, the army set up a shout of joy. When Sigurd heard it he said, "Many a bad man will rejoice over my head this day." Then Thjostolv Aaleson went to where Sigurd was sitting, struck from his head a silk hat edged with a gold band, and said, "Why wert thou so impudent, thou son of a slave! to dare to call thyself King Magnus Barefoot's son?"

Sigurd replied, "Presume not to compare my father to a slave; for thy father was of little worth compared to mine."

Hall, a son of the doctor Thorgeir Steinson, King Inge's hird-man, was present at this circumstance, and told it to Eric Oddsson, who afterwards wrote these accounts in a book, which he called "Back Pieces." In this book is told all concerning Harald Gille and his sons, and Magnus the Blind, and Sigurd Slembedegn, until their deaths. Eric was a sensible man, who was long in Norway about that time. Some of his narratives he wrote down from Hakon Mage's account. He was one of the lendermen of Harald's sons; and Hakon and his sons were in all this feud, and in all the councils. Eric names, moreover, several men of understanding and veracity, who told him these accounts, and were so near that they saw or heard all that happened. Something he wrote from what he himself had heard or seen.

CHAPTER XII. TORTURES OF SIGURD SLEMBEDEGN.—Hall says that the chiefs wished to have Sigurd killed instantly; but the men who were the most cruel, and thought they had injuries to avenge, advised torturing him; and for this they named Bentein's brothers, Sigurd and Gyrd the sons of Kolbein. Peter Byrde-Svein would also avenge his brother Finn. But the chiefs and the greater part of the people went away. They broke his shin-bones and arms with an axe-hammer. Then they stripped him, and would flay him alive; but when they tried to take off the skin, they could not do it for the gush of blood. They took leather whips and flogged him so long, that the skin was as much taken off as if he had been flayed. Then they stuck a piece of wood in his back until it broke, dragged him to a tree and hanged him; and then cut off his head, and brought the body and head to a heap of stones and buried them there. All acknowledge, both enemies and friends, that no man in Norway, within memory of the living, was more gifted with all perfections, or more experienced, than Sigurd; but in some respects he was an unlucky man. Hall says that he spoke little, and answered only a few, and in single words, under his tortures, although they spoke to him. Hall says further, that he never moved when they tortured him, more than if they were striking a stock or a stone. This Hall alleged as a proof that he was a brave hero, who had courage to endure tortures; for he still held his tongue, and never moved from the spot. And farther, he says that he never altered his voice in the least, but spoke with as much ease as if he was sitting at the ale-table; neither speaking higher nor lower, nor in a more tremulous voice than he was used to do. He spoke until he gave up the ghost, and sang between whiles a third part of the Psalter, which Hall considered beyond the powers and strength of ordinary men. And the priest who had the church in the neighbourhood let Sigurd's body be transported thither to the church. This priest was a friend of Harald's sons; but when they heard it they were angry at him, had the body carried back to where it had been, and made the priest pay a fine. Sigurd's friends afterwards came from Denmark with a ship for his body, carried it to Aalborg, and interred it in Mary church in that town. So said Dean Ketel, who officiated as priest at Mary church, to Eric; and that Sigurd was buried there. Thjostolv Aaleson transported Magnus the Blind's body to Oslo, and buried it in Halvard's church, beside King Sigurd his father. Loden Saupprud, Thorleiv Brynjolfson, and Kolbein were transported to Tunsberg; but the others of the slain were buried on the spot.

CHAPTER XIII. EYSTEIN HARALDSON AND MAGNUS HARALDSON [1142].—When the kings Sigurd and Inge had ruled over Norway about six years, Eystein, who was a son of Harald Gille, came in spring from Scotland. Arne Sturleson, Thorleiv Brynjolfson, and Kolbein Ruge had sailed westward over the sea after Eystein, accompanied him to Norway, and sailed immediately with him to Drontheim. The Drontheim people received him well; and at the Öre-thing[1] of Ascension-day he was chosen king, so that he should have the third part of Norway with his brothers Sigurd and Inge. They were at this

[1] Held on the Rogation Days of Ascension Week (25–7 May, 1142).

time in the east part of the country; and men went between the
kings who brought about a peace, and that Eystein should have
a third part of the kingdom.   People believed what he said of
his paternal descent, because King Harald himself had testified
to it.   King Eystein's mother was called Bjadauk, and she
accompanied him to Norway.   Magnus was the name of King
Harald Gille's fourth son, who was fostered by Orm Kyrping.
He also was chosen king, and got a fourth part of the country;
but Magnus was deformed in his feet, lived but a short time,
and died in his bed.   Einar Skuleson speaks of him:

> The generous Eystein money gave;
> Sigurd in fight was quick and brave;
> Inge loved well the war-alarm;
> Magnus to save his land from harm.
> No country boasts a nobler race
> The battle-field, or Thing, to grace.
> Four brothers of such high pretence
> The sun ne'er shone upon at once.

CHAPTER XIV. MURDER OF OTTAR BIRTING.—After King
Harald Gille's death, Queen Ingerid married Ottar Birting,
who was a lenderman and a great chief, and of a Drontheim
family, who strengthened King Inge's government much while
he was in his childhood.   King Sigurd was not very friendly
to Ottar; because, as he thought, Ottar always took King
Inge's side.   Ottar Birting was killed north in Kaupangen, in
an assault upon him in the twilight as he was going to even-
song.   When he heard the whistling of the blow he held up
his cloak with his hands against it; thinking, no doubt, it was
a snowball thrown at him, as young boys do in the streets.
Ottar fell by the stroke; but his son, Alv Rode, who just at the
same moment was coming into the churchyard, saw his father's
fall, and saw that the man who had killed him ran east about
the church.   Alv ran after him, and killed him at the corner
of the chancel; and people said that he had good luck in avenging
his father, and afterwards was much more respected than he
had been before.

CHAPTER XV. OF KING EYSTEIN HARALDSON.—King Eystein
Haraldson was in the interior of the Drontheim district when
he heard of Ottar's murder, and summoned to him the bonder-
army, with which he proceeded to the town; and he had many
men.   Ottar's relatives and other friends accused King Sigurd.
who was in the town, of having instigated this deed; and the
bonder were much enraged against him.   But the king offered
to clear himself by the ordeal of iron, and thereby to establish

the truth of his denial; and accordingly a peace was made. King Sigurd went to the south end of the country, and the ordeal was never afterwards heard of.

CHAPTER XVI. OF ORM THE KING-BROTHER.—Queen Ingerid had a son to Ivar Sneis, and he was called Orm, and got the surname of King-brother. He was a handsome man in appearance, and became a great chief, as shall be told hereafter. Ingerid afterwards married Arne of Stodreim,[1] who was from this called King-consort; and their children were Inge, Nicolas,[2] Philip of Herdla,[3] and Margaret, who was first married to Bjorn Buk, and afterwards to Simon Kaareson.

CHAPTER XVII. JOURNEY OF ERLING SKAKKE AND EARL ROGNVALD TO FOREIGN PARTS.—Orm Kyrping, and Ragnhild a daughter of Sveinke Steinarson, had a son called Erling. Orm Kyrping was a son of Svein Sveinson, who was a son of Erlend of Gerde. Earl Orm's mother was Ragnhild, a daughter of Earl Hakon the Great. Erling was a man of understanding, and a great friend of King Inge, by whose assistance and counsel Erling obtained in marriage Christina, a daughter of King Sigurd the Crusader and Queen Malmfrid. Erling possessed a farm at Studla [now Stöle] in South Hordaland. Erling left the country [1150]; and with him went Eindride Unge and several lendermen, who had chosen men with them. They intended to make a pilgrimage to Jerusalem, and went across the West sea to Orkney. There Earl Rognvald and Bishop William[4] joined them; and they had in all fifteen ships from Orkney, with which they first sailed to the South Hebudes, from thence west to Valland, and then the same way King Sigurd the Crusader had sailed to Nörvasund; and they plundered all round in the heathen part of Spain. Soon after they had sailed through the Nörvasund, Eindride Unge and his followers, with six ships, separated from them; and then each was for himself. Earl Rognvald and Erling Skakke fell in with a large ship of burden at sea called a dromund,[5] and gave battle to it with nine ships. At last they laid their cutters close under the dromund; but the heathens threw both weapons

---

[1] Now Staareim in Eid, Nordfjord.

[2] Afterwards Bishop of Oslo, 1190–1225.

[3] Philip fell in 1180 against Sverre.

[4] Bishop of the Orkneys from 1112, or perhaps from 1102, until his death in 1168

[5] Dromund was the name of a large class of merchant vessels in use in the Mediterranean in the Middle Ages, although the word was also used of warships. The word is ultimately derived from Greek *dromon*, runner, and probably came into Norse from French or Anglo-Norman.

and stones, and pots full of pitch and boiling oil. Erling laid
his ship so close under the dromund, that the missiles of the
heathens fell beyond his ship. Then Erling and his men cut
a hole in the dromund, some working below and some above
the water-mark; and so they boarded the vessel through it. So
says Thorbjorn Skakkescald. in his poem on Erling:

> The axes of the Northmen bold
> A door into the huge ship's hold
> Hewed through her high and curved side,
> As snug beneath her bulge they ride.
> Their spears bring down the astonished foe,
> Who cannot see from whence the blow.
> The eagle's prey, they, man by man,
> Fall by the Northmen's daring plan.

Audun Rode, Erling's forecastle-man, was the first man who
got into the dromund. Then they carried her, killing an immense number of people; making an extraordinarily valuable
booty, and gaining a famous victory. Earl Rognvald and
Erling Skakke came to Palestine in the course of their expedition, and all the way to the river Jordan. From thence they
went first to Constantinople, where they left their ships, travelled
northwards by land, and arrived in safety in Norway, where
their journey was highly praised. Erling appeared now a much
greater man than before, both on account of his journey and of
his marriage; besides he was a prudent sensible man, rich, of
great family, eloquent, and devoted to King Inge by the
strictest friendship more than to the other royal brothers.

CHAPTER XVIII. BIRTH OF HAKON HERDEBREID.—King
Sigurd went to a feast east in Viken along with his court, and
rode past a house belonging to a great bonde called Simon.
While the king was riding past the house, he heard within
such beautiful singing that he was quite enchanted with it,
and rode up to the house, and saw a girl singing at work at
the handmill and grinding. The king got off his horse, and
went to the girl and courted her. When the king went away,
the bonde Simon came to know what the object of the king's
visit had been. The girl was called Tora, and she was Simon
the bonde's servant-girl. Simon took good care of her afterwards, and the girl brought forth a male child, who was called
Hakon, and was considered King Sigurd's son. Hakon was
brought up by Simon Torbergson and his wife Gunhild. Their
own sons also, named Onund and Andreas, were brought up
with Hakon, and were so dear to him that death only could
have parted them.

CHAPTER XIX. OF EYSTEIN AND THE PEASANTS OF HISINGEN.
—While King Eystein Haraldson was in Viken, he fell into
disputes with the bonder of Ræne[1] and the inhabitants of
Hisingen, who assembled to oppose him; but he gave them battle
at a place called Leikberg,[2] and afterwards burnt and destroyed
all around in Hisingen; so that the bonder submitted to his
will, paid great fines to the king, and he took hostages from
them. So says Einar Skuleson:

> The Viken men
> Won't strive again,
> With words or blows
> The king to oppose.
> None safety found
> On Viken's ground,
> Till all, afraid,
> Pledge and scatt paid.

And further:

> The king came near;
> He who is dear
> To all good men
> Came down the glen,
> By Leikberg hill.
> They who do ill,
> The Ræne folk, fly,
> Or quarter cry.

CHAPTER XX. THE WAR EXPEDITION OF KING EYSTEIN
HARALDSON.—Soon after, King Eystein began his journey out
of the country over sea to the West, and sailed first to Caithness. Here he heard that Earl Harald Maddad's son was in
Thurso, to which he sailed directly in three small boats. The
earl had a ship of thirty banks of oars, and nearly eighty men
in her. But they were not prepared to make resistance, so
that King Eystein was able to board the ship with his men;
and he took the earl prisoner, and carried him to his own ship,
but the earl ransomed himself with three marks of gold: and
thus they parted. Einar Skuleson tells of it thus:

> Earl Harald in his stout ship lay
> On the bright sand in Thurso bay;
> With fourscore men he had no fear,
> Nor thought the Norse king was so near.
> He who provides the eagle's meals
> In three small boats along-shore steals;
> And Maddad's son must ransom pay
> For his bad outlook that fair day.

From thence King Eystein sailed south along the east side
of Scotland, and brought up at a merchant town in Scotland

---

[1] The inhabitants of Ranrike.   [2] This place has not been located.

called Apardjon,[1] where he killed many people, and plundered the town. So says Einar Skuleson:

> At Apardjon, too, I am told,
> Fell many by our Norsemen bold;
> Peace was disturbed, and blue swords broke
> With many a hard and bloody stroke.

The next battle was at Hjartapoll[2] in the south, with a party of horsemen. The king put them to flight, and seized some ships there. So says Einar:

> At Hjartapoll, in rank and row,
> The king's court-men attack the foe.
> The king's sharp sword in blood was red,
> Blood dropped from every Norse spear-head
> Ravens rejoice o'er the warm food
> Of English slain, each where he stood;
> And in the ships their thirst was quenched:
> The decks were in the foe's blood drenched.

Then he went southwards to England,[3] and had his third battle at Whitby, and gained the victory, and burned the town. So says Einar:

> The ring of swords, the clash of shields,
> Were loud in Whitby's peaceful fields;
> For here the king stirred up the strife—
> Man against man, for death or life.
> O'er roof and tower, rose on high
> The red wrath-fire in the sky:
> House after house the red fiend burns;
> By blackened walls the poor man mourns.

Thereafter he plundered wide around in England, where Stephen[4] was then the king. After this King Eystein fought with some cavalry at Skarpa-sker.[5] So says Einar:

> At Skarpa-sker the English horse
> Retire before the Norse king's force:
> The arrow-shower like snow-drift flew,
> And the shield-covered foemen slew.

---

[1] Aberdeen.
[2] Hartlepool.
[3] The king is stated to have gone south to England from Hartlepool. As explained in previous notes the England of these sagas did not include the country north of the Tees.
[4] Icelandic annals place this attack in 1151; it could not have been earlier, cf. *Libellus de . . . Beati Cuthberti virtutibus* (Surtees Society, 1835), pp. 65–6; *Symeonis monachi opera* (Rolls Series 75, 1882–5), I, xl–xli. Stephen reigned from 1135 to October 1154.
[5] This place is unknown.

He fought next at Pilavik,[1] and gained the victory. So says Einar:

> At Pilavik the wild wolf feeds,
> Well furnished by the king's brave deeds:
> He poured upon the grass-green plain
> A red shower from the Perthmen [2] slain.
> On westward to the sea he urges,
> With fire and sword the country purges:
> Langtown he burns; the country rang,
> For sword on shield incessant clang.

Here they burnt Langatun,[3] a large town; and people say that the town has never since risen to its former condition. After this King Eystein left England in autumn, and returned to Norway. People spoke in various ways about this expedition.

CHAPTER XXI. OF HARALD'S SONS.—There was good peace maintained in Norway in the first years of the government of Harald's sons; and as long as their old counsellors were alive, there was some kind of unanimity among them. While Inge and Sigurd were in their childhood, they had a hird together; but Eystein, who was come to age of discretion, had a hird for himself. But when Inge's and Sigurd's counsellors were dead—namely, Saade-Gyrd Baardson, Ottar Birting, Aamunde Gyrdson, Thjostolv Aaleson, Ogmund Svifte, and Ogmund Dengir, brother of Erling Skakke (Erling was not much looked up to while Ogmund lived)—the two kings Inge and Sigurd divided their hirds. King Inge then got great assistance from Gregorius Dagson, a son of Dag Eilivson by Ragnhild a daughter of Skofte Ogmundsson. Gregorius had much property, and was himself a thriving, sagacious man. He presided in the governing the country under King Inge, and the king allowed him to manage his property for him according to his own judgment.

CHAPTER XXII. OF THE HABITS AND MANNERS OF HARALD'S SONS.—When King Sigurd grew up he was a very ungovernable, restless man in every way; and so was King Eystein, but Eystein was the more reasonable of the two. King Sigurd was a stout and strong man, of a brisk appearance; he had light brown hair, an ugly mouth; but otherwise a well-shaped

---

[1] Pilavik is not known, unless it be Welwick or Balivick, two places situated near the Spurn Head; or it may be Filey Bay, south of Scarborough. (There is no evidence to support these suggestions.)
[2] The word translated Perthmen is *Partar* in the original (it occurs again in a verse by Sigvat, see *Olaf Sagas*, p. 126, where it is translated "porters"). Who they were is unknown—certainly not men from Perth.
[3] The place has not been certainly identified; Langton is a fairly common place-name in England.

countenance. He was polite in his conversation beyond any man, and was expert in all eloquence. Einar Skuleson speaks of this:

> Sigurd, expert in every way
> To wield the sword in bloody fray,
> Showed well that to the bold and brave
> God always luck and vict'ry gave.
> In speech, as well as bloody deeds,
> The king all other men exceeds;
> And when he speaks we think that none
> Has said a word but he alone.

King Eystein was dark and dingy in complexion, of middle height, and a prudent able man; but what deprived him of consideration and popularity with those under him were his avarice and narrowness. He was married to Ragna, a daughter of Nicolas Maase. King Inge was the handsomest among them in countenance. He had yellow but rather thin hair, which was much curled. His stature was small; and he had difficulty in walking alone, because he had one foot withered, and he had a hump both on his back and his breast. He was of cheerful conversation, and friendly towards his friends; was generous and allowed other chiefs to give him counsel in governing the country. He was popular, therefore, with the public; and all this brought the kingdom and the mass of the people on his side.

King Harald Gille's daughter Brigitta was first [1] married to the Swedish king Inge Halsteinson, and afterwards to Earl Karl of Gotland, and then to the Swedish king Magnus. He and King Inge Haraldson were children of the same mother. At last Brigitta married Earl Birger Brose,[2] and they had four sons; namely, Earl Philip,[3] Earl Canute, Folke, and Magnus. Their daughters were Ingigerd, who was married to the Swedish king Sörkve,[4] and their son was King Jon [5]; a second daughter was called Christina, and a third Margaret. Harald Gille's second daughter was called Maria, who was married to Simon Skaalp, a son of Halkel Huk; and their son was called Nicolas. King Harald Gille's third daughter was called Margaret, who was married to Jon Halkelson, a brother of Simon. Now many things occurred between the brothers which occasioned

---

[1] These two marriages are not historic. King Inge died about 1124 and Earl Karl is not mentioned after 1137, whilst Brigitta was a mere child in 1136.

[2] Earl in Sweden, 1170; ob. 1202.

[3] Earl in Norway with King Sverre and fell in 1200.

[4] King in Sweden, 1195–1210.

[5] King, 1216–22.

differences and disputes; but I will only relate what appears to me to have produced the more important events.

CHAPTER XXIII. CARDINAL NICOLAS COMES TO THE COUNTRY [1152].—In the days of Harald's sons Cardinal Nicolas came from Rome to Norway, being sent there by the pope. The cardinal had taken offence at the brothers Sigurd and Eystein, and they were obliged to come to a reconciliation with him; but, on the other hand, he stood on the most affectionate terms with King Inge, whom he called his son. Now when they were all reconciled with him, he moved them to let Jon Birgerson be consecrated archbishop of Drontheim, and gave him a vestment which is called a pallium; and settled moreover that the archbishop's seat should be in Nidaros, in Christ church, where King Olaf the Saint reposes. Before that time there had only been suffragan bishops in Norway. The cardinal introduced also the law, that no man should go unpunished who appeared with arms in the merchant town, excepting the twelve men who were in attendance on the king. He improved many of the customs of the Northmen while he was in the country. There never came a foreigner to Norway whom all men respected so highly, or who could govern the people so well as he did. After some time he returned to the South [1] with many friendly presents, and declared ever afterwards that he was the greatest friend of the people of Norway. When he came south to Rome the former pope [2] died suddenly, and all the people of Rome would have Cardinal Nicolas for pope, and he was consecrated under the name of Adrian; and according to the report of men who went to Rome in his days, he had never any business, however important, to settle with other people, but he would break it off to speak with the Northmen who desired to see him. He was not long pope, and is now considered a saint. [3]

CHAPTER XXIV. MIRACLE OF KING OLAF.—In the time of Harald Gille's sons, it happened that a man called Haldor fell into the hands of the Vendland people, who took him and mutilated him, cut open his neck, took out the tongue through the opening, and cut out his tongue-root. He afterwards sought out the holy King Olaf, fixed his mind entirely on the holy man, and weeping besought King Olaf to restore his speech and

[1] Snorri evidently did not know that the cardinal went from Norway to Sweden first and then returned to the south.
[2] Anastasius IV died 3 December, 1154
[3] This was the Englishman, Nicholas Breakspear, born soon after 1100, abbot of St. Rufus Abbey (Avignon), 1137; Pope as Adrian IV, 1154-9.

health. Thereupon he immediately recovered his speech by the good king's compassion, went immediately into his service for all his life, and became an excellent and devout man. This miracle took place a fortnight before the last Olaf's mass upon the day [20 July, 1152] that Cardinal Nicolas set foot on the land of Norway.

CHAPTER XXV. MIRACLE OF KING OLAF ON RICHARD.—In the Uplands were two brothers, men of great family, and men of fortune, Einar and Andreas, sons of Guttorm Graabard, and brothers of King Sigurd Haraldson's mother; and they had great properties and udal estates in that quarter. They had a sister who was very handsome, but did not pay sufficient regard to the scandal of evil persons, as it afterwards appeared. She was on a friendly footing with an English priest called Richard, whose lodging was at the house of her brothers, and on account of their friendship for him she did many things to please him, and often to his advantage; but the end of all this was, that an ugly report flew about concerning this girl. When this came into the mouth of the public, all men threw the blame on the priest. Her brothers did the same, and expressed publicly, as soon as they observed it, that they laid the blame most on him. The great friendship that was between the girl and the priest proved a great misfortune to both, which might have been expected, as the brothers were silent about their secret determination, and let nothing be observed. But one day they called the priest to them, who went, expecting nothing but good from them; enticed him from home with them, saying that they intended to go to another district, where they had some needful business, and inviting him to go with them. They had with them a farm-servant who knew their purpose. They went in a boat along the shore of a lake which is called Randsfjord, and landed at a ness called Skiftesand,[1] where they went on shore, and amused themselves a while. Then they went to a retired place, and commanded their servant-man to strike the priest with an axe-hammer. He struck the priest so hard that he swooned; but when he recovered he said, "Why are ye playing so roughly with me?" They replied, "Although nobody has told thee of it before, thou shalt now find the consequence of what thou hast done." They then upbraided him; but he denied their accusations, and besought God and the holy King Olaf to judge between them. Then they broke his leg-bones, and dragged him bound to the forest with them;

[1] This place has not been located.

and then they put a string around his head, and put a board under his head and shoulders, and made a knot on the string, and bound his head fast to the board. Then the elder brother, Einar, took a wedge, and put it on the priest's eye, and the servant who stood beside him struck upon it with an axe, so that the eye flew out, and fell upon his beard. Then he set the pin upon the other eye, and said to the servant, "Strike now more softly." He did so, and the wedge sprang from the eye-stone, and tore the eyelid loose. Then Einar took up the eyelid in his hand, and saw that the eye-stone was still in its place; and he set the wedge on the cheek, and when the servant struck it the eye-stone sprang out upon the cheek-bone. Thereafter they opened his mouth, took his tongue and cut it off, and then untied his hands and his head. As soon as he came to himself, he thought of laying the eye-stones in their place under the eyelids, and pressing them with both hands as much as he could. Then they carried him on board, and went to a farm called Sæheimrud,[1] where they landed. They sent up to the farm to say that a priest was lying in the boat at the shore. While the message was going to the farm, they asked the priest if he could talk; and he made a noise, and attempted to speak. Then said Einar to his brother, "If he recover and the stump of his tongue grow, I am afraid he will get his speech again." Thereupon they seized the stump with a pair of tongs, drew it out, cut it twice, and the third time to the very roots, and left him lying half dead. The housewife in the farm was poor; but she hastened to the place with her daughter, and they carried the priest home to their farm in their cloaks. They then brought a priest, and when he arrived he bound all his wounds; and they attended to his comfort as much as they were able. And thus lay the wounded priest grievously handled, but trusting alway to God's grace, and never doubting; and although he was speechless, he prayed to God in thought with a sorrowful mind, but with the more confidence the worse he was. He turned his thoughts also to the mild King Olaf the Saint, God's dear favourite, of whose excellent deeds he had heard so much told, and trusted so much more zealously on him with all his heart for help in his necessity. As he lay there lame, and deprived of all strength, he wept bitterly, moaned, and prayed with a sore heart that the dear King Olaf would help him. Now when this wounded priest was sleeping after midnight, he thought he saw a gallant man

[1] Called Askeims herad (Hadeland) in the *Passio et miracula beati Olavi*.

coming to him, who spoke these words, "Thou art ill off, friend Richard, and thy strength is little." He thought he replied to this assentingly. Then the man accosted him again, "Thou requirest compassion?" The priest replies, "I need the compassion of Almighty God and the holy King Olaf." He answered, "Thou shalt get it." Thereupon he pulled the tongue-stump so hard that it gave the priest pain; then he stroked with his hands his eyes, and legs, and other wounded members. Then the priest asked who he was. He looked at him, and said, "Olaf, come. here from Drontheim"; and then disappeared. But the priest awoke altogether sound, and thus he spoke: "Happy am I, and thanks be to the Almighty God and the holy King Olaf, who have restored me!" Dreadfully mishandled as he had been, yet so quickly was he restored from his misfortune that he scarcely thought he had been wounded or sick. His tongue was entire; both his eyes were in their places, and were clear-sighted; his broken legs and every other wound were healed, or were free from pain; and, in short, he had got perfect health. But as a proof that his eyes had been punched out, there remained a white scar on each eyelid, in order that this dear king's excellence might be manifest on the man who had been so dreadfully misused.

CHAPTER XXVI. THE KINGS INGE AND SIGURD HOLD A THING IN THE HOLM [1154–5].—King Eystein and King Sigurd had quarrelled, because King Sigurd had killed King Eystein's hirdman Harald, the Viken man, who owned a house in Bergen, and also the priest Jon Tabard, son of Bjarne Sigurdson. On account of this affair, a conference to settle it was appointed in winter in the Uplands. The two sat together in the conference for a long time, and so much was known of their conference that all the three brothers were to meet the following summer in Bergen. It was added, that their conference was to the effect that King Inge should have two or three farms, and as much income as would keep thirty men beside him, as he had not health to be a king. When King Inge and Gregorius heard this report, they came to Bergen with many followers. King Sigurd arrived there a little later, and was not nearly so strong in men. Sigurd and Inge had then been nineteen years kings of Norway. King Eystein came later still from the south than the other two from the north. Then King Inge ordered the Thing to be called together at Holmen [1] by sound of trumpet; and Sigurd and Inge came to it with a great many people.

[1] Now Bergenhus.

Gregorius had two long-ships, and at the least ninety men, whom he kept in provisions. He kept his house-men better than other lendermen; for he never took part in any entertainment where each guest brings his liquor, without having all his house-men to drink with him. He went now to the Thing in a gold-mounted helmet, and all his men had helmets on. Then King Inge stood up, and told the assembly what he had heard; how his brothers were going to use him, and depose him from his kingdom; and asked for their assistance. The assembled people made a good return to his speech, and declared they would follow him.

CHAPTER XXVII. OF GREGORIUS DAGSON. — Then King Sigurd stood up and said, it was a false accusation that King Inge had made against him and his brother, and insisted that Gregorius had invented it; and insinuated that it would not be long, if he had his will, before they should meet so that the golden helmet should be doffed; and ended his speech by hinting that they could not both live. Gregorius replied, that Sigurd need not long so much for this, as he was ready now, if it must be so. A few days after, one of Gregorius's house-men was killed out upon the street,[1] and it was Sigurd's house-men who killed him. Gregorius would then have fallen upon King Sigurd and his people; but King Inge, and many others, kept him back. But one evening, just as Queen Ingerid, King Inge's mother, was coming from vespers, she came past where Sigurd Skrudhyrne, a hird-man of King Inge, lay murdered. He was then an old man, and had served many kings. King Sigurd's hird-men, Halvard Gunnarson, and Sigurd a son of Eystein Travala, had killed him; and people suspected it was done by order of King Sigurd. She went immediately to King Inge, and told him he would be a little king if he took no concern, but allowed his hird-men to be killed, the one after the other, like swine. The king was angry at her speech; and while they were scolding about it, came Gregorius in helmet and armour, and told the king not to be angry, for the queen only spoke the truth. "And I am now," says he, "come to thy assistance, if thou wilt attack King Sigurd; and here we are, above a hundred men in helmets and armour, and with them we will attack where others think the attack may be worst." But the most dissuaded from this course, thinking that Sigurd would pay the mulct for the slaughter done. Now when Gregorius saw that there would be no assault, he accosted King

[1] Övregate.

Inge thus: "They are plucking thy men from thee in this way; for first they lately killed my house-man, and now thy hird-man, and afterwards they will chase me, or some other of thy lendermen whom thou wouldst feel the loss of, when they see that thou art indifferent about such things; and at last, after thy friends are killed, they will take the royal dignity from thee. Whatever thy other lendermen may do, I will not stay here longer to be slaughtered like an ox; but Sigurd the king and I have a business to settle with each other to-night, in whatever way it may turn out. It is true that there is but little help in thee on account of thy ill-health, but I also believe that thou hast little will to hold thy hand over thy friends, and I am now quite ready to go from hence to meet Sigurd, and my banner is flying in the yard."

Then King Inge stood up, and called for his arms, and ordered every man who wished to follow him to get ready, declaring it was of no use to try to dissuade him; for he had long enough avoided this, but now steel must determine between them.

CHAPTER XXVIII. OF KING SIGURD'S FALL.—King Sigurd sat and drank in Sigrid Sæte's house ready for battle, although people thought it would not come to an assault at all. Then came King Inge with his men down the road from the smithy shops against the house. Arne, King Inge's stepfather, came out from the Sand-bridge,[1] Aslak Erlendsson from his own house, and Gregorius from the street [Övregate] where all thought the assault would be worst. King Sigurd and his men made many shots from the holes in the loft, broke down the fire-places, and threw stones on them. Gregorius and his men cut down the gates of the yard; and there in the port fell Einar, a son of Laxe Paal, who was of Sigurd's people, together with Halvard Gunnarson, who was shot in a loft, and nobody lamented his death. They hewed down the houses, and many of King Sigurd's men left him, and surrendered for quarter. Then King Sigurd went up into a loft, and desired to be heard. He had a gilt shield, by which they knew him; but they would not listen to him, and shot arrows at him as thick as snow in a snow-shower, so that he could not stay there. As his men had now left him, and the houses were being hewn down, he went out from thence and with his hird-man Tord Husfreya from Viken. They wanted to come where King Inge was to be found; and Sigurd called to his brother King Inge, and begged him to grant him life and safety; but both Tord and

---

[1] This bridge led from the king's meadow to Övregate.

Sigurd were instantly killed, and Tord fell with great glory. King Sigurd was interred in the old Christ church out on the Holm [Bergenhus]. King Inge gave Gregorius the ship King Sigurd had owned. There fell many of King Sigurd's and King Inge's men, although I only name a few; but of Gregorius's men there fell four; and also some who belonged to no party, but were shot on the piers, or out in the ships. It was fought on a Friday [10 June, 1155], and fourteen days before Saint John the Baptist's day. Two or three days after, King Eystein came from the eastward with thirty ships, and had along with him his nephew Hakon, a son of King Sigurd. Eystein did not come up to the town, but lay in Florevaag, and good men went between to get a reconciliation made. But Gregorius wanted that they should go out against him, thinking there never would be a better opportunity; and offered to be himself the leader. "For thou, king, shalt not go, for we have no want of men." But many dissuaded from this course, and it came to nothing. King Eystein returned back to Viken, and King Inge to Drontheim, and they were in a sort reconciled; but they did not meet each other.

CHAPTER XXIX. OF GREGORIUS DAGSON.—Somewhat latei than King Eystein, Gregorius Dagson also set out to the eastward, and came to his farm Bratsberg in Havund[1]; but King Eystein was up in the fjord at Oslo, and had his ships drawn above two miles over the frozen sea, for there was much ice at that time in Viken. King Eystein went up to Hovund to take Gregorius; but he got news of what was on foot, and escaped to Telemark with ninety men, from thence over the Fjelds, and came down in Hardanger; and at last to Studla [now Stöle] in Etne, to Erling Skakke's farm. Erling himself had gone north to Bergen; but his wife Christina, a daughter of King Sigurd, was at home, and offered Gregorius all the assistance he wanted; and he was hospitably received. He got a long-ship there which belonged to Erling, and everything else he required. Gregorius thanked her kindly, and allowed that she had behaved nobly, and as might have been expected of her. Gregorius then proceeded to Bergen, where he met Erling, who thought also that his wife had done well.

CHAPTER XXX. RECONCILIATION OF THE KINGS EYSTEIN AND INGE.—Then Gregorius went north to Drontheim, and came there before Yule. King Inge was rejoiced at his safety, and told him to use his property as freely as his own, King Eystein

1 Now Gjerpen, to the east of the town of Skien.

having burnt Gregorius's house, and slaughtered his stock of cattle. The ship-docks which King Eystein the Elder had constructed in Kaupangen, and which had been exceedingly expensive, were also burnt this winter, together with some good vessels belonging to King Inge. This deed was ascribed to King Eystein and Philip Gyrdson, King Sigurd's foster-brother, and occasioned much displeasure and hatred. The following summer [1156] King Inge went south with a very numerous body of men; and King Eystein came northwards, gathering men also. They met in the east at the Sel Isles,[1] near to the Naze; but King Inge was by far the strongest in men. It was nearly coming to a battle; but at last they were reconciled on these conditions—that King Eystein should be bound to pay forty-five marks of gold, of which King Inge should have thirty marks, because King Eystein had occasioned the burning of the docks and ships; and, besides, that Philip, and all who had been accomplices in the deed, should be outlawed. Also that the men should be banished the country, against whom it could be proved that they gave blow or wound to King Sigurd: for King Eystein accused King Inge of protecting these men; and that Gregorius should have fifteen marks of gold for the value of his property burnt by King Eystein. King Eystein was ill pleased with these terms, and looked upon the treaty as one forced upon him. From that meeting King Inge went eastward to Viken, and King Eystein north to Drontheim; and they had no intercourse with each other, nor were the messages which passed between them very friendly, and on both sides they killed each other's friends. King Eystein, besides, did not pay the money; and the one accused the other of not fulfilling what was promised. King Inge and Gregorius enticed many people from King Eystein; among them, Baard Standale Brynjulfson, Simon Skaalp a son of Halkel Huk, Haldor Brynjulfson, Jon Halkelson, and many other lendermen.

CHAPTER XXXI. OF EYSTEIN AND INGE [1157].—Two years after King Sigurd's fall both kings assembled armaments; namely, King Inge in the east of the country, where he collected eighty ships; and King Eystein in the north, where he had forty-five, and among these the Great Dragon, which King Eystein Magnusson had built after the Long Serpent; and they had on both sides many and excellent troops. King Inge lay with his ships south at Moster Isle,[2] and King Eystein a little

---

[1] On the west of Lindesnes.
[2] Mosterö in Sunnhordland.

to the north in Gröninga Sound.[1] King Eystein sent the young Aslak Jonsson, and Arne Sturle, whose father was Sæbjorn, with one ship to meet King Inge; but when the king's men knew them they assaulted them, killed many of their people, and took all that was in the ship belonging to them. Aslak and Arne and a few more escaped to the land, went to King Eystein, and told him how King Inge had received them. Thereupon King Eystein held a House-thing, and told his followers how ill King Inge had treated his men, and desired the troops to follow him. "I have," said he, "so many, and such excellent men, that I have no intention to fly, if ye will follow me." But this speech was not received with much favour. Halkel Huk was there; but both his sons, Simon and Jon, were with King Inge. Halkel replied, so loud that many heard him, "Let thy chests of gold follow thee, and let them defend thy land."

CHAPTER XXXII. KING EYSTEIN'S DEATH.—In the night many of King Eystein's ships rowed secretly away, some of them joining King Inge, some going to Bergen, or up into the fjords; so that when it was daylight in the morning the king was lying behind with only ten ships. Then he left the Great Dragon, which was heavy to row, and several other vessels behind; and cut and destroyed the Dragon, started out the ale, and destroyed all that they could not take with them. King Eystein went on board of the ship of Eindride a son of Jon Mörnef, sailed north into Sogn, and then took the land-road eastwards to Viken. King Inge took the vessels, and sailed with them outside of the isles to Viken. King Eystein had then got to the east of Folden,[2] and had with him twelve hundred men; but when they saw King Inge's force, they did not think themselves sufficiently strong to oppose him, and they retired to the forest. Every one fled his own way, so that the king was left with but one man. King Inge and his men observed King Eystein's flight, and also that he had but few people with him, and they went immediately to search for him. Simon Skaalp met the king just as he was coming out of a willow bush. Simon saluted him. "God save you, sire,[3]" said he.

The king replied, "I do not know if thou art not sire here." Simon replied, "That is as it may happen."

The king begged him to conceal him, and said it was proper

---

[1] On the west side of the Bergen peninsula.
[2] The Oslofjord district.
[3] The word used is lávarðr (Old English hlaford, now lord).

to do so. "For there was long friendship between us, although it has now gone differently."

Simon replied, it could not be.

Then the king begged that he might hear mass before he died, which accordingly took place. Then Eystein laid himself down on his face on the grass, stretched out his hands on each side, and told them to cut the sign of the cross between his shoulders, and see whether he could not bear steel as King Inge's followers had asserted of him. Simon told the man who had to put the king to death to do so immediately, for the king had been creeping about upon the grass long enough. He was accordingly slain, and he appears to have suffered manfully. His body was carried to Fors, and lay all night under the hill at the south side of the church. King Eystein was buried in Fors church, and his grave is in the middle of the church floor, where a fringed canopy is spread over it, and he is considered a saint. Where he was executed, and his blood ran upon the ground, sprang up a fountain, and another under the hill where his body lay all night. From both these waters many think they have received a cure of sickness and pain. It is reported by the Viken people that many miracles were wrought at King Eystein's grave, until his enemies poured upon it soup made of boiled dogs' flesh. Simon Skaalp was much hated for this deed, which was generally ascribed to him; but some said that when King Eystein was taken Simon sent a message to King Inge, and the king commanded that King Eystein should not come before his face. So King Sverre has caused it to be written [1]; but Einar Skuleson tells of it thus:

> Simon Skaalp, the traitor bold,
> For deeds of murder known of old,
> His king betrayed; and ne'er will he
> God's blessed face hereafter see.

[1] In what book Sverre caused this account to be written is not known.

HAKON THE BROAD-SHOULDERED

[1157–61]

CHAPTER I. OF HAKON HERDEBREID.[1]—Hakon, King Sigurd's son, was chosen chief of the troop which had follówed King Eystein, and his adherents gave him the title of king. He was ten years old. At that time he had with him Sigurd, a son of Havard Hold of Reyr,[2] and Andreas and Onund, the sons of Simon, his foster-brothers, and many chiefs, friends of King Sigurd and King Eystein; and they went first up to Gotland. King Inge took possession of all the estates they had left behind, and declared them banished. Thereafter King Inge went to Viken, and was sometimes also in the north of the country. Gregorius Dagson was in Konghelle, where the danger was greatest, and had beside him a strong and handsome body of men, with which he defended the country.

CHAPTER II. OF GREGORIUS DAGSON [1158].—The summer after Hakon came with his men, and proceeded to Konghelle with a numerous and handsome troop. Gregorius was then in the town, and summoned the bonder and townspeople to a great Thing, at which he desired their aid; but he thought the people did not hear him with much favour, so he did not much trust them. Then Gregorius set off with two ships to Viken, and was very much cast down. He expected to meet King Inge there, having heard he was coming with a great army to Viken. Now when Gregorius had come but a short way north he met Simon Skaalp, Haldor Brynjulfson, and Gyrd Amundeson, King Inge's foster-brothers. Gregorius was much delighted at this meeting, and turned back with them, being all in one body, with eleven ships. As they were rowing up to Konghelle, Hakon, with his followers, was holding a Thing without the town, and saw their approach; and Sigurd of Reyr said; "Gregorius must be *fey* to be throwing himself with so few men into our hands." Gregorius landed opposite the town to wait for King Inge, for he was expected; but he did not

---

[1] Broad-shouldered.   [2] Reyrir, now Rör in Ringsaker, Hedemark.

come. King Hakon put himself in order in the town, and appointed Torljot Skavescale, who was a viking and a robber, to be captain of the men in the merchant ships that were afloat in the river; and King Hakon and Sigurd were within the town, and drew up the men on the piers, for all the townspeople had submitted to King Hakon.

CHAPTER III. KING HAKON'S FLIGHT.—Gregorius rowed up the river, and let the ships drive down with the stream against Torljot. They shot at each other a while, until Torljot and his comrades jumped overboard; and some of them were killed, some escaped to the land. Then Gregorius rowed to the piers, and let gangways be cast on shore at the very feet of Hakon's men. There the man who carried his banner was slain just as he was going to step on shore. Gregorius ordered Hall, a son of Audun Hallson, to take up the banner, which he did, and bore the banner up to the pier. Gregorius followed close after him, held his shield over his head, and protected him as well as himself. As soon as Gregorius came upon the pier, and Hakon's men knew him, they gave way, and made room for him on every side. Afterwards more people landed from the ships, and then Gregorius made a severe assault with his men; and Hakon's men first moved back, and then ran up into the town. Gregorius pursued them eagerly, drove them twice from the town, and killed many of them. By the report of all men, never was there so glorious an affair as this of Gregorius; for Hakon had more than 4000 [4800] men, and Gregorius not full 400 [480]. After the battle, Gregorius said to Hall Audunson, "Many men, in my opinion, are more agile in battle than ye Icelanders are, for ye are not so exercised as we Norwegians; but none, I think, are so bold under arms as ye are." King Inge came up soon after, and killed many of the men who had taken part with Hakon; made some pay heavy fines, burnt the houses of some, and some he drove out of the country, or treated otherwise very ill. Hakon fled at first up to Gotland with all his men; but the winter after he proceeded by the upper road to Drontheim, and came there before Easter [12 April, 1159]. The Drontheim people received him well, for they had always served under that shield. It is said that the Drontheim people took Hakon as king, on the terms that he should have from Inge the third part of Norway as his paternal heritage. King Inge and Gregorius were in Viken, and Gregorius wanted to make an expedition against the party in the north; but it came to nothing that winter, as many dissuaded from it.

CHAPTER IV. FALL OF GYRD AND HAVARD.—King Hakon left Drontheim in spring with thirty ships nearly; and some of his men sailed before the rest with eight ships, and plundered in North and South Möre. No man could remember that there ever before had been plundering between the two towns (Bergen and Nidaros). Jon the son of Halkel Huk collected the bonder in arms, and proceeded against them; took Kolbein Ode prisoner, and killed every woman's son of them in his ship. Then they searched for the others, found them all assembled in seven ships, and fought with them; but his father Halkel not coming to his assistance as he had promised, many good bonder were killed, and Jon himself was wounded. Hakon proceeded south to Bergen with his forces; but when he came to Stjornvellta,[1] he heard that King Inge and Gregorius had arrived a few nights before from the east at Bergen, and therefore he did not venture to steer thither. They sailed the outer course southwards past Bergen, and met three ships of King Inge's fleet, which had been outsailed on the voyage from the east. On board of them were Gyrd Amundeson, King Inge's foster-brother, who was married to Gyrid a sister of Gregorius, and also lagman Gyrd Gun-hildsson, and Haavard Klining. King Hakon had Gyrd Amundeson and Haavard Klining put to death; but took lag-man Gyrd southwards, and then proceeded east to Viken.

CHAPTER V. OF THE CONSULTATIONS OF KING INGE.—When King Inge heard of this he sailed east after them, and they met east in the Gotha river. King Inge went up the north arm of the river, and sent out spies to get news of Hakon and his fleet; but he himself landed at Hisingen, and waited for his spies. Now when the spies came back they went to the king, and said that they had seen King Hakon's forces, and all his ships which lay at the stakes in the river, and Hakon's men had bound the stems of their vessels to them. They had two great East-country trading vessels, which they had laid outside of the fleet, and on both these were built high wooden stages [top castles]. When King Inge heard the preparations they had made, he ordered a trumpet to call a House-thing of all the men; and when the Thing was seated he asked his men for counsel, and applied particularly to Gregorius Dagson, his brother-in-law Erling Skakke, and other lendermen and ship-commanders, to whom he related the preparations of Hakon and his men.

Then Gregorius Dagson replied first, and made known his

[1] An unknown place, possibly in Stadtland.

mind in the following words: "Sometimes we and Hakon have met, and generally they had the most people; but, notwithstanding, they fell short in battle against us. Now, on the other hand, we have by far the greatest force; and it will appear probable to the men who a short time ago lost gallant relatives by them, that this will be a good occasion to get vengeance, for they have fled before us the greater part of the summer; and we have often said that if they waited for us, as appears now to be the case, we would have a brush with them. Now I will tell my opinion, which is, that I will engage them, if it be agreeable to the king's pleasure; for I think it will go now as formerly, that they must give way before us if we attack them bravely; and I shall always attack where others may think it most difficult."

This speech was received with much applause, and all declared they were ready to engage in battle against Hakon. Then they rowed with all the ships up the river until they came in sight of each other, and then King Inge turned off from the river-current under the island [Hisingen]. Now the king addressed all the commanders, and told them to get ready for battle. He turned himself especially to Erling Skakke, and said, what was true, that no man in the army had more understanding and knowledge in fighting battles, although some were more hot. The king then addressed himself to several of the lendermen, speaking to them by name; and ended by desiring that each would give his opinion, and say what he thought would be of advantage, and thereafter all would act together.

CHAPTER VI. ERLING'S SPEECH.—Erling Skakke replied thus to the king's speech: "It is my duty, sire, not to be silent; and I shall give my advice, since it is desired. The resolution now adopted is contrary to my judgment; for I call it foolhardy to fight under these circumstances, although we have so many and such fine men. Supposing we make an attack on them, and row up against this river-current; then one of the three men who are in each half room [1] must be employed in rowing only, and another must be covering with the shield the man who rows; and what have we then to fight with but one third of our men? It appears to me that they can be of little use in the battle who are sitting at their oars, with their backs turned to the enemy. Give me now some time for consideration, and

[1] The whole room was apparently the space between two benches of rowers, in which the men lived; and these were divided into half rooms, viz. on the starboard and larboard sides, and the men belonged to the starboard and larboard oars of the bench.

I promise you that before three days are over I shall fall upon some plan by which we can come into battle with advantage."

It was evident from Erling's speech that he dissuaded from an attack; but, notwithstanding, it was urged by many, who thought that Hakon would now, as before, take to the land. "And then," said they, "we cannot get hold of him; but now they have but few men, and we have their fate in our own hands."

Gregorius said but little; but thought that Erling rather dissuaded from an attack that Gregorius's advice should not have effect, than that he had any better advice to give.

CHAPTER VII. OF HAKON'S FLEET.—Then said King Inge to Erling, "Now we will follow thy advice, brother, with regard to the manner of attacking; but seeing how eager our counsellors are for it, we shall make the attack this day."

Erling replied, "All the boats and light vessels we have should row outside the island, and up the east arm of the river, and then down with the stream upon them, and try if they cannot cut them loose from the piles. Then we, with the large ships, shall row from below here against them; and I cannot tell, until it be tried, if those who are now furiously warm will be much brisker at the attack than I am."

This counsel was approved by all. There was a ness stretched out between their fleet and Hakon's, so that they could not see each other. Now when Hakon and his men, who had taken counsel with each other in a meeting, saw the boat-squadron rowing down the river, some thought King Inge intended to give them battle; but many believed they did not dare, for it looked as if the attack was given up; and they, besides, were very confident, both in their preparations and men. There were many great people with Hakon: there were Sigurd of Reyr, and Simon's sons, Onund and Andreas; Nicolas Skjaldvarson; Eindride, a son of Jon Mörnef, who was the most gallant and popular man in the Drontheim country; and many other lender-men and captains. Now when they saw that King Inge's men with many ships were rowing out of the river, Hakon and his men believed they were going to fly; and therefore they cut their land-ropes with which they lay fast at the piles, seized their oars, and rowed after them in pursuit. The ships ran fast down with the stream; but when they came farther down the river, abreast of the ness, they saw King Inge's main strength lying quiet at Hisingen. King Inge's people saw Hakon's ships under way, and believed they were coming to attack them; and now there was great bustle and clash of arms, and they encouraged each other by a great war-shout. Hakon with his fleet turned northwards a little to the land, where there was a turn in the bight of the river, and where there was no current. They made ready for battle, carried land-ropes to the shore, turned the stems of their ships outwards, and bound them all together. They laid the large East-country traders without the other vessels, the one above, the other below, and bound them to the long-ships. In the middle of the fleet lay the king's ship, and next to it Sigurd's; and on the other side of the king's ship lay Nicolas, and next to him Eindride Jonson. All the smaller ships lay farther off, and they were all nearly loaded with weapons and stones.[1]

CHAPTER VIII. SIGURD OF REYR'S SPEECH.—Then Sigurd of Reyr made the following speech: "Now there is hope that the time is come which has been promised us all the summer, that we shall meet King Inge in battle. We have long prepared ourselves for this and many of our comrades have boasted that they would never flee or flinch before King Inge and Gregorius, and now let them remember their words. But we who have sometimes got the toothache in our conflicts with them, speak less confidently; for it has happened, as all have heard, that we very often have come off without glory. But, nevertheless, it is now necessary to fight manfully, and stand to it with steadiness; for that is the only way to bring victory. Although we have somewhat fewer men than they, yet luck determines which side shall have the advantage, and God knows that the right is on our side. Inge has killed two of his brothers; and it is obvious to all men that the mulct he intends to pay King Hakon for his father's murder is to murder him also, as well as his other relatives, which will be seen this day to be his intent. King Hakon desired from the beginning no more of Norway than the third part, which his father had possessed, and which was denied him; and yet, in my opinion, King Hakon has a better right to inherit after his father's brother King Eystein, than Inge or Simon Skaalp, or the other men who killed King Eystein. Many of them who would save their souls, and yet have defiled their hands with such bloody deeds as Inge has done, must think it a presumption before God that he takes the name of king; and I wonder God suffers such monstrous impudence as this:

---

[1] The importance of stones, and the enormous quantity required in the battles of those ages, form an element in the military movements of great bodies of men in the countries in which stones are scarce, not sufficiently considered by historians.

but it may be God's will that we shall now put him down. Let us fight then manfully, and God will give us victory; and, if we fall, will repay us with joys of all kinds for now allowing the might of the wicked to prevail over us. Go forth then in confidence, and be not afraid when the battle begins. Let each watch over his own and his comrade's safety, and God protect us all." There was great applause made at this speech of Sigurd, and all promised fairly, and to do their duty. King Hakon went on board of the great East-country ship, and a shield-bulwark was made around him; but his standard remained on the long-ship in which he had been before.

CHAPTER IX. OF KING INGE'S MEN.—Now must we tell about King Inge and his men. When they saw that King Hakon and his people were ready for battle, and the river only was between them, they sent a light vessel to recall the rest of the fleet which had rowed away; and in the meantime the king waited for them, and arranged the troops for the attack. Then the chiefs consulted in presence of the army, and told their opinions: first, which ships should lie nearest to the enemy; and then where each should attack.

Gregorius spoke thus: "We have many and fine men; and it is my advice, King Inge, that you do not go to the assault with us, for everything is preserved if you are safe. And no man knows where an arrow may hit, even from the hands of a bad bowman: and they have prepared themselves so, that missiles and stones can be thrown from the high stages upon the merchant ships; so the danger is little less for those who are farthest from them. They have not more men than we lendermen can very well engage with. I shall lay my ship alongside their largest ship, and I expect the conflict between us will be but short; for it has often been so in our former meetings, although there has been a much greater want of men with us than now." All thought well of the advice that the king himself should not take part in the battle.

Then Erling Skakke said, "I agree also to the counsel that you, sire, should not go into the battle. It appears to me that their preparations are such, that we require all our precaution not to suffer a great injury from them; and whole limbs are the easiest cured. In the council we held before to-day many opposed what I said, and ye said then that I did not want to fight; but now I think the business has altered its appearance, and greatly to our advantage, since they have hauled off from the piles, and now it stands so that I do not dissuade from giving battle; for I see, what all are sensible of, how necessary it is to put an end to this robber band who have gone over the whole country with pillage and destruction, in order that people may cultivate the land in peace, and serve a king so good and just as King Inge who has long had trouble and anxiety from the haughty unquiet spirit of his relatives, although he has been a shield of defence for the whole people, and has been exposed to manifold perils for the peace of the country." Erling spoke well and long, and many other chiefs also; and all to the same purpose—all urging to battle. In the meantime they waited until all the fleet should be assembled. King Inge had the ship Bökesuden[1]; and, at the entreaty of his friends, he did not join the battle, but lay still at the island.

CHAPTER X. BEGINNING OF THE BATTLE.—When the army was ready they rowed briskly against the enemy, and both sides raised a war-shout. Inge's men did not bind their ships together, but let them be loose; for they rowed right across the current, by which the large ships were much swayed. Erling Skakke laid his ship beside King Hakon's ship, and ran the stem between his and Sigurd's ship, by which the battle began. But Gregorius's ship swung upon the ground, and heeled very much over, so that at first she could not come into the battle; and when Hakon's men saw this they laid themselves against her, and attacked Gregorius's ship on all sides. Ivar, Hakon Mage's son, laid his ship so that the poops struck together; and he got a boat-hook fastened on Gregorius, on that part of his body where the waist is smallest, and dragged him to him, by which Gregorius stumbled against the ship's rails; but the hook slipped to one side, or Gregorius would have been dragged overboard. Gregorius, however, was but little wounded, for he had on a plate coat of armour. Ivar called out to him, that he had a "thick bark." Gregorius replied, that if Ivar went on so he would "require it all, and not have too much." It was very near then that Gregorius and his men had sprung overboard; but Aslak Unge threw an anchor into their ship, and dragged them off the ground. Then Gregorius laid himself against Ivar's ship, and they fought a long while; but Gregorius's ship being both higher sided and more strongly manned, many people fell in Ivar's ship, and some jumped overboard. Ivar was so severely wounded that he could not take part in the

---

[1] *Bœkisúðin,* "the beech-ship." The word *súð* (from the same root as English "sew") means "the joining of planks in a clinker-built ship"; from this it is used, as here, as a word for ship.

fight. When his ship was cleared of the men, Gregorius let
Ivar be carried to the shore, so that he might escape; and from
that time they were constant friends.

CHAPTER XI. KING HAKON'S FLIGHT.—When King Inge and
his men saw that Gregorius was aground, he encouraged his
crew to row to his assistance. "It was," he said, "the most
imprudent advice that we should remain lying here, while our
friends are in battle; for we have the largest and best ship in
all the fleet. But now I see that Gregorius, the man to whom
I owe the most, is in need of help; so we must hasten to the
fight with all fierceness. It is also most proper that I should
be in the battle; for the victory, if we win it, will belong to me.
And if I even knew beforehand that our men were not to gain
the battle, yet our place is where our friends are; for I can do
nothing if I lose the men who are justly called the defence of
the country, who are the bravest, and have long ruled for me
and my kingdom." Thereupon he ordered his banner to be set
up, which was done; and they rowed across the river. Then
the battle raged, and the king could not get room to attack, so
close lay the ships before him. First he lay under the East-
country trading ship, and from it they threw down upon his
vessel spears, iron-shod stakes, and such large stones that it
was impossible to find protection there, and he had to haul
off. Now when the king's people saw that he was come they
made place for him, and then he laid alongside of Eindride
Jonson's ship. Now King Hakon's men abandoned the small
ships, and went on board the large merchant vessels; but some
of them sprang on shore. Erling Skakke and his men had a
severe conflict. Erling himself was on the forecastle, and called
his forecastle-men, and ordered them to board the king's ship;
but they answered, this was no easy matter, for there were
beams above with an iron comb on them. Then Erling himself
went to the bow, and stayed there a while, until they succeeded
in getting on board the kings ship; and then the ship was
cleared of men on the bows, and the whole army gave way.
Many sprang into the water, many fell, but the greater number
got to the land. So says Einar Skuleson:

> Men fall upon the slippery deck—
> Men roll off from the blood-drenched wreck;
> Dead bodies float down with the stream,
> And from the shores witch-ravens scream.
> The cold blue river now runs red
> With the warm blood of warriors dead,
> And stains the waves in Karmt Sound
> With the last drops of the death-wound.

All down the stream, with unmann'd prow,
Floats many an empty long-ship now.
Ship after ship, shout after shout,
Tell that King Hakon can't hold out.
The bowmen ply their bows of elm,
The red swords flash o'er broken helm:
King Hakon's men rush to the strand,
Out of their ships, up through the land.

Einar composed a song about Gregorius Dagson, which is
called the River-song. King Inge granted life and peace to
Nicolas Skjaldvarson when his ship was cleared, and thereupon
he went into King Inge's service, and remained in it as long
as the king lived. Eindride Jonson leaped on board of King
Inge's ship when his own was cleared of men, and begged for
his life. King Inge wished to grant it; but Haavard Klining's
son ran up, and gave him a mortal wound, which was much
blamed; but he said Eindride had been the cause of his father's
death. There was much lamentation at Eindride's death, but
principally in the Drontheim district. Many of Hakon's people
fell here, but no other chiefs. Few of King Inge's people fell
but many were wounded. King Hakon fled up the country,
and King Inge went north to Viken with his troops; and he, as
well as Gregorius, remained in Viken all winter. When King
Inge's men, Bergljot and his brothers, sons of Ivar of Elda,[1]
came from the battle to Bergen, they slew Nicolas Skegg, who
had been Hakon's recorder, and then went north to Drontheim.

King Hakon came north before Yule, and Sigurd was sometimes home at Reyr; for Gregorius, who was nearly related to
Sigurd, had obtained for him life and safety from King Inge,
so that he retained all his estates. King Hakon was in Kaupangen in Yule; and one evening in the beginning of Yule his
men fought in the guard-room, and in this affray seven men were
killed, and many were wounded. The eighth day of Yule
[1160], King Hakon's man Alv Rode, son of Ottar Birting, with
about eighty men, went to Elda, and came in the night unexpectedly on the people, who were very drunk, and set fire
to the room; but they went out, and defended themselves
bravely. There fell Bergljot, Ivar's son, and Ogmund his
brother, and many more. They had been nearly thirty altogether in number. In winter died, north in the merchant
town, Andreas Simonson, King Hakon's foster-brother; and his
death was much deplored. Erling Skakke and Inge's men,
who were in Bergen, threatened that in winter they would

[1] Now Elden, between Namdal and Beitstadfjord.

proceed against Hakon and his men; but it came to nothing. Gregorius sent word from the east, from Konghelle, that if he were so near as Erling and his men, he would not sit quietly in Bergen while Hakon was killing King Inge's friends and their comrades in war up in the Drontheim country.

CHAPTER XII. THE CONFLICT UPON THE PIERS [1160].—King Inge and Gregorius left the east in spring, and came to Bergen; but as soon as Hakon and Sigurd heard that Inge had left Viken, they went there by land. When King Inge and his people came to Bergen, a quarrel arose between Haldor Brynjulfson and Bjorn Nicolasson. Bjorn's house-man asked Haldor's when they met at the pier, why he looked so pale.

He replied, because he had been bled.

"I could not look so pale if I tried, at merely being bled."

"I again think," retorted the other, "that thou wouldst have borne it worse, and less manfully." And no other beginning was there for their quarrel than this. Afterwards one word followed another, till from bawling they came to fighting. It was told to Haldor Brynjulfson, who was in the house drinking, that his house-man was wounded down on the pier, and he went there immediately. But Bjorn's house-men had come there before, and as Haldor thought his house-man had been badly treated, he went up to them and beat them; and it was told to Bjorn Buk that the people of Viken were beating his house-men on the pier. Then Bjorn and his house-men took their weapons, hurried down to the pier, and would avenge their men; and a bloody strife began. It was told Gregorius that his relative Haldor required assistance, and that his house-men were being cut down in the street; on which Gregorius and his men ran to the place in their armour. Now it was told Erling Skakke that his sister's son Bjorn was fighting with Gregorius and Haldor down on the piers, and that he needed help. Then he proceeded thither with a great force, and exhorted the people to stand by him; saying it would be a great disgrace never possible to wipe out, if one man from Vik should be able to trample on them in their native place. There fell fourteen men, of whom nine were killed on the spot, and five died of their wounds, and many were wounded. When the word came to King Inge that Gregorius and Erling were fighting down on the piers, he hastened there, and tried to separate them; but could do nothing, so mad were they on both sides. Then Gregorius called to Inge, and told him to go away; for it was in vain to attempt coming between them, as matters now stood. He said it would be the greatest misfortune if the king mixed himself up with it; for he could not be certain that there were not people in the fray who would commit some great misdeed if they had opportunity. Then King Inge retired; and when the greatest tumult was over, Gregorius and his men went to Nicolas church, and Erling behind them, calling to each other. Then King Inge came a second time, and pacified them; and both agreed that he should mediate between them.

When King Inge and Gregorius heard that King Hakon was in Viken, they went east with many ships; but when they came King Hakon fled from them, and there was no battle. Then King Inge went to Oslo, and Gregorius was in Konghelle.

CHAPTER XIII. MUNAN'S DEATH.—Soon after Gregorius heard that Hakon and his men were at a farm called Saurbö,[1] which lies up beside the forest. Gregorius hastened there; came in the night; and supposing that King Hakon and Sigurd would be in the largest of the houses, set fire to the buildings there. But Hakon and his men were in the smaller house, and came forth, seeing the fire, to help their people. There Munan fell, a son of Aale Oskeynd, a brother of King Sigurd, Hakon's father. Gregorius and his men killed him, because he was helping those whom they were burning within the house. Some escaped but many were killed. Asbjorn Jalde, who had been a very great viking, escaped from the house, but was grievously wounded. A bonde met him, and he offered the man money to let him get away; but the bonde replied, he would do what he liked best; and, adding that he had often been in fear of his life for him, he slew him. King Hakon and Sigurd escaped, but many of their people were killed. Thereafter Gregorius returned home to Konghelle. Soon after King Hakon and Sigurd went to Haldor Brynjulfson's farm of Vettaland,[2] set fire to the house, and burnt it. Haldor went out, and was cut down instantly with his house-men; and in all there were about twenty men killed. Sigrid, Haldor's wife, was a sister of Gregorius, and they allowed her to escape into the forest in her nightshift only; but they took with them Amunde, who was son of Gyrd Amundeson and Gyrid Dag's daughter, and a sister's son of Gregorius, and who was then a boy about five years old.

CHAPTER XIV. OF THE FALL OF GREGORIUS DAGSON [1161]. —When Gregorius heard the news he took it much to heart, and inquired carefully where they were. Gregorius set out from

[1] Sörbygden in Bohuslen.   [2] Wætteland in Skee, Bohuslen.

Konghelle late in Yule, and came to Fors [1] the thirteenth day of Yule [6 January], where he remained a night, and heard vespers the last day of Yule [7 January], which was a Saturday, and the holy Evangel was read before him. When Gregorius and his followers saw the men of King Hakon and Sigurd, the king's force appeared to them smaller than their own. There was a river called Befja [2] between them, where they met; and there was unsound ice on the river, for there went a stream under the ice from it. King Hakon and his men had made holes in the ice, and laid snow on top, so that nobody would know. When Gregorius came to the ice on the river the ice appeared to him unsound, he said; and he advised the people to go to the bridge, which was close by, to cross the river. The bonder-troops replied that they did not know why he should be afraid to go across the ice to attack so few people as Hakon had, and the ice was good enough. Gregorius said it was seldom necessary to encourage him to show bravery, and it should not be so now. Then he ordered them to follow him, and not to be standing on the land while he was on the ice; and he said it was their counsel to go out upon the dangerous ice, but he had no wish to do so, or to be led by them. Then he ordered the banner to be advanced, and immediately went out on the ice with the men. As soon as the bonder found that the ice was unsound, they turned back. Gregorius fell through the ice, but not very deep, and he told his men to take care. There were not more than twenty men with them, the others having turned back. A man of King Hakon's troop shot an arrow at Gregorius, which hit him under the throat, and thus ended his life. Gregorius fell, and ten men with him. It is the talk of all men that he had been the most gallant lenderman in Norway that any man then living could remember; and also he behaved the best towards us Icelanders of any chief since King Eystein the Elder's death. Gregorius's body was carried to Hovund, [3] and interred at Gimsö, in a nunnery which is there, [4] of which Gregorius's sister Baugeid was then the abbess.

CHAPTER XV. KING INGE HEARS OF GREGORIUS'S FALL.— Two bailiffs went to Oslo to bring the tidings to King Inge. When they arrived they desired to speak to the king; and he asked what news they brought.

"Gregorius Dagson's death," said they.

[1] Now Fossum, near Uddevalla.
[2] Now Bäfveraa, at the mouth of which Uddevalla lies.
[3] See p. 369, note 1.
[4] By Gimsö, near Skien.

"How came that misfortune?" asked the king.

When they had told him how it happened, he said, "They prevailed most who understood the least."

It is said he took it so much to heart that he cried like a child. When he recovered himself he said, "I wanted to go to Gregorius as soon as I heard of Haldor's murder; for I thought that Gregorius would not sit long before thinking of revenge. But the people here would think nothing so important as their Yule feasts, and nothing could move them away; and I am confident that if I had been there, he would either have proceeded more cautiously, or I and Gregorius would now have shared one lodging. Now he is gone—the man who has been my best friend, and more than any other has kept the kingdom in my hands; I thought it would be but a short space between us. Now I make an oath to go forth against Hakon, and one of two things shall happen: I shall either come to my death, or shall walk over Hakon and his people; and such a man as Gregorius is not avenged, even if all were to pay the penalty of their lives for him."

There was a man present who replied, "Ye need not seek after them, for they intend to seek you."

Christina, King Sigurd's daughter and King Inge's cousin, was then in Oslo. The king heard that she intended going away. He sent a message to her to inquire why she wished to leave the town.

She thought it was dangerous and unsafe for a female to be there.

The king would not let her go. "For if it go well with me, as I hope, you will be well here; and if I fall, my friends may not get leave to dress my body; but you can ask permission, and it will not be denied you, and you will thereby best requite what I have done for you."

CHAPTER XVI. OF KING INGE.—On Saint Blasius' day [3 Feb., 1161], in the evening, King Inge's spies brought him the news that King Hakon was coming towards the town. Then King Inge ordered the war-horns to call together all the troops up from the town; and when he drew them up he could reckon them to be nearly 4000 [4800] men. The king let the array be long, but not more than five men deep. Then some said that the king should not be himself in the battle, as they thought the risk too great; but that his brother Orm should be the leader of the army. The king replied, "I think if Gregorius were alive and here now, and I had fallen and was to be avenged, he would not lie concealed, but would be in the battle. Now, although I, on account of my ill health, am not fit for the combat as he was, yet will I show as good will as he would have had; and it is not to be thought of that I should not be in the battle."

People say that Gunhild, who was married to Simon, King Hakon's foster-father, had a witch employed to sit out[1] all night and procure the victory for Hakon; and that the answer was obtained, that they should fight King Inge by night, and never by day, and then the result would be favourable. The witch who, as people say, sat out was called Tordis Skeggia; but what truth there may be in the report I know not.

Simon Skaalp had gone to the town, and was gone to sleep, when the war-shouts awoke him. When the night was well advanced, King Inge's spies came to him, and told him that King Hakon and his army were coming over the ice[2]; for the ice lay the whole way from Oslo to Hovedöen.[3]

CHAPTER XVII. KING INGE'S SPEECH.—Thereupon King Inge went with his army out on the ice, and he drew it up in order of battle in front of the town. Simon Skaalp was in that wing of the army which was towards Trælaborg[4]; and on the other wing, which was towards the Nunnery,[5] was Gudrod, the king of the South Hebudes, a son of Olaf Klining,[6] and Jon, a son of Svein, a son of Bergthor Buk. When King Hakon and his army came near to King Inge's array, both sides raised a war-shout. Gudrod and Jon gave King Hakon and his men a sign, and let them know where they were in the line; and as

[1] At sitja úti, "to sit outside," was an expression denoting a certain kind of witchcraft. The witch went out at night to get in touch with spirits. It was a practice expressly forbidden by law.

[2] Over the Bundefjord and between the islands.

[3] The island to the south of the town.

[4] Under Ekeberg at the present Grönlien.

[5] The nunnery at Leret, now 73 Oslo Street.

[6] The Chronicle of the Kings of Man coincides with the saga. Godredus, son of Olaf king of the Hebrides, went in 1152, in the lifetime of his father, to Inge (called Hinge in the Manx Chronicle), king of Norway, to do homage for Man. His father was slain in his absence, and he returned from Norway in 1154 and was proclaimed king after his father. As he treated the chiefs of the island harshly, they joined Sumarlid, with whom after a sea-fight in 1158 he was obliged to share his kingdom; and in 1159 he was obliged to flee from Man and seek assistance from Norway. Sumarlid fell in a war with the Scottish king, and in 1164 Gudrod's sovereignty was seized by his brother Reginaldus (Rognvald). Then Gudrod returned with forces from Norway, took his brother prisoner, mutilated him and held the sovereignty until his death in 1187. From this account, derived from the Manx Chronicle, Gudrod appears to have been in Norway from 1159 to 1164. The battle described above was fought on 4 February, 1161. Gudrod's father, Olaf Klining, had ruled from 1113 to 1153. Olaf Klining was brother of King Lagmadr (Lawman), son of Gudrod, on whom see p. 262.

soon as Hakon's men in consequence turned thither, Gudrod immediately fled with 1500 [1800] men; and Jon, and a great body of men with him, ran over to King Hakon's army, and assisted them in the fight. When this news was told to King Inge, he said, "Such is the difference between my friends. Never would Gregorius have done so in his life!" There were some who advised King Inge to get on horseback, and ride from the battle up to Raumarike; "where," said they, "you would get help enough, even this very day." The king replied, he had no inclination to do so. "I have heard you often say, and I think truly, that it was of little use to my brother King Eystein that he took to flight; and yet he was a man distinguished for many qualities which adorn a king. Now I, who labour under so great decrepitude, can see how bad my fate would be, if I betook myself to what proved so unfortunate for him; with so great a difference as there is between our activity, health, and strength. I was in the second year of my age when I was chosen king of Norway, and I am now twenty-five; and I think I have had misfortune and burdens with my kingly dignity, rather than pleasure and peaceful days. I have had many battles, sometimes with more, sometimes with fewer people; and it is my greatest luck that I have never fled. God will dispose of my life, and of how long it shall be; but I shall never betake myself to flight."

CHAPTER XVIII. KING INGE'S FALL.—Now as Jon and his troops had broken the one wing of King Inge's array, many of those who were nearest to him fled, by which the whole array was dispersed, and fell into disorder. But Hakon and his men went briskly forwards; and now it was near daybreak [4 February, 1161]. An assault was made against King Inge's banner, and in this conflict King Inge fell; but his brother Orm continued the battle, while many of the army fled up into the town. Twice Orm went to the town after the king's fall to encourage the people, and both times returned, and went out again upon the ice to continue the battle. Hakon's men attacked the wing of the array which Simon Skaalp led; and in that assault fell of King Inge's men his brother-in-law, Gudbrand Skafhoggson. Simon Skaalp and Halvard Hikre went against each other with their troops, and fought while they drew aside past Trælaborg; and in this conflict both Simon and Halvard fell. Orm, the king's brother, gained great reputation in this battle; but he at last fled. Orm the winter before had been contracted with Ragna, a daughter of Nicolas Maase, who had been married before to King Eystein Haraldson; and the wedding was fixed for the Sunday [5 February] after Saint Blasius' mass, which was on a Friday. Orm fled east to Sweden, where his brother Magnus [1] was then king; and their brother Rognvald was an earl there at that time. They were the sons of Queen Ingerid and Henrik Halte,[2] who was a son of the Danish king Svein Sveinson. The princess Christina took care of King Inge's body, which was laid in the stone wall of Halvard's church, on the south side without the choir. He had then been king for twenty-five years. In this battle many fell on both sides, but principally of King Inge's men. Of King Inge's people fell Arne Fredrikson. Hakon's men took all the feast and victuals prepared for the wedding, and a great booty besides.

CHAPTER XIX. OF KING HAKON AND QUEEN CHRISTINA.— Then King Hakon took possession of the whole country, and distributed all the offices among his own friends, both in the towns and in the country. King Hakon had meetings with his men in Halvard's church, where they had private conferences concerning the management of the country. Christina the princess gave the priest who kept the church keys a large sum of money to conceal one of her men in the church, so that she might know what Hakon and his counsellors intended. When she learnt what they had said, she sent a man to Bergen to her husband Erling Skakke, with a message that he should never trust Hakon or his men.

CHAPTER XX. OF KING OLAF'S MIRACLE IN FAVOUR OF THE VÆRINGER OF CONSTANTINOPLE.—It happened once in the Greek country, when Kirialax was emperor there, that he made an expedition against Blökumannaland.[3] When he came to the Petzina plains,[4] a heathen king came against him with an innumerable host. He brought with him many horsemen, and many large wagons, in which were large loop-holes for shooting through. When they prepared for their night quarters they drew up their wagons, one by the side of the other, without their tents, and dug a great ditch without; all which made a defence as strong as a castle. The heathen king was blind. Now when the Greek king came, the heathens drew up their array on the plains before their wagon-fortification. The

---

[1] Magnus Henrikson was king in Sweden, 1160–1.

[2] Henrik Halte (ob. 1134) had been the husband of Ingerid before she married Harald Gille.

[3] The land of the Blökumenn, who were the inhabitants of Wallachia (modern Rumania), Greek Blachoi.

[4] The plains of the Pechenegs, a tribe on the lower Danube.

Greeks drew up their array opposite, and they rode on both sides to fight with each other; but it went on so ill and so unfortunately, that the Greeks were compelled to fly after suffering a great defeat, and the heathens gained a victory. Then the king drew up an array of Franks and Flemings, who rode against the heathens, and fought with them; but it went with them as with the others, that many were killed, and all who escaped took to flight. Then the Greek king was greatly incensed at his men-at-arms; and they replied, that he should now take his wine-bags, the Væringer.[1] The king says that he would not throw away his jewels, and allow so few men, however bold they might be, to attack so vast an army. Then Tore Helsing, who at that time was leader of the Væringer, replied to the king's words, "If there was burning fire in the way, I and my people would run into it, if I knew the king's advantage required it." Then the king replied, "Call upon your holy King Olaf for help and strength." The Væringer, who were 450 [540] men, made a vow with hand and word to build a church in Constantinople, at their own expense and with the aid of other good men, and have the church consecrated to the honour and glory of the holy King Olaf; and thereupon the Væringer rushed into the plain. When the heathens saw them, they told their king that there was another troop of the Greek king's army come out upon the plain; but they were only a handful of people. The king says, "Who is that venerable man riding on a white horse at the head of the troop?" They replied, "We do not see him." There was so great a difference of numbers, that there were sixty heathens for every Christian man; but notwithstanding the Væringer went boldly to the attack. As soon as they met, terror and alarm seized the army of the heathens, and they instantly began to fly; but the Væringer pursued, and soon killed a great number of them. When the Greeks and Franks who before had fled from the heathens saw this, they hastened to take part, and pursue the enemy with the others. Then the Væringer had reached the wagon-fortification, where the greatest defeat was given to the enemy. The heathen king was taken in the flight of his people, and the Væringer brought him along with them; after which the Christians took the camp of the heathens, and their wagon-fortification.

CHAPTER XXI. OF OLAF'S MIRACLE.—It happened at the battle of Stiklestad, as before related,[2] that King Olaf threw

---

[1] This miracle is misplaced. It belongs to the reign of Alexios I Comnenos, 1081–1118.   [2] *Olaf Sagas*, p. 375.

from him the sword called Neite when he received his wound
A Swedish man, who had broken his own sword, took it up,
and fought with it. When this man escaped with the other
fugitives he came to Sweden, and went home to his house.
From that time he kept the sword all his days, and afterwards
his son, and so relative after relative; and when the sword
shifted its owner, the one told to the other the name of the
sword, and where it came from. A long time after, in the
days of Kirialax the emperor of Constantinople, when there
was a great body of Væringer in the royal castle, it happened
in the summer that the emperor was on a campaign, and lay
in the camp with his army. The Væringer who had the guard,
and watched over the emperor, lay on the open plain without
the camp. They changed the watch with each other in the
night, and those who had been before on watch lay down and
slept; but all completely armed. It was their custom, when
they went to sleep, that each should have his helmet on his
head, his shield over him, sword under the head, and the right
hand on the sword-handle. One of these comrades, whose lot
it was to watch the latter part of the night, found, on awaking
towards morning, that his sword was gone. He looked after
it, and saw it lying on the flat plain at a distance from him.
He got up and took the sword, thinking that his comrades who
had been on watch had taken the sword from him in a joke;
but they all denied it. The same thing happened three nights.
Then he wondered at it, as well as they who saw or heard of it;
and people began to ask him how it could have happened. He
said that this sword was called Neite, and had belonged to King
Olaf the Saint, who had himself carried it in the battle of
Stiklestad; and he also related how the sword since that time
had gone from one to another. This was told to the emperor,
who called the man before him to whom the sword belonged,
and gave him three times as much gold as the sword was worth;
and the sword itself he had laid in Saint Olaf's church, which
the Væringer supported, where it has been ever since over the
altar. There was a lenderman of Norway while Harald Gille's
sons, Eystein, Inge, and Sigurd, lived, who was called Eindride
Unge; and he was in Constantinople when these events took
place. He told these circumstances in Norway, according to
what Einar Skuleson says in his song about King Olaf the
Saint, in which these events are sung.

XVII

MAGNUS ERLINGSON[1]

CHAPTER I. OF MAGNUS ERLINGSON'S BEGINNING. — When
Erling got certain intelligence of the determinations of Hakon
and his counsellors, he sent a message to all the chiefs who,
he knew, had been steady friends of King Inge, and also to his
hird-men and his retinue, who had saved themselves by flight,
and also to all Gregorius's house-men, and called them together
to a meeting. When they met, and conversed with each other,
they resolved to keep their men together; and this resolution
they confirmed by oath and hand-shake to each other. Then
they considered whom they should take to be king. Erling
Skakke first spoke, and inquired if it was the opinion of the
chiefs and other men of power that Simon Skaalp's son, the
son of the daughter of King Harald Gille, should be chosen
king, and Jon Halkelson be taken to lead the army; but Jon
refused it. Then it was inquired if Nicolas Skjaldvorson, a
sister's son of King Magnus Barefoot, would place himself at
the head of the army; but he answered thus: It was his opinion
that some one should be chosen king who was of the royal
race; and, for leader of the troops, some one from whom help
and understanding were to be looked for; and then it would
be easier to gather an army. It was now tried whether Arne
would let any of his sons, King Inge's brothers, be proclaimed
king. Arne replies, that Christina's son, as she was daughter
of King Sigurd the Crusader, was nearest by propinquity of
descent to the crown of Norway. "And here is also a man to
be his adviser, and whose duty it is to take care of him and
of the kingdom; and that man is his father Erling, who is both
prudent, brave, experienced in war, and an able man in governing the kingdom: he wants no capability of bringing this
counsel into effect, if luck be with him." Many thought well
of this advice.

Erling replied to it, "As far as I can see or hear in this

[1] From about 1162 to 1177, when the *Heimskringla* ends; King Magnus
Erlingsson did not die until 1184.

meeting, the most will rather be excused from taking upon themselves such a difficult business. Now it appears to me altogether uncertain, provided we begin this work, whether he who puts himself at the head of it will gain any honour; or whether matters will go as they have done before when any one undertakes such great things—that he loses all his property, and possibly his life. But if this counsel be adopted, there may be men who will undertake to carry it through; but he who comes under such an obligation must seek, in every way, to prevent any opposition or enmity from those who are now in this council."

All gave assurance that they would enter into this confederacy with perfect fidelity. Then said Erling, "I can say for myself that it would almost be my death to serve King Hakon; and however dangerous it may be, I will rather venture to adopt your advice, and take upon me to lead this force, if that be the will, counsel, and desire of you all, and if you will all bind yourselves to this agreement by oath."

To this they all agreed; and in this meeting it was determined to take Erling's son Magnus to be king. They afterwards held a Thing in the town; and at this Thing Magnus Erlingson, then five years old, was elected king of the whole country. All who had been servants of King Inge went into his service, and each of them retained the office and dignity he had held under King Inge.

CHAPTER II. KING MAGNUS GOES TO DENMARK. — Erling Skakke made himself ready to travel, fitted out ships, and had with him King Magnus, together with the household-men who were on the spot. In this expedition were the king's relatives— Arne; Ingerid, King Inge's mother, with her two sons; besides Jon Kutissa, a son of Sigurd Stork, and Erling's house-men, as well as those who had been Gregorius's house-men; and they had in all ten ships. They went south to Denmark to King Valdemar and Buris Henrikson, King Inge's brother. King Valdemar was King Magnus's blood-relation; for Ingeborg mother of King Valdemar, and Malmfrid mother of Christina, King Magnus's mother, were sisters. The Danish king received them hospitably, and he and Erling had private meetings and consultations; and so much was known of their counsels, that King Valdemar was to aid King Magnus with such help as might be required from his kingdom, to win and retain Norway. On the other hand, King Valdemar should get that domain in Norway which his ancestors Harald Gormson and Svein Forkbeard had possessed; namely, the whole of Viken as far north as Rygiarbit.[1] This agreement was confirmed by oath and a fixed treaty. Then Erling and King Magnus made themselves ready to leave Denmark, and they sailed out of Skagen.[2]

CHAPTER III. BATTLE OF TUNSBERG.—King Hakon went in spring, after the Easter week [16 April, 1161], north to Drontheim, and had with him the whole fleet that had belonged to King Inge. He held a Thing there in Kaupangen, and was chosen king of the whole country. Then he made Sigurd of Reyr an earl,' and gave him an earldom, and afterwards proceeded southwards with his followers all the way to Viken. The king went to Tunsberg; but sent Earl Sigurd east to Konghelle, to defend the country with a part of the forces in case Erling should come from the south. Erling and his fleet came to Agder, and went straight north to Bergen, where they killed Arne Brigdar-scalle, King Hakon's officer, and came back immediately against King Hakon. Earl Sigurd, who had not observed the journey of Erling and his followers from the south, was at that time east in the Gotha river, and King Hakon was in Tunsberg. Erling brought up at Rossaness,[3] and lay there some nights. In the meantime King Hakon made preparations in the town. When Erling and his fleet were coming up to the town, they took a merchant vessel, filled it with wood and straw, and set fire to it; and the wind blowing right towards the town, drove the vessel against the piers. Erling had two cables brought on board the vessel, and made fast to two boats, and made them row along as the vessel drove. Now when the fire was come almost abreast of the town, those who were in the boats held back the vessel by the ropes, so that the town could not be set on fire; but so thick a smoke spread from it over the town, that one could not see from the piers where the king's array was. Then Erling drew the whole fleet in where the wind carried the fire, and shot at the enemy. When the townspeople saw that the fire was approaching their houses, and many were wounded by the bowmen, they resolved to send the priest Roald Long-speech to Erling, to beg him to spare them and the town; and they dissolved their array, as soon as Roald told them their prayer 'was granted. Now when the array of the townspeople had dispersed, the men on the piers were much thinned: however, some urged Hakon's men to make

[1] Now Jernestang, between Nedenes and Bratsberg.
[2] The northernmost tip of Jutland.
[3] The north point of Nöterö off Ramberg.

resistance; but Onund Simonson, who had most influence over the army, said, "I will not fight for Earl Sigurd's earldom, since he is not here himself." Then Onund fled, and was followed by all the people, and by the king himself; and they hastened up the country. King Hakon lost many men here; and these verses were made about it:

> Onund declares he will not go
> In battle 'gainst Earl Sigurd's foe,
> If Earl Sigurd does not come,
> But with his house-men sits at home.
> King Magnus' men rush up the street,
> Eager with Hakon's troop to meet;
> But Hakon's war-hawks, somewhat shy,
> Turn quick about, and off they fly.

Thorbjorn Skakke-scald also said:

> The Tunsberg men would not be slow
> In thy good cause to risk a blow;
> And well they knew the chief could stain
> The wolves' mouths on a battle-plain.
> But the town champion rather fears
> The sharp bright glance of levelled spears;
> Their steel-clad warrior loves no fight
> Where bowstring twangs, or fire flies bright.

King Hakon then took the land-road northwards to Drontheim. When Earl Sigurd heard of this, he proceeded with all the ships he could get the sea-way northwards, to meet King Hakon there.

CHAPTER IV. OF ERLING AND HAKON.—Erling Skakke took all the ships in Tunsberg belonging to King Hakon, and there he also took the Bökesuden which had belonged to King Inge. Then Erling proceeded, and reduced the whole of Viken in obedience to King Magnus, and also the whole country north wheresoever he appeared up to Bergen, where he remained all winter. There Erling killed Ingebjorn Sipel, King Hakon's lenderman, in the north part of the Fjords district. In winter King Hakon was in Drontheim; but in the following spring he ordered a levy, and prepared to go against Erling [1162]. He had with him Earl Sigurd, Jon Sveinson, Eindride Unge, Onund Simonson, Philip Peterson, Philip Gyrdson, Ragnvald Kunta, Sigurd Kaapa, Sigurd Hjupa, Frederik Köna, Askel of Forland, Thorbjorn, a son of Gunnar the Recorder, and Strad-Bjarne.

CHAPTER V. OF ERLING'S PEOPLE.—Erling was in Bergen with a great armament, and resolved to lay a sailing prohibition on all the merchant vessels which were going north to Nidaros;

for he knew that King Hakon would soon get tidings of him, if ships were sailing between the towns. Besides, he gave out that it was better for Bergen to get the goods, even if the owners were obliged to sell them cheaper than they wished, than that they should fall into the hands of enemies and thereby strengthen them. And now a great many vessels were assembled at Bergen, for many arrived every day, and none were allowed to go away. Then Erling let some of the lightest of his vessels be laid ashore, and spread the report that he would wait for Hakon, and, with the help of his friends and relatives, oppose the enemy there. He then one day called a meeting of the shipmasters, and gave them and all the merchant ships and their steersmen leave to go where they pleased. When the men who had charge of the traders, and were all ready to sail away with their goods, some for trade, others on various business, had got leave from Erling Skakke to depart, there was a soft and favourable wind for sailing north along the coast. Before the evening all who were ready had set sail, and hastened on as fast as they could, according to the speed of their vessels, the one vying with the other. When this fleet came north to Möre, Hakon's fleet had arrived there before them; and he himself was there fully engaged in collecting people, and summoning to him the lendermen, and all liable to serve in the levy, without having for a long time heard any news from Bergen. Now, however, they heard with every arrival, that Erling Skakke had laid his ships up in Bergen, and there they would find him; and also that he had a large force with him. King Hakon sailed from thence to Veö,[1] and sent away Earl Sigurd and Onund Simonson to gather people, and sent men also to both the Möre districts. After King Hakon had remained a few days at the town he sailed farther, and proceeded to the South, thinking that it would both promote his journey and enable new levies to join him sooner.

Erling Skakke had given leave on Sunday to all the merchant vessels to leave Bergen; and on Tuesday, as soon as the early mass was over, he ordered the war-horns to sound, summoned to him the men-at-arms and the townsmen, and let the ships which were laid up on shore be drawn down into the water. Then Erling held a House-thing with his men and the people of the levy; told them his intentions; named ship commanders; and had the names called over of the men who were to be on board of the king's ship. This Thing ended with

[1] A town and island in Romsdal.

Erling's order to every man to make himself ready in his berth
wherever a place was appointed him; and declared that he who
remained in the town after the Bökesuden was hauled out,
should be punished by loss of life or limb. Orm, the king's
brother, laid his ship out in the harbour immediately that
evening, and many others, and the greater number were afloat
before.

CHAPTER VI. OF ERLING SKAKKE.—On Wednesday, before
mass was sung in the town, Erling sailed from Bergen with all
his fleet, consisting of twenty-one ships; and there was a fresh
breeze for sailing northwards along the coast. Erling had his
son King Magnus with him, and there were many lendermen
accompanied by the finest men. When Erling came north,
abreast of the Fjords district, he sent a boat on shore to Jon
Halkelson's farm, and took Nicolas, a son of Simon Skaalp,
and of Maria, Harald Gille's daughter, and brought him out to
the fleet, and put him on board the king's ship. On Friday,
immediately after matins, they sailed to Steinavaag [1]; and King
Hakon, with fourteen ships, was lying in a harbour in the
neighbourhood. He himself and his men were up at play upon
the island, and the lendermen were sitting on the hill, when
they saw a boat rowing from the south with two men in it,
who were bending back deep towards the keel, and taking hasty
strokes with their oars. When they came to the shore they
did not belay the boat, but both ran from it. The great men
seeing this, said to each other, "These men must have some
news to tell"; and got up to meet them. When they met,
Onund Simonson asked, "Have ye any news of Erling Skakke,
that ye are running so fast?"

They answered, as soon as they could get out the words, for
they had lost their breath, "Here comes Erling against you,
sailing from the south, with his twenty ships, or thereabouts,
of which many are great enough; and now ye will soon see
their sails."

Then said Eindride Unge, "Too near to the nose, said the
peasant, when his eye was knocked out."

They went in haste now to where the games were playing,
and immediately the war-horns resounded, and with the battle-
call all the people were gathered down to the ships in the
greatest haste. It was just the time of day when their meat
was nearly cooked. All the men rushed to the ships, and each
ran on board the vessel that was nearest to him, so that the

[1] Now the westmost part of Aalesund.

ships were unequally manned. Some took to the oars; some raised the masts, turned the heads of the vessels to the north, and steered for Veö, where they expected much assistance from the townspeople.

CHAPTER VII. FALL OF KING HAKON.—Soon after they saw the sails of Erling's fleet, and both fleets came in sight of each other. Eind-ide Unge had a ship called Draglön, which was a large buss-like long-ship, but which had but a small crew; for those who belonged to her had run on board of other ships, and she was therefore the hindmost of Hakon's fleet. When Eindride came abreast of the island Sekk, the Bökesuden, which Erling Skakke himself commanded, came up with her; and these two ships were bound fast together. King Hakon and his followers had arrived close to Veö; but when they heard the war-horn they turned again to assist Eindride. Now they began the battle on both sides, as the vessels came up. Many of the sails lay midships across the vessels; and the ships were not made fast to each other, but they lay side by side. The conflict was not long before there came disorder in Hakon's ship; and some fell, and others sprang overboard. Hakon threw on a grey cloak, and jumped on board another ship; but when he had been there a short time he thought he had got among his enemies; and when he looked about him he saw none of his men nor of his ships near him. Then he went into the Bökesuden to the forecastle-men, and begged his life. They took him in their keeping, and gave him quarter. In this conflict there was a great loss of people, but principally of Hakon's men. In the Bökesuden fell Nicolas, Simon Skaalp's son; and Erling's men are accused of having killed him. Then there was a pause in the battle, and the vessels separated. It was now told to Erling that Hakon was on board of his ship; that the forecastle-men had taken him, and threatened that they would defend him with arms. Erling sent men forwards in the ship to bring the forecastle-men his orders to guard Hakon well, so that he should not get away. He at the same time let it be understood that he had no objection to giving the king life and safety, if the other chiefs were willing, and a peace could be established. All the forecastle-men gave their chief great credit and honour for these words. Then Erling ordered anew a blast of the war-horns, and that the ships should be attacked which had not lost their men; saying that they would never have such another opportunity of avenging King Inge. Thereupon they all raised a war-shout, encouraged each other, and rushed to the assault. In this tumult King Hakon received his death-wound. When his men knew he had fallen they rowed with all their might against the enemy, threw away their shields, slashed with both hands, and cared not for life. This heat and recklessness, however, proved soon a great loss to them; for Erling's men saw the unprotected parts of their bodies, and where their blows would have effect. The greater part of Hakon's men who remained fell here; and it was principally due to want of numbers and the small heed they paid to their own defence. They could not get quarter, also, excepting those whom the chiefs took under their protection and bound themselves to pay ransom for. The following of Hakon's people fell: Sigurd Kaapa, Sigurd Hjupa, and Ragnvald Kunta; but some ships' crews got way, rowed into the Fjords, and thus saved their lives. Hakon's body was carried to Raumsdal, and buried there; but afterwards his brother, King Sverre, had the body transported north to Kaupangen, and laid in the stone wall of Christ church south of the chancel.

CHAPTER VIII. FLIGHT OF THE CHIEFS OF KING HAKON'S MEN.—Earl Sigurd, Eindride Unge, Onund Simonson, Frederik Köna, and other chiefs kept the troop together, left the ships in Raumsdal, and went up to the Uplands. King Magnus and his father Erling sailed with their troops north to Kaupangen, and subdued the country as they went along. Erling called together an Öre-thing, at which King Magnus was proclaimed king of all Norway. Erling, however, remained there but a short time; for he thought the Drontheim people were not well affected towards him and his son. King Magnus was then called king of the whole country.

King Hakon had been a handsome man in appearance, well grown, tall and thin; but very broad-shouldered, and on this account his men called him Herdebreid. As he was young in years, his lendermen ruled for him. He was cheerful and friendly in conversation, playful and youthful in his ways, and was much liked by the people.

CHAPTER IX. OF KING SIGURD'S BEGINNING.—There was an Upland man called Marcus of Skog,[1] who was a relative of Earl Sigurd. Marcus brought up a son of King Sigurd Haraldson, who was also called Sigurd. This Sigurd was chosen king by the Upland people, by the advice of Earl Sigurd and the other chiefs who had followed King Hakon. They had yet a great army, and the troops were divided in two bodies; so that Marcus

[1] In Bröttum, Ringsaker.

and the king were less exposed where there was anything to do, and Earl Sigurd and his troop, along with other leaders, were most in the way of danger. They went with their troops mostly through the Uplands, and sometimes eastwards to Viken. Erling Skakke had his son King Magnus always with him, and he had also the whole fleet and the land defence under him. He was a while in Bergen in autumn; but went from thence eastward to Viken, where he settled in Tunsberg for his winter quarters, and collected in Viken all the taxes and revenues that belonged to Magnus as king; and he had many and very fine troops. As King Sigurd had but a small part of the country, and kept many men on foot, he soon was in want of money; and where there was no chief in the neighbourhood he had to seek money by unlawful ways—sometimes by unfounded accusations and fines, sometimes by open robbery.

CHAPTER X. EARL SIGURD'S CONDEMNATION.—At that time the realm of Norway was in great prosperity. The bonder were rich and powerful, unaccustomed to hostilities or violence, and the oppression of roving troops; so that there was soon a great noise and scandal when they were despoiled and robbed. The people of Viken were very friendly to Erling and King Magnus, principally from the popularity of the late King Inge Haraldson; for the Viken people had always served under his banner. Erling kept a guard in the town, and twelve men were on watch every night. Erling had Things regularly with the bonder, at which the misdeeds of Sigurd's people were often talked over; and by the representations of Erling and his adherents, the bonder were brought unanimously to consider that it would be a great good fortune if these bands should be rooted out. Arne the king's relative spoke well and long on this subject, and at last severely; and required that all who were at the Thing — men-at-arms, bonder, townsmen, and merchants—should come to the resolution to sentence according to law Earl Sigurd and all his troop, and deliver them to Satan, both living and dead. From the vehemence and uproar of the people, this was agreed to by all; and thus the unheard-of deed was adopted and confirmed by oath, as if a judgment in the case was delivered there by the Thing according to law. The priest Roald Long-speech, who was a very eloquent man, spoke in the case; but his speech was to the same purpose as that of others who had spoken before. Erling gave a feast at Yule in Tunsberg, and paid the wages of the men-at-arms at Candlemas [2 February, 1163].

CHAPTER XI. OF ERLING.—Earl Sigurd went with his best troops down to Viken, where many people were obliged to submit to his superior force, and many had to pay money. He drove about thus widely higher up the country, penetrating into different districts. But there were some in his troop who desired privately to make peace with Erling; but they got back the answer, that all who asked for their lives should obtain quarter, but they only should get leave to remain in the country who had not been guilty of any great offences against Erling. And when Sigurd's adherents heard that they would not get leave to remain in the country, they held together in one body; for there were many among them who knew for certain that Erling would look upon them as guilty of offences against him. Philip Gyrdson made terms with Erling, got his property back, and went home to his farm; but soon after Sigurd's men came there and killed him. They committed many crimes against each other, and many men were slain in their mutual persecution; but here only what was committed by the chiefs is written down.

CHAPTER XII. ERLING GETS NEWS OF EARL SIGURD [1163]. —It was in the beginning of Lent[1] that news came to Erling that Earl Sigurd intended to come upon him; and news of him came here and there, sometimes nearer, sometimes farther off. Erling sent out spies in all quarters around to discover where they were. Every evening he assembled all the men-at-arms by the war-horn out of the town; and for a long time in the winter they lay under arms all night, ready to be drawn up in array. At last Erling got intelligence that Sigurd and his followers were not far distant, up at the farm Re.[2] Erling then began his expedition out of the town, and took with him all the townspeople who were able to carry arms and had arms, and likewise all the merchants; and left only twelve men behind to keep watch in the town. Erling went out of the town on Thursday afternoon [19 February, 1163], in the second week of Lent; and every man had two days' provisions with him. They marched by night, and it was late before they got out of the town with the men. Two men were with each shield and each horse; and the people, when mustered, were about 1300 [1560] men. When they met their spies, they were informed that Sigurd was at Re, in a house called Ramnes, and had 500 [600] men. Then Erling called together his people; told them the news he had received; and all were eager to hasten their march, fall on them in the houses, or engage them by night.

[1] Lent began on 10 February.   [2] To the north-west of Tönsberg.

Erling replied to them thus: "It is probable that we and Earl Sigurd shall soon meet. There are also many men in this band whose handiwork remains in our memories; such as cutting down King Inge, and so many more of our friends, that it would take long to reckon them up. These deeds they did by the power of Satan, by witchcraft, and by villainy; for it stands in our laws and country rights, that however highly a man may have been guilty, it shall be called villainy and cowardly murder to kill him in the night. This band has had its luck hitherto by following the counsel of men acquainted with witch-craft and fighting by night, and not in the light of day; and by this proceeding have they been victorious hitherto over the chiefs whose heads they have laid low on the earth. Now we have often said, and proved, how unsuitable and improper it is to go into battle in the night-time; therefore let us rather have before our eyes the example of chiefs better known to us, and who deserve better to be imitated, and fight by open day in regular battle array, and not steal upon sleeping men in the night. We have people enough against them, so few as they are. Let us, therefore, wait for day and daylight, and keep together in our array in case they attack us."

Thereafter the whole army sat down. Some opened up bundles of hay, and made a bed of it for themselves; some sat upon their shields, and thus waited the day-dawn. The weather was raw, and there was a wet snow-drift.

CHAPTER XIII. OF EARL SIGURD'S BATTLE ARRAY.—Earl Sigurd got the first intelligence of Erling's army when it was already near to the house. His men got up, and armed them-selves; but not knowing how many men Erling had with him, some were inclined to fly, but the most determined to stand. Earl Sigurd was a man of understanding, and could talk well, but certainly was not considered brave enough to take a strong resolution; and indeed the earl showed a great inclination to fly, for which he got many stinging words from his men-at-arms. As day dawned, they began on both sides to draw up their battle array. Earl Sigurd placed his men on the edge of a ridge between the river and the house, at a place at which a little stream runs into the river.[1] Erling and his people placed their array on the other side of the river; but at the back of his array were men on horseback well armed, who had the king with them. When Earl Sigurd's men saw that there was so great a want of men on their side, they held a council, and were

[1] The brook flows into the Auli river below the farm of Ramnes.

for taking to the forest. But Earl Sigurd said, "Ye alleged that I had no courage, but it will now be proved; and let each of you take care not to fail, or fly, before I do so. We have a good battle-field. Let them cross the bridge; but as soon as the banner comes over it let us then rush down the hill upon them, and none desert his neighbour."

Earl Sigurd had on a red-brown kirtle, and a red cloak, of which the corners were tied and turned back; shoes on his feet; and a shield and sword called Bastard. The earl said, "God knows that I would rather get at Erling Skakke with a stroke of Bastard, than receive much gold."

CHAPTER XIV. EARL SIGURD'S FALL.—Erling Skakke's army wished to go on to the bridge; but Erling told them to go up along the river, which was small, and not difficult to cross, as its banks were flat; and they did so. Earl Sigurd's array proceeded up along the ridge right opposite to them; but as the ridge ended, and the ground was good and level over the river, Erling told his men to sing a Paternoster, and beg God to give them the victory who best deserved it. Then they all sang aloud "Kyrie Eleison," and struck with their weapons on their shields. But with this clamour 300 [360] men of Erling's people slipped away and fled. Then Erling and his people went across the river, and the earl's men raised the war-shout; but there was no assault from the ridge down upon Erling's array, but the battle began upon the hill itself They first used spears, then edge weapons; and the earl's banner soon retired so far back, that Erling and his men scaled the ridge. The battle lasted but a short time before the earl's men fled to the forest, which they had close behind them. This was told Earl Sigurd, and his men bade him fly; but he replied, "Let us on while we can." And his men went bravely on, and cut down on all sides. In this tumult fell Earl Sigurd and Jon Sveinson, and nearly sixty men. Erling lost few n.en, and pursued the fugitives to the forest. There Erling halted his troops, and turned back. He came just as the king's slaves were about stripping the clothes off Earl Sigurd, who was not quite lifeless. He had put his sword Bastard in the sheath, and it lay by his side. Erling took it, struck the slaves with it, and drove them away. Then Erling, with his troops, returned, and sat down in Tunsberg. Seven days after Earl Sigurd's fall [i.e. 27 February] Erling's men took Eindride Unge prisoner, and killed him, with all his ship's crew.

CHAPTER XV. OF MARCUS OF SKOG, AND KING SIGURD
SIGURDSON.—Marcus of Skog, and King Sigurd his foster-son,
rode down to Viken towards spring, and there got a ship; but
when Erling heard it he went eastwards against them, and they
met at Konghelle. Marcus fled with his followers to Hisingen;
and there the country-people came down in swarms, and placed
themselves in Marcus's and Sigurd's array. Erling and his
men rowed to the shore; but Marcus's men shot at them. Then
Erling said to his people, "Let us take their ships, but not go
up to fight with a land force. The Hisinger are a bad set to
quarrel with—hard, and without understanding. They will
keep this troop but a little while among them, for Hisingen is
but a small spot." This was done: they took the ships, and
brought them over to Konghelle. Marcus and his men went
up to the forest districts, from which they intended to make
assaults, and they had spies out on both sides. Erling had
many men-at-arms with him, whom he brought from other
districts, and they made attacks on each other in turn.

CHAPTER XVI. BEGINNING OF ARCHBISHOP EYSTEIN [1161].
—Eystein, a son of Erlend Himalde, was elected to be archbishop, after Archbishop John's death; and he was consecrated
the same year King Inge was killed. Now when Archbishop
Eystein came to his see, he made himself beloved by all the
country, as an excellent active man of high birth. The Drontheim people, in particular, received him with pleasure; for most
of the great people in the Drontheim district were connected
with the archbishop by relationship or other connection, and
all were his friends. The archbishop brought forward a request
to the bonder in a speech, in which he set forth the great want
of money for the see, and also how much greater improvement
of the revenues would be necessary to maintain it suitably, as
it was now of much more importance than formerly when the
bishop's see was first established. He requested of the bonder
that they should give him, for determining law-suits, an öre of
silver value, instead of what they had before paid, which was an
öre of judgment money,[1] of that kind which was paid to the king
in judging cases; and the difference between the two kinds of
öre was, that the öre he desired was a half greater than the
other. By help of the archbishop's relatives and friends, and
his own activity, this was carried; and it was fixed by law in

---

[1] Few coins had been struck since Harald the Stern's reign, and the
percentage of silver in his coins decreased as his reign progressed. The
recipients of fixed dues and statutory fines, chiefly the Church and the
Crown, suffered most from this depreciation.

all the Drontheim district, and in all the districts belonging to his archbishopric.[1]

CHAPTER XVII.—OF MARCUS AND KING SIGURD.—When Sigurd and Marcus lost their ships in the Gotha river, and saw they could get no hold on Erling, they went to the Uplands, and proceeded by land north to Drontheim. Sigurd was received there joyfully, and chosen king at an Öre-thing; and the sons of many men of standing attached themselves to his party. They fitted out ships, rigged them for a voyage, and proceeded when summer came southwards to Möre, and took up all the royal revenues wheresoever they came. At this time the following lendermen were appointed in Bergen for the defence of the country: Nicolas Sigurdson, Nokkve [2] Paalson, and several military leaders; as Thoralf Dryll, Thorbjorn Treasurer, and many others. As Marcus and Sigurd sailed south, they heard that Erling's men were numerous in Bergen; and therefore they sailed outside the coast-rocks, and southwards past Bergen. It was generally remarked, that Marcus's men always got a fair wind, wherever they wished to sail to.

CHAPTER XVIII. MARCUS AND KING SIGURD KILLED.—As soon as Erling Skakke heard that Sigurd and Marcus had moved northwards, he hastened to Viken, and drew together an armed force; and he soon had a great many men, and many stout ships. But when he came farther in Viken, he met with a strong contrary wind, which kept him there in port the whole summer. Now when Sigurd and Marcus came east to Lister, they heard that Erling had a great force in Viken; so they turned to the north again. But when they reached Hordaland, with the intention of sailing to Bergen, and came opposite the town, Nicolas and his men rowed out against them, with more men and larger ships than they had. Sigurd and Marcus saw no other way of escaping but to row away southwards. Some of them went out to sea, others got south to Sund, and some got into the fjords. Marcus, and some people with him, sprang upon an isle called Skarpa.[3] Nicolas and his men took their

[1] The penalties on offences against the law, and the fees for determining cases in the Things, appear to have been a main source of the revenues of the kings. On the establishment of bishops there appear to have been bishops' courts for judging of cases coming within clerical jurisdiction, of which the fees and penalties belonged to the bishopric revenue. It does not appear that the king's courts ceased in those districts which had bishops; but only that the fees and penalties in certain cases belonged to the bishop, not to the king.

[2] It has been conjectured that Nokkve Paalson and Nicolas Kuvung (p. 417) are the same man, but this seems unlikely.

[3] Now Skorpa on the south side of the Korsfjord, near Bergen.

ships, gave Jon Halkelson and a few others quarter, but killed the most of them they could get hold of. Some days after, Eindride Heidafylja found Sigurd and Marcus, and they were brought to Bergen. Sigurd was beheaded outside of Gravdal,[1] and Marcus and another man were hanged at Hvarvnes.[2] This took place on Michaelmas day [29 September, 1163], and the band which had followed them was dispersed.

CHAPTER XIX. OF ERLING AND THE PEOPLE OF HISINGEN.— Frederik Köna and Bjarne the Bad, Onund Simonson and Ornolf Skorpa, had rowed out to sea with some ships, and sailed outside along the land to the east. Wheresoever they came to the land they plundered, and killed Erling's friends. Now when Erling heard that Sigurd and Marcus were killed, he gave leave to the lendermen and people of the levy to return home; but he himself, with his men, set his course eastward across the Folden fjord,[3] for he heard of Marcus's men there. Erling sailed to Konghelle, where he remained the autumn; and in the first week of winter[4] Erling went out to Hisingen with his men, and called the bonder to a Thing. When the Hising people came to the Thing, Erling laid his law-suit against them for having joined the bands of Sigurd and Marcus, and having raised men against him. Ossur was the name of one of the greatest of the bonder on the island, and he answered Erling on account of the others. The Thing was long assembled; but at the close the bonder gave the case into Erling's own power, and he appointed a meeting in the town within one week, and named fifteen bonder who should appear there. When they came, he condemned them to pay a penalty of three hundred head of cattle; and the bonder returned home ill pleased at this sentence. Soon after the Gotha river was frozen, and Erling's ships were fast in the ice; and the bonder kept back the mulct, and lay assembled for some time. Erling made a Yule feast in the town; but the Hising people had joint-feasts with each other, and kept under arms during Yule. The night after the fifth day of Yule [i.e. on 29 December, 1163] Erling went up to Hisingen, surrounded Ossur's house, and burnt him in it. He killed one hundred men in all, burnt three houses, and then returned to Konghelle. The bonder came then, according to agreement, to pay the mulct.

CHAPTER XX. OF THE DEATH OF FREDERIK KÖNA AND

[1] A creek inside Kvarven.
[2] Kvarven, south-west of Bergen.
[3] Folden fjord was the mouth of Oslo fjord.
[4] i.e. the week after 14 October, Winter Day.

BJARNE [1164].—Erling Skakke made ready to sail in spring as soon as he could get his ships afloat for ice, and sailed from Konghelle; for he heard that those who had formerly been Marcus's friends were marauding in the north of Viken. Erling sent out spies to learn their doings, searched for them, and found them lying in a harbour. Onund Simonson and Ornulf Skorpa escaped, but Frederik Köna and Bjarne the Bad were taken, and many of their followers were killed. Erling had Frederik bound to an anchor and thrown overboard; and for that deed Erling was much detested in the Drontheim country, for the most powerful men there were relatives of Frederik. Erling ordered Bjarne the Bad to be hanged; and he uttered, according to his custom, many dreadful imprecations during his execution. Thorbjorn Skakke-scald tells of this business:

> East of the Fjord beyond the land,
> Unnoticed by the pirate band,
> Erling stole on them ere they knew,
> And seized or killed all Köna's crew.
> Köna, fast to an anchor bound,
> Was thrown into the deep blue Sound;
> And Bjarne swung high on gallows-tree,
> A sight all good men loved to see.

Onund and Ornolf, with the band that had escaped, fled to Denmark; but were sometimes in Gotland, or in Viken.

CHAPTER XXI. CONFERENCE BETWEEN ERLING SKAKKE AND ARCHBISHOP EYSTEIN.—Erling Skakke sailed after this to Tunsberg, and remained there very long in spring; but when summer came he proceeded north to Bergen, where at that time a great many people were assembled. There was the legate from Rome, Stephanus; the Archbishop Eystein, and other bishops of the country. There was also Bishop Brand, who was consecrated bishop in Iceland,[1] and Jon Loftsson, a daughter's son of King Magnus Barefoot; and on this occasion King Magnus and Jon's other relatives acknowledged the relationship with him.

Archbishop Eystein and Erling Skakke often conversed together in private; and, among other things, Erling asked one day, "Is it true, sir, what people tell me—that you have raised the value of the öre upon the people north in Drontheim, in the law-cases in which money-fees are paid you?"

"It is so," said the archbishop, "that the bonder have allowed me an advance on the öre of law casualties; but they did it willingly, and without any kind of compulsion, and

[1] Brand Sæmundsson was consecrated bishop of Hólar, the northern diocese in Iceland, on 8 September, 1163; he died in 1201.

have thereby added to their honour for God and the income of the bishopric."

Erling replies, "Is this according to the law of the holy Olaf? or have you gone to work more arbitrarily in this than is written down in the law-book?"

The archbishop replies, "King Olaf the Holy fixed the laws, to which he received the consent and affirmative of the people; but it will not be found in his laws that it is forbidden to increase God's right."

Erling: "If you augment your right, you must assist us to augment as much the king's right."

The archbishop: "Thou hast already augmented enough thy son's power and dominion; and if I have exceeded the law in taking an increase of the öre from the Drontheim people, it is, I think, a much greater breach of the law that one is king over the country who is not a king's son, and which has neither any support in the law, nor in any precedent here in the country."

Erling: "When Magnus was chosen king, it was done with your knowledge and consent, and also of all the other bishops here in the country."

Archbishop: "You promised then, Erling, that provided we gave you our consent to electing Magnus king, you would, on all occasions, and with all your power, strengthen God's rights."

Erling: "I may well admit that I have promised to preserve and strengthen God's commands, and the laws of the land with all my power, and with the king's strength; and now I consider it to be much more advisable, instead of accusing each other of a breach of our promises, to hold firmly by the agreement entered into between us. Do you strengthen Magnus in his dominion, according to what you have promised; and I will, on my part, strengthen your power in all that can be of advantage or honour."

The conversation now took a more friendly turn; and Erling said, "Although Magnus was not chosen king according to what has been the old custom of this country, yet can you with your power give him consecration as king, as God's law prescribes, by anointing the king to sovereignty; and although I be neither a king, nor of kingly race, yet most of the kings, within my recollection, have not known the laws or the constitution of the country so well as I do. Besides, the mother of King Magnus is the daughter of a king and queen born in lawful wedlock, and Magnus is son of a queen and a lawfully married wife. Now if you will give him royal consecration, no man can take royalty from him. William Bastard was not a king's son; but he was consecrated and crowned king of England, and the royalty in England has ever since remained with his race, and all have been crowned. Now we have here in Norway an archiepiscopal seat, to the glory and honour of the country; let us also have a crowned king, as well as the Danes and Englishmen."

Erling and the archbishop afterwards talked often of this matter, and they were quite agreed. Then the archbishop brought the business before the legate, and got him easily persuaded to give his consent. Thereafter the archbishop called together the bishops, and other learned men, and explained the subject to them. They all replied in the same terms, that they would follow the counsels of the archbishop, and all were eager to promote the consecration as soon as they saw that this was what the archbishop wanted.

CHAPTER XXII. KING MAGNUS'S CONSECRATION.—Erling Skakke then had a great feast prepared in the king's house. The large hall was covered with costly cloth and tapestry, and adorned with great expense. The hird-men and all the attendants were there entertained, and there were numerous guests, and many chiefs. Then King Magnus received the royal consecration from the Archbishop Eystein; and at the consecration there were five other bishops and the legate, besides a number of other clergy. Erling Skakke, and with him twelve other lendermen, joined Magnus in taking the oath of the law; and the day of the consecration the king and Erling had the legate, the archbishop, and all the other bishops as guests; and the feast was exceedingly magnificent, and the father and son distributed many great presents. King Magnus was then eight years of age, and had been king for three years.

CHAPTER XXIII. KING VALDEMAR'S EMBASSY.—When the Danish king Valdemar heard the news from Norway that Magnus was become king of the whole country, and all the other parties in the country were rooted out, he sent his men with a letter to King Magnus and Erling, and reminded them of the agreement which Erling had entered into, under oath, with King Valdemar, of which we have spoken [p. 393]; namely, that Viken from the east to Rygjarbit should be ceded to King Valdemar, if Magnus became the sole king of Norway. When the ambassadors came forward and showed Erling the letter of the Danish king, and he heard the Danish king's demand upon Norway, he laid it before the other chiefs by whose counsels he usually covered his acts. All, as one man, replied that the Danes should never hold the slightest portion of Norway; for never had times been worse in the land than when the Danes had power in it. The ambassadors of the Danish king were urgent with Erling for an answer, and desired to have it concluded; but Erling begged them to proceed with him east to Viken, and said he would give his final answer when he had met with the men of most understanding and influence in Viken.

CHAPTER XXIV.—OF ERLING AND THE PEOPLE OF VIKEN. —Erling Skakke proceeded in autumn to Viken, and resided in Tunsberg, from whence he sent people to Sarpsborg to summon a Thing of four districts; and then Erling went there with his people.

When the Thing was opened Erling made a speech, in which he explained the resolutions which had been settled upon between him and the Danish king, the first time he collected troops against his enemies. "I will," said Erling, "keep faithfully the agreement which we then entered into with the king, if it be your will and consent, bonder, rather to serve the Danish king than the king who is now consecrated and crowned king of his country."

The bonder replied thus to Erling's speech: "Never will we become the Danish king's men, as long as one of us Viken men is in life." And the whole assembly, with shouts and cries, called on Erling to keep the oath he had taken to defend his son's dominions, "should we even all follow thee to battle." And so the Thing was dissolved.

The ambassadors of the Danish king then returned home, and told the issue of their errand. The Danes abused Erling, and all Northmen, and declared that evil only proceeded from them; and the report was spread, that in spring the Danish king would send out an army and lay waste Norway. Erling returned in autumn north to Bergen, resided there all winter, and gave their pay to his people.

CHAPTER XXV. OF THE LETTERS OF THE DRONTHEIM PEOPLE.—The same winter some Danish people came by land through the Uplands, saying they were to go, as was then the general practice, to the holy King Olaf's festival. But when they came to the Drontheim country, they went to many men of influence, and told their business; which was, that the Danish

king had sent them to desire their friendship, and consent, if he
came to the country, promising them both power and money.
With this verbal message came also the Danish king's letter
and seal, and a message to the Drontheim people that they
should send back their letters and seals to him. They did so,
and the most of them received well the Danish king's message;
whereupon the messengers returned as Lent passed on.[1] Erling
was in Bergen; and towards spring [1165] Erling's friends told
him the loose reports they had heard by some merchant vessels
that had arrived from Drontheim, that the Drontheim people
were in hostility openly against him; and had declared that if
Erling came to Drontheim, he should never pass Agdaness in
life. Erling said this was mere folly and idle talk. Erling now
made it known that he would go to Unarheim [2] to the Gangdage-
thing [3]; and ordered a cutter of twenty rowing benches to be
fitted out, a boat of fifteen benches, and a provision-ship. When
the vessels were ready, there came a strong southerly gale. On
Thursday [11 May] of the Ascension week, Erling called his
people by sound of trumpet to their departure; but the men
were loath to leave the town, and were ill inclined to row against
the wind. Erling brought his vessels to Biskopshavn.[4] "Well,"
said Erling, "since ye are so unwilling to row against the wind,
raise the mast, hoist the sails, and let the ships go north." They
did so, and sailed northwards both day and night. On Wednesday, in the evening, they sailed in past Agdaness, where
they found a fleet assembled of many merchant vessels, rowing
craft, and boats, all going towards the town to the celebration
of the festival [5]—some before them, some behind them; so that
the townspeople paid no attention to the long-ships coming.

CHAPTER XXVI. OF ERLING AND THE PEOPLE OF DRONTHEIM.
—Erling came to the town just as matins were being sung in
Christ church. He and his men ran into the town, to where it
was told them that the lenderman Alv Rode, a son of Ottar
Birting, was still sitting at table, and drinking with his men.
Erling fell upon them; and Alv was killed, with almost all his
men. Few other men were killed; for they had almost all gone
to church, as this was the night before Christ's ascension day.
In the morning early, Erling called all the people by sound of
trumpet to a Thing out upon Öre. At the Thing Erling laid

[1] Lent in 1165 lasted from 14 February till 4 April.
[2] Now Onareim on the island Tysnes, Sunnhordland.
[3] Held on the Rogation Days of Ascension week; cf. p. 350, note 2.
[4] On the By-fjord, north of Bergen.   [5] Ascension Day, 13 May.

a charge against the Drontheim people, accusing them of intending to betray the country, and take it from the king; and named Baard Standale, Paal Andreson, and Rasse-Baard, who then presided over the town's affairs, and many others. They, in their defence, denied the accusation; but Erling's writer stood up, produced many letters with seals, and asked if they acknowledged their seals which they had sent to the Danish king; and thereupon the letters were read. There were also those Danes with Erling who had gone with the letters in winter, and whom Erling for that purpose had taken into his service. He told to these men the very words which each of them had used. "And you, Rasse-Baard, spoke, striking your breast; and the very words you used were, 'Out of this breast are all these counsels produced.'" Baard replied, "I was wrong in the head, lord, when I spoke so." There was now nothing to be done but to submit the case entirely to the sentence Erling might give upon it. He took great sums of money from many as fines, and condemned all those who had been killed as lawless, and their deeds as lawless; making their deaths thereby not subject to mulct. Then Erling returned to Bergen.

CHAPTER XXVII. OF KING VALDEMAR'S EXPEDITION TO NORWAY.—The Danish King Valdemar assembled in spring a great army, and proceeded with it north to Viken. As soon as he reached the dominions of the king of Norway, the bonder assembled in a great multitude. The king advanced peacefully; but when they came to the mainland, the people even when there were only two or three together shot at them, from which the ill-will of the country people towards them was evident. When they came to Tunsberg, King Valdemar summoned a Haugar-thing; but nobody attended it from the country parts. Then Valdemar spoke thus to his troops: "It is evident that all the country people are against us; and now we have two things to choose: the one to go through the country, sword in hand, sparing neither man nor beast; the other is to go back without effecting our object. And it is more my inclination to go with the army to the East against the heathens, of whom we have enough before us in the East country, than to kill Christian people here, although they have well deserved it." All the others had a greater desire for a foray; but the king ruled, and they all returned back to Denmark without effecting their purpose. They pillaged, however, all around in the distant islands, or where the king was not in the neighbourhood. They then returned south to Denmark without doing anything.

CHAPTER XXVIII. OF ERLING'S EXPEDITION TO JUTLAND.— As soon as Erling heard that a Danish force had come to Viken, he ordered a levy through all the land, both of men and ships, so that there was a great assemblage of men in arms; and with this force he proceeded eastward along the coast. But when he came to Lindesness, he heard that the Danish army had returned south to Denmark, after plundering all around them in Viken. Then Erling gave all the people of the levy permission to return home; but he himself and some lendermen, with many vessels, sailed to Jutland after the Danes. When they came to a place called Dyrsaa,[1] the Danes who had returned from the expedition lay there with many ships. Erling gave them battle, and there was a fight, in which the Danes soon fled with the loss of many people; and Erling and his men plundered the ships and the town,[2] and made a great booty, with which they returned to Norway. Thereafter, for a time, there was hostility between Norway and Denmark.

CHAPTER XXIX. OF ERLING'S EXPEDITION TO DENMARK.— The princess Christina went south in autumn to Denmark, to visit her relative King Valdemar, who was her cousin. The king received her kindly, and gave her fiefs in his kingdom, so that she could support her household well. She often conversed with the king, who was remarkably kind towards her. In the spring following [1166] Christina sent to Erling, and begged him to pay a visit to the Danish king, and enter into a peace with him. In summer Erling was in Viken, where he fitted out a long-ship, manned it with his finest lads, and sailed (a single ship) over to Jutland.[3] When he heard that the Danish king Valdemar was in Randaros,[4] Erling sailed thither, and came to the town just as the king sat at the dinner-table, and most of the people were taking their meal. When his people had made themselves ready according to Erling's orders, set up the ship-tents, and made fast the ship, Erling landed with eleven men, all in armour, with hats over their helmets, and swords under their cloaks. They went to the king's lodging, where the doors stood open, and the dishes were being carried in. Erling and his people went in immediately, and drew up

[1] The easternmost point in Jutland, north-east of Aarhus.
[2] It was called Grindhög and now Grenaa.
[3] Erling's journey to Jutland and reconciliation with King Valdemar must be placed in 1170 (not 1166).
[4] Randers in North Jutland.

in front of the high seat. Erling said, "Peace and safe conduct we desire, king, both here and to return home."

The king looked at him, and said, "Art thou here, Erling?"

He replies, "Here is Erling; and tell us, at once, if we shall have peace and safe conduct."

There were eighty of the king's men in the room, but all unarmed. The king replies, "Peace ye shall have, Erling, according to thy desire; for I will not use force or villainy against a man who comes to visit me."

Erling then kissed the king's hand, went out, and down to his ship. Erling stayed at Randaros some time with the king, and they talked about terms of peace between them and between the countries. They agreed that Erling should remain as hostage with the Danish king; and that Asbjorn Snara, Bishop Absalon's [1] brother, should go to Norway as hostage on the other part.

CHAPTER XXX. CONVERSATION BETWEEN KING VALDEMAR AND ERLING.—In a conference which King Valdemar and Erling once had together, Erling said, "Sire, it appears to me likely that it might lead to a peace between the countries if you got that part of Norway which was promised you in our agreement; but if it should be so, what chief would you place over it? Would he be a Dane?"

"No," replied the king; "no Danish chief would go to Norway, where he would have to manage an obstinate hard people, when he has it so easy here with me."

Erling: "It was on that very consideration that I came here; for I would not on any account in the world deprive myself of the advantage of your friendship. In days of old other men, Hakon Ivarson and Finn Arneson, came also from Norway to Denmark, and your predecessor King Svein made them both earls. Now I am not a man of less power in Norway than they were then, and my influence is not less than theirs; and the king gave them the province of Halland to rule over, which he himself had and owned before. Now it appears to me, sire, that you, if I become your man and vassal, can allow me to hold of you the fief which my son Magnus will not deny me, by which I will be bound in duty, and ready, to undertake all the service belonging to that title."

Erling spoke such things, and much more in the same strain, until it came at last to this, that Erling became Valdemar's man and vassal; and the king led Erling to the earl's seat one

[1] Bishop in Roskilde, 1158-91, archbishop from 1178.

day, and gave him the title of earl, and Viken as a fief under
his rule. Earl Erling went thereafter to Norway, and was
earl afterwards as long as he lived; and also the peace with the
Danish king was afterwards always well preserved. Earl
Erling had four sons by his concubines. The one was called
Reidar, the next Ogmund, who were by two different mothers;
the third was called Finn; the fourth Sigurd: these were younger,
and their mother was Aasa the Fair. The princess Christina
and Earl Erling had a daughter called Ragnhild, who was married
to Jon Torbergsson of Randaberg.[1] Christina went away from
the country with a man called Grim Rusli; and they went to
Constantinople, where they were for a time, and had some
children.

CHAPTER XXXI. BEGINNING OF OLAF.—Olaf, a son of Gudbrand Skafhoggsson and Maria, daughter of King Eystein Magnusson, was brought up in the house of Sigurd Agnhatt in the
Uplands. While Earl Erling was in Denmark, Olaf and his
foster-father gathered a troop together, and many Upland
people joined them; and Olaf was chosen king by them. They
went with their bands through the Uplands, and sometimes
down to Viken, and sometimes east to the forest settlements;
but never came on board of ships. Now when Earl Erling got
news of this troop, he hastened to Viken with his forces; and
was there in summer in his ships, and in Oslo in autumn, and
kept Yule there. He had spies up the country after this troop,
and went himself, along with Orm the King-brother, up the
country to follow them. Now when they came to a lake in
Sweden called . . .,[2] they took all the vessels that were upon
the lake.

CHAPTER XXXII. OF ERLING [1167].—The priest who performed divine service at a place called Rydjokul,[3] close by the
Glommen, invited the earl to a feast at Candlemas.[4] The earl
promised to come; and thinking it would be good to hear mass
there, he rowed with his attendants over the river the night
before Candlemas day. But the priest had another plan on
hand. He sent men to bring Olaf news of Earl Erling's arrival.
The priest gave Erling strong drink in the evening, and let him
have an excessive quantity of it. When the earl wished to lie
down and sleep, the beds were made ready in the drinking-room;

[1] In the extreme north-west of Jæderen.
[2] The name is missing here in all the manuscripts.
[3] Identified as a farm called Rjodaakul in Sörum, Romerike.
[4] 2 February, 1167, but a more reliable account in *Sturlunga Saga* gives it
as the day after All Saints' Day, i.e. on 2 November, 1166.

but when they had slept a short time the earl awoke, and asked if it was not the hour for matins. The priest replied, that only a small part of the night was gone, and told him to sleep in peace. The earl replied, "I dream of many things to-night, and I sleep ill." He slumbered again, but awoke soon, and told the priest to get up to sing matins. The priest told the earl to sleep, and said it was but midnight. Then the earl again lay down, slept a little while, and, springing out of bed, ordered his men to put on their clothes. They did so; took their weapons, went to the church, and laid their arms outside while the priest was singing matins.

CHAPTER XXXIII. BATTLE AT RYDJOKUL.—As Olaf got the message in the evening, they travelled in the night six miles,[1] which people considered an extraordinarily long march. They arrived at Rydjokul while the priest was yet singing matins, and it was pitch-dark. Olaf and his men went into the room, raised a war-shout, and killed some of the earl's men who had not gone to the early mass. Now when Erling and his men heard the war-shout, they ran to their weapons, and hastened down to their ships. Olaf and his men met them at a fence, at which there was a sharp conflict. Erling and his men retreated along the fence, which protected them. Erling had far fewer men, and many of them had fallen, and still more were wounded. What helped Earl Erling and his men the most was, that Olaf's men could not distinguish them, it was so dark; and the earl's men were always drawing down to their ships. Are Thorgeirson, father of Bishop Gudmund,[2] fell there, and many others of Erling's hird-men. Erling himself was wounded in the left side; but some say he did it himself in drawing his sword. Orm the King-brother was also severely wounded; and with great difficulty they escaped to their ships, and instantly pushed off from land. It was generally considered as a most unlucky meeting for Olaf's people, as Earl Erling was in a manner sold into their hands, if they had proceeded with common prudence. He was afterwards called Olaf the Unlucky; but others called his people Hat-lads. They went with their bands through the Uplands as before. Erling again went down to Viken to his ships, and remained there all summer. Olaf was in the Uplands, and sometimes east in the forest districts, where he and his troops remained all the next winter.

CHAPTER XXXIV. BATTLE AT STANGE [1168].—The follow-

[1] Probably from thirty-five to forty English miles.
[2] Gudmund the Good, bishop of Hólar in Iceland, 1203-37.

ing spring Olaf and his men went down to Viken, and raised the
king's taxes all around, and remained there long in summer.
When Earl Erling heard this, he hastened with his troops to
meet them in Viken, and fell in with them east of the Fjord,
at a place called Stange[1]; where they had a great battle, in
which Erling was victorious. Sigurd Agnhatt and many others
of Olaf's men fell there; but Olaf escaped by flight, went south
to Denmark, and was all winter in Aalborg in Jutland. The
following spring [1169] Olaf fell into an illness which ended
in death, and he was buried in the Maria church[2]; and the
Danes call him a saint.

CHAPTER XXXV. HARALD'S DEATH.—King Magnus had a
lenderman called Nicolas Kuvung, who was a son of Paul
Skofteson. He took Harald prisoner, who called himself a son
of King Sigurd Haraldson and the princess Christina, and a
brother of King Magnus by the mother's side. Nicolas brought
Harald to Bergen, and delivered him into Earl Erling's hands.
It was Erling's custom when his enemies came before him, that
he either said nothing to them, or very little, and that in all
gentleness, when he had determined to put them to death; or
rose with furious words against them, when he intended to
spare their lives. Erling spoke but little to Harald, and many,
therefore, suspected his intentions; and some begged King
Magnus to put in a good word for Harald with the earl: and the
king did so. The earl replies, "Thy friends advise thee badly.
Thou wouldst govern this kingdom but a short time in peace
and safety, if thou wert to follow the counsels of the heart
only." Earl Erling ordered Harald to be taken to the North-
ness, where he was beheaded.

CHAPTER XXXVI. OF EYSTEIN EYSTEINSON AND THE BIRKE-
BEINER [1174].—There was a man called Eystein, who gave
himself out for a son of King Eystein Haraldson. He was at
this time young, and not full-grown. It is told of him that he
one summer appeared in Sweden, and went to earl Birger
Brose, who had married Eystein's aunt, Brigitta, daughter of
King Harald Gille. Eystein explained his business to them,
and asked their assistance. Both Earl Birger and his wife
listened to him in a friendly way, and promised him their
confidence, and he stayed with them a while. Earl Birger
gave him some assistance of men, and a good sum for travelling

---

[1] In Vaaler, in Smaalenene.
[2] The convent church at Aalborg, on the same site as the present Church
of Our Lady; cf. p. 355.

expenses; and both promised him their friendship on his taking leave. Thereafter Eystein proceeded north into Norway, and when he came down to Viken people flocked to him in crowds; and Eystein was there proclaimed king, and he remained in Viken in winter. As they were very poor in money, they robbed all around, wherefore the lendermen and bonder raised men against them; and being thus overpowered by numbers, they fled away to the forests and desolate hill grounds, where they lived for a long time. Their clothes being worn out, they wound the bark of the birch-tree about their legs, and thus were called by the bonder Birkebeiner.[1] They often rushed down upon the settled districts, pushed on here or there, and made an assault where they did not find many people to oppose them. They had several battles with the bonder with various success; and the Birkebeiner held a few battles in regular array, and gained the victory in them all. At Krokaskoven [2] they had nearly made an unlucky expedition, for a great number of bonder and men-at-arms were assembled there against them; but the Birkebeiner felled brushwood across the roads, and retired into the forest. They were two years in Viken before they showed themselves in the northern parts of the country.

CHAPTER XXXVII. OF THE BIRKEBEINER, KING EYSTEIN, AND ERLING SKAKKE [1176].—Magnus had been king for thirteen years when the Birkebeiner first made their appearance. They got themselves ships in the third summer, with which they sailed along the coast gathering goods and men. They were first in Viken; but when summer advanced they proceeded northwards, and so rapidly that no news preceded them, until they came to Drontheim. The troop of Birkebeiner consisted principally of hillmen and river-borderers, and many were from Thelemark; and all were well armed. Their king, Eystein, was a handsome man, with a little but good countenance; and he was not of great stature, for his men called him Eystein Meyla.[3] King Magnus and Earl Erling were in Bergen when the Birkebeiner sailed past it to the north; but they did not hear of them.

Earl Erling was a man of great understanding and power, an excellent leader in war, and an able and prudent ruler of the country; but he had the character of being cruel and severe. The cause of this was principally that he but seldom let his enemies remain in the country, even when they prayed to

---

[1] Birch legs.   [2] In Saurbö, now Sörbygden in Bohuslen.
[3] Meyla, a little girl.

him for mercy; and therefore many joined the bands which were collected against them. Erling was a tall, strong-made man, somewhat short-necked and high-shouldered; had a long and sharp countenance of a light complexion, and his hair became very grey. He bore his head a little on one side; was free and agreeable in his manners. He wore the old fashion of clothes—long body-pieces and long arms to his coats, foreign cloak, and high shoes. He made Magnus wear the same kind of dress in his youth; but when he grew up, and acted for himself, he dressed very sumptuously.

King Magnus was of a light turn of mind, full of jokes; a great lover of mirth, and not less of women.

CHAPTER XXXVIII. OF NICOLAS.—Nicolas was a son of Sigurd Raneson and of Skjaldvor a daughter of Brynjolf Ulvalde, and a sister of Haldor Brynjolfson by the father's side, and of King Magnus Barefoot by the mother's side. Nicolas was a distinguished chief, who had a farm at Ongul [1] in Halogaland, which was called Steig. Nicolas had also a house in Nidaros, below Saint John's church, where Torgeir the chaplain later dwelt. Nicolas was often in the town, and was the president of the townspeople. Skjaldvor, Nicolas's daughter, was married to Eric Arneson, who was also a lenderman.

CHAPTER XXXIX. OF ERIC AND NICOLAS.—As the people of the town were coming from matins the last day of Marymas [8 September, 1176], Eric came up to Nicolas, and said, "Here are some fishermen come from the sea, who report that some long-ships are sailing into the fjord; and people conjecture that these may be the Birkebeiner. It would be advisable to call the townspeople together with the war-horns, to meet under arms out on the Öre."

Nicolas replies, "I don't go after fishermen's reports; but I shall send out spies to the fjord, and in the meantime hold a Thing to-day."

Eric went home; but when they were ringing to high mass, and Nicolas was going to church, Eric came to him again, and said, "I believe the news to be true; for here are men who say they saw them under sail: and I think it would be most advisable to ride out of the town, and gather men with arms; for it appears to me the townspeople will be too few."

Nicolas replies, "Thou art persistent now, son-in-law: let us first hear mass, and then take our resolution."

Nicolas then went into the church. When the mass was

---

[1] Now Engelöen in Stegen, Nordland.

over Eric went to Nicolas, and said, "My horses are saddled; I will ride away."

Nicolas replies, "Farewell, then: we will hold a Thing to-day on the Öre, and examine what force of men there may be in the town."

Eric rode away, and Nicolas went to his house, and then to dinner.

CHAPTER XL. THE FALL OF NICOLAS.—The meat was scarcely put on the table, when a man came into the house to tell Nicolas that the Birkebeiner were rowing up the river. Then Nicolas called to his men to take their weapons. When they were armed Nicolas ordered them to go up into the loft. But that was a most imprudent step; for if they had remained in the yard, the townspeople would have come to their assistance; but now the Birkebeiner filled the whole yard, and from thence scrambled from all sides up to the loft. They called to Nicolas, and offered him quarter, but he refused it. Then they attacked the loft. Nicolas and his men defended themselves with bow-shot, hand-shot, and stones of the chimney; but the Birkebeiner hewed down the houses, broke up the loft, and returned shot for shot from bow or hand. Nicolas had a red shield in which were gilt nails, and about it was a border of stars. The Birkebeiner shot so that the arrows went in up to the arrow-feather. Then said Nicolas, "My shield deceives me." Nicolas and a number of his people fell, and his death was greatly lamented. The Birkebeiner gave all the towns-people their lives.

CHAPTER XLI. EYSTEIN PROCLAIMED KING.—Eystein was then proclaimed king, and all the people submitted to him. He stayed a while in the town, and then went into the interior of the Drontheim land, where many joined him, and among them Torfin Swart of Snaas [1] with a troop of people. When the Birkebeiner, in the beginning of winter, came again into the town, the sons of Gudrun from Saltness,[2] John Ketling, Sigurd, and William, joined them; and when they proceeded afterwards from Nidaros up Orkedal, they could number nearly 2000 [2400] men. They afterwards went to the Uplands, and on to Toten and Hadeland, and from thence to Ringerike, and subdued the country wheresoever they came.

CHAPTER XLII. THE FALL OF KING EYSTEIN.—King Magnus went eastward to Viken in autumn with a part of his men, and

[1] Snaasa, near the boundary between North Tröndelag and Namdal.
[2] A farm in Buvik, about twenty miles south of Trondheim.

with him Orm the King-brother; but Earl Erling remained
behind in Bergen to meet the Birkebeiner in case they took the
sea route. King Magnus went to Tunsberg, where he and Orm
held their Yule. When King Magnus heard that the Birkebeiner were up in Re, the king and Orm proceeded there with
their men. There was much snow, and it was dreadfully cold.
When they came to the farm [1] they left the home-fields for the
road, drew up their array outside of the fence, and trod a path
hard in the snow with their men, who were not quite 1500
[1800] in number. The Birkebeiner were dispersed here and
there in other farms, a few men in each house. When they
perceived King Magnus's army, they assembled and drew up
in regular order; and as they thought their force was larger
than his, which it actually was, they resolved to fight; but
when they hurried forward on the road only a few could advance
at a time, which broke their array, and the men fell who first
advanced upon the beaten way. Then the Birkebeiner banner
was cut down; those who were nearest gave way, and some
took to flight. King Magnus's men pursued them, and killed
one after the other as they came up with them. Thus the
Birkebeiner could never form themselves in array; and being
exposed to the weapons of the enemy singly, many of them fell,
and many fled. It happened here, as it often does, that although
men be brave and gallant, if they have once been defeated and
driven to flight, they will not easily be brought to turn round.
Now the main body of the Birkebeiner began to fly, and many
fell; because Magnus's men killed all they could lay hold of,
and not one of them got quarter. The whole body became
scattered far and wide. Eystein in his flight ran into a house,
and begged for his life, and that the bonde would conceal him;
but the bonde killed him, and then went to King Magnus, whom
he found at Ramnes,[1] where the king was in a room warming
himself by the fire along with many people. Some went for
the corpse, and bore it into the room, where the king told the
people to come and inspect the body. A man was sitting on a
bench in the corner, and he was a Birkebein, but nobody had
observed him; and when he saw and recognised his chief's body
he sprang up suddenly and actively, rushed out upon the floor,
and with an axe he had in his hands made a blow at King
Magnus's neck between the shoulders. A man saw the axe
swinging, and pulled the king to a side, by which the axe
struck the shoulders, and made a large wound. The Birkebein

[1] See p. 401, text and note 2.

then raised the axe again, and made a blow at Orm the King-brother, who was lying on a bench, and the blow was directed at both his legs; but Orm, seeing the man about to kill him, drew in his feet instantly, threw them over his head, and the blow fell on the bench, in which the axe stuck fast; and then the blows at the Birkebein came so thick that he could scarcely fall to the ground. It was discovered that he had dragged his entrails after him over the floor; and this man's bravery was highly praised. King Magnus's men followed the fugitives, and killed as many as they were able to catch. Torfinn of Snaas, and a very great number of Drontheim people, fell there.

CHAPTER XLIII. OF THE BIRKEBEINER.—The faction which called itself the Birkebeiner had gathered together in great numbers. They were a hardy people, and the boldest of men under arms; but wild, and going forward madly when they had a strong force. They had few men in their faction who were good counsellors, or accustomed to rule a country by law, or to head an army; and if there were such men among them who had more knowledge, yet the many would only allow of those measures which they liked, trusting always to their numbers and courage. Of the men who escaped many were wounded, and had lost both their clothes and their arms, and were altogether destitute of money. Some went east to the borders, some all the way east to Sweden; but the most of them went to Telemark, where they had their families. All took flight, as they had no hope of getting their lives from King Magnus or Earl Erling.

CHAPTER XLIV. OF KING MAGNUS ERLINGSON. — King Magnus then returned to Tunsberg, and got great renown by this victory; for it had been an expression in the mouths of all, that Earl Erling was the shield and support of his son and himself. But after gaining a victory over so strong and numerous a force with fewer troops, King Magnus was considered by all as surpassing other leaders, and that he would become a warrior as much greater than his father Earl Erling as he was younger.

HERE THE HEIMSKRINGLA ENDS

APPENDIX I
SOME ADDITIONAL NOTES

APPENDIX I

SOME ADDITIONAL NOTES

20 [1] sacrifice of expiation: *sonarblót*, sacrifice of a boar, an animal particularly associated with the cult of Frey; see G. Turville-Petre, *Hervarar Saga* (Viking Society, 1956), p. 78, note to 36/6.

40 [9] the Vendel domain; i.e. Vendsyssel, north Jutland.

75 [2-3] Gunhild, Eric Bloody-axe's wife, was in fact a daughter of King Gorm of Denmark, a fact mentioned only in the *Historia Norvegiae* (see Introduction, p. xvi). The transformation of her origin in the Icelandic sources must depend on the evil reputation she enjoyed there. The fostering of Harald Greycloak by King Harald Gormsson and the support the sons of Eric had from Denmark (pp. 90-1, 100, 106) are easily understandable when the royal houses of Norway and Denmark were so nearly related in this way.

91 note 3 The name in Eid- is probably due to the influence of the place-name Eidsvoll (at the southern end of Lake Mjösen), the site of the assembly from the eleventh century onwards.

92 [10] Onund: the name does not occur in any manuscript of the *Heimskringla*, but is supplied from another source.

95 [28-9] generous with their money, but sparing with their diet: cf. p. 41 [1-4] above.

106 note 3 It depends whether the original word is read as *arhjalmr* ("eagle-helmet") or *árhjalmr* ("bronze-helmet"; *ár* from Old English *ār*, cogate with Latin *aes*).

109 [33] and wished him in Valhalla: literally, "and directed him on his way to Valhöll." The phrase occurs elsewhere as a form of dedication (of one's enemies) to Odin, see G. Turville-Petre, *Hervarar Saga* (Viking Society, 1956), p. 74, note to 7/10.

109-11 The stanzas quoted on pp. 106 and 107 [16-27] also belong to the poem *Hákonarmál* (they come between the present first and second stanzas, pp. 109-10).

127 [26] Onund Olafson: Onund is doubtless the correct name, although all the manuscripts of the *Heimskringla* except one read Emund.

149 note 1 On Hrafn Sveinbjarnarson, chieftain in the north-west of Iceland, see *The Saga of Hrafn Sveinbjarnarson*, trans. Anne Tjomsland (*Islandica*, XXXV; Cornell University Press, 1951).

205 [15] Sealand: all manuscripts except one have *Smálönd* ("small lands"), which is taken to mean the small islands lying south of Fyen and Sealand.

234 [33] Walthjof's ballad: on Walthjof (i.e. Earl Walter, as he is elsewhere referred to in the translation) see F. S. Scott, 'Valþjófr jarl," *Saga-book of the Viking Society*, XIV (1953-7), 78-94.

245 [34] Lower Long Street: the original has simply "the street," but the identification is certainly correct.

264 [20] Moriartak (Icelandic Mýrkjartak) is Irish Muircheartach, son of Toirdhealbhach. He was king of Munster in the south of Ireland, 1086–1119 (not Connaught, although he laid claim to the high kingship of Ireland). Sigurd's marriage with the Irish princess did not take place until 1102, after which King Magnus made Sigurd king of Man.

271 [38–9] Skofte may have been the first Norwegian to sail through the Straits of Gibraltar, but the passage had been made by (Danish) vikings long before, in the ninth century.

292 Chapter xx follows chapter xxiii (p. 297) in the *Heimskringla*. For *Jon* in line 41, read *Sörkve*.

299 [36–301 8] The text here translated is an expansion, and to some extent a rearrangement, of the text in the *Heimskringla*. Correction would be too complex. Snorri's briefer text is less stylized and more forceful.

329 [17–18] six hundred and sixty Vendland cutters: some manuscripts read "two hundred and eighty," which may seem a more likely figure.

389–91 Chapters xx and xxi appear in the reverse order in the *Heimskringla*.

405 [33] Sund is not certainly a place-name; it may mean simply the channel (through the leads).

APPENDIX II

CORRECTIONS TO THE TRANSLATED TEXT

APPENDIX II

CORRECTIONS TO THE TRANSLATED TEXT

In the following a more accurate translation of the text of the *Heimskringla* is given after the bracket mark:

5 [10] are considered by many men of knowledge] seem to me. 22 [23-4] so as not to waken him] he said he would not stay awake waiting for her. 25 [20], [26], [30], [33] twenty-five] twenty. 79 [35] seventy] nearly seventy. 82 [36] The grave—there to the present day] In the middle of the mound was King Harald's grave. One large stone was placed at his head, another at his feet, and a large flat stone was raised above them, with other smaller stones piled up underneath it on both sides. The great stones that were in the mound now stand in the churchyard there. 85 [23] able] highborn and wise. 132 [26-9] Sigvat the scald—south to Rome] Sigvat the scald had gone south on pilgrimage to Rome. 135 [26-9] Under it was an arched way—locked with a key] It rested on columns, and its top was shaped like a roof with a decorated strip along the roof-ridge and with a head at each end. The top is hinged at the back, and has hasps in front which can be locked with a key. (The shrine was built like a model wooden church; carved wooden animal-heads were used to ornament the projecting ends of the main beams.) 163 [32], [39] box] *skaut*, a square of cloth. 202 *passim* earth-worms] earth-worm, snake. 221 [24] Ulv—and Gyda—were brother's and sister's children] Ulv—and Gyda—were brother and sister. 243 [8-10] King Olaf—merchant towns] King Olaf had the "Great Guild" established in Nidaros, and many other guilds in the towns. 273 [20] and there were paths cut through] where planks of timber were laid down to make the path. 274 [36] "Thus we break spear-shafts—] "This is the way we break every hobble—". 279 [32-4] but it lay—projected over it] he took up his station on a crag, but a great height had still to be traversed to get up to the stone wall, which was protected from above by an overhanging rock. 280 [2] spread them out before the Northmen] waved them at the Northmen. 284 [8-12] for in all his sails—side wind] for his sails were decorated with strips of precious stuff. These were moreover worked both into the front and the back of the sails, for both his foredeck-men and his poopdeck-men refused to have the less beautiful side of the sail before their eyes. 292 [41]-293 [2] Karl Sörkvison—Malmfrid] Karl Sörkvison, and their son was Sörkvi (king of Sweden 1196-1210). 314 [14] at the second mass for Olaf before matins] at the time of matins on the second feast of St. Olaf (3 August). 326 [15-16] the passage—to the Monks' bridge] the channel from the king's house. 338 [27-8] had passed the ness, and had come nearly to Mjolk-a] were passing a certain ness. 341 [7] Gyrd] Saade-Gyrd. 345 [7-8] where they fought—but he fled] But when King Eric heard that, he fled. 347 [33-4] which of his lads

—brave man's work] why they did not go in after him. 355 [36] Sturleson] Sturle (a nickname, cf. p. 371 [2]). 362 [28] of Gotland] Sonason. 363 [10-11] he moved them to let Jon Birgerson be consecrated] he permitted them to have Jon Birgerson consecrated. 374 [2] Skavescale] *Skaufuskalli* (a nickname). 377 [9-11] Gregorius said—advice to give] Gregorius said little; but he plainly hinted that he thought Erling dissuaded them from attacking in order to frustrate Gregorius's plans, and not because Erling himself had better counsel to offer than anyone else. 377 [13] brother] brother-in-law. 378 [16] all the summer] for a long time. 385 [21] or to be led by them] "yet I will not put up with your taunts." 391 [36-8] There was —in Constantinople] Eindride Unge was in Constantinople. 393 [7-9] But if this counsel—must seek] But if this plan meets with any success, then there may be men who will wish that they had undertaken this task themselves. But he who enters on this difficult course must seek—. 396 [18] evening] mid afternoon (*nón*, 3–4 p.m.). 398 [13-15] King Hakon—Eindride] King Hakon and his followers had arrived close to Veö when they heard the war-horns, for the nearest ships to Eindride had turned back to help him. 402 [12-13] have they been—laid low] they have gained their victory over such a chieftain as he was, whose head they have laid low. 402 [36-7] on the edge of a ridge] on a slope above the bridge. 403 [34] halted his troops] reviewed the state of his troops. 421 [16-17] which broke—beaten way] and any who left the road fell into such deep drifts that they could hardly advance. This broke their array, and those men who were foremost on the road itself were killed.

APPENDIX III

INTERPOLATIONS IN THE TRANSLATED TEXT

APPENDIX III

INTERPOLATIONS IN THE TRANSLATED TEXT

In addition to the passages in the text printed in square brackets the following should also be dismissed as interpolations in the text of the *Heimskringla* (cf. the Introduction, p. xxx):

37 [10-11] and then fled—Evil-worker. 57 [34-5] or not—kings. 61 [2] and they gave—kiss. 61 [31] and dwelt there awhile. 96 [37] by himself, or. 103 [28-9] where they stopped—expedition. 122 [20] after passing—Uplands. 122 [21] and lived five years with him. 131 [2-4] King Svein—Hardacanute. 131 [5] forty years old. 132 [30-8] He made these verses—many a land. 140 [43-51] This verse—kind. 141 [1-2] In this song—had established. 146 [26-31] King Magnus married—Olaf the Saint. 148 [32-7] It is told in the Bremen Book—men with them. 157 [42]-158 [17] While King Magnus—the king's friend. 160 [3-4] and was fifteen years old. 160 [6-7] in the poem—"Sexstefia." 160 [26-9] My wounds—rightful lord. 161 [30-6] Arnor—shield. 168 [35] fixed a bar—open. 179 [15] an intelligent man. 179 [17] according to Torgils' account. 190 [28] as well as his father. 190 [29] which the sagas—show sufficiently. 199 [28] was long earl, and. 223 [34-5] Some say—Agdaness. 225 [36] of Hundatunir. 233 [29-31] Olaf Haraldson—remained. 235 [24-7] William died—William the first. 238 [14-17] and this Skopte—Bjorn Buck. 241 [7-8] in Gudbrandsdal—mother's side. 241 [34-5] And by the intervention—Konghelle. 241 [37-40] The agreement—Norway. 242 [11-12] and loving—all things. 243 [10-13] and in his time—the king's protection. 243 [28-9] which was introduced—foreign kings. 245 [2-4] because he sat—dominions. 251 [26-27] thanked—given him, and. 252 [4-5] and Hakon—two years. 254 [23-34] And some one—make me so." 264 [11] of the Hebudes. 264 [21-3] Magnus gave—Hakon Paulson. 264 [29-30] who carried—he fell. 268 [44]-269 [2] This was proclaimed—best of friends. 269 [35]-270 [26] It is said—true and kind. 275 [11-12] leaving the Irish king's daughter behind. 279 [27-9] It was high—missile weapons. 281 [28-35] It is written—et Afer. 283 [24] which some—Sidon. 283 [27] with all his men and sixty ships. 284 [29-30] The emperor—to meet them. 284 [32-5] It is told—regard it. 284 [36]-285 [21] and when King Sigurd's men—equitably among his men. 287 [3-4] and appointed—food and drink. 287 [27-8] He had a large hall—in Norway. 292 [28-9] Valdemar—Olaf the Swede. 309 [30-1] although—counsel. 310 [5-11] and invoking—laid in bed, and. 310 [25-8] but King Sigurd—drinking together. 310 [36-9] Magnus had got—opinion. 321 [4] by Tora. 323 [1-10] and he sang—Ash to see. 323 [13-30] So says Halldor—he tries. 333 [9] the Bible. 337 [41-3] many gave—accordingly. 338 [5-11] When—put to death. 339 [34-5] killed the watchmen first. 339 [42]-340 [1] The men—an Icelander. 342 [1-4] At that time—friends. 343 [3-6] Shield—

433

thrown away. 344 [28-9] It was carried—three months. 345 [17-24] Now we shall—expeditions. 346 [32-40] So says Ivar—that day. 347 [8-9] Many—Aslak Smidsson. 347 [35]–348 [5] Bentein, who heard —his head. 350 [13-15] Afterwards—everywhere. 353 [41] and Gyrd. 355 [30-1] Thorleiv Brynjolfson, and Kolbein. 370 [39] after the Long Serpent. 373 [12-13] had beside him—with which he. 374 [37-8] The Drontheim people—shield. 379 [20] and then—attack. 400 [32-3] and merchants. 401 [25] in the winter. 401 [26] ready to be. 403 [42-3] with all his ship's crew. 415 [27] in Sweden. 418 [14] They had— success. 419 [38-9] for it appears—too few. 420 [38-9] and subdued— he came. (Cf. also p. 343, note 1.)

APPENDIX IV
OMISSIONS IN THE TRANSLATED TEXT

APPENDIX IV

OMISSIONS IN THE TRANSLATED TEXT

In this list a passage following the sign + is in the original text of the *Heimskringla* and should be inserted after the word given before the bracket mark:

22 ¹³ expeditions] + He was called Elfsi. 25 ³¹ Upsal] + for twenty years. 30 ³ Uplands] + from Norway. 30 ³⁵ roof-timbers] + and never drank by the corner of the hearth. 35 ⁴¹ warforce] + from all the lands he had brought under his sway. 46 ³⁸ Sigurd the Snake-eyed] + son of Ragnar Lodbrok. 69 ² Tore Roaldson] + in Firdafylke. 71 ²³ the two vikings] + Then this verse was made: "Tree-beard he gave to trolls,/Turf-Einar slew Skurfa." 79 ¹⁹ peace] + On these events Jorunn the poetess composed some stanzas in the poem called *Sendibit*: "Harald heard the Fairhaired/Of Halfdan's deeds all warlike;/But the poem's praises/ Pall in the fighter's hearing" [the second couplet is obscure]. 93 ¹⁰ intercourse] + and trade. 97 ²⁵ eight chiefs] + those who had chief control over the pagan sacrifices in all the Trondheim districts. 98 ⁹ filled for him] + without making the sign of the cross over them. 100 ¹⁶ fired] + because it had been usual to look for them lighted from the east onwards, and nobody had observed them [Eric's sons] from the east coast [omitted in error from Laing's own translation]. 106 ⁹ island] + and landed and drew up in battleorder. 108 ²⁷ king-killer"] + and shot the flein at Hakon. 109 ²⁰ friends] + and kinsmen. 113 ² her mother was] + Ingibjorg. 138 ³⁹ among themselves] + "What is this king thinking of when he breaks our laws, the ones established by Hakon the Good? Has he forgotten that we have never tolerated injustice?" 154 ³ straight down] + to Skaane. 197 ²⁶ face] + Then Hakon went away. 229 ²³ black horse] + with a blaze on his forehead. 262 ¹¹ to all men] + and their belongings. 276 ⁸ a year older] + King Sigurd left the Irish king's daughter behind in the west. 288 ¹⁶ allegiance]+ He began by saying that the Jemteland people had put themselves under the rule of King Hakon, Athelstan's foster-son, and had been subject to the kings of Norway for a long time after that. 290 ³¹ well grown] + and brisk. 328 ¹⁷ time] + Helga was the daughter of priest Andreas and Solveig; her husband was Einar. 343 ¹⁶ Earl Karl] + Sonason. 357 ¹⁶ Erlend of Gerde] + Orm's mother was Ragna, daughter of Earl Orm Eilivsson and Sigrid, daughter of Earl Finn Arneson. 361 ³⁶ of the two] + but he was an extremely avaricious and miserly man. 385 ¹⁶ good enough] + and they said they thought his luck had deserted him. 393 ³⁷ sisters] + daughters of King Harald of Gardar, son of Valdemar [son of Vissevald], son of Jarisleiv. 396 ²⁸ sent away] + into Romsdal. 403 ³⁷ lifeless] +

but unconscious. 405 [19] a fair wind] + that summer. 409 [6] crowned] + Svein Ulfsson in Denmark was not the son of a king, yet he was a crowned monarch himself, and his sons were after him and each of his line ever since. [The first Danish king to be crowned was in fact Knut Valdemarsson in 1170.] 420 [22] red shield] + the work of William [probably the name of the maker].

INTRODUCTION TO INDEXES

(i) Icelandic *á* (Scandinavian *å*, *aa*) is represented by *a* and *aa*, sometimes by *o*; Icelandic and Scandinavian *ö* normally by *o*, sometimes by *ö*, *a* or *au*. Medial and final *f* in Icelandic (Scandinavian *v*) appears as both *f* and *v*. Icelandic *þ* (= *th* as in *thin*) is represented by both *th* and *t* (the Scandinavian equivalent); Icelandic *ð* (= *th* as in *then*) by *d*.

In the alphabetical order *ä* is included as if it were *a*, *æ* as if it were *ae*; *ö* is found under *o*.

The name John appears in this form and also as Jon and Joan (from Johan(nes)). Paul (Icelandic Páll) appears both as Paal and Paul.

(ii) Under each separate name are first listed those individuals who are not denoted as somebody's son or daughter, and the alphabetical order here depends on their description (nickname, place-name, relationship to some other person). Then come the individuals whose father's or mother's name is given, arranged in alphabetical order according to the parent's name.

(iii) Place-names that are only used to identify persons (as e.g. Hall of Sida, p. 5) are not generally included in the Index of Places, but they naturally figure in the description of the individual in the Index of Persons.

(iv) The following abbreviations are used: abp., archbishop; bp., bishop; d., daughter; D., Denmark, Danish; E., earl; Emp., Emperor, Empress; Eng., England, English; Eric Ba., King Eric Bloody-axe; f., father; Harald Fh., King Harald the Fairhaired; I., Iceland, Icelandic; Ir., Ireland, Irish; K., king; m., mother; N., Norway, Norwegian; O., Orkney; Q., queen; s., son; S., Sweden, Swedish; w., wife.

Names of Norwegians and of places in Norway and well-known place-names outside Scandinavia are not normally distinguished by any sign in the Indexes.

INDEX

PERSONS

PLACES

GROUP-NAMES

THINGS AND LAWS

MYTHICAL AND ANTIQUARIAN